MORE TH
ENTHRALLING NOVEL
GENESIS
AN EXPERIENCE YOU WILL NEVER FORGET!

In these pages you will enter a world of little-known but indisputable fact woven into explosive, spellbinding fiction. . . . A world of superscience and global conspiracy that will fill you with horror and fascination. You will see the hidden forces of technological evil massing to obliterate those who discover and threaten to reveal their appalling existence. You will bear witness to the outer reaches of man's imagination and to his indomitable spirit.

Once in a long while comes a novel designed to grip the reader relentlessly from first page to last. Once in a long, long while comes a book that can change the way you look at the world . . . at the universe . . . forever!

Books by W. A. Harbinson

GENESIS
REVELATION
OTHERWORLD

GENESIS

W. A. Harbinson

A DELL BOOK

Published by
Dell Publishing Co., Inc.
1 Dag Hammarskjold Plaza
New York, New York 10017

For Ursula

A slightly different edition of this book was published in
Great Britain by Corgi Books.

Dell ® TM 681510, Dell Publishing Co., Inc.

ISBN: 0-440-12832-3

Printed in the United States of America
January 1982

10   9   8

It began when the B-25 had crossed the Rhine and was starting its bombing run over darkened Germany. The other aircraft had already made their first run when Lieutenant Tappman, twenty-one years of age and out of Denver, Colorado, studied the cross hairs of his bombsight, watched the last of the indices join, and prepared to trip away his load of 500-pounders.

The first bombs were already exploding, tiny flames in the black void, the flak drifting far below, the tracer bullets like fireworks, when Tappman blinked and saw the pulsating red lights winking on and then vanishing. "What the hell—?" the pilot said. "Jesus Christ!" a gunner added. The intercom crackled, voices rising and falling, then the Plexiglas nose was briefly filled with crimson light as three globes of spinning flame shot up vertically and vanished above.

Tappman blinked and shook his head, heard the coughing of the engines, felt the plane shuddering strangely and leveling out and heading away from the target zone. A spasm of fear lanced through him, an instinctive dread of the unknown, and he promptly pressed the button of his throat mike and said, "What the hell's happening there?" The intercom crackled. "What was *that*?" the copilot said. "I don't know," the tail-gunner's voice replied, "I saw lights—three red lights." Tappman looked into his bombsight, saw the cross hairs over darkness, cursed softly when the engines malfunctioned and the plane shuddered again. "You're going off course!" he shouted. "What the hell are you up to? I can't see a damned thing from here! Is it enemy aircraft?" The plane shook and dropped down, climbed back up, leveled out, the intercom crackling, metallic voices colliding, *"Red lights! Something burning! No, they're climbing! Jesus Christ!"* and then Tappman was dazzled, the night filled with spinning flames, and the burning globes spread out around the plane and then started to pace it.

The plane shuddered and rolled, went into a shrieking dive, barreling down through streams of tracers and black mushrooms of flak, the blazing buildings of Germany far below, illuminating the darkness. "Pull her up!" Tappman shouted, his eyes blinded by purple flares. "What the hell's going on? We're cutting out! *We're going down, you dumb bastards!"* The plane roared and shook violently, leveling out, its wings quivering, and Tappman saw his jack plug dangling loose and jammed it back into the intercom. "They're still with us!" the pilot was shouting. "What *are* they?" the gunner wailed. The nose shuddered and pointed upwards, heading through the tiers of flak, the plane's engines sounding healthy again as it started to climb.

Tappman looked for the balls of fire, saw nothing, rubbed his eyes, felt isolated in the bombardier's compartment at the end of the crawl-way. "What are you doing?" he bawled, seeing yellow fires below, the ugly black clouds of flak around him, hearing muffled explosions. "We cut out!" he shouted. "We went dead! *What's going on out there?"*

The intercom crackled, the tailgunner's voice wailing, fading in and out, back in again, sounding close to demented. "What are they?" the gunner wailed. "They're right beside me! I can't hit them! I can't make them out! They're not planes! *What the hell are those things?"* Tappman cursed and glanced around him, not believing what he had seen, wishing he could see them again, filled with dread and excitement. *"What?"* the pilot bawled. "Spinning balls!" the gunner wailed. "Balls of fire! I'm not sure! They look like balls of fire and they're spinning! Oh my God, *now there's more of them!"*

A sudden silence, then the static, then the roaring of the guns, someone screaming and then the plane rolling as if out of control. Tappman cursed and shook his head, flicked his eyes up, saw the sky, the dark clouds and the smaller clouds of flak, the silvery web of the tracers. *"Drop the bastards!"* the pilot bawled, wanting the bombs to be released, wanting the plane to be freed of its load and climb out of the chaos. *"I can't!"* Tappman hissed, working the controls and getting nothing, the fear racing in and smashing his senses when the engines cut out again. *"We're going down!"* someone screamed.

The plane shuddered and went silent, started rolling, falling fast, Tappman trapped in the Plexiglas nose with the earth far below him. He heard the static, someone wailing—the tailgunner, the copilot—looked below, following the line of the falling plane, and saw the fires of the air raid. "What *are* they?" the gunner cried. "The engines are dead!" the pilot bawled. "They're not planes!" the gunner cried. "They're balls of fire! Jesus Christ, *now they're climbing!*"

The engines roared back into life, as if controlled by the balls of fire, the plane leveling out and heading through the tracer bullets and the black clouds of flak. Tappman groaned and licked his lips, simply forgot to release his bombs, jerked his head around and saw a crimson light that fanned out through the dark sky. *"What's that?"* Tappman shrieked, his own voice unrecognizable, his heart pounding as he searched for the German fighters and saw only the crimson light. "I don't know!" the pilot bawled. "They're right behind us!" the gunner screamed. "They're pacing us!" the copilot joined in, his voice high and distorted. *"They're killing our engines!"*

Tappman glanced all around him, closed his eyes, looked again, saw the crimson glow spreading through the darkness at the side of the nose cone. Then the engines malfunctioned, started spluttering into silence, coughed into life yet again and made the plane jerk dementedly. Tappman shrieked some mindless plea, hardly aware of his own voice, staring out through the glinting Plexiglas to see a strange ball of fire. "Jesus Christ!" he hissed at no one, his eyes wide and disbelieving, seeing that spinning ball of fire, then another, then a third, suddenly remembering all the stories he had heard and never dared to believe. *"Foo fighters!"* the gunner screamed, his voice distorted by the intercom, reverberating in Tappman's head and fading away as the plane hurtled earthwards.

"We're going down! *Pull her up!"*

Tappman grabbed hold of himself, closed his eyes, embraced the nightmare, felt his body being pressed back into the chair as the plane kept on falling. The plane fell an endless mile, shuddering violently, spinning wildly, but it reached the ground eventually, plunging into it, exploding, Tappman hearing a crazed voice wailing *"Foo!"* which was where it all ended.

CHAPTER ONE

Shortly after noon on March 6, 1974, a battered, two-toned Pontiac passed through the gates of Winslow Air Base, Arizona, and headed directly for the Air Traffic Control Tower. The car moved leisurely but smoothly past the administration blocks and hangars, sunlight flashing off its windows, its wheels churning up red dust, the soft droning of its engine drowned out by the roaring of the aircraft either taking off or landing. There were white clouds in the blue sky, the planes glittered above the mountains, and the clouds were like banks of pure snow in a clear, azure lake.

When the car eventually stopped at the glass and concrete control tower, the driver climbed out slowly, closed the door with some care, locked it, then glanced vaguely around him. This man was short and bulky, insignificant in his dark suit, his white shirt disheveled and his green tie hanging loose, the tanned fingers of his right hand reaching up to stroke a gray, Vandyke beard. He was no longer young, was in fact over sixty, and his face was a webbed, sunburned map of fatigue and reflection.

After glancing briefly at the surrounding mountains, the man reached into his jacket pocket, pulled out a billfold, flipped it open and dangled it before the civilian guard. The guard was tall and impassive, dressed in black shirt and pants, and he studied the identity card, fingered the holster on his hip, gently stroked the peaked cap on his head and then nodded assent. The old man smiled bleakly, returned his billfold to his pocket, winced when a plane roared overhead, passed the guard, went inside.

The stairs were made of concrete, uncovered, painted white, and they led up through silence and a dim half-light to the more pronounced semidarkness of the approach control room. The old man glanced at the elevator, considered it, rejected it, took a deep breath and climbed up the stairs, breathing fitfully, wearily. Finally reaching the top, facing a steel-plated door, he let his racing heart settle, tied the knot in his tie, buttoned his jacket and then pushed the door open and closed it quietly behind him.

The approach control room was dimly lit, the numerous radarscopes flashing, the walls banked with computers and flight maps and schedule charts, the air traffic controllers bunched around the consoles, their hair short, their sleeves rolled up. The old man blinked and coughed, his hazel eyes scanning the gloom, then he raised one hand and gently stroked his beard, the noise and dim light confusing him. The air controllers all talked at once, telephones rang, radios crackled, and the colored lights of radarscopes and computers flashed on and off brilliantly.

The old man coughed again, raised a hand and waved slowly, watched his friend detaching himself from a group and walking over toward him. His friend was young and flashy, his flowered shirt open-necked, the chain belt on his white trousers gleaming as he shook the old man's hand. He did this and then stepped back, glanced around him, smiled and shrugged, then stepped forward again, took the old man by the shoulders and shook him.

"You look fine," he said.

The old man smiled wearily, smoothed his thinning gray hair, looked around him, eyes squinting, bathed in muted orange light, stroked his beard and then loosened his tie and looked back at his younger friend.

"I don't feel as fine as I look," he said. "Now what's this emergency?"

"I'm sorry I had to—"

A weathered hand waved. "It's all right," the old man said. His accent was faintly European, his voice soft, almost hesitant. "Just tell me what's happening."

The young man was slow to answer, his fingers playing with the gleaming belt. He glanced uneasily around him and then reluctantly looked back at the older man.

"We found Irving," he said.

Something happened to the old man, something almost imperceptible, a spasm of shock, a fleeting fear or despair, before he blinked and rubbed slowly at his beard and then quietly controlled himself.

"You found him?"

"Yes, Frederick. He's dead."

The old man looked at the floor, rubbed his eyes, glanced around him; he saw the glowing radarscopes, their orange light on men's faces, the men casting long shadows on the floor, on the humming computers. He felt fear at that moment, the dry, familiar fear, a hopeless dread that had enveloped his past and now mapped out his future. He looked back at his young friend, at the blond hair and blue eyes, saw the multicolored darkness all around him, making him unreal.

"Suicide?" the old man said.

"So it seems," the young man said. "They found him an hour ago, on U.S. 66—in his car, just beyond Valentine, a gun in his hand."

"U.S. 66?"

"That's right. Apparently Mary never even saw him leaving. She's staying in the house on Camelback Hill, and I just rang her and she didn't sound too well."

"No," the old man murmured. "Obviously not."

"Anyway," the young man said, "the usual. Mary says he hadn't been sleeping well lately, that he'd been getting up in the middle of the morning and just wandering about the house, looking out the windows, looking up, obsessed by the whole thing. She thinks he must have done that this morning—got up when she was asleep—only this time he didn't walk around: he took the car and drove off. The cops found him an hour ago. He'd shot himself in the mouth. I told them to hold off till we got there. We better go now."

The old man closed his eyes, shook his head from side to side, opened his eyes again and glanced around him, strain and grief on his face.

"Poor Mary," he murmured.

The young man took his elbow, led him out of the control tower, down the stairs, through the door, past the guard, around the dusty old Pontiac. The noon sun blazed down upon them, upon the airstrip across the road, burned a monstrous white hole in the sky above the hazed, blue-ridged mountains.

"Leave your car here," the young man said. "We won't be gone very long. We'll just fly out there and find out what we can and then I'll bring you right back."

The old man stroked the Pontiac, rubbed the dust from his hand, glanced around him, eyes squinting against the sun, then followed the younger man. The air base was busy, planes taking off and landing, a constant noise and movement above them as they crossed the hot tarmac. The old man was sweating, mopped his forehead, felt the wind—a fierce wind that emanated from a roaring and made his eyes narrow. His young friend was just ahead, ducking low, waving hands, urging him on toward the red and white 47G helicopter that had just burst into life on its landing pad.

The rotor blades whirled, became a blur that whipped the dust up, turned the dust into a localized whirlwind that enveloped the old man. He almost stumbled, righted himself, covered his mouth and cursed softly, then his free hand held his jacket against his chest as he followed his friend.

The helicopter roared and shuddered, its short steel ladder rattling, and the younger man, already inside, reached down with one hand. The old man was pulled up, stumbled in behind the pilot, and quickly strapped himself into his seat as his friend closed the door. Then his friend sat down beside him, the helicopter shook and climbed, and the old man, visibly relieved, stared out through the Perspex.

He felt grief and outrage, a cold, uncoiling fear, looking down, Winslow shrinking beneath him, remembering other days, other deaths. Suicide, he thought. We all finally commit suicide. There is never a reason nor a motive, but it's always a suicide. Of course he didn't believe it, never had, never would; he looked down on the mountains, on the bare, rockstrewn earth, on the saguaros and ocotilla and barrel cacti, and felt the fear creeping over him.

"How do you feel?" the young man said.

"About what you'd expect." The old man stroked his beard and rubbed his eyes. "I feel for Mary. How awful."

The helicopter dipped and climbed, sunlight flashing all around it, and the engine made a fierce, relentless roaring that drummed in their ears.

"We have a flap on," the young man said. "That's why I'm out at the air base. There's been sightings all over the goddamned place, and they're keeping us busy."

The old man glanced through the Perspex, saw the buttes and wind-carved valleys. "There's been a flap for the past *fifteen months*," he said, looking up, smiling gently.

"White Sands," his friend continued. "Los Alamos and Coolidge Dam. Visual sightings and radar reports, all unidentified returns solid." The young man shrugged his shoulders, gently ruffled his blond hair. "I don't know," he said. "It just makes me shiver. These things know where they're going." He looked at the old man. His bearded friend did not reply. "Weird," he said. "So how did your year go? How are things at the institute?"

The old man sighed. "Very busy," he said. "It's been the biggest flap since 1967 and we haven't had breathing space."

"Anything solid?".

"Too much to discuss." The old man saw mountains far below, the desert stretching around them. "I just wish we could catch one."

The young man didn't smile. "I want to pay you a visit," he said. "But you keep all these things in your head; just tell me a few."

"There were hundreds," the old man said. "Every conceivable kind. High-level, low-level, distant, actual contact; electrical and mechanical interference, numerous car-chasing incidents; mental and physical effects on people, animals similarly affected; landings with genuine traces left behind, the materials still unidentified. So, there were plenty."

"Jesus," the young man said. "Jesus Christ."

"Good witnesses," the old man said. "All reliable witnesses. We've never had such quality before. Most encouraging. Most heartening."

"Irving said that," the young man said.

"Irving's dead," the old man said. "Irving told me he had found something important . . . now Irving is dead."

"I can't hear you," the young man said.

"All right. I'm sorry."

"Tell me about some sightings," the young man said. "Who in hell are your witnesses?"

"Policemen," the old man said. "We're running a survey on police sightings. A policeman isn't prone to hysteria— and he's trained to observe."

The old man scratched his beard, gave a sigh, looked at his hands. The helicopter roared in his ears, making his head throb.

"October 17, 1973," he said. "In Waverly, Illinois, in the early hours of the morning, the police chief and three citizens observe an object with green and red flashing lights. They watch the object with binoculars for an hour and a half; it gives out glowing embers that fall to the ground, then disappears as quickly as it arrived . . . Los Angeles: police officers are summoned to investigate an object on the east side of the city; on arrival the officers see an oblong, bluish-white, very bright object which, when their car moves toward it, rises at a 45 degree angle to a height of about 1,500 feet and then speeds off . . . Palmyra, Missouri: several high-school students report that a bizarre object with flashing lights has appeared over the Missouri River, beamed a spotlight on a passing barge, lit up the entire river bottom, circled the river quite a few times, and approached onshore spectators before taking off vertically and disappearing. Four days later, Palmyra citizens *and* police observe an object with red, white and amber lights on it, plus two very powerful headlights in front; this object silently and slowly circles the whole town at low level, and only when police officers shine a spotlight on it, does it finally move away and disappear . . ."

"Okay. You've convinced me." The younger man grinned, shook his head from side to side, glanced sideways at the old man, looked away, saw the silvery-blue sky. "Any contact? Anything verifiable?"

"Not with the police."

The old man sighed, a muted hint of defeat, played abstractedly with the collar of his rumpled shirt, his gray eyes on the desert. The helicopter vibrated, roared and rattled around him, lifting up and then dropping down again in a sickening fashion. The old man looked down below, saw the mountains and valleys, the red earth, the scorched, writhing rocks, a world untouched by time . . . No, that wasn't so: nothing left had remained untouched. He looked down on Two Guns, Winona, Humphreys Peak, through all that had lived there and passed away because it no longer mattered. The land below was haunted, the dust settling over history, erasing the Apache and the Mojave, the Papago and the Pima, the Hopi and the Hualapai and the Yavapai, the Maricopa and Paiute. The Spanish *ricos* had disappeared but lonely missions remained, their walls bleached by the sun and eroded by fierce, swirling winds, the ancient bells red with rust. Arizona was unreal, a dream of legend and myth, its prairies crossed by Kit Carson and Billy the Kid and Wyatt Earp, still sheltering the reservations and pueblos, the sad remains of the Indians. The old man glanced down and shivered, felt the clinging, familiar fear, tried to reconcile the past with the present and its possible future. He thought of the White Sands Proving Ground, of Alamogordo, New Mexico, of Los Alamos and what it represented: the ever-threatening Atomic Age. Yes, the future was here and now—in aeronautics and atomic research. It was also in the lights in the sky that now obsessed the whole world.

"There has of course been contact," the old man said. "But alas, not with policemen."

"The Air Force?"

"Doubtless. But not announced."

"No. Those bastards wouldn't."

The old man rubbed his beard, seeming more tired each minute, a slight, almost imperceptible shiver running through his short body.

"Still," the young man said, "I think we're becoming more respectable. Did you know that on February 21 this year Monsieur Robert Galley, the French Minister of Defense, gave an interview on *France-Inter* in which he stated categorically that UFOs exist, that the phenomenon over France was massive, that they were considered of definite interest to national defense, and that since 1970, in collaboration with the *Gendarmerie*, all information regarding French sightings has been passed over to the *Groupment d'Etude des Phenomenes Aeriens* for investigation? I also note that this very month the American Institute of Aeronautics and Astronautics has revitalized its UFO committee. So, not to pun, things are looking up."

The old man seemed lost in thought, fingers scratching his beard, looking slightly impoverished beside the more colorful presence of his younger friend. When he finally spoke, his voice was soft and remote, as if divorced from himself.

"I'm tired," he said. "I'm growing old and I'm tired. I've been at this business for twenty-five years and I've seen too many friends kill themselves. I'm not tired. I'm just frightened."

His young friend did not reply, merely gazed down at the desert, momentarily embarrassed into silence, knowing what the old man meant.

"You've heard of Calvin Parker and Charles Hickson?"

"Yes," the young man said. "The Pascagoula case."

"Remarkable," the old man said. "The publicity was astonishing. A close encounter of the third kind that even Hynek was inclined to believe. When was that? Was it last year?"

"Yes," the young man said. "You've got your year right. The mouth of the Pascagoula River in Mississippi. A hell of a buzz."

"Some can't be broken down," the old man said. "Some are just beyond reasoning." He closed his fist and coughed into it, shook his head as if disgusted, rubbed at his eyes and glanced down, saw the stark, shadowed mountains. "Route 114A near Manchester, New Hampshire. November, 1973, four o'clock in the morning. Driving home from work a twenty-five year old woman—checked out, highly intelligent—notices a bright orange light that continually vanishes and reappears in the sky ahead. About seven miles further on, the object is much closer than before, much lower, much larger. Estimated as being about 1,600 feet in front of her, it is ball-shaped and honeycombed with various hexagons. The object has a translucent quality about it, with red, green and blue rays emanating from its center; and it is making a steady, high-pitched whining sound which makes her whole body tingle. Briefly as follows: Though frightened, the woman is unable to remove her hands from the steering wheel and feels that the object is actually drawing her car toward it. There is a memory loss during a half-mile stretch. Recovering, the woman finds her car hurtling toward the object, which is now about thirty feet above the ground. Still driving, and about 500 feet from the hovering object, the woman notices a window and an occupant inside, the occupant framed waist-up by the window. Description: head grayish, round, dark on top; eyes: large and egg-shaped; skin under the eyes loose or wrinkled. The witness didn't notice any ears or nose, though this may not mean anything . . . The witness seemed to be genuine."

"Any trace cases?"

"Too many to recount."

"Actual contact?"

"Yes, your Pascagoula case."

"That," the young man said, "was a humdinger."

"Grayish skin again. Conical appendages for nose and ears. Round feet and hands, crablike claws, lots of wrinkles, no eyes recalled."

"But five feet tall."

"Yes."

"Almost human."

"That's right. Almost human . . ."

The old man's voice trailed off, was drowned out by the roaring chopper, the chopper turning and dipping toward the earth, sunlight flashing around it. The old man felt ill, his stomach rumbling, heart fluttering, and he looked down on Dinosaur City, a gleaming maze in the desert.

"We'll soon be there," his young friend said.

"Good," the old man said. "I want to get it over and done with. I'm not as young as I used to be."

"Well, you're still working. You've kept the institute going. I'm glad you haven't given up yet. You're doing valuable work there."

"I hope so. I'm not sure. We can only do a limited amount. On the other hand, we *are* more organized—and nowadays they cooperate."

"The Air Force?"

"Yes. To a certain extent. However, what's more important—indeed, as you've just said—is the fact that witnesses from all walks of life are coming forward more willingly. The crank reports are now almost at zero, while reports from flight personnel, astronomers and even astronauts are being received at an astonishing rate. We now have a computer data bank for analysis of reports and storage of information. Areas covered include medical examinations of people and animals affected, psychological studies of witness reliability, theoretical studies of UFO movements and properties, photographic and special graphic analysis of UFOs, and analysis of plants that a UFO may have affected. In short, we're covering the subject pretty thoroughly."

The young man laughed, flicked blond hair from his blue eyes, glanced briefly at the pilot in front, then turned back to his friend.

"I believe it," he said.

"And now Irving."

"Jesus Christ . . . yes . . . I'm sorry."

They fell silent after that, both plunged into gloom, each locked into his personal concept of what might have happened. The helicopter rolled and dipped, started shuddering and falling, and looking down they saw U.S. 66, curving back toward the mountains. The old man rubbed his eyes, the sun blinding him, dazing him, then he reached for the knot in his tie and automatically tightened it.

"There they are," his friend said.

The old man looked down, saw the dark line of the

road, a ribbon winding around buttes and through valleys, shades of green, rose and lavender. Panic came and then departed, left him drained and forlorn, silvery sunlight exploding around him and then disappearing, leaving blue sky, white haze, a dark flock of birds, a jagged barrier of mountains in the distance, a stream of dense clouds above them.

The taste of death and its aftermath; the accumulation of fresh pain . . . his heart pounded and he let the fear depart and opened himself to his anger. He was old, most assuredly, growing older every day, but gazing down on the highway, seeing it widen and rush up toward him, seeing the police cars and the ambulance and the men around the other car, he let the rage wash away his grief and fear and charge his blood with new life. That was Irving down there. Back in Phoenix, Mary wept. The old man coughed and muttered an oath and sat back looking grim.

"I don't believe it," he said.

The helicopter dropped lower, roared louder, shuddered roughly, brown rock and parched grass and yellow cacti moving up to enfold it. Looking down he saw the police cars, the ambulance, the milling men, the latter gazing up, waving hands, shading eyes, the red dust being swept up by the chopper and swirling around them. The chopper moved away, crossed the road, dropping lower, shuddered again and then settled down two-hundred yards from the road. There was a bump, a brief shaking, a subsidence, then peace, the engine whining down into silence, the rotor blades finally stopping.

"Okay, you guys," the pilot said loudly. "Here we are. It's all yours."

The young man with the blond hair and colorful clothes unsnapped his safety belt and stood up. The older man was slower, fumbling clumsily with his belt, finally managing to unsnap it and rise, breathing harshly; laboriously. There was a rattling and banging, a beam of sunlight poured in, then the pilot slid the ladder through the door and motioned them outside. The young man went out first, held his hand up to the old man, took his elbow and guided him down the ladder to the safety of drifting dust. The old man coughed and blinked, one hand shading his eyes; he felt the sudden, claustrophobic, burning heat and then followed his young friend. They kicked sand and trampled shrubs, saw a lizard, a line of ants, then they arrived at the edge of the road and saw their friend, Irving Jacobs.

Irving was in his car, his face flattened against the steering wheel, the back of his head blown away, a bloody mess all around him. His arms hung down by his sides, the wind rippling his shirt-sleeves, and his face was turned slightly toward them, staring at them with dead eyes.

"Oh my God," the young man said.

The old man said nothing, simply shuddered and turned aside, tightened his tie and then took a deep breath and looked slowly around him. He saw police cars, the ambulance, the white medics, the milling cops, then a fat man wiping sweat from his forehead walked over toward them.

"Stanford?"

"No, I'm Stanford." The young blond man stepped forward. "I'm sorry to have kept you all this time. I had a bit of a hold-up."

The fat man looked at Stanford, wiped more sweat from his face; he was big, but that didn't stop his gut from flopping over his belt.

"I'm Toland," he said, "Captain Toland. Homicide. I don't know what you birds want out here, but you better be quick. He's startin' to stink already. He's been cooked by the sun. He shot himself early this morning. Put the gun in his mouth."

"What gun?" the old man said.

"Who are you?" Toland said.

"I'm sorry," Stanford said. "This is Dr. Frederick Epstein. Of the Aerial Phenomena Investigations Institute in Washington. I told you I'd bring him."

"Washington, eh?" Toland said, mopping sweat from his brow. "He must be a big fish."

"Not big at all," Epstein said. "He was just a close friend. Now what's this gun you're talking about? My friend didn't own a gun. In fact he didn't even know how to shoot one, I can assure you of that."

"You don't have to know how to shoot one to blow your own head off." The captain pulled out a handkerchief, mopped the back of his neck, glancing around at the cops taking measurements and photographing the dead man. "You just unclip the safety catch," he said, looking down at Dr. Epstein, "and stick the barrel in your mouth and pull the trigger. That's all there is to it."

"He didn't own a gun," Epstein repeated stubbornly. "He wouldn't know where to buy one."

"What are you, Doc? A scientist?"

"That's right. I'm a scientist."

"You sound pretty melodramatic for a scientist. You can buy a gun anywhere."

Epstein glanced at Stanford, saw him shrugging his shoulders; he glanced briefly at the dusty red Ford; at the policemen around it. The policemen were dressed in tan, wore dark glasses and brimmed hats, seemed threatening with their pistols and clubs, murmuring jokes, laughing raucously. Epstein saw the side of the car, the door open, an arm dangling; beneath a limp hand the sand was stained with a patch of dried blood. Epstein shuddered and turned away, felt anguish and choking rage rising out of himself and floating back to take a grip on his future. Captain Toland was staring at him, towering above him, gazing down, his fat face burned by sun and desert wind, his shirt rumpled and sweat soaked.

"It was a Luger," Toland said. "A German Luger. We've wrapped it up for the lab boys."

"He wouldn't buy a gun," Epstein said.

"Then he stole it," Toland said. "He got a Luger and he shoved it in his mouth and that's all there is to it."

"I don't believe that," Epstein said.

"Jesus Christ," Toland said. He turned his head and looked appealingly at Stanford. "The Doc thinks it was murder." The thought obviously amused Toland, made him grin and scratch his belly; then he turned back to Epstein, took his shoulder and said, "Here, come with me, Doc."

They walked around some lounging cops, past the ambulance, toward the Ford, Epstein feeling a deep surge of revulsion at the sight of that dangling arm. Then he gazed down at his friend, saw the bloody, shattered head, turned aside and looked down at the ground and saw a dark stain on red earth.

"Don't look at him," Toland said. "Just take a good look around you. Tell me what you see or what you don't see . . . Just have a good look."

Epstein did as he was told, a small man, tired and grim, rubbing slowly at his beard and staring around him, his gray eyes lined with age. The desert lay there before him, scorched eternally by the sun, rolling away through the buttes, into valleys, the distant mountains in blue haze. Stillness. Desolation. His gaze returned to the men around him: the medics were pulling a stretcher from the ambulance and walking toward the red Ford. They were dragging his friend out, a dead thing, meat and bone, and he choked back his rage and revulsion, looked once, turned away again. The sky, the white clouds, the ocher mountains beneath them; the mountains fell to the wilderness floor that stretched across to his feet.

"I don't know what you mean," he said.

The captain sighed with satisfaction, twisted his body and glanced around him, then waved one hand languidly at the road, at the tracks of the vehicles.

"Those tracks there," he said. "The tracks right in front of you. They belong to your friend's car and there isn't a trace of a skid mark: he drove up here and stopped." The captain waved his hand again, indicating more tracks— tracks crisscrossing each other and spreading out to the police cars and ambulance. "He was found by our patrol car. There were no other tracks here. Those tracks you see belong to our vehicles—before we came there was nothing. Just one set of tracks—your friend's tracks—there were no other vehicles. Our own car was the first to reach him. No other cars had passed this way. No tire tracks, no footprints, no nothing . . . He did it all on his own, Doc."

Epstein didn't reply, simply stood there deep in thought, his unfocused eyes becoming more alert when they fell on the medics. They were at the back of the ambulance, one inside, one on the ground, Irving Jacobs strapped tightly to

the stretcher that was tilted between them. Dr. Epstein
stepped forward, touched his friend's face with his fingers,
shook his head from side to side as if bewildered, then
stepped back and just watched. The stretcher was hoisted
up, the gleaming doors were slammed shut; the remaining
medic ran around to the driver's seat and waved a hand
and climbed in. The engine roared into life, the wheels
churned the dust up, then the ambulance reversed and
turned around and drove along the deserted road. Epstein
watched it drive away, didn't move till it disappeared, then
finally sighed and walked back to young Stanford, who
was looking perturbed.

"Jesus," Stanford said, "that was awful. How the hell
could he do it?"

Epstein opened his mouth to speak, changed his mind,
shrugged his shoulders, glanced around and tightened his
lips with distaste when Captain Toland approached him.

"That's it," the captain said. "We're going back now.
They'll do the autopsy in Phoenix. You got any more
questions?"

"No, Captain," Stanford said. "No more questions.
Thanks for your help."

"No sweat," the captain said, the sweat pouring down
his face, dabbing at his neck with the handkerchief, his
grin directed at Epstein. "It's all part of the service."

He turned and walked away, his large hips rolling
rhythmically, a pistol slapping up and down on one thigh,
a hand mopping his forehead. The other cops were in their
cars, the cars reversing in clouds of dust, then screeching,
wheels churning up more dust as they shot down the road.
The captain turned back and waved, his flushed face split
by a grin, then he chortled and climbed into his car and
the car rumbled away. Stanford stood beside Dr. Epstein.
They watched the cops drive away. They waited until all
the cars had disappeared in the distance, then they turned,
the dust settling around them, and walked back to the helicopter.

"Okay?" the pilot said.

"Okay," Stanford said. "Homeward bound."

They strapped themselves into their seats and Epstein

loosened his tie, wiping sweat from his neck with his hand as the chopper took off. They climbed straight up toward the sun, the sky dazzling, a blinding haze, Epstein gazing down on U.S. 66, the drifting dust of the wilderness.

"How's your love life?" Epstein said.

"Pretty regular," Stanford said.

"You're picking up a bad reputation."

"I know. I just love it."

"I thought you were marrying some girl."

"Yes. I was. I changed my mind."

"You could never make decisions," Epstein said. "That's your one human weakness."

Stanford grinned and shook his head. Epstein smiled and patted his arm. The chopper climbed higher, the land spreading out below, and Epstein suddenly leaned forward, his eyes widening, filled with shock, and reached out and took Stanford by the shoulder and shook him impatiently.

"Your flap!" he snapped. "New Mexico and Arizona. You mentioned the Coolidge Dam."

"That's right," Stanford said.

"Any more?" Epstein snapped. "Apart from Coolidge! *Did you have any more?*"

Stanford was startled. "Shit, yes," he said. He stared hard at his old friend, at his flushed, impatient face, and was amazed to see the brightness in his eyes, an almost fevered intensity. "All over the place," he said. "A constant flap the past three days. Over Glendale, over Prescott, over Tucson and Eloy, over Flagstaff and Sedona and Sunset Crater—the whole goddamned show."

"Look down there!" Epstein hissed.

Stanford looked down. He saw U.S. 66. He saw the spot where Irving Jacobs had been found, the rocky earth all around it. Then he blinked and looked harder. A shiver ran down his spine. He suddenly saw the rippling earth, the concentric rings of dust and sand, the rings surrounding the spot where Irving had been found and running out a great distance. It was like the thumbprint of a giant, the rings like whorls on the earth, as if the dust and sand had been blown away by some awesome explosion. Stanford blinked and kept looking. He couldn't believe what he was seeing. The huge thumbprint was half a mile in diameter, the earth scorched at its edges.

"Oh my God!" Stanford said.

The helicopter climbed higher, turned away from the sun, and neither Stanford nor Epstein said a word as they flew back to Winslow.

CHAPTER TWO

The man who stepped off the luxury cruiser onto the Puerto Banus yacht harbor near Marbella, southern Spain, was tall and sophisticated, wearing a black shirt and slacks, his eyes hidden behind dark glasses, his hair silvery but plentiful, parted neatly on the left and falling down over an unusually seamless forehead. He stood briefly on the dock, surveying the massed boats of the rich, then he turned in a sharp, decisive manner and walked alongside the restaurants. The tables were crowded, the clientele suntanned and elegant, wearing bikinis and sport shirts and sunglasses, gazing up at the mountains' haze. The man in black ignored them, walking slowly and carefully, only stopping when he arrived at the Sinatra Bar, looking in, entering warily.

The bar was bright and cool, almost empty, very quiet, one young lady at the far end of the counter, another man near the entrance. This man was middle-aged, rather plump, dressed in a white suit, the suit bulging slightly over his left breast to which a pistol was strapped. He looked up and smiled, a practiced smile, nervous, then he lightly patted the chair to his left, his fingers glittering with rings.

"Ah," he said. "Mr. Aldridge!"

The man in black nodded curtly, remained standing in the doorway, removed his glasses and blinked azure eyes and stared along the bright room. The young woman was

tanned and lovely, brown hair trailing down her spine,
breasts and crotch emphasized by her bikini, the long legs
crossed invitingly. Aldridge looked at her, studied her, saw
the indolence of the rich, and then, satisfied that she was
harmless, he sat beside the white-suited man.

"Buenas días," the white-suited man said. "It's been a
very quiet time, *señor."*

"That sounds promising," Aldridge said.

"I think so, Mr. Aldridge. There's been nothing unusual
at all. The work's all been routine."

"No visitors?"

"Not a knock on the door."

"I feel better each minute."

A short, dark Spanish girl emerged from a door behind
the bar, saw Aldridge and started to move toward him. Aldridge smiled pleasantly, but shook his head from side to
side, and the girl, with a slight, knowing nod, turned away
to clean glasses.

"You're not drinking?" the man in white said. "I
thought your trip would have made you thirsty."

"Not for wine, Fallaci. Just for rest. I am here to
relax."

Fallaci nodded and sipped his *vino*, his fingers glittering
around the glass, then he glanced at the young lady along
the bar and slowly turned back to Aldridge.

"I had a telephone call this morning. From our friends
in Arizona. They said to tell you that Irving Jacobs is
dead. It's been announced as a suicide."

"How unfortunate," Aldridge said. "At least for him. I
would like to leave now."

Fallaci licked his lips, turned around and snapped his
fingers, and the Spanish girl smiled and walked toward
him, blue-jeaned hips swaying sensually. *"Cuanto?"* Fallaci
said.

"Ciente pesetas, señor."

Fallaci put his money down on the counter. *"Muchas
gracias,"* he said.

He slid his legs off the stool and followed Aldridge
through the doorway, the sun blinding, flashing off the
white walls, the rolling boats, the blue water. Fallaci
blinked and glanced around him, saw tanned thighs, a

brief bikini, then he saw the upraised hand of Mr. Aldridge, heard the snap of his fingers.

"Where's the car?" Aldridge said.

"This way," Fallaci said.

"We're not in public now," Aldridge said.

"Sorry, sir. This way, sir."

They walked along a narrow street, the high walls painted white, the balconies of the apartments overhead casting shadows around them. The street was cool but very short, opening out to a monstrous heat, a fierce white haze that enveloped the waste ground and shimmered over the dusty cars. Fallaci walked on ahead, his leather shoes kicking stones, a glittering hand upraised and waving, flicking sweat from his brow. He finally stopped at a black limousine, opened the rear door, waited patiently, let Aldridge slip inside and settle down and then closed it again. When this was done he glanced around him, a portly figure, no longer suave, then he opened the driver's door and climbed in and switched on the ignition.

"How was Paraguay, sir?"

"It was hot," Aldridge said. "Now please get me there as quickly as possible. I have much work to do."

Fallaci flushed and turned away, released the hand brake, stepped on the gas, and the car moved off slowly, winding out of the parking lot, eventually turning onto the road to Fuengorola and picking up speed.

Aldridge sighed and sat back, looked outside, saw the traffic, the parched blue and ocher hills rolling up to the sky, desecrated by white-walled *urbanizationes,* the influx of foreign wealth. Aldridge grimaced with distaste, dropped his eyes, looked straight ahead, saw the dark hair on the back of Fallaci's head, the road racing toward him. Then he smiled and sat forward, pressed a button on Fallaci's seat, heard a humming as the glass pane slid down and cut him off from his driver.

The back of the car was soundproofed, air-conditioned, well cushioned, a bar, telephone and Video-TV recording system all built into the back of the front seats. There was a mirror above the cabinet. Aldridge studied his own reflection. He saw a deeply tanned, strangely ageless face, blue eyes cold with intelligence. Aldridge sighed, felt removed from all his years, then he unhooked the cassette recorder microphone and started to talk.

"One. General. The British Mercantile Airship Transportation Company, in collaboration with Plessey, are currently working on an experimental prototype of a Thermo Skyship. The Skyship, which has been developed under the general leadership of Rear Admiral David Kirke, is shaped like a flying saucer with the engines positioned right around the rim. Estimated diameter: 650 feet. Approximate weight: 500 tons. The machine is reputed to get its lift partly from helium and partly from hot air generated by the swiveling jet engines. Envisaged speed at the moment is 100 miles per hour, but most certainly this will be improved upon. The British Defense Ministry has expressed interest in this machine with a view to speeding the Rhine Army into battle, and it has been confirmed that the Royal Navy has also expressed interest in the possibility of using the Skyships for North Sea Oil defense . . . File for review.

"Confirmation received that for the past ten years the United States Air Force has been watching and photographing the secret Soviet laboratory at Semipalitinsk where it is believed that the Russians are developing an extremely powerful beam weapon capable of destroying intercontinental missiles at almost the speed of light. The beam is thought to comprise atomic or sub-atomic particles—electrons, protons or ions—equivalent to billions of volts of electricity and accelerated toward the target at just under 180,000 miles per second. John Allen, senior U.S. government scientist, has stated that a weapon of this type now appears to be possible; and both George J. Keegan, head of USAF Intelligence, and Dr. Willard Bennett, member of the U.S. team that was obliged to abandon beam weapon work in 1972, believe that the Russians are well ahead of the Americans in this field . . . Regular surveillance of the Semipalitinsk laboratory is recommended.

"In July of 1985 NASA plans to launch a new, solar powered, ion engine spacecraft whose purpose is to fly to Halley's Comet and circle Temple 2. A space shuttle will carry the spacecraft into earth orbit and then a dual-engine Inertial Upper Stage booster will propel the 1,600-kilogram probe into an interplanetary orbit, after which the fuel boosters will drop off and the solar-powered ion engine will take over the three year, low-thrust voyage to Temple 2 . . . File for review."

Aldridge switched the mike off, pursed his lips, glanced outside, watched the huge apartment blocks sweeping past, the mountains soaring beyond them. This stretch of road was ugly, scarred by building sites and hotels, the old villages now bustling, gaudy towns, filled with tourists and souvenirs. The old Spain was dead and the new expanded every day, spreading out along the Costa del Sol like some hideous cancer. It was the dawn of Democracy, that old dream that devoured itself, and Mr. Aldridge, with his ruthless intelligence, was appalled by the sight of it. He sighed, pursed his lips, listened to the humming of the limousine, then sank back into his seat and switched the mike on and started to talk again.

"Two. Prosthetics. Work is progressing at an uncomfortable rate on the artificial heart, lung, gut and gill, not to mention artificial cells, blood vessels, intestines and even skin. Artificial bones, joints and sockets are being used with increasing success, the main alloys being of the cobalt and chromium variety: tantalum, titanium, niobium and molybdenum. Blood vessels, heart valves, bone, skin, blood and the cornea of the eye have all been preserved artificially. Skin, stored in DSMO for periods of years, has been successfully grafted to the human body by researchers at the University of Pennsylvania School of Medicine. Bone frozen for years and then revived with cobalt radiation has also taken when grafted to the body. Likewise, red blood cells have been freeze-dried for years, and now tissue banks are disturbingly common. Indeed, it has been pointed out that the U.S. Navy tissue bank recently supplied some 3,000 square inches of human skin to Brazilian fire victims . . . Request further research.

"External prosthetics. Myoelectric control is advancing every day, with the Soviets reportedly making the greatest advances in this field. Apparently the Soviets have already perfected a hand-arm prosthesis in which all five fingers are capable of closing around objects of variable shape with the precision of the human hand. British scientists have developed, among other things, myoelectric arms with interchangeable hands; while in the United States a team of scientists and engineers from Harvard, MIT and Massachusetts General Hospital have developed a sophisticated myoelectric arm that moves at any angle, speed or force simply by being *thought* into action. This arm picks up muscle signals generated to the natural stump, transmits these to a small amplifier and uses them to drive a compact electric motor; the machinery for all this is housed inside a flesh-colored, fiber-glass casing that resembles a real arm . . . Researchers at the Powered Limbs Unit of West Hendon Hospital in England have come up with what amounts to an implantable electrode or transmitter, called an Emgor. This uses a resonator circuit that does not require batteries to detect myoelectric signals, thus obviating the need for frequent surgical intervention to replenish the power source. It is to be noted that amputees so treated are actually capable of *unconscious* gesticulations—and that similar lower body prostheses have now been developed to the point where some surgeons are willing to perform himicorporectomies—amputation of the entire lower half of the body, including legs, rectum and genitalia. This procedure has already been offered to patients in a prominent New York hospital as an alternative to death by abdominal cancer . . . Request further research."

The car turned off the main road, bumping over rough ground, and Aldridge looked out and saw the surrounding hills, the fields of olive trees and wheat. They passed a scattered *urbanization*, the walls whitewashed and gleaming, their gardens parched by the sun, the earth hard, a fine dust on the Moorish walls. Aldridge studied the place casually, noted the swimming pools and bikinis, the tanned limbs of the expatriates lounging around the deck chairs and tables. Oblivious. And superfluous. The real world would pass them by. Aldridge smiled and settled back, observed Mijas high above, then his blue eyes turned bright and intense as he started to talk again.

"Three. Gerontology. Dr. Richard Hochschild of the Microwave Instrument Company of Del Mar, California, has discovered that by adding DMAE to the water of mice one increases their life span significantly. Other investigators have successfully employed centro-phenoxine to delay lipofuscin buildup in the brain of guinea pigs; likewise, Phenoxene is being used experimentally in France to improve the mental abilities of senile patients.

"Along the same lines, Dr. Horace T. Poirier is close to developing a number of compounds that increase life by as much as 50 percent in mice. These include Vitamin E, mercaptothylemine, BHT, Santoquin and sodium hypophosphite, an old drug used for the treatment of tuberculosis. Also being utilized is DMAE, dimethylaminoethalol, a lysome membrane stabilizer which strengthens cells against damage caused by lipofuscin accumulations . . . Eliminate Poirier.

"An increasing number of scientists now believe that the program for aging is encoded in the hypothalamus-pituitary system. Among these are Dr. Joseph R. Wiseman of Chicago, who has successfully reactivated the estrus of aged female rats by stimulating the hypothalamus with electric impulses; he has also reactivated the ovarian cycles of the old females by feeding them L-Dopa, a dopamine stimulator also used in the treatment of Parkinson's disease, and hormones such as progesterone, epinephrine and iproniazid . . . Eliminate Wiseman.

"Dr. Saul A. Terkel, director of the Gerontology Research Institute, Richmond, Virginia, now believes that if life-extension were to become a national priority like the space program, and if the Americans, Russians and Japanese were to join hands in a billion dollar assault on aging and death, this could produce dramatic results in five years. Terkel has pointed out that such a program would cost no more than these countries now spend on the maintenance of old age homes. Now, backed by the full authority of the Gerontology Research Institute, Terkel is lobbying Washington with disturbing success . . . Eliminate Terkel."

The car climbed the mountain road, bouncing over large stones, passing immaculate *urbanizationes* and dilapidated farmhouses, just occasionally passing a Spaniard on a donkey, the field hands bent in labor. Aldridge frequently glanced out, observed the white haze of the sky, a thin ribbon of gray cloud above the mountains, the dizzying sweep of the valleys. The past was crumbling beneath the present, the future racing to devour them both, and Aldridge sat there, trying to remember all his years, the broad terrains he had traveled. Then the limousine slowed down, took the left fork of the road, headed away from Mijas, toward Alhaurin el Grande, as Aldridge closed his eyes and opened them again and talked into the microphone.

"Four. Telesurgery and telepsychiatry. Telediagnosis is now being utilized between Massachusetts General Hospital and Boston Logan International Airport, between numerous California hospitals, and between two hospitals in Edinburgh, Scotland. Also, a telesurgery linkup has been established between Massachusetts General Hospital and the Bedford Veteran's Administration Hospital eighteen miles away. In all these areas the computer becomes more predominant.

"It is also to be noted that many bioengineers are now claiming that computer and human brain will soon be directly linked. Said R. M. Page of the U.S. Naval Research Laboratory: 'The information which a machine can obtain and store from a person in a few minutes will exceed the fruits of a lifetime of man-to-man communications.' As to method: 'The coupling mechanisms to carry out the functions will be myriad, including in some cases electrical connections to the body and to the brain. Some connections may be wireless, with imperceptible transmitting elements implanted in the body.'

"Further note: Geneticists Harold P. Klinger and Orlando J. Miller, speaking before an international symposium on fetology, suggested that what was needed in the United States was a national registry of hereditary abnormalities to help prevent the conception of defective children. This system would have to be implemented via all newborn children when their skin and blood samples would, as a matter of course, be fed into a computerized genetic scanner which would immediately establish the presence of any chromosomal abnormalities and print them out on data cards that would be kept on permanent file in

Washington D.C. Computer analysis of current ethical attitudes on this subject is required. Please action."

Aldridge switched off the microphone and gazed through the window to see the archaic village of Coin. The car went through the village, past the dark eyes of the Spaniards, and traveled on down a steep, winding road, between two rows of olive trees. Aldridge leaned toward the console, pressed a button, ejected the cassette tape, took the tape and slipped it into his shirt pocket and then sat back impatiently. The car eventually emerged to sunlight, to flat fields strewn with rubble, and moved uphill and then leveled out and drove straight toward the house.

The house was buried between barren hills, well protected by a high-walled compound, the walls featureless, made of square concrete blocks that had never been painted. The walls were twenty feet high, their tops covered with barbed wire, the only entrance being a large wooden door broad enough for the car. The whole compound was solid, completely hiding the house inside, standing four-square between the surrounding hills like some stark, lunar fortress.

The car stopped before the compound and Aldridge stayed in the back while Fallaci got out and walked up to the door. Aldridge sat there and watched him, saw him pressing a metal buzzer, read his lips when he talked into the box and gave the code word for entrance. Fallaci then returned to the car, got inside, waited patiently; then the large wooden door slid up on metal grooves and Fallaci drove inside.

"Here we are, sir," he said.

Aldridge sat there impatiently, drumming his fingers on the seat, and Fallaci flushed and climbed out of the car and opened the rear door. Aldridge sighed and climbed out, stretched himself, looked around him, neither pleased nor disturbed to be back, simply checking the compound.

The compound was empty, graveled earth between walls and house, no shrubbery, no trees, no outbuildings . . . just open space to be crossed. There were cameras on all the walls and they swiveled back and forth, high up, their lenses shaded from the sun, with infrared beams for nighttime.

The house was linear, functional, a rectangle of brick and glass, about a hundred feet long, about fifty feet wide, the roof flat, the structure two stories high, the two doors made of solid steel. The numerous windows were large, made of bulletproof, one-way glass, and constantly moving above each of these windows were more scanning devices.

Fallaci walked up to the front door, pressed a button, glanced at Aldridge; the door opened and Aldridge walked inside and Fallaci then followed him. Fallaci closed the door behind him, pressed a button to set the alarms, and then he stood there with his hands behind his back, his full attention on Aldridge.

"I'll have a fruit and nut cereal," Aldridge said. "And a glass of white wine. Very dry. Very cold."

Fallaci nodded and departed, disappeared through a nearby door, and Aldridge walked along the corridor to his study. The walls were bland and impersonal, covered in spray-on felt fabric, no decoration, just digital control panels filled with flickering green numerals. Aldridge studied them as he walked, noting temperatures, power levels, then he went into his study, into silence, subdued lighting, the fiber glass Jacobean oak panels looking just like the real thing. He sat down behind his desk, beside a panel of tiered buttons, pressed a button and then sat back in the chair and studied the screens above.

There were six screens in all, banked in two rows of three, all set into the wall before the desk and wired up to the scanner. The scanners were all over the building, outside and inside the compound walls, in the bedrooms, in the toilets, in the garage, and they were all wired for sound. Aldridge surveyed the whole place from here, controlled its temperature and lighting, could open and shut any door at will, could plunge the place into darkness.

The screens flickered into life, the pictures sharp and precise, showing the kitchen, the servants' quarters, the laboratory, each from two different angles. The scanning cameras moved constantly, showing the whole of each room, and Aldridge switched the different receivers off and on, thus surveying the whole house. For the most part it was empty, the rooms vague in subdued lighting, the walls covered in fiber glass and spray-on felt, the furniture func-

tional and sparse. The building was almost futuristic,
strangely sterile and impersonal, a luxury abode for transient inhabitants, the silence heightening the strangeness.

Aldridge switched back to the kitchen, observed Fallaci
and the crippled dwarf, both standing before the gleaming
cooker unit, Fallaci mopping his sweaty brow. The dwarf
was a disgusting sight, his spine bent, his legs twisted, his
right hand a metal claw that was strapped to his arm with
wires running into a small pack at his waist, the pack
bulky and heavy. It was a primitive prosthetic and the
dwarf was tired of it, forever begging Aldridge to fit him a
new one, always being refused. Now Aldridge smiled
slightly, reached down and pressed a button, saw Fallaci
and the dwarf look up promptly at the camera above
them.

"Hello, Rudiger," Aldridge said to the dwarf. "How are
you feeling?"

"Ah, ah," the dwarf stuttered, his metal claw opening
and closing, his eyes blinking above a queerly flattened
nose and thick, dribbling lips. "Ah, ah . . . all right . . .
you know, sir . . . ah, *all right* . . . I think . . . I mean
. . . *sleepless*."

"Sleepless?" Aldridge said. "You mean nightmares?"

The metal claw waved indecisively, hinges opening and
closing, passing over the luminous, frightened eyes and
scraping saliva from the lips.

"Ah . . . nightmares . . . ah, *yes*, sir . . . bad, ah . . .
very bad . . . every night, *all* nights, ah, nightmares . . .
can't *sleep* at nights."

"That sounds terrible," Aldridge said with a smile.
"When did this start?"

The metal claw waved more frantically, the blubbering
lips opening and closing, the crippled dwarf in a positive
anguish of speaking, trying to force the words out.

"Ah, ah . . . *start*? When you left . . . *always*, sir, always then . . . when you leave . . . the fear . . . dreadful
nightmares . . . too frightened to leave here."

Aldridge smiled again. "You should have gone out," he
said. "I told you, you could leave when you wished. I'm
sure the break would have helped you."

"Ah, ah . . . *grateful*, sir . . . tried to go out . . .

couldn't *do* it . . . too frightened . . . *very* frightened
. . . of what's out there . . . all the nightmares . . . too
many bad dreams." The claw opened and closed, snapped
at air, clenched steel teeth, the dwarf's head rolling help-
lessly on stooped shoulders, lips dribbling saliva. "So glad,
sir . . . you're back . . . so relieved . . . *Please*, sir . . .
want you . . . *help me*!"

"Go to your room," Aldridge said. "Just lie down. Close
your eyes. Go to sleep."

"Please, sir . . . please, no . . . the *nightmares*!"

"No more nightmares," Aldridge said soothingly. "I am
back. No more bad dreams."

The dwarf shook with emotion, waved his claw, muttered gratitude, then turning around, glancing nervously at
Fallaci, he shuffled out of the kitchen. Fallaci stood where
he was, still looking up at the camera, a sharp image on
the television screen above Aldridge's blue eyes.

"He's been orderly?" Aldridge said.

"Yes, sir, he's been fine. I tried to force him out once or
twice, but he was too scared to go. It worked just like you
said it would."

"Good," Aldridge said "I'll have my food in ten
minutes. I'll relax for half an hour after that. You can
send the girl up then."

"Yes, sir," Fallaci said.

Aldridge pressed another button, putting the receivers
on automatic, then he pulled the cassette tape from his
shirt pocket and slotted it into the console. The recorder
turned itself on and Aldridge sat back and started to talk
again.

"Five. Brain research. Electrical stimulation of the
brain, ESB, has recently become dangerously innovative.
The suggestion that computer-controlled electrodes be implanted in the brains of babies a few months after birth,
thus robotizing them for life, has already been made by
Curtiss R. Schafer in a paper he presented before the National Electronics Conference in Chicago some time
ago—and while such a suggestion may have been made
half in fun, it is now clear that such devices have moved
out of the realms of animal experimentation and into the
human arena with volunteer subjects wired for electro-

sleep, electroprostheses, electrovision, electroanalgesia, electroanesthesia and, increasingly, electrosociology.

"Dr. Jose M. R. Delgado, professor of physiology at the Yale University School of Medicine, and Dr. James Olds of McGill University in Canada, have both experimented with the so-called pleasure centers of the human brain, as has Dr. Robert G. Heath of Tulane University. Meanwhile, Dr. C. Norman Shealy, chief of neurosurgery at the Gundersen Clinic in La Crosse, Wisconsin, has perfected electroanalgesic techniques to the point where they are now being applied to humans, mainly through the implanting of a .8 to 1.2 stimulating electrode in the spine rather than the brain. Regarding electrosociology, a team of doctors at Massachusetts General Hospital and Boston General Hospital have pacified violent human subjects by the implantation of electrodes into the rostral part of the caudate nucleus of the brain. It is requested that all these people be placed under immediate surveillance."

Aldridge switched the recorder off and sat back looking thoughtful, then he stood up and walked across the room and passed his hand over a control box. The opaque box glowed red and the paneled walls slid apart to reveal a linked audiovisual computer system, a mass of screens and controls. Aldridge pressed the MODE switch, another switch marked VISUAL/RECORD, and a receiver screen, 6' × 6', started crackling and glowing. Aldridge then turned a knob, saw a door, a white wall, kept turning until he saw the crippled dwarf stretched out on his bed. The dwarf was still wearing his clothes, a pair of blue jeans, checkered shirt, and he twisted and turned uncomfortably on the bed, moaning loudly and sweating. His eyes were luminous with fear, his metal claw opening and closing; and when he glanced around the room he seemed to shrink from the empty white walls.

"Stay still," Aldridge said, speaking softly. "Relax. Just lie quietly."

The dwarf froze where he lay, his large eyes fixed on the camera, and Aldridge slowly turned another knob marked ZOOM and saw the dwarf's face in close-up. The dwarf's eyes were filled with hope, beads of sweat shone on his nose, and his tongue crept out tentatively from his lips to lick up the saliva. Aldridge studied the screen and smiled, flicked a switch, turned a knob; and the dwarf's head started jerking, the eyes widening, then closing, until his head seemed to sink into the pillow, the lips shaped in a crooked smile.

Aldridge studied the large screen, observed the dwarf in sleep, turned the sound up and heard even breathing, a heart beating more normally. He then looked at the ECG, noted the subdued, irregular flickering, and satisfied that the dwarf would sleep well, he turned the screen off.

Moving away from the console, Aldridge walked across the study and went through a door into an adjoining, L-shaped lounge. Filling up the narrow wall of this room was an enormous ITT television set, a Neal tape recorder, a Philips video recorder and a bank of expensive Revox hi-fi equipment. Facing this luxurious system, about fifteen feet from it, was a low settee with a bank of switches on one arm. Aldridge sat down here, found a prepared list of video programs, studied them and then pressed the switch that was wired to the kitchen. There was a soft humming sound and part of the paneled ceiling descended, dropping down until it covered Aldridge's legs and formed a small table. Sitting on the table was a bowl of fruit and nut cereal, with a glass of very dry, very cold wine.

Aldridge pressed another switch marked VIDEO/PLAY/3, then he picked up his spoon and started eating as the television screen brightened. He watched the program as he ate, his blue eyes sharp and intense, occasionally rubbing his very smooth, unlined forehead, concentrating ferociously. It was a prerecorded tape, a compilation of various programs, a condensed survey of all the scientific and political events that he had missed during his absence. He finished his meal but kept watching, his brain recording, calculating, and only when the program had finished did he seem to relax. He pressed another button, the table ascended into the ceiling, and then he stood up and languidly stretched himself and went into his bedroom.

This room was like all the others, the lighting subdued, the temperature modest, a few expressionist paintings decorating the walls, more control panels flickering. Aldridge undressed himself, his body lean but tense with muscle, enormous scars running across his back and chest, and stepped into the shower. Like all else in this building, the water's temperature was preset; the water also contained an olive-based detergent that negated the need for soap. Aldridge stood there for some time, his brain disseminating information, then he stepped out, dried himself with a warmed towel, and lay down on the bed.

There were glass panels in the ceiling, hiding a Nordic solarium, and Aldridge pressed another button, the glass panels slid apart, and the solarium came on automatically, pouring down infrared rays. He lay very still, his eyes covered by protective glasses, breathing deeply, holding his breath for long periods, letting it out very slowly. His tense muscles relaxed, his scarred body seemed to glow, and then, precisely thirty minutes later, the solarium switched itself off.

The girl arrived shortly after, opening the door with some care, looking across at him and seeing him nod and padding quietly toward him. She was in her bare feet, her body wrapped in a loose sarong, her jet-black hair trailing down her spine, shining under the soft lights. Aldridge still lay on the bed, completely naked, looking up at her, his azure eyes revealing no more than a cool curiosity. The girl was slim, very young, probably in her late teens, her brown eyes and copper-toned skin suggesting a half-caste Eurasian. She stood beside Aldridge's bed, her head bowed, her hands clasped, and Aldridge lay there and studied her at length, quietly pleased by her beauty.

"What's your name?" he finally said.

"Rita," the girl whispered.

"You know what I require?"

"Yes, sir."

"Good. Please proceed."

The girl loosened her sarong, let it fall to the floor, and stood there, her naked body gleaming, covered lightly with oil. Her legs were long and slim, her waist tiny, her breasts full, the triangle of hair slightly shaved, rather smooth, almost velvety. Aldridge looked her up and down, his eyes calm, analytical, then he nodded and the girl smiled with gratitude and got to her knees.

She leaned over the bed, her hair falling across his loins, then she held his flaccid penis in one hand and slid it into her mouth. He watched her, smiling thinly, feeling her lips, her rolling tongue, her teeth pinching gently, imperceptibly, her mouth wet, a warm glove. Aldridge lay there and smiled, a remote smile, half regretful, then he reached out and touched the girl's head, felt it move up and down. Her wet lips, her rolling tongue: he tried to feel her and respond, gazing down at her shining, outspread hair, trying to will himself into her. The girl was expert, well schooled, her mouth working its way on him, but the distance he had traveled, all the years, again rendered him impotent. The girl finally raised her head, his flaccid penis in her hand, her brown eyes very large, lit by fear, her face begging forgiveness.

"It's all right," he said quietly. "It's not your fault. Just use the machine."

The girl was visibly relieved, standing upright, smiling nervously, then she went to the wall beside the bed and pressed an imbedded button. Two paneled doors slid apart, exposed a bright walk-in cupboard, and the naked girl walked in and emerged with a neat, mobile console. Aldridge closed his eyes and lay there, heard her movements, felt her hands; she dabbed the paste on his forehead, on his cranium and temples, then she fixed the small electrodes to his skull and switched on the machine.

An imperceptible current. A flow of energy through his brain. He relaxed, gave himself to the machine and felt his body responding. Opening his eyes, he saw himself: his erect, engorged penis; the naked girl was bending over his penis, tying something around it. He closed his eyes and surrendered, his years falling away from him, voluptuous visions and perverse, buried fantasies rising up to envelop him. Fierce reality and heat; the sublime, unraveled flesh . . . he surveyed it and touched it and felt it and returned to his youth. The girl breathed in his face, her tongue slithering between his lips, traveled down him, her tongue and lips working, sliding over him, burning him. The visions filled him and released him, engorged his flesh and drained it, and he gasped and slowly opened his eyes and felt the inflowing peace.

The room seemed a lot brighter. The naked girl was very real. He watched her as she soaped his sperm-drenched loins, washed him clean, dried him carefully. When she had finished, she straightened up, her dark, oil-slicked body gleaming, looking at him, hesitation in her face, her head bowed automatically. Aldridge smiled at her and nodded, indicating that she could leave, and she pushed the console back into the cupboard, closed the doors and walked out.

Aldridge put the dark glasses on, pressed a button and lay stretched out; the glass panels in the ceiling slid apart to expose the solarium. Aldridge lay there for some time, his eyes closed, trying to relax, but eventually his restless intellect forced him upright and made him start work again. He rolled off the bed, put his dressing gown on, walked into the study and sat down and turned on the tape recorder, speaking quietly, precisely.

"Dr. George D. Schroeder of the American Institute of Orgonomy, Seattle, writing in the English magazine *New Scientist*, has stated that orgone energy weather engineering techniques are an important new element in the environmental struggle. Schroeder has finally received government backing for a lengthy program of investigations into weather engineering possibilities. Already he had discovered that orgone energy exists as mass-free energy in the soil, water and atmosphere of earth, and that it is manipulable by mechanical cloud-busters, commonly called CLBs. It is to be noted that so-called tuned CLBs have proved their value not only in weather engineering, but in more than one UFO investigation. This has to be stopped."

Aldridge stopped talking, sat back, stroked his chin, his silvery-gray hair falling over his blue eyes, across that smooth, unlined forehead. He gazed at the opposite wall, at the banked screens and video recorders, and his bright, mathematical brain considered all of the options. He had once met Schroeder, had found him tough and intelligent, a possibility that might yet be tapped, a candidate for the future. It was a pity to lose Schroeder, but he didn't have much choice: the good professor now had government backing and that smacked of progress. Aldridge gazed across the room, pursed his lips, stroked his chin, then he sighed and ran his fingers through his hair and spoke quietly, implacably.

"Eliminate Schroeder."

CHAPTER THREE

The Audi 100 GL, all white and polished and gleaming, came up over the top of the hill and rolled down through the narrow, gray street in no particular hurry. Richard stepped forward quickly, his thumb high in the air, but the gleaming white Audi purred past, splashing water across him.

"Oh, shit," Richard murmured.

He pulled his thumb down and wiped rain from his forehead, glancing up to see the leaden gray sky and the dark, drifting clouds. At least the rain had stopped; there was that if nothing else. Richard shivered, adjusted his knapsack, checked the camera around his neck, then soaked to the bone, his hair plastered to his head, he turned and walked along the village street, past the small, silent houses.

The road opened out at the end of the village, curving uphill past a 17th century church, dominated by green hills. The Audi had stopped in front of the church, its engine cutting in and out, the car jerking roughly as it misfired and tapered off into silence.

"Good for you," Richard murmured.

He wiped rain from his beard, adjusted the knapsack on his shoulders, then sauntered in a casual manner toward the stalled car. An arm emerged from the driver's window, suntanned, definitely feminine, the fingers fanning out to drop a cigarette just where Richard was walking.

"Jesus!" a woman's voice said very softly.

Richard stopped immediately, looked down, saw her green eyes, a wave of very red, shining hair tumbling past pouting lips. The woman clenched her left fist and lightly hammered the steering wheel, then licked her upper lip and glanced at Richard, her fine eyebrows raised. Richard smiled encouragingly at her, ran his fingers through his long hair, his blue denims and jacket still wet, the cold creeping into him.

"Can I help you?" he said.

The woman studied him a moment, gently biting her lower lip, then, satisfied that he looked sane, she shrugged her shoulders and nodded.

"I haven't a clue what happened," she said. "It just suddenly cut out."

Richard shivered and glanced around him, saw the green hills of Devon, then he let the knapsack slide from his shoulders and fall to the ground.

"It might be nothing," he said. "A bit of damp. Something jammed. It probably isn't anything serious. I'll look under the hood."

The woman stared at him. Her gaze seemed to be unfocused. She had a thin, suntanned face, sophisticated, rather weary, fine eyebrows arching above the green eyes, lips unpainted and moist.

"Get it started and I'll give you a lift," she said. "Cars quite simply baffle me."

"It didn't cut out gradually?"

"No," the woman said. "I saw the lightning and then the car cut out. Does that make any sense to you?"

Richard glanced at the gray sky. "Lightning?" he said. "Are you sure? *I* didn't see any lightning. I don't think it was that."

The woman shrugged again. "It *looked* like lightning," she said. "Anyway, that's when the car cut out. I just don't understand it."

"Not lightning," Richard said. "I don't think it was lightning. You probably saw the lights of a plane. Let me look at the engine."

The woman shrugged again and leaned across to her left, her thin hand reaching down to the floor beneath the passenger seat. Richard shivered, feeling cold, hearing the snapping of the lock, then he walked to the front of the car and raised the wide, heavy hood. The engine looked normal. He told the woman to try the ignition. She did so and the car roared into life and then ticked over smoothly.

Richard stepped back, surprised. He glanced past the raised hood. The woman was leaning out of the window, the wind blowing her red hair.

"What did you do?" she said.

"Nothing," Richard said.

"You must have done *something*," the woman said.

"I just looked at it," Richard said. He shrugged and grinned at her, stepped forward and slammed the hood down, then walked back and leaned toward the woman, his eyes fixed on the warning lights.

"It looks okay," he said. "The battery light's out. It must have been something pretty simple, and it's obviously cured itself."

The woman smiled at him, her green eyes unfocused. "You just looked at it," she said, "and it worked. You must be a charmer."

Richard blushed and grinned shyly. "I don't think so," he said. "Anyway, it's working okay, so do I get that lift now?"

"Where are you going?"

"St. Ives."

"You've got it," she said. "Put your knapsack in the trunk. It's not locked. Let's go while the going's good."

Richard grinned with pleasure, a boyish grin, blue eyes gleaming, then he picked up his knapsack, glanced briefly at the gray church, and walked to the rear of the car, very glad it had stalled. He opened the trunk, heaved the knapsack in, closed the trunk and then returned to the woman, looking down at her upturned face. She had lit another cigarette, her lips pouting, blowing smoke, and the green of her eyes was slightly bloodshot, her gaze still unfocused.

"Okay," she said. "Get in."

"Front or rear?" Richard said.

"I don't like to talk over my shoulder, so get in beside me."

Richard walked around the car, opened the door and

climbed in, closed the door and sank back into the seat, appreciating the luxury. The dashboard was polished wood, the seats a deep maroon velours, and the woman, in her knee-length dark dress, seemed to match it all perfectly. Her red hair was long and lustrous, tumbling down around her shoulders, emphasizing the shifting green of her eyes when she glanced at him briefly. She put her foot on the clutch, the dress tightening, drawing upward, and Richard saw the shadowed outline of her thighs as she turned the ignition on.

"It's still working," she said.

Richard nodded, smiled at her, clasped his hands and then unclasped them, as the woman put her foot on the accelerator and the car started moving. The green hills, the dripping trees, the brooding clouds above the road . . . Richard kept his eyes fixed on the scenery, feeling tired and unreal.

The woman drove in a careless manner, keeping at fifty miles an hour, her right hand on the steering wheel, her left holding the cigarette, her lips pouting when she exhaled the smoke, her breasts rising and falling. Richard kept glancing sideways, attracted to her, feeling furtive, surprised that he could harbor such notions for a woman so old. Not really so old: probably in her late thirties. Nevertheless she was sexy, her legs long, her breasts firm, and Richard flushed when she suddenly stared at him with her green, slightly bloodshot eyes.

"What's your name?" she said.

"Richard . . . Richard Watson."

"A student?"

"Yes," Richard said. "I go to the Art College in Hornsey. I want to be a designer."

"Hornsey?" the woman said.

"London," Richard said.

"Ah, yes," the woman said. "North London. I'm not keen on the area."

She drove in silence for another minute, breathing deeply, inhaling smoke, and Richard shifted uneasily in his seat, trying to keep his eyes off her.

"A designer," she said finally. "What kind of designer?"

"Magazines," Richard said. "That kind of thing. At least that's what I'll start at."

The woman glanced at him and smiled, blinked her green eyes, coughed a little. Richard glanced down to see her silken legs tapering into the high-heeled shoes.

"Why are you going to St. Ives?" she asked.

"Just a holiday," Richard said. "A friend of mine owns a small cottage and he's letting me use it."

The woman smiled again, lips pouting, blowing smoke; the smoke swam in a haze around Richard, making him cough.

"An art student," the woman said.

"That's right," Richard said.

"All art students drink," the woman said. "At least that's what I've heard." She put her cigarette in her mouth, inhaled, blew the smoke out, held the steering wheel lightly in her other hand, the green hills whipping past her. "Well?" she said abruptly.

"What?" Richard said.

"Is it true that all art students drink?"

"I wouldn't know," Richard said.

He coughed into his fist, a bit embarrassed by her conversation, and tried not to look at the breasts thrusting out from her tight dress. The woman was obviously wealthy, a bit jaded, worldly wise, but her strange, oblique statements filled Richard with a sense of foreboding. He thought the woman might be drunk. He glanced briefly at her eyes. The woman looked drawn and very tired, but he still thought her sexy, Richard shifted uncomfortably. A guilty flush burned his cheeks. He thought of Jenny back in London, of the two weeks ahead of him, and he silently cursed his primitive lust and wondered how men survived it.

"Do *you* drink?" the woman said.

"When I can afford it," Richard said.

"Good," the woman said. "I'd rather not drink alone. You'll find a flask of gin in the glove compartment. I think we should share it."

Richard turned his head slightly, glanced at her, saw her eyes, twin pools of green flecked with red, and was convinced of her drunkenness. He turned away just as quickly, attracted to her, feeling foolish. pulled the glove compartment down and saw two flasks, one on top of the other.

"The bottom flask," the woman said. "The top one's empty. I get tired when I drive."

Richard blushed at that remark, removed the top flask, withdrew the bottom, unscrewed the cap, held the flask out to the woman, saw her shaking her head from side to side, her red hair like a flame.

"You first," she said quietly.

Richard shrugged and drank some gin, felt it burning down inside him, warming him, making his head swim, alleviating his weariness. He wiped his lips and burped a little, passed the flask to the woman; she stubbed her cigarette out, took the flask, her right hand on the steering wheel. Richard watched her drinking. The shining red hair framed her face. When she finished, she passed the flask back and put her hand on the steering wheel.

"Have another," she said.

They both drank much too fast. They passed the flask back and forth. The A30 ran past Dartmoor, through Featherford and Fowley, stretched ahead through the green hills and fields, climbing up, rolling down again. They saw little of all this, both involved in their drinking, time dissolving as the drink took command and made them feel more unreal. Richard studied the woman. He thought of Jenny back in London. This thought, with its residue of guilt, crossed his mind and then passed.

"You never saw the lightning," the woman said. "I just don't understand that."

Richard reached into his pocket, pulled out a cigarette, lit it and then glanced at the woman, wondering what she was talking about. The woman returned his gaze, her green eyes vague and bloodshot, and the car, making a smooth, rhythmic humming, rolled on through the quiet countryside.

"Where are you going?" Richard said.

"To Bodmin," the woman said. "I live in St. Nicholas. It's a very small place, very quiet . . . Without London I'd die."

Richard didn't reply. The woman seemed a bit distracted. He scratched his forehead and glanced out the window, saw the drifting clouds thinning. A pearly gray haze broke through, striations of weak light beaming down, fanning out, falling over the wet field sand, the stark, neolithic remains.

"What time is it?" the woman said.

Richard looked at his watch. "Ten to six," he said. "Around that . . . give or take a few minutes."

"You didn't see it," the woman said.

"The lightning?"

"The light. It was obviously some kind of bright light. I keep thinking about it."

Richard shivered. "There was no lightning," he said. "No thunder, no lightning—just the rain. You must have seen an aircraft."

"With lights?"

"With lights."

"In the daylight?"

"That's right." Richard shrugged and drank some gin and passed the flask to the woman, saw the skepticism clearly in her eyes and looked back at the road. "Okay," he said. "So you saw a bright light. You saw a flash—a plane reflecting the sunlight. I think that's what it was."

He sighed much too loudly. The woman's eyes turned toward him. She shrugged and put the flask to her lips, driving dangerously fast.

"No," she said. "It was too quick for that. It just came and then disappeared."

Richard shook his head wearily, feeling drunk, a bit disturbed, gazing out at the cold, descending evening, at the vast, bloody sky. The sun was sinking beyond the moors, a fiery orb, large and luminous, melting slowly, spreading out along the hills in two streams of pulsating flame.

"Not possible," Richard murmured. "Just not possible. You must have imagined it."

The woman didn't reply. Her red hair reached her breasts. The car hummed and vibrated, an abstract, seductive rhythm, the bleak hills of the moors rolling past, the road unwinding in front of them. Richard looked and was held, saw the marshlands and quarries, the neolithic stones silhouetted in that fierce, bloody sky. It was the landscape of a dream, serenely beautiful, strangely ominous, and it made Richard shiver and drop his eyes, wondering why it disturbed him.

"I think I'm drunk," he murmured.

"Already?" the woman said.

"Yes," Richard said.

"You must have been tired," the woman said. "Lie back ... try to sleep."

Richard stubbed his cigarette out, put his head back on the seat, closed his eyes and felt the drowsiness creep over him, almost embalming him. His thoughts scattered and spun, became streaming stars, dark shapes, the past and the present in one, as a shifting kaleidoscope: the cluttered rooms of the art college, a nude model in a chair, Jenny's brown eyes, the woman's flaming hair, the swirling mists over shadowed hills. He fell in and out of sleep, felt a langorous desire, saw the tight dress on the woman's shapely thighs, Jenny's darkly accusing gaze. Guilt and lust made him restless. His eyes fluttered and opened. He felt the woman's fingers at his elbow, tugging sharply, incessantly.

"There it is!" she hissed. *"Look!"*

Richard shook himself awake. The car vibrated beneath him. He glanced briefly at the woman, saw her green eyes, her red hair, saw the pink bud of her tongue between her teeth and then looked at the sky. The sun was sinking in the west, a crimson orb above the hills, the sky a molten stream of red and blue, the clouds drifting away from him. Richard looked all around him. He saw nothing unusual. He looked back at the woman, saw her bloodshot, glinting eyes, and wondered just how much she had drunk before picking him up.

"There's *what*?" he said.

The woman hissed something, shook her head and smacked the steering wheel. "Damn it," she said. "It was there! I just saw it! *That light!*"

Richard rolled his eyes mockingly. "The lightning?" he said.

"No," she snapped. "Not lightning. Something else. A streak of light. It just passed us."

"Passed us?"

"It crossed us. It flew east to west. A long streak of light. Like a tadpole. I just blinked and it disappeared."

"A meteor," Richard said.

"You think so?"

"I think so."

"Maybe you're right," the woman said. "I don't know . . . it seemed strange."

She shook her head slowly, her eyes brighter, less bloodshot, flitting from left to right in nervous movements, surveying the twilight sky. Richard stared at her, disturbed, wondering if she was hallucinating, now aware that the woman had drunk a lot and was dangerously tired. Then he looked up at the sky. He did it almost against his will. He saw drifting gray clouds, the crimson fire of the sinking sun, vaporous ribbons of mist along the hills, the lonely splendor of Bodmin Moor.

"We're in Cornwall," he said.

"You're a bright boy," the woman replied. "We've been in Cornwall for the past thirty minutes and you've finally noticed it."

Richard flushed at her sarcasm. "I'm pretty sleepy," he said. "I'm tired and the gin just knocked me out. I can hardly keep my eyes open."

The woman appeared not to have heard him. She kept looking all around her. Her green eyes were very bright, framed by flaming red hair, and she kept licking nervously at her upper lip, her tanned brow furrowed anxiously. Her tension was contagious, reaching out and touching Richard; he glanced around and saw the moors, the hills rushing past the car, rolling up and falling away into shadow, looking ancient and ominous. Richard shivered again. He suddenly felt a bit haunted. He stared directly at the sun, at that sinking ball of fire, and the light spread out and filled his whole vision and made his eyes sparkle.

"Why strange?" he said.

"Pardon?" the woman said.

"You said that the light you saw seemed strange. What did you mean by that?"

The woman's green eyes turned toward him, very bright, no longer bloodshot, took him in and then turned back to the road and blinked repeatedly, nervously.

"I don't know," she said.

"Think," Richard said. "Let's assume it wasn't a meteor or a plane. What did you *think* you saw?"

The woman took a deep breath, slowly licked her upper lip, then raised her left hand, spread her fingers and patted her glinting hair.

"It was very fast," she said. "It was very close the first time. The first time I just saw a bright flash and I thought it was lightning. The next time it was different: it was farther away. It was fast—a lot faster than a plane—and it seemed very bright. It flew from east to west. It shot across and disappeared. And it didn't really fly out of sight: it just seemed to wink out. It wasn't a plane. I know it couldn't have been a plane. It was strange. It wasn't a meteor . . . I think it was climbing."

Richard felt a bit ill. His head was light and he felt feverish. He wiped his lips with the back of his right hand, glancing vaguely around him.

"*Climbing?*" he said.

"You're always repeating what I say."

"It was faster than a plane and it was climbing? Are you sure you saw right?"

"I'm not *that* drunk," the woman said. "I think I know what I saw. That light was very bright, very fast, and the damned thing was *climbing*."

"Any noise?" Richard said.

"Not a sound," the woman said. "It just shot across and then it winked out . . . making no sound at all."

Richard shrugged and glanced around him, saw the desolate, timeless moors, dark clouds drifting over the misty hills, the sky a darkening crimson haze. There was nothing up there. The woman was probably hallucinating. She was obviously very tired, she had drunk far too much, and now she was starting to fall apart and see things that weren't there.

This thought disturbed Richard. He wanted to get out of the car. He didn't want to end up in a ditch with his head through the windshield. He decided to avoid the subject, closed his eyes and tried to sleep. He slipped in and out of consciousness, his head spinning, stomach churning, thought of Jenny back in London, of the cottage in St. Ives, of the woman's red hair and green eyes, her tongue licking her trembling lips. These visions were relentless, materializing and disappearing, giving way to streaming stars and spinning suns, to white lights in a black void. Richard shivered and muttered something. A bolt of panic lanced through him. He almost groaned and checked himself, shook his head and licked his lips, then spiraled back up through the darkness and opened his eyes again.

"What on earth . . . ?"

The woman glanced at Richard, shook her head in bewilderment, pressed her foot on the gas pedal and changed gears as the car coughed and spluttered. The engine roared and then cut out. The woman cursed and pumped the pedal. The engine spluttered again and then was silent as the car rolled downhill. She turned the ignition key, changed gears and nothing happened. The car rolled down the hill, its wheels hissing in the silence, then it stopped at the bottom of the hill and its headlights went off.

"I don't believe this. *What's wrong?*"

The woman shook her head and angrily smacked the steering wheel. She turned the ignition key once or twice and still nothing happened. Cursing, she looked at Richard. Richard shrugged and glanced around him. He saw the bloody-red sky, the gnarled silhouetted trees, a nearby circle of neolithic stones that seemed strangely ominous. Richard felt himself shivering. The silence seemed to be vibrating. He gulped and licked his lips, his heart racing inexplicably, then he turned and stared hard at the woman and imagined a roaring.

Not a roaring . . . something else . . . a strange, nerve-tingling humming. Richard blinked and saw that huge pulsating sun, the light shifting, expanding. "Oh my God!" Richard murmured. He suddenly forgot what he was doing. The sun expanded and became a white sheet that blotted out the whole sky. Richard gasped and felt fear, pushed the woman against the door, saw her hands darting up to cover her ears, the sky beyond her a silver haze.

"Jesus Christ!" Richard hissed.

It came over the nearest hill, over the neolithic stones, a fierce incorporeal luminescence that spread out and moved forward. Richard stared and was blinded, turned away, looked again, heard a loud, almost physical humming, *felt* the sound, was crushed by it. The woman shrieked and shook her head, her hair whipping around her face, bent forward, huddled up on hands and knees, trying to hide in her seat. The noise increased and the light expanded, swept across them, filled the car, and Richard gasped and felt a sudden scorching heat that made him howl and fall down.

His head touched the woman's head. The whole car started shaking. The engine roared and then cut out again and left the woman's loud sobbing. Richard retched. He felt the burning of his face, touched the woman and felt her jerk away as if stung by a whip. The vibration; the noise . . . Oh my God, it was cutting through him . . . His body trembled as his mind slipped into chaos, an intense, choking fear. What was it? Jesus Christ! Something roared and shook the car. He glanced up and saw the woman's red hair, the blinding white light beyond her. Richard felt his heart pounding. The sweat was pouring down his face. The car rocked from side to side, shrieked in protest, and then settled down again. Leaving silence . . . and fear.

Richard shivered and shook, reached out slowly, touched the woman; she recoiled and looked at him with wide eyes, still crouched low on the seat. They just stared at one another. Neither knew what to say. The interior of the car was very bright and then it suddenly darkened. Richard wiped sweat from his head, licked his lips, gasped for breath, his chest heaving, lungs scorched and sucked dry, arms and legs shaking terribly. The woman's green eyes were glazed, looking at him and through him; and then, as if by order, as if reading each other's thoughts, they both sat up and turned and looked out at that brilliant white haze.

"Oh my God!"

"Jesus Christ!"

The fear crawled up Richard's spine, took a hold, shook him viciously, left him limp and drained, a hollow shell, almost mindless with disbelief. The woman obviously felt the same, body twitching, dress soaked, her two hands rising up to her face, the fingers outspread and trembling.

They both sat there in the car, looking out, their eyes glazed, taking in the impossible dream, their senses flying away from them.

The white haze was receding. Beyond the white haze: a dark mass. The mass, that great featureless body, was blocking off the whole sky Richard stared and was hypnotized, terrified and fascinated, looking out across that field of white light to where it eclipsed the sinking sun. He couldn't believe it. He kept looking and it remained. The white haze seemed to shimmer and fade, and then he saw it more clearly.

It was hovering above the ground, about a hundred feet up, an enormous dark mass, a dark mass containing lights, sequential flashes of green, blue and orange, very bright, very fast. The lights went from left to right, illuminating the ground below. Richard gasped and saw an immense, silvery disc stretching over the whole field. It was several stories tall, three hundred feet in diameter, an enormous, kaleidoscopic apparition that rendered him speechless.

Fear and fascination; disbelief and stunned awareness: Richard felt his brain slipping and sliding into dark, swirling chaos. Was he drunk? Hallucinating? The woman's red hair: Was she real? He gasped for breath and tried to stop himself shaking, tried to keep himself sane. The woman trembled beside him, her hair falling around her shoulders. Her spine was arched and she seemed to shake in spasms and then settle down again. Richard stared past her head, saw that huge, floating mass, its colored lights flashing on and off brilliantly, illuminating the field below.

Richard sobbed and bit his lip. He looked again and saw it changing. It flared up and went dark, became one with the evening sky, then two panels of yellow light, a good three hundred feet apart, materialized to silhouette two black pupils, two bright eyes staring down at him. The woman gasped and bit her knuckles. Richard held on to his seat. The shimmering panels disappeared, the black pupils became metallic, then they flew down from that vast inky mass and headed straight for the car.

"Jesus, no!" Richard hissed.

A whipping sound; the car shook. A brief silence; a sudden humming. Richard closed his eyes and opened them again and saw the discs at both sides of him. They were miniature flying saucers, about three feet in diameter, and they circled the car slowly, first humming, then whistling, and then a beam of light shone from each one, cutting down through the darkness.

The car began to shake. Richard groaned and clenched his fists. He glanced quickly at the woman, saw her sitting up straight, and understood, rather than saw, her paralyzed fascination. Richard couldn't believe it: he felt no fear from her at all. Then a disc dropped by her window, shone a bright light on her face, and she gasped, seemed to twitch, settled down, closed her eyes and just sat there. Richard dropped down to his seat. The blade of light burned his neck. It moved away and he sat up again and saw the discs disappearing.

"It's all right," the woman whispered, opening her eyes, looking peculiar. "Don't be frightened. It's all right. It's all right."

Richard stared at her and shivered, disbelieving, wracked by fear, his breath coming in large, anguished gulps, his heart pounding, his head on fire. Against his will he looked up. The panels of light blazed in the sky. He saw the immense, much darker mass above the field, the panels of light at each end of it. Then the panels swallowed the discs, blinked out, leaving darkness; then the black mass, that enormous floating shape, started glowing and flashing.

Richard sat up and stared.

The great disc was solid, a silvery craft in a white haze, towering high and spread out across the field, flashing green, blue and orange lights. It now had shape and dimension. It had long, narrow windows. Silhouettes moved back and forth across the windows, very small, faraway. The colored lights continued flashing, illuminating the field below; the tall grass and shrubs had been flattened and scorched. Richard looked up in awe. He saw the panels at either end. They were doors and they opened up again, looking larger, more ominous. Then Richard froze with fear, put his hand out, touched the woman. He saw another two discs, silvery-gray, coming out of the panels. There were searchlights on these discs, beaming down toward the car. The discs hovered just in front of the larger craft, then flew toward Richard.

He sobbed and stared around him. He felt unreal, dislocated, stripped of every defense, crouched there on the seat, feeling naked, dispossessed from the living world. What was happening? Was it real? Where was he? *Hallucinating!* He tried to think of who he was and what he was, but then it all fell away from him. A whipping sound, a sudden wind, the car shrieking and shaking, then silence, the other discs at each side of him, their gray metal gleaming.

Richard almost stopped breathing. He couldn't believe what he was seeing. He reached out and grabbed the woman by the shoulder and she turned and stared at him. He saw the suntanned face, the red hair, the wet lips; her green eyes were staring at him and through him as if he didn't exist. Richard shivered and turned away. He saw a disc outside the car. It was about thirty-five feet wide, hovering just above the ground, and its perimeter swept up to form a dome made of something like glass. Richard stared, paralyzed. A strange creature stared back. The opaque dome distorted its features, made it look quite grotesque. The eyes were two slits, the nose seemed to be metallic, and Richard shivered with revulsion when he realized that it didn't have lips. The creature's skin was gray and wrinkled. It lifted up a clawlike hand. Richard screamed and then a beam of light hit him and made him oblivious.

Darkness. Streaming light. A sudden nausea and dread. Richard retched and shook his head and sat up and hardly looked at the woman. No point looking: she was frozen. Richard stared straight ahead. He blinked and started to scream and then stopped and just crouched back in terror.

He was still in the car. The dark night stretched around him. The mother ship, the enormous craft, was coming down and blocking out the whole view. It seemed incredible, almost magical—its very silence made it awesome: it was spread across the field right ahead, its colored lights flashing on and off. Richard licked his lips and murmured, rubbed his eyes and shook his head. The enormous craft settled down above the ground, fifty yards from the car.

Then the car started moving. It also started going wild. Richard's camera-strap snapped, the camera smashed against the dashboard, then his ball-point pen shot out of his pocket and fixed itself to the windshield. Richard couldn't believe it. The air was sucked from his lungs. The woman's bracelets suddenly shot off her wrists and also stuck to the windshield. Richard gasped and tried to breathe, felt himself jerking forward, grabbed the dashboard and pushed himself back, had to hold himself there. The car continued moving forward. Richard couldn't believe his senses. The car was silent, but it moved forward slowly toward that huge, flashing mass. Richard tried to scream again; he opened his mouth and nothing happened. He glanced at the woman, saw blind eyes, and then he looked at the smaller discs. They were at both sides of the car, hovering level with the car, each shooting a beam of light down upon it, drawing it with them. Magnetism? *Oh my God!* Quite impossible. *Jesus Christ!* Richard held himself into his seat and looked ahead and knew terror.

The enormous craft was there before him. It filled all of his vision. The colored lights flashed on and off, left to right, right to left, then they suddenly flickered off, leaving gray metal gleaming, then the metal seemed to split along the bottom and a long, thin white light emerged.

Richard sobbed and started shaking. His eyes were wide and disbelieving. He saw a huge metal door sliding up and then his senses were shattered. A glaring white light all around him. Silhouettes in the haze. The car was picked up and drawn toward the light and then surrounded on all sides. Richard drained out of himself. He let his senses fly away. He opened his mouth to scream but nothing happened, so he simply collapsed.

All white.

Everything.

CHAPTER FOUR

It is important that I remember. My time will soon be up. The plastic surgery and the pacemaker and the prosthetics have all been useful, but the liver still manages to elude us and so I must die. I remain philosophical. I have had more than most. I have lived a long time, made the dream a reality, and I cannot complain because nature still shelters its secrets.

We never conquered the liver. Perhaps we never will. Now I start to degenerate, feel the hardening of my veins, and my memory is not what it was and too often betrays me. No matter: it is done; we cannot be stopped now. The sun glitters off the ice as I write, and the ice is the new world.

It is important to remember. Some fragments, if nothing else. It was all so long ago, so far away, and now it seems like a dream. My parents: not important. We are blessed and cursed by birth. Two very ordinary people heading nowhere, myself growing under them.

I detested my childhood. That much I do remember. Long days in the Midwest, clouds of dust over the flatlands, my father and mother in the fields, bending over their crops. They were simple, decent people. I can hardly remember them. They talked little and they worked very hard and received scant reward. Detested it. Yes. The days stretched out forever. As a boy, still a child, how young I don't remember, I spent hours gazing up at the stars and wondering how I could get there.

I've never understood emotions. An aberration of the weak. I am thinking of what they call "love" and its attendant illusions. They would call me a genius. By their terms they must be right. From the beginning. (I remember this well) I was always obsessed. An emotion of a different sort. Not a need for human warmth. I saw humans in biological terms and thought the world a laboratory. The obsession was with knowing. It was all within the mind. Anything outside the mind—the need for love, for material gain—was no more than a degrading manifestation of our primitive origins. What matters in Man is mind. I have always believed that. Even then, as a child, about ten years old I think, I believed that (or felt it) and lived it and would not let it go.

They would call me a genius. I would say "integrated." My mind and emotions were fused to perform in calm harmony. No weakness. No digressions. My flesh never defeated me. Even later, as a young man, in the offensive throes of puberty, I would hold my yellow semen in my hand and try to sniff out its properties. The vas deferens and the seminal vesicles, the bulbo-urethral and prostate glands: my ejaculations were examined biologically and found to be normal. I thus conquered such distractions. I took the semen on my tongue. Various liquids and sperm, two hundred million spermatozoa; orgasm thus became a form of research and lost its great mystery.

Hard to believe it now. All so very long ago. My parents ignorant with a Bible on the table, my head in the stars. The small farm was a prison. My decent parents were viewed as wardens. A teenager, isolated, my head bursting at the seams, the lack of books, of the means of education, drove me close to insane. I knew I was exceptional. I felt trapped by circumstances. Two or three times I ran away from home. but was always brought back. So, I detested it. I just had to get away. This much I remember about my childhood: I grew up in Iowa.

Such a long time ago. The late 1800s. I remained a prisoner by lieu of my background and suffered accordingly. A genius, by their terms. Had to be, even then. For my birthday I received a microscope and then exam-

ined my own sperm. Fourteen? Fifteen? I can't remember the age. In my room I took my penis in my hand and let the semen stain slides. The mystery of life was in biology. Ejaculation was mere phenomena. I thus reduced my shifting yearnings and dreams to their most basic nature. The human body was just a vessel. Without the mind it was superfluous. I learned early, and had no cause to doubt, that the mind took precedence.

Science. That is all. The pursuit of knowledge was all that mattered. Even then, growing up in Iowa, I had no other yearnings. The death of my mother pleased me. There was nothing personal in it. A good woman, she died as people do, and that gave me release. My father sold the farm. He took a job in Massachusetts. A small place, I don't remember the name, quite close to Worcester. Thus was I set free. Universities and libraries. My mind was filled with energy and light and I crammed it with knowledge. The Worcester Polytechnic Institute. I wonder what they called it then. I remember that I came alive there and realized my potential.

What year? Does it matter? I think 1888. Then the Massachusetts Institute of Technology and the thrill of pure logic. I was an outstanding student. I was not very popular. The thrill was in logic, but the nightmare was in people: my genius isolated me completely from most of the students.

I don't remember caring much. I don't think I cared at all. (Goddard would later suffer the same, and he, too, was a genius.) The behavior of fluids at MIT. Wind pressure on surfaces. The dream of flight was what kept me alive and made the world seem more bearable. I rarely socialized. I only stopped for food and sleep. The dream of flight was my dream, aerodynamics my taskmaster, and my genius drove me forward relentlessly and would not let me rest.

Inhuman? I wonder. I have often thought about it. Not then, but later, when I succeeded, when the skies shed their secrets. Yes, only then. I remember thinking about it then. Repulsed by abstract emotions, by the human need for self-esteem, by what was known as love and affection, I lived without women.

I think I tried once. There are vague recollections. Not inhuman, I must have been concerned that they would see I was different. A girl with dark hair. Perhaps a redhead or a blonde. Spreadeagled, their flesh white as snow, their soft words unbearable. I tried, but I failed. I saw their bodies as meat. The act of love was as primitive and functional as eating or shitting. I do not recall passion. My rhythmic thrusting was demeaning. My partners' groanings drove me back into myself and made me think scientifically. I surveyed my probing penis. The parting vulva held no charms. Their heaving bodies and my downward thrusting loins lacked aesthetic refinement. The caves are just behind us: this one thought I remember. Perhaps I thought of the spermatozoa in the womb and wondered how to control them. So much for the act of love. My mind would not let me succumb. I gave up and returned to masturbation of a functional kind. This act was not for pleasure. The point was to kill the need. And my hand, which touched my flesh without guilt, was just a means to this end.

As for love: a mere illusion. Love is nature's slyest trick. The emotion called love is but a tool in nature's great building plan. Love encourages procreation. It protects the helpless young. Its true purpose is not to exalt us but to make us continue. Thus did I view it. I reduced it to biology. Love was no more than the semen in my palm, but it could be destructive. Men lived their lives for love. This made them weaker men. The need for love and admiration (for self-effacement and power) was the need that made them abuse their full potential and remain close to primitive.

The possibility was intolerable. I never wanted to let it happen. My genius, the ruthless brilliance of my mind, would not let me accept it. Thus I lived for my studies. I never let my flesh defeat me. My sexual needs were appeased by my own hands or by whores; my body's hungers were not confused with love and could not then distract me. No, I wasn't popular. The other students thought me strange. I think now of that time, of the bliss of isolation, and realize that my devotion to my mind made me someone unique.

My fondest memories are not of people. My fiercest pleasures all came from facts. Angles of wind attack, lift, drag and airspeed: the experiments with the wind tunnel in the basement of Eng A, the revelations of the vane anemometer, the Lawrence Hargraves experimental reports, Sir Hiram Maxim and his engines and propellers, my mind glowing, expanding. The dream took root then. I wanted the conquest of all knowledge. I had a dream of a society devoid of conflict and dissension, a society subordinated to science and its ultimate truths. I had that dream and lived it. I devoted my whole life to it. And now, looking out at the glittering ice caps, I feel great contentment.

I never accepted the impossible. I refused to recognize it. I learned with a speed that was thought to be abnormal, living only for the lectures. for the libraries and wind tunnel, my hands black with oil, my eyes red from too much reading, breaking down and analyzing my masters, then racing ahead of them.

My father died in that time. I can't remember the funeral. A kind man, he had lived an aimless life and the lesson was clear to me. Nothing mattered but the mind. Human emotions were mere distractions. What mattered was the grandeur of science and where it might lead us. And so I continued studying. My genius left me no choice. Then Sibley College, Cornell University, in Ithaca, New York.

All things were possible there. More than most of the students knew. I do not remember faces, but I do remember names: Rolla Clinton Carpenter, Octave Chanute, Oliver Shantz and Aldred Henry Eldridge and quite a few others. Machine design and construction, experimental engineering, electrical and mechanical engineering and aerodynamics. These courses were in their infancy, were the products of the New Age. It was an age of scientific innovation and grand aspirations. A Bachelor of Science in Aeronautics. I remember that from Sibley. I think I obtained it in 1894, but I cannot be sure of that.

How stupid people are. How stupid they always were. The only emotion I can still entertain is that of contempt. For what they did to me. For what they later did to Goddard. They tried to use us and cast us aside and then con-

trol our creations. I think of the businessmen. I also think of politicians. Commerce walks hand in hand with politics, and both are corrupt. Man's purpose is to build upon his past and thus conquer the unknown. All other aspirations are pointless; they are only of the moment. This is the dream of science. It is logic, not emotion. It is a logic that is not shared by businessmen or politicians—nor by the mass of normal men who mostly live without purpose. Such men have no real logic. They are moved by base hungers. They are blinkered and retain a narrow view that will never be broadened. They think only of the present. Their future is here and now. They take genius and fear it and use it and then cast it out. I did not know this soon enough.

Within the ice is the new world. Beyond it is the old. I look beyond the glinting plateaus and think of where I came from.

What an age it was then! So magnificent, so blind. An age of flowering genius, of corrupt commerce and politics; an age of the most insoluble contradictions, of builders and wreckers. I did not know soon enough. They financed me and used me. They took my enthusiasm and genius and then tried to pervert it. Yet what if I had known? Out of college, a B.S. in Aeronautics, I had to take whatever they offered me.

Finance. Equipment. The world opened up to me. The secret hangars in the wilds of Illinois formed my bridge to the future. Myself and some others. The very cream of young scientists. Sworn to secrecy, we worked night and day and made miracles commonplace. We tolerated the businessmen. We rarely thought of the politicians. With the innocence of all passionate dreamers, we just worked for our pleasure. What year was that? I think it was 1895. A full year before Langley's first successful test flights, we had already surpassed the airships and were moving toward greater things.

The work never ceased. The secrecy was total. More hangars in Iowa, in the Gulf of Mexico, yet another in a place near Fort Worth, all producing components. My first lesson in secrecy: a wide spreading of the work force. Who would know in Iowa or New Mexico or Fort Worth *what the individual parts they were making would ultimately form? Thus we moved forward. Thus did I create them. The skies opened up and gave me their secrets and the dreams became real.*

The second lesson in secrecy: that men will not believe their eyes. Or that men, if they do believe their eyes, will be ridiculed for it. We flew all across the country. The great wings and rotors glinted. They were very primitive flying machines, but they must have looked awesome. And so we could land. Our crude creations needed water. And like all young men who feel they are conquerors, our mood was ebullient. We played jokes on those who saw us, told the truth and then told lies, and later, when we read the newspapers, we knew the ruse had succeeded.

Such a secret cannot be kept. Nevertheless, it can be protected. To protect a secret you must give away part of it and turn it into a rumor. We mixed half-truths with lies. Speculation did the rest. Who believes what they now see in the skies and can say so with ease? The world's governments understand this. It is a tactic they learned from me. We flew across the length and breadth of America and were never discovered.

All else was superfluous. It was fodder for the masses. Langley's flying machines, the Wright brothers' manned flight, the later flights of Wilbur Smith and Louis Bleriot—all were publicized trifles. Such events were mere distractions. The real progress was made in secret. By 1904 we had crossed the Pacific, and our lights, which were seen by the Navy, were called natural phenomena. Such descriptions were reassuring. I had no desire for glory. My one wish was to continue my life's work without interruptions.

How stupid they are. How stupid they always were. They now see us in the skies and close their eyes and still refuse to believe it. That's why we are winning. That's why we could never lose. They can never accept what is possible—but for us, all things are.

CHAPTER FIVE

Epstein stood quietly before the open door, hesitant, his heart beating uncomfortably, feeling nervous and childish. He was nervous because the door was open, because the house was in darkness, because Irving Jacob's death and his own failing health had reminded him of life's callous betrayals, its indiscriminate brutality. Now, in the darkness, in the silence of Camelback Hill, preparing to step inside and loathing the thought of doing so, he trembled with a youngster's baseless fear and was ashamed of himself . . . Irving's death and Mary's grief; his own mortality and passing time: he grew old and his childhood returned with all its haunting uncertainties . . . Was it suicide? Had he been murdered? Why was Mary's door wide open? Dr. Epstein, stoop-shouldered and disconsolate, felt close to ridiculous.

Too melodramatic for a scientist. Perhaps the chief of police had been right. Epstein stood on the porch and looked up and saw the sweeping night sky. The stars glittered above the clouds, the clouds wispy and dark, drifting languidly, serene and mysterious, the black sky over all. It was quiet up there. Empty. Epstein shivered and dropped his eyes. He saw his shadow trailing out from his feet, his grotesque, faceless second half. We are not what we appear. We live and die in ignorance. Epstein felt a deep grief, an aching loss, then he knocked on the open door.

"Mary? Are you in there?"

There was no reply. The darkness led into silence. Epstein shivered and then stepped inside, wondering what he would find there. The hall led past closed doors, through the kitchen, into the living room; he saw the back of Mary's head above a chair, the chair facing the garden. Mary's head was very still, her hair dark and turning gray, and Epstein stood there, transfixed, seeing moonlight in the garden, then coughed and slowly whispered Mary's name, the pain twisting inside him.

"Frederick?"

"Yes."

"I thought you would come."

"Is that why you left the door open?"

"Yes."

"That was dangerous."

Mary chuckled sardonically, still sitting in the chair, facing the moonlight that fell on the garden beyond the glass doors. Perhaps it was the grief, a release from her shock; nevertheless the chuckle cut through the silence and made Epstein wince. He had come prepared for tears, for hysteria or vicious rage, but now, in the presence of that ghostly chuckling, he felt simply bewildered.

"Dangerous?" she said bitterly. "You think an open door is dangerous? Irving kept the doors closed all the time—but then he went for a drive. What's a closed door these days?"

Moonlight fell on the chair, glinting off her gray-black hair, the back of the chair bisecting her neck, the space around her all dark. Epstein coughed into his fist, feeling slightly absurd, then he nodded, a silent gesture of agreement, and sighed and sat down.

"You saw him?"

"Yes, I saw him." Epstein sniffed and rubbed his beard. He was staring at the back of Mary's head, at the dark, silent room. "He's been brought into Phoenix."

Mary sat forward and sobbed, covering her face with her hands, bent over in the chair, in the moonlight, trying to stifle the weeping. Epstein watched her, feeling helpless, filled with longing and grief, remembering better days, her smiling face, before the work became dangerous.

"*Please*, Mary," he said.

"It's all right. I'm all right." She sat up and wiped her eyes with one hand. "Oh, my God, what a day it's been."

"If I can do anything . . . *anything*."

"You can't do anything. He's dead."

"I just thought . . ."

"There's nothing to think. He's dead. It's all over."

She was sitting up straight again, staring into the moonlit garden, a clenched fist shoved into her mouth, lightly tapping her teeth. Then she sighed and stood up, went to the window and walked back, turned her chair around and shook her head sadly and sat down facing Epstein. The moonlight reached out to her face, illuminating her tear-washed eyes. She was in her middle forties but her face retained its beauty, an elegant mask now ravaged by loss, the eyes brown, very large. Epstein sat there before her, feeling crushed and defeated, his love for her and Irving boiling up and turning rancid with guilt.

"Here in Phoenix," she said softly.

"Yes," he said. "The autopsy."

"And presumably they'll ring me tomorrow?"

"Yes," he said. ". . . the arrangements."

She nodded and sighed, her gaze roaming around the room, her white hands twitching restlessly in her lap, trying to hold on to something.

"What did you come here for?" she said.

"You knew I'd come, Mary."

"To offer your condolences?"

"Yes."

"And to ask me some questions."

It was a mean, honest statement, making Epstein recoil, flushing, the guilt rushing through him as he stared at her grim face.

"Yes," he said. "I can't help that."

Mary nodded, smiling bitterly. "You just never give up," she said. "*All* of you—you just can't give up no matter what happens. I suppose I should accept it—the good wife supporting the cause—but I can't. And now Irving is dead. To hell with your institute."

"I have to know, Mary."

"You have to know what? That my husband was driven

mad by his work and now he's found peace at last? There's your answer. Go home with it."

"No," Epstein said. "I don't think that's the answer."

"Yes it is," she said. "It's the only answer available."

"I don't think it was suicide," Epstein said. "I feel I should tell you that."

The anger was quick to come, flashing out of her brown eyes, her head shaking from side to side in denial as she climbed to her feet. She looked down at him, this old man, this professor who felt his age, and her lips, a tight line below the pert nose, spat out all her grief.

"Damn you!" she snapped. "Damn you and your pride! It's not that you don't believe it—it's that you *can't* . . . because you need your obsession. My husband committed suicide. Your work drove him half crazy. He couldn't sleep, he couldn't eat, he started to ignore his whole family, and it happened because of your damned obsession, your belief in conspiracies. Of *course* he didn't kill himself! Of course it *had* to be murder! You've been at this game for twenty-five years, so now it has to be *something*!"

"Please, Mary . . . that's unfair."

She shook her head and turned away, went to the windows and came back, started walking to and fro in agitation, her hands slapping her thighs.

"He was a scientist," she said. "He wasn't cut out to be a detective. He studied physics at Berkeley, designed nuclear reactors, worked for NASA and the American Nuclear Society, was written up in *Who's Who*. My husband was a fine man—an intelligent and decent man—then you involved him in your UFOs, in your speculations and intrigues, and he fell for it and became obsessed with it and paid the full price. Do you know what it was like watching him? Seeing him crack and fall apart? Can you possibly understand what it's like to see your husband go down that way?"

"He was frightened," Epstein said.

"Damn right, he was frightened. You and your bloody institute, your associates, you all frightened him to death."

"It wasn't us," Epstein said.

"It was you," Mary said. She stopped walking and just stood there, looking down at him, her brown eyes bright with tears.

"Damn you," she said.

Epstein had to look away, his gaze roaming around the dark room, taking in the familiar paintings, the furniture and ornaments, all the items he had seen through the years that he had visited this place. Those days were gone now. They had gone with Irving's death. It could never possibly be the same again—not for him, not for Mary. Epstein shivered with grief and rage that matched the woman's, and he wanted to reach out and console her, to soothe both their wounds.

"I saw it coming," Mary said. "It had been coming a long time. He wasn't capable of fighting his old friends, and it tore him apart. I saw it back in 1968, during that House Science and Astronautics Committee Symposium, when he stood up and stated that he had come over to your side and now believed in the existence of the UFOs. He should never have done that."

Epstein didn't reply. There was nothing he could say. He simply had to let her talk it out, no matter how much it hurt him. Knowing this he just sat there, watching her carefully with his tired eyes, as she walked to and fro across the room, from the darkness to moonlight.

"It was after that," she said. "That was when it began. He believed in it all, gave lectures and interviews, and then, when he started losing his credibility, he simply *had* to believe it. Why not indeed? It was all he had left. First thing he was a senior physicist at the University of Arizona, next thing he was a member of your institute, another crank chasing UFOs . . . You think I'm being cruel? Most perceptive. Quite correct. He fell in with a bunch of scientific quacks, and was ridiculed for it."

"You don't believe that," Epstein said.

"Yes, damn you, I believe it. Irving was a physicist, a man of some authority, and then, when he championed your cause, he lost everything . . . *everything!*" She almost choked on the last word, actually had to catch her breath, then she blinked her eyes rapidly, looking dazed, and slumped into her chair. "Jesus Christ, I feel ill," she said.

Epstein flinched when she sobbed again, felt himself recoil with shame, averting his gaze when she reached for her handkerchief and dabbed at her eyes. He thought briefly of Irving, of his passion for the truth, of how that passion had led him inexorably into the UFO controversy. Epstein hadn't seduced him. Irving had joined of his own accord. And then, as it had happened to so many, something had happened to Irving . . . Epstein thought about it briefly, tried to cast it from his mind, and looked up, feeling pained and confused, to see Mary's dark eyes.

"It was you," Mary said. "I don't want you to forget that. If it hadn't been for you and your institute, he would still be alive."

She burst into tears again, crouching over in the chair, moonlight falling on the back of her head as she shook it from side to side. The sobs were loud and wracked, filled with pain and despair, and she pressed both her hands to her face as if to blot out the truth. Epstein sat there saying nothing, too stricken to offer sympathy, deeply wounded by what she had said, wondering how he could live with it. Then she sobbed even louder, her body shaking in a fever, and he stood up and went to her chair, bent down to her, embraced her.

"Oh God!" she sobbed brokenly. "It's a lie! It's all a lie! It's tearing me apart and I can't take it and I have to strike out! It wasn't you—I know it wasn't you . . . *God, it's all such a mess!*" She pressed her face against his thigh, her tears flowing, head shaking, holding on to him as if he might depart and leave her with nothing. Then she looked directly at him, her face white and distraught, and he saw the brown, luminous eyes, wild with incomprehension. "What was it?" she sobbed. "How did it happen? Was it me? *Was it me?*"

He got down on his knees beside her, held her face in his hands, shook her head from side to side, murmuring words he would not recall. Eventually she calmed a little, wiped her eyes, gave a sigh, sinking slowly back into the chair, staring up at the ceiling.

"No," Epstein said. "It wasn't you. It had nothing to do with you."

"It was suicide," she whispered.

"It wasn't suicide," Epstein said. "Irving wasn't the type to commit suicide. We both know that's a fact."

"Then what . . . ?" She shook her head, "I just don't understand . . . Why on earth . . . ? Who would want to . . . ?" She shook her head again, bit her lip. *"I just don't understand!"*

Epstein sighed and stood up, disappeared into the darkness, returned with two glasses of bourbon and handed her one of them. She took it gratefully and drank it down, gasped for breath, put her head back, stared up at him as if not quite awake, moonlight touching her white face. Epstein sipped at his own drink, looking thoughtful, undecided, then he sat in his chair and stared at her, and spoke quietly, convincingly.

"Listen to me," he said. "I didn't encourage Irving to join the institute; he wrote to me on his own and suggested we work together. In fact, Irving had been privately interested in the UFOs from about 1955, and the 1965 wave had merely strengthened his growing conviction that the phenomenon had definite scientific importance. Irving never officially joined the institute; his only connection was that he would trade information with us and help us by proxy with his specialized knowledge. It *is* true that he visited us in Washington quite a few times, and that by the time he had gone through our files he had become convinced of the reality of the phenomenon. But I repeat: Irving did all this on his own—not because we encouraged him."

Mary studied him carefully, her brown eyes in the moonlight, the remainder of her face in the shadows, darkness swimming around her. She seemed a lot calmer now, more thoughtful and alert, and she studied Epstein's face as if deciding whether to talk or keep silent. The tension between them was uneasy, filled with doubt and recrimination, but eventually she sighed and leaned forward and gave him her glass.

"I need another," she said.

Epstein nodded and stood up, disappeared into the darkness, returned with two glasses of bourbon and handed her one of them. She didn't say anything, simply turned the glass around, watched the moonlight flashing on and off it like tumbling diamonds. Epstein sighed and sat down, crossed his legs, sipped his drink, determined not to push her too far, to let her take her own time. Finally she sipped her bourbon, licked her moist upper lip, then slowly sank back into her chair, her face lost in the shadows.

"All right," she said. "What do you want to know?"

"I want to know what frightened Irving," Epstein said. "Or what you *think* might have frightened him."

Mary shook her head and sighed. "God," she said. "I don't know. At least I'm not very sure. It just seems too ridiculous."

"Ridiculous?"

"Yes, ridiculous." She sighed again, almost mockingly. "He never really told me what frightened him. I can only make guesses."

She sat forward in her chair, her elbows resting on her knees, the moonlight falling over her brown eyes, glinting off the small bourbon glass.

"You've heard of Dr. James E. McDonald?"

"Of course," Epstein said.

"Then you'll know that McDonald was once at the University of Arizona, senior physicist in the Department of Atmospheric Sciences and a leading proponent of the extraterrestrial hypothesis."

"Yes," Epstein said. "It's common knowledge."

"Okay. Now Irving certainly didn't agree with all of McDonald's theories, but he *did* respect McDonald enormously for his courage in putting forward his unpopular opinions. Indeed, if anyone may be said to have influenced Irving, McDonald would have to be that man."

"So?"

Mary shrugged. "Back in 1967, when the Condon Committee was being set up, McDonald was on a visit to the Wright-Patterson Air Force Base in Dayton, Ohio, when he accidentally saw the classified version of the 1953 Robertson Panel report. McDonald was shocked to discover that the CIA had had a large hand in that report, and that the classified version of the report, apart from deliberately ignoring some of the most positive UFO sightings, had secretly recommended what amounted to a national brainwashing program and a complete cover-up of official UFO investigations. So, in early 1967, after seeing the classified version of this report, McDonald linked the Air Force's notorious secrecy policies to the CIA and, on the same day that the Air Force announced the establishment of the Condon Committee, made this controversial information public. Naturally, Irving—who had widespread connections with the scientific community and the media—helped him in this. And from that day on, both he and McDonald became loudly vocal critics of the Air Force *and* the CIA."

"Are you trying to tell me that Irving was frightened of the CIA?"

Mary shrugged again, sighed loudly, gazed around her, the bourbon glass resting on one palm, her other hand lightly stroking it.

"I don't know," she said. "I think he was certainly worried about it. I think that by this time he was beginning to understand that you couldn't wade too deep in those waters. You know, McDonald was in the forefront of all this, and Irving was well aware of what was happening to McDonald. McDonald attacked the Air Force and the CIA relentlessly, and by 1969 the word was out that these organizations wanted to silence him. Whether this was true or not, it was certainly quite obvious that McDonald was not having an easy time. The major defenders of the Air Force's attitudes toward UFOs were Harvard astronomer and author Donald H. Menzel, and Philip Klass, avionics editor of *Aviation Week*. Menzel had repeatedly explained most of the sightings—including the famous 1952 Washington sightings—as reflections, mirages, ice crystals floating in clouds, or the results of refraction and temperature inversion. On the other hand, Klass, a man fervently opposed to the extraterrestrial hypothesis and particularly opposed to McDonald, continually tried to ridicule McDonald and put forward his own theory that all UFO sightings were due to coronal discharges in the atmosphere. Anyway, McDonald tore these theories to shreds and made himself a couple more enemies. According to McDonald, Klass tried to ruin him by telling the Office of Naval Research that he. McDonald, had used Navy funds on a trip to Australia to study UFOs. This caused a hell of a scandal, and led to the Navy sending an auditor to look at McDonald's contract. The Navy found nothing to pin on McDonald, but it still caused McDonald embarrassment and gave him a lot of problems with the university administration. Then, as McDonald continued to expose Air Force and CIA shenanigans, things grew progressively worse for him. More and more professional ridicule was heaped on him until, in 1971, the House Committee on Appropriations called him to testify about the SST supersonic transport plane, during which testimony he was constantly mocked as the man who saw little green men flying around in the sky. McDonald's work on the SST was his last project. In June 1971, at the age of fifty-one, McDonald drove himself into the desert and shot himself in the head—exactly like Irving."

Mary suddenly shivered and shook her head from side to side, a clenched fist going to her mouth as if to stifle a sob. She took a deep breath and sank back, her face disappearing in darkness, then the glass of bourbon glinted in the moonlight as she had a stiff drink. There was silence for a long time. A clock ticked on the wall. Epstein hadn't heard the ticking before and it made him feel strange.

"Do you think there's a connection?" he said.

"I don't know," Mary said. "It just seems too ridiculous. But I do know that *Irving* thought about it . . . and it started to frighten him."

"Why?"

"Oh . . . various things." The glass came down from her lips, rested lightly on one knee, her fingers curving lightly around it, her wedding ring glinting. "You know, some strange things have happened to a lot of people involved in UFOs—accidents, suicides, the loss of good careers—and Irving started taking an interest in such cases. This was shortly after Dr. McDonald's suicide—and also after Irving had started drinking."

"The drinking was bad?"

"Yes, *very* bad," she said. "I'd never seen him drinking before, but then he started to drown in it." She shivered again, shook her head in a dreamy manner, raised her glass to her lips and had a drink, sighing deeply, forlornly. "Irving was particularly fascinated by the career of Captain Edward Ruppelt, who headed the Air Force's UFO investigations from 1951 to 1953. According to Irving, Ruppelt was the best man the Air Force ever used during their twenty years of UFO investigations; however, during his three years as head of Project Blue Book, Ruppelt became more and more convinced that the UFOs were real and of extraterrestrial origin, and that the Air Force was antagonistic to such a hypothesis. According to Irving, this was why, when the Robertson Panel submitted its formal conclusions to the CIA, the Pentagon and the higher echelons of the Air Force, the CIA refused to give a copy to Ruppelt and his staff. And from this point on, Ruppelt, who was critical of the whole Robertson Panel, found the ground being cut from under his feet. Apparently Ruppelt had been determined to mount a full-scale UFO investigation but faced a lot of opposition from the Pentagon, until, by mid-1953, the Blue Book staff had been stripped down to a total of three people: Ruppelt and two assistants. Consequently, Ruppelt left Blue Book permanently in August of that year, went to work as a research engineer for the Northrop Aircraft Company, and also wrote his famous book on UFOs."

"The Report on Unidentified Flying Objects."

"Right. Now what bothered Irving about this case was the fact that Ruppelt's book was a forthright attack on the Air Force's handling of the UFO phenomenon and a plea for a more honest and intensive investigation of it. Obviously Ruppelt was a believer . . . but then, in 1959, three years after he had first published his book, Ruppelt revised it, totally reversed his previous stand, and stated in the new edition that UFOs as a unique phenomenon did not exist. One year later he died of a heart attack."

Mary finished off her bourbon, placed the glass on the floor, and leaned forward until her face was in the moonlight, her brown eyes large and misty.

"Irving was bothered by the case," she said. "He couldn't understand Ruppelt's reversal. He investigated the case thoroughly, interviewed a lot of people, but couldn't really come up with anything definite. There was the possibility that Ruppelt had just become fed up with it, with the constant controversy that surrounded the subject, with the media and the crackpots who hounded him day in and day out. A possibility. A thin one. Certainly Irving could never accept this as an answer, and he never stopped pondering the riddle. Possibly because of this he became involved with a similar case, that of Dr. Morris K. Jessup, the noted astronomer and selenographer."

"I thought *he* was a crackpot," Epstein said.

"Well, he may or may not have been. In his defense, it's worth noting that he was a teacher of astronomy and mathematics at the University of Michigan and a researcher whose work led to the discovery of thousands of binary stars. In short, Jessup was an astronomer of considerable repute—until he became obsessed with the UFOs. Apparently, once that started, his ideas became a little crazier, more speculative and bizzare, some derivative but some strikingly original. As Irving frequently said, this wasn't all that unusual: a lot of people who developed an interest in UFOs tended to turn pretty strange. Anyway . . . Irving was interested in Jessup because Jessup had been conducting a lot of investigations into possible Naval experiments with field forces that could temporarily dematerialize matter or somehow make it invisible. While this sounded pretty crazy to me—a sort of Flash Gordon fantasy—it interested Irving in the sense that he often felt that the UFOs might work on just such a principle. So . . . Dr. Jessup had been investigating what had been known in books, magazines and various scientific journals as the Philadelphia Experiment. Allegedly, during 1943, the United States Navy had conducted a series of tests at the Philadelphia Navy Yard, at Norfolk-Newport News, Virginia, and at sea to the north of the Bermuda Triangle. Reportedly the experiment was at least partially successful, the ship used being the U.S.S. *Eldridge,* and its disappearance allegedly being seen from the decks of the Liberty ship S.S. *Andrew* and a cargo ship, S.S. *Malay*. Apparently, after disappearing, the ship reappeared at its berth at Norfolk, then mysteriously turned up at its original dock in the Philadelphia Navy Yard. And according to other unsubstantiated reports, some of the crew died, many had to be hospitalized and more than a few had gone mad . . . As I said, Irving was interested in this because he thought that the seemingly incredible materialization and dematerialization of UFOs might somehow be based on unusual, controlled magnetic conditions in which the attraction between molecules could be altered temporarily to cause the transmutation or transference of matter."

"A sort of space-time machine."

"Exactly. Matter simply dematerializes and materializes elsewhere—hey presto! space and time don't exist."

Epstein raised his eyebrows. "Go on," he said.

"Okay. I know. It sounds crazy. Anyway, Irving followed this up and discovered that in 1959, the same year Ruppelt performed his abrupt about-face with the revised edition of his book, Jessup informed Dr. J. Manson Valentine—currently curator honoris of the Museum of Science of Miami and research associate of the Bishop Museum of Honolulu—that he had reached some definite conclusions regarding the Philadelphia Experiment and wanted to show Valentine his manuscript. Valentine says that he arranged for Jessup to come for dinner on the evening of April 20 that year—but Jessup never made it that far. According to the Miami police, Jessup, some time before 6:30 that evening, drove his car to Matheson's Hammock in Dade County, Miami, and committed suicide by attaching a hose to the exhaust of his car and running the hose inside the vehicle."

"Was the manuscript found in the car?"

"According to the Miami police report, no."

Mary rubbed at her forehead and swept the hair from her eyes, then she stood up and visibly shivered and started pacing the room. Epstein watched her, entranced. She was lovely, and she was also a stranger to him, a hazy figure in the moonlight.

"It made Irving worse," she said. "He started to drink

even more. He wouldn't talk about it unless he was drunk, and then he seemed incoherent. Incoherence or craziness? I swear to God, I don't know. He was obsessed by the idea that important UFOlogists were marked men, that they always ended up in a bad way: either crazy or dead. He pointed out to me that Ruppelt had had a lot of problems during his final few years and that those problems might have contributed to his heart attack. He reminded me constantly about McDonald's last few years, about the Air Force's fear of him, about his low standing in the eyes of the CIA and the ridicule heaped upon him by his fellow scientists. Then, on June 12, 1972, precisely one year after McDonald's suicide, another proponent of the UFO phenomenon, scientist and inventor Rene Hardy, was found dead, apparently a suicide by a bullet—and this made Irving paranoid."

She stopped pacing and stared around her, eyes blinking, slightly vague, then she bent down and picked up her glass and disappeared in the darkness. Epstein listened to the bourbon pouring, felt the tension within himself, wondered how they had all come to this, to this fear and confusion. Then Mary returned, the glass already at her lips, and she drank and gazed around her and sat down, her legs crossed, her hands shaking.

"You want to know what frightened *me*?" she said. "Well, I'll tell you . . . And it's every bit as crazy as the rest of it."

She had another drink, licked her lips, put her head back, her brown eyes gazing up at the ceiling, looking through it, beyond it.

"Irving had problems sleeping. He started pacing the house each night. He would get up and walk around his study, muttering under his breath. He often looked out the windows. He always looked up at the sky. He started thinking They were coming to get him . . . I never found out who *They* were. He'd been working on something special. He was very secretive about it. The more he worked on it, the more he grew frightened, the less he could sleep. Then one night he was really drunk. I drank with him and we talked. I asked him what it was that had him scared, and he attempted to tell me. It wasn't easy for him. The drink had made him incoherent. He started babbling about his colleagues, about how the ridicule had increased; he said the university was putting pressure on him and he might have to leave. Naturally I was shocked. God knows, I was shocked. Then he said that he thought he was being followed, that he just had this feeling."

Mary shook her head and sighed. She seemed remote and somehow lost. She gazed at Epstein and he saw her brown eyes, the pain buried behind them.

"There are a lot of stories," she said, "about mysterious men who often contact people investigating UFOs. Since most of these stories come from the lunatic fringe, they are rarely given serious attention. Nevertheless, Irving was worried about them. He told me that in 1955, during that famous UFO flap, Dr. Jessup had been called in for an interview at the ONR—the Office of Naval Research in Washington, D.C. There it was explained to him that one of his books had been mailed to the Chief of ONR, Admiral F. N. Furth, and had subsequently been examined by both the ONR Special Projects Office and the Aeronautics Projects Office. Precisely what was then said between the ONR and Dr. Jessup remains unclear, but according to Irving, Jessup started having severe personal problems from then on, and those problems led directly to his suicide . . . Crazy, yes? Well, *I* thought it was crazy. No matter: the story fascinated Irving and fitted in with his theories."

She had another drink. The clock ticked on the wall. Epstein thought of what the police chief had said . . . something about melodrama.

"Irving thought he was being followed by three men," Mary said. "He had seen them in a car, outside the house, outside his office, and he felt that they were coming to get him and take him away. Of course I didn't believe a word of it. I put it down to his illness. I just thought that all these stories about mysterious, nameless visitors had sunk into his subconscious and mixed in with his increasing paranoia. But Irving was adamant. He couldn't let the subject go. He talked about how a lot of the UFOs were described as being surrounded by a glowing, plasmalike

cloud; about how the U.S.S. *Eldridge* had also been described as disappearing within a luminous green cloud;
about how the Bermuda Triangle and the Devil's Jaw are
on approximately the same line of longitude and how
many of the planes and ships that were lost in those
areas were often described as disappearing in similar
clouds. Irving thought there was a connection. He thought
Jessup had found the connection. He thought that the
disappearing ships and planes were tied in with the
UFOs, and that the Navy might have stumbled onto the
truth through the Philadelphia Experiment. Irving also
talked a lot about McDonald, about Rene Hardy and Edward Ruppelt, about how a lot of reputable people had
come to a sticky end—and about the mysterious men who
harassed UFO witnesses, often claiming they were from
the CIA. All of this scared Irving. It made him pace the
house at nights. Then, just a few days ago, Irving read
about Chuck Wakely . . . and that bit of news was too
much for him."

"Chuck Wakely?"

"Yes. Chuck Wakely was a young Miami pilot who almost lost himself in a luminous cloud above the Bermuda
Triangle. He was so shaken by this experience that he
started to investigate the whole subject—writing about it,
lecturing about it, appearing on TV and radio, and generally digging up a lot of old bones. A few days ago Chuck
Wakely was shot through the window of his apartment in
Miami, apparently while working on his research. The motive and assailant are still unknown."

"Coincidence," Epstein said.

"Maybe," Mary said. "But that coincidence didn't particularly help Irving. In the end he just thought of the men
following him—and became paranoid."

Epstein sat forward, feeling cold, a bit unreal, his eyes
drawn to the moonlight in the garden, to the stars in the
night sky. What could he say? What could *anyone* say?
The story was too bizzarre to be accepted and contained
by mere logic.

"What was Irving working on?" he asked.

"I don't know," Mary said. "That's what frightens me

most. I went through his study today and couldn't find a damned thing."

"No papers?"

"Nothing."

"But he *must* have kept a file!"

"He had a file as thick as *War and Peace*, but it's just disappeared."

Epstein sank into his chair, feeling cold, disorientated, the fear creeping over him slowly and making the silence sing . . . Death. Suicide. Careers broken and good men lost. He thought of Irving in the car in the desert, of McDonald and Hardy. Suicide by the bullet. Or carbon monoxide inhalation. Suicide and murder and madness: an inexplicable catalogue . . . Epstein had to know the answers. There was nothing else left to know. He grew old and his time was growing short and that invited obsession. Yes, that was the word. Obsession: the only word. It was what had taken hold of them all and then driven them ruthlessly. Epstein sighed and sat forward, his stubby fingers interlocked, his knuckles forming a broken white ridge that displayed a great tension.

"A strange story," he said.

Mary laughed bitterly, shook her head and looked away, slowly raised the glass of bourbon to her lips, her brown eyes wet and vague.

"That's the story," she said. "That's my legacy from Irving. God knows, it's too insane to be true . . . but that's what it came to."

She drank deeply of the bourbon, threw her head back and gasped, her brown eyes focused vaguely on the ceiling and seeing nothing at all. Epstein watched her, entranced, thinking of days long ago, of when his wife had been alive and they had sat in this room and felt young and beyond the reach of time, their ambitions before them. A great innocence had filled those days, had colored Epstein's fondest memories; now that innocence lay shattered about him and left him with old age. His wife had died five years ago, Irving had killed himself yesterday, and here, in the timeless, moonlit silence, he and Mary were parting. All the dreams had turned to dust. Each possibility had reached its limit. What was left was a teasing, frustrating mystery that might yet make him mad. Epstein studied Mary carefully, saw the fading of her beauty, the spreading of her flesh, the falling breasts, the glint of gray in her dark hair. Life approached and then withdrew. It bled away into the night. It was merciless, taking beauty and hope, leaving nothing to cling to.

Epstein sighed. He felt old and very tired. He stood up and gazed nervously around him and then stared at Mary. She was still in the chair. He saw the moonlight in her eyes. The eyes were luminous and wet with rampant grief, and they tore at his pounding heart.

"It's getting late," he said. "I'll have to go. I'll try to drop in tomorrow."

"No," she said. "Don't drop in tomorrow. I'll be packing tomorrow."

Her voice was flat and remote, a stranger's voice, a chilling sound, and Epstein stood there and blinked and stared at her, not quite comprehending.

"Packing?" he said.

"Yes, packing," she replied. "I don't want to see you again. I don't want to see anyone."

He almost sat down again, the shock shaking him, draining him; but instead he simply lifted one hand and lightly brushed his beard.

"It's not you," she said. "It's everything you represent. It's the UFOs and their victims, Irving's hopes and their destruction; and, most of all, it's my fear that he might have been right. I'm too old for this, Frederick. I can't live within these walls. I want to run from all his friends, from his work and his associates, and I never want to see this house again, to hear a knock on the door. I'm frightened, Dr. Epstein. Irving's fear is getting to me. I'm too weary to stay here and fight it, so I'm packing my bags. I'll attend to the funeral. I don't want you to be there. I'll leave as soon as Irving is buried, and I'll never come back. Give me a kiss, Frederick. Do that and then go. Don't talk to me. Don't say another word. Kiss me once and then leave."

The moonlight fell on her face. Her brown eyes were wet with tears. Epstein felt a searing pain, a crippling loss, and then he stepped over to her. The darkness surrounded them, dissolved them and made them one. Epstein leaned down and kissed her on the cheek and then he walked from the house.

CHAPTER SIX

The air-conditioning in the Fontainebleau Hilton, as in most hotels, condominiums and fleabags in Miami Beach, smacked the flesh with a refrigerated chill that stopped sweat in its tracks. Aldridge stood in the lobby, glancing around him, gaze thoughtful, taking in the milling people, the WASP residents and tourists, not amused by the superfluous extravagance and inane conversations. He nodded briefly at Fallaci, who stood beside him, looking elegant, and together they pushed their way through the crowds and went up to the desk clerk.

There was a large mob at reception, all waving hands and shouting, drunk already and flushed with excitement, trying to sort out their room keys. Aldridge stepped back, disdainful, thinking how unreal they were, and Fallaci, apparently cool in his white suit, pushed his way to the desk.

"Excuse me—" he began.

The desk clerk raised one hand and brushed blond hair from his eyes, the eyes swiveling toward Fallaci, very blue, opaque with panic, then returning to stare blindly at a man whose elbows straddled the counter. The man had short-cropped red hair, a blotched face, squinting eyes, a garish terry cloth shirt on his large frame, a cigar in his lips.

"No!" he bawled. "You listen to me! You keep your crap for your hookers!"

"Excuse me—" Fallaci said.

"No fucking way!" the big man bawled. "We've just been to the Ivanhoe, to the Bal Harbour on North Bay Causeway, we've been up and down that road, from Hallandale Beach to Lincoln Mall, and we haven't been offered as much as a fucking john and now we're just goddamn tired of it. What sort of jerk offs do you think we are? You think we'll sleep on the goddamned beach? What the hell do you mean you've got a convention? We come here every year, bud!"

"I'm sorry, sir, but—"

"Don't fucking 'but' me, bud! I'm not here for a goddamned snow job. I've got a bus full of people, a fucking Eastern Airlines bus, and I'm not about to drive off again. Fuck you, bud. Where's the manager?"

"Excuse me," Fallaci said, very polite, very firm, taking the desk clerk's coat sleeve and jerking the elbow toward him, both his voice and his insistent brown eyes making the desk clerk take notice. "A Mr. Vale," Fallaci said. "He's coming to see Mr. McKinley. Mr. McKinley and I have just been for lunch and wondered if he'd arrived."

"Goddamned lunacy!" the big man said. "Where the hell's the goddamned manager?" The desk clerk glanced at him quickly, licked his lips, stared at Fallaci, looked down at his desk pad and whispered, "No, sir. There's no message."

"Fucking madness!" the big man said.

"Excellent," Fallaci said. "Mr. McKinley is in his room, and when Mr. Vale arrives he wants him to be sent up immediately. Don't bother to phone."

"Yes, sir," the desk clerk said, scribbling the message down.

Fallaci retreated, smiling politely at the desk clerk, watching the big man slam his fist on the desk and start bawling again, his passengers milling around him.

"Well?" Aldridge said.

"He hasn't arrived yet," Fallaci said. "I told the desk clerk to send him straight up without using the phone."

"Good," Aldridge said. "Let's go up there. Let's see Mr. McKinley."

Together they walked across the flamboyant, rococo lobby, passing bikinis and bathing suits, feet in sandals and clodhoppers, hair bleached blond and purple, piled high, hanging low, plastic bracelets on thin, suntanned wrists, rhinestone sunglasses gleaming. Aldridge was not impressed, never had been, never would be, now just wanting to collect his man and get out and leave Miami behind him. Nevertheless he seemed part of it—silvery haired, deeply tanned, his light suit businesslike—he might well have been a native of Broward County, just in town for the day.

"What did you tell him?" Aldridge said.

"I said we'd just had lunch with McKinley. He's going to send Professor Vale right up. We won't have any trouble."

They took the elevator to the sixth floor, a very crowded elevator, the people noisy and in a holiday mood: young girls in paper dresses, paunchy men in Bermuda shorts, the girls giggling, the men dabbing at sweat as they cruised gently upward. Aldridge stepped out with relief, surveyed the corridor, the garish walls, then he turned and walked along to 605, Fallaci walking beside him.

"This is worse than Las Vegas," Aldridge said.

"I've never been there, sir. I keep meaning to go there every year, but I never get around to it."

"This McKinley," Aldridge said. "You're sure he's never met Professor Vale?"

"He wouldn't know Vale from my mother. That's a hundred percent."

Aldridge nodded his head. "I hope you're right," he said. "I'd rather not have anything messy. I don't want any accidents."

"This is it: 605."

They both stopped at the door, a white door with gold embossing, and Fallaci glanced at Aldridge, saw the nod, and then pressed the doorbell. Obviously Vale was expected—they heard the footsteps immediately; the door opened without hesitation and McKinley stared at them. He was ruddy-faced, gray-haired, wearing slacks and a flowered shirt, a steely glint in the green of his eyes, no smile on his face.

"Professor Vale?" he said, looking from Aldridge to

Fallaci, his right hand still resting on the door, as if preparing to close it.

"I'm Vale," Aldridge said. He put his hand out to Mc-Kinley. They shook hands and McKinley indicated Fallaci. "Who's this?" he said bluntly.

"My assistant," Aldridge said. "Mr. Fallaci. You don't mind? He's quite clean."

"You said you'd come alone."

"My personal assistant. I'm sorry. But Mr. Fallaci travels with me everywhere. He knows everything . . . *everything*."

Aldridge stepped into the apartment, brushing casually past McKinley, and Fallaci followed with a smile on his lips, a polite smile, remote. McKinley shrugged and closed the door, looking thoughtfully at Aldridge, then he waved at the mock-Renaissance chairs and said, "Fine. Take a seat." Aldridge didn't sit. Fallaci circled the room. McKinley said, "You guys want a drink?" and headed straight for the bar. He was a big man, but muscular, very fit, his movements light. "I'm sorry about that," he said, "but I'm sure you understand: in this business we have to be careful; we have to know who we're dealing with." He reached the bar and turned around. "The government watches us—" he began. His eyes flicked to the right, saw Fallaci, an upraised hand, and he cursed and tried to duck to the side and then knew it was too late.

Fallaci's hand chopped through the air, turned on edge, the fingers closed, a small guillotine that snapped McKinley's neck with a fearsome precision. McKinley gasped and went down, his legs buckling, his body spinning, and Fallaci stepped out and caught him in his arms before he fell to the carpet. It had happened very quickly, very quietly, without fuss, and the dead man now lay in Fallaci's arms, body sagging, legs outstretched.

Aldridge stepped forward and examined him. McKinley's chin lay on his chest. He had urinated in his pants and the stain was spreading out around the crotch.

"Quickly," Aldridge said. "Get him into the bathroom. I don't want him dripping on the carpet. Get him in there immediately."

Fallaci slid his arms deeper under McKinley's armpits

and then, with the lifeless head against his chest, dragged him into the bathroom. The walls were a lurid pink, the toilet seat covered in fur, and Fallaci slung the body over a bath that was made of white marble.

"Christ, he's heavy," he said.

Aldridge didn't reply, his gaze curious, academic, as Fallaci took a short rope from his pocket and tied it around the steel curtain rail. Then he made a small noose. "You'll have to help me," he said. Aldridge stepped in and tugged at the corpse, his arms under its armpits. Together they lifted the body up, the lifeless arms around their shoulders, held it up until its feet were off the floor, the head under the noose. "Hold him there," Fallaci said. He stepped away and turned around. He opened the noose and slipped it over the dead man's head and then tightened the knot. "That's it," he said. Aldridge let go of the corpse. The dead man dropped down abruptly, then stopped, spinning slightly, his head jerked up by the rope, his neck stretched, the face bloating, his slippered feet dangling just above the floor, swinging gently from left to right. "Suicide," Fallaci said. "He reached the end of his tether." He took a small stool and set it on its side just in front of the dead man's swinging feet. Then he stood up and smiled.

"Okay, sir?"

"Okay."

They left the bathroom and closed the door, went back into the other room, and stood there, glancing around in a casual fashion, intrigued by the decor. The colors were flamboyant, the furniture a bizarre mixture of styles, imitations of late-Renaissance and Victoriana and Art Nouveau, an enormous chandelier in the ceiling, intricate moldings, poor paintings. Aldridge sat down in a chair, crossed his legs, checked his creases, his azure eyes calm but remote, as if focused elsewhere. He looked up at Fallaci, saw him standing by the windows, framed by the glinting green of Biscayne Bay and the sky's sweeping white haze.

"I hope he's punctual," Aldridge said.

"He should be here any minute."

"And you're sure he's never met that McKinley?"

"It was all done by phone."

Aldridge checked his cuff links, crossed his legs the other way. "What about my voice?" he said coldly. "He might notice the difference."

"No, sir," Fallaci said. He started wandering about the room. "The arrangement was made through a third party. Your voice won't mean a thing."

Aldridge studied his watch. "We were informed that he was punctual."

"That checks," Fallaci said. "He's a punctual man. He won't be very late."

The bell rang a minute later. Aldridge got to his feet. Fallaci looked at him, nodded, went to the room door, opened it and took a step back and said, "Yes? Can I help you?"

"I'm Professor Vale," a man said. "Are you Mr. Mc-Kinley?"

"No, sir. I'm his secretary."

Fallaci stepped aside and Vale walked into the room, a slim man, quite short, beard and hair flecked with gray, wearing white pants and a colorful flowered shirt, a tennis racket in his right hand.

"McKinley?" he said.

"Yes," Aldridge said. "Hello." He stepped forward and shook Professor Vale's hand. "I'm glad you could come."

Professor Vale smiled slightly. He seemed young for his fifty years. "Your man was very persuasive," he said. "If a little oblique."

Aldridge returned the smile. "Yes," he said. "I'm sure he was. But I'm sure you'll understand our discretion when we finish our talk." He nodded at the bar. "Would you like a drink, professor?" The professor wiped sweat from his brow and said, "Thanks. Rum and Coke."

Aldridge nodded at Fallaci. "A white wine for me," he said. Fallaci went to the bar as Aldridge pointed to a chair and said, "Sit down, professor. Relax. It must have been a good game."

The professor nodded and sat down, placed his tennis racket on the table, stretched his legs and wiped the sweat from his face with a folded white towel. "It kills me," he said. "I don't know why I do it." He patted his stomach and said, "I've got to keep it down. An academic's obsession." Aldridge smiled at the self-mockery. Fallaci brought them both drinks. Aldridge sat down and Fallaci walked away and stood behind the small bar.

"You play often?" Aldridge said.

"Only on vacation," the professor said. "I don't like vacations all that much, so it helps pass the time." He drank his rum with some relish, wiped his lips with one hand, then sighed and stared directly at Aldridge, quietly sizing him up. "All right," he said eventually. "What do you want, Mr. McKinley? Your man said it was an offer of work, and at the moment that interests me."

"Just how much did my man tell you?" Aldridge said.

"He told me that you represented a European-based commercial organization dealing in electronics, aerospace technology, communications satellites and assorted areas of high energy research. He also said that you had produced components for ASAT warheads and European and American ICBMs. He said, further, that you were under contract to NASA for the production of various rocket components, but that you were intending to expand quite dramatically. Finally, he said that you were desperately in need of civilian scientists and technicians with experience in aerospace technology, and were willing to pay well for their talents. He said no more than that."

Aldridge smiled. "He was told to be brief."

"He was brief," the professor said. "*Much* too brief. But I must say I'm interested."

Aldridge smiled again and put his chin in his hands, his elbows resting lightly on his knees, on his immaculate pants.

"Well, Professor Vale, your information is essentially correct. I represent Air Communications and Satellite Systems, better known as ACASS, a Frankfurt-based, internationally financed company that specializes in the production of advanced electronic communications and spy satellite components under contract to European and U.S. government defense establishments."

"I know about ACASS," the professsor said. "I've often used your components."

"Yes," Aldridge said, "that stands to reason. You've

worked in the past for the USAF Space and Missiles System Organization in San Diego, California; for the Linear Accelerator Center of Stanford University; and for the Lawrence Livermore Laboratory near San Francisco. You are, at the moment, an Advanced Space Programs Coordinator at the top secret Aerospace Defense Command Cheyenne Mountain Complex in Colorado Springs, Colorado. At these various posts you have specialized in research on advanced ICBMs and anti-satellite weapons, and you're currently engaged in research into high energy laser beams and particle beam weapons, with particular interest in the Semipalatinsk plant in Russia . . . Given this, you would have certainly used our components. We'd now like to use you."

Professor Vale smiled a little, crossed his legs, glanced at Fallaci. Fallaci took his glass and topped up the rum and then handed it back to him.

"You've certainly done your homework," the professor said.

"Yes. We're efficient."

The professor smiled at Aldridge, his eyes glinting above his glass. He sipped his rum and then sat back in the chair, his boyish face looking thoughtful.

"I'm under contract to USAF," he said.

"That contract ends in two months."

Professor Vale grinned, his vanity stroked with such attention, then he had another sip of his drink and sat up and said, "Talk."

Aldridge leaned forward, smiling, just a little amused, thinking first of the professor's understandable human vanity, thinking next of the man hanging in the bathroom, his neck snapped where the rope would scar.

"Professor Vale," he said, "we need men like you because we are, as you said, expanding dramatically. Put simply, ACASS is planning to set up an overseas satellite launching base which will break the superpowers' monopoly of space by launching spy satellites for any Third World country willing to pay what we ask. At the moment this capability is available only to America and the USSR, so there is, as we see it, an open market for the sale of such satellites to any smaller developing country that is

concerned with protecting its borders and wants a sophisticated early warning system at a reasonable price. We can
fill that need. We can construct simple, efficient rockets.
We can launch those rockets for anyone who pays, and
there are plenty of customers."

"No doubt you'll have plenty of customers, but where
will your base be?"

"A certain Third World leader in Africa has leased us
approximately 100,000 square kilometers of his country in
return for a rent of $50 million a year to be paid in local
currency after our first commercial launch, which will be
five years from now. Given that this country's inflation is
running at about 85 percent a year, the payment will be
relatively negligible by the time it is due. We have also offered to launch a satellite free of charge, but on the condition that the president pays for the actual production of
the rocket. In short, what we have been given by this
black lunatic, virtually for free, is 100,000 square kilometers of territory, total autonomy over that territory, full
immunity from any prosecution by the state, full control
over who is allowed to remain in the territory, and absolute disciplinary control over all natives within our desig-
nated area."

"That's insane," the professor said.

"That's a fact," Aldridge said. "That's the deal that was
worked out between ACASS and the president in Africa,
and the contract has been signed, sealed and delivered.
Photocopies of the contract are on my boat and await
your inspection."

The professor studied Aldridge carefully, tapping his
teeth with his glass, obviously startled by what he had
heard, just as obviously intrigued.

"You can't build a rocket that cheap," he said.

"Yes," Aldridge said promptly, "we can. The basic idea
for the rocket came from some German scientists who
originally worked on the V-2 rocket for Hitler. After the
war one of those scientists went to Egypt to design rockets
for President Nasser, retired to Austria, and then came to
ACASS. Another came to the United States with Wernher
von Braun, became an American citizen and leading light
of the Kennedy Space Center, retired three years ago and

has since worked for ACASS. The ACASS rocket is very much like a model the Nazis were perfecting when the war ended: easy to build, cheap, but efficient. Its basic unit consists of a tube filled with an oxidizing agent and another filled with diesel fuel; when these liquids combine they ignite and the rocket takes off. Also, instead of mounting rocket stages on top of one another, the ACASS rocket is simply a large bundle of standard units: the greater the load, the more units you include. It is, in short, a mass-produced rocket, quite functional and operative."

"I'd want to see the plans."

"You can see them. They're on the boat also."

The professor sat back in his chair, tapping his glass against his teeth, studying Aldridge and then gazing around the room, trying to take it all in. Aldridge sat there saying nothing, thinking of the dead man in the bathroom, thinking also of what could happen to the world if ACASS had their way. Would the idiocy never cease? Could the fantastic be controlled? Aldridge thought of the dead man, of the commercial company he had represented, of all the scientists who would take on any work so long as the price was right. Professor Vale would not be one of them. Professor Vale would not be paid. The good professor, with his vanity and greed, would be put to use elsewhere.

"I'm interested," Vale said, "but I want to see some documentation. I want to see all your contracts, I want to study the rocket designs, and after that, if I'm satisfied that you're legit, I might discuss my own terms."

"Excellent." Aldridge said. "I'm sure you'll find it quite impressive. All you need is the safe on my boat. Could you go there right now?"

"Now?" the professor said.

"Why not?" Aldridge said. "You're only here on vacation, you said yourself that you were bored—so let's go to my boat, take a trip, some food and wine, and you can study all the documents at your leisure then go home and decide."

"I don't know . . ." the professor said.

"Is your wife here?" Aldridge said.

"Yes."

"Then why don't we collect her? I'm sure she'll enjoy it."

That was enough for the good professor. "I think I'll go on my own," he said. "I mean, I don't want her hanging around when we're talking our business. What the hell, let's just go. . . ." He finished his drink and stood up, licked his lips and nodded his head, then walked to the bar, past Fallaci, and set his glass down. "Where's your boat docked?" he said.

"Another drink, sir?" Fallaci said.

"No, thanks," the professor said.

"Pompano Beach Marina," Aldridge said. "It should take about an hour."

"You got a john?" the professor said. Fallaci touched his elbow lightly. "Yes, sir," Fallaci said. "That door there. At the far end of the room. The first door on your left." The professor thanked him and walked away, turning into the second bathroom. Fallaci then looked at Aldridge, grinning nervously. "That was close," Aldridge said.

They all left shortly after, left the dead McKinley dangling, closed the door and went down in the elevator and walked out through the lobby. The sudden brightness was dazzling, beating off the white walls, off tall buildings and sidewalks and streets, the sea beyond the palm trees. Fallaci walked on ahead. He led them into a parking lot. Aldridge sat in the rear, talking casually to Professor Vale, and Fallaci drove the car onto Collins Avenue, his eyes fixed on the road.

Professor Vale was loquacious. The two rums had affected him. He kept looking out the window, at the condominiums and hotels, at the surfers and executives, at the restless wives and gaudily brazen whores and the flesh-littered sands. Miami Beach glided past them.

"You know Miami, Mr. McKinley?"

"No, I don't," Aldridge said. "I used to have the boat docked in Norfolk; I only came here this year."

"You picked the wrong year," the professor said. "You picked the year of the pig. I've been coming to this place for fifteen years, but it's not what it used to be. Cubans and blacks, homosexuals and hookers: you get these kids from the University of Miami and they're wrecking the place. I swear to God, it's unbelievable. You wouldn't believe what goes on. I'm a white, Anglo-Saxon American, and I don't mind admitting it. Take a good look around you. What the hell do you see? Drive through 79th Street or Biscayne Boulevard or Kennedy Park; you'll get a blowjob in the front seat of your car before you know where your billfold's gone. I mean these hookers are everywhere. They own Lincolns and Cadillacs. You just go into the Boom-Boom Room or the Poodle Lounge in the Fontainebleau and you'll see them shaking their tails for all they're worth, picking up on the tourists. Either that or it's the fags, from Coconut Grove to Fort Lauderdale: they've got it organized so well that the Twenty-first Street sea wall is no longer the place to go for a broad—they've just cleared out the area. The future America is in Miami; the Brave New World is around the corner: prostitution, male and female; a lot of porno movie houses; filthy bookstores and V.D. and drugs and organized crime. That's Miami, Mr. McKinley. That's the world delivered by science. I look around me and I wonder what it means and then I look to the future. Fuck America, I say. What's America given me? It's given me radicals and communists and anarchists and degenerates, and it's offering me Miami and Las Vegas and cesspits like New York. Fuck America. Who needs it?"

The professor shook his head and chortled, short and slim, almost boyish, his bearded face denying his fifty years, the lines good humored and ageless. Aldridge looked at him, amused, a cold amusement, and then the car came to a halt.

"Here we are," Aldridge said.

They climbed out of the car onto the blinding white marina, blinking eyes and then stretching themselves and getting used to the tropical heat. Fallaci led them to the boat, a neat Italian, walking quickly, his eyes darting left and right, their delicate brown disguising ice, double-checking every human, every movement that could represent trouble. Bronzed girls in bikinis, blond youths in tight shorts, gawking tourists and surfers and lifeguards: Fallaci watched them all carefully. The sky above was a dazzling haze, the water went from blue to green, and the boats in the harbor, all sizes, all shapes, reflected sunlight from chrome and polished wood, their colored sails flapping rhythmically.

Professor Vale was impressed. He was particularly impressed by the boat they stopped at. A high-powered luxury cruiser, about sixty feet long, it had the air of a floating penthouse and was obviously a rich man's toy. Fallaci led them over the gangplank, onto the highly polished deck, and a servant wearing an immaculate starched white jacket stepped forward and bowed to them. Aldridge followed them aboard, his eyes quickly scanning the boat, then he waved to the door of the cabin and said, "In there, professor."

The professor glanced around him, at the blue sky and sea, and said, "If you don't mind I'd like to stay out here and pretend that I'm healthy."

Aldridge smiled understandingly. "That's fine with me," he said. "We'll just take the boat out a few miles and discuss business then. We can talk over lunch."

The waiter stepped forward, bowed slightly at Professor Vale. He had dark skin and Oriental eyes, his face curiously smooth.

"A drink, sir?"

"Rum and Coke."

"White rum?"

"No, dark."

The waiter bowed again and then retreated, backing in through the cabin door.

"Where does he come from?" the professor asked.

"Hawaii," Aldridge said.

"For a moment there I thought he was Korean, but then he seemed a bit different. Hawaii . . . should have known." The professor shrugged and rolled his eyes, grinned at Aldridge and turned around, looking over the other boats, the gleaming white walls of the marina, at the shimmering haze above the horizon where the sky met the sea. "This is some boat," he said.

"Thank you," Aldridge said.

"If you meant to impress me, you've succeeded."

"Good." Aldridge said. "We like to please. It's all part of the service."

The waiter returned with two drinks on a tray while Fallaci, who had been standing near the cabin, disappeared through the door. The professor and Aldridge took their drinks, the waiter bowed low and departed, then Professor Vale leaned against the railings and stared around him with interest.

The boat had a large crew, all dressed in white, all moving back and forth at their tasks, working methodically and silently. There was something strange about them. The professor didn't know what it was. They were all small and slim, dark-skinned, with narrow eyes; and the professor couldn't truly accept that they came from Hawaii. He watched them with interest. They made him feel a bit unreal. They never glanced at one another, never spoke, and they kept their heads down. The professor suddenly shivered. He felt decidedly odd. He drank his rum and grinned at Aldridge, still not knowing who he was, then the boat's engines rumbled and the boat moved slowly out of the harbor.

"Where are we going?" the professor asked.

Aldridge shrugged. "Nowhere special. We'll just go out a little bit, about ten or fifteen miles, and then anchor. We'll have lunch and you can study the documents."

The boat cruised out of the harbor, past white buildings and other boats, the palmettos casting shadows on the people wandering lazily back and forth. Eventually the marina fell behind them, revealing the immense sweep of the coastline, yellow beaches dominated by condominiums and baroque, white-washed hotels. Finally there was the sea, green and blue, reflecting sunlight, the waves washing in pearly lines around the boat and streaming out in their wake.

"Beautiful, isn't it?" Aldridge said.

"Yes, it is," the professor said. "But I always feel pretty weird out here. You can't ignore all the stories."

"Of course . . . the Bermuda Triangle."

"You sound skeptical," the professor said.

"Oh, I'm not really that. When so many boats and planes just disappear, one can't help feeling curious."

"Right," the professor said. "You simply can't ignore the facts. Sinking boats you can accept. Crashing planes you can accept. But other things have never been explained, and they make your flesh creep. What I mean is, I'm a scientist. I try not to believe in magic. But cases like that . . . I don't know . . . we still don't know the answers."

"What about UFOs?" Aldridge said.

"What about them, McKinley? I won't buy it that UFOs are the problem here or anywhere else. I draw the line at flying saucers. The proof for UFOs is negligible. I'll believe they exist when I see one . . . and I don't think I'll see one."

"Really?" Aldridge said, sipping his wine and smiling slightly, gazing over the railings at the sea, at the cloudy horizon. "I thought you might have seen one over the Cheyenne Mountain Complex."

"Why would I see one over there?"

"Oh, I don't know . . ." Aldridge gazed at the clouds on the horizon, coming closer, expanding. "It's just that I'd heard that UFOs were frequently observed over scientific and military establishments. Given that, I thought they might have been seen over the Aerospace Defense Command."

"Balls," the professor said. "Anyway, the Cheyenne Mountain Complex has been built to survive a nuclear war—no matter how destructive—and as such it can't be seen from the air. In fact, the Cheyenne Complex is a complete underground city, existing right inside the mountain, resting on giant shock absorbers, webbed with miles of underground tunnels, and completely sealed off from the outer world. Believe me, McKinley, when you work in that damned place you're not able to see *anything* in the sky—you don't see a damned thing. Our job is to track spy satellites. Those are all we've *ever* tracked. Neither the radar nor the telescopes have ever picked up anything else. UFOs just don't exist."

Aldridge smiled and sipped his wine, let the cool breeze fan his face, kept his gaze fixed on the sea, on the clouds near the horizon, that horizon which forever receded and led out to Bermuda. They would never reach Bermuda. They would anchor and then wait. The good professor, in an intoxicated dream, would find that facts have no credence.

"I don't believe it," the professor said.

"What?" Aldridge said.

"Spy satellites being sold in the marketplace. That's just fucking incredible."

Aldridge simply smiled. He watched the land disappearing. The sea was calm and the sky was a blue sheet, with white clouds drifting under it. Professor Vale continued talking. He seemed unsteady on his feet. He sipped his drink and kept blinking his eyes and glanced vaguely around him. Aldridge listened attentively. The professor was talking about pulse power weapons. The boat stopped and the anchor went down and the professor kept talking. The crew took up their positions. Fallaci reappeared on the deck. The sea washed around the boat, rolled away to the horizon, and Aldridge smiled when he saw a dark mass spreading out just below them. Professor Vale kept talking. He suddenly seemed very drunk. Jets of steam were rising up from the sea and forming into a cloud. This cloud surrounded the boat.

"We didn't invent the pulse power beam. The Russians didn't invent it either. The British invented it eighteen years ago and kept it under tight wraps. Now we're expanding its potential. We're running a race with the Russians. We're utilizing it as a defensive weapon, for communications and reconnaissance, and we're making quantum jumps in our technology, quietly forging ahead. These laser beams are amazing. Their possibilities are limitless. They can knock out spy satellites, zero in on flying rockets, and they can show the number plate of a car from two hundred miles up—they can pinpoint just about anything. Think of what that means, McKinley. The Cold War has been superseded. What we now have is a Balance of Terror in a post-nuclear age. People don't know what's happening."

Aldridge didn't reply. The silence rang in the professor's ears. He shook his head and saw the shifting of the clouds, a silvery haze all around him. He didn't know what was happening. He felt very peculiar. Quite suddenly, sweeping away his ebullience, he felt a fierce, senseless dread. What the hell was going on? He felt drunk and disorientated. His throat went dry and his eyes went out of focus and the deck seemed to tilt.

The professor dropped his glass. He watched it falling toward the sea. It took a long time going down, spinning over, reflecting sunlight, the light flashing off in dazzling striations of incredible beauty. He never saw it hit the water. The hot air beat all around him. He looked sideways at McKinley—McKinley?—and saw blue eyes and gray hair.

Not gray: silvery. Not silvery: a shimmering white. He was here, Professor Vale, I am here to make a deal with McKinley. Then fear. The inexplicable. The white hair and azure eyes. Professor Vale tore himself from the vision and glanced wildly around him. The boat was silent and still. The sea was boiling up around it—roaring and boiling up around them all in immense walls of green steam.

"Jesus Christ! What the hell—?"

The professor grabbed hold of the railings, the deck shuddering beneath his feet. The huge clouds of steam were rising from the sea and surrounding the boat. The professor couldn't believe his eyes. The clouds of steam blocked out the sky. They had formed a perfect circle around the boat, half a mile in diameter. He suddenly wanted to scream. The deck shuddered and groaned. He looked over the railing, down the side of the boat, saw an enormous dark mass below the surface, spreading out, slowly surfacing.

"The Triangle! Oh Jesus . . . !"

He beat his forehead with his hand, the terror sweeping away his senses, glanced around and saw McKinley, azure eyes and white hair, saw the crew, the Orientals, coming toward him, also white, moving silently. He tried to run but it was useless: he was paralyzed with fear. He gripped the railing, his eyes darting left and right, trying to take in the nightmare.

"Oh fuck! *Oh my God!*"

The sea suddenly roared. He stared wildly at the distant clouds. They boiled up from the waves and formed a wall that blocked out the whole sky. Then the spiraling waves exploded, the spray sweeping around glinting steel. A perimeter of spikes surfaced, faraway, beneath the steam, all triangular, splitting the water like metal fins, thrusting up, growing larger.

He heard the sound of his own blubbering, saw the white ridge of his knuckles, his rational self stunned by disbelief and a throttling terror. All that and something else: an unreality that drained his senses; his head was spinning and he remembered the falling glass and realized he was drugged.

He tried to focus on McKinley, wondered who McKinley was, saw McKinley's blue eyes and white hair, the wall of clouds far beyond him. The boat was trapped inside those clouds. The green steam swirled and glided. The triangular grids rose from the sea, growing larger, spitting water, a great circle of glinting steel teeth that surrounded the boat.

He couldn't believe what he was seeing. The only reality was his fear. The deck shuddered beneath his feet, the boat rocking and rumbling, and he glanced down and saw an enormous mass rising up to the surface.

"Grip the railing! Hold tight!"

Someone was shouting at him. He licked his lips and saw McKinley. The blue eyes were very bright and intense, hypnotizing him, chilling him. The professor did as he was told. He saw the wall of steel around him. He felt the presence of the massed crew behind him, but he didn't dare look at them.

The monster's steel jaws were closing. His eyes were drawn to the boiling sea. The dark mass was rising up and spreading out, and then it hit the boat's hull. The professor felt it and heard it: the deck shuddered and screeched. There was a harsh, metallic rumbling, water rushing and hissing, then the boat suddenly rocked from side to side, settled down, finally steadied.

The professor stared, mesmerized. The whole boat was rising up. The sea poured away between the climbing walls, and an enormous steel deck broke the surface. This steel deck was smooth and solid, a quarter mile in diameter, and the walls that had looked like huge fins went right around its perimeter. The sea poured out through these

walls, the enormous deck pushed the boat up, and the triangular walls of the perimeter started moving toward one
another, sweeping up and curving in above the boat like
interlocking, giant fingers.

The professor gazed up in awe. The steel walls curved
high above him. They were roaring and hissing, water
rushing down their sides, and they moved in toward one
another and blocked out the green clouds. The professor
stood there, mesmerized. The deck was steady beneath his
feet. The triangular walls came together high above and
formed a huge, empty hangar.

The walls locked and reverberated. A bright light filled
the gloom. The professor looked across that great floor of
steel and saw nothing but curved walls. Then the floor began to rumble. The professor almost gagged with fear. The
floor started to sink, like some enormous elevator, and the
walls soared all around him, an immense globe of steel,
until the light formed a blinding white haze that turned
the dream to reality.

Sweeping vistas of steel and glass. A maze of ladders
and catwalks. Silhouettes moving through the white haze,
the air vibrating and humming. The professor saw it and
felt awe and choking horror. Something cold touched his
neck and then scorched it and he dropped into Hell.

CHAPTER SEVEN

Richard was standing before the large windows of the front room of the apartment, a glass of cheap red wine in his shaking right hand, his eyes bloodshot and blinking, slightly glazed with constant fear, looking over the adventure playground, the grimy rooftops of Finsbury Park, the gray sky that seemed to smother the distant maze of the City of London. The sky obsessed him, hypnotized him, filled him with fear and fascination, flitted through his dreams and colored his waking hours with the promise of horror. It was six in the evening, darkness crept across the skyline, and Richard raised his glass of wine to his lips and drank deeply, compulsively.

All white. Everything. He closed his eyes and saw the nightmare. His hand shook as he drank some more wine and then opened his eyes again. He saw the maze of the city, the distant dome of St. Paul's, and above it, the darkening, cloud-filled sky that took him back to the start of it.

Richard shivered violently, finished his drink and turned away, then he walked out of the room, into the kitchen, and poured some more wine. He had a sip and glanced around him, at empty bottles and unwashed dishes, crumpled newspapers on the table, on the floor, the signs of total neglect. He had been here five days, and had only gone out for the papers. He couldn't eat, he couldn't sleep, he rarely washed, and the wine made the days dissolve.

He walked out of the kitchen, stood a moment in the hall, drank some wine and stared at each of the rooms in turn, at the comforting brightness. Every light in the apartment was on. They had been on all the time. He didn't dare turn them off in case the nightmares returned and jerked him awake screaming wildly, his head bright with phantoms.

All white. Everything. He couldn't believe that it had happened. He could believe even less that he had awakened three days later, alone, on the hills of Dartmoor, thirty miles from Bodmin Moor, the woman and her car no longer there, the missing days a dark void. Richard shuddered at the very thought of it, put the glass to his lips, drank deeply and walked back to the lounge and wished that Jenny would come.

He had phoned her an hour ago, the first call since his return, and had noticed the confusion in her voice, the hint of anger beneath it. In truth he couldn't blame her, more precisely he didn't care; now driven by the singular, desperate need to talk it out of his system.

All white. Everything. His last memory was of the whiteness. He remembered the flying discs, the enormous mother ship, the silhouettes moving slowly in the burning haze—then nothing; oblivion. A nauseous awakening on Dartmoor; stumbling down the hill and hitching a lift and being told it was Sunday. He hadn't understood that at all—his last memory was of Thursday—and sitting there in the truck beside the farmer he had thought himself mad.

Now he stood by the window, drinking wine, shaking in spasms, rubbing his unshaven chin and looking out as the city's lights winked on. The lights were floating in darkness, a silvery web, a sparkling mosaic, and they merged with the lights in his head and took shape as the nightmare . . .

His feverish thoughts had filled the nights, and he had prowled from room to room through the apartment, trying to hide from his nightmares. The fear was always present, all around him, deep inside him, a living thing that breathed against his neck and made him reach for the wineglass. Exhausted, terrified, he dreaded sleep yet had to sleep, sitting upright in a chair, groping blindly for the bottle, muttering vague and incoherent protestations as the silence surrounded him.

Richard couldn't understand it, couldn't reach it or see it. What it was, what it meant or might mean was something concealed from him. So he drank and relived it. He wondered constantly about the woman. He saw the enormous flashing mass, the flying discs, the jolting car; and he sobbed as the white light flared up and sent him into oblivion.

It had started five days ago. He had paced the apartment all that time. The world outside, that web of light and darkness, now seemed alien and threatening. Richard thought about reality. He wondered what reality was. He was pondering this riddle, drowning gradually in labyrinths, when the ringing of the doorbell cut through him and made his nerves twitch.

"Jesus Christ!" he hissed.

He turned away from the window, stepped forward, then stopped, took another sip of wine and licked his lips and let his nerves settle down. It was all too much for him: at eighteen he felt like fifty. He glanced around the cluttered room at the debris of his hibernation, and he felt the shame reaching up to stroke him and make his cheeks burn. Then he licked his lips again, shook his head and stepped forward, left the room and walked along the straight hall, the lights stinging his eyes.

The front door had stained-glass windows, pretty mosaics of lead and wire, and he saw her silhouette through the glass, an indistinct, smokey form. He stopped, suddenly frightened, the fear followed by shame, briefly wondering if it really was her, wondering why he should doubt it. Then he shook his head again, cursing softly, trying to grin, and the grin died pathetically on his face when the bell rang for a second time.

"Jenny?"

"Yes! What's the matter? Let me in! Why in God's name are you whispering through the door? What on earth's going on in there?"

Richard unlocked the door, fumbling clumsily, nervously, then stepped back and pulled the door open and studied her carefully. Jenny didn't move forward, simply stared at him, shocked, her right hand reaching up to her forehead, brushing dark hair from brown eyes.

"What on earth . . . ?"

"Come in."

"*What?*"

"I said come in."

"What on earth have you been doing to yourself?"

"Don't just stand there. *Come in!*"

She stared at him, brow furrowed, a forefinger to her lips, then she shrugged and stepped laconically inside, her shoulder brushing against him. This slight contact seemed electric, jolting through him like a shock—not sexual; more a sudden awareness of a being outside himself. He closed the door and turned around, saw brown eyes, a moon face, her dark hair a tangled web of curls, her long legs in blue jeans. She stared at him, studying him, then shrugged and walked away, wandering lazily along the hall, looking into all the rooms, raising eyebrows when she saw the awful mess: the empty, discarded bottles.

"Very nice," she said, nodding.

She raised her eyebrows and looked at him, a quiet appraisal, frankly mocking, then she shrugged and walked into the room and he dutifully followed her. She stood a moment in the doorway, surveying this further desecration, then she sighed and slumped into a chair, her legs outstretched, disgusted.

"I don't believe this," she said.

Richard didn't reply, simply raised his glass and drank, then walked to the window and looked out and saw the lights of the city. The whole of London was ablaze. The lights defied the early darkness. They then merged and fused into his nightmare, and he turned away, shivering. Jenny sat there in a chair, her shabby parka across her lap, her legs outstretched, very long, very slim, lethargically mocking him.

"Five days," she said. "You said you've been here five days. I didn't really believe it when you told me, but now I'm convinced." She raised both her hands, lazily indicating the squalid room, then the hands dropped down to rest on one another as her brown eyes looked up at him. "You and the apartment both look the same," she said. "You both look fucking terrible."

Richard tried to grin and failed; instead he shrugged and glanced around him before slowly, reluctantly looking at Jenny, wondering what he could say to her.

"It's a mess all right," he said.

"Yes," she said. "A bloody mess. What the hell have you been doing all this time? Supervising an orgy?"

Richard managed to grin, a weak offering, not his usual, then his blue eyes, which normally were candid, slid furtively sideways.

"What are you looking at?" Jenny said.

"Nothing," he replied.

"Take a good look," she said. "It's worth studying. I've never seen it like this before." Her brown eyes, brown and lively, their languid depths flecked with steel, wandered over the patterned armchair, the stained settee, the cluttered tables, the bottles lying on the floor, the unwashed glasses, the newspapers and magazines. "You only got this apartment so cheap," she said, "because my friend is still holding the lease. Now it's not a great apartment, but it *is* pretty good, and I don't think you'll impress him too much by turning it into a pigsty."

Richard finished off his wine, visibly shuddered and turned away, picking a bottle off the table and filled his glass and drank again, breathing deeply.

"Don't offer me a drink," Jenny said. "The sight of you puts me off it."

"Sorry. Didn't think. You want one?"

"No." She smiled bleakly and looked at him. "Even your parents think you're still down in Cornwall. What the hell's going on?"

Richard turned away abruptly and went to the window, stood there for some time, staring out, methodically sipping his wine.

"I don't know," he said finally. "It seems crazy. I don't think you'll believe me."

"Try me."

He turned around to face her, his eyes bloodshot, remote, the light shining on the wine in his glass, the glass visibly shaking.

"All right," he said. "I never got to St. Ives. Something happened on the way to St. Ives that I just can't explain. You'll probably think I've gone mad."

"And have you?"

"What?"

"Gone mad."

"I don't know. I'm not sure."

He shivered again, his eyes sliding furtively sideways, the ghost of himself in this squalor, trembling lips stained with wine. Then he told her the story, talking hurriedly, frantically, pacing to and fro, his hands shaking, spilling wine, running nervous fingers through his uncombed hair, his eyes avoiding her face. It was suddenly easy to tell it—more than easy; a fierce necessity—and as he listened to his own voice, as the words came tumbling out, he felt as if he was coming apart, losing his old protected self, changing into someone wiser, less assured, aware of life's hidden mysteries . . .

"That was near King Arthur's Hall. King Arthur's Hall is on Bodmin Moor. The last thing I remembered was the white light and those strange silhouettes . . . Like a dream, a sort of vision, not real; and I screamed and then heard myself groaning and had nightmares and woke up . . . I was right back on Dartmoor.

"Can you imagine the feeling? I was dazed and scared shitless. It was cold, but I was burning all over—my hands were burned red. I mean, I couldn't accept it. I didn't know what had happened. I walked down to the road, hitched a lift with a farmer, and when I tried to tell him what had happened, he thought I was crazy . . .

"I caught a train and came back here. I saw my burned face in the mirror. That made me believe it and I got frightened, so I just kept on drinking. I didn't know what to do. I didn't want to tell anyone. I felt frightened and the fear was something else, something living inside me. What I mean is, it seemed *real*. The fear seemed to be a presence. I could feel it there beside me, right behind me, something tangible: living . . . Then I thought about the woman. What had happened to her? She was real, had to be—we spent hours in her car—then the both of us, inside that car, were drawn into the spaceship.

"Spaceship? I don't know. I know that sounds crazy
. . . but something, something enormous, came down and
opened up and then swallowed us . . . Unbelievable. Ridiculous. I can't believe that it happened. I can't believe it
but it had to be real . . . it just had to be; *had* to be . . .

"So, I stayed here. I was scared and couldn't sleep. I
forced myself out every morning, but I couldn't stay out
long. I kept imagining things. I always felt I was being followed. I'd come back to the apartment and start drinking
and hear all the walls creaking. I was terrified of sleeping.
At night I'd fall asleep anyway. I'd dream that they were
coming to get me, but they'd never materialize.

"I wanted to phone you, phone my folks or the cops,
but every time my hand reached for the phone the fear
would come back in spades. I think it's going away now.
It's still here, but not so bad. I think the booze is starting
to burn the fear out, but I still feel uneasy. What happened out there? What happened to that woman? I awakened three days later on Dartmoor. I have to know where
those days went . . ."

He stopped talking and blinked his eyes, saw the light
bulb above him, a dazzling sun, blinding him, making him
melt. He shook his head and licked his lips, glanced at
Jenny, turned away, picked a bottle from the table and
poured more wine, let it splash on his wrist. He had a
drink and gasped loudly, his head back, eyes on the ceiling, then he shuddered and slumped into a chair, facing
Jenny's cold gaze.

"You're drunk," Jenny said.

"Jesus Christ, is that your answer?"

"You're drunk and you've been drunk for five days and
the drink is now talking."

"I don't believe this," Richard said.

"I'm no idiot," Jenny said. "What the hell were you doing with that woman in a parked car at night?"

"What?"

"Your lady friend. Red hair and green eyes. You and
some bitch in her car in the middle of Bodmin Moor."

"Damn it, Jenny—"

"Bodmin Moor, my love? The middle of desolate Bodmin Moor? Do you really expect me to believe that this

woman's car just broke down? Come *on,* love, pull the other leg."

"It *didn't* break down," Richard said. "That flying saucer made it cut out! Believe me, there was nothing wrong with the car; those things just made it stop!"

"Oh, my God, what a story!"

Richard's head began to swim, his hands shaking even more, as the logic of her feminine reason mocked his pitiful fears. He suddenly felt a strange mirth, a bitter, self-wounding humor, bubbling up to his throat and sticking there, almost making him choke. It was just too ridiculous—could she really be jealous?—and he licked his lips and blinked and stared at her, trying to keep her in focus.

"Fuck you," she said. "That's why you've been drinking. You hitchhike to Cornwall, you get picked up by some tart, you get drunk and she makes you an offer that you just can't refuse. God, you miserable bastard! What a Puritan you must be! You had a bit on the side, a little fling, and now you just can't admit it . . . But UFOs . . . Oh, Jesus!"

She shook her head and rolled her eyes, crossed her legs in rejection, then gazed around the room with studied interest, as if thinking of other things.

"It was a UFO," Richard said.

"Filled with little green men?"

"All right, Jenny, fuck it, just forget it. Go to hell. Just go home."

"You're drunk."

"So I'm drunk."

"You should have tried to stay sober. At least sober you'd have thought of a decent story. Now you know what the wine can do."

Richard stood up and swayed, the room spinning around him, then he steadied himself and stepped to the table and poured some more wine.

"I'm going home," Jenny said.

She sighed and stood up, walked across to the bookshelves, ran her finger through the dust, held it up and examined it thoroughly. She was attractive standing there, slim in blue jeans and blouse, but he studied her with no real desire, suddenly feeling removed from her. It was odd to feel that way. He felt no desire at all. He then realized that he had not thought once of sex during the whole nightmare week. Jenny's presence had not changed that. He still felt sexually dead. He was ruled by his head, by the fear, and all else had been killed in him. What did he feel? He felt nothing beyond himself. He no longer felt anything but dread, his ever present, cold horror. Jenny turned around to face him. She was tense and antagonistic: a pretty girl, someone from his past, with no place in his future . . . someone talking from faraway.

"I don't believe this," she said.

"Neither do I," Richard said.

"Did you really think I'd fall for that story? Or is the drink just too much for you?"

Richard suddenly felt rage, an unreasonable, brutal hatred, recalling the woman in the car, the flying discs outside the windows, the beams of light that shone over her eyes and turned her to stone, his own burned hands and face . . . Then he stepped toward Jenny, jerked his shirt collar down, bent his head and then pointed to his neck with a stained, shaking finger.

"Look!" he hissed. *"Damn you, look!"*

Jenny was startled by his vehemence, almost pushing him away, her tiny hands flapping loosely in the air and then cupping her face. She glanced briefly at his neck, her brow furrowed, eyes confused, and she saw the livid scar beneath his ear, running under his jawbone.

"It's a burn mark," she said.

"Damn right, it's a burn mark! They shot a beam of light into the car and that's what it did to me."

"Oh, Richard, for God's sake—"

He let his shirt collar go and looked at her with wild eyes, his glass of wine spilling on the floor, further staining the carpet.

"Fuck it, Jenny, *it's true*! These lights shone into the car. They hypnotized the woman, burned the back of my neck, and then, I swear to God, they did something to the car, took a hold of it somehow, pulled it forward, right into that spaceship. *You* explain it! *You tell me!*"

He was shouting, all flushed, a demented gleam in his eyes, those blue eyes that normally were wild and filled with good humor. Jenny watched him, transfixed, not quite frightened but nervous, seeing someone other than Richard, some stranger . . . a threatening presence. At that moment it became unreal—the room's squalor, his fierce temper—and she pursed her lips and picked up her parka and tried to hide behind anger.

"I don't *have* to explain it," she said. "I don't believe it and I won't listen. I'm not sure why you're acting this way, I'm not sure of anything. But you're drunk. You're talking crazy. I won't accept this bloody nonsense. When you're sober just pick up the phone and give me a call. I'm going home now."

Richard stumbled toward her, his hand raised to hurl his glass, then he cracked his shin against the low table and dropped the glass and cursed loudly. Jenny stepped back, slightly frightened, staring at him with big eyes, then she shook her head sadly from side to side and walked out of the room. Richard followed her, enraged, almost stunned by his own violence, then raised his hand and shook his fist wildly as she opened the front door.

"We're asleep!" he shouted after her. "*All* of us—we're asleep! You listen to me, Jenny, we're asleep! We'll all have to wake up soon!"

He hardly knew what he was shouting, didn't listen, didn't care, simply wanted to hear his own voice raging into her silence. The slamming door was his reply—slamming hard; a rebuke—and Richard cursed and turned back into the room, suddenly shaking and horrified.

What had happened with Jenny? What the hell had he done? Already the scene was dreamlike, unreal, slipping out of his reach. The light bulb burned above him, strangely bright, hypnotizing, and he blinked and rushed across the silent room to look down through the window. He saw her just below him, walking along the tarmac path, slinging her parka loosely across her shoulders as she passed the parked cars. It was dark in the driveway, moonlight filtering through the trees, the fallen leaves drifting around her feet as she walked toward the broken gate. Then she was gone. She had not looked back once. Richard stood there and studied the darkness and let the silence surround him.

Fear. The inexplicable. Dread returned, creeping slyly.
Richard found another glass on the table, poured more
wine, started drinking. What the hell was he doing? He
hadn't been a drunkard before. It was funny how quickly
you got to need it, how the fear made your throat go dry.
Richard drank and paced the room, his hands shaking,
eyes flickering, seeing shadows, hearing whisperings in his
head, sensing things all around him.

Jenny had left. She had departed and he felt dead. This
death was not in Jenny's departure, but in something
much larger. He had died a week ago. The other Richard
had disappeared. The new Richard, a haunted man,
sweaty with fear and confusion, was the matrix of something to be formed and prepared for an alien world.

Dread and disbelief. A past rendered obsolescent. He
glanced up and saw the burning electric bulb, the rings of
light all around it. All white. Everything. It had ended and
started there. His whole history, his structured life, his
child's illusion of an orderly world, had been shattered in
the blinding white haze and would never return. He was
sane or he was mad. If he was sane the world was mad.
The most fantastic possibilities now arose and left him
feeling defenseless.

Richard went to the window, looked up at the stars, and
was drawn to the vast sweep of the sky. It had happened:
he had lived it. Looking up, he knew the fear. It was the
fear that it might happen again—or that it might not have
happened. He couldn't separate the two. The two were one
and the same. He dreaded knowing what the experience
might have meant, but feared his ignorance more.

And what had he shouted at Jenny? What exactly had
he meant? *We're asleep. We'll all have to wake up soon
. . .* What in God's name did *that* mean? Richard shook
his head in wonder. He didn't know what he had meant
. . . a belief, possibly just a suspicion, that the fantastic
was actual. His farewell. His defiance.

Richard shivered and turned away and saw the room's
revealing squalor. The white telephone gleamed on the
table and offered its challenge. Fear. The inexplicable. He
couldn't do it: he couldn't talk. He thought of Jenny, of
her reaction and her departure, and he knew what it

meant. The whole world would think he was mad. No rational being could understand. Richard shivered and then felt a great hunger that overrode his concern. He had to get out or collapse. He had to drag his sanity back. He felt spectral, asexual, drained of life, and he had to defeat that. He shivered again and shook his head, placed his wineglass on the table. He glanced around the squalid room, heard the silence, felt the fear, then he reached out and picked up the telephone and dialed the police.

Someone spoke.

Faraway.

CHAPTER EIGHT

I retain my contempt. This one emotion is strength. I have needed that strength for many years and will not let it go. What age was I at the time? I think I must have been forty. I still think it was the explosion over Russia that led to the troubles.

That was 1908. We made a simple mistake. We had a crude form of atomic propulsion and we couldn't control it. So, we had an explosion. The Tunguska region was devastated. The accident frightened the stock company in New York and that started the problem. Some executive panicked, his panic reached the U.S. Government, and they were frightened that the project would be exposed and reacted accordingly. They demanded control of the project. Talked of national security. They made a deal with the corporation in New York and placed us under the military.

The military mind is a perversion. It destroys all it touches. Once the military took over our project I knew it was doomed. An immediate clash of interests. I presented my case and was rejected. I had dreamed of the Atomic Age, of exploration and research, but the military had only one aim, which was national defense. I knew what that meant: they wanted machines for future wars. And despising them, I nevertheless worked with them to keep my plants open.

The following years were a nightmare. My contempt for

the military deepened. A complexity of paperwork, inter-departmental conflicts, interference of the most ignorant kind, then a cutback in funds. All governments are the same. They lumber along like dinosaurs. Shortsighted, un-imaginative, existing only for the moment, they make de-mands and then cry at the cost, thinking only of votes. Yes, I despised them. That emotion was a luxury. It burned in me all of those years and gave me strength to continue. My contempt lacked morality. I have never believed in such. Morality, that conceit of free men, is no aid to their progress. So, not moral outrage. No, it wasn't that. My contempt was for the cowardice and ineptitude that ham-pered my work.

My one interest was science. My major passion was flight. I was dreaming of a voyage to the stars and their infinite mysteries. This dream was not common. Those fools thought it was madness. I realized that they were draining my brain for their own pointless purposes. And so finally I revolted. Withheld vital information. Over two or three years I sabotaged my own projects, deliberately causing failure after failure, feeling pain for the first time.

Such anguish to endure. The first and last time I felt it. The knowledge that I was destroying my own work to keep it safe for the future. And for all that, I did it. My contempt was my protection. I now knew that the cost of the research had filled them with panic. My great machines would not be built: they would rot while the weapons grew. The men in charge were men moved by formless fears: they lacked vision and courage. I did not need such men. Such men were a menace. Only heroes or madmen, History's undefiled dreamers, would be capable of backing my vision and making it real.

Thus I sabotaged the project. I said our hopes had been misguided. They stared at me from behind their long table and showed great relief. My apologies were accepted. A few murmured their regrets. Then my atomic propulsion project was aborted and the hangars closed down. World War I had already started. The Dark Ages had returned. They wanted aircraft of a functional nature, so I quietly resigned.

The worst years of my life. I was forty-five years old. My genius for technology kept me working, but frustration was choking me. Years of drifting around the country. Working here, working there. Disguising genius and displaying mere competence, thus avoiding attention. How did I survive it? With contempt. With my will. Democracy, that catch phrase of the West, became something to laugh at. Democracy was incompetence. The right to vote meant poor leadership. What was needed in the world, and what I wanted most desperately, was a government of heroes or madmen who sought the impossible. Such a government did not exist. The U.S. government was run by cowards. Thus for years, with a pain that turned to rage, I kept my dreams to myself.

Years of cold anguish. The first and last time. Sustained by omniferous curiosity and indomitable will. My contempt for their blindness. My refusal to accept defeat. Every scientific library in the country falling under my scrutiny. All that plus the work. The demeaning jobs I did for money. My genius for engineering, electronics and aeronautics offered up in the disguise of mere competence as a means of survival. But I used even that. Used laboratories and workshops. Created small things here and there, the minor offshoots of my genius, and sold them to the moguls in suits for the freedom I needed.

Then I found a resting place. The facilities were exceptional. I stayed with an aircraft company in Texas as the chief of their research lab. All those nights spent alone. The white sheets of the draftsman. All the experiments I conducted in secret while designing their aircraft. (My head aches as I think this. I find it difficult to remember. The prosthetics and artificial heart cannot help me forever.) Electrostatic repulsion. Photosensitive cell steerage. The reaction of streams of ions to furnish rocket propulsion, then a means of neutralizing the decrease of gravity and other such matters. I never cared about their aircraft. Already they were obsolete. Already I had moved beyond mere flight and was tackling the boundary layer. The boundary layer was everything. Conquer that and the dream was mine. Thus I worked and theorized, the labora-

tory, the wind tunnel, but the theories still remained on the paper and could never be tested.

My dream was of evolution. Man's place in the universe. My dream was of Man as a mind that could transcend the body.

Yet how to achieve this? Man meant individual men. And such men, being imperfect tools, were distracted by hungers. The hunger for love. For admiration and power. I then tried to understand what such things meant and found them all in myself.

The hunger for love. In my loneliness I felt it. Somewhere, sometime, a memory almost gone, I wasted nights trying to heal my own wounds in a more common flesh. What was found was soon lost. The vulva's folds were a threat. The rigid shaft of my penis in their flesh gave no more than a spasm. Such a spasm shapes the world. People live and die for such. And that spasm represents what people want: admiration and power.

Knowing this, I retreated. Love's deceits showed the way. I understood in my moment of grace that their needs were illusions. I retreated and found myself. I took myself in my own hands. When my need, when my sex, became a threat I gave my semen release. Thus I understood men. They were feelings, not thought. Whereas Man, that outpouring of separate men, held the promise of greatness.

Science represents the mind. It is what we must live by. It is logic and towers above the chaos of outmoded emotions. I learned this and lived by it. I stood above my crude desires. When my flesh seduced my mind from its work, I gave it instant release. A shaft of meat in the hand. The ejaculation of semen. It meant then, and to this day still means, the mere appeasement of hunger. And knowing this, I was released. The call of science was my soul. From then on I neither entered another being nor believed in men's sanctity.

Inhuman? Perhaps. But then what does "human" mean? It means fear and confusion and doubt and emotional chaos. To be human is to err. More: to stagnate. Men are impulse encased in flesh and bone, and alone they are nothing. But Man is something different. Man is mind

*over matter. Man is imperfection crawling from the slime
to evolve into Superman.*

I met Goddard in Massachusetts. I remember returning
there. I was fifty years of age at the time, but feeling
younger than that.

How I envied Goddard! Both envied and pitied him.
Another genius humiliated by his countrymen, slowly turning eccentric. Envy. Admiration. Both share the same bed.
And so I envied his achievements, respected them, analyzed them, and felt pity for the future he would have at
the hands of his fellows.

It was 1929. I looked upon him as a child. A suspicious, secretive, brilliant child with more instinct than
logic. And yet he was a genius. There were things I
learned from Goddard. Not much; just the odd, bizarre in-
sight, some small things I had missed: peculiarities of steering systems, gyroscopic controls, various kinds of
self-cooling combustion chambers—small things, all quite
priceless. In return he learned from me. We worked together for two years. My presence unannounced, Goddard
sworn to keep me secret, we spent days in the deserts of
New Mexico, unraveling mysteries. Goddard sent his rockets skyward. My soul soared aloft with them. It was
1932, a troubled year, and I knew that my time had come.

Tsiolkovski and Goddard. Both still alive then. One
older, one much younger than myself, both true pioneers.
The basic principles of space flight: the deaf Russian's
great achievement. Then the liquid-fueled rocket of young
Goddard, abused beyond mention. Both stood at the
threshold. Both failed the same way. Both depended on
honorable men and were thus chained by small minds.
Their mistake was not repeated. I did not trust honorable
men. What I wanted were heroes or madmen—and the
latter sufficed.

I never dwell on morality. Never did, never will. Morality is the crutch of the cripple, the mask of the weak.
What of Wernher von Braun? What of Walter Dornberger? Such men were neither sinners nor saints; they were
quite simply scientists. Can a scientist think of morals?
Should he split peas in a pod? No, what the scientist must
do is pursue his great calling. By himself he has no means.

He must depend on those with power. And in doing so, he must stand aloof from all concepts of right and wrong. I always believed that. I believe it to this day. And gazing out at the wilderness, at the world of snow and ice, I think of how, after working with Goddard, I accepted this truth.

There were madmen back in power. They were obsessed and visionary. To me, they represented the possibility of limitless facilities. I never thought of right or wrong. I simply took my opportunity. I left Goddard and America behind me—and I never returned.

CHAPTER NINE

They drove out of Galveston as the evening fell about them, a fiery sun bathing the Gulf of Mexico in a red, incandescent light. The city soon fell behind them, gave way to impoverished flatlets, old shacks and houses leaning on stilts, silhouetted in crimson haze. Stanford wiped sweat from his brow: the April winds outside were hot; he swore softly and glanced briefly at Epstein, saw him framed by the sinking sun. The professor looked very tired; he rubbed his eyes and coughed a lot. Stanford grinned at him and then watched the road that cut through the bleak countryside.

"I got a call from a friend," he said. "He told me it happened this afternoon. He works in the Manned Spacecraft Center just outside Houston and he wants us to go there when he's finished. He said he would talk to us."

Epstein smiled wearily. "You're such an operator," he said. "I never imagined I'd get into MSC, so you've just made my day."

Stanford laughed at that. "Well, you know me, professor. I had this sweet girl and this girl knows this guy and this guy wants what I get from the girl and so he's very obliging."

"You're a bastard," Epstein said.

"I have a mom and a pa."

"You really should settle down, Stanford. You're too old for that nonsense."

Stanford laughed again. "I can't make decisions," he said. "You told me that about two weeks ago, and I think you were right. I'm an irresponsible sonofabitch. I can't let my cock go hungry. If it wasn't for that I'd have been a good scientist instead of troubleshooting for your institute. We all have our place in life."

Epstein almost laughed but instead a cough came out, making him cover his mouth with a handkerchief and spit the phelgm out. When he had finished he cursed softly, shook his head from side to side, then glanced out of the window of the speeding car, his eyes slightly unfocused.

"You should see a doctor," Stanford said.

"I'm too busy, young man."

"You've had that goddamned cough a long time."

"I've been alive a long time."

"You're not so old."

"I grow younger every day." Epstein studied the bloody sunset in the west, the starkly shadowed flatlands. "Where on earth are we going?"

"Someone's ranch," Stanford said. "About halfway between here and Houston. It's supposed to be just off this road. We should be there real soon."

"What sort of rancher?"

"A struggling one-man band. A few crops and a hundred head of cattle. Now he's left with the crops."

Epstein nodded sympathetically, closed his eyes and put his head back, sinking luxuriously into the seat, trying to sleep. The sun had almost gone, the crimson dusk turning to darkness, a ragged ribbon of mountains in the distance, suffused in an ocher haze. The wind was growing stronger, howling around the speeding car, clouds of dust racing across the flatlands and whipping the cactus trees.

"What did you find out about Irving?"

"I thought you were sleeping," Stanford said.

"No," Epstein said, "I'm just resting. Now what about Irving?"

Stanford sighed. "Not a thing," he said. "The loss of his papers is still a mystery—and that doesn't help much."

"The police?"

"No papers. They didn't find anything in the car. Apparently the only thing Irving took with him was that fucking pistol."

"We checked the terrain," Epstein said. "That area was definitely radioactive. I think something came down above Irving and made that scorched circle."

"That was one hell of a scorch mark."

"Yes, it was huge. But assuming that something descended, that would explain the lack of tire tracks."

"A UFO."

"Precisely."

"It's too incredible," Stanford said. "I just can't bring myself to believe it. I try, but I can't."

"There were UFOs over the area. They were all tracked on radar. Three of them—one large and two small—and they were tracked near that area."

"I checked on Mary's info. A lot of what she said was true. Dr. Jessup committed suicide. Rene Hardy committed suicide. James McDonald drove himself into the desert and shot himself in the head—exactly like Irving. She was also right about Chuck Wakely. He'd been stirring things up a bit. He was shot in his room in Miami a couple of weeks back."

"I think there's a connection."

"I think you may be right."

"And the Philadelphia Experiment?"

"All the doors are closed tight. The Navy categorically denied that it ever existed . . . it's just one of those rumors."

"Maybe," Epstein said. "And then again, maybe not. It's a known fact that the Navy has been working for some years to develop a form of magnetic cloud that can temporarily render ships invisible. It's also widely rumored, though not yet proven, that NASA has been engaged in researching the possibilities of antigravity. Who knows *what* they've accomplished. They keep a lot of their achievements quiet. As both of us know, their denials don't mean a damned thing."

The sun sank behind the mountains, the bloodred dusk dissolving, the sky starry, the wind howling around the car as it headed toward Houston. Epstein sank into his seat, his hands folded primly in his lap, trying not to think of

Irving or Mary or the passage of time. He wasn't really growing younger. In fact his age weighed upon him. He glanced out of the speeding car, saw the swirling of the sand, the black night stretched out all around them, hybrid with mystery.

"What do you know about the CIA?"

"Odds and ends," Stanford said.

"UFO investigations?"

"They've been involved," Stanford said. "No one really knows how long or how much, but they *have* been involved."

"Is it possible to check it out?"

"It wouldn't be too difficult."

"No," Epstein said. "I mean to check it out in detail. I want to know the whole history, from the end of the war to the present. I want to know when it started. I want to know why. I want to know if their concern is just for national security or if they're really concerned with something much bigger. I don't want the usual rumors, the speculations and guesswork; I want the facts straight from the horse's mouth: the complete, detailed picture."

"Why?" Stanford said.

"Because I think the answer's there. Because too many of those people have come to bad ends after having a lot of trouble with the establishment, scientific or military. Why was Jessup called to Washington? Why did Ruppelt revise his book? Why did Irving and Dr. James McDonald both go down the same way? McDonald was harassed and humiliated. Irving had to endure the same. Mary claims that Irving thought he was being followed, and that might well be true. Others have made similar claims. Many retired or disappeared. There's no doubt that investigating UFOs can lead to bad trouble. Does the government know something? Is the CIA involved? If the UFOs exist, and if they're extraterrestrial, that would certainly put the wind up any government, might frighten the hell out of them. I think the UFOs exist. I also think they're extraterrestrial. It's possible that the government thinks the same and is just running scared. That would explain the harassment. It would explain all their denials. They might be scared of people getting too close and revealing the truth."

Stanford shook his head wearily. "You're getting carried away." he said. "You've been at this game too many years and it's all getting through to you. Of *course* the CIA is interested—they're involved in national security. They're interested in the UFOs because they don't know what they are and because *any* unidentified objects could be dangerous. It doesn't matter what UFOs are; what matters is what they *do*. And what the UFOs do is cause panic and confusion, distracting pilots and tying up communications every time there's a sighting. In short, they're a fucking nuisance. They cost time and a lot of bread. If we could identify them positively as atmospheric phenomena, the pilots would no longer be distracted and the phones would stop ringing . . . thus the CIA's interest."

"But the CIA has denied that they're interested."

"God, you're stubborn," said Stanford.

He grinned and rolled his eyes, turned the car off to the right, left the main road in favor of a narrow track that cut obliquely through flat fields. The track was very rough, making the car bounce and groan, its headlights almost useless in the dust clouds that howled all around them. Stanford cursed and slowed down, trying to see through the darkness, the moon and stars almost blotted out by the thick swirling dust.

"Jesus," Stanford said, "that's some wind out there."

Epstein coughed and rubbed his eyes, feeling strangely suffocated, aggravated by the howling of the wind and the dense, swirling dust clouds. They were in the middle of nowhere, the storm raging through a void; he caught a glimpse of barbed wire, a gnarled tree, the black hump of a distant hill. The dust seemed to be alive, racing at them and around them, smacking the car and then exploding obliquely and spraying back down upon them. This night had no boundary, stretching as far as the eye could see, filled with nothing but clouds of dust and the odd, indistinct tree.

"There they are," Stanford said.

Epstein stared into the storm, saw some lights far ahead, rather dull and suspended in space, the dust racing across them. He blinked and looked again, saw the lights coming closer, separating, gliding away from one another until they formed a long line. Epstein strained to see better. The lights were now a lot brighter. The car shuddered and then rolled down an incline and the lights changed again. They were actually raised up on trucks. The trucks surrounded a large field. The lights were like the lamps of a football stadium, beaming down on the ground below. The whole scene was very strange. He saw the circle of lights, the dust racing across the field, indistinct figures wandering back and forth, waving arms, bending over. The sand blew all around them, clumps of sagebrush rolled and danced, and the arc lamps formed an immense globe of light surrounded by black night.

They drove up to the field, parked behind one of the trucks, and the lamps threw down a monstrous white glare that temporarily blinded them. Epstein closed his eyes a moment, opened them, looked again: he saw the dust sweeping through the bright light, around the men walking back and forth. All the men seemed very odd: they seemed to have no eyes nor lips. Epstein shivered and tried to concentrate and then saw the reality. The men were wearing protective glasses, their mouths covered with white filter masks. They were waving at one another, trying to shout against the wind, bending over the dark, motionless bundles that littered the ground.

"Here we go," Stanford said. He handed Epstein a mask and glasses. "Put them on. You'll need them out there. That stuff could choke you to death."

Epstein did as he was told, sniffed the mask, felt claustrophobic, then he stared at Stanford through the dark glasses and beheld a strange creature. No eyes. No lips. Epstein thought of his UFO reports. There were connections wherever you cared to look and it was best not to think of them. Stanford opened the car door. He pointed ahead and then jumped out. Epstein opened his own door and jumped out and felt the fist of the wind.

The wind smacked his face, punched his chest, pushed him back; he reached out and grabbed the door of the car and then pulled himself forward. The noise was eerie, bizarre, a constant, deathly howling, the blowing sand making a separate, hissing sibilance that tortured his eardrums. Epstein felt that he was dreaming: demoniac shapes formed in the dust. A grotesque, faceless figure materialized and reached out to grab hold of him. Epstein was pulled forward. He followed Stanford toward the lights. The dust spiraled around the trucks, around the lights, around the men in the bright field. They walked past the nearest truck, saw a man kneeling down. He was dressed in coveralls, wore the mask and dark glasses, and was studying the intestines of a cow that had been disemboweled.

Stanford waved his right hand. "All dead," he said. "A hundred head of cattle. All dead. Every last one of them."

Epstein looked around the field, recognized the dark bundles, saw the dust covering blood, bone and tripe, the hides slashed and peeled back. It was a scene of incredible carnage. The wind carried the stench away. The masked men walked back and forth, looking here, looking there, kneeling down and then standing up again with their hands dripping blood. They were carrying surgical instruments, probing flesh and dismembered limbs, moving to and fro as if in a trance, still not fully believing it. Epstein suddenly shivered. It was hot, but he felt cold. He saw the gleam of white bone, a slashed udder, a pool of blood; the wind howling, the dust sweeping over all, trying to bury the horror.

Stanford led him across the field, walking between the dead cattle, around the bulldozer that was roaring into life, past the blood-covered men. The cattle were everywhere, scattered over the whole field, some stripped of their hides, the rib cages gleaming dully, throats slashed, legs and udders chopped off, eyeballs torn from their sockets. Epstein had never seen anything like it—it was a shocking, bloody sight. The wind threw the sand around the men, around the trucks and the blazing lamps.

Stanford walked on ahead, skirting around blood-soaked pits, then turned his head and pointed toward a nearby truck, telling Epstein to follow him. Epstein nodded and continued walking. The wind tugged at his body. He put his head down and stumbled toward the truck, trying to see through the twisting sand. Eventually he reached the truck, walked around it and saw a car, a group of men squatting in the narrow space where the wind was less fierce.

Epstein walked up to this group and knelt down beside Stanford, noticed the tripe on the dusty coveralls, the men minus their masks. These men seemed very weary and were drinking cans of beer. The narrow space between the truck and the car afforded modest protection. Stanford pulled his mask off and Epstein gratefully did the same, then Stanford opened a can of beer, had a drink, wiped his lips and grinned at another squatting man as if they were old friends.

"Help yourself to a beer," this man said. "Don't wait to be asked."

Stanford grinned boyishly. "A fine brew," he said. "I only come out nights like this on the chance of a free beer."

"What the hell are you doing here, Stanford? I thought this was a secret. We only got the word an hour ago, and we haven't told anyone."

Stanford winked. "An old MSC friend. He gave me the word on the hot line and I just came right over."

"He?"

"Oh, well . . ."

"You've been poking some cutey."

"A man has to give something in return; it's the least I could do."

The squatting man grinned and shook his head from side to side. "Oh, boy," he said, "you really are a mover . . . you're some scientist, Stanford." He spat dust from his mouth, wiped some grime from his eyes, had another slug of beer and glanced around him, shook his head again, slowly. "You ever seen anything like that? It's happening all over the country. Cattle and sheep and sometimes horses: a real butcher's paradise."

"Bless the wind," another man said.

"Yeah," another said. ". . . the stench."

"Stanford, you better keep your mouth shut; we don't want this discussed."

Stanford nodded and sipped some beer. "That's understood," he said. "We had a case like this three months ago; the very same thing."

"Where was that?"

"Lubbock."

"I think I remember it." The squatting man looked lazily at Epstein. "Who's this?" he said.

Epstein flushed a little, feeling a bit out of place, but he looked the squatting man in the eyes and said, "Frederick Epstein."

"Who?"

"Dr. Epstein's from the Aerial Phenomena Investigations Institute in Washington," Stanford said. "He's been on a few cases like this before and he doesn't talk much."

"The Aerial Phenomena Investigations Institute? Why the hell are you interested in this?"

"Come *on*, Miller!" Stanford said.

"Come on *nothing*," Miller replied. "I don't know what you birds want out here. It's got nothing to do with you."

"Yes, it has," Epstein said. "There's been a number of cases like this right around the whole country, and they usually occur when UFOs have been reported. Cattle mutilation isn't common: there might be a connection."

Miller drank some beer, wiped his lips with one hand, shook his head wearily from side to side and sighed in despair.

"I don't believe this," he said. "You fucking dogs stop at nothing. The slightest chance to pin something on a UFO and you just rush to grab it. This has nothing to do with UFOs. There's no connection at all. What you have here is the work of a gang of rural deviants—or possibly some bizarre religious ritual. It may be sick, but that's all it is: a gang of nuts on the loose."

"I don't believe that," Epstein said.

"You come from Washington," Miller said. "You don't know what some of these country boys are like. The lack of sex drives them crazy."

Stanford laughed at that. "Not *my* problem," he said.

"No," Miller said. "Not your problem. You're a clean living city boy." He sighed again and stood up, finished off his can of beer, threw the can on the ground at his feet and then held up his face mask. "We've got work to do," he said. "We've got to bury these carcasses. I can't sit here and talk to you lunatics. Go on home. On your feet, boys."

The other men cursed and groaned, wearily climbed to their feet, started putting on their face masks and glasses, the dust whirling around them. Stanford stood up as well, handed his beer can to Epstein, walked up to Miller, tugged his elbow and leaned very close to him, hissing into the wind.

"Just tell me one thing," he said quietly. "Have you had any UFO reports?"

Miller looked at him coolly, turned away and surveyed the field, his shadow stretching out from his feet, emphasized by the bright lights.

"I don't know what you're talking about," he said.

Stanford wasn't smiling. "I'm talking about fucking UFOs. I'm wondering what you boys are doing here if what you told me is true."

"*What* did I tell you?"

"You told me this was nothing. You told me it was the work of some crazies. If so, it's a police case."

"We're burying the bodies," Miller said.

"You work for NASA," Stanford said. "You work for a decontamination unit and you've done this before."

"So, what's your bitch? Dead cattle can contaminate. We came out because we don't want this mess causing any disease. We're the nearest available people. That's all there is to it. We got called out because there's no one else and because we're equipped. The local health officer called us out. He said he wanted this mess cleaned up. He said it would take too long to get civilians, and he asked us to help. There's no mystery about it."

"Horseshit," Stanford said.

"Suit yourself," Miller said.

"That apartment in Austin," Stanford said. "It's booked up from this moment."

Miller sighed, shook his head in despair, walked a little bit away from the men, tugging Stanford along with him. They stood at the edge of the field, the carnage spread out behind them, the lamps on the trucks beaming down, the sand spiraling and hissing.

"You've got a friend in MSC?"

"That's right," Stanford said.

"And he's the one who told you about this?"

"You hit the nail on the head."

Miller nodded and glanced around him, the wind tugging at his clothes, the dust sweeping across the flat field and the slumped bloody cattle.

"So, you're going to see him."

"Right," Stanford said.

"Then presumably he'll tell you about it and I've nothing to lose." Miller glanced around him carefully. Epstein moved a little closer. The wind made it difficult to hear, and Miller spoke softly. "There's a rancher and his daughter. The rancher seems to be in shock. The daughter's about eighteen years old and she doesn't seem too bright. The rancher's still babbling. The daughter doesn't say much at all. The rancher says he was in the house, having dinner with his daughter, when they heard a humming sound, the whole place went bananas, and a strange light, much brighter than the sun, almost blinded them both. The rancher dived to the floor. Apparently his daughter just sat there. The light faded and the rancher got up and grabbed his rifle and rushed outside. At first he saw nothing. Then the humming began again. His daughter joined him on the porch as he looked up, so she looked up as well. There was something over his grazing land. He's pretty vague on what it was. All we know is that he thinks it was huge and that it glowed and climbed slowly. I don't think he's all there. I think they're both a bit nuts. He says the object was as big as the field, that it was silvery and disc-shaped. It hummed and climbed slowly. There were lights right around its rim. It climbed vertically to a hundred feet or so and then it shot off obliquely. His daughter smiles when he mentions it."

"What about MSC?"

"They've had radar lock-ons. The blips appeared then disappeared, kept returning and disappearing, and we sent some jets up to pursue them but there wasn't a hope. Those unidentified's were moving fast. They made the jets seem like toys. They were doing 7,000 miles an hour, and the jets never saw them. The radar located them here. Same place and same time. The rancher jumped in his truck and came out here and almost went crazy. He called the sheriff and the sheriff called us and here's what we found."

Miller waved his right hand, indicating the floodlit field, the men stooped and working hard in the churned-up dust, the roaring mass of the bulldozer.

"Are these storms usual?" Epstein asked.

"Not at this time of the year."

"It might be electrical," Stanford said.

"It might be anything," Miller said. He waved at the nearby men, told them to get back to work, then he put on his mask and dark goggles and said, "Come with me."

Stanford and Epstein followed him, skirting the edge of the field, both wearing their face masks and goggles, bent against the fierce wind. Miller climbed into a jeep, told them to get in the back, and when they did so he shot off down the road, the dust defeating his headlights. He drove for five minutes, driving blindly and dangerously, bouncing over potholes and mounds of earth until he came to the ranch. It was large and dilapidated, an overgrown shack on stilts, creaking in the wind and hissing dust, its lights piercing the darkness.

Miller drove up and stopped, killed his headlights and jumped out, waited for Stanford and Epstein, then walked up to the steps. The house lamps were lit, framed by shuddering windows, and the light fell from the windows to the porch, illuminating the silent girl. The girl was unkempt, her long hair whipping her face. She was wearing a cheap cotton dress, her legs and arms were bare, and she stood there with a thumb in her mouth, staring up at the sky.

"Hello, Emmylou!" Miller shouted. "What are you doing, standing out here? You're going to choke in this dust!"

The girl moved very slowly, turning her head with some reluctance, gazing down at them, her thumb still in her mouth, her brown eyes very large. She didn't say anything, simply studied Miller and Epstein. She glanced at Stanford and her eyes flicked away and then came back toward him. She smiled, the thumb still in her mouth, looking lazily at Stanford.

"Can we come in?" Miller said.

The girl blinked and then nodded. The three men walked up the steps to the porch and then stood by the front door. They all stared at the girl. The howling wind pressed her dress to her body, revealing large breasts and hips. The dress had buttons up the front; these buttons were undone up to her thighs. The dress was blown back, exposing her legs which were brown and quite muscular.

Stanford studied her carefully. He couldn't take his eyes off her. She had the insolence of a child, a sort of lazy sensuality, standing there and sucking her thumb, staring at him and smiling. Stanford wanted to put it into her. He suddenly saw himself doing it. The lust took him with immediate, startling force and stripped his senses away. He shook his head and checked himself. He was sweating and felt feverish. The girl sucked her thumb and stared at him, smiling slightly, ambiguously.

"You're the daughter," Stanford said.

The girl smiled at him and nodded.

"We want to talk to you and your father. We want to know what you saw out there."

The girl stood five feet away. Stanford wanted to touch her. He could hardly stop himself from doing it. The girl sucked at her thumb and stared at him and made no reply.

"Can we go inside?" Miller said.

The girl nodded dumbly. Miller knocked on the door and then opened it and they followed him in. The house was brightly lit, with oil lamps near the windows, casting shadows on the dusty, wooden floor and the makeshift furniture. Stanford stood beside Epstein, the girl inching in behind him; he felt that she was pressing against him, and it made him uncomfortable. The shadows fell down flaking walls, crept over handmade wooden chairs. The old rancher was at the table, his hair white, his chin unshaven, a bottle of whiskey close to his left hand, most of it gone. Miller touched him on the shoulder, shook him gently, murmured to him; the old man raised his head, licked his lips, gazed around him, stared at Miller and went very red and then reached for the bottle.

"Not again," he growled. "No!"

Miller stepped back a little. "Just once more," he said. "Just tell these men what you think you saw. It could be important."

The old man drank from the bottle, slammed it down and glared at Miller; his eyes were bloodshot and he had the glazed look of someone not in control of himself. He wiped his lips with one hand, the fingers blistered and grimy, flicking whiskey from his lips and then slipping down to scratch at his chin. Miller's shadow fell across him, blotting out half his face, and he moved out of the shadow and glared at Epstein, finally settled on Stanford. The girl was standing behind Stanford. He heard the rustling of her dress. He thought of her dress sticking to her skin, to her hot thighs and soft breasts. Stanford felt very strange, obscurely threatened by the girl, having to force himself not to turn around and touch her flesh with his hands. He couldn't understand the feeling: it was something more than lust; it was like a dream carried in on the wind and now surrounding his being. Stanford felt sick with longing; he had a hard, pulsating erection. He stepped back into the shadows to hide it, and the girl moved back with him. The old man was staring at him, glaring at him, snorting contemptuously, then he glared at Miller and Epstein in turn and started drinking more whiskey. His hand was shaking a lot. He was not as fierce as he looked. He spilled some whiskey down his shirt and then cursed and slammed the bottle back down.

"I saw nothing," he said. "*Nothing!*"

"Please," Miller said.

"Go to hell," the old man said.

"It's important that you try to remember."

"Go to hell. I saw nothing."

The girl moved away from Stanford, slipping quietly through the shadows, pressed herself against the window's wooden frame and gazed up at the sky. She wasn't sucking her thumb: she was biting her tongue and humming softly, her belly pressed against the windowpane, her spine arched, her breasts outthrust. Stanford tried not to stare; his eyes were drawn against their will. Shadows flickered over the girl, over Miller and Epstein, over the old man who sat at the table and spilled whiskey and cursed.

"It was silvery," Miller prompted.

"I saw nothing," the old man growled.

"You said it was as big as the field."

"Jesus Christ . . . *Fucking Jesus!*"

The old man kicked his chair back, stood up straight, clutched his head, then he let out a terrible anguished scream that lacerated them all. Miller and Epstein jumped back. Stanford glanced at the girl. She smiled and slid her thumb into her mouth, then turned her eyes toward her father. The old man was clutching his head, shaking it wildly and screaming. He suddenly slammed his fist down on the table, swung it back, swept the bottle off. The bottle flew across the room, hit the wall and exploded, the whiskey spraying over Miller and Epstein as they moved toward the door. Miller pulled the door open. The girl sucked her thumb and hummed. The old man screamed again and grabbed the table and then tipped it over. Epstein followed Miller out. Stanford edged along the wall. The old man grabbed his rifle, swung it wildly around his head, and started sweeping cups and plates off a shelf that ran above the fireplace. Stanford glanced at the girl. She was smiling and humming softly. She was still sucking her thumb and her brown eyes were luminous and teasing. Stanford edged out through the door. The old man screamed and smashed things. Stanford backed into the wind and blowing sand and stumbled down the porch steps. Miller and Epstein were in the jeep, the engine running, the headlights on, and Stanford got in the back beside Epstein, pouring sweat, his heart pounding. The old man lurched through the door, a silhouette in yellow light, rushed forward and put his hand on an upright and then glared at them all.

"I saw light!" he shrieked. *"Light!"*

Stanford drove along NASA Highway 1 toward the Manned Spacecraft Center. Stanford felt very strange. He felt terribly alone. Epstein was sitting in the seat right beside him, but he didn't seem real. Stanford drove fast and recklessly, now ignoring the storm, oppressed by the heat and the noise, obsessed with the girl.

He thought back on what had happened, turned it over in his head, tried to cast it out and concentrate on his driving, but returned to the mystery . . . What had happened back there? What had drawn him to the girl? Was there a connection between the girl's calm abstraction and her father's wild outburst? He remembered the old man clutching his head, shaking it wildly from side to side, screaming as if trying to break loose from a terrible anguish. What had actually made him scream? What had made him turn so violent? And what secret did he share with the girl who sucked her thumb and smiled mindlessly? Stanford tried to think it out. He could think only of the girl. He saw her standing on the porch, in the light from the window. Stanford couldn't understand it. His lust was almost supernatural. It was not based on her breasts and full thighs, but on her luminous, empty eyes. Stanford felt himself shivering. The sound of the wind tore at his nerves. He glanced at Epstein, at that lined, bearded face, and wondered what he was thinking.

"What do you think they saw?" he said.

"I don't know," Epstein said.

"They sure as hell were acting pretty strange."

"Yes, they were," Epstein said.

"I think what they saw affected them."

"Yes, no doubt it did."

"I mean, I think it might have *physically* affected them."

"You think so?" Epstein said.

Stanford didn't reply to that. He didn't know what to say. He looked ahead and saw the clouds of dust sweeping over the dark road. The storm was fierce and unrelenting, blotting out the moon and stars, the spinning sand forming into shapes that seemed almost alive. Stanford cursed again softly. The noise and darkness were getting to him. He thought he saw some lights far ahead, and that made him feel better.

"That looks like it," he said.

"The Manned Spacecraft Center?"

"Yes," Stanford said. "Straight ahead. You can't see much from here."

Epstein sat up and looked ahead. He thought he saw

lights in the distance, but he couldn't be sure. The dust was everywhere, racing at them and around them, hammering at the car and making it vibrate. Epstein didn't feel very well. He kept thinking of the hundred butchered cows, the men in goggles and masks. Epstein shivered and coughed and glanced briefly at Stanford; his friend was just a dark form in the black night, a faint light in his eyes. Epstein wondered what was wrong: his young friend was too quiet; he sensed a great tension in Stanford and he wondered what caused it. Not the hundred butchered cows. Not the raving old man. Stanford was much tougher than that, was much stronger than he was. Epstein looked at his young friend, heard him murmuring something. He wondered what Stanford was thinking, then he studied the road ahead. He saw the distant lights, shining weakly through the storm, emphasizing the awful desolation of this dark, empty area.

"That man Miller," Epstein said. "How did you get him to talk? I heard you saying something about an apartment. What on earth did you mean?"

That finally got a laugh from Stanford. "God, you're sharp," he said. "It's an apartment that I've had for years in Austin, and I let some friends use it. Miller's a married man. He's not a happily married man. I've been letting him use the place this past few months for his one great *affaire*. He's not experienced at that game. That's the only place he can go. He doesn't want to lose his little bit of action, so his tongue started wagging."

"That's blackmail," Epstein said.

"Don't be sordid," Stanford said. He laughed again and looked at the lights ahead and then he started to frown. "Jesus Christ," he said. "What the hell . . . ?"

Epstein looked ahead and saw the lights through the murk. The car was racing toward them, but the lights remained unchanged: the same size, the same distance away, as if actually pacing them. Epstein sat up very straight. Stanford stepped on the gas. The car roared and raced into the storm, heading straight for the distant lights. Epstein suddenly felt unreal. He bent forward and strained to see: there were twenty or thirty lights, very weak, not too big, spread out at equal distances in a long line that straddled the road. Stanford cursed and gunned the engine. The distance between the car and the lights remained exactly the same.

"Goddammit, *they're moving!*"

Stanford almost screamed the words. He kept his eyes on the lights. The car raced into the murk, doing sixty miles and hour, and the distance between it and the lights didn't alter the least.

"They're above the road," Epstein said.

"Fucking right!" Stanford exclaimed. "They're a good hundred feet above the road and they're definitely *moving!*"

"How far away do you think they are?"

"About a quarter of a mile."

"Then that line of lights is half a mile wide."

"Jesus Christ . . . *Jesus Christ!*"

Stanford put his foot right down and the car leaped ahead, throwing Epstein back into his seat in an untidy heap. He quickly pushed himself back up, heard the mournful, howling wind, saw the lights in the sky far ahead, glowing through the fierce dust clouds. Stanford just kept on driving, his eyes bright and intense; he went all out, but the distance remained the same, the lights luring them on.

Stanford cursed and kept driving. Epstein held on to his seat. The line of lights was very straight, very wide, and it kept the same distance. There was something weird about it. The car was roaring against the wind. The line of lights appeared not to be moving, but it stayed well ahead of them. Then it suddenly stopped: the lights rushed at them and grew larger, glowing down through the dense dust, illuminating the road below.

"Jesus Christ!" Stanford hissed.

He slammed his foot on the brake pedal, and the car shrieked and started skidding around in a spiraling cloud of dust, almost turning full circle. Epstein's head hit the windshield, bounced back into the seat, his hands darting out to grab the dashboard as the car skidded around, its rear facing the motionless lights. Stanford cursed and killed the engine, opened his door and jumped out, was pummeled by the wind and sand and saw the lights rising vertically. Epstein followed him out, wiping blood from his forehead; and they stood there, one at each side of the car, looking up disbelievingly.

The long line of lights was rigid and didn't sway from side to side. It was not too far away, about two hundred feet up, the separate lights yellow and weak, glowing through the dust storm. The lights rose very slowly, making no discernible sound, growing smaller, moving closer together, then finally merging as one. This one light was long and thin and gradually shrank to a glowing sphere. The glowing sphere slowly climbed above the storm and disappeared in the black sky.

Stanford and Epstein were stunned, glancing briefly at one another. They stood there for a long time. They both stared up at the sky. Eventually, being pummeled by wind and dust, they went back to the car.

"Where are we?" Epstein said.

"About a mile from MSC. I thought that thing was heading straight for it. I thought it was going to smash through it."

"It was low enough," Epstein said.

"Damned right, it was low enough. It was low enough and big enough to level MSC to the ground."

"They must have seen it," Epstein said.

"They couldn't have missed it," Stanford said. "Let's go. I want to find out what's happening. Those fuckers can't deny this one."

Stanford drove more carefully now, feeling strangely disorientated, his nerves flayed by the wind and the dust and the night's weird events. He thought of the girl on the porch, of her luminous, empty eyes, of her firm breasts and brown, naked thighs, her belly pressed to the windowsill. His lust returned immediately, a primitive, unreasoning lust, and he shook his head and tried to think of something else: the old man's sudden violence . . . What had descended over the field? Just what had the old man seen? Stanford tried to think it through and failed dismally, his lust growing and blinding him.

Epstein remained silent, feeling stunned and exhilarated, thinking of the vertically climbing lights and their serene, silent beauty. It all seemed fantastic. The whole night was like a dream. He felt a bit dizzy, coughed a lot and rubbed his eyes, exhausted and excited all at once, his heart pounding dramatically. It was his first UFO sighting and it had filled him with awe. He thought of the butchered cattle, of the old man screaming, *"Light!"*, and he wondered if what he had just seen had also materialized over the grazing field.

The storm was almost unnatural, certainly unprecedented; it had emerged from a placid, crimson dusk and showed no signs of abating. Epstein thought of the ascending lights—that line of lights that never swayed—and wondered what kind of object it was that could hide in this storm.

Epstein glanced ahead and saw another line of lights, hazed behind the dense clouds of dust, hanging dimly in black space. He rubbed his eyes and looked again, feeling decidedly odd. The lights grew larger and illuminated a fence and a wide metal gate. It was the Manned Spacecraft Center. The lights shone from white buildings. Epstein sighed with relief and then coughed and wiped his lips with a handkerchief.

Stanford drew up to the gate and stopped the car and a guard came toward them. The guard was stooped against the wind, pressing his cap to his head, the dust whirling around him and covering his uniform. Stanford rolled the window down and the dust roared in through the car. The guard's masked face appeared at the window, his eyes hidden by goggles.

"Dr. Stanford!" Stanford shouted. "This here's Professor Epstein! We have an appointment with Captain Armstrong of the Space Science and Technology Administrative Office!"

"I'm sorry, sir," the guard said. "Your appointment's probably been canceled. We're in the middle of a special security exercise, under strictest security."

"You don't understand, corporal . . . we have an *appointment*."

"I'm sorry, sir. Your appointment has been canceled. You'll have to leave now."

Stanford looked beyond the guard, saw the closed gate and fences, the roads between the buildings filled with troops, all heavily armed.

"A *security* exercise?"

"That's right, sir. Just routine."

"That's an awful lot of men for a security exercise. What the hell's going on here?"

The guard's face was impassive. "I'm sorry, sir. You'll have to leave."

"Listen, corporal, we've got an *appointment*. Now just get on that telephone."

The corporal straightened up, waved his hand at the guard's box, and another man, a sergeant, walked out, carrying a rifle.

"What's up?" he said.

"We've got an appointment," Stanford said.

"All appointments have been canceled," the sergeant said. "You're not allowed in."

Stanford looked past the sergeant, past the fence, into the Space Center, saw the troops lined along the linear roads, all studying the sky.

"Sergeant," he said, "we just saw some very strange lights across the road about a mile or so back. They were moving, and then when we approached them, they started to climb. Any idea what they were?"

"Probably a helicopter, sir."

"Too big to be a helicopter, sergeant. Try something else."

"I don't know, sir."

"You should have seen them from here, sergeant."

"No, sir, we didn't."

"You couldn't have possibly missed them, sergeant; they formed a very long line."

"We haven't seen anything."

"Why are your men studying the sky, sergeant?"

"They're looking for helicopters, sir. It's a security exercise. They're supposed to report the helicopters as soon as they see them."

"You have helicopters up there in this storm?"

"That's right, sir."

"You think helicopters can fly in this weather?"

"Yes, sir. I suppose so."

"And you're not going to report the lights we saw?"

"We haven't seen any lights, sir. Now please leave the area."

Stanford sighed, studied the soldiers behind the fence, saw them all staring up at the sky.

"Sergeant, please get on that telephone and tell Captain Armstrong that we're here."

"I can't do that."

"What the hell do you mean, you can't do that?"

"Captain Armstrong isn't here, sir. No administrative personnel are allowed in until the end of the exercise."

"But he *told* us to meet him here!"

"That was probably before he knew about this exercise. He's not here anymore, sir."

"Sergeant, that was only two hours ago."

"Sorry, sir."

"You mean you pulled this security exercise without giving anyone any notice?"

"I'm sorry, sir. You'll have to leave now."

The sergeant straightened up and held his rifle across his chest, trying to see through the dense sand, unprotected by goggles. Stanford glared at him, unwilling to move, then the corporal placed his right hand on his pistol and reached out for the door handle. Stanford noticed the gesture, cursed softly and shook his head, then he turned on the ignition, reversed the car sharply, and headed back along NASA Highway 1, cutting through the fierce storm.

"God*dammit!*" he exclaimed. "What the *hell's* going on? Those bastards were lying through their teeth. They know something is up there."

"They were studying the sky," Epstein said.

"Damned right, they were studying the sky . . . They've seen something up there and now they've locked the fucking gates and they've got that place looking like a battle zone. And now Armstrong . . . Oh, *Jesus!*"

He smacked the steering wheel with one hand, shook his

head from side to side, and glanced at Epstein with a drugged gleam in his eyes.

"Where are we going?" Epstein said.

"Clear Lake," Stanford said. "Armstrong lives in Nassau Bay and I think he's probably hiding out there now. I want to talk to that bastard."

Epstein sank back into his seat and closed his eyes, his exuberance giving way to exhaustion. The car roared and vibrated, pummeled constantly by the storm, and Epstein floated in a weird, light-flecked darkness, now removed from himself. He saw the long line of lights, rising slowly and silently, gliding up through the wind and dust with a startling majesty. Then he imagined the rancher's field, the same lights descending quietly, the cattle bellowing in panic and confusion as the dust beat about them . . . What had happened after that? What had caused the terrible carnage? Indeed, had anything descended at all or had the rancher imagined it? . . . Epstein coughed and wiped his lips, opened his eyes and surveyed the storm. Clouds of dust swept around the speeding car and raced across the dark flatlands.

"It's not like Armstrong," Stanford said. "I've known that guy for years. He's been passing me information for years, and he's always reliable. He told me to meet him at MSC. He's never missed an appointment. If that was just a security exercise he'd have certainly known about it and he wouldn't have sent us out there in the first place. Those guards are looking for something. They sealed that place off at the last moment. They must have sealed it off just after Armstrong rang me, and there must be a reason for that. Armstrong said he had something to tell me. That usually means unidentifieds. I think those guards in MSC and the NASA decontamination team are part and parcel of the very same thing: there's something over this area."

He slowed the car down, pointing his finger at murky lights, turning into the sleepy suburb of Nassau Bay and cruising along empty streets. There were lights on in the houses, silhouettes framed by windows, the lights beaming out and falling on neat lawns, the shrubbery bent by the wind. Stanford cruised for some time, studying the left side of the road, straining to see through the clouds of dust and muttering under his breath.

"That's it," he said eventually, pulling over to the right, stopping the car on a graveled drive that fronted a chalet-styled, charcoal brown house. He killed the engine and switched the lights off, opened the door and climbed out, and Epstein followed him and joined him on the porch as he was pressing the doorbell. They heard the sounds of revelry from inside, a lot of laughing and shouting. Stanford pressed the bell again, looking angry and impatient. The door opened and a man stared at them, his face flushed with alcohol, red eyes blinking and settling on Stanford, opening wide with surprise.

"Oh, Christ," he said softly.

"We had an appointment," Stanford said.

The man seemed reluctant to open the door further, his shoulder leaning against it.

"Get out of here," he said.

"Let us in," Stanford said.

"I can't talk to you, Stanford. Go away. I've got people in here."

"Your buddies from MSC?"

"That's right," Armstrong said. "It's a private party, Stanford. I can't talk now. Just get the hell out of here."

He started to shut the door, but Stanford stopped it with his foot, leaned forward and stared directly at Armstrong, breathing into his face.

"We've come a long way," he said. "We came just to see you. You said you had something to tell us—now you're slamming the door. What the hell's going on?"

"Nothing," Armstrong said.

"Then let us in," Stanford said.

"I can't," Armstrong said. "It's a private party. For chrissakes get out of here."

"I love parties," Stanford said.

"You can't come in, Stanford."

"Why not? What the fuck are you worried about? I've been in there before."

"You know damned well why not."

"You brought us out here," Stanford said.

"I told you I'd meet you at MSC."

"You weren't there," Stanford said.

There was a lot of laughter from inside, a lot of shouting, someone singing, and Armstrong glanced nervously over his shoulder and then looked back at Stanford.

"Goddammit," he said.

"What's going on?" Stanford said. "How come you suddenly throw a private party when you knew we'd be here?"

"It just happened," Armstrong said.

"That's horseshit," Stanford said. "You threw that party because you didn't want us to come here and find you alone. You don't want to talk, Harry. You're suddenly frightened of something. You were going to tell me something and now you're shitless, and I want to know why."

"I'll give you a call," Armstrong said.

"I don't want a goddamned call. I'm not leaving here until I know what's happening, so you better start talking."

"Give me a break, for chrissakes!"

"Why?" Stanford said.

"I've got the CIA on my back!"

"We're coming in," Stanford said.

He started to push the door open, but Armstrong pressed his shoulder against it, glancing nervously back into the house and wiping his lips. Then he looked back at Stanford. *"Okay, okay!"* he hissed. He slipped outside and closed the door behind him, looking briefly at Epstein. He was a small man, potbellied, his hair thinning and turning gray; he glanced back over his shoulder, at the closed door behind him, then he shivered and turned into the howling wind and spoke directly to Stanford.

"This is the last time," he said. "I won't talk anymore. Don't ask me why—I won't tell you—but this is the last time."

"You mentioned the CIA."

"No, I didn't," Armstrong said. "Remember that. I didn't say a word. I didn't mention the CIA."

"Okay. I never heard it."

"Good," Armstrong said. "Now listen to the rest of this very carefully and don't ever forget it. You don't call me anymore. You understand that, Stanford? What I say to you tonight is the finish. I'll only talk on those terms."

"Christ, Armstrong, we're old friends!"

"Shut up. There's something else . . . This conversation never happened. The last time we talked was two hours ago. We haven't spoken since then."

They stood facing one another, the dust sweeping between them, the wind shaking the railings of the porch. Epstein said nothing, feeling embarrassed and guilty, ashamed of his complicity in the matter, trying to avoid Armstrong's frightened gaze.

"It's a deal," Stanford said.

"Okay," Armstrong said. He licked his lips and nodded, glancing nervously left and right, ascertaining that there was no one else on the porch, seeing only the swirling dust. He was still holding his drink, a half empty glass of bourbon, and he finished it off and wiped his lips and looked directly at Stanford.

"There's a flap on," he said. "It's a very big flap. In fact, it's the biggest flap we've ever had and that place is bananas. It all started three hours ago. We received some calls from our pilots. They reported seeing unidentifieds over the Gulf of Mexico, traveling in a northerly direction at incredible speeds. These objects were silvery lights. The pilots refused to comment further. These sightings occurred an hour before sunset and continued till darkness. Meanwhile, we were getting radar lock-ons. These lock-ons located the unidentifieds not over the Gulf of Mexico, but over that old farmer's ranch. According to the radar, something enormous had come from the direction of the Gulf of Mexico, circled around at 40,000 feet over the Manned Spacecraft Center, and was now descending as three separate blips over the ranch. These objects went off the scopes when they entered the radar's ground clutter."

Armstrong glanced around him, left and right along the porch, his eyes wandering to the far side of the street as if searching for someone. There was no one in the street. The storm was keeping them all inside. Armstrong spat dust from his mouth and rubbed his eyes and then looked up at Stanford.

"We were going to scramble some jets," he said, "but

just as we gave the order this dust storm blew up out of nowhere. That effectively grounded the jets—the wind over the strip was incredible—but we still kept getting lots of unidentifieds. These reports were coming in by telephone from other radar stations located at White Sands, Los Alamos and the whole Gulf of Mexico area—and according to our own radar readings, they were right above us. Naturally, because of the dust storm, we still couldn't scramble the jets, so we just had to sit there and tear our hair out. Then, about half an hour before I called you, the three objects above the ranch reappeared on the radar scopes, merged and became one, and this object started flying toward the Manned Spacecraft Center, doing no more than thirty miles an hour."

"Did you say *thirty* miles an hour?"

"That's what I said."

"And it wasn't just a weather balloon?"

"No, Stanford, it wasn't."

The sounds of the party continued inside, growing louder each minute. Armstrong listened at the door, nodded his head in satisfaction, then glanced along the porch once again, his red eyes flickering nervously.

"We all went outside," he said. "We watched this thing flying over us. It was flying above the storm, it was pitch black out there, and all we could see were its lights. The lights formed a perfect circle. They were pretty hazy through the dark. There was nothing to measure them against, but that circle seemed monstrous . . . it must have been a few hundred feet up and it *still* seemed enormous. It just glided right over us, hardly moving at all, then it moved off in an easterly direction and its lights just blinked out. When we got back inside there were unidentifieds all over the radarscopes."

Armstrong took a deep breath and gazed up at the sky and saw nothing but a curtain of dust. He shook his head wearily from side to side and started talking again.

"Shortly after that we received a call from the local sheriff, telling us to get out to that ranch. Remembering what we had seen, we complied pretty quickly and soon received a phone call from our boys. No need to recount the message—you've already been out there—but when they found out what was happening, the MSC Intelligence promptly ordered us all off the base. Naturally we were furious. We wanted to know what was going on. What we were told was that we hadn't seen or heard anything, that loose talk would lead to trouble, and that we were to go to our homes and remain there until further notice. That's why we're all here. That's why I can't talk to you again. What happened out there is unprecedented and we're all pretty scared."

"The CIA?"

"I didn't say that."

"Right: you didn't say it. Just tell me about that field of dead cattle. Where does all that fit in?"

"I don't know," Armstrong said. "I swear to God, I don't know. All I know is that it's happened before—all over the country."

"One of your men said it was a bunch of local crazies, but I can't really buy that."

"One final thing, Stanford, and that's all . . . I won't talk anymore."

"Okay, one last thing."

"It wasn't a bunch of crazies. That wasn't amateurish butchery. Whatever the reason for the butchery, it was done with a frightening efficiency. Those cattle were killed by an unknown nerve gas, they were sliced up with tools that must have been razor sharp; and their tongues and their eyes, their genitals and their udders, were removed with a surgical precision, and then spirited away. Don't ask me why. It doesn't make sense to me. But those cattle weren't slaughtered by a bunch of nuts—they were professionally butchered."

"The decontamination unit?"

"The area's radioactive. That's why coyotes or buzzards won't touch the carcasses. It's always the same."

"And the old man and girl?"

"That's as far as I go, Stanford. That's it. I'm not saying any more. Don't ever call me again."

Armstrong opened the door, started into the house, hesitated, then turned back to face them, his eyes focused on Stanford.

"We're old friends," he said, "so I'll give you some advice. Don't go back to that ranch. I warn you, don't be tempted. Whatever you do, don't go back there. It's not worth the trouble."

He stepped in and slammed the door. Stanford stood there, his eyes fixed on the closed door, then he turned and gazed at Epstein, shrugged his shoulders and shook his head, stepped down to the dark, graveled lawn and walked back to the car. Epstein followed him reluctantly, feeling dazed and exhausted, fighting against the wind and the dust and wondering when it would end. Once in the car, he stared at Stanford, now pale and too tense. Stanford angrily started the car, drove out into the street, and turned back the way they had come, looking very determined.

"I'm going back there," he said.

"To MSC?" Epstein said.

"No," Stanford said. "To the ranch."

"Oh, my God," Epstein murmured.

He put his head back on the seat, closed his eyes and embraced the darkness, quietly cursing the wind and the dust and the night's teeming mysteries. He kept his eyes closed, refusing to look outside the car, letting the anger take hold of him and shake him and return him to wakefulness. He then thought of the butchered cattle, of the old man and his daughter, of the lights in the sky and the guards at MSC, of Armstrong's inexplicable reluctance to talk and Stanford's consequent fury. Something odd was definitely happening. It was causing panic and fear. He and Stanford had been lied to, locked out and warned off: the events of the night were being suppressed and that meant they were real.

Epstein coughed and muttered an oath, opened his eyes and stared at Stanford, saw his profile silhouetted in the window, the storm raging beyond him. Stanford's good humor had deserted him. He had never looked so cold. The wind and dust were pummeling the car, but he just kept on driving.

They finally turned off the road, went along the familiar track, passed the flat fields that stretched into the darkness on either side, and stopped near the crest of the hill that led down to the ranch. Stanford killed his headlights and they both stared straight ahead. A ghostly light formed a huge fan in the sky beyond the crest of the hill.

"What the hell—?" Stanford said.

He glanced briefly at Epstein, opened his door and tumbled out, and the wind swept the dust through the car. Epstein coughed and cleared his throat, covered his eyes with his hands, then he followed Stanford out of the car, into the storm's awful fury.

The storm seemed worse than ever, much louder, more violent, the dust lashing their faces with extraordinary strength. They had to force themselves forward, protecting their eyes with their hands, stooped over as if pushing against a wall, being shaken from side to side. Epstein felt suffocated, a bit unreal, slightly frightened; he saw Stanford on the hill, his clothes flapping about him, silhouetted in the large fan of light that split the darkness ahead. Epstein struggled up to him, reached out to grab his shoulder, and they stood there, neither saying a word, looking down on the ranch.

The area surrounding the ranch was floodlit, filled with trucks and armed troops, some of the soldiers wearing goggles and masks, staring up at the sky. Other soldiers were hard at work, crouched low and gesticulating, hammering posts into the ground and running barbed wire along them, erecting a fence that ran right around the ranch in an enormous rectangle. The lights in the ranch were on. The wind howled and hurled sand over all and made the whole scene unreal.

"Jesus Christ," Stanford said. "Do you see that? They're being fenced in!"

"Damn them," Epstein hissed. "The bastards won't get away with this."

"They're carrying weapons and studying the sky," Stanford said. "They must be waiting for *something*."

Epstein suddenly exploded, his throttled anger breaking loose; he smacked the palm of one hand with his fist and turned back toward the car. The wind lashed him, tugged at him, tried to throw him on the ground, and he cursed and shouted into the storm.

"Damn them!" he shouted. "The bastards won't get away with it! We've been given the runaround once too often, and the buck stops right here. I want to know about this, Stanford! I want to know about *all* of it! I want the Air Force checked out, I want the facts on the CIA, I want to know what's been happening all these years and why they're keeping it quiet. The Air Force say they're not involved! The CIA say the same! They're both lying and now we have the proof, so let's find out the truth. You understand, Stanford? It's time to stop playing around! I want to know what's been going on, I want the facts and not their fiction, and I want to take those facts and break them down and tear this whole thing apart!"

He stopped shouting and stared at Stanford. His friend was gazing up at the sky. Epstein suddenly realized that it was quiet, that the fierce wind was dying. Startled, he looked around him: the blowing sand was settling down, spiraling gently, drifting down all around him in the stark, abrupt silence. Epstein couldn't believe it. He looked up at the sky. He saw the dust clouds thinning out, the moon and stars reappearing, the soft moonlight illuminating the fields and the parched, shivering trees.

Epstein stared down at the ranch. The dust no longer obscured the porch. The girl was standing there and sucking her thumb, gazing up at the sky. Everyone was gazing up. The soldiers had switched off the floodlights. They were standing around the house, clearly visible in the moonlight, neither moving nor making a sound, staring up at the sky.

"There they go," Stanford said.

Epstein followed Stanford's gaze. He saw the three lights in the sky. They were very high up, very small, very bright, one of them the size of a dime, the other two a lot smaller. Epstein watched, mesmerized. He felt Stanford's presence beside him. The lights formed a perfect triangle, climbing vertically, moving slowly, each composed of a luminous outer layer that surrounded a darker core. Epstein felt his heart pounding. He couldn't tear his eyes away. The two smaller lights changed, glowing brighter, accelerating, then they raced with a silent, serene grace toward the large light above them. The three lights merged together, became one, a brilliant star, then this star flared up and shot off to the south and disappeared almost instantly.

Stanford looked down at the ranch. He saw the girl on the porch. She was bathed in the moonlight, her dress fluttering against her legs, her feet bare, her thumb still in her mouth, her eyes fixed on the sky. Then she slowly turned toward him. She appeared to be staring directly at him. Stanford shivered and looked at Epstein, shivered again and shook his head, then they both returned silently to the car and headed back toward Galveston.

"I'll find out," Stanford said.

CHAPTER TEN

Richard sat up straight on the hard wooden chair and stared nervously at the window beyond the desk. The desk was long and solid, its surface badly scarred, supporting a telephone and a couple of empty trays, all covered in dust. The window was equally dusty, one of its panes badly cracked, now vibrating with the traffic that raced along Tottenham Court Road. Richard sat there for five minutes. It seemed longer than that. He was still studying the window, watching the rain splash the glass, when the door behind him suddenly opened and was slammed shut again.

Richard jerked his head around, but the two men were already past him, walking around him and sitting down behind the desk on two more wooden chairs. The men were both middle-aged, one with dark hair, one bald, both wearing nondescript suits and ties and carrying briefcases. The bald-headed man smiled, opened his briefcase and removed some papers, placed the papers fastidiously on the desk and then unclipped a ball-point pen.

"Awful weather," he said.

The other man seemed humorless, patting his dark hair with long fingers, opening his briefcase and pulling out a tape recorder which he set down before him. Only then did he look at Richard, his dark eyes expressionless, his face sallow, his chin badly shaved, his fingers scratching the table.

"Feeling all right?" the bald-headed man said.

"Uh?" Richard grunted.

"I said, are you feeling all right? You seem a bit tired."

"Yes, I'm tired," Richard said. "I haven't had any sleep. I came yesterday to report seeing a UFO, and I've been here all night."

"Sorry about that," the bald man said. "Must have been a bit uncomfortable. But the police can't touch cases like this—they always have to call us."

"Who are you?" Richard said.

"Data processors," the man said. "We specialize in aeronautical phenomena and we work for the government."

"What department?" Richard said.

"I don't think that's important. We're just here to assess what you think you saw and write it up for the record."

"What I *think* I saw?"

"Don't be offended. We're not insulting you. But the sky is not as simple as it seems, and it plays tricks with people."

"Such as?"

"St. Elmo's fire can turn a perfectly ordinary airplane into a bright, multicolored halo of twisting light. The planet Venus, when viewed under certain conditions, will appear as a glowing orb that moves in the most extraordinary patterns. Comets, meteors, balloons, satellites, flares, fireworks, noctilucent clouds, plasmoids and corona discharges can all look like bright, solid objects. For instance, a high altitude balloon, if struck at a low angle by the rays of the setting sun, will resemble an enormous disc flying at tremendous speed. What will appear to the observer to be the blazing exhaust of the disc will actually be the swirl of dust and ice crystals left in the wake of the balloon and also reflecting the sunlight. Likewise with temperature inversions. These are various layers of air, all at different temperatures, which bend and twist and generally distort the rays of light to create what is best termed a mirage. Did you know that a temperature layer can pick out a boat at sea, project it as a mirage in the sky, and that that mirage will be viewed by a competent pilot as a long, dark shape filled with bright windows? Similarly, somewhere in the country a long line of cars may be crawling up a hill, all beaming their headlights into the night sky; given the proper temperature inversion, these lights will be bent and sent traveling, will bounce off another temperature inversion thirty or forty miles away, and will appear to the observers as a mass of glowing, disc-shaped objects, all flying in perfect formation through the sky. As for plasmoids and ball lightning, both are basically formed by electrified gas that when burning brightly oscillates, vibrates, wobbles, flies horizontally, climbs vertically, glows in blue and red colors, and can look like a sphere or a disc or a gigantic torpedo; they also hum and make other strange sounds and are *very* impressive . . . Shall I continue?"

"No," Richard said.

"Good," the man said.

"I didn't see any of those things."

"Possibly not. Let's find out."

The bald man smiled pleasantly and sat back in his chair, tapping his teeth with his ball-point pen and nodding his head. The dark-haired man leaned forward, resting one hand on his tape recorder, not smiling, speaking in clipped, measured speech, his dark eyes fixed on Richard.

"The following questions have been designed to give the government as much information as possible concerning the unidentified aerial phenomenon that you have reported. Please try to answer the questions as accurately as possible. The information that you give will be used for research purposes and will be regarded as confidential material. Your name will not be used in connection with any statements, conclusions or publications without your permission. Now please confirm that you understand and accept this."

"Yes," Richard said.

The bald-headed man sat forward and leaned over the desk, his pen hovering just above his notepaper, preparing to write. The other man turned his tape recorder on and then started the questioning.

"When did you see the object?"

"The seventh of March."

"1974?"

"Yes."

"Time of day?"

"About eight thirty."

"In the evening?"

"Yes."

The bald man was making annotations in a large form, filling in the blank spaces.

"Where were you when you saw the object?"

"In Cornwall."

"Precisely."

"The A30 through Bodmin Moor. It was near King Arthur's Hall. That's between Bolventor and Bodmin. That's all I can tell you."

"How long did you see the object?"

"Pardon?"

"The duration of the sighting."

"I dunno. A good five minutes, I think. I blanked out after that."

"You're certain you saw it that long?"

"I'm not certain of anything."

"Five minutes is a long time."

"A lot of things were happening. They couldn't have happened in under five minutes; it must have been at least that."

"What was the condition of the sky?"

"I don't know what you mean."

"Bright daylight? Dull daylight? Bright twilight? Just a trace of daylight? No trace of daylight? Don't remember . . . ?"

"Bright twilight. A very red sky. The sun was just sinking."

"Where was the sun located as you looked at the object?"

"I don't know. I can't remember . . . Yes, it was behind the object. In fact, I thought the object was the sun. I thought the sun was exploding."

"It eclipsed the sun?"

"Yes."

"What did you notice concerning the sky?"

"Sorry?"

"The stars . . . None? A few? A lot? Can't remember . . . ?"

"I can't remember. There was just this silvery haze. I don't think I saw stars."

"And the moon?"

"I didn't see it. There was just the silvery haze, then this faded and I saw the object. This object was so big that it seemed to blot out the whole sky."

"The object was brighter than the background of the sky?"

"Yes, it was at first. It was the brightest thing I'd ever seen. Then it darkened and lights flashed all around it and it blotted out the sky."

"How dark was the dark shape?"

"I don't know what you mean."

"Was it darker than the sky at that time?"

"The sky was red. This thing was dark."

"Did the object appear to stand still at any time?"

"It came up over the rocks and then stopped, just floating there in the sky."

"Did it speed up and rush away at any time?"

"No, it just stayed there. It was enormous and it stayed there. It just hung there in the sky and then dropped lower and then opened up and we were—"

"Did it break up into parts or explode?"

"These questions are ridiculous. What happened was—"

"Please just answer the questions."

"No, it didn't explode. It didn't break up either. These panels opened and two other discs flew out and—"

"Did the object give off smoke?"

"There were *three* objects!"

"Did the large object give off any smoke?"

"No. Not that I noticed."

"The smaller objects?"

"No. Definitely not."

"Why definite?"

"They were close. They were right outside the car. They just drifted around the car very slowly and I didn't see smoke."

"Did any of the objects change shape?"

"No. I mean, I'm not too sure of that. When I first saw the large object it just looked like a light—a very bright explosion of light that filled the whole sky. Then it changed to the dark shape. There were flashing lights all around it. I kept thinking it was changing its shape, but I think the lights did that. It didn't change as it rested there."

"Rested? On what?"

"It was just floating in the air."

"How high up?"

"I don't know. It seemed about a hundred feet or so, but I couldn't be sure of that. Then it came down. It dropped almost to ground level. That's when it opened along the bottom and then drew us toward it."

"Did the object flicker, throb or pulsate?"

"It was just a sudden flaring light that faded away and was replaced by the dark shape."

"You mentioned various lights."

"That's right. Colored lights. They were green, blue and orange, they stretched the length of the machine, and they flickered on and off in sequence, from left to right, then right to left, flickering on and off very fast, almost making one color."

"Where were the lights positioned?"

"I don't know. I'm not sure. I think they were near the bottom of that thing. I think they went right around it."

"Did the object move in front of something at anytime?"

"I told you: the sun."

"Anything closer?"

"It came over the nearby rocks and stopped in front of them. It just blotted them out."

"Rocks?"

"The neolithic stones."

"Did it move *behind* anything at any time?"

"No."

"Did the object appear solid or transparent?"

"Solid. Definitely solid."

"Were you wearing glasses or sunglasses?"

"No."

"Did you observe the object through the windshield or windows?"

"Yes."

"Did you roll the windows down at any time?"

"No."

"Any reflections on the windshield or windows?"

"I don't know."

"Did you view the object at any time through binoculars, a telescope, a theodolite or any other optical instrument?"

"No. There was no need for that. It was practically on top of us."

"Did the object make any sound?"

"I don't know. I'm not sure. I think it made a humming sound. At first I thought I heard an explosion, but now I don't think I did. I think I *felt* something. It was a sort of vibrating noise. I don't know. I can't answer that one. There was noise. A vibrating . . ."

"The smaller discs?"

"A humming sound. They sometimes made a whistling noise. When they whistled, they shot beams of light over us . . . I've never heard noise like that before."

The dark-haired man sat back and turned the tape recorder off while the bald man pushed a sheet of paper at Richard and passed him a pencil.

"I want you to draw a picture that will show the general shape of the objects," the bald man said. "Label and include in your sketch any details of the objects that you saw, such as wings and other protrusions, and including exhaust and vapor trails. Use arrows to show the direction the various objects were traveling. Also include in the picture any motion that the object or objects made. Place an 'A' at the beginning of the path, a 'B' at the end of the path, and show any changes in direction during the course."

Richard did as he was told. His hands were shaking a lot. The room was very cold but he was sweating, and he felt a bit feverish. The two men watched him quietly. They never took their eyes off him. He heard the rain beating on the window just beyond their two heads. He did the drawing very quickly. It was a neat and accurate sketch. He then pushed the paper back to the bald man, who studied it carefully.

"That's a good drawing," he said.

"I'm an art student," Richard said.

"Ah, yes, the Hornsey Collge of Art."

"That's right," Richard said.

The bald man passed the sketch to his more serious

companion, who studied it, passed it back, turned the tape recorder on again, and then spoke directly to Richard.

"Okay. Were the edges of the object fuzzy or blurred, or sharply outlined?"

"The smaller discs were sharply outlined. They were disc-shaped and silvery. I couldn't see the edges of the big one. Its flashing lights were too bright. The body was just a dark mass and the flashing lights made the edges invisible."

"What length would you estimate the various discs to be?"

"Not length: diameter. The big one was three hundred feet in diameter and at least several stories high. The other discs came in two sizes: the first two were about three feet in diameter, the second two about thirty-five feet. The first two discs were completely solid. The second two had a perimeter that swept up to form a dome. The dome was made of something like glass. I remember seeing people in there. And I didn't imagine that . . ."

"Never mind the occupants. What do you think the objects were made of?"

"Some sort of metal."

"You mentioned the word 'silvery.' "

"Silvery or metallic gray."

"What were you doing at the time you saw the first object, and how did you happen to notice it?"

"I was in the passenger seat. The woman was driving the car. The engine spluttered and died, the headlights went out, and the car rolled to the bottom of the hill and came to a stop. Then I thought I heard something. I didn't hear it: I *felt* it. Then the car was filled with light—the whole area was filled with light—and that light swept over the stones in the field nearby and materialized as the object."

"What direction were you moving before the car stopped?"

"Southwest."

"What direction were you looking when you first saw the object?"

"At the sinking sun. West."

"Are you familiar with angular direction?"

"No."

"What were the weather conditions at the time you saw the objects?"

"It had been raining most of the day, but the clouds were disappearing, and the sky was red and gradually turning dark. There was mist coming over the hills, but none around us."

"There was no mist near the car when you were driving?"

"No."

"Any mist during your encounter with the objects?"

"No. Just the white haze."

"You're convinced that this haze wasn't mist?"

"Yes. It was light."

"Wind?"

"I don't think so."

"Temperature?"

"Pretty cold."

"What was the speed of the large object in flight?"

"I'm no good at judging speeds."

"Roughly."

"About thirty miles an hour."

"*Thirty?*"

"Yes."

"You know that's impossible?"

"Yes. It's impossible, but that's what it was doing. I mean that thing was just *drifting.*"

"The smaller discs?"

"I couldn't say. They were fast. They could sit in midair, just drift gently around the car, or shoot off in the blinking of an eye. I couldn't give you a speed."

"Can you give me an estimation of how far away the large object was from you?"

"When it came down, it was about fifty yards from the car, give or take a few yards."

"Did it give off any heat?"

"Yes, I think it did. I remember feeling hot and suffocated . . . but I *was* pretty frightened."

"Was this the first time you had seen an object or objects like this?"

"Yes."

"Ever thought about them?"

"Not much."

"Did anyone else see the objects?"

"The woman driving the car."

"Apart from her."

"No."

"When did you first report this officially?"

"Yesterday."

"Why did you wait that long?"

"I was frightened."

"Frightened? Of what?"

"I didn't think anyone would believe me."

"Anything else?"

"I was just frightened in general. I was frightened by what had happened. I couldn't really believe it at first—I didn't *want* to believe it. Also, I had nightmares. I kept dreaming about it. I thought maybe I was going a little crazy. I didn't want to tell anyone."

"What did you dream about?"

"I'm not sure. I could never remember them clearly . . . just dreams of the white haze, silhouettes all around me, strange creatures, not saying a word, just crowding around me."

The dark-haired man nodded and switched the tape recorder off while his bald friend pushed more paper toward Richard.

"I want you to draw the occupants," he said.

"I can't remember," Richard said.

"Just try," the bald man said. "Try to remember. Just to give us some idea."

Richard did as he was told. His hands were shaking worse than ever. He was sweating, and the fear was coming back as he drew the weird faces. It took him longer than before. He was finding it hard to concentrate. He heard the rain against the window, the steady breathing of the two men, and his heart was racing faster than it should, as if succumbing to panic. He finally finished the drawing. It looked childish and ridiculous. He pushed it back to the bald-headed man and watched him study it carefully.

"A little Picasso," the man said.

"That's what it looked like," Richard said.

"Do you think they were wearing some kind of mask?"

"Yes, I do," Richard said.

The bald man smiled at him, passed the drawing to his partner, and the other man studied it for some time before setting it down. He then looked directly at Richard, not smiling, and switched on his tape recorder.

"Is that nose supposed to be metal?"

"That's what it looked like," Richard said.

"And a mask could account for the lack of lips?"

"That's right," Richard said.

"Did the glass dome distort them?"

"I think so," Richard said. "I couldn't really see beyond their heads—that dome blurred the interior."

"They stared at you?"

"Yes."

"Did they make any gestures?"

"The creature in one of them raised his hand. It looked like a claw."

"A metal claw?"

"Yes."

"Any flesh?"

"Gray and wrinkled. The skin around the eyes was very wrinkled, but I can't be too sure of that."

"Why?"

"The transparent dome. I think it distorted their features. It was bright but it wasn't all that clear. It had a rippling effect."

"What did you do when it raised its hand?"

"I sort of blanked out. A beam of light suddenly shot over me and I think that's what did it."

"And then?"

"I don't think I was unconscious long. I think it was just a few seconds. I woke up and saw the big ship coming down and blocking out the whole view. Then our car was drawn toward it. The car was dead, but it was moving. The thirty-five foot discs were at either side of the car, shooting beams of light down on the car and just drawing it forward."

"You say thirty-five feet. That's a rather precise estimate."

"I know. I don't know why I think that . . . But I always feel sure of it."

"Okay. Continue."

"That was it," Richard said. "We were pulled toward the big ship. The colored lights flickered off, the ship split along the bottom, we were drawn right inside, saw white light and silhouettes, and after that I don't remember a thing . . . I guess I just fainted."

"Then you recovered three days later."

"That's right. Thirty miles away."

"And you've absolutely no idea how you got there?"

"No. No idea."

"Have you ever suffered from amnesia?"

"No, of course not."

"We can check on your medical records."

"You won't find amnesia." Richard scratched his beard, studying the two men in turn, wondering what the both of them were thinking, feeling frightened again. "The doctor," he said. "That guy examined my neck. The cops said they would give you the report. What did it say?"

"There was a burn mark all right. Unfortunately it was nearly gone. It's impossible at this stage to say what caused it. Otherwise you're unchanged."

"Unchanged?" Richard said.

"Your blood sample revealed nothing."

"What did you expect to find?" Richard said.

"Nothing," the man said. He switched the tape recorder off, folded his hands beneath his chin, drummed the fingers of both hands together and kept staring at Richard.

"Well, what do you think?" Richard said.

"What do you expect us to think?"

"I want to know what happened out there."

"I think you probably imagined it."

"Imagined it?"

"Yes. It's not credible," the man said. "I'm afraid the pieces don't fit together. It just doesn't make sense."

"*What* doesn't make sense?"

"None of it," the man said. "What you said cannot be real because such things don't exist."

"But I *saw* them!"

"You *think* you saw them. You possibly saw a mirage.

You saw the reflection of an airplane or ship, caused by temperature inversion."

"It was *real*!"

"No, it wasn't. It couldn't have been real. No object that big can travel thirty miles an hour and then hover without a sound above the ground. It's scientifically impossible."

"*What's* scientifically impossible? What the hell does *that* mean? All I know is that it *happened*, that it happened to *me*, and that I came here to get an explanation because that's what I need."

"What can *we* explain?" the man said. "Do you want us to *confirm* it? Unidentified lights we can discuss, but what you saw is pure fantasy. It's not possible. There's no way we can accept it. The facts would seem to speak for themselves: your whole story is nonsense."

"Oh, shit!" Richard said.

"Not shit—facts. Just one question to ask and then we're finished: Were you drunk when you saw it?"

"Drunk?" Richard said.

"That's right. Were you drunk? According to the report you gave to the police, you were drinking that evening."

"Well, yes, but . . ."

"You were drunk."

"I don't think it has relevance—"

"The woman herself said you drank a lot. In fact, she said you were plastered."

Richard jerked his head up, suddenly feeling disoriented, remembering the gleaming white Audi and the woman with red hair and green eyes. That woman had disappeared. She was gone when he awakened. But she had been there and had seen all that happened . . . It just didn't make sense.

"The woman?" Richard whispered.

"That's right: your driver. We located her at her home in St. Nicholas and she told us her story. She remembered picking you up. She said you helped fix her car. She said that you drank a lot, that you became extremely drunk, and that she had to tip you out close to Bodmin when you became too offensive. She didn't see any flying saucers. She saw nothing at all. She said she dropped you off at

Bodmin, that you were swaying from side to side, and that you staggered back the way you had come—heading straight back for Bodmin Moor. That's the last she saw of you. Her journey was otherwise uneventful. In short, she saw nothing unusual—and neither did you."

"But she's lying!" Richard shouted.

"I don't think so," the man said. "I think you got exceptionally drunk, that you hitchhiked back to Dartmoor, and that there you saw Venus or ball lightning or a mirage, and that in your drunken state you thought it was real and then imagined the rest. It's not that uncommon. People see things all the time. In a drunken condition a natural occurrence can shock you and make you see what's not there. It was all in your head, lad."

"You don't believe that," Richard said.

"Yes, I do," the man said.

"Christ, mister, I'm telling you the truth!"

"Or what you *think* is the truth."

Richard silently collapsed, feeling crushed and defeated, the fear rushing back and swallowing him whole, leaving him senseless. The two men cleared the desk, snapping the locks on their briefcases, then they walked around Richard without a word and opened the door of the room. Richard jerked his head back and stared up at both the men. The dark-haired man was slipping from the room, but the bald man still stood there. Richard didn't know what to say. The walls were closing in on him. The bald man was just standing there, smiling, as Richard stared up beseechingly.

"Sonny," the bald man said with a smile, "you better see your psychiatrist."

CHAPTER ELEVEN

Professor Vale was paralyzed. He knew that almost immediately. He opened his eyes and flicked them left and right because his head wouldn't move. The room was all white, shaped like a geodesic dome, its triangular plates made of aluminum, joined by thin, steel-gray tubing. The professor licked his dry lips. The paralysis didn't bother him much. He felt dreamy and unreal, a bit removed from himself, content just to lie there on the bed and let events take their course.

His eyes flicked left and right. The circular wall was white and featureless. The one door was molded into the wall as if it couldn't be opened. The professor was impressed. He had never seen a room like it. He gazed up at the bright, dome-shaped ceiling and saw two porthole windows. The windows were very beautiful. Exotic fish were swimming past. The professor realized that he was under the ocean, probably down on the sea bed.

None of this bothered him. In fact it filled him with interest. He heard the breathing of someone nearby, but he couldn't quite see them. It didn't really matter: he would find out soon enough. He tried to move, but the paralysis was total, so he just lay there quietly. The whole room was very quiet. There was a distant humming sound. He heard the breathing of the person nearby and tried turning his head. This time he could move it.

There was another bed in the room, about twelve feet

away, made from shiny white plastic, sweeping down to
the floor, and apparently molded to the body of the man
who lay sleeping on top of it. This man was wrapped in a
surgical gown and had a metalic skullcap on his head,
small electrodes joining the skullcap to the various colored
wires that ran back into a panel behind the bed. The professor studied the man at length. The man was in some
sort of coma. There were straps running around his wrists
and ankles, with more wires running out of them.

The room was like a gigantic eggshell. The professor
looked up at the ceiling. He saw strange fish staring down
through the portholes and disappearing in green murk. It
was eerily beautiful. The silence was serene. The room's
antiseptic whiteness, its seamless circular wall, gave it the
appearance of an enormous, sheltering womb and made
him feel almost childlike.

The professor raised a hand and touched the hair on his
head and felt his fingers scratching his scalp. He wasn't
wearing a skullcap. The paralysis was going away. He
moved his toes and felt the muscles in his legs and then he
slowly sat upright. He felt dizzy and weak, his stomach
nauseous and rumbling, but he took a deep breath and
glanced around him and soon felt much better.

The other man was still asleep, hardly moving, breathing
evenly, his face lean and pasty, almost deathly, his chin in
need of a shave. The professor studied the strange bed. It
was molded out of the floor. Thrusting out of the wall behind it, and looming over the bed itself, was a unit containing lamps and plasma jars and an X-ray camera, this
whole unit also molded with abstract grace from the shiny
white plastic.

The professor gazed around the room. The shining
whiteness stung his eyes. He glanced up and saw the fish
at the portholes and then remembered the boat . . . The
sea had turned to green steam. The metal jaws had closed
above them. The metal jaws had become a giant version of
the room now surrounding him . . . The professor was
fascinated. He understood that he was drugged. He swung
his legs off the bed, placed his feet on the floor, then stood
up, swaying slightly from side to side, making sure he was
strong enough.

The white floor wasn't moving. It didn't sway or vibrate. It appeared to be made of white fiber glass and was reasonably warm. The professor wondered where he was, wondered what was expected of him; he no longer felt in charge of himself and wanted someone to guide him.

The humming came from the distance. He thought it came from beyond the door. The door had no handle, no keyhole or lock, but the professor walked up to it and touched it and it slid open silently, sliding into the wall. The professor just stood there. He kept rubbing his eyes. He tried to tear himself from what he saw, but he couldn't escape it.

He was staring along a corridor that curved gently out of view, its walls shaped like a tunnel, gleaming brightly, and broken up with large windows. These windows were rectangular, revealing the bottom of the ocean, beams of light boring through the murky depths, illuminating a wonderland.

The professor stepped into the corridor, gazed through the nearest window, saw writhing rocks and multicolored plants and bizarre, drifting creatures. It was awesome, incredible, the landscape of a dream; the fish monstrous and minute, stunningly beautiful and grotesque—throbbing gills, swaying tails, eyes like prisms and stars, their colors changing as they merged with one another and formed wavering rainbows. The ocean bottom was stone and sand and had a fathomless mystery; the sand swept out and rippled around the rocks which were alive with primordial life. The professor almost stopped breathing. He was stunned by what was out there. He saw a huge uncoiling eel, a web of glistening, writhing tentacles, a gelatinous mass of gold, green and violet sniffing petrified plants. He saw it all in the beams of light. The lights were fixed outside the windows. The beams of light were the only illumination in those dark, vitreous depths.

The professor walked along the corridor. The floor warmed his bare feet. He was still wearing his flowered shirt and shorts, and that worried him slightly. How long had he been down here? Had he slept for hours or days? The questions flickered through his mind and then departed without having quite touched him. He felt only curiosity, an overwhelming sense of awe, obsessed by the need to go farther and make contact with someone. He didn't question this desire: the need itself was enough. He kept walking, passing windows and the ocean's teeming life, and the corridor kept curving away from him in a long, endless circle.

The humming sound grew louder. There was a rhythmic vibration. The professor arrived at an open door at the left side of the corridor, and stopped there, momentarily transfixed, before stepping up to it. The noise here was much louder and had a hollow, echoing ring. He looked through to an immense geodesic dome filled with ladders and catwalks.

The professor stood there a long time. He remembered seeing all this before. He glanced up at the silvery-gray dome and remembered it closing. Then he looked down again, saw the ladders and catwalks. There were glittering floors and platforms, modules made from steel and glass, shining mazes of pipes and generators, bright lights flashing off white walls. There were people down there, very small and faraway, all dressed in coveralls, climbing ladders, crossing catwalks, moving up and down those dizzying depths in elevators like cages. The professor walked toward the door. It hissed loudly and slammed shut. He touched it but it didn't open again, so he shrugged and walked off.

He was amazed but not frightened. He understood that he was drugged. This thought filled him with a strange, dry amusement that never quite came to life. The corridor stretched out before him, kept curving away from him. He passed the windows overlooking the murky depths and then he came to another door. He tried to step through it, but it slammed shut in his face. He shrugged and turned away, feeling calm, unperturbed, understanding that he had to keep walking and that the closed doors were guiding him.

He finally reached the end of the corridor, arriving at a large white room. The professor stepped into the room and stood there and looked around him. The room was circular and dim, without windows, very cool, the molded beds going right around the wall and melting into the smooth floor. All the beds were occupied, filled with men, women and children; they were all lying quietly, wrapped in surgical gowns, the wires running from electrodes on their heads, hands and legs and coiling up to the ECG machines that were fixed to the wall. The rhythmic breathing of the people on the beds was quite loud in the silence.

The professor suddenly shivered. He wasn't frightened, but he felt odd. He walked across to the far side of the room and passed through to another room.

This room also was circular, much bigger, very bright, the wall lined with glass cabinets and winking digital control panels, with two prop-up surgical beds, surrounded by tall equipment units, standing on the center of the floor, their headrests slightly raised. There was a dwarf at one of the beds, his spine bent, his legs twisted; he was wearing a white gown, working swiftly and silently, his extraordinarily pale and delicate hands flipping back a white sheet.

"Where am I?" the professor said. "Who are you? Where's Mr. McKinley?"

The dwarf finished his job, unconcerned, working lovingly, then he turned and stared up at the professor with large, slightly glazed eyes. He then sniffed and scratched an ear, shuffled forward laboriously, his head rolling loosely from side to side, buried between his raised shoulders.

"Ah," he said, "you're awake!"

"Where am I?" the professor said.

"We were expecting you," the dwarf replied.

"Who are you?"

"I stayed here. I was waiting."

"Where's Mr. McKinley?"

The dwarf nodded understandingly, his head rolling from side to side, then he went to what looked like a dentist's chair and started raising the headrest. The professor looked at the glass cabinets, which were about six feet long, every cabinet containing a naked body, all apparently dead. The glass seemed lightly frosted. The control panels were flickering. The professor realized that they were cardiograph and ECG readouts, and that the people in the cabinets were still alive. He returned his gaze to the crippled dwarf, who was grinning inanely, waving at him.

The professor walked over to the chair and sat down and didn't ask himself why.

"You are comfortable?" the dwarf said.

"Yes," the professor said.

"No fear," the dwarf said. "Fear is foolish."

"Where's Mr. McKinley?"

The dwarf nodded understandingly. "Mr. Aldridge comes soon," he said. "I press a button to call Mr. Aldridge, and your fear . . . fear is over."

The professor sat in the chair, studying the dwarf, intrigued by him, saw him walking across the floor and pressing a button that was fixed to the wall. The dwarf grinned at him and nodded, shuffled along to some cabinets, pressed his nose to a pane of frosted glass and stared at a naked man. The man appeared to be dead. The readouts said he was alive. The dwarf turned around and waved his delicate hands and then came back to the chair. He looked right at the professor, his eyes large and very brown, grinned stupidly and then pointed to the spot just above the professor's head.

The professor looked up and saw a circular white canopy. Sunken into the base of the canopy were surgical lamps and convex lenses, all surrounding a stereotaxic skullcap and loosely hanging electrodes. The professor studied the canopy carefully. It obviously housed an X-ray camera. He studied the electrodes and the stereotaxic skullcap, then he looked at the dwarf.

"Who are you?"

"I stay and wait."

"Who *are* you?"

"I work good." The dwarf grinned and waved his delicate hands. "No need fear . . . fear is over."

The professor looked at the domed ceiling. It seemed to shine with natural light. Feeling unreal, but not at all frightened, he looked back at the dwarf. The pathetic creature was still grinning. His hands clashed with the rest of him. Compared to the crippled legs, and to the curved, distorted spine, the extraordinarily pale and delicate hands were almost movingly lovely. The dwarf grinned and shook his head, pointing excitedly to the door ahead. The profes-

sor looked up as McKinley walked in, his blue eyes clear
and steady.

"I'm Aldridge," he said.

"I thought you were McKinley."

"McKinley came to an unfortunate end. I am Aldridge.
Remember that."

Aldridge looked neat and cool, his shirt and trousers
black, standing starkly against the white of the circular
room, a slight smile on his face. The professor just sat
there, feeling a strange, distant fear; he wondered why he
didn't feel it more and then remembered the drug. Aldridge nodded and stepped forward, leaned over the professor. He placed his thumb on the professor's eyelid,
pulled it up and examined the eye, then nodded, removed
his hand and stepped back, glancing briefly around him.

"You find this interesting?" he said.

"Yes," the professor said.

"And you don't feel any fear?"

"I don't think so."

"Well, that's as it should be."

The professor glanced around him, at the white walls
and glass cabinets, trying to feel fear and not succeeding,
his curiosity predominant.

"Was I drugged?"

"Of course."

"I don't really feel much different."

"You *are* different . . . you don't feel any fear, and that
should be enough to confirm it. Think about it. What
you've just been through would normally have made you
crazy, but you still act as if you're untouched by it. Think
of what happened on the boat. Think of where you awakened. Think of what you've just seen as you walked here
and ask yourself why you're sane. Of *course* you were
drugged. Otherwise you would be mad. Even now, as you
sit there, you're still drugged, which is why you're so
calm."

"What kind of drug is it?"

"More advanced than any you know. Scientifically, your
world is antiquated. You will soon find that out."

Aldridge walked to the glass cabinet, raised a hand and
pointed gently. "Observe," he said, "the wonders of our

science. They will sleep till I waken them." He turned and looked down at the dwarf, who was grinning and nodding wildly. Aldridge patted the dwarf lightly on the head and then offered a bleak smile. "This is Rudiger," he said. "He has wonderful hands. We removed his hands and gave him metal claws and then we gave him his hands back. Of course they're not his old hands. In fact, they're not flesh and blood. Nevertheless, they are as good as the old, and the patient is happy." He returned to the professor, leaned close to him, stared at him. "And you still don't feel any fear?" he said.

"No, I don't. I don't think so."

Aldridge smiled and straightened up, moving slowly and carefully, going back to the glass cabinets against the wall and surveying the bodies. "They're all alive," he said. "We're killing them off very slowly. We want to preserve them for the future, so they'll have to die gently. We will drain all their blood, fill them with glycerine and dimethyl-sulfoxide to prevent ice crystals forming in their tissues, then wrap them in aluminum foil, place them in cryonic storage chambers, and only resurrect them when we need them." He turned away from the cabinets, walked leisurely across the room, leaned over the professor once again and offered his bleak smile. "And you *still* feel no fear?" he said.

The professor gazed around the room, at the smooth, circular wall, at the solid, geodesic dome that glowed brightly above him. Then he looked at the glass cabinets. The frosted glass distorted the bodies. The jagged white lines jumped erratically above them, moving slower each minute. The professor looked up at Aldridge, saw the cold, intelligent eyes, the tanned, strangely seamless forehead under the shock of white hair.

"Who are you?" he said.

"You know that. I'm Aldridge."

"Where do you come from?" the professor said.

"You'll learn that when you need it."

"And the bodies in the cabinets?"

"What about them?"

"Where do they come from?"

"From earth," Aldridge said. "From all over. We picked them up here and there."

"I'm not frightened," the professor said.

"No. You're still drugged."

"What do you want from me?" the professor said.

"I want your brain," Aldridge said.

The professor felt nothing. The hint of fear had come and gone. He just sat there, staring around the strange room, wondering just where he was. He remembered the triangular steel spikes, rising up, closing above him, remembered sinking down through the white haze, past steel ladders and catwalks. All that and much more: the long walk along the corridor; the large windows, the ocean bed, the great dome that soared above the huge decks and workshops, dwarfing the men in the modules of steel and glass, reverberating with phantom sounds. He was at the bottom of the ocean. This room was part of something enormous. He was possibly in an undersea city, but he couldn't be sure of that.

"Put your head back," Aldridge said.

"Pardon?"

"Put your head back. I want to place this skullcap on your head. It won't take very long."

The professor did as he was told. Aldridge pulled the skullcap down. The professor felt the cold metal against his scalp, and then he felt a slight pressure.

"You don't have to shave my head?"

"No, my dear professor. We're no longer as primitive as that. The operation is simple."

Aldridge adjusted the skullcap. It tightened around the professor's head. The professor raised his eyes and saw a tangle of electrodes dangling down just in front of him. A pair of hands came into view, both extraordinary pale and delicate: the crippled dwarf was leaning over his shoulder and inserting the electrodes. The professor didn't move. His own serenity was vaguely surprising. He knew that what was happening was a nightmare, but he couldn't break free of it. The dwarf inserted the electrodes. There was a distant ringing sound. The professor tried to raise his hands to his head but found them stuck to the armrest. His hands and forearms tingled. The chair's armrests were vibrating. The professor sat there, unable to move a muscle, reconciled to his fate.

"No fear," the dwarf hissed. "Fear is over . . . No fear in your future."

The professor couldn't see the dwarf. The dwarf was obviously right behind him. Aldridge was standing directly in front of him, a bleak smile on his face.

"In 1932," he said, "Dr. Walter Hess devised the modern technique of electrode implantation, thereby demonstrating that nearly all of man's functions and emotions can be influenced by stimulation of specific areas of the brain. A state of constant drowsiness can be brought about by the simple electric stimulation of the caudate nucleus, the nucleus reticularis or the inferior thalamus; conversely, a similar stimulation of the mesencephalic reticular formation will induce instant arousal. Man is thus just a machine, to be utilized, controlled, operable by simple laws of give and take, without will of his own. The philosopher's stone has been shattered. Philosophy itself has become redundant. The mysteries of the human mind, its creativity, its moral imperatives, have been reduced to a set of components which we endlessly play with. Man is not a magical creature—he is a container of various impulses. These impulses can be rearranged to a pattern that will change his behavior."

Aldridge flicked a switch, bathing the professor in bright light, filling his head with an unusual incandescence and making it vibrate. The professor blinked his eyes, but had no will to resist. He understood that what was happening was hideous, yet he still felt no fear. He drifted out of himself, observed himself succumbing quietly, his head trapped in the stereotaxic cap beyond which there was nothing.

"The hypothalamus," Aldridge continued, "is that area of the brain which controls your most basic and primitive needs. By stimulating the appropriate areas of the hypothalamus with submicroelectronic electrodes I can regulate your blood pressure, your heart rate and respiration; your sleep, your appetite, even the diameter of your pupils; I can place you in suspended animation or make you work till you drop . . . Do you understand that?"

"Yes," the professor said.

"Excellent," Aldridge said. "Now, the rather simple bio-cybernetic system into which you are now plugged consists of a fifteen-channel programmable brain stimulator and a normal LINC-8 digital computer with the appropriate interfacing equipment. At the moment, radiopaque materials are being injected into the intracerebral spaces inside your skull to facilitate, by X ray, the visualization of various parts of your brain. The stereotaxic machine, utilizing minute spikes that have already pierced your scalp, is now taking the X rays from numerous different angles. At this precise second the stereotaxic apparatus is making geometrical calculations using the X rays and reference point grids to give me three-dimensional coordinates for the positioning of the electrodes . . . You will feel none of this."

The professor sat quietly, his eyes closed in surrender. His whole head was vibrating, was glowing and warm, and he felt that he was crouched up in there, his own skull surrounding him. It made him think of the great dome. His own skull was such a dome. It was immense and he was crouched low at its center . . . overwhelmed by the dark space.

"The desired targets have been fixed. I am drilling into your skull. The steel electrodes are as thin as hairs, the micromanipulators are guiding them in, and in a moment you will feel an electric current as light as a feather. You will not feel any pain. You will experience a brief panic. This panic will pass away very quickly, after which you'll feel nothing . . . I am taking your mind now."

The professor sat very still, almost welcoming what was coming. His eyes were closed and he crouched in a darkness lit by tiny white flashes. His brain's interior was enormous. He actually thought he could see it. It was an immense, crenellated, dark dome rising up all round him. There was silence. A humming. A distant rumbling reverberated. He crouched alone in the wilderness of his mind and saw the holes in the sky. That sky was vast and utterly black. The holes appeared as tunnels of light. The light burned through the sweeping black curtain and exploded around him.

The professor shrank within himself, feeling helpless, totally naked, suddenly whipped by a sudden, shocking terror that returned him to childhood. Then he heard his own voice, a strangled sound, cracked and pitiful, gasping out its anguished plea for release, its final expression of will:

"Please don't," he whimpered.

It didn't matter after that. The fear passed and he was calm. The light receded and he saw the dark walls of his chained, captured mind. There was a glowing in the darkness: the light of mindless peace. The walls retreated and dissolved all around him and he opened his eyes. He saw the radiant white room, the grinning dwarf, the glass cabinets, a seamless face staring at him, the cold blue eyes reflecting him.

"I'm not from ACASS," Aldridge said. "Mr. McKinley was from ACASS. Mr. McKinley wanted to hire you for his project, but we needed you more. We need people everywhere. We have to know what's going on. We need someone in the Cheyenne Mountain Complex, and you are that person. You will do what we tell you, without question, without fear; you will do it because you won't have a choice, because you'll feel that you want to. Your will is our will. What we will, you will do. You will live just for service, and that service will be to us—and in doing that service you will experience the most complete satisfaction."

"I understand," the professor said.

"Good," Aldridge said. "Understanding is enough. We will now take you back to Miami and deposit you there. You will go back to your room and have a sleep and awaken refreshed. You will not go to see Mr. McKinley. Mr. McKinley is dead. You will continue your vacation as before, as if nothing has happened. You will then return home. As usual, you will go to work. You will renew your contract with USAF, continue your work in the Cheyenne Complex, and then do whatever your head tells you to do, without fear or regret. You are not responsible for your actions. Your will is our will. You will do what we tell you to do and through that know contentment. Now stand up, professor."

The professor stood up. He surveyed the circular room. The white walls and the bodies in the cabinets both offered him comfort. He looked at Mr. Aldridge and felt a warm, transcendent peace. The blue eyes of Mr. Aldridge were his will and he felt a great freedom. The crippled dwarf shuffled toward him, his head rolling, hands outstretched; the professor saw the hands, pale and beautiful, waving him forward.

"Can I go now?" the professor said.

"We'll take you back," Aldridge said.

"I feel very tired," the professor said. "I think I need a good sleep."

The dwarf shuffled out first, his legs jerking mechanically, leading the professor into another white corridor that curved out of view. Aldridge followed the professor, walking slowly and carefully. They all went along the corridor, past the white walls, through silence, eventually reaching a high, narrow door that led into another room.

"We'll wait here," Aldridge said.

The dwarf nodded, shuffled away and stopped before a closed door; there was a hissing and the steel door slid open to reveal a small room. The professor recognized it as an elevator. The dwarf stepped in and the door closed. Aldridge pointed to a chair of flowing lines and the professor sat down.

"It won't take long," Aldridge said.

The professor gazed around the room. It was white and rectangular. One whole wall was a sheet of convex glass that looked out on the ocean bed. Bright lights beamed through the murk, streams of green and silver shimmered, shoals of transparent fish and giant squid and monstrous eels drifted back and forth as if in slow motion, colors glinting and merging. It was a scene of unearthly beauty. The professor thought it was wonderful. He saw grotesque eyes, bizarre fins and rainbow tails, teeth that gleamed like new razors in jaws as round and smooth as the rocks. The sand formed extraordinary patterns, tiny stones flashed like diamonds, the rocks sensual, alluvial, starkly shadowed, mysterious, alive with a primordial life that defied all description. It was too much for the professor: he let his gaze cleave to the walls which were white and had a pure, glacial sheen that reflected his shadow. He turned his head and glanced behind him. Another window revealed the dome. Below the dome were the canyons of glass, steel and plastic, that materialization of a science beyond all normal reckoning. The professor felt close to tears, wanting never to leave this place. He turned again and looked directly at Aldridge and knew what he must do.

"You understand?" Aldridge said.

"Yes," the professor said.

"Your work will be important. Most valuable. You will always be warmed by that."

"I understand," the professor said.

"Understanding is enough. We will always be with you to guide you. What we need, you will get for us."

"I understand," the professor said.

The elevator door opened. Aldridge motioned with one hand. The professor stood up and felt a great peace as he walked through the door. Aldridge stepped in behind him. The steel walls shone like glass. The doors closed and the elevator descended, dropping smoothly and silently. The professor studied his own reflection, saw a shadow on polished steel: he felt calm and alert and in control, and out of this sprang his pleasure. Aldridge offered him a smile. The professor felt a quiet pride. The doors opened and he followed Aldridge out and saw the high, curving steel walls.

"This is a wonderful place," he said.

"I'm glad you like it," Aldridge said.

"I hope I can come back here some day."

"You will," Aldridge said.

The steel floor was enormous, the dome sweeping up and over. Around the wall, scaling dizzying heights, were the ladders and catwalks. Hidden lights cast long shadows, modules gleamed upon other modules, and there were enormous generators and pumps and miles of coiling steel pipes. Most of the workers seemed faraway and wore different colored coveralls, moved up and down ladders, crossed the catwalks and balconies, and were silhouetted behind the long windows that glowed orange and blue. All this was bathed in the white haze. The professor's shadow was stark. He looked ahead, across the immense lower floor, and saw the boat on the platform.

"That's some boat," the professor said.

"Thank you," Aldridge said.

"If you meant to impress me, you've succeeded."

"We always do," Aldridge said.

They walked across the steel floor, their footsteps ringing with a hollow sound, eventually stopping at the platform that was raised off the floor on hydraulic supports. The professor looked up at the boat and saw the crew hard at work. The domed roof was high above, a monstrous jigsaw of shadow and light, and the eighty-five foot boat seemed small beneath it, isolated in open space. The crew was working in silence and seemed vaguely Oriental. The crippled dwarf was at the top of the ramp that ran down to the floor.

"After you," Aldridge said.

The professor walked up the ramp and stepped down onto the deck, the dwarf reaching out and touching his wrist and then darting away again. The professor stepped off the ramp, leaned on the railings, glanced around him, his gaze taking in Aldridge as he came up the ramp, then roaming across the dome's sweeping wall to the vast working space. The light glinted off the modules, off the catwalks and ladders, then fused and became a white haze that spread across the machinery. The professor thought it was beautiful. He didn't really want to leave. Turning around, he saw Fallaci, still dressed in his white suit, leaning casually against the door of the cabin and talking to Aldridge.

Someone tugged at the professor's trousers. He glanced down and saw the dwarf. The dwarf was grinning up at him, his head bobbing, his delicate hands waving.

"You feel good?" the dwarf said. "You feel better? No fear for your future?"

"No fear," the professor said.

Aldridge looked directly at him. "We're going up now," he said. "You won't feel anything until we reach the surface, then the boat may rock slightly. Hold on to the railing."

The professor did as he was told. It seemed a natural thing to do. He felt a very light vibration, heard a muffled droning noise, then the steel floor under the boat began to

rise, moving up toward the domed roof. The professor
glanced around him, saw the ladders and catwalks, felt a
sudden, immeasurable loss as it all fell away from him.
The steel floor kept rising, the boat rocking imperceptibly.
The professor glanced down below, at the workshops and
modules, and wished that he could stay here forever and
explore all these wonders.

"Hold on now," Aldridge said.

The steel floor stopped rising. The silence was broken
by muffled rumblings. The noise came from the encircling
wall of the dome, reverberating and echoing. The professor knew it was the sea. The dome was nearing the surface.
He had a final look around him, saw that technological
marvel, then put his head back and stared above him at
the shadow-streaked metal dome.

There was a sudden roaring sound, an insane hammering and hissing, as the sea exploded around the surfacing
dome and rushed down its curved outer wall. The professor held on to the railing. The boat rocked from side to
side. The dome seemed to sway above him, then it
steadied, reverberating with hollow sounds.

The professor kept looking up, the roof of the dome still
high above him, then he saw thin lines of light, getting
brighter, growing longer, spreading out like the ribs of a
giant umbrella and exposing the vivid sky. The professor
was enthralled. He stared up in growing wonder. The dome
was splitting apart, becoming four monstrous triangles,
then these triangles themselves split in two and moved
away from each other.

A shocking brightness poured into the dome. The light
exploded like an enormous star. The striations blazed
down around the boat and swept out through the gloom.
The professor felt the burning sun, saw the vast arch of
the sky. The immense, sun-reflecting, triangular walls were
sinking down all around him. Then he saw the hazed horizon, the white sheet of the sky above. The sea boiled
around the circle of sinking steel fins, then it swallowed
them totally, poured across the great steel deck, and soon
the deck was nothing more than a black mass below the
turbulent waves. There was a brief, hollow ringing, the
boat rocked violently and steadied, then the black mass

sank deeper, grew smaller, disappeared, and then the boat was drifting lazily in the sea which swept out on all sides.

Professor Vale stared all around him. The sea was calm and very beautiful. The green waves rolled away to the horizon and a thin wedge of dark land. It was the coastline of Miami. The boat was heading straight toward it. The crew was moving back and forth, working silently at their tasks, the late afternoon sun beating down, flashing off steel and glass.

The professor leaned against the railing, saw Fallaci near the cabin. The dwarf had disappeared somewhere inside, but Mr. Aldridge was still there. The professor felt good about that. He was very fond of Mr. Aldridge. Smiling, the professor leaned on the railing and took in the fresh sea air.

Mr. Aldridge finally approached him. There was a waiter by his side. Mr. Aldridge smiled a little and nodded while the waiter bowed low.

"What would you like to drink?" Aldridge said.

"Rum and Coke," the professor said.

CHAPTER TWELVE

*The dream of the Thousand Year Reich had all the gran-
deur of lunacy. Nothing was impossible. They firmly believed that. They had their volkish socialism, their need for
an Aryan Utopia, and with the passion of all mad visionaries, they stepped forth to create it. Mysticism? Yes. The
Reich was born from mysticism: the Cosmic Circle of
Munich, the Anthrosophy of Rudolph Steiner, the Theoso-
phy and Rosicrucianism of Vienna and Prague, the ancient dreams of Atlantis and Lemuria, of the undefiled
German. Mysticism and racism: the "pure" blood decreed
by Schuler; the Third Reich sprang out of a vision of a
Utopia devoid of Jews and subhumans.*

*Such dreams have no limits. Simple logic cannot contain
them. In such dreams the Third Reich saw the light over
limitless vistas—and ignored the impossible. The whole
world would be changed. Cities and nations would be
erased. The earth would be cleansed of Jews and subhumans and other vermin; and in isolated colonies, in new
cities of glass and stone, a chosen hierarchy of masters and
slaves would create the New Order.*

*No doubt, they were madmen. Their strongest leaders
were grotesque. They were men who lived their dreams,
who were divorced from reality, who like children felt that
all things were possible and that nothing could stop them.*

*Science is logic. Mysticism is the opposite. I despised
the mysticism of the Nazis, but could see its potential. My*

*own dreams were grandiose. No democracy could afford
them. I needed money and equipment and labor on a staggering scale. No democracy could sanction it. Only lunatics would. And the lunatics, all those mad visionaries, were
the Reich's leading lights.*

*I knew this when I met Himmler. It was in 1935. Be-
hind his spectacles his eyes had the mildness of a priest or
a fool. We were in his office in Berlin. I spread my
drawings on his desk. He glanced down and stroked his
thinning dark hair and touched his nose with one finger.
He had once been a chicken farmer. Now he headed the
S.S. A mild and modest killer, puritanical, quietly spoken,
he was seeking to resurrect Atlantis through a Reich filled
with supermen. I had checked him out beforehand. What I
found was enough. He believed in mesmerism, in reincarnation and clairvoyance, in Horbinger's cosmic world of ice
and fire, in gods and god-men. His S.S. was a religious order. His men were bound by blood and oath. Himmler
wanted to isolate them, to brainwash them and remold
them, to mate them with the purest German women and
produce blond perfection. He had once processed chickens; now he wanted to process people: he had a dream of
a disciplined Order of masters and slaves. I wanted a similar Order—but one devoted to science. And when
Himmler raised his eyes from my drawings, I knew that I
could have it.*

*Himmler checked me out thoroughly. He couldn't be-
lieve why I had come. He first thought me an eccentric
American who ought to be shot. I was held prisoner in Berlin. They interrogated me for months. In the Gestapo prison, in the Prinz Albrechtstrasse, I heard the screams of the
tortured. My own interrogations were more casual. My cell
was very comfortable. They fed me and supplied me with
books and let me work on my notes. The interrogations
were conversational. The less fortunate continued screaming. For two months I kept repeating my history, as they
jotted down details. The prison was always busy. Bleeding
people were dragged down corridors. I told my questioners
of the project in Iowa and of how I had sabotaged it. The
Americans don't know, I said. They thought the project
was a disaster. My questioners tapped their pencils on the*

*table and smiled at each other. Quite often I heard gun-
fire. It always came from the basement. I saw soldiers carrying bodies wrapped in shrouds and putting them into the
trucks. Such scenes did not disturb me. My hopes lived on
undiminished. After two months, they concentrated on my
drawings, still unsure of their value. I don't know who first
studied them. I think the Italian, Bellonzo. Nevertheless, I
was shortly released and taken back to see Himmler.*

*No point in even dwelling on the blood that had stained
Himmler's hands. Such a quiet man he was. His good
manners were impressive. A modest face with round
glasses, his hair thinning and neatly parted, he sat behind
his desk like a minor clerk offering help. He asked me
what I wanted. I explained my requirements. He nodded
in a slow, thoughtful manner, sometimes stroking his nose.
We are very impressed, he said. Indeed, he added, we are
astonished. He then told me that some technical advisors
had thought my drawings miraculous.*

*I asked who these men were. He mentioned Bellonzo
and Schriever. He said Bellonzo was getting too old, but
that Schriever was brilliant. They wished to work on my
project. Himmler thought it a good idea. I realized that he
wanted to have me watched, so I nodded agreement. You
are committed, he said. You must now bend to our will.
You will never return to your own country; if you try we
will kill you. I reassured him immediately. I would report
directly to him. My whole project would be wrapped in
strict secrecy and controlled by the S.S.*

*I will never forget that day. My dream came alive then.
Even now, the pain biting, my poor liver in disarray, I
gaze out upon the glinting ice caps and remember it vividly.*

*I was driven to Kummersdorf West. It was sixty miles
south of Berlin. We both sat in the back of the car and
looked out at the city. Himmler obviously loved Berlin.
The sunlight flashed off his glasses. He stroked his nose
and pointed out the sights with a quiet, clear excitement.
The city was indeed majestic. The streets were filled with
smiling people. The walls were decorated with swastikas
and flags and obscene propaganda. The word Juden was
prominent. I saw few on the pavements. Soldiers sauntered*

*up and down and laughed loudly, in love with themselves.
The very air seemed to smile. It was the triumph of the
will. In its own perverted way it was the proof of Man's
awesome potential.*

*Perverted? Most certainly. With that truth I would live.
Behind those walls were the high priests of a demoniac
Order: Hermann Goering, Josef Goebbels, Rudolph Hess,
Martin Bormann—alcoholics, drug addicts, occultists and
degenerates—the very epitome of that gross irrationalism
which I so much abhorred. There, too, the Gestapo butchers, the drilled ranks of the S.S., and all the torture and
murder that went on every day in the basements.*

*Yet I had to accept it. Science cannot moralize. Those
irrational brutes were no more than the means to achiev-
ing my ends. Progress needs its trampled bones. Death
gives way to more life. Evolution knows neither right nor
wrong and transcends transient matters. So, I would work
with them. In doing that, I could use them. And looking out upon Berlin, glancing sideways at Himmler, I felt
nothing but hope for the future, the glow of fulfilment.*

*We drove out of the city. Planes roared overhead. Sit-
ting beside me, very stiff and upright, Himmler started to
talk. He was suddenly like a child. His eyes gleamed behind the glasses. The words poured out and splashed
around my ears as if they couldn't be stopped. He said the
rocket teams had left. They had been moved to Peenemunde. The research center at Kummersdorft was empty
and now it was mine. We passed troops on the roads. The
tanks growled through swirling dust. Himmler talked of
Aryan blood and German might, of the world of the future. We will cleanse the earth, he said. We will purify the
blood. We will exterminate the Jews and the infirm and
maladjusted, use the lesser races as slaves to the Reich,
create a race of pure Nordics. There was no need to reply.
Right or wrong did not touch me. When Himmler talked
of his New Order, of his masters and slaves, I had the
feeling that it just might succeed and that I could utilize it.*

*Unlimited labor was what I needed. No democracy
could supply it. But here, in this country where all
freedom had been destroyed, where the will of the people
was one will—the Volk—and where discipline and slavery*

walked hand in hand—here, at the dawn of the new era, I could do the impossible. Yes, I grabbed at it. I was fifty-seven years of age. I thought then, before I knew what could be done, that my time was too short. Thus I didn't moralize. Not then and not now. I looked out at the air-craft, at the tanks and machine-gun carriers, at the troops who were numbered in their thousands, and accepted it all.

History will exonerate me. What I did, I did for progress. I sit now in my mountain lair, the white wilder-ness below me, and I know with the certainty of faith that my life has meant something. I am changing the course of history. I am aiding evolution. When I go, as I now know I must, my achievements will live on.

I knew this at the time. The sight of the proving range convinced me. The experimental station was between two artillery ranges, safely isolated from the surrounding towns and villages, all the hangars in good shape. Here Wernher von Braun had worked. And Walter Dornberger and Klaus Riedel. Those names, and those of Grottrup and Becker, made me smile condescendingly. The A-3 and A-5 rockets. So highly praised, so primitive. And the V-1 and V-2 would be feared when I thought them mere toys. Nev-ertheless those men had gone. They had been moved to Peenemunde. They would not be here to view what I was doing, would not know I existed. In this I agreed with Himmler. Even the Fuhrer would not know. Himmler had his own plans for the future and did not want them men-tioned.

Himmler showed me around the hangars. He introduced me to the workers. I met the Italian, Bellanzo, who was old and gray-haired, and the younger Flugkapitan Ru-dolph Schriever, who seemed dangerously ambitious. The old Italian was a physicist. Rudolph Schriever was an en-gineer. Both men were engaged in aeronautical research, both were keen on my drawings. I didn't really want those men. They had been around too long. I was disturbed by their knowledge of my work, and by their closeness to Himmler. They obviously wanted to impress him: bowed and scraped in his presence. I knew immediately that they would try to pick my brains and then usurp my authority.

I could not allow that. What I needed was total secrecy. After my experience in Iowa, aware that no one could be trusted, I had already planned to strengthen my position by becoming invaluable. I would hide the most vital facts. I would doctor all the drawings. I would split the work up, spread it widely among the work force, and thus insure that no single individual could duplicate my success. In this way I would protect myself. I would become indispensable. And so, as I shook hands, as I talked to Schriever and Bellonzo, I decided not to let them get too close to whatever was workable.

Yes, I was ruthless. I had to protect myself. I was aware of my dependence upon the Nazis—and of how weak that made me. Sooner or later they might disown me—the war might drain their resources—and if that happened, I had to be ready to make good my escape. I would take my secrets with me. I would leave them useless toys. But by then, if I made use of my time, I would have what I wanted.

Such thoughts were not expressed. Himmler smiled and led me out. We returned to his car and climbed in and headed back to Berlin. There was paperwork to be completed. Requisition forms and orders: more manufacturers, more instruments, more pyrotechnicists, more welding experts and laborers. I did not think it was possible. The required numbers seemed awesome. I wondered if even Himmler, with his frightening, godlike powers, could requisition workers in such numbers for a clandestine project. Himmler smiled at my obvious doubts. He stroked his nose and blinked his eyes. He said that I had no need to worry, that he had something to show me.

The fields of Germany were green. I heard aircraft overhead. We passed columns of troops and growling tanks, but the peace soon returned. This memory remains vivid. The sun shone from a blue sky. It was difficult to believe that war would come and devastate all of Europe. Then we passed barbed wire fences. Beyond the wire were smoking chimneys. We drove through guarded gates, beneath watchtowers and guns, kept driving toward the long, wooden buildings, passed a series of gallows. The wind made the ropes dance. Ragged people were digging

ditches. We drove on and reached the center of the camp
and saw the Reich's buried nightmare.

Himmler made the driver stop. A nervous soldier let us
out. We stood together in the mud of the compound, surrounded by prisoners. Himmler smiled and rubbed his
nose. I saw the guards with the bullwhips. The hundreds
of men, women and children were filthy and silent. Nearly
all had shaved heads. Their bones showed through their
flesh. Their large eyes were filled with anguish and despair
and a hopeless submission. I heard the crack of the whips.
The dogs snarled and someone screamed. Himmler blinked
and rubbed his nose, smiled with quiet, modest pride, and
then waved one hand languidly in the air to take in all the
misery.

"Your workers," he said.

CHAPTER THIRTEEN

"You don't go too close to UFOs. It's a dangerous thing to do. If you go too close to UFOs you get burned, and you rarely recover. Just look at me, Stanford. I run this flea-pit in Albuquerque. I was a World War Two pilot, decorations up the ass; I fought in the Pacific and Europe and returned home a hero. What the hell am I doing here? You must have asked yourself that question. I ask the same question every night and I just wake up screaming."

Goldman was bent across the table, his right hand waving wildly, his left hand holding a glass of neat bourbon, the bottle in front of him.

"Well, I tell you," he continued, "I'm not the only one like this. There are a lot of us hiding out, lying low, running scared, and we're doing it because we haven't a choice, because the doors have been closed to us. You don't talk about UFOs. If you do, strange things happen. You can never pin down what it is, but things start going haywire."

He raised his glass and drank some bourbon, slopping it down his shirt front, then he put his glass back on the table and glanced all around him. The bar was noisy and crowded, a real homegrown honky-tonk, a jukebox blaring out of one corner, the lights mercifully dim. Stanford reached out for the bottle, filled up Goldman's glass, glancing casually at the women along the bar to see if one was worth having.

"You knew Ruppelt?" Stanford said.

"Sure," Goldman said. "You wouldn't be here if you didn't know that. We worked a long time together, we respected one another, and even when he left, when those bastards pushed him out, he still came to see me now and then, very quiet, just for old time's sake. Ruppelt was a believer. I've no doubts about that at all. He was a believer and he died a believer, no matter what his book said."

"You mean he took the UFOs seriously?" Stanford said.

"Fucking right," Goldman said.

Stanford studied Goldman's face, the hollow cheeks, the bloodshot eyes, took note of the stubble on his chin and his darkly stained teeth. Something had happened to Goldman—something not very nice—and now the Air Force hero was a wreck, always drunk in his own bar.

"I thought Ruppelt was a career man," Stanford said. "I didn't think he'd believe that."

"He believed in the Air Force," Goldman said. "And the *Air Force* believed it."

"I'd always thought the opposite," Stanford said.

"That's bullshit," Goldman said. "A PR's diarrhea. The Air Force believed in UFOs from as far back as 1947."

"Really?" Stanford said.

"Yeah, really. I was with the Air Technical Intelligence Center at the time—then based at Wright Patterson AFB in Dayton, Ohio—and believe me, we were in a state of near panic. And why? Because contrary to their own publicity, the military was being plagued with their own sightings: first over Maxwell Air Force Base in Montgomery, Alabama, then, to our horror, over the White Sands Proving Ground—right smack in the middle of our A-bomb territory. Finally, what really got us going was a whole series of sightings on July 8, 1947, over Muroc Air Base—now Edwards AFB—our top secret Air Force test center in the Mojave Desert."

"I know about those sightings," Stanford said. "They really were something."

"Fucking A," Goldman said.

He put his glass to his lips, had a drink, topped it up,

cursed the noise of the blaring jukebox and put his glass on the table. Stanford topped his own glass up, glanced around the crowded bar, taking note of the Stetsons and boots and the girls in tight dresses.

"I'm told that those sightings led to Project Sign."

"Right," Goldman said. "No less a luminary than General Nathan Twining, commander of the Air Material Command, wrote to the commanding general of the Army—Air Forces stating that the phenomenon was something real, that it wasn't visionary or fictitious, and that the objects were disc-shaped, as large as aircraft, and *controlled*. Shortly after that, about December '47, we established Project Sign, gave it a 2A classification, and handed it over to Wright-Patterson Air Force Base."

"That was just before the death of Captain Mantell."

"Oh, yeah," Goldman said. "A famous case."

"I'm told he died chasing a UFO, but the Air Force denies it."

"Right," Goldman said. "Those fuckers tried to wipe it out. But that case, and a lot of other unknown sightings, really shook the hell out of us."

"How do you mean?" Stanford said.

Goldman had another drink, licked his lips and glanced around him, waved at a couple of friends and then looked back at Stanford.

"Well," he said, "it prompted Project Sign to write an official, top-secret Estimate of the Situation—and we didn't piss around when we did it. That Estimate traced the whole history of UFO sightings, included the fireballs and ghost rockets and American sightings before 1947, and concluded, I kid you not, that the UFOs were of extraterrestrial origin. We then sent the report through channels, all the way to the Chief of Staff, General Hoyt Vandenberg, but the good general, to our amazement, sent it back with instructions to bury it."

Stanford sipped his bourbon and saw a girl at the bar, her blond hair tumbling down to her shoulders, her tits pointing at him. Stanford smiled at the girl, the girl smiled right back, and Stanford placed his glass on the table and scratched his right ear.

"You run a good bar," Stanford said. "Lots of action, I notice."

"Yeah," Goldman said. "Lots of action. I gotta admit that."

"General Vandenberg sounds pretty odd to me. He must have caused you some problems."

Goldman nodded his agreement, drank some bourbon and burped, then waved his left hand in the air, his eyes bleary and bloodshot.

"It was there and then," he said, "when that report was sent back, that we realized just how shitty the job was. In fact, word filtered back to us that Vandenberg had called us all mad—and the repercussions from that story were pretty rough. Fear of further offending Vandenberg quickly led to a whole new policy: in the future all Sign personnel were to assume that *all* UFO reports were misidentifications, hallucinations or hoaxes. Not only that, but we had to check with FBI officers, and with the criminal and subversive files of police departments, looking into the private lives of the witnesses to see if they were *reliable*. No need to say it: that was fair warning to us all that it wasn't wise to open your mouth too wide . . . And shortly after, the Sign Estimate was incinerated."

"Then Project Sign became Project Grudge."

"Right," Goldman said. "A sure sign of General Vandenberg's displeasure."

Stanford looked at the bar and saw the girl with blond hair, now talking to a very large brunette, the pair of them giggling. The blond girl turned and stared, smiled at him and stroked her hair, then she turned away and whispered to the other girl and they giggled again.

"I've heard bad stories about Grudge," Stanford said. "A real shitty assignment."

"Right," Goldman said. "We were told to kill the whole affair. Now our job was to shift the investigation away from the actual UFOs and on to the poor bastards who reported them—we had to prove that the UFOs did *not* exist."

"That must have been pretty difficult," Stanford said. "I mean, according to the Grudge Report, snow job though it was, a good twenty-three percent of your sightings were still classed as unknowns."

"Big deal," Goldman said. "That was obviously still too much for General Vandenberg. The same day we released that report, the Air Force announced the termination of the project, all the Grudge records were stored, a few officers walked the plank, and the rest of our personnel were widely scattered."

"But you remained."

'Yeah."

"You must have felt pretty bad."

"Fucking right," Goldman said. "I began to think that the Air Force was only making a pretense at investigating UFOs, when in fact they didn't want us to find out anything. I couldn't figure out their attitude. It just didn't make sense. All I knew was that reported unknowns led to really bad trouble."

Stanford studied Goldman's face, saw the dark, bloodshot eyes, and was awed by how far the man had fallen. It was best not to think about it. Men like Goldman were the victims. It was hard to think of Goldman as a highly decorated fighter pilot, hard to think of him working on Project Blue Book when the project was honorable. Goldman and Ruppelt: they had both paid the price. Now Goldman talked like a man without a future, still glancing behind him.

"Tell me about Ruppelt," Stanford said. "There's a real mystery there."

"Not a mystery," Goldman said. "Clear as glass. They just slid the blade in."

He topped up his glass, emptied the bottle and put it down, picked it up again and waved it at the barman and demanded another. Stanford sat back and waited. He didn't want to push too hard. It was supposed to be a casual conversation and it had to remain that way. Stanford glanced around the room. The air was filled with blue smoke. High-heeled boots stomped the floor, Stetsons clashed, the tight dresses were glittering. Stanford saw the blond girl. She smiled at him and raised her glass. Stanford thought she might soften up Goldman, so he nodded and grinned. The barman brought them another bottle. He slapped Goldman on the back. When he left, Goldman poured them both drinks and then started to talk again.

"Ruppelt was assigned to the Air Technical Intelligence Center in January 1951—and like me, he was working under Lieutenant Jerry Cummings. Now, up to that time Ruppelt hadn't paid too much attention to UFO reports, but what he read in our files turned him on. As I remember, he was particularly impressed by two reports that involved movies taken at the White Sands Proving Ground. Now bear in mind that the White Sands Proving Ground was fully instrumented to track high-altitude, fast moving objects—namely, the guided missiles—and had camera stations equipped with cinetheodolite cameras located all over the area. So, on two different days in June 1950, two UFOs were actually shot by two different cameras, and the guys who performed the analysis were, by putting a correction factor in the data gathered by the two cameras, able to arrive at a rough estimation of speed, altitude and size. According to their reports, those UFOs were higher than 40,000 feet, traveling at over 2,000 miles an hour, and were over 300 feet in diameter."

"Jesus," Stanford said.

"Fucking right. Now those reports really got Ruppelt going. He was hooked on the UFOs, started working like a beaver, and that's when we really got together, going through the old files."

Goldman stared around the room. He was obviously growing restless. He owned the whole bar, it was his, and he wanted to use it. Stanford recognized the signs. Goldman seemed a little petulant. Stanford thought of Epstein waiting in Washington, and decided to push it.

"What led to Project Blue Book?" Stanford said.

"The Lubbock lights," Goldman said. "Those and the Fort Monmouth sightings. They really stirred the shit up."

"This must be boring you," Stanford said.

"I don't mind," Goldman said.

"Let's have a little company," Stanford said. "That blond and brunette."

Stanford swiveled around and raised his glass to the blond girl, then waved his left hand in an inviting gesture. The blond glanced at the brunette, looked at Stanford, feigned surprise, then pointed her finger at herself and watched Stanford's head nodding. Goldman looked on, amazed. He thought Stanford was pretty cool. The girls giggled and then walked toward the table, holding on to each other. The juke box was still shrieking. Couples danced without touching. The two girls pushed through the crowds, reached the table and stopped, looked at Stanford and Goldman in turn and gave them broad, street-wise smiles.

"Hi," the brunette said.

"Peace on earth," Stanford said. "We thought you might like a little drink with two honorable men."

"Oh, Jesus," the brunette said.

"Don't pray," Stanford said. "We don't hold with religion on Friday nights. Just set yourself down."

They both giggled and sat down. They looked different up close. The blonde wore jeans and halter, her tanned belly exposed, her breasts thrusting forward in challenge, her nose upturned, her eyes hard. The brunette was much bigger, far heavier, less pretty, her loose dress hiding unwanted flesh, her face masked in thick makeup. Goldman figured them for hookers. Stanford knew that for a fact. The girls flicked their eyes at Stanford, looked away, giggled once and then sighed.

"I'm Joanna," the blonde said. "This here's my friend Carol. We both live on the other side of town. We've never been here before."

"I'm Stanford," Stanford said. "This gentleman is Mr. Goldman. We're both bored with the sound of our own voices and we thought you'd distract us."

The girls giggled again. "That's a shame," the brunette said. "I thought you guys loved one another. So *involved* with each other."

"What were you talking about?" the blonde said.

"UFOs," Goldman muttered.

"UFOs?"

"Flying saucers," Stanford said. "Mr. Goldman's an expert."

The large brunette shivered. "Christ, they're creepy," she said.

"Fantastic," the blonde said. "My favorite subject. Are you *really* an expert?"

She stared straight at Goldman. Her eyes were large and blue. Goldman grinned and sat up in his chair, almost preening himself.

"I guess so," he said.

"He's being modest," Stanford said. "This guy was chasing UFOs for the Air Force. He knows all about them."

The blonde moved close to Goldman, her breasts brushing against his arm, her blue eyes very large and excited, her knee touching his knee. Goldman couldn't resist it, acted more drunk than he was, put his arm around the girl and then hugged her, slyly touching her left tit.

"Tell her about the Lubbock lights," Stanford said. "Give her all of the details."

Goldman grinned at the blonde. "Okay, sweetheart," he said. "Let me give you a display of expertise that'll boggle your mind."

Stanford poured them all drinks. Goldman drank and hugged the blonde. The brunette glanced around her and shivered and hissed, "This is creepy." The blonde giggled and hugged Goldman. Stanford watched them both carefully. Goldman grinned at the three of them in turn and then started to talk.

"The Lubbock affair began on the evening of August 25, 1951, when an employee of the Atomic Energy Commission's supersecret Sandia Corporation—one with a top 'Q' security clearance—looked up from his garden on the outskirts of Albuquerque to see a huge aircraft flying swiftly and *silently* over his home. He later described it as having the shape of a 'flying wing,' about one and a half times the size of a B-36, with six to eight softly glowing bluish lights on the aft end of its wings. On that same night, about twenty minutes after this sighting, four professors from the Texas Technological College at Lubbock observed a formation of lights streaking across the sky: about fifteen to thirty separate lights, all a bluish-green color, moving from north to south in a semicircular formation . . . Then, early in the morning of August 26, only a few hours after the Lubbock sightings, two different radars at an Air Defense Command radar station located

in Washington State showed an unknown target traveling
at 900 miles an hour at 1,300 feet and heading in a northwesterly direction. Nor did it end there. On August 31, at
the height of the flap, two ladies were driving near Mata-
dor, seventy miles northeast of Lubbock, when they saw a
'pear-shaped object' about 150 yards ahead of them, about
120 feet in the air, drifting slowly to the east at less than
the take-off speed of a Cub airplane. One of those
witnesses was pretty familiar with aircraft—she was married to an Air Force officer and had lived near air bases
for years—and she swore that the object was about the
size of a B-29 fuselage, had a porthole on one side, made
absolutely no noise as it moved *into* the wind, and that it
suddenly picked up speed and then climbed out of sight,
seemingly making a tight, spiraling motion. That same
evening an amateur photographer took five photos of a V
formation of the same bluish-green lights as they flew over
his backyard. And finally, a rancher's wife told her husband—who related the story to Captain Ruppelt—that she
had seen a large object gliding swiftly and *silently* over her
house. That object was viewed about ten minutes after the
Sandia Corporation viewed *his* object, it was described as
'an airplane without a body', and the woman said that on
the aft edge of the wing were pairs of glowing bluish lights
—an exact description of the Albuquerque sighting by the
Sandia employee."

"Christ," the blonde said.

"I don't believe this," the brunette said. "I mean, people
see things all the time. You can't prove they exist."

"Not so," Goldman said. "We investigated all the Lubbock sightings thoroughly. First, we discovered that the
Washington State radar lock-on was a solid target—not a
weather target—and it was then easy to work out that an
object flying between that radar station and Lubbock
would have been on a northwesterly course at the time it
was seen at the two places—and that it would have had a
speed of approximately 900 miles an hour, as calculated
by the radar. Next, we analyzed the five photographs
taken by the amateur photographer. The lights had crossed
about 120 degrees of open sky at a 30-degree-per-second
angular velocity—which corresponded exactly to the angu-

lar velocity carefully measured by the four professors from
the tech college at Lubbock. Analysis of the photos also
showed that the lights were a great deal brighter than the
surrounding stars and that their unusual intensity could
have been caused by an exceptionally bright light source
which had a color at the most distant red end of the
spectrum, bordering on infrared."

"Jesus," the brunette said, "he sounds like Einstein.
What the hell does that *mean?*"

Goldman preened at her bewilderment, grinned at each
of them in turn, then fixed his bleary gaze upon Stanford,
ignoring the girls.

"Well," he said, "since the human eye isn't sensitive to
such a light, the light could seem dim to the eye—as many
of the Lubbock lights did—but be exceptionally bright on
film—as they were on our photographs. And, according to
the Photo Reconnaissance Laboratory, at the time there
was nothing flying that had those pretty magical characteristics. However, what *really* knocked us out was the discovery that the lights on the photos were amazingly
similar to the description given by the Atomic Energy
Commission employee of the lights on the aft edge of the
huge UFO that passed over his house."

"So," Stanford said, leaning forward, "*did* something fly
over Albuquerque and travel 250 miles to Lubbock at a
speed of 900 miles an hour? And did the radar station in
Washington State pick up that same object?"

"According to the witnesses," Goldman said, "and to
our radar and visual tracking calculations, it did. Our Lubbock files were also studied by a group of rocket experts,
nuclear physicists and intelligence experts, and they were
all convinced that the Lubbock lights were of extraterrestrial origin."

"Oh, God," the blonde said, "they must be real. I mean,
you hear that, they've *got* to be."

"Shit," said the brunette. "It's all shit. Let's talk about
sex." She reached out for her glass, had a drink, put the
glass down, gave them all a look of disgust and then lit up
a cigarette. Stanford smiled understandingly, reached out
and stroked her cheek. "Sex," he said. "I like the sound of
that. I think we might even try it." He sat back and smiled

at her. His smile was returned. The blonde pouted in a
theatrical fashion and gave Goldman a hug. "Just ignore
them," she said. "I think it's really far out. I mean, stuff
like this you don't hear every day. I feel shivery all over."
Her breasts moved when she shivered. Goldman seemed a
lot brighter. Stanford shrugged as if he didn't really care,
and then topped up their glasses.

"It's all shit," the brunette repeated.

"Is it?" Stanford said. "Well I heard that the Pentagon
was involved. Is that true, Mr. Goldman?"

"Right," Goldman said. "Not many people know that.
The Pentagon, no matter what you hear, was fucking involved all right. The Fort Monmouth sightings started it.
All the witnesses were top brass. Those sightings caused a
fucking sensation and really got the ball rolling. I mean,
within hours of those sightings we received a call from the
Director of Intelligence of the Air Force, Major General
Cabell, telling us to get someone from ATIC to Jersey fast
and find out what the hell was going on. Shortly after that,
the T-33 pilot and an Air Force major who had tried to
pursue the UFO were on a plane to New York where they
were grilled by two of our best men. By the following day
our two men, Lieutenant Cummings and Lieutenant
Colonel Rosengarten, were sitting down in the Pentagon,
having words with Major General Cabell. Every word of
that meeting was duly recorded—but according to our
sources the recording was considered so hot it was later
destroyed. No matter . . . now totally convinced of the le-
gitimacy of the UFO problem, Major General Cabell ordered ATIC to establish a new UFO project. And, since
Cummings was due for release from active duty, Captain
Ruppelt was put in charge of the operation. In April
1952, Project Grudge was renamed Project Blue Book,
and Ruppelt really took that project seriously."

Stanford stared straight at Goldman. This was what he
wanted to hear. More accurately, it was what Epstein
wanted to hear, and Stanford had to deliver.

"Business," the brunette said. "I'm fed up with all this
shit. I think you two guys should make an offer. I've got a
living to make."

"Oh, for God's sake," the blonde said, "that can wait. I mean, we both need a break."

"That's right," Stanford said. "Let's all have another drink. Don't worry: we're both here for the night. And we're not short on bread."

The brunette puckered her lips, glared at her friend and then shrugged. Stanford picked the bottle up and poured more drinks and then looked straight at Goldman.

"This is amazing," he said. "I can hardly believe my ears. I mean, I never thought they took it that serious. The Pentagon! *Jesus!*"

He was stroking Goldman's vanity and the response was immediate: Goldman slid his arm away from the blonde and talked directly to Stanford.

"Not only the Pentagon," he said. "The fucking CIA, too."

"What?" Stanford said.

"You heard me right," Goldman said. "By June of that year Project Blue Book was really going strong and had received more official reports than it had received in any previous month in its history. In fact, the number of reports coming in at that time was fucking astonishing—and Air Force officers in the Pentagon became frantic. In July, ATIC received over five hundred reports—more than three times the number received in June—and then, when one of the top dogs in the CIA—and most of his guests—saw a silent, vertically climbing UFO over his home in Alexandria, Virginia, General Samford, Director of Intelligence, called Ruppelt to a secret meeting in Washington. At that meeting were General Samford, members of his staff, intelligence officers from the Navy and, according to Ruppelt, quite a few CIA officers. That was the first time the CIA officially stepped into the picture—and it was also the start of all our troubles."

"You mean that's when Ruppelt started to get screwed."

"Right," Goldman said. "What finally blew the balloon was the unprecedented number of July sightings, peaking in the famous UFO invasion of Washington in 1952. After that, it was murder."

"I'm filing my fingernails," the brunette said. "I've got

nothing else to do. I'm sitting on my fanny getting numb, so I'm filing my fingernails."

Everyone glanced at her. She was filing her fingernails. There were people dancing close to the table, and the juke-box was wailing. The blonde shook to the rhythm, looked at Stanford and winked. Stanford smiled, but kept his eyes fixed on Goldman, trying to keep him pinned down. "The Washington sightings were incredible," he said, "but what went on in the background? I mean, what's the connection with Ruppelt? I think you said it affected him."

"Yeah," Goldman said. "It did. Ruppelt wasn't in Washington during the night of the sightings, but he got the flak right in the face. In fact, Ruppelt hadn't even been informed of the sightings, and he only found out when he bought a newspaper at the Washington National Airport Terminal Building when he got off an airliner from Dayton, Ohio. He rushed immediately to the Pentagon where he had an urgent meeting with Major Dewey Fournet and Colonel Bower, an intelligence officer from Bolling AFB. They told him that throughout the night the restricted air corridor around the White House had been filled with interceptor jets trying to chase UFOs, that the UFOs had been radar tracked all around Washington, that an analysis of the sightings had completely ruled out temperature inversions, and that the radar operators at Washington National Airport and Andrews AFB—plus at least two veteran airline pilots—had all sworn that their sightings were caused by the radar waves bouncing off hard, *solid* objects."

"So," Stanford said, "what happened to Ruppelt?"

"Well," Goldman said, "on behalf of the Air Force, Al Chops gave the press an official 'No Comment' on the sightings. In the meantime, Captain Ruppelt tried to set up a thorough investigation, but was shafted wherever he turned. He planned to go all over the area, to every sighting location, but he hardly got his foot out of the Pentagon. First, he called the transportation section for a car—and was refused. Next, he went down to the finance office to see if he could *rent* a car—and was refused. Next, he was reminded that he was supposed to be on his way back to Dayton, and that if he didn't leave he would be technically AWOL. Ruppelt gave up in disgust and returned to Wright-Patterson in Dayton."

"Are you trying to tell me that the Air Force deliberately got rid of their most competent investigator?"

"What the hell do you think it sounds like?"

"Okay," Stanford said. "So within a week to the hour of the first major flap, another invasion took place over Washington."

"Right," Goldman said. "And this time it was even worse. At about ten thirty on the evening of July 26, the same radar operators who had seen the UFOs the week before picked up several of the very same objects . . . and this time the UFOs were spread out in a huge arc around Washington—from Virginia to Andrews AFB. In short, they had Washington boxed in."

Stanford glanced at the brunette, saw her filing her fingernails, then glanced at the bare-bellied blonde and received an excited grin.

"So," Stanford said, "the White House took the invasion pretty seriously."

"They sure did," Goldman said. "Throughout that night there was chaos in Washington. The press was furious because all reporters and photographers had been ordered out of the radar rooms at the time our interceptors were chasing the UFOs. However, once the press had gone arguments really blew up in all those radar towers and in the Pentagon itself. According to Dewey Fournet, the Pentagon liaison man, everyone in the radar rooms had been convinced that the targets had been caused by solid, metallic objects and couldn't possibly have been anything else. And whatever those things were, they could literally hover in the air, then abruptly accelerate to 7,000 miles an hour."

"*Jesus,*" the blonde said. "To think I read about those saucers! Is it true President Nixon actually saw them?"

"It was 1952," the brunette said. "You got your presidents wrong."

"Yeah," Goldman said. "When I was there, word came down the grapevine that President Truman himself had almost gone apeshit when he saw UFOs skimming right around the White House. That story was quickly squashed by some of the President's aides, but shortly after, about ten that morning, the President's air aide, Brigadier General Landry, called Intelligence at Truman's personal request to find out what the hell had been going on. Ruppelt himself took that call and he had to hedge his answers, because he couldn't explain the sightings at all."

The brunette opened her shoulder bag, put her nail file away, then stared at the three of them in turn, her lips puckering distastefully.

"I'm finished," she said. "My fingernails are all filed. I'm sitting here trying to make a living, but I'm not getting action."

"Oh, *Carol*!" the blonde snapped.

"I'm just a working girl," Carol said. "I need to live just like anyone else, and these two guys aren't helping."

"We've got rooms," Goldman said.

"I *know* that," Carol said.

"Okay," Stanford said. "It's a deal. Just give us five minutes."

Carol sniffed and then nodded, had a drink and glanced around her. "Right," she said. "As long as that's settled. I mean, we've got other customers."

The blonde smiled at Stanford. Goldman smiled at the blonde. Stanford winked at the blonde and then leaned forward and stared straight at Goldman.

"What do you think it all meant?" Stanford said.

Goldman sighed. "It was the Washington sightings, more than anything else, that made all of us at Blue Book a bit suspicious of the Air Force's stance on UFOs. In fact, we spent over a year investigating those sightings, and what we came across really shook us. For a start, when the tower operators at Andrews AFB were later interrogated about the 'large, fiery, orange-colored sphere' they had reported over their radio, they completely changed their story and said that what they had really seen was a star and that they had just been *excited*. Now, apart from the fucking idiocy of highly skilled radio operators describing a normal star as a 'large fiery, orange-colored sphere' right over their control tower, Ruppelt also found out that according to astronomical charts there were *no* exceptionally bright stars where the UFO was reported to have been seen. Ruppelt then found out, from what he claimed was a reliable source, that the tower operators had been 'persuaded' a bit. Likewise, the pilot of an F-94C, who had told us about vainly trying to intercept unidentified lights, later stated in his *official* report that all he had seen was a ground light reflecting off a layer of haze—an equally ridiculous statement since both the pilot and the radar had confirmed that the lights had repeatedly disappeared and reappeared in the sky before finally shooting away. Then, regarding the Air Force's continuing stance that the lights had been caused by temperature inversions, we checked out the strength of the inversions through the Air Defense Command Weather Forecast Center—and at no time during the flap was there a temperature inversion remotely strong enough to show up on the radar. Finally, no weather target makes a 180 degree turn and flies away every time an airplane reaches it. The Washington sightings, according to Blue Book, are still unknowns."

Stanford started to forget the girls. He felt a cold, clear excitement. He thought of Epstein in the office in Washington, waiting patiently to hear from him. Epstein had been right. The Air Force had covered up. Why they had covered up was a mystery that Ruppelt might solve.

"As I said," Goldman continued, "it was the official reaction to the Washington sightings that made a lot of us suspicious of the Air Force. Too many people were telling us one thing and then changing their story for their 'official' reports. Also, it became more and more obvious that the top brass of the Air Force were trying to blind us with some dodgy maneuvers. After the Washington sightings, Ruppelt became convinced that pilots reporting UFOs were being intimidated into either changing their reports or simply remaining silent, that a lot of information was being withheld from Blue Book, and that the CIA was stepping into the picture for unexplained reasons."

"You were *really* worried about the CIA?"

"Yeah. The person who worried us most during this time was General Hoyt Vandenberg. Bear in mind that it was Vandenberg who had buried the original Project Sign Estimate, who had reportedly called us all mad, and who had directly or indirectly caused the fear of ridicule that has ever since hindered all UFO projects. It was also because of Vandenberg that the Sign Estimate was incinerated and that Project Sign was insultingly renamed Project Grudge. Now, while none of us could be sure of just how *much* Vandenberg was influencing either the Air Force or the CIA, the knowledge that he had been head of the Central Intelligence Group—later the CIA—from June 1946 to May 1947, that his uncle had been chairman of the Foreign Relations Committee—then the next most powerful committee in the Senate—that Vandenberg obviously still had great influence in those areas, and that pressure was always coming from those areas to suppress knowledge of UFO investigations, did nothing to make us trust him anymore. It therefore came as no surprise when we heard that the CIA and some high-ranking officers, including Generals Vandenberg and Samford, were, against the objections of the Battelle Memorial Institute, convening a panel of scientists to 'analyze' all the Blue Book data. Nor did it surprise us to discover that this panel was to be headed by Dr. H. P. Robertson, director of the Weapons System Evaluation Group in the Office of the Secretary of Defense—and a CIA classified employee."

"What do you know about the Robertson Panel?" Stanford said.

Goldman glanced at the two hookers, glanced at Stanford, licked his lips, now excited and wanting to continue, but nervous of doing so. He looked at the girls again. The blonde smiled and licked her lips. The brunette had her chin in her hand, her lips puckered in boredom.

"I'm getting impatient," she said. "I think you're giving us a snow job. I don't think you intend taking us upstairs. A pair of fags, I got sitting here."

"I can't afford you," Goldman said.

"It's on me," Stanford said. "I've got a pocketful of bread and I'm horny, so let's fix something up."

"Jesus, thanks," Goldman said. "I mean, that's really fucking decent. Tell you what, send the girls up to the room and then we'll finish the talk."

"Oh, shit," the blonde said.

"This is confidential," Goldman said. "I wanna finish this story with my buddy, so just wait for us upstairs."

"How long?" the brunette said.

"About five minutes," Goldman said.

"Here," Stanford said. "It's a deposit. It guarantees we'll be up there."

He passed over fifty dollars. The brunette put it in her bag. She stood up and then looked down at the blonde and said, "Okay, let's go." The blonde sighed and stood up, turned her nose up at them both. "What room?" she said. "We have to know what room. We can't fuck in the corridor." Goldman told her the room number. She sniffed loudly and walked away. The brunette grinned at them both, followed the blonde across the room, and they both passed the screaming jukebox and disappeared in the crowd. Goldman sighed and filled his glass, had a drink and glanced around him, then he leaned across the table and stared at Stanford, his dark eyes intense.

"Okay," he said. "The only thing I really know about the Robertson Panel is that it was convened in secrecy in Washington in 1953, and that *contrary* to the evidence submitted by Project Blue Book it wrote a totally negative report which led to the virtual dissolving of our operation. First, the panel submitted its report to the CIA, the higher echelons of the Air Force and the Pentagon, but refused to give a copy to Ruppelt or any of the Blue Book staff. Next, Ruppelt and Captain Garland were summoned to CIA headquarters where it was explained to them that the Robertson Panel had recommended *expanding* Blue Book's staff and terminating all secrecy in the project. This naturally encouraged Ruppelt, but his pleasure turned sour when he discovered that the CIA had been lying to him. In fact, it later transpired that the Robertson Panel had recommended a *tightening* of security, a mass 'debunking' of the phenomenon, and a subtle ridiculing of UFO witnesses and the phenomenon in general."

Goldman looked around him. The room was smokey and packed. The jukebox was screaming in the corner, surrounded by dancers.

"So," he said. "When it became obvious that the CIA had lied to us and that the Air Force was in fact trying to strangle Blue Book, a lot of us at ATIC got very nervous. Ruppelt himself began to feel that he was facing growing opposition from the Pentagon to his plans for expanding Blue Book's activities. This feeling was confirmed when he asked for a transfer, but agreed to stay on with Blue Book until a replacement could be found. He had asked for that transfer in December 1952, but by the following February no replacement had materialized. Nor were there any replacements when Lieutenant Flues was transferred to the Alaskan Air Command, when Lieutenant Rothstein's tour of active duty ended, or when others on the staff left or were transferred out. In short, Ruppelt left a drastically reduced Blue Book organization in February 1953, and by the time he returned, in July of that same year, he found that the Air Force had reassigned most of his remaining staff, that they had sent no replacements, and that Blue Book now consisted of only himself and a mere two assistants. To put it bluntly, Project Blue Book had been fucked."

"And you think it was intentional?" Stanford said.

"Yeah," Goldman said. "It was deliberate. I was out of the Air Force by the time Ruppelt returned, and what happened to me wasn't uncommon. In fact, once Ruppelt had left for Denver, it became clear to us all that the Air Force had deliberately not replaced him because they wanted to strip Blue Book of its one remaining figure of authority. With no competent officer in charge, Blue Book had little means of resisting the numerous transfers and subtle pressures that eventually strangled it. Of course, a few of us tried to speak out against all that, but it was the worst fucking thing we could have done. More and more I saw guys getting harassed for no good reason, having their confidence shattered, their good records ruined, and then getting transferred out by way of punishment—or being asked to resign. That happened to me. Those fuckers just went out to get me. I started getting picked up for negligence, for dumb insolence and other shit, and then they started moving me around from place to place, from one hole to another. After that, I gave up. I couldn't take it anymore. I was drinking like a fish, my wife packed up and left, and then eventually, like a lot of the others, I just

had to resign . . . You don't go too close to UFOs. It's a
dangerous thing to do. If you go too close to UFOs you
get burned—and you rarely recover."

Goldman picked his glass up and finished it off with one
gulp, then wiped his lips with the back of his free hand
and glanced wildly around him.

"Jesus," he said, "I'm drunk. I think I need a good fuck.
I have to blow this out of my system. Let's hit those two
whores."

He stood up and swayed, grabbed the table and steadied
himself, then Stanford stood up and took him by the elbow and turned him around. They pushed their way
through the noisy crowd, passed the dancers around the
jukebox, emerged from the haze of blue smoke and found
the dark, narrow stairs.

"What happened to Ruppelt?" Stanford said. "You
haven't told me. You never finished the story."

Goldman stumbled on the stairs. The drink had suddenly hit him hard. Stanford slid his arm around him and
helped him up, wondering how he had come to this.

"I don't know," Goldman said. "He just got fucked up
like me. He came to see me just after he'd left the Air
Force, and we drank beer and talked. Ruppelt's head was
filled with questions. He couldn't let the subject go. He
had left, but the subject still obsessed him and kept him
awake at night. He wondered what had gone wrong with
Blue Book. He wondered why they had run it down. He
wondered why the Air Force had played a double
game—and he kept asking questions."

They reached the top of the stairs. The corridor was
short and dark. Goldman snorted and lurched forward,
swaying dangerously from side to side, but Stanford
grabbed him and turned him around and pressed him into
the wall.

"*What* questions?" Stanford said.

Goldman coughed into his fist. He stared at Stanford
with bloodshot eyes. Then he spoke, his voice harsh and
self-mocking, releasing his bitterness.

"Why, when the Air Force was telling the whole world
that the study of UFOs hadn't produced enough evidence
to warrant investigation, did they secretly order all reports

to be investigated? Why, when all of us had actually read General Twining's statement that the phenomenon was something real, did they deny that such a statement had ever been submitted? Why, when they themselves initiated Project Sign and received its official report concluding that the UFOs were of extraterrestrial origin, did they dissolve the project and then burn the report? Why, when Project Sign was changed to Project Grudge, did they go all out to ridicule the reported sightings and then disperse most of the staff on that project? Why, when the Air Force continued to claim that they had absolutely no interest in UFOs, did they insist that all reports be sent to the Pentagon? Why, when Lieutenant Cummings and Lieutenant Rosengarten discussed UFOs in the Pentagon with the Director of Intelligence of the Air Force, was the recording of that meeting destroyed? Finally, why did the CIA lie to Ruppelt, why was the Robertson report kept from him, and why was Project Blue Book run down? Those questions haven't been answered."

Stanford opened the bedroom door. The light beamed into the corridor. The two hookers were sitting up on the bed, drinking bourbon and giggling. The room was small and shabby. The double bed was unmade. Stanford pushed Goldman in, shut the door with a bang, then he turned and walked along the dark corridor until he came to the stairs. He stood there a long time. The bar below seemed far away. The darkness was alive with possibilities and strange, formless mysteries.

"Why?" Stanford said.

CHAPTER FOURTEEN

"Why?" Epstein said. "We always come back to why. There are too many contradictions and ambiguities. We have to know a lot more."

Stanford sighed and nodded wearily. The Caribbean sun stung his eyes. He glanced back at St. Thomas, at the bubbling white wake of the boat, felt the deck shaking under his feet and heard the engine's dull rumblings.

"I haven't finished yet," he said. "That Goldman was just the start. I've got this old CIA friend in Washington, and he's promised to talk to me."

"He's still in the CIA?"

"You've got to be kidding," Stanford said. "No. He left ten years ago . . . but he was pretty high up."

"I want to know more about Ruppelt. I want to know what happened to him. I want to know what the Robertson Panel actually said behind closed doors. I want to know who was on that panel. I think that's fairly important. I want to know who they were and I want to know their precise recommendations. We were wrong about the Air Force. We've been fooled for twenty years. The Air Force and the CIA and the Pentagon have been involved, and that involvement has been kept a tight secret. I want to know why."

"This friend was in on it," Stanford said. "He assured me of that much. He said there were strange things going on and that they didn't make sense to him. He's willing to talk. He'll pick up where that tape left off. I'll go see him as soon as we get back and then give you a tape."

Stanford glanced around the ferry. There weren't many passengers aboard. He saw a blonde-haired Dutch girl with the brown skin of a *vahine,* a couple of dusky workers arguing loudly in Creole French, a few American holidaymakers, waving hands, snapping pictures, and a black woman of African descent selling mangoes and pineapples. They were all framed by the sea, very calm, a dazzling blue, sweeping out to the cays and islets of the American Virgin Islands, their rolling hills blue-gray and parched green, a few clouds in the silvery sky.

"This is some place," Stanford said.

"What did you think of St. Thomas?"

"It looked like 42nd Street," Stanford said.

"You should know," Epstein said.

Stanford squinted against the sun. "Is that the hotel?" he said. He was looking at a sprawling white complex dominating an islet.

"That's it," Epstein said.

Stanford nodded and turned around, leaned against the iron railing, let the trade winds blowing in from the northeast dry the sweat on his face. His gaze fell on the black woman. She was selling her fruit from a woven basket. She was wearing a white blouse and a skirt, a colorful apron over the skirt, and had a bright orange turban on her head, her black hair pulled up under it. Stanford kept looking at her. She saw him staring and smiled back. She had laughing brown eyes, a sort of innocent sensuality, and he immediately thought of the girl on the porch in the ranch outside Galveston. He thought a lot about that girl and still couldn't understand it. He thought about that girl night and day, and was becoming obsessed.

"Remember Galveston?" Stanford said.

"Could I ever forget it?" Epstein replied.

"I'm thinking of going back there," Stanford said. "I want to talk to those people."

"That was a year ago," Epstein said.

"So, it was a year ago."

"That's a very long time," Epstein said. "You won't do any good."

"Why do you say that?"

"They wouldn't talk when we were there. The old man was mad and the girl was dumb. I don't think they'll talk now."

"I don't care," Stanford said. "I want to try anyway. I want to know what those people really experienced, and this time I'll just push them."

"The Army might still be there."

"I don't think so," Stanford said.

"All right," Epstein said. "Please yourself. We've got nothing but time."

Epstein shrugged and glanced around him, his gray hair blown by the breeze, his jacket hanging over his left arm, his grubby tie hanging loose. He had aged a lot in the past year, had thinned down and was coughing more, the lines on his face more predominant, his movements slow and exhausted. Stanford had noticed the change. It had started with Irving's death. Dr. Epstein now looked his true age and was shrinking each day.

Stanford was also changing, was more tense, less ebullient, now driven by forces beyond his comprehension, lured by riddles and mysteries. He thought constantly about the flatlands, about the lights in the sky, about the dust and the wind and the dead cattle and the girl on the porch. Stanford couldn't understand it. It was much more than sex. He had thought about the girl for a year and now she seemed to be part of him. There was something unreal about it. He felt as if the girl was calling him. He was losing track of time, losing touch with reality, and often felt that he was trapped in a frozen present, still blinded by dust clouds.

Life was an illusion. He believed that more and more. He had pursued the invisible for too long and now was paying the price. Nothing seemed real anymore, nothing here, nothing immediate; his one reality was a night of wind and dust and strange lights and masked figures. What did it all mean? Why was he now so driven? Stanford glanced around the ferry, saw the faces black and white, saw the blue sea and cays and islets that burned under a white sun. He felt hot and suffocated, slowly dissolving where he stood, and he turned toward the prow of the boat as it approached the small island.

"That's some hotel," he said.

"It collects the vacation crowds."

"It looks like a fucking Moorish castle."

"A touch of Hollywood," Epstein said.

The ferry was nearing the islet, heading straight for the rocks, then it turned and drifted toward a wooden dock and then bumped alongside it. One of the crew jumped off the boat, started tying the ropes, and Stanford gazed up the climbing parched land and saw the walls of the hotel. The walls were whitewashed and gleaming, broken up by horseshoe arches, rising up in tiers above a swimming pool and lined with colorful flowers. It was a single-story building, sprawling across the upper slopes, dominating the sunbleached, rocky island with serene gradiosity. The ferry bumped against the dock. The crew put the gangplank down. Stanford looked along the dock, saw a bus and some cars, a few people milling about in the dust, examining the disembarking passengers.

"Is he there?" Stanford said.

"Yes," Epstein said. "The man in the sport shirt and shorts."

"They *all* look like that," Stanford said.

Epstein nodded and smiled, watched the passengers disembark, waited until the last stepped off the ferry and then followed them down. He walked slowly and carefully, as if not sure of his footing, gazing down past the gangplank at the water which eddied and rippled. Stanford followed him down, glancing vaguely around him, at the crystal clear blue of the sea, the green islands, the silvery sky. The heat was incredible. The air shimmered before his eyes. He stepped onto the wooden dock, followed Epstein's stocky form, and a short man wearing a sport shirt and shorts stepped forward to meet them.

"Long time no see," he said to Epstein. "You look pretty exhausted."

The man was small and too fat, his shirt loosened around his belly, his white hair blowing over bright green eyes and a tanned, humorous face. He and Epstein shook hands, exchanged a few jocular pleasantries, then Epstein turned to introduce Stanford who also shook the man's hand.

"Robert Stanford," Epstein said. "I just call him Stanford. The name has a certain crass elegance that suits him quite well."

"You're still young," the man said.

"Is that surprising?" Stanford said.

"I suppose not," the man said with a grin. "I just didn't expect it." He waved his hand all around him. "How do you like it?" he said.

"A good place for a vacation," Stanford said.

"That's what *I* thought," the man said.

Epstein looked up at the hotel. "Do we have to walk up?" he said.

"No," his friend said, indicating a dusty Volkswagen Beetle. "I didn't think you'd make it that far, so I've brought my own transport."

The other passengers were climbing into the small hotel bus that was sitting just beyond the Volkswagen. The car and the bus were both parked on a tract of flat earth that overlooked the shimmering azure sea. Beyond the bus, and across that broad expanse of clear blue water, was St. Thomas and the capital, Charlotte Amalie.

"I come here every year," Professor Gerhardt said. "I come because there's nothing to do and that suits me just fine . . . At least it did until *this* year."

He opened the door of the Volkswagen and then pulled the front seat forward. Stanford scrambled into the back, placing his small suitcase on his knees, and sat there, bunched up in the cramped space, feeling highly uncomfortable. Gerhardt got in behind the steering wheel and Epstein sat beside him, slamming the door as the car roared into life and started up the steep hill. The road snaked around the islet, climbing toward the hotel, passing coco palms and divi-divi trees and tracts of parched, windblown grass. Stanford looked out the window. The sea was spread out far below him. He saw the cays and scattered islets, the sea blue and sun-reflecting, motor launches racing around coral reefs, helicopters above them. Then the car reached the hotel, spluttering angrily before falling silent, stopping between dazzling white walls and high, horseshoe-shaped arches.

"Home sweet home," Gerhardt said.

He opened the door and climbed out, pulled the seat up for Stanford, and Stanford, pushing his suitcase out ahead of him, emerged gratefully to the patio. Epstein got out the other side, stretched himself and glanced around him, gently nodding his head in appreciation and then smiling at Stanford.

"The one advantage about this job," he said quietly, "is that a man gets to travel."

"It's damned hot," Stanford said.

"It'll soon get cooler," Gerhardt said. "The sun will be gone in half an hour, and then you'll feel a lot better."

"We better sign in," Epstein said.

"I've already done that," Gerhardt said. "I did it as soon as I got your cablegram. Now do you want to go to your rooms for a rest or would you rather we talked?"

"I'd like a drink," Stanford said.

"We better talk now," Epstein said. "We're hoping to leave in the morning, so let's go to the bar."

"Have you eaten?"

"No."

"Then let's eat," Gerhardt said. "I'll tell you the whole story over dinner, and then you can sleep on it."

They left their suitcases at the reception desk, felt the breeze from the spinning fans, then walked out and went along a cobbled courtyard and emerged into the gardens. Gerhardt led them up some steps, across a cool, covered patio, then guided them into the open-air restaurant overlooking the sea. The restaurant looked like a large terrace, its white walls strewn with flowers; lanterns hung from the ceiling, glowing red, green and blue, their light rendered obsolete by the sunlight pouring over the verandah wall. Gerhardt sat them on the verandah, at a table against the wall, and Stanford looked down and saw the parched earth falling to a large, crowded swimming pool. There was a small bar by the pool. Girls in bikinis sucked on straws. Beyond their distant, shadowed figures was the sea and the red, sinking sun.

"Apart from fish," Gerhardt said, "I couldn't recommend the menu. Most of the food in the Caribbean comes in cans. The fruit and fish are both fresh."

"I'll have lobster," Epstein said.

"I fancy crayfish," Stanford said. "And I'll start with a very tall rum and Coke to make myself feel at home."

They spent some time perusing the menu, enjoying their brief role as tourists; Gerhardt ordered and he and Epstein talked of old times until the food came. Stanford studied Gerhardt carefully. He liked the man a lot. Gerhardt had a sense of humor, a natural openness and ebullience, but beneath his spontaneity was a tension that was finely suppressed. He discussed old times with Epstein, told them both about the Caribbean; he didn't mention what he had brought them both here for until they had all finished eating. The sun was going down by then. The sea looked like flowing lava. The islets dotting the crimson water were casting shadows that undulated and deepened. Gerhardt sat back in his chair. A yellow lantern shone in his eyes. He sipped his wine and glanced uneasily around him and then stared straight at Epstein.

"All right," he said. "As you know I'm still working for NORAD in the Cheyenne Mountain Complex. Now for the past year things have been going wrong there: computers malfunctioning, data cards disappearing, the printouts from our worldwide network of radar stations coming in either erratically or not at all. Even worse: we have quite a few spy satellites whose sole purpose for being is to photograph the Semipalitinsk laboratory in Russia, where we think they're creating some extraordinary pulse beam weapons. So, what happens? Our damned satellites start malfunctioning. A couple get knocked out of the sky—we don't even know where they went—and the rest take their turn at malfunctioning in inexplicable ways. We don't know what's happening. We just can't pin it down. We've checked that whole complex from top to bottom, but we can't find a fault.

"Okay, so I'm in trouble. I'm supposed to be in charge of the data imput. Eyes are pointed suspiciously in my direction and my nerves start to twitch . . . I *should* know what's causing it—it's my field; my speciality—but I'm sitting in the Operations Center, just chewing my nails off. I haven't a goddamned clue, I can't find a single reason, and now I'm being checked out by the CIA and my credit is zero."

"This all started a year ago?"

"That's right, Epstein: a year ago."

"Have you taken on any new staff since then?"

"Not a one. They're all old hands."

"Okay. Go on."

"Right. Now listen to this. For the past three months this has all been getting on top of me—my nerves playing up, too many sleepless nights, sweating and trying to work out my problems and then just sweating more. Then I get a phone call. It's from a guy named James Whitmore. He tells me that he works for ACASS, that they've heard I'm having a bad time, and that they want me to work for them in Europe and will pay me a lot. I tell him to put it in writing. He says he can't do that. He says that I'm to meet him in a hotel for a drink and a chat. I tell him I'm not interested. He becomes very insistent. I get angry and tell him to shove off, but that just makes him laugh. Things won't get better, he says. Things will get worse at NORAD. He then says that he'll get me sooner or later, then he laughs and hangs up."

Gerhardt poured himself more wine, picked the glass up, set it down, sighed and looked over the low white wall at the sun's dying rays.

"I started worrying about that call," he said. "It seemed an odd way to approach a scientist. I also wondered how ACASS, a European-based commercial company, could know about the problems we were having in our top-secret establishments. So, I called ACASS. I rang their personnel manager. He said he hadn't heard about me, that he hadn't planned to offer me a job, that they didn't have a Whitmore on their staff and that I'd just had my leg pulled."

Gerhardt picked up his glass, sipped some wine and then shrugged, set the glass back on the table and started drumming his fingers.

"I couldn't forget that guy," he said. "I wondered who he might be. If he knew about my problems, he either worked right there with me or had a friend planted in

NORAD, passing back information. I told this to the FBI.
They ran a check and came up with nothing. They
thought it might be a practical joke—a silly and dangerous
practical joke—and they told me to keep my eyes on my
own staff and then report my suspicions. I just couldn't accept that. None of my staff are that dumb. I then thought
of what that guy had said—that he would get me sooner
or later—and I couldn't shake that statement from my
head, and my nightmares increased."

"Do you mean nightmares literally?"

"I mean a nightmare is a nightmare is a nightmare—
and that's what I was having." Gerhardt sat forward in his
chair, his face ghostly in the yellow light, the lanterns
growing brighter in the falling darkness, the restaurant filling. "What happened next was very strange," he said.
"First, my wife's at home on her own one day when she
hears a knock on the door. She opens it to find these three
guys on the porch, all dressed in dark suits, businesslike,
all extremely polite. These guys then start taking turns at
asking my wife various questions—Is she the wife of Professor Gerhardt? Is Professor Gerhardt at home? When
would be the best time to come and see him?—and so on
and so forth. My wife is unnerved. She asks the men
who they are. They say they're from the Federal Bureau
of Investigation, but that's all they can tell her. Then my
wife gets angry and demands to know what they're after.
The men just nod politely, back away to a waiting limousine, climb in and then drive off down the street . . . My
wife tells me about all this and I start wondering what's
going on. I have a friend in the FBI, he's a hundred percent loyal, so I ring him and ask him to check it out and
he tells me he will. He rings me back the next day. He
says the CIA are worried about the foul-ups in NORAD,
but that neither they, nor the Federal Bureau of Investigation, sent men around to my house. This turns out to be
true. We get a visit from the FBI. They spend a couple of
hours grilling my wife, trying to find out who those men
were . . ."

Darkness had fallen. The stars were glittering like diamonds. The restaurant was nearly full, the clientele ele-

gantly dressed, and the lanterns glowed green, blue and yellow on blond hair and bronzed shoulders.

"That was the first thing," Gerhardt said. "It wasn't to be the last . . . Three days later I get a phone call. It's Mr. Whitmore again. He asks me if I'm willing to reconsider his previous offer. I don't mention ringing ACASS. I'm too confused to think about it. I ask him if he knows about the men who dropped in on my wife. The bastard just laughs. I demand to know who he is. He replies that he'll get me pretty soon, and then he laughs and hangs up . . . The next night it's even worse. I'm on my way home from work. The car suddenly cuts out, its headlights go off, and I'm stranded in the middle of the desert wondering what the hell's happened. Then I see three men. They're walking along the road toward me. It's so dark I can't make out what they look like, but they're definitely moving. I look beyond them and see nothing. I'm trying to work out where they came from. They come closer and they're wearing coveralls, but I can't see their faces. Then I get frightened. I suddenly start to panic. I try to start the car and nothing happens and I just don't believe it. I look at the men again. They're very close to the car. I look behind me and see another car coming out of the distance. There's a sudden strange noise. I turn back to the front. The men are gone and then the other car passes and my own car starts up again . . . I didn't touch the ignition. I didn't touch a damned thing. The car just started and I put my foot down and then drove home like crazy."

Gerhardt sat back in his seat. The shadows fell across his face. Epstein and Stanford stared at him, neither saying a word. The darkness was now complete. The stars glittered in lonely splendor. The restaurant was noisier, a steel band played calypso, and the lanterns glowed green, blue and yellow on the flushed, happy faces.

"I was frightened," Gerhardt said. "I still can't forget that night. Shortly after, the nightmares began—one nightmare each week. That's how they came. They were as regular as clockwork. Every Wednesday, the same night every week, I would have this same nightmare. The car broke down on a Wednesday. Every Wednesday I'd relive that. The dream would always end just as the men were about to reach me, and my wife would have to shake me awake to cut short my screaming."

Gerhardt shrugged and glanced around him, his face bathed in the yellow light, a gleaming white arch beyond his head, the black sea beyond that.

"That's why I came here alone," he said. "I just had to get away. I was hoping that if I came here I'd relax and the nightmares would go away."

"But they didn't," Epstein said.

"No," Gerhardt said. "They suddenly started coming every night, and then something else happened."

"Three days ago?"

"That's right."

"That was Wednesday."

"That's right. It happened at midnight on Wednesday— and it scared the shit out of me."

Stanford glanced over the wall, looking down on the swimming pool, saw the water reflecting the string of lanterns that were strung up around it. The bar down there was closed. There was only one person in the pool. It was a girl in a red bikini, swimming slowly up and down, her long blond hair trailing out behind her like ribbons of gold. Stanford turned back to Gerhardt. He was leaning across the table. His green eyes were slightly hazed in the yellow light that glowed out of the lantern.

"I couldn't sleep that night. I was just lying on top of the bed. It was hot and the room was pretty bright because of the moonlight. Then the moonlight disappeared. It just seemed to blink out. The room was plunged into darkness and I looked through the window and I couldn't see a star in the sky. That sky was pitch-black. I couldn't see a thing out there. I couldn't see the walls of the room, and then it suddenly went cold. Then the fear came. I remembered the nightmare. The fear increased and I tried to sit up, but I just couldn't move. That really terrified me. I was completely paralyzed. I tried to scream, but I couldn't make a sound and I seemed to be freezing. Then there was a sudden light. It poured in from the balcony. The doors opened and two figures came in and walked straight to the bed. I couldn't see them very well. They were silhouetted in the blinding light. They were wearing

one-piece suits, were no taller than five feet, and their
heads were tilted toward me, looking at me, neither saying
a word. I just lay there, paralyzed. I'd never known such
fear before. I just lay there and watched them as they
walked up to the bed, as one started to lean over toward
me, his right hand reaching out for me. He pressed something against my neck. It was cold and then it burned. I
tried to scream, but I couldn't make a sound, and then the
pain went away. I stared up at the two men. I couldn't
think through my fear. Both men made a little bow, a sort
of curtsy, and then they walked from the room. 'Saturday,'
I thought. I thought one of them said, 'Saturday.' I don't
think they said anything at all, but that word filled my
head. Then they were gone. There was a strange vibrating
sound. The light from the balcony blinked out and the
moonlight returned. I remember the moonlight. I remember wanting to sit up. I fell asleep and I didn't have
dreams and I awakened refreshed. Then I went to the mirror. I examined myself. There was an ugly red scar on my
neck where that man had placed something. That scar has
gone already. Maybe it was never really there. But I don't
feel any fear anymore . . . I feel a strange, calm elation."

Stanford looked at Gerhardt's eyes, thought of the girl
on the porch, shivered and then turned away and looked
down at the swimming pool. The blue water reflected the
lanterns. The golden girl had disappeared. The pool was a
rectangle of light in a vast, sweeping darkness. Stanford
turned to glance at Epstein. Epstein thoughtfully scratched
his beard. Stanford returned his gaze to Gerhardt, saw the
green eyes in yellow light, and he thought of the girl on
the porch and felt the mystery deepening.

"This is Saturday," Stanford said.

"That's right, Dr. Stanford. This is Saturday and I'm
talking to you and I don't feel a thing."

"Anything else?" Epstein said.

"Yes, there's something else. I think that something's going to happen tonight, and I think it concerns you."

Epstein scratched his beard, glanced thoughtfully
around him, saw the diners at the tables, the couples dancing on the floor, the silk shirts and snap brims of the Trin-

idadian band members, the colored lanterns swaying in the breeze that trickled through the large restaurant.

"Why call *us?*" he said. "There must be more than that."

"There is," Gerhardt said. "There's something else . . . and it's right up your street." He leaned further across the table, his chin propped up in his hands, his green eyes diffused in yellow light, the gleaming white arch behind him. "There's a Limey film crew here," he said. "They're making a movie about Captain Cook. Now the morning after the incident I was talking to their stills photographer, a young guy who was looking pretty stunned. He knew I worked for the government, that I was some kind of scientist, so he thought I was the best man to talk to. Apparently, the night before—about the same time I was having my little experience in my room—he had been down on the beach trying to take some low-speed shots in the moonlight. He was taking some pictures of the film company's replica of the *Endeavour* and he managed to shoot one roll in color. Now, the next morning, when he developed that film in his room, he was startled to see what appeared to be a very large, blurred, milky-white, disc-shaped object hovering in the night sky above the boat. What really stunned him about this was his conviction that at no time during the shooting of those pictures had he seen anything but stars in that sky. He was absolutely convinced of this. He was willing to swear to it. And yet that disc was in nine of his thirty-six photos, a little higher up in each single picture, finally cut off by the top of the frame in the very last one."

Stanford looked over the wall, saw the dark sea and sky, the stars glittering above the gliding moon, a few clouds drifting silently. He then looked at Gerhardt's eyes, thought of the girl on the porch, remembered the lights in the sky and felt a chill passing through him.

"Any estimation of size?" Epstein said.

"Pretty rough," Gerhardt said. "Judging by the land behind it, and by the boat just below it, we both thought it was at least a hundred feet wide—but we couldn't be sure of that."

"What was the duration between each of the pictures?"

"I've no idea."

"Anything else on the photographs?"

"No. There was just a sort of glowing around the disc. The disc itself was quite blurred."

Stanford knew what was coming. He looked directly at Epstein. The restaurant behind Epstein was crowded and romantically lit. The lanterns glowed with different colors, candles flickered on all the tables, and the musicians on the stage were very excited, sweating over their instruments. The whole scene was enchanting, was too good to be true, and Stanford turned his gaze back toward Epstein, knowing what he would say.

"We'll have to stay," Epstein said. "I think we should hang around for a while. I seriously doubt that anything else will happen, but we can't be too sure of that. I also want to talk to that photographer. I want copies of all his photographs. I want the photographer to take me down to the beach and show me just where it happened. I guess we'll just have to stay."

Gerhardt slumped into his chair, spread his hands and shook his head, then leaned forward again and looked right at Epstein, his green eyes very bright.

"That's the whole point," he said quietly. "The photographer's vanished."

The rain started just before midnight, splashing in large drops on the verandah outside Stanford's room and making him open his eyes. There was a distant clap of thunder. The verandah doors rattled. Stanford cursed and glanced around the silent room and saw the white walls in darkness.

The thunder rumbled again. The rain fell more heavily. The doors rattled and Stanford stared at them, feeling strangely uneasy. The doors were still closed. The shutters revealed no moonlight. The thunder rumbled and the doors shook and rattled, and the rain poured down heavily. Stanford thought he heard the sea, a muffled noise far below, the waves rushing in and washing over the rocks and then pouring back out again. It was an unexpected sound; he hadn't anticipated such weather. Stanford closed his eyes and tried to fall asleep and thought again of the girl.

Stanford groaned aloud. He opened his eyes and saw the ceiling. There was a wooden fan spinning above his bed, blowing cool air upon him. He heard the rain on the verandah, falling very heavily now. The thunder rumbled and the double doors rattled as if being pushed open. Stanford felt strangely nervous, unreal, disorientated, trying to sleep and thinking often of the girl . . . and of Gerhardt's green eyes.

"Goddammit," he muttered.

He closed his eyes and saw the girl. Her luminous eyes drew him in. He saw the thumb between her lips, the breasts thrusting against her dress, the triangle of her thighs and shadowed crotch, her belly pressed to the windowsill. Stanford felt himself hardening. He reached down and touched himself. He saw Gerhardt's green eyes, filled with fear and strange elation, and he cursed and sat up on the bed and shook his head in despair.

The room was very dark. No moonlight came through the shutters. Stanford wondered what was happening, thought of Gerhardt's fearful calm, then thought of the girl on the porch and of her empty, revealing eyes. She and Gerhardt had something in common: an unnatural calm, a sheltered secret; they had both seemed like people not quite real, couched in awed expectation. What had they both experienced? What dreams did their eyes conceal? Stanford sat up very straight and gazed around him, seeing white walls in darkness.

He suddenly felt frightened. He hadn't felt that before. The thunder rumbled and the double doors rattled as if being pushed open. Stanford shook his head disgustedly, rubbed his face, glanced around him, then reached out and switched on the light and sat back with a sigh.

Then he heard the footsteps. They were coming toward the door. He sat up as if he had been stung, and just looked straight ahead. The footsteps stopped outside the door. He felt his throat drying. He held his breath and stared straight at the door and tried to hold his fear down.

"Stanford?" Knuckles hammered on the door. "Are you still awake?"

Stanford exhaled his breath, took it in again and sighed, leaning his head back on the pillow and felt very relieved.

"Yes, Epstein, I'm awake."

"Can I come in?"

"Why not?"

The door opened and Epstein entered.

"I saw the light under the door," he said. "I couldn't sleep either."

He was wearing an old dressing gown, a bit frayed at the edges, obviously purchased in 1955 and now much too tight for him.

"I brought a bottle," he said.

"So I see," Stanford said.

"I thought you could do with a drink . . . keep the rain from your doors."

Stanford grinned at that, swung his legs off the bed, rubbed his eyes, and then looked at the rattling doors.

"That's some storm," he said.

"It certainly is," Epstein said. "I'm wondering if there's any connection. Where are the glasses?"

"Why a connection?"

"I can't drink without a glass."

"You'll find a couple of glasses in the bathroom. Now why a connection?"

Epstein went into the bathroom, reappeared with two glasses, unscrewed the bottle of Scotch and poured two stiff shots.

"Here," he said, passing one to Stanford. "It'll settle your nerves."

Stanford took the glass. "What makes you think I'm nervous."

"Aren't you?"

"Yes."

"So am I. That's why I'm here."

They both sipped their whisky. Epstein sat down in a chair. Stanford remained on the edge of the bed, observing the rattling doors.

"You think there's a connection?"

"There might be," Epstein said. "That storm just blew up out of nowhere—and it's unusually violent."

"You're thinking of Galveston."

"We're *both* thinking of Galveston."

Stanford had another sip of whisky. "I feel weird," he said quietly.

The thunder rumbled again. They heard the crackling of lightning. The rain poured down on the verandah, whipped across by the groaning wind, the wind making the double doors rattle, trying to force them both open.

"How is Gerhardt?" Stanford said.

"I think he's sleeping," Epstein said. "I had a look before I came here. His room lights were off."

"There's something strange there," Stanford said.

"You think so? I hadn't noticed."

"I'm thinking of his conversation. He said the experience terrified him. A minute later he said he felt nothing, then he said he felt elated. Those are contradictory words. His face was also contradictory. His eyes were very bright, very eager and excited, yet the rest of his face was tense with fear . . . it doesn't really add up."

"Is that what you saw?"

"That's what I *think* I saw."

"He seemed calm when he went into his bedroom."

"He seemed *unnaturally* calm."

Epstein sighed. He put his glass to his lips and sipped some whisky, his gray eyes roaming restlessly.

"Maybe you're right," he said. "I *did* think he was a bit odd. I couldn't quite put my finger on it, but that might have been it. It's a rather strange story. He mentioned Saturday night. Given the nature of his experience, he should be more frightened than he is." Epstein drank some more whisky. He splashed a little on his wrist. "I would love to have seen those photos," he said. "I wonder where that man went."

"It's interesting," Stanford said. "I was thinking about it later. The photographer said he didn't see a thing when he was taking the pictures. I got to thinking of Goldman. That guy mentioned a similar case. I think he was talking about the Lubbock lights and the photographs taken then."

"That's right," Epstein said. "It was definitely the Lubbock photographs. He said that what the photographer picked up was an exceptionally bright light source which had a color at the most distant red end of the spectrum.

That means it was infrared—or something similar to infrared. That in turn means that the object would seem dim to the human eye, but be very bright and clear on a photograph. It's an interesting possibility. That's what we could have here. That disc could have been solid, giving off infrared light, and thus would have been invisible to the photographer while coming out on his photographs."

"Take it further," Stanford said. "Go beyond the known spectrum. If these objects could produce such light, if they could produce it at will, that would explain why they could materialize and disappear in the wink of an eye."

"It's possible," Epstein said. "It's within the bounds of probability. The UFOs are usually described as being surrounded by *glowing* colors: blue, green, yellow, orange, red. Assuming that we're dealing with a metal composed of already known elements—possibly of unusual purity and radical mixtures, but known elements nevertheless—then we can also assume that what we are *not* dealing with is a magical metal that can actually transmit light."

"I'll buy that."

"Thank you." Epstein sipped his whisky, cocked an ear to the rumbling thunder, and shivered when the double doors rattled. "So," he said. "Electrical discharges of unusual strength will sometimes lead to a soft white glow, a corona, near high-voltage transmission lines. This leads one to assume that our UFO may have either some sort of negative potential that causes electrons to leak into the atmosphere surrounding it, an alternating potential that agitates gas atoms in the surrounding atmosphere to their ionization potential, or even an alternating current within its own shell which draws radiate energy from that same surrounding atmosphere."

"A neat theory," Stanford said. "But that only accounts for a *white* glow."

Epstein smiled. "Very true," he said. "However, what we're now assuming is that the UFO's luminosity is not caused by its own unique composition, but by the natural air closely surrounding it. Let us now bear in mind the fact that if atoms are sufficiently agitated by the absorption of electromagnetic radiation, a few of their electrons will be elevated out of their normal orbits or possibly removed from the atom completely; then, as further electrons fall back into these empty spaces, a certain amount of energy will be released and radiated away as photons. That being said, I need only point out that within the visible region a stream of such photons having the same wavelength and frequency will be seen by the human eye as an unusual, glowing color, ranging all the way from violet to red."

"Electromagnetic radiation?"

"It fits in with our trace cases. We have often found unusual traces of electromagnetic radiation upon examination of reported landing sites."

"Right. And assuming that such craft were made of some exceptionally pure composition of white metals—say aluminum, magnesium, titanium or strontium—and that this unusually pure metal was electromagnetically charged, that would account for the fact that our UFO often appears to be white or silvery up close, a dull or dark gray when viewed through atmospheric haze, or is just as often surrounded by a glowing halo of various colors."

"Precisely. And of course, as you've just said, should it be able to create a color source beyond the known spectrum—and turn that source on and off at will—it could be invisible to the human eye, show up on normal film, and yet materialize in our visible spectrum whenever it wishes."

Stanford shook his head and whistled. "That would explain a lot," he said.

"The whole subject is a mystery," Epstein said. "And it's driving me crazy."

The thunder roared outside and was followed by crackling lightning. The doors rattled and Epstein glanced up, then stared down at the floor. His own words were meaningless to him. They were words to bridge the silence. He was frightened and he didn't know why, and that made him more frightened. He glanced up at Stanford. His young friend obviously felt the same. They were both very frightened at this moment, neither knowing the reason. Epstein thought of Professor Gerhardt, thought of what Stanford had said; Professor Gerhardt had changed in a subtle manner, and was hiding some secret. Epstein sighed

and sipped his whisky, heard the beating of the rain. He
thought of the night at Galveston, of the strange girl on
the porch, of her smile and her ambiguous gaze, her eyes
fixed on the sky. He wondered what the girl had experienced, wondered how it had affected her; wondered if
Gerhardt had been effected, and if so, to what extent. Epstein glanced across at Stanford. His young friend was
very pale. He had never seen Stanford so tense before, and
he cursed the whole mystery.

"We should go to sleep," he said.

"I can't sleep," Stanford said.

"What on earth do you think is going to happen?"

"I don't know," Stanford said.

Epstein stared at the shuttered doors. They were rattling
dementedly. The thunder roared and lightning flashed
through the shutters and the doors shook again. Epstein
suddenly shivered. The storm seemed to be unnatural. He
saw Stanford rising slowly to his feet and then putting his
glass down. Epstein couldn't think straight. He saw Stanford turning around. The lights suddenly went out, plunging the room into darkness, then the locks on the shuttered
doors snapped and the doors were blown open.

The wind howled and rushed in, sweeping Epstein from
his chair, filling the air with flying sheets and pillowcases
and papers and bottles. Epstein rolled across the floor,
heard the sound of exploding glass. A fierce light filled the
room, very warm, almost blinding, and he gasped and then
rolled into Stanford and they both hit the wall. Stanford
cursed and grabbed the bed. A bottle exploded above his
head. The wind roared and pressed Epstein to the wall
with debris flying around him. The heat. The white light.
He covered his eyes with his hands. The heat receded and
he opened his eyes and saw a black, streaming darkness.

"Gerhardt!" Epstein screamed.

He crawled toward the front door. A spinning sheet
coiled around him. He cursed and clawed wildly at the
sheet while the wind roared about him. Then it hissed and
receded. He looked up, disbelieving. The wind still swept
the rain across the porch, but the storm seemed more
natural. Lightning flashed across the sky, briefly illuminating the room; he saw Stanford rolling away from the bed

and clambering back to his feet. "Jesus Christ!" Stanford said. He glanced dazedly around him. Epstein clambered to his feet and shook his head and then rushed for the front door.

"It's Gerhardt!" he bawled.

Epstein pulled the door open. The whole corridor was in darkness. He and Stanford both raced along the corridor till they reached Gerhardt's room. The room door was open. There was no one inside. Epstein cursed and looked wildly at Stanford and then they both started running.

The whole hotel was in darkness, doors opening and closing, people shouting and hurrying back and forth, a few carrying torches. Stanford and Epstein rushed outside. The wind howled along the terraces. The coco palms were bent low and groaning, silhouetted in faint light.

"The beach!" Stanford shouted.

They both ran along the terrace, passed Reception, crossed the patio, the wind howling and sweeping the rain about them, almost bowling them sideways. Stanford reached out for Epstein. They held on to each other. They stumbled through the rain and beating wind and found themselves in the gardens. Stanford pointed a finger. *"—down there! Somewhere there!"* He moved forward and then pulled Epstein with him, the thunder rolling above them.

The storm was demoniac, lightning ripping through the sky. They leaned forward and headed into the wind, circling around the hotel. Torches shone and winked out. The gleaming white walls receded. They found the track at the back of the hotel and headed off toward the beach. Epstein kept his head down. The thunder roared in his ears. He glanced up as the lightning ripped through the night, a giant skeleton hand. Stanford was shouting at him. Epstein couldn't hear what he said. The wind howled beneath the roaring of the thunder and the rain poured down brutally.

"—there he is!—over there."

Lightning flashed across the sky, briefly illuminated the ground below. Epstein looked ahead and saw Professor Gerhardt, a white ghost in the distance. The professor was wearing his pajamas. He was not looking back. He was hurrying toward a grove of coco palms that led down to the beach, his pajamas flapping wildly about him, both his hands on his head. The lightning flashed across the sky. A fierce glare flared up and died. The winding track and the surrounding earth and trees materialized and then vanished.

"—what the hell is he after?"

Stanford shouted against the wind, the rain hissing and sweeping across him. The lightning lit up the night and the distant palm trees. Professor Gerhardt had vanished. Stanford cursed and raced head. The lightning passed and he saw a strange glow fanning out in the sky.

"—over there! That's the path!"

Stanford pulled Epstein forward. They stumbled toward the palm trees. The thunder roared and the lightning ripped the sky in jagged fingers of yellow flame. Then the darkness returned. They saw the glow above the sea. Stanford cursed again and Epstein groaned. The wind whiplashed the rain. The thunder roared and the wind howled through the trees and the mud made a squelching sound. It all seemed like a nightmare. The land flared up and vanished. They were blinded by lightning and lost in the darkness, and they stumbled through the howling wind and rain as if running in circles.

Then they reached the palm trees, which were quivering, pouring rain. The lightning flashed and they saw a stretch of sea, a black sheet streaked with silver. Then it was dark again. Thunder rolled above their heads. Stanford pointed to the left and stepped forward and pulled Epstein with him. They passed between the creaking trees. The branches shivered and drenched them. They left the shelter of the trees and found the path that ran down to the beach. Lightning burst suddenly and disappeared. They had not seen the beach. To their right, between them and the beach, was a high bank of earth.

"—we're going down! Watch your step!"

The steep track was running mud. They both slipped and tripped on stones. The track curved to the right, broadened out and then narrowed, climbed a little and then plunged on down and started leveling out again. The thunder rumbled above them, the wind howled and then receded, the rain lashed them in a final bout of rage and then suddenly eased.

Epstein looked up, surprised, saw a dark cloud drifting by, saw the stars and then gazed down sloping earth and saw a white stretch of beach. Epstein couldn't believe it. There was no wind there at all. Stanford jerked on his wrist and pulled him forward and they both raced down-hill.

"There he is!" Stanford hissed.

They both stopped on the instant, saw a broader expanse of beach, Professor Gerhardt hurrying across the sand, his pajamas windblown. The moonlight fell upon him, elongating his shadow; he was drenched and his hands were by his sides and he seemed very fragile. Then he stopped walking. He was near the coco palms. Another man came into view, unusually small, very slim, wearing a one-piece suit of silvery material, a strange cap on his head.

Stanford and Epstein were both stunned. They stood in silence, staring down. The banked earth limited their vision to a triangular stretch of beach, the long line of trees forming one side, the other formed by the moonlit sea. Professor Gerhardt was near the trees. The small man had stopped in front of him. Epstein blinked and felt a pressure in his head, an imperceptible vibrating. The small man stepped up to Gerhardt, his suit gleaming in the moonlight. He reached out with his left hand, touched Gerhardt on the neck, then they both walked to the right and disappeared behind the high, muddy bank.

"Jesus Christ," Stanford said. "Did you see that? *Gerhardt didn't resist!"*

They both started running again, slipping and sliding down the track, the mud squelching beneath their bare feet, the branches shivering and dripping rain. Epstein felt cold and frightened, his head tight and vibrating. He thought he heard a very deep humming sound, but he couldn't be sure. They both stumbled down the track, passed through moonlight and shadow, gasping as the branches dripped rain, further soaking their clothes. Stanford cursed and then fell, tumbled down the last of the hill. He rolled over and then climbed to his feet and they both raced to the beach.

"Oh my God!" Epstein murmured.

They both slithered to a halt. The beach was stretched out before them. It was fringed with coco palms and those trees formed a wall that stretched in a semicircle toward the sea. They both looked out at the sea, saw a seventeenth-century ship. Its huge white sails were billowing in the breeze, illuminated in white haze. The great disc was above the ship, was twice as long as the ship. It just sat there in the sky, about two hundred feet up, a dark mass in a plasmalike glow, the stars winking around it.

Stanford and Epstein just stood there. They were stunned by this vision. They saw the past and the future before their eyes and were dazed by its beauty. The white sails of the ship billowed. The great disc glowed and pulsated. The air hummed and vibrated and seemed alive with some mysterious force. Epstein rubbed his stinging eyes. Stanford shook his head in wonder. The great disc hovered over the ship and they were both bathed in silvery haze.

"It's the *Endeavour*," Stanford murmured.

"What?" Epstein said.

"It's a replica of Captain Cook's ship."

"What the hell's that *above* it?"

Stanford didn't reply, merely stood there, gazing up. The great disc was a dark mass in glowing light, its details obscured. The wind ruffled Stanford's hair. He glanced briefly at Epstein. They stared at one another, both speechless, wondering what they could do. The beach vibrated beneath them. They both heard the humming sound. The sound was all around them and above them and had no fixed direction. They both stared at the *Endeavour*. Its huge white sails billowed out. They raised their eyes and saw the great disc above it, its glow hazing the stars.

Then Epstein remembered Gerhardt. He turned around and surveyed the beach. The sand stretched out to the curved wall of a cove at the end of the beach.

"Gerhardt must have gone there," he said. "There's

nowhere else they could have gone. That creature must have taken him over there. I think we better go look."

He started running along the beach, heard Stanford running behind him. The light falling on the beach wasn't moonlight: it came from the hovering disc. Epstein gasped but kept running, his heart pounding uncomfortably. The silvery haze fell across the surrounding trees and made them look artificial. Epstein heard the lapping water, a rhythmic, timeless sound. He kept running, feeling hollow and unreal, his head vibrating and tightening. He wondered what that was. He knew it came from the enormous disc. Stanford raced up to his side and then passed him and rushed on ahead. They were nearing the wall of the cove. Epstein felt a great fear. He saw a curved line of trees, a wall of stone, and then a roar split his eardrums.

The ground shook beneath him, sand swirling, sky tilting, and he felt the ground under his back and then rolled toward the trees. A fierce light swept across him. He covered his eyes with his hands. The sand hissed and then rained down upon him and his ears started ringing. Epstein cursed and smacked his forehead, blinked his eyes and looked up, saw Stanford scrambling back to his feet, bathed in light. Epstein pushed himself up, fell weakly against a tree. The tree shivered and poured rain down upon him and then he stepped forward. Stanford's eyes were very bright, looking stunned and confused. The air around him was red, blue and yellow, the colors flickering and merging.

They both looked out to sea and saw the stately *Endeavour,* moon-bathed in a ghostly rainbow haze, the light flickering crazily. They both looked at the disc above it. The surrounding haze had disappeared. What they saw was an immense, silvery disc rimmed with windows and flashing lights. The windows were long and narrow, curving strips of fierce bright light, broken up by imperceptible black dots that moved backward and forward. The colored lights were below the windows, running around the enormous base, flashing from left to right, right to left, with incredible speed. The lights formed a dazzling kaleidoscope, flickering on and off brilliantly, turning the dark sea into blood and yellow lava and streaming green, changing the ship's sails into billowing rainbows, obliterating the black sky.

Stanford gasped and turned away, shook his head and stared at Epstein. His friend looked like a translucent ghost, materializing and vanishing. Then they ran between the palm trees, scrambled over the wall of earth, slithered down to the cove on the other side and saw the flat, empty sand.

"We're too late," Stanford said.

Epstein closed his eyes and sighed, his head vibrating painfully. The humming sound was all around him and above him and it seemed to dissolve him. He opened his eyes again. The shadows rippled with numerous colors. He moved forward and saw a large sunken circle, the sand curled at its edges. Epstein looked up at the sky and saw a globe of white light. It was shooting obliquely toward the great disc, moving slowly and gracefully.

"Oh, God," he said. "They've got him."

Then the great disc disappeared. The night was plunged into starlight. The large sails of the *Endeavour* were gleaming white in the moonlight. Epstein didn't remove his gaze. His tight head was still vibrating. He kept looking and he saw an enormous black patch where the stars should have been. Then he saw two squares of light. They were three hundred feet apart. They were windows of vivid white light floating there in the sky. Then one of them disappeared. The glowing orb flew toward its partner. The glowing orb became a black silhouette in that square frame of blazing light. Then the light went out, became a black hole in the sky, and the great disc materialized, filled up the black hole, and the colored lights flickered on and off and then became a white haze.

The humming grew louder. The beach vibrated with some violence. The great disc became a dark mass within a pulsating glow, rising vertically toward the drifting clouds with serene, stately grace. The ship below it was untouched. Its sails billowed in the breeze. The white glow illuminated the blue sea and hazed the stars nearest to it. The great disc continued rising. There was a faint humming sound. The ground vibrated and then settled down and the silence was total. The great disc rose and shrank, eventually became a glowing ball; it reached the clouds and then it suddenly winked out and the stars reappeared.

Stanford and Epstein were speechless. They stayed close to the lapping water. They stood there a long time, looking up, breathing deeply, bathed in the warm, silky moonlight, the stars sweeping over them. The sea washed on the sand, splashing lazily around their feet. They lowered their eyes and looked across at the *Endeavour*. There was no one on the boat. Its rigging shook in the breeze. Its wooden hull was rolling from side to side, the boards creaking in protest. Stanford and Epstein stared at it. The white sails were bathed in moonlight. They looked up and saw the stars in the sky, and then they both walked away.

CHAPTER FIFTEEN

"Okay, Stanford, I want you to understand one thing: I'm going to give you the information, I won't ever do it again, and if you breathe my name even in your sleep I'll have your head in a doggie bag. It's a very dangerous subject. I like to think it's all behind me. So when we're finished, when you walk out that door, make sure it's the last time."

O'Hara looked very prosperous, his tie straight, his cuff links gleaming, his face lined to match the graying of his hair, his blue eyes cold as ice. He was framed by a plate glass window, his backdrop Manhattan, and his broad frame seemed strangely out of place in the neat, paneled office.

"Okay," Stanford said, "that's fine with me. First the Robertson Panel."

"According to my notes the panel met from January 14, 1953 to January 17, in Washington, D.C., and the meeting at the time was top secret. The seriousness with which the subject was to be treated may best be illustrated not only by the credentials of the men involved—all specialists in the physical sciences, with particular emphasis on atomic research and advanced weaponry—but also by the fact that the group's written verdict was to be given to the National Security Council and then—if the decision was that the UFOs were of extraterrestrial origin—to the President himself."

"That sounds like a heavy number," Stanford said.

"It was," O'Hara said. "And what later intrigued me about the panel was that—at least according to the concrete evidence that *I* was seeing and hearing—the extraterrestrial hypothesis was in fact a grim reality and that the existence of the UFOs had been proven. Nevertheless, and pretty much to my amazement, the panel rejected the findings."

"What findings?"

"I'll just give you a few," O'Hara said. "They'll be enough to convince you." He opened a box on the desk, took out a fat cigar, clipped the end off and put a match to it, then sat back and smoked. "For the first two days Ruppelt reviewed the Blue Book findings for the scientists, and what he said was pretty damned impressive. First, he pointed out that Blue Book received reports of only ten percent of the UFO sightings made in the United States, which meant that in five and a half years about 44,000 sightings had been made. He then broke the sightings down into the percentage that was composed of balloons, aircraft, astronomical bodies, and other misinterpretations such as birds, blowing paper, noctilucent clouds, temperature inversions, reflections and so forth, and pointed out that this still left 429 as definite 'unknowns.' Of those unknowns, it was clear that the most reported shape was elliptical, that the most often reported color was white or metallic, that the same number of UFOs was reported as being seen in daylight as at night, and that the direction of travel equally covered the sixteen cardinal points of the compass. Seventy percent of those unknowns had been seen visually from the air—in other words, by experienced pilots and navigators; twelve percent had been seen visually from the ground, ten percent had been picked up by airborne and ground radar, and eight percent were combination visual-radar sightings. Ruppelt then disturbed us all greatly by confirming that the UFOs were frequently reported from areas around places like our atomic energy installations, harbors and manufacturing areas. Finally, he begged us to take note of the fact that according to radar readings there were recorded flight speeds of up to 50,000 miles an hour."

"You were right," Stanford said. "It sounds impressive."

"Indeed," O'Hara said, puffing smoke. "And even more impressive was the fact that Ruppelt and Major Dewey Fournet had completed an analysis of the *motions* of the reported unknowns as a means of determining if they were intelligently controlled. Regarding this, Major Fournet, who had an exemplary reputation, told us of how—by eliminating every possibility of balloons, airplanes, astronomical bodies and so forth from the hundreds of reports studied, and by then analyzing the motions of the UFOs in the remaining unknown category—his study group had been forced to conclude that the UFOs were, in the words of the group report: 'intelligently controlled by persons with brains equal to or far surpassing ours.' The next step in the study, the major explained, had been to find out where those beings came from; and, since it would seem unlikely that their machines could have been built in secret, the answer was that the beings were from outer space. Surprised, Dr. Stanford? So were we . . . And we were even more surprised when, the next morning, we were shown four strips of movie film that had been assessed as falling into the definite unknown category."

"You mean the cinetheodolite movies taken by scientists at the White Sands Proving Ground in 1950?"

"Bright boy. Those plus the Montana Movie taken on August 15, 1950, by the manager of the Great Falls baseball team and the Tremonton Movie, taken on July 2, 1952, by Navy Chief Photographer, Warrant Officer Delbert C. Newhouse."

"And?"

"The Montana Movie showed two large, bright lights flying across the blue sky in an echelon formation; the lights didn't show any detail, but they certainly appeared to be large, circular objects. The Tremonton Movie showed about a dozen shiny, disclike objects fading in and out constantly, performing rather extraordinary aerial maneuvers, and darting in and out and circling one another in a cloudless blue sky. Any possibility that the objects might have been astronomical phenomena was dispelled when the film clearly showed them heading in the same tight cluster toward the western horizon, and, more specifically, when one of them left the main group and shot off to the east."

"Anything more positive than that?"

"Yep. The Montana Movie had been subjected to thousands of hours of analysis in the Air Force lab at Wright Field, and their analysis proved conclusively that the objects weren't birds, balloons, airplanes, meteors or reflections—in short, they were unknowns. As for the Tremonton Movie, it had been studied for two solid months by the Navy lab in Anacostia, Maryland, and their conclusion was that the unidentifieds were not birds or airplanes, were probably traveling at several thousands of miles an hour, and were, judging by their extraordinary maneuvers, intelligently controlled vehicles."

Stanford gave a low whistle and sat forward in his seat, thinking back on what had happened in St. Thomas and of how it had affected him. It had left him in a state of wonder, overawed and disbelieving, but now, as he listened to O'Hara talking, he began to accept it.

"That was the evidence," O'Hara said, "and it seemed pretty damned conclusive, but the Robertson Panel still managed to reject it. The panel members duly spent two days going over the evidence, but the results of their ponderings were preordained. Guided by myself and my fellow CIA members, the panel simply concluded in their report that the evidence was not substantial, that the continued emphasis on the reporting of the phenomenon was resulting in, quote, 'a threat to the orderly functioning of the protective organs of the body politic,' and that the reports clogged military channels, could possibly precipitate mass hysteria, and might encourage defense personnel to misidentify or ignore actual enemy aircraft. In short: the real problem wasn't the UFOs—it was the *UFO reports.*"

Stanford stared past O'Hara, saw the skyscrapers of Manhattan, raised his eyes and surveyed the blue sky and the drifting white clouds. The sky revealed nothing. Stanford sighed and dropped his gaze. His friend O'Hara, a private detective, once a CIA officer, was sitting forward with his elbows on the desk, blowing smoke through his nostrils.

"So," he said, "we made some recommendations. First, we recommended that the two major private UFO organizations—the Aerial Phenomena Research Organization and the Civilian Saucer Intelligence—be watched because of what we described as their 'potentially great influence on mass thinking' in the event of widespread sightings. Regarding this, I believe we also inserted the sentence: 'The apparent irresponsibility and the possible use of such groups for subversive purposes should be kept in mind.' Next, we recommended that national security agencies take immediate steps to strip the UFO phenomenon of its importance and eliminate the aura of mystery it had acquired, the means being a public education program. Finally, we outlined a program of public education with two purposes: training and debunking. The former would help people identify known objects and thus reduce the mass of reports caused by misidentification; the latter would reduce public interest in UFOs and thereby decrease or eliminate UFO reports."

"The liberal conscience," Stanford said, "would call that brainwashing."

"The liberal conscience," O'Hara said, "would be right." He smiled coolly at Stanford, leaned back in his chair, gazed up at the ceiling and kept talking, still puffing blue smoke. "As a means of pursuing this education—or in the vernacular, brainwashing—program, the panel suggested that the government hire psychologists familiar with mass psychology, military training film companies, Walt Disney Productions and personalities such as Arthur Godfrey to subtly convey this new thinking to the masses. They also—contrary to what we were later to tell Ruppelt—decided *not* to declassify the sighting reports, and implied—again, contrary to what we were to tell poor Ruppelt—that the Air Force should further *tighten* security and continue to deny nonmilitary personnel access to UFO files. In other words: Kill it."

Stanford sat back in his chair, thinking of Goldman in Albuquerque, realizing that Goldman, though a drunkard, had been telling the truth.

"I think it was shortly after that," O'Hara continued, "that I began to wonder what the hell was going on. As

you can judge for yourself, the whole point of the Robertson Panel was to enable the Air Force to state for the next
decade or so that an *impartial* scientific body had examined the UFO data and found no evidence of anything unusual in the skies. While this was an obvious distortion of
fact, it *did* mean that the Air Force could now avoid discussing the nature of the objects and instead concentrate
on the public relations campaign to eliminate the UFO reports totally. And given the nature of the panel's recommendations, there's no doubt that they were directly
responsible for the policy of ridicule and denial that has
inhibited an effective study of the phenomenon ever since,
and that has had—to put it mildly—some *unfortunate* effects on the lives of a lot of perfectly responsible civilians
and Armed Forces personnel."

"You mean, humiliation of UFO witnesses was fairly
standard."

"More or less," O'Hara said. "Anyway, given our brief
about national security—we were still fighting the war in
Korea, the Soviets had exploded their first hydrogen bomb,
and the Cold War was still at its chilliest phase—I could
understand the need for such a charade. However, what I
couldn't figure out was why our superiors wanted us to lie
to Ruppelt—wanted us to tell him that Blue Book was
being expanded instead of run down, that UFO info was
going to be freed of restrictions instead of being further
restricted—and why they wanted him to believe that he
could carry on with his plans when in fact we intended
stopping him in his tracks."

"Did you ever find out?"

"I'm not sure, but let me tell you what happened. As
you've already indicated, you know what happened to Project Blue Book: it was practically wiped out. Also, by that
time, the recommendations of the Robertson Panel were in
full swing—and the most credible UFO witnesses, namely
aircrews and radar operatives, had been successfully
frightened out of submitting their UFO reports. Worse was
to come. In August 1953—the same month Ruppelt left
the Air Force—the Pentagon issued Air Force Regulation
200–2. AFR 200–2 was drafted purely as a public relations
weapon in that it prohibited the release of *any* information

about a sighting to the public or media, except when the sighting was *positively* identified as natural phenomena. In addition, while AFR 200–5, the previous regulation, had stated that sightings should not be classified higher than restricted, the new regulation insured that *all* sightings would be classified as restricted. Then, much worse, in December 1953 the Joint Chiefs of Staff followed 200–2 with Joint Army-Navy-Air Force Publication 146, and this made the releasing of any information to the public a crime under the Espionage Act, punishable by a one to ten year prison term or a fine of ten thousand dollars. And the most ominous aspect of JANAP 146 was that it applied to anyone who knew it existed—including commercial airline pilots. Needless to say that regulation effectively put a stop to the flow of information to the public. To all intents and purposes, and contrary to public Air Force pronouncements, the UFO project had been plunged into secrecy."

Stanford thought of Albuquerque, of what Goldman had told him, of himself at the top of the stairs, dazed by incomprehension. That feeling was with him now, a growing fear that had no shape, and he began to understand that the facts were never what they appeared to be. He stared at O'Hara, his old CIA friend, wondering how such men managed to flourish without guilt or pain.

"Wait a minute," Stanford said. "I'm getting a bit confused. You say that the CIA virtually directed the Robertson Panel, but that their main concern was national security—not a belief in the UFOs."

"No," O'Hara said. "I'm saying that our superiors hoodwinked us."

"I don't understand," Stanford said.

"Listen," O'Hara said. "According to our superiors, the reason they wanted the interest in UFOs killed off was that the UFO *reports* were a threat to national security: first, because a deliberately confused American public might think attacking enemy bombers were merely UFOs; second, because a foreign power could exploit the UFO craze to make the public doubt official Air Force statements about UFOs and thereby undermine public confidence in the military; and, third, because in terms of psychological warfare, particularly in 1952, the communi-

cations lines of the whole country could be saturated by a
few hundred phone calls, and such calls—which *always*
came after a rush of UFO sightings—were putting the defense network in jeopardy. Those were the reasons they
gave us for the need for suppression."

"But you thought it was bullshit," Stanford said.

"Right," O'Hara said. "If national security was the issue, then the suppression had a certain amount of logic.
However, if national security was the *only* concern, why
were we humiliating so many UFO witnesses and harassing
our own ground and air crews into keeping their mouths
shut? The only logical explanation was that the higher
echelons of the Air Force were more concerned about the
phenomenon than they were willing to admit, that they
possibly *knew* more about it than they were willing to admit, and that for reasons of their own they were actively
discouraging their most competent personnel from investigating the subject."

"Ruppelt seems to be the perfect example of all this."

"Right," O'Hara said. "It seemed to me that the more
proven unknowns Ruppelt came up with—and most of his
unknowns *were* unknowns—the more nervous the Air
Force became. I first realized this when the CIA told us to
lie to him about the recommendations of the Robertson
Panel. I was even more convinced when they neglected to
replace him when he went to Denver, and when they
stripped Blue Book of its staff in his absence."

"Still," Stanford said, "that doesn't necessarily mean too
much. As you said, if they were genuinely worried about
the sheer number of UFO reports clogging their communications network, they would have wanted those reports
reduced to the minimum."

"Let me give you a better example," O'Hara said.
"Shortly after scaring the hell out of the Air Force with
the evidence presented to the Robertson Panel, Ruppelt
came up with a couple of cases that virtually confirmed
that the UFOs were intelligently controlled. The first was a
sighting that occurred over Haneda AFB, now Tokyo International Airport, in Japan. This UFO was first observed
by two control tower operators who saw a large, brilliant
light in the northeast over Tokyo Bay. The light, which

was moving, was observed through 7 × 50 binoculars; it had a constant brilliance, was circular in shape, and appeared to be the upper portion of a large, round, dark shape which was about four times the diameter of the light itself. Then, when it moved, the tower operators saw a second and dimmer light on the lower edge of the dark, shadowy portion. This particular UFO was simultaneously tracked by radar and observed by intelligence officers as it flew back and forth across the central part of Tokyo Bay, sometimes almost hovering, then abruptly accelerating to 300 miles an hour. It was pursued by, and deliberately eluded, an F-94 plane."

"Deliberately?"

"So it seemed," O'Hara said. "That sighting was thoroughly investigated by the FEAF intelligence officers in the area, then later investigated just as thoroughly by Ruppelt. Both agreed that it was definitely not a weather target, that it definitely wasn't a star, that both visual and radar lock-ons had proved that it was solid *and* moving. They also proved that each turn the UFO made was constant, and that the straight 'legs' between the turns were about the same length. Indeed, Ruppelt later wrote that the sketch of the UFO's flight path reminded him very much of the crisscross patterns he used to fly during World War Two—and that the only time the UFO had seriously deviated from this pattern was when the F-94 tried to pursue it."

"And the second sighting?"

"The second sighting was one that had occurred on the night of July 29, 1952, when an F-94 attempted to intercept a UFO over eastern Michigan. This sighting was even more interesting in that there was a definite reason for every move the UFO made. First, it made a 180-degree turn because the F-94 was closing in on it. Next, it alternately increased and decreased its speed—but only increased its speed when the airplane was closing in on it, and always slowed down when it was just out of range of the airplane's radar. Then, adding weight to his argument that such movements could not have been random, Ruppelt submitted a third report—the one he called the best unknown ever—of an F-84 pilot who chased a visually and radar located object right across Rapid City. According to the pilot *and* the radar operatives, that target accelerated and decelerated so that there was always *precisely* three miles between it and the F-84—and it kept this up until the F-84 ran out of fuel. Later, both the pilot and the tower controller told Ruppelt that the UFO seemed to have some kind of automatic warning radar linked to its power supply."

"Okay," Stanford said, "let's assume the UFOs were intelligently controlled . . . but what's this got to do with the CIA?"

"Think," O'Hara said, studying his dwindling cigar, forming his lips into an O and blowing smoke, his blue eyes clear and mocking. "If, as the CIA claimed, national security was their only concern, such sightings should have scared the hell out of them and made them want to know more. That, however, was not remotely the case. Instead of encouraging Ruppelt or utilizing his information, they went all out to stop him in his tracks—and they put a watch on him."

"So," Stanford said. "What you're saying is that they claimed to be concerned with national defense, yet they didn't want people watching the skies—a contradiction in terms."

"That's right," O'Hara said.

Stanford sighed and rubbed his eyes, feeling weary and a bit unnerved, convinced that he was getting out of his depth and approaching a danger zone. The contradictions were now obvious: national security did not explain them. It was clear that the Pentagon, the CIA and the Air Force were more concerned with the UFOs than they admitted and were still trying to hide that fact. He sighed again and studied O'Hara. His old friend's blue eyes were clear. Stanford shook his head wearily from side to side and wondered if he was dreaming.

"Keep going," he said.

"Okay," O'Hara said. "I'll stick to Ruppelt for the moment. Because what Ruppelt did, and how the Air Force reacted, are representative of the whole shady story and might tell you a lot." He stubbed his cigar out, put his hands behind his head, then leaned very far back in the chair, the sun flashing around him. "I had in fact been watching Ruppelt from about August the previous year—1952—and the order to report his movements simply intrigued me. Bear in mind that at that particular time there was a sudden rash of UFO sightings. Now, those sightings were mainly the build up to the beginning of September, when every morning for about two weeks there were half a dozen or so new reports from the southeastern United States, notably Georgia and Alabama, a lot of them from the vicinity of the new, top secret Atomic Energy Commission complex at Savannah River, many more over Brookley Air Force Base near Mobile, Alabama. That same month the NATO naval forces were holding maneuvers off the coast of Europe, namely, Operation Mainbrace. On September 20, an American newspaper reporter and a group of pilots and flight deck crew on board an aircraft carrier in the North Sea watched a perfectly clear, silvery sphere moving across the sky just behind the fleet of ships. The object was large and appeared to be moving rapidly, and the reporter shot several pictures of it. The pictures were developed straight away and immediately studied by the intelligence officers aboard the carrier. The pictures were excellent, and the object looked like a large balloon—but no balloons were in the area and an analysis of all the photos proved conclusively that the object had been moving very fast. Then, the following day, six Limey Air Force pilots flying a formation of jet fighters over the North Sea saw a shiny, spherical object coming from the direction of the NATO fleet. They took after it and lost it, but when they neared their base one of the pilots noticed that the UFO was following them. He turned back toward it, but the UFO also turned away and outdistanced the RAF plane in a matter of minutes. Finally, on the third day, a UFO was observed near the fleet, this time over the Topcliffe Aerodrome in England. A pilot in a British jet was sent in pursuit and managed to get close enough to describe the object as 'round, silvery and white' and to note that it 'seemed to rotate around its vertical axis and sort of wobble.' Then, when he tried to get closer, the UFO shot off . . ."

O'Hara sat forward again, removed his hands from behind his head, propped his elbows firmly on the desk and cupped his chin in his hands.

"Naturally those sightings disturbed NATO," he said. "In fact, according to an RAF intelligence officer in the Pentagon, it was the Mainbrace sightings that finally forced the RAF to recognize the UFO phenomenon—a fact they have denied to this day. However, Ruppelt investigated the case and assessed all those sightings as unknowns. Unfortunately, this encouraged him to think that he could now pin down the UFOs for good . . . and it was this very enthusiasm that led to the destruction of the most important system ever devised for UFO research."

"Don't look so pleased," Stanford said. "Just tell me what happened."

"Okay. For a long time Ruppelt and Brigadier General Garland, then chief at ATIC, had been looking for a way of getting concrete information about the UFOs. What they finally came up with was a plan for visual spotting stations to be established all over northern New Mexico—an area that had consistently produced more UFO reports than any other area in America. The visual spotting stations would be equipped with specially designed sighting devices, all of which would be linked with an instantaneous interphone system: any two stations could then track the same object and, from their separate readings, compute the UFO's altitude and speed. Also at each visual spotting station would be instruments to measure the passage of any body that was giving off heat, any disturbance in the earth's magnetic field, and any increase in nuclear radiation at the time of the sighting."

"I never even heard of it," Stanford said, "but it sounds pretty impressive."

"Well, it was," O'Hara said. "In fact, that was the first time that a proper, scientific system had been designed and submitted to the Air Force. It was virtually foolproof and if it had been adapted, we could have tracked, photographed and measured UFOs with unprecedented precision."

"And you're going to say the Air Force killed it off."

"Right."

"Why?"

O'Hara shrugged. "I'm not sure. All I know is that in December of that year—when Ruppelt's plans went to Washington for approval—the U.S. Navy was going to shoot the first H-bomb during Project Ivy, and some folks in the Pentagon, remembering the unidentifieds over Operation Mainbrace, directed Ruppelt to fly out to the test area and organize a UFO reporting team." O'Hara grinned laconically, spread his hands out in the air, then gently kicked his chair back again, his legs lazily outstretched. "As it is with the CIA, so it is with the Pentagon: there are wheels within wheels and somewhere there's a wheel you can't reach. What I mean by this is that the order for Ruppelt to fly to Project Ivy came down in November, but by December his plans for the visual radar sighting network were received in Washington . . . and shortly after that I received a phone call from the Pentagon, suggesting that I axe Ruppelt's trip—which naturally I did."

"So what you're suggesting is that certain people in the Pentagon are genuinely concerned with the UFOs, but that others, for some unknown reason, don't want the UFOs to be investigated."

"What a bright boy you are."

Stanford stared past O'Hara's head and saw the tops of the skyscrapers, the sun a silvery ball in the clear sky, the white clouds drifting languidly.

"So," he said eventually, "*were* UFOs seen over Project Ivy during the shooting of the H-bomb?"

"I don't know," O'Hara said, "and neither did Ruppelt. Shortly after that came the Robertson Report and its consequences, and a few months later, in August '53, Ruppelt, doubtless feeling bitter, left the Air Force for good. By the end of that year, Project Blue Book had a mere three staff members left, its investigating authority had been handed over to the 4602d—the inexperienced Air Intelligence Service Squadron—and most of its projects had been strangled systematically through a reduction of funds. Ruppelt, Fournet and Chops were no longer involved, and General Garland, once a strong Ruppelt supporter, never again raised his voice in defense of any UFO investigation."

Stanford sat there, saying nothing, not knowing what to say. He thought of Ruppelt and Goldman, of the deception and suppression, then he thought of Irving Jacobs in the desert and wondered what it all meant. The Air Force was covering up. The Pentagon was involved. The whole of Washington was concerned with the UFOs, but didn't want them investigated. Stanford didn't understand it. Nothing seemed to add up. The mystery deepened and swirled there before him like a black hole in space.

"It just doesn't make sense," he finally said. "What was the purpose of all that?"

"I'm not sure," O'Hara said. "I kept asking myself that question. The only thing I came up with was the thought that maybe there *was* something in the UFO phenomenon—and, more intriguing, that maybe the Air Force actually knew what the UFOs were and therefore wanted to keep the lid tight on the matter."

"That could make sense," Stanford said. "Why else would they set out to ridicule their own pilots and ground crew? Why else would they encourage officers like Ruppelt to investigate the matter and then, when they came up with firm evidence, harass them out of the scene?"

"Right," O'Hara said. "And bear in mind how the defense forces operate. The Navy, the Army and the Air Force all run research projects independently of one another—and they usually keep their secrets to themselves. Likewise, in the Pentagon, there are departments so secret that even *the President* doesn't know what they're up to. The same could be said for the FBI and the CIA: behind the names there are numbers and those numbers can't be checked—those numbers represent the nameless men who create their own laws."

"So," Stanford said, "there are always rumors."

"Right," O'Hara said. "For instance, just before I left the CIA there were rumors going around that there had been actual UFO landings on Air Force bases, one at Cannon AFB, New Mexico, on May 18, 1954, another at Deerwood Nike Base on September 9, 1957, and a third at Blaine AFB on June 12, 1965. Now the automatic response to such stories is to say that they couldn't be true—that such events couldn't possibly be kept secret, not only from the public, but from the vast majority of FBI, CIA and Pentagon staff."

"Not true," Stanford said. "Some of our most startling scientific discoveries have been kept under wraps with incredible efficiency for as long as fifty years. Antibiotics were discovered as far back as 1910, but weren't truly applied until 1940. Likewise, nuclear energy was discovered in 1919, but not generally announced until 1965. In short, no matter how big the secret, we can make sure it stays that way."

"Right," O'Hara said. "So . . . could the fact that UFOs have landed on at least three different Air Force bases be kept a secret for almost a decade? I think it could. I think so because the Air Force, the Navy, the Army, the CIA or the higher echelons of the Pentagon could, if not *totally* suppressing such a fact, reduce that fact to a mishmash of vague speculation and rumor . . . And a very good example of that is the renowned Flying Flapjack."

"That," Stanford said, "sounds familiar."

"It should be," O'Hara said. "The most interesting thing about the Flying Flapjack is that no one in the CIA had ever mentioned it until 1950, yet it had been designed back in 1942. The Flapjack, originally known as the Navy Flounder, was a circular aircraft being built by the U.S. Navy during the Second World War. At that time what the Navy desperately needed was an airplane that would not require long airfields, could rise almost vertically from an aircraft carrier, and could be used from any cleared area just behind frontline troops. What they came up with was a combination of helicopter and jet plane, a saucer-shaped machine powered by two piston engines and driven by twin propellers. The prototype, designed by Charles H. Zimmermann of the National Advisory Committee for Aeronautics and constructed by Chance-Voight, had a maximum speed of 400 to 500 miles an hour, could rise almost vertically, and could practically hover at thirty-five miles an hour. Apparently, because the aircraft was wingless, the lessened stability presented problems, but a later model—the one since reported to be the XF-5-U-1—solved that problem and was rumored to be circular in shape, over a hundred feet in diameter, and with jet nozzles—which resembled the glowing windows observed on so many UFOs—arranged right around its outer rim. Further, it was built in three layers, with the central layer slightly larger than the other two; and, since the saucer's velocity and maneuvering capabilities were controlled by the power and tilt of the separate jet nozzles, there were no ailerons, rudders or other protruding surfaces."

"A genuine flying saucer," Stanford said.

"Right," O'Hara said. "Now, as I've already stated, no one in the CIA—at least no one I dealt with—knew a damned thing about that machine until early 1950 when the Air Force, in a bid to legitimize their December 1949 termination of Project Grudge, released photographs and vague technical information about the Navy Flounder and Flying Flapjack, adding in their press release that they had dropped the project back in 1942 when they had generously passed it over to the U.S. Navy, who had more interest in it."

"Christ," Stanford said.

"Okay," O'Hara said. "Information about the Flounder and Flapjack was released to the public in April 1950 via the *U.S. News and World Report,* and it touched off some interesting speculations. The first of these arose from the retrospective knowledge that the U.S. Navy had always expressed more interest in a vertically rising aircraft than the Air Force, that it had, up to 1950, spent *twice* as much money as the Air Force on secret guided missile research, that their highly secret missile-research bases were located around the White Sands Proving Ground—where the majority of the military UFO sightings had occurred—and that, because they were not involved officially in UFO investigations, they could conduct their own research in a secrecy unruffled by the attentions of the public or the media. The next interesting point was that the measurements taken by Navy Commander R. B. McLaughlin and his team of Navy scientists of the UFO they tracked over the White Sands Proving Ground in early 1950 corresponded very closely, except for the speed, with the details of the legendary XF-5-U-1, that those details were more or less made known to the general public through

McLaughlin's published article of that year, and that the U.S. Navy, while refusing to make any comment about the Flying Flapjack project, promptly shipped Commander McLaughlin back to sea."

"Christ," Stanford said.

"Okay, Stanford, let's look at what we have here. First question: Were the rumors that passed around the CIA about flying saucers having landed on at least three Air Force bases based on fact? Second question: Could it be that the same machines which either landed on, or possibly were being *tested* on, those Air Force bases were the same objects that were frequently being observed over the White Sands Proving Ground area? In short, do we have here a scenario which says that the so-called unidentified flying objects are just what they appear to be—and that rather than being of extraterrestrial origin, they are in fact the products of the U.S. Navy's secret research activities since the Second World War?"

Stanford tried to control himself. He felt a cold, hard excitement. The facts tumbled like ball bearings in his head with confusing rapidity.

"Was anyone else involved in this?" he said.

"I don't know," O'Hara said. "What I *do* know is that in 1954 the Canadian government announced publicly— after having examined the Project Blue Book evidence on the Lubbock sightings of 1951—that the UFO observed over Albuquerque was exactly like a flying saucer they were then trying to construct but had since, due to lack of know-how and facilities, passed over to the U.S. Air Force. The U.S. Air Force naturally claimed that they'd eventually dropped this project as being unworkable."

Stanford bent forward and put his face in his hands, rubbed his eyes and then sat up again and stared straight at O'Hara.

"This all sounds impossible," he said.

"Impossible?" O'Hara said. "Then let's review the facts, Stanford. We have the fact that the majority of the proven unknowns are observed either over desolate countryside or over top-secret military and civilian establishments. We have the fact that crude flying saucers were once constructed by the National Advisory Committee on Aeronautics, that they were one of the U.S. Navy's research projects from at least 1942 to 1947, that similar machines were rumored to have landed on military bases around the White Sands Proving Ground area, and finally, that the Canadian government claimed to have worked on a flying saucer that was eventually passed on to the U.S. Air Force. And last but not least, we have the fact that when a U.S. Navy commander and his Navy scientists tracked and measured an unidentified flying object over the White Sands Proving Ground—and when that object turned out to correspond very closely to the Navy's Flying Flapjack— that Navy commander was removed from White Sands and transferred back to sea.

"Now let's look at how the Air Force reacted to the most successful UFO investigations. We had, during that time, only three scientifically sound methods of analyzing the speed and dimensions of the UFOs, and, more important, of ascertaining whether or not they were intelligently controlled. The first was Major Fournet's maneuver study of 1952, the second was the Project Blue Book compilation of official unknowns, and the third was Ruppelt's planned visual-radar sighting network. Regarding these, the Air Force denied that Fournet's maneuver study ever existed, secreted Project Blue Book's findings behind the Espionage Act, and killed off Captain Ruppelt's visual-radar sighting plan.

"What else did we have? We had an Air Force that insisted that UFOs did not exist, yet made the release of information on that subject to the public a crime under the same Espionage Act. We also had, in that regulation, a threat not only to military personnel, but to civilian airline pilots and any civilian who happened to know that the regulation existed. We had, more mysteriously, an Air Force which claimed that national security was its only concern, yet insured that its own air crews and ground crews would *not* report unidentified objects in the sky . . . What do *you* think it means?"

He stared straight at Stanford, his eyes blue and unblinking, as Stanford sat up straight in his chair, feeling strangely unreal.

"That still begs the question," Stanford said. "Is all this *possible?*"

"And the answer must be yes," O'Hara said. "*All* things are possible. As you yourself said: in this context we only have to think of the extraordinary innovations in today's science and technology—and then remember that such miracles are only the tip of the iceberg, and that what goes on behind the guarded fences of our top-secret establishments is probably decades ahead of what we officially know about. Given this, the speed and capability of the unidentified flying objects are not beyond the bounds of possibility. Also, given this, it is not beyond reason that the UFOs rumored to have landed on various Air Force bases are the products of a military program so secret that only the personnel on those bases know what's going on."

O'Hara looked at his watch, pressed a button on the desk. The door of the office opened and a secretary walked in, moving over to stand beside Stanford, very sleek and efficient. Stanford stood up, feeling dazed. He also felt a growing rage. He glanced at the girl, at the paneled walls of the room, at the clear sky beyond O'Hara's head, at O'Hara's broad outline. The facts were amazing. The possibilities were frightening. Stanford looked at O'Hara's blue eyes and let the rage become part of him.

"There the case rests," O'Hara said. "Don't come back, Doctor Stanford."

CHAPTER SIXTEEN

The New Order was planned and executed with the sort of ferocious drive that only the mystically inclined can possess. Albert Speer was the architect; he created the environment for their vision. In the works of Albert Speer and the other Nazi architects, I could see the realization of Lebensraum in its most concrete form. Lebensraum—space—German conquest and expansionism: the great buildings and the underground factories were signposts to my future.

Himmler showed me Hitler's teahouse. It was on top of the Kehlestein Mountain. The five-mile road that ran up from the Berghof had been hacked out of the side of the mountain by the sweat of slave labor. In the peak of the mountain was an underground passage; at the end of the passage was a copper-lined elevator, its shaft, about four hundred feet deep, hacked out of the solid rock. That elevator dropped down to an immense, high-walled gallery, supported by baroque Roman pillars. At the end of the gallery, also hacked out of the mountain, was a dazzling, glassed-in, circular hall. And standing in that great hall, looking out through the windows, I saw nothing but the other mountains and the sky—an overwhelming experience.

The impossible made possible—such was constantly accomplished. If the dreams were grandiose, the actual achievements were more so: the achievements of men who could make the impossible quite commonplace.

The German genius was for organization. In that area it had no peer. Add to this the fact that their well of slave labor was bottomless, and what one had was the dream as a reality. Who built the mighty pyramids? The thousands of Egyptian slaves. The Third Reich had the genius and seven and a half million slaves, and given the combination of these two, all things became possible.

Seven and a half million slaves. Slaves who worked an endless day. Slaves who hacked out the mountains and dug tunnels through the earth and moved rocks and equipment and stores, and never complained. Such were my resources. I could have made Egypt envious. And given that, plus my own grandiose ambitions, there was little I couldn't do.

I was very close to Himmler. He unveiled his great dream. It was a dream of Atlantis reborn from the ashes of war. No Jews or subhumans. A blond S.S. would rule. In a society of masters and slaves there would be no dissension. Great cities of steel and glass. The pure Aryan predominant. Himmler told me of his dream of a wilderness populated by supermen.

"How do you build Atlantis? You need masters and slaves. The masters will be the elite of my Death's Head S.S., and the slaves will be the Poles and the Czechs and all the other low races. And how do we do it? It is easy, mein freund. We keep building the camps, we ship the Jews there by their thousands, and when the wires of the camps begin to bulge we build more crematoriums. Gas the schweine and burn them; let them turn to smoke and ash. When the camps have been cleared of the Jews we bring the subhumans in. The subhumans are the workers. They exist as mere slaves. They live just to work and that work is for the glory of the Reich—the slaves will build the new temples."

The new temples would be the factories, the laboratories and universities; the new religion would be knowledge and conquest: the return of the Superman. How grandiose the dream! How impressive the rehearsal! Himmler wanted cities under the earth and set out to create them. He drove me all around Germany. He showed me what could be *achieved. I saw the great underground factories and I learned what was possible.*

I remember Nordhausen well. It had been hacked out of the Kohnstein Mountain. Thirteen thousand slaves from Buchenwald had done it with muscle and sweat. It was empty when I saw it. The V-2 complex had yet to come. It had tunnels 1,800 meters long, and nearly fifty side chambers. I gazed around me in wonder. Himmler scratched his nose and smiled. The work area was 125,000 meters square, buried deep in the mountain. Himmler showed me around. His voice echoed in the silence. There were twelve ventilation shafts, huge generators supplied the light, and special heating insured a constant temperature, day in and day out.

"Here thousands will work. The slaves will live in a separate camp. That camp, which now exists, is hidden deep in a mountain valley, less than a kilometer from the entrance to one of the tunnels. It has every facility. Lots of barracks, a brothel. It has a sports ground and a hospital, a kitchen and a laundry, a psychological and vocational selection unit, a crematorium and prison. There is also the town of Bleicherode. It's twenty kilometers from here. There, the new tunnels, sixteen kilometers deep, will house several more missile factories and living quarters for thousands. What else are mountains for? How else do we use the slaves? The new temples will be underground cities that are virtually impregnable."

I still remember his every word. His voice echoed in that vast silence. I knew that the whole area, from the Harz Mountains to Thuringia, south of Prague and across to Mahren, was littered with similar tunnels and underground factories. Only a few were known to Hitler. Himmler controlled them all. They were cloaked in the strictest of secrecy and ruled by the S.S. The work went on night and day. All slackers were shot or hung. The underground factories were totally insular colonies, worked by masters and slaves, unrestricted by moral laws, and yet very few Germans knew about them or would ever set eyes on them.

Thus were my problems solved. I saw what could be achieved. Standing there beside Himmler, in that enor-

mous, silent cave, I thought of all the thousands who
would work there, and knew where my future lay.
Himmler dreamed of ice and fire. He dreamed of cities
beneath the earth. He saw the sun flashing off the frozen
peaks that showed nothing but emptiness. I would take
what Himmler offered. I would hide in glass and stone. I
turned around and stared at Himmler's modest eyes and
saw his madness as sanity.

"The New Order needs its masters and they have to be
Aryan: blond-haired and blue-eyed and strong—and absolutely obedient. Such are found in the Jungvolk—the boys
of ten to fourteen—and they are formed in the Hitler
Youth, given the Blood and Honor dagger, retrained to
worship the Fuhrer and the Nation, and then join my S.S.
Once there, they are mine. I do with them what I will.
They no longer belong to Hitler, but to me—and they
worship me slavishly."

Himmler dreamed it and did it: he gave birth to his
acolytes. The mild chicken farmer blinked his modest eyes
and saw a world of godmen. The S.S. was Himmler's
church, his bed and his altar; it was an Order run on
Jesuit principles and run with an iron fist. All its members
were racially pure. They were bound together by sacred
oaths. They were stripped of their history, given numbers
instead of names, indoctrinated with the myths of the Volk
and emerged as disciples. No questions would be asked.
No order would be ignored. Their blind obedience would
let them wade through hell without shame or revulsion.

I believed in this approach. Without discipline there is
dissension. Himmler's ultimate aims struck me as religious,
but his methods were sound. We cannot progress with
freedom. Free men are a curse. Such men resist change
because it leaves them exposed as superfluous. Himmler
understood that much. He feared individuals. Himmler felt
that individuals were a threat to his great masterplan. And
what was his plan? He wanted gods, not normal men. He
believed in obedience, in controlled breeding and vivisection, believed in biological mutation and its product, the
Superman. Such a dream is not uncommon. Modern
science still pursues it. Out there, in the world beyond the
ice, primitive surgeons hack bone for it. As for myself, I

accepted it: men were meat to be used. I believed in biological mutation and used all that was offered.

"The New Order will be purified. The subhumans will be slaves. All dissenters will be stripped of their resistance until they, too, obey. Failing that, they will be removed—by gas, gun or blade—and even then, we will insure that they contribute to the good of the Order. Gouge the gold from their teeth. Use their skin for lampshades. We will turn their bones to ashes and dust in the great crematoriums. It is necessary to do so. We must affirm that we are serious. We must let them know that discipline is all, and that their ash can be useful. The New Order will be strict. Its one goal will be progress. It will be dedicated to experiment and research, to the advancement of knowledge. Most laboratories have limitations; in the New Order this won't be so. The subhumans, who are useful as slaves, will also serve us as specimens."

Not all aeronautics. That went on at Kummersdorft West. In the hangars of Kummersdorft West my other dream took fruition. I worked with Schriever and Bellonzo. Perhaps Miethe and Habemohl. I remember the names, not the faces, and I feel no affection. Nonetheless, I worked with them. My restless genius drove me. The vicissitudes of the war did not touch me and my project expanded. How many nights did I go sleepless? I think back on that with pride. I was in my early sixties at the time, but I drove them relentlessly. The first disc took shape slowly. There were many imperfections. I traveled north and south, east and west, stealing men and ideas. Factories hidden in the Schwarzwald. The R-Laboratory in Volkenrode. Heated discussions about electrostatic fields and gyroscopic controls. The great disc filled the hangar. Schriever's eyes were filled with greed. The four legs that housed the gas turbine rotors reflected the bright lights. Schriever studied it with wonder. This very memory makes me smile. What Schriever gazed upon with such greed and wonder was a primitive toy. The real achievements were in my files. What Schriever saw was nothing. In the hangar in Kummersdorft West I was building a useless thing.

The deceit was necessary. There was no one I could trust. The Third Reich was filled with frightened, ambi-

tious men who wished to make an impression. I did not
trust Rudolph Schriever. I saw the death in Himmler's
eyes. I remembered my past, the great hangars in Iowa, all
the businessmen and cowardly politicians who had smothered my life's work. The same thing could happen again.
The war would not last forever. Already, in 1941, I saw
the Reich's trickling wounds. Just how long would
Himmler last? And how long could he keep his secret? I
wanted to utilize his masterplan, but what guarantee had
I? The Nazis devoured their own kind. They might well
devour Himmler. Either that, or the Reichsfuhrer would
turn on me, destroying all I had gained. Heinrich
Himmler: the Reichsfuhrer. His mild eyes did not deceive
me. His neat fingernails were polished with blood and his
smile hid hysteria. No, I didn't trust him. There was no
one I could trust. And so I gave him just a little, a prototype that would not work, kept explaining that I needed
more time and that the problems were many.

A delicate maneuver. A great cunning was required.
The disc had to fool the other engineers while still lacking
in something. I used obsolete technologies. I gave the engineers their head. Gas turbines and liquid-fuel rockets
were the fruits of their labors. Such creations kept them
happy. Schriever's eyes shone with triumph. Young and
lean, he showed his drawings to Himmler while I went my
own way. Their great disc had been surpassed. The real
achievement was in my files. I gave a little and took a
great deal and listened always to Himmler.

"We have our underground factories. We have our
chosen location. We have our masters, the S.S., and our
slaves and your own crystal genius. But that isn't enough.
We need more than normal men. What we need is a biological mutation that will lead to true greatness. We must
learn to control the workers. Not with whips and not with
guns. What we need is automatic control of their minds
and their bodies. The human brain must be examined. The
body's secrets must be explored. We must try to steal their
will and their strength and leave them just what they need.
The democracies cannot do this. Regressive morals would
forbid it. But here, at the dawn of the new era, there is
nothing to hinder us. We must use the Ahnenerbe. We

must use the Lebensborn. *We must study racial characteristics and breed only the purest. This will solve the first
problem. In this way, we will find the Superman. Nevertheless, that leaves the problem of the workers, and we
must solve that also. Control of mind and body. We must
find a whole new method. I think of medical and psychological experiments of the most extreme kind. The camps
are yours to command. The* schweine *there are useless
meat. The New Order needs a wealth of mindless muscle
and your genius must find it."*

The concentration camps were the laboratories. The
camp inmates were the guinea pigs. The whole mystery of
human life was explored as it writhed on the tables . . .
What are the limits of human pain? How long before the
lungs collapse? Will scorched flesh, if left unattended,
renew itself or turn gangrenous? Inject this woman with
jaundice. Inject that child with typhoid. Shoot this creature
with poison bullets, graft a bone, transfer a limb, remove
testicles and ovaries and intestines, but don't use anesthet-
ics. Was it the surgery that led to death? Was it death
through shock or pain? Put that frozen man between those
two whores and then check his responses. More work. (It
rarely stopped.) The Ahnenerbe needs human heads. The
Institute for Research into Heredity needs anthropological
measurements. Take these filthy Jews and Poles. Strip
them naked and measure them. If suitable, put them into
the gas chamber and then chop off their heads. Ship the
heads off in cannisters. Use extreme care when packing.
Peel the flesh from the bones of the corpse, dissolve the
bones, use the healthy flesh. This strip decomposed already.
A good piece of material there. These tattoos would make
a nice lampshade in Frau Koch's bedroom . . . But such
was Nazi frivolity. My true research never stopped. The
concentration camps, with their abatoirs and crematoria,
were extraordinary laboratories.

"Do you understand at last? The New Order is very
real. It will be broken into colonies, each separate, each
with its work, all divided into masters and slaves, existing
just for the future. What's a colony in our wilderness? It's
just another Nordhausen. You ship the subhumans in to
build your underground complex, you control them with

*your implants and the Death's Head S.S., you then move
in your scientists and technicians and administrators, and
you bind them all together with fear of the all-seeing masters. And once there, where can they go? There is no way
in or out. They will live underground, cowed by fear,
seduced by power, the masters bound by their oaths, by
their religious convictions, the subhumans by torture and
death and the lack of all exits. Yes, American, it is possible. We are halfway there already. You must work, you
must complete your great disc, before we settle the matter."*

So I listened to Himmler. So his droning words encouraged me. Not for long did I think he would survive, but
his ideas were valuable. I used him and his facilities. We
filled the trains with nameless thousands. The slaves were
shipped to the harbor of Kiel and then they just disappeared.

Yet I had to be careful. I couldn't hold back too much.
Himmler pressed me for a test flight of the disc, and I had
to oblige. It was 1941. I am certain it was June. The
great doors of the hangar were pulled open and the sunlight poured in. That much I remember. The disc flashed
in the sunlight. Schriever climbed into the dome-shaped pilot's cabin, his eyes bright with excitement. The engineers
all retreated. They all shielded their eyes. Himmler joined
me behind the sandbags, his glasses high on his nose. The
disc looked like a metallic mushroom. It perhaps looked
like a spider. Its four legs housed the gas turbine rotors
and ran down obliquely. Himmler rubbed at his nose. The
sun flashed off his spectacles. There was a roar as the hollow legs spewed fire and filled the air with dark smoke.
Yellow flame spat from the tarmac. The roaring changed
and became a numbing sibilance as the disc left the
ground. Himmler covered his ears. His body seemed to be
shrinking. The disc shuddered and shrieked, lifted gently
from the ground, hovered briefly and swayed from side to
side and was hazed by the swirling smoke. Himmler
turned and stared at me. His mild eyes were like the sun.
The disc roared and hovered just above the ground as
Himmler reached for my hand.

CHAPTER SEVENTEEN

Richard licked his forefinger and ran it around the rim of his glass. The cigarette smoke curled about him, stinging his bleary, bloodshot eyes, and the noise in the crowded, lunchtime pub was too much for his ears. He kept his gaze on the glass, on the ice cubes in the Coke, but glanced occasionally, with a twisted, bitter smile, at Jenny's unfinished lager.

"Just one drink," he said.

"No," Jenny said.

"Just let me have half a pint of bitter. It won't affect me a bit."

Jenny sighed and shook her head, her brown eyes devoid of humor, abstractly tugging at a lock of her curly hair and gently biting her lower lip.

"No," she repeated. "You're not supposed to drink anything. And once you start, you won't know how to stop—you never do anymore."

"A half pint," Richard said.

"No. Go to hell."

"Just give me a sip of yours, for chrissake."

"Drink your Coke and shut up."

Richard rolled his eyes despairingly, picked his glass up and saw it shaking, held it to his lips with great care, had a drink, put it down again.

"You're still shaking," Jenny said.

"What do you expect?" Richard replied. "I haven't had a drink for five days. I'm going out of my skull."

"You're already out of your skull. You've been that way for a year now. I couldn't take another year like that, so just keep your mouth shut."

Richard didn't reply to that. There was little he could say. He had drowned the past year in a sea of liquor, trying to kill off the nightmares. Now he glanced around the pub, the smoke stinging his eyes, taking in the pinstripe suits, the black shoes and umbrellas, the pretty secretaries with their hair trailing loosely down their backs, their cheeks flushed with gin and Campari, their breasts thrusting ambitiously. They all seemed remote to him, superfluous, unreal, their beauty and vigor redundant, diffused behind frosted glass. Then he looked at Jenny: brown eyes in a moon face. She was wearing her shabby parka and faded blue jeans, her blouse unbuttoned just above her breasts, the skin creamy and smooth. She seemed slightly more real, a bit closer, part of him, and the fact that she was still trying to help him filled him with shame.

"A hypnotist!" he exclaimed. "Jesus Christ, I don't believe it!"

"He's not a crackpot," Jenny said. "He's a psychiatrist and neurologist, a Harley Street specialist, and since he can't possibly make you feel worse, you've nothing to lose."

"A psychiatrist?" Richard said.

"Don't look mortified," Jenny said.

"You think I need a psychiatrist?" Richard said. "You think I've gone crazy?"

"And what would *you* call it?"

"I'm not crazy," Richard said.

"All right," Jenny said, "you're not crazy . . . but you're not healthy either."

"Ah," Richard said, touching his temple with a finger and turning the finger around like a screwdriver. "I am sick in the head!"

"Very funny," Jenny said.

"Yes, *very*," Richard said.

"Listen, Richard, you're not going to see a witch doctor. He won't beat on his jungle drums." She reached into her shoulder bag, pulled out a pack of cigarettes, used her lighter with a quick, suppressed anger and threw it back in her bag. "What's bugging you?" she said. "The man's just a fucking doctor. This is 1975, for God's sake: it's a normal occurrence."

Richard flushed and looked away and studied the glasses above the bar, hurt and embarrassed by her statement, recognizing the truth in it. The past year had been a horror, a gradual dissolving into madness, the days viewed through the filter of liquor, the nights strung out on nightmares. The police interview hadn't helped, had in fact made it worse, their disbelief filling him with shame and deepening confusion. Now the wheel had turned full circle: he was himself loath to accept it; more and more he was resisting the idea it had actually happened.

"Listen," Jenny said, "I don't happen to think you're crazy. I just happen to think you're pretty sick and you have to be cured. You used to drink like a normal person. I mean, you had the odd wild night. But you never *needed* to drink like you need it now—and you need it too much. You just can't go on like this. It won't do you any good. You've already given up art school, you're living off unemployment, and you haven't seen your family or friends in close to a year. What kind of life's that? You're only nineteen, for God's sake! You've been seeing your doctor for mysterious rashes and headaches, and you're washing the pills down with red wine . . . you've got to sort yourself out, kid."

Richard sipped his iced Coke, ran his finger around the glass, looked up and shrugged his shoulders in defeat, his smile modest and painful.

"I suppose you're right," he said.

"No bloody question about it."

"I haven't seen too much of you either."

"Don't blame that on me."

Richard glanced around the pub, saw the beer glinting golden, the flushed faces of the men and the women lined along the packed bar. Their conversation was noisy, a meaningless lunchtime repartee, and he felt a sudden sweeping isolation, as if no longer part of them. Had it ever happened at all? Had he dreamed the whole damned thing? The instant he thought of this he felt a fear that made his heart start to pound. He returned his gaze to Jenny, saw her stubbing the cigarette out. She glanced up at him and smiled, her brown eyes large as spoons, and again he felt that secret, gnawing shame that had now become part of him.

"I'm getting better," he said.

"Don't talk shit," Jenny said.

"No, really," he said. "I'm getting better. I don't think I need this."

"Richard, he's a *psychiatrist*."

"I don't care. I feel stupid."

"Damn it, he's used to *crazy* people . . . you'll probably seem halfway normal."

"It's all bullshit," Richard said.

"What's bullshit?"

"This hypnosis."

"You ever tried it?"

"No, I haven't tried it."

"Then how the hell do you know?"

Richard shrugged and gazed around him, saw the upper class brigade, the men with pinstriped suits and umbrellas, the women cleansed with deodorants. What was he doing here? He didn't want to be here. He felt a slowly uncoiling desperation that threatened to strangle him.

"What good will it do me?"

"You won't know until you try."

Jenny pushed her chair back and stood up with a determined movement, brushing the dark hair from her forehead and avoiding his gaze. Richard sighed and raised his hands, an indecisive, weak gesture, but Jenny, ignoring him, turned away and walked out of the pub. He cursed quietly and followed her out, found her standing on the pavement, exhaling cigarette smoke, her lips pouting attractively, her parka falling below her thighs, around the faded blue jeans.

She flounced off along the street, shaking her head in an angry gesture, turning the corner at Baker Street station as if no longer caring. Richard cursed and hurried after her, pushing his way through the lunchtime crowds, caught up with her as she passed the Planetarium and Madame Tussaud's.

"Okay!" he said, spreading his hands. "I apologize. *Okay?*"

"Don't bother," she said. "I don't want your fucking apology. I just want you to visit that psychiatrist. That's all I ask."

"You ask? I *surrender*."

She stopped at York Gardens, the wind blowing her hair, her face pale and her lips a tight line, the brown eyes large and luminous. "Okay," she said. "Fine."

They crossed Marylebone Road, passing a wall of waiting traffic, then walked silently along the opposite pavement, neither touching the other. Richard stayed a little behind, feeling nervous and confused, glancing along the gray streets, the stately rows of Georgian buildings, his throat dry and crying out for a drink, for the soothing oblivion. He needed that oblivion. He didn't want to go back. What had happened was in the past and should remain there, buried deep and forgotten. He didn't want to relive it, didn't think he could stand it, and yet walking behind Jenny, following her into Harley Street, he knew that she was right, that he had to face the problem, that he had to tear away the veil of mystery that kept him in terror.

"This is it," Jenny said.

She had stopped before a tall, flat-fronted Georgian house with a black door and polished brass handle. Richard stared at the door, at the names on a brass plate, and a tremor of dread rippled through him and congealed in his throat.

"Oh, well," he said.

"Are you going in?" she said.

"Yes," he said. "I guess I'm going in. Jesus Christ, I feel dumb."

Jenny pressed the bell, her face close to a small speaker, and a voice, indistinct and distorted, lazily drawled the word, "Yes?" Jenny gave Richard's name, the tinny voice said, "Come up," then the door made an irritating buzzing sound that signified they could open it. Richard pushed the door open, letting Jenny pass through first, then he stepped

in and closed the door behind him and the buzzing noise
ceased.

"The third floor," Jenny mumbled.

They stood together in the hall, its walls paneled and
darkly varnished, a lavish velvet carpet on the floor, a
potted plant near the front door. Richard stared at the elevator, at its polished metal door, and experienced a fleeting claustrophobia that made him shake slightly. He
glanced uneasily at Jenny, at the high, ornate ceiling, at
the stairs that curved behind the elevator and climbed past
faded paintings. The fear crept up over him, devoured him
and made him numb, and he felt himself dissolving where
he stood, drifting free from his body. He didn't want to go
up there, didn't want to relive it; he wanted to turn
around and walk out, but he just couldn't do it.

"We'll use the stairs," Jenny said.

Richard nodded his head, a dumb gesture of agreement,
saw her brown eyes through a film of panic, her head
turning away from him. Then he followed her up the
stairs, moving slowly and reluctantly, his eyes fixed on her
blue-jeaned legs, on the high heels of her boots, on the
wrinkles where the parka curved out around her broad,
swaying hips. It was coming back to him already, the
white haze, the silhouettes, the woman with red hair and
green eyes—the whole nightmarish catalogue, Richard felt
himself shaking, felt ashamed and confused, glancing
down and seeing his feet on the carpet, his heart pounding
dramatically. Then they reached the third floor, an elevator gate gleaming, a stricken silence surrounding them.
Jenny stopped at a door, raised her hand, let it hang there,
then turned around and took a step toward him and gently
embraced him.

It was a sad, instinctive gesture, a sudden confession of
tension, the first time she had actually held him in
months: her confession of need. Richard stood there, confused, his hands hanging down by his sides, feeling the
warmth of her body, her love, and wondering what he
could do with it. Then he slid his arms around her, felt
her shoulder blades, her spine, spread his fingers and
pressed her closer to him and laid his cheek on her head.

"It's all right," he whispered.

She clung to him for another moment, her fingers
scratching his back, her thighs and firm breasts molded to
him before moving away. Then she glanced at him
quickly, her smile hesitant, eyes shadowed, and nodded
and disappeared down the stairs, leaving scent in the air.

Richard stood there for some time, feeling shaken, re-
awakened, closed his eyes and covered his face with his
hands and took a deep, painful breath. He then put his
head back, studied the ceiling's moldings, shrugged and
knocked lightly on the door and heard a voice bid him
enter.

He stepped inside, closed the door quietly behind him,
saw walls of pale green, a glass table, comfortable arm-
chairs, a middle-aged lady behind the desk, looking up,
smiling pleasantly.

"Mr. Watson?"

"That's right."

"You're a very punctual patient," she said. "Dr. Campbell's expecting you."

She pressed a buzzer on the desk, her hand milky white
and elegant, and announced Richard's presence to the
speaker, her voice soft but precise. Richard glanced
around the office, not listening, not really present, still
aware of Jenny's warmth in his clothes, touched again
with emotion. Then the woman stood up, a white blouse, a
neat gray skirt, and quietly opened the door to another office and motioned him in. Richard coughed into his fist,
trying to orientate himself, then he walked past the
woman, smiling at her, avoiding her eyes, and heard the
door closing behind him with a sharp, clicking sound.

"Ah! Mr. Watson!"

"Yes," Richard said.

"Do you mind if I call you Richard?"

"No."

"Good. Please sit down."

The man wore a gray-striped suit, a white shirt, a bright
tie, his hands spread out on the desk, cuff links glittering,
a large ring on one finger. His hair was dark and rather
long, tumbling carelessly on his forehead, lines of humor
around bright blue eyes, his teeth obviously capped. He
was in his late thirties, looked suntanned and healthy,

a white handkerchief protruding from one pocket, neatly folded and pressed.

"Please," he said. "Sit down."

Richard did as he was told, sitting in front of the desk, crossing his legs and then uncrossing them again and putting his hands in his lap. He glanced quickly around the office, saw the same pale green walls, some reproductions of Turner, a few diplomas, the doctor framed by the window.

"Have you ever been to a psychiatrist before?"

"No," Richard said.

"Have you ever been *hypnotized* before?"

"No," Richard said.

"And does any of this bother you?"

"Yes," Richard said.

"Why?"

"I don't know. It just seems stupid. I don't think it will work."

"You don't think you can be hypnotized?"

"No," Richard said.

"Why not?"

"I just don't think so," Richard said. "I just don't believe in it."

Dr. Campbell smiled. "You don't believe in it," he said. "And is that why you think you can't be hypnotized?"

"Yes."

"Well, we'll see."

The doctor looked down at his desk, at a gray manila folder, opened the folder and pulled out some papers and studied them carefully. Richard just sat there, feeling nervous and slightly vague, trying to seem a lot more casual than he was, wanting to get up and run.

"An interesting case," the doctor said, glancing up and smiling brightly. "You've obviously had a rather bad year. How do you feel now?"

"Okay," Richard said.

"Are you nervous?"

"Yes."

"Well, that's normal. It means you're still human." The doctor smiled at Richard, raised his hand and studied his ring, glanced down at the papers again and then looked back up. "It says here you've been drinking a lot."

"Yes," Richard said.

"And you still have to drink?"

"Yes."

"Why?"

"I don't know."

"And the nightmares?"

"What about them?"

"According to these notes, all your nightmares are exactly the same."

"So?"

"So you're not just dreaming—you're reliving that exact same incident."

"You mean, *you* think it happened?"

"Not necessarily," the doctor said. "It *could* be a case of autosuggestion brought on by great stress."

"You think I'm crazy, is that it?"

"Not remotely. I'm just saying that whatever happened during your period of amnesia could have led to this particularly vivid hallucination."

"Okay, I'll accept that. That's fine. Now how do you cure me?"

"You really accept that statement?"

"Yeah. Sure."

"Rubbish. Of course you don't. You're just saying that because you want to get out of here and go for a drink."

Richard shrugged and put his hands out. "Okay, Doc, have it your way. Just tell me what you want me to say and I'll gladly oblige."

"I just want you to say what you believe."

"I don't believe anything. I don't *know* what to believe. The whole business happened a year ago, and that's a very long time. I told the cops about it. They laughed me out of the office. When I tried to tell anyone else, they just thought I was crazy—and I think they were right. It couldn't have happened. Things like that just don't happen. So I really think you're right—that I had a sort of blackout, and that during that time I hallucinated and then thought it was real. I don't *care* what it was. I just want to forget it. I want to get rid of those nightmares and sleep good again."

"I didn't say it was hallucination; I said it *might* be."

"I hallucinated. Believe me, that's what happened. Now how will you cure me?"

"You said you felt okay."

"I was lying. I feel rotten."

"You mean physically?"

"I mean mentally . . . I mean, I have trouble sleeping, I have the nightmares when I *do* sleep, and I keep breaking out in rashes and getting very bad headaches, and I think it's all part of the same thing."

"Yes," the doctor said. "I have your medical records here. You never had such ailments before the incident . . . and they *are* quite peculiar."

"Peculiar? What do you mean?"

"They're not caused by anything physical. The rashes and the headaches are psychosomatic: brought on psychologically."

"That's ridiculous," Richard said.

"No, Richard, it's not ridiculous. People can *will* headaches and fevers and ulcers and heartburn and stomach upsets and skin diseases . . . in fact, just about anything."

"I'm not a hypochondriac."

"I wasn't suggesting that at all."

"That's what it sounded like to me."

"No. Not hypochondria."

The doctor sat back in his chair, placed his hands behind his head, put his feet up on the desk and smiled pleasantly.

"Let me tell you about the human brain," he said. "The first thing to note is that the human brain, while being a remarkable instrument, is rarely used at even a *tenth* of its full potential. Now, most of our bodily functions are actually controlled by the brain—the brain tells us what to do, when to do it and how to do it—so what we see, hear, smell and we feel are merely the colors, sounds, smells and sensations that the brain has *selected* as being most necessary. This selection is not arbitrary—the brain selects what it thinks we need—but there are other sensations which, though being actual, are beyond the limited range of our immediate senses. However, by awakening certain dormant areas of the brain, either electrically, by the use of drugs or through hypnotic suggestion, the scope of both our senses and our capabilities can be dramatically expanded."

"I can't see what that's got to do with me."

"Well, I'll tell you. Would you agree that drugs or electrical stimulation of the brain can change human behavior?"

"Yes."

"Fine. Now did you know that these methods of affecting the brain can also *induce* pain and similar experiences?"

"Yes, I knew that."

"Okay. Well, regarding hypnotherapy we can apply the same principles, the only difference being that the sensations are induced—or recalled—by a process of suggestion rather than physical means. In other words, just as through hypnotism a patient can be directed to go to sleep or awaken, feel a nonexistent pain or ignore applied pain, turn as rigid as a plank or relive long forgotten experiences, and generally do things that he would not normally contemplate—so, too, can the average human being actually *will* himself into pain, into depression or serious illness, not believing for the slightest moment that he's doing it, convinced that it's physical."

"I don't believe that," Richard said.

"Don't you?" the doctor said. "Do you know that a perfectly normal person, if told under a hypnotic trance that he has just been scalded, will actually come out in blisters? Do you know, further, that that same person, still in the hypnotic trance, can be burned or pierced with needles, experience no pain at all, and not be marked by the burning or piercing when snapped out of the trance state?"

"No, I don't believe that."

"Believe me, Richard, if I hypnotized you and told you that you were a wooden plank, you would turn as stiff as a plank, could be stretched out across two supports, and wouldn't budge if a couple of people used your groin as a springboard . . . you would simply *become* a plank."

"Bullshit," Richard said.

"No, lad, not bullshit. These are the realities of autosuggestion, tested and verified; so when I tell you that your ailments might be psychosomatic, I'm not suggesting for a moment that you're a hypochondriac . . . I'm merely saying that the ailments are symptoms of a deeper disturbance."

Richard crossed his legs, uncrossed them, scratched his knee, then looked down at the floor for a moment and looked up again.

"So," he said, "what are you going to do about it?"

"I'm going to try to take you back to when you suffered the amnesia, find out just what happened during that missing three days, record what you tell me while you're in the trance state, and then play that recording back to you."

"I don't want to know," Richard said.

"You have to," the doctor said.

"I don't give a fuck," Richard said. "I don't want to know."

He was shocked by his own vehemence, sitting upright in the chair, flushed, his heart pounding dramatically, his throat suddenly constricting. The doctor looked at him thoughtfully, not very surprised, then placed his feet back on the floor and propped his chin in his hands.

"What frightens you?"

"I just don't want to do it."

"Why?"

"I'm not dumb enough to be hypnotized. I don't believe it. It won't work."

The doctor smiled patiently. "Well, now," he said, "I think you're antagonistic because you feel that being hypnotized is degrading. Let me therefore assure you, Richard, that any intelligent adult and most children over the age of seven can be hypnotized, that only the mentally retarded and the psychotic can *resist* being hypnotized, and that hypnotizability is in no way a sign of weak will. Indeed, the more intelligent and imaginative the individual, the better a subject he'll be. You therefore needn't be ashamed. There's nothing *wrong* in being hypnotized. Just think of it as another branch of medicine, and try to accept it."

Richard crossed his legs, uncrossed them, scratched his

knee, licked his lips and glanced vaguely around the office and then studied the floor. He thought of the past year, of the nightmares and the drinking, of the loss of his friends, of Jenny's rage, of his own failing health. He couldn't live like that much longer; it just didn't make sense. He wanted to kill it off, to be cured, but the fear held him back. He glanced across at the doctor, tried to speak and did not succeed, finally stood up and scratched his left ear and then shrugged in defeat.

"What do I do?" he said.

The doctor smiled and stood up. "Excellent," he said. "I just want to try a few of your reactions and see if you're suitable." He walked around the desk and stood just in front of Richard, gazed in his eyes then stepped away and said, "Look at your watch." Richard did as he was told. The time was three thirty. "Keep your hands by your sides," the doctor said, "and just relax, just hang loose." Richard did as he was told. He thought the doctor was pretty foolish. He felt sorry for the doctor and decided to humor him to save him embarrassment. The doctor kept talking. He kept telling Richard to relax. He said, "Clasp your hands together," and Richard did so, still wanting to humor him. The doctor kept on talking. He told Richard to relax more. He said, "Your hands are clasped together and you won't be able to open them no matter how hard you try." Richard didn't bother trying. He wanted to humor the doctor. The doctor told him he could pull his hands apart, so Richard pulled them apart. The doctor told him to raise his right arm. Richard did as he was told. The doctor pinched his right arm and Richard didn't feel a thing because he didn't want the doctor to be embarrassed. The doctor told him to lie down. Richard lay down on the couch. The doctor told him to relax and Richard lay there and felt a bit amused. The doctor told him to close his eyes. Richard grinned and closed his eyes. The doctor told him to open his eyes again and look at his watch. Richard opened his eyes. He raised his hand and studied his watch. He blinked and then looked at his watch again and just couldn't believe it. The time was four thirty. A whole hour had passed. Richard shook his head and sat up on the bed, feeling vague but refreshed.

"How do you feel?" the doctor said.

"Fine," Richard said.

"How long do you think you've been asleep?"

"I haven't been sleeping."

Richard looked at his watch again. It was definitely four thirty. He shrugged and grinned foolishly, stood up and stretched himself, then walked behind the desk and sat down and scribbled his name on the notepad.

"Why did you do that?" the doctor said.

"I don't know," Richard said. He stood up and walked back around the desk and stopped in front of the doctor. "Did you tell me to do it?"

"Yes," the doctor said. "You've been asleep for an hour. You were obedient and you talked an awful lot and it's all down on tape."

"Can I hear it?"

"No."

"Why not?"

"You're not ready yet." The doctor went to his desk, switched the tape recorder off, then sat down and scribbled something on the notepad and then looked up at Richard. "I want you to go home now," he said. "You should go to bed early. With a bit of luck, you won't have any nightmares and you'll get a good sleep. I want you to come back here next week. My secretary will give you an appointment. When you return, I'll say something that will put you to sleep immediately, and the experience will be as painless as it was today. I'm taking you back gradually. I can't do it too quickly. That means you'll be coming here on a regular basis, for quite a few months. I don't think this will bother you. In fact, you'll probably want to come. At the end of the sessions, when all the pieces are together, you can hear what happened during those missing days. Okay? See you next week."

The doctor smiled and Richard left. The secretary gave him another appointment. He took the elevator down and walked out into the street and headed straight for Baker Street station, melting into the jostling crowds. The journey home was uneventful. He changed trains at Kings Cross. The train was crowded and the light stung his eyes and he felt very calm. He got out at Finsbury Park, feeling bright and exhilarated. There were drunks in the long, tunneled exits that led up to the buses. Richard boarded the W7, bought his ticket and sat down, looked outside and saw the darkness falling, the street lights flickering on. The bus took him to Crouch Hill. He stepped out and felt the cold. He walked along the dusty pavement, turned into a driveway, passed the parked cars and entered the apartment blocks, feeling strangely lightheaded. He opened the front door and closed it quietly behind him, then he walked along the corridor and stopped when he came to the bedroom. Jenny was stretched out on the bed, fully dressed, her eyes open. Richard walked up to the bed and stood there, saying nothing, just smiling. Jenny reached up for his hand. Their fingers locked and she pulled him down. Their tears mingled as they undressed one another and melted together. Richard poured himself into her. His remaining fear was drained away. He was surrounded by her arms, by the cradle of her thighs, and there, on that bed of flesh and bone, he slept the sleep of a child.

CHAPTER EIGHTEEN

James S. Campbell, B.A., M.A., M.D.,
c/o Society of Medical Hypnotists,
4, Victoria Terrace,
Kingsway, Hove
Sussex, England
February 14, 1976

Dr. Frederick Epstein,
Aerial Phenomena Investigations Institute,
Massachusetts Avenue,
Washington, D.C.,
U.S.A.

Dear Frederick,

Further to our telephone conversation of this morning, I am enclosing a transcript of the most recent taped hypnotic session with young Richard Watson.

I should remind you again that there have been a total of eighteen hypnotic sessions over a period of approximately six months, that the editing of the transcripts has been undertaken as a means of eliminating repetitions and verbal ambiguities, and that the complete tapes of all the sessions can be heard in my Harley Street office upon your arrival in London. In the meantime, here is the background you requested.

Richard Watson first presented himself at my office on September 9, 1975, at the recommendation of a professional colleague (the father of the young man's girl friend) and with the approval of his personal physician. The patient had been suffering from persistent nightmares, insomnia and acute anxiety, all originating in a three-day period of amnesia which apparently began on the evening of March 7, 1974, when the young man, and the unknown lady who was driving him, experienced what he believed was a close encounter with extraterrestrials. The alleged incident took place on the A30 on Bodmin Moor in Cornwall.

According to the young man's original story to both his doctor and the Tottenham Court Road police (the medical records and a photocopy of the police interview are enclosed), the incident began when the car, being driven by the female owner, cut out and rolled to a standstill in a desolate area between Bodmin and Bolventor. Almost immediately, a strange aircraft described by the patient as "enormous" descended and released two three-feet diameter flying discs. These discs circled the car, appeared to be examining it by remote control, then shot "beams of light" into it, allegedly stunning the woman, and then flew away to re-enter the "mother" ship.

Shortly after this, two larger flying discs emerged from the mother ship and also circled the car. According to the patient, these discs were piloted by strange creatures, they also shone beams of light into the car, and those beams of light appeared to *pull* on the car and draw it toward the mother ship. At this point the mother ship descended almost to ground level, appeared to split along the bottom, and then the car, by mysterious means, was drawn up into it.

The period of amnesia appears to have started at this moment, ending three days later when the patient awakened and found himself on a hill in *Dartmoor*—approximately thirty miles from the scene of the alleged incident. Neither the woman nor her car were to be seen.

According to the medical report, the patient could

remember nothing of his "missing" three days, but was suffering numerous nightmares, all of which were obviously related to the period immediately prior to the beginning of amnesia. As a consequence of the amnesia, or of the alleged incident itself, the patient became alcoholic, suffered either insomnia or nightmares, developed severe headaches and skin inflammations (usually around the face and neck) and also succumbed to acute depression and anxiety.

Regarding this, it is to be noted that the young man's physician described him as being, prior to the incident, highly intelligent, emotionally stable, and imaginative.

The patient was, at the time of the incident, a student at the Hornsey College of Art in North London, where he was studying to be a graphic designer, but he dropped out shortly after the incident and is now living off what you Americans call Welfare.

According to the police report, young Richard reported the incident about a week after it allegedly occurred. According to Richard himself (a story repeated under hypnosis), he was held in the police station all night and then interviewed, the following morning, by two men in plain clothes who claimed they were from a government data department. Also, according to Richard's conscious and unconscious statements, the men who interviewed him told him that they had already located the female driver of the car, that she had denied the whole incident, and that she described Richard as being extremely drunk when she dropped him off near Bodmin. Richard was, in fact, drunk at the time, but insisted, even under hypnosis, that the incident had actually occurred and that the woman had been a witness to it.

It was shortly after his interviews with the police and government officials that Richard, obviously depressed and less confident about the reality of his experience, began to develop the headaches and skin inflammations. As you can judge from the transcripts, the skin inflammations might well be psychosomatic manifestations of the "burn mark" on his neck which he believes was caused by one of the so-called ex-traterrestrials.

For the following sixteen months Richard contin-ued suffering the nightmares and attendant insomnia, and subsequently his drinking increased. During this period he was regularly seeing his doctor for unsuc-cessful treatment of the headaches and skin inflam-mations. Dissatisfied with Richard's progress, his doctor recommended psychiatric treatment, which Richard was reluctant to undertake. Then, in late Au-gust, 1975, his girl friend's father, my friend and col-league Dr. Robert C. Parker, recommended that he come to me for hypnotherapy. The first session was, as I have stated, on September 9, 1975, and there were eighteen further sessions, the most recent being on February 10 this year.

The reality or nonreality of UFOs is hardly my province; I therefore centered my treatment on the patient's anxiety reaction to the amnesia which formed part of the alleged experience. Since Richard had obviously developed a strong aversion to the thought of reliving the experience, I was forced to at-tempt a penetration of the amnesia by taking him gradually through the three prime stages of hyp-notism: light, medium and heavy, the latter being a state of somnambulism.

The treatment has so far been successful only to a limited degree. As you will notice when you read the transcript of the most recent hypnotic session, there is a point beyond which the patient simply refuses to go—and to try to force him to do so could be dan-gerous.

Whether the amnesia was a means of obliterating a real experience or an extremely painful fantasy is, in a certain sense, immaterial; what matters is that the memory appears to be real to the patient and that the climax of the experience, or hallucination, was obvi-ously traumatic. It is therefore to be noted that in the period between the last two hypnotic sessions—during which I attempted by suggestion to break down the patient's resistance to a total recall—his mental and

physical condition have degenerated, with a full return of the headaches and skin inflammations. These
symptoms have naturally led to a return of the patient's former acute anxiety.

This regression, brought about by the patient's fear
of a total recall, has so far made me reluctant to use
Sodium Amytal or Pentothal to facilitate the breakthrough. However, should such a breakthrough fail to
occur during the forthcoming hypnotic session, which
is tomorrow, I feel that these alternatives will have to
be risked.

Since the events leading up to the period of amnesia are detailed in the enclosed police and doctor's
reports—and since these events have been corrobo-
rated by the patient's recall under hypnosis—the attached transcript covers only the most recent
hypnotic session, during which the patient finally discussed what happened during part of the period of
amnesia. As you will note, there is a point beyond
which the patient still refuses to go.

I look forward to seeing you on your arrival,

Yours fondly,

James S. Campbell

PATIENT: Richard Alexander Watson
AGE: 19 yrs. 7 mths.
SYMPTOMS: Nightmares, attendant insomnia and
acute anxiety centered around a three-
day period of amnesia.
HISTORY: See attached police and medical reports.
DOCTOR: James S. Campbell.

SESSION 18/February 10, 1976

DOCTOR

You are relaxing, relaxing, you are very relaxed.
You are sleeping, deep sleep, sleeping deeper, very
deep. You are sleeping, very comfortable, relaxed,
very relaxed, you are deeper and deeper in sleep, very
comfortable, deeper. You are relaxed and comfortable. You are deep, deep in sleep. You are relaxed and

you will remember everything and you will answer
my questions.
RICHARD
     Yes.
DOCTOR
     All right, Richard. You are going back to the eve-
ning of the 7th of March, 1974. You are going back
now.
RICHARD
     Yes.
DOCTOR
     Do you know where you are?
RICHARD
     I am in the car. The woman is beside me. The car
has stopped . . . a roaring sound . . . a humming, I
don't know . . . and the light . . . Oh my God, it's
all white! *The whole sky is exploding!*
DOCTOR
     It's all right. It won't harm you. Calm down.
Relax. You can see it. Are you all right? Can you see
it?
RICHARD
     Yes.
DOCTOR
     All right, Richard, we've already discussed how
you were given a lift by the woman in the Audi, how
the car stalled in the middle of Bodmin Moor, how
the sky became bright, and how the car was eventually drawn into the large saucer. Before discussing
what happened inside the saucer—
RICHARD
     I don't want to remember that.
DOCTOR
     Before discussing what happened inside the saucer,
I would like to clarify some points about the previous
period. I want us to do this, Richard.
RICHARD
     Yes.
DOCTOR
     I want to start with the emergence of the two

smaller, three-foot diameter discs from the larger craft.

RICHARD

Yes.

DOCTOR

You said that the two smaller discs flew around the car as if they were examining it.

RICHARD

Yes.

DOCTOR

Why did you think they were examining the car?

RICHARD

They were humming. They made some whistling sounds . . . not whistling: strange, high-pitched beeps, almost like Morse code. They made me think of computers. I was thinking of computers. I had the feeling they were examining the car, photographing it, making some sort of calculations.

DOCTOR

That's a strange thing to think. Why did you think that?

RICHARD

Because of the way they circled the car. Because of the sounds they were making. Because they shone lights into the car and the car began to shake and a beam of light fell on the woman's eyes and made her act strange.

DOCTOR

She changed when the beam of light hit her?

RICHARD

Yes.

DOCTOR

How?

RICHARD

She was very frightened at first. She was almost paralyzed with fear. Then the beam of light caught her in the eyes and she changed almost instantly. I remember this clearly. I was fascinated by it. The woman gasped and then shuddered, closed her eyes and settled back, then, when she opened her eyes again, she was incredibly calm. She told me not to be frightened. She kept saying, "It's all right." She stared at me as if I didn't exist, and she seemed almost happy. I thought that was strange.

DOCTOR

And why didn't the light effect you that way?

RICHARD

It didn't get near my eyes. I fell down on the seat. The light passed over the back of my head and just burned my neck.

DOCTOR

I see. Please continue.

RICHARD

Then the small discs flew away. They returned to the large object. Each disc went into a separate opening. Then the panels at each end of the large object winked out, leaving darkness.

DOCTOR

Describe the large saucer again.

RICHARD

It was dark, but it grew bigger. It was surrounded by a glowing haze. The colored lights along the bottom started flashing on and off, and I could see the object itself very clearly. It was definitely solid. It seemed to be made of white metal. It had long, narrow windows running right along the front, curving back on either side as if running right around the whole object. There were people at those windows. I couldn't see them—they were silhouettes. They were moving back and forth across the windows, very small, faraway. The large saucer was immense. It wasn't large—it was enormous. It was three or four hundred feet wide, two or three stories high.

DOCTOR

Fine, Richard. Then the two panels opened again and two more ships emerged.

RICHARD

Yes.

DOCTOR

Describe them, please.

RICHARD

They flew straight toward the car. They hovered

just above the ground. There was one at either side of the car, and they were different from the previous ones. They were an awful lot bigger. They were thirty-five feet in diameter. Their perimeters swept up to form a dome made of something like glass. There were people inside.

DOCTOR

That's right. You mentioned two people.

RICHARD

Two people in each saucer.

DOCTOR

How far away was the saucer nearest to you?

RICHARD

The part of the perimeter closest to me was about three feet from the car; and the glass dome, about fifteen feet away, was just a little above me.

DOCTOR

You more or less looked directly at the pilots?

RICHARD

Yes. I looked directly at the pilots.

DOCTOR

You are relaxed. You are very relaxed. You have nothing to fear. I want you to remember. I want you to remember it clearly. I want you to tell me what the pilots looked like.

(The patient does not immediately respond.)

DOCTOR

There is nothing to fear. You are relaxed. Tell me what the pilot looked like.

RICHARD

Strange. They look strange. They look strange and I'm scared.

DOCTOR

There is nothing to fear. You are relaxed. What do they look like?

RICHARD

No lips. A mask. It must be a mask. The glass has a rippling effect, so it must be a mask.

DOCTOR

What else?

RICHARD

It has to be a mask. The nose is metallic. The nose is made of metal—it's covered in metal—so it must be a mask.

DOCTOR

Go on.

RICHARD

The eyes are just slits. They seem a bit Oriental. I think they're slits, but this could be the rippling effect. They seem Oriental.

DOCTOR

And their faces?

RICHARD

White. Very wrinkled. Sort of gray.

DOCTOR

White or gray? Be specific.

RICHARD

Sort of gray. Very wrinkled. It looks like dead skin. It doesn't look like human skin at all. I have the feeling it's dead skin.

DOCTOR

Dead skin?

RICHARD

I don't know. It made me think of a corpse.

DOCTOR

Think very hard. Is there anything else you can tell me about the pilots?

RICHARD

Oh Jesus, he lifted up his hand. He's lifting it up now! Oh, Jesus, *the hand is a metal claw!*

DOCTOR

Easy, relax, deep deep sleep, very deep sleep, very deep, you are very relaxed, you have nothing to fear . . . Now can you tell me anything else about the pilot?

RICHARD

He raised his hand. No hand. A metal claw. A sort of metal replacement.

DOCTOR

A prosthetic hand?

RICHARD

I don't know what that is.

DOCTOR

Never mind. He raised his hand and you looked at him. Then what?

RICHARD

I woke up.

DOCTOR

What do you mean, you woke up?

RICHARD

I woke up.

DOCTOR

You weren't asleep.

RICHARD

I must have fallen asleep. He raised his hand and a beam of light hit me and then I blanked out.

DOCTOR

All right, let's assume you blanked out. How long do you think you were unconscious?

RICHARD

Not long. Just a few seconds.

DOCTOR

How did you know that?

RICHARD

The saucers were still outside the car. They were still in the same position. The woman was still in the same position. She seemed in a trance.

DOCTOR

Fine. What happened next?

RICHARD

Oh God, it's coming down! The big mother ship's coming down! Its colored lights are all flashing and it doesn't make a sound and it's dropping down slowly, very slowly, not making a sound. Oh God, *there it is!*

DOCTOR

Where is it?

RICHARD

Oh God! *Oh my God!*

DOCTOR

Relax, relaxed, you are relaxed, you are comfort-

able, you have nothing to fear, you are relaxed, you
can tell me.

RICHARD

Yes.

DOCTOR

Where is the mother ship, Richard?

RICHARD

It's settled down above the ground. It's sitting just
above the road. It's close to the road, but not on it—
it's just sitting above it.

DOCTOR

It's now in front of the car?

RICHARD

Yes.

DOCTOR

It's straddling the road?

RICHARD

Yes.

DOCTOR

How far away is it?

RICHARD

It goes right across the road. It's resting just above
the road. It's about fifty yards from the car and it's
really enormous . . . Oh, God, *the car's shaking
again!*

DOCTOR

It's all right, it's all right, the car's shaking. Why is
it shaking?

RICHARD

Everything's shaking. The whole car is going wild.
Everything's flying about inside the car and sticking
itself to the windshield . . . I can't breathe, I'm almost choking, all this stuff is flying around me, the
car's shaking and moving forward, no sound, just
moving forward, being pulled by the saucers at both
sides, being drawn toward the mother ship.

DOCTOR

What's pulling the car forward, Richard?

RICHARD

The saucers. The saucers on both sides. They're
pulling us forward.

DOCTOR

How are they pulling you forward?

RICHARD

I don't know. I think it's the beam of light. The beams of light come from the saucers, they're shining on both sides of the car, and the saucers are moving toward the mother ship and pulling us with them.

DOCTOR

Beams of light or cables?

RICHARD

Not cables. Not rope. Nothing. Just beams of light.

DOCTOR

Do you believe that, Richard?

RICHARD

Yes, I believe it. The beams of light are pulling us forward and . . . Oh, Jesus, *it's opening up!*

DOCTOR

The mother ship is opening up?

RICHARD

Yes, the mother ship is opening up. It's splitting along the bottom, just above the flashing lights . . . It's *not* splitting open, it's forming a ramp—the bottom's forming a ramp leading up into the mother ship and the car is being pulled up inside . . . Oh, my God, *it's all white in there!* All those people . . . *Oh, Jesus!*

DOCTOR

All right, you are very relaxed, very rested, deep deep in sleep, very relaxed, very comfortable, very peaceful, you have nothing to fear. You are being pulled up into the mother ship. You have nothing to fear. You are relaxed and can remember everything. You are being drawn up into the mother ship. What happened next?

(The patient does not immediately respond.)

DOCTOR

What happened next, Richard?

RICHARD

I am on the hill. I am cold. I don't know where I am. I—

DOCTOR

You are not on the hill, Richard. You are jumping ahead. You are in the car with the woman and you are being drawn into the mother ship. Now what happened next?

(*The patient does not immediately respond.*)

DOCTOR

Can you hear me, Richard?

RICHARD

Yes.

DOCTOR

What happened next, Richard?

RICHARD

I am on the hill. I am cold. I don't know where I am. I—

DOCTOR

You're skipping ahead, Richard. You are three days ahead. Go back to when you were pulled into the mother ship. What happened then?

RICHARD

Oh, God, it's all white! It's all white, it's so bright! All the people! Silhouettes! This is crazy! Oh, Jesus, oh God, I don't want to! *I don't want to! I don't want to!*

DOCTOR

Relax, you will relax, you are relaxed, you have nothing to fear. You are sleeping, deep sleep, sleeping deeper, very deep. You are deep, deep in sleep. You are relaxed and comfortable. You are relaxed and you will remember everything and you will answer my questions.

RICHARD

Yes.

DOCTOR

I want you to tell me what you think happened during the missing three days.

RICHARD

I don't know.

DOCTOR

But you think about it a lot?

RICHARD

Yes.

DOCTOR

Would you like to know what happened?

RICHARD

Yes. No. I don't want to know.

DOCTOR

You just said you would like to know.

RICHARD

I want to know. I don't want to know. It frightens me.

DOCTOR

It won't frighten you if you discuss it. It won't frighten you anymore. You can remember without feeling any fear. You will remember. You are remembering.

RICHARD

Yes.

DOCTOR

You are in the car. You are in the car with the woman. The car is being drawn into the mother ship and you see the white light. Do you see the white light?

RICHARD

Yes.

DOCTOR

The car is being drawn into the mother ship and you see the white light and silhouettes. Do you see the white light and silhouettes?

RICHARD

Oh Jesus!

DOCTOR

Do you see the white light and silhouettes?

RICHARD

Oh Jesus! Oh no!

DOCTOR

You are relaxed, very relaxed, deeply relaxed. There is nothing to fear. You are deep, deep in sleep, you are relaxed, and nothing can harm you. You are all right. You can answer my questions. Do you see the white light and silhouettes?

(The patient does not immediately respond.)

DOCTOR

Can you hear me, Richard?

RICHARD

Yes.

DOCTOR

The car is being drawn into the mother ship. You can see the white light and silhouettes. Now I want you to recall everything that happened. Tell me what happened.

RICHARD

All white.

DOCTOR

White?

RICHARD

Everything.

DOCTOR

Please explain that, Richard.

RICHARD

The walls are all white and the place is filled with light and the light is so bright it nearly blinds me. That's all I can see. The white walls, the bright haze. The silhouettes are moving all around me, moving in toward the car.

DOCTOR

Go on.

RICHARD

I'm beginning to see better. The place is really very bright. The silhouettes are men in coveralls, moving in around the car. Most of the men seem very small. They all seem about five feet tall. They're wearing one-piece coveralls, some black, some a silvery gray, and they have this sort of gray, wrinkled skin, metal noses, no lips.

DOCTOR

All right. You are very comfortable. You have nothing to fear. You say they had metal noses, no lips. Just what do you mean by that?

RICHARD

Metal noses. No lips.

DOCTOR

They were wearing masks like the pilots?

RICHARD

I don't know. I'm not sure. They looked like masks, but they seemed permanent. The masks covered their nose and the lower half of the chin and seemed to be molded out of one piece of very thin metal. That's why there were no lips. The metal covered their lips. I could see the wrinkled skin on their foreheads and around their strange eyes.

DOCTOR

Strange eyes?

RICHARD

Oriental.

DOCTOR

You mentioned that before. Anything else?

RICHARD

The eyes were like the skin—they seemed dead.

DOCTOR

They were blind?

RICHARD

No. The eyes were looking at me, but they seemed dead.

DOCTOR

All right. So these men surrounded the car.

RICHARD

Yes.

DOCTOR

What happened then?

RICHARD

They opened the car doors and pulled us out.

DOCTOR

They had to pull you out?

RICHARD

I don't understand.

DOCTOR

Did they pull you out because you were frightened?

RICHARD

They didn't actually pull us out. This man opened

the door and took me by the arm and just sort of assisted me.

DOCTOR

You didn't resist?

RICHARD

No.

DOCTOR

I thought you were frightened.

RICHARD

I was just numb. I think I was numb with fear. I was dazed and felt weak. I got out automatically.

DOCTOR

And the woman did the same?

RICHARD

I don't know. I wasn't looking. I assume she did the same. I saw her standing beside me, fascinated, looking around her, smiling with that strange gleam in her eyes.

DOCTOR

Could she have been in a trance?

RICHARD

She could have been. Not quite. She was wide-awake.

DOCTOR

Posthypnotic suggestion?

RICHARD

I don't know what that means.

DOCTOR

It doesn't matter. The men pulled you out of the car. Where was the car?

RICHARD

The car was inside the mother ship.

DOCTOR

You're sure of that?

RICHARD

Yes. I looked around me and saw the ramp swinging up and forming part of the wall. The ramp swung from the floor. It closed and formed part of the wall. It didn't make a sound when it closed, and then I saw the wall. The wall was white. It was very slightly curved. It curved horizontally and vertically and formed part of a dome. It was only part of a dome. It was shaped like a slice of orange. It was very large, very white, very bright, like part of an aircraft hangar.

DOCTOR

What made you think of an aircraft hangar?

RICHARD

I was in an aircraft hangar once. I remember that hollow ringing noise. The car was on the sort of ramp that you see in a garage, and the whole place looked like a hangar, a sort of large workshop.

DOCTOR

You saw machinery?

RICHARD

Yes.

DOCTOR

What sort of machinery?

RICHARD

I don't know. I don't know much about machinery. It just seemed like an aircraft hangar because it had all this machinery and because it was big and sort of echoing. Also, all the men were wearing the coveralls.

DOCTOR

And the curved wall. What did you think that was?

RICHARD

It was just a curved wall. It was the inside of the outer wall of the mother ship, where the ramp had come down.

DOCTOR

All right, so the car was drawn up the ramp into the mother ship, the ramp was drawn up and became part of the wall, and the car came to rest on a sort of platform close to the inner wall.

RICHARD

Yes.

DOCTOR

Fine. Now you and the woman are standing beside the car, surrounded by the men in coveralls.

RICHARD

Yes.

DOCTOR
    What happened next?
RICHARD
    I looked at the men around me, wondering if they
were wearing masks, and my fear got worse and I
started to shake. Then one of the men walked up to
me. Oh Jesus, those dead eyes! He stared at me and
passed his hand across my face and then I felt a lot
better.
DOCTOR
    You weren't frightened anymore?
RICHARD
    I went sort of limp. I mean, I went limp inside. I
just emptied out, felt drained and light-headed, felt a
bit removed from it all—it became like a dream.
DOCTOR
    Yet you still felt awake?
RICHARD
    I was aware of where I was. It just seemed more
distant and unreal, as if I was dreaming.
DOCTOR
    Were there any distinct sounds in the hangar?
RICHARD
    A humming. A sort of humming vibration. All the
time. It was constant.
DOCTOR
    Was this similar to what you had experienced in-
side the car?
RICHARD
    Similar, but almost imperceptible. I hardly heard it
at all.
DOCTOR
    Heard it or felt it?
RICHARD
    Both.
DOCTOR
    Did the men talk to you?
RICHARD.
    No. No lips.
DOCTOR
    ˙ They made no sound?

RICHARD

No.

DOCTOR

Go on.

RICHARD

There was an escalator near the car. They made us go up the escalator. One man walked ahead of us, another stayed behind us, and a third took my elbow and helped me to walk to the escalator.

DOCTOR

What did the others do?

RICHARD

They surrounded the car.

DOCTOR

Why did they surround the car?

RICHARD

I don't know. I didn't look back.

DOCTOR

All right. The man led you and the woman up the escalator.

RICHARD

Yes. The escalator took us up past plain bright white walls to a corridor that curved out of sight.

DOCTOR

Was the corridor curved to the wall of the mother ship?

RICHARD

Yes, I think so. I think it ran around the rim of the whole ship.

DOCTOR

Any windows?

RICHARD

No windows on the outside wall of the corridor. There were doors on the left. These doors were the kind that slide in and out—they didn't swing back on hinges.

DOCTOR

Go on.

RICHARD

We stood for a moment at the top of the escalator, and then one of the men told us to keep walking. We all walked along the corridor, past a lot of closed doors, and then, when we reached a certain door, the leading man made us stop.

DOCTOR

Just a moment, Richard. You just said that one of the men told you to keep walking.

RICHARD

He told us both to keep walking.

DOCTOR

But you said that these men never spoke.

RICHARD

They never spoke. They had no lips. The metal covered their lips.

DOCTOR

Yet you say one of the men spoke to you.

RICHARD

He told us to keep walking.

DOCTOR

How did he tell you? Did he speak to you?

RICHARD

He didn't talk. He just told us. I just knew.

DOCTOR

Did you actually *hear* him?

RICHARD

He told us to keep walking. I must have heard him.

DOCTOR

You think you heard him? You heard a voice in your head?

RICHARD

I don't know. I just heard him.

DOCTOR

But you're convinced that this man didn't actually speak?

RICHARD

He didn't talk. I just heard him.

DOCTOR

All right. You are standing at one of the doors.

RICHARD

The door opens. It seems to open automatically. It slides open, disappearing into the wall, and we walk

through the doorway. The door makes me think of
ships. It's like the hatchway of a ship. We walk
through and the door closes behind us and we're all
in a dimly lit room, a circular room, the walls white
. . . Oh, my God . . . *I don't want to!*

DOCTOR

It's all right, you are relaxed, you are very relaxed,
deep, deep in sleep and relaxed, you can see it and
tell me.

RICHARD

It's eerie.

DOCTOR

Yes. The room is circular and dimly lit.

RICHARD

The wall is white and completely circular. The
beds form a circle around us. There are people on the
beds, there are men, women and children, and they're
all wrapped in surgical gowns and have wires running
out of them.

DOCTOR

Wires?

RICHARD

The wires are taped to them. There are wires and
rubber tubes. All these things run back to the wall behind the beds and are fixed to machines. The
machines have colored screens. Not colored, a sort of
monochrome. I thought they were colored because I
saw the lines of bright light jumping up and down.

DOCTOR

Have you ever seen an ECG machine?

RICHARD

I think so. In the movies.

DOCTOR

Is that what these machines looked like?

RICHARD

Yes. The room looked like a hospital ward—except
for its shape.

DOCTOR

The circular shape.

RICHARD

Yes.

DOCTOR

All right. Go on.

RICHARD

We were led to the far side of the room and taken through another door, and we entered another circular room, much bigger, very bright. There were a couple of surgical beds—no, like operating tables. There are people around the beds, and the walls are all lined with long glass cabinets . . . Oh please God, *I don't want to!*

DOCTOR

It's all right, you are relaxed, you are deep, deep in sleep, you are very relaxed and you can tell me, you have nothing to fear. What is it that you don't want to do?

RICHARD

I don't want to look at them.

DOCTOR

At what?

RICHARD

I don't want to look at the glass cabinets.

DOCTOR

Why don't you want to look? What do you see in the glass cabinets?

RICHARD

People. Naked people. There are naked people in the glass cabinets. The glass cabinets are like coffins, the glass seems to be lightly frosted, and the naked people are lying in the cabinets with tubes running out of them. *Oh God, I can't look at them!*

DOCTOR

All right, Richard, it's all right, you're relaxed, you don't have to look at them. Relax, Richard. I just want to go over something I might have missed. In the room you've just come from, where the people were lying on the beds, did any of those people actually talk to you?

RICHARD

No. They couldn't. They were unconscious.

DOCTOR

And the people in the glass cabinets?

RICHARD

I don't want to look at them!

DOCTOR

It's all right. You don't have to look at them again. Just tell me: Were they unconscious?

RICHARD

They were unconscious or dead.

DOCTOR

Did you see anything that looked like an ECG machine?

RICHARD

Yes. There were machines like that above and between the glass cabinets.

DOCTOR

Were the lights on the screens jumping up and down?

RICHARD

Yes.

DOCTOR

Fine. That means they were alive.

RICHARD

They were alive. They were unconscious.

DOCTOR

Fine, Richard. Now tell me about the people in the room.

RICHARD

They were ordinary.

DOCTOR

They looked like normal human beings?

RICHARD

Yes.

DOCTOR

All right. Go on. You are facing the people in the room.

RICHARD

They are both pleasant. They are smiling at me and the woman. One is tall and slim, white hair, suntanned, I think in his fifties or late forties, but his forehead unlined.

DOCTOR

That was the only odd thing you noticed?

RICHARD

He was normal, but his forehead was unlined.

DOCTOR

And the other man?

RICHARD

He has no hair on his head. He looks normal, but he's bald. He seems older than the other man—not much, but a bit older—and the skin on his face seems unreal, as if he's had plastic surgery.

DOCTOR

Do you know what plastic surgery looks like?

RICHARD

Yes. I had a friend who got burned.

DOCTOR

Were there any other men in the room?

RICHARD

Yes. There were three or four other men, all wearing white smocks and trousers, very young, adolescents, quite small, a bit foreign looking.

DOCTOR

Explain that, please.

RICHARD

They looked like Vietnamese. Something like that. I'm not sure. They had strange eyes, narrow, Oriental . . . I'm not sure. It seemed unreal.

DOCTOR

You still felt as if you were dreaming?

RICHARD

I never felt I was dreaming. It was just different. I didn't feel frightened anymore. I felt nothing. Removed from it.

DOCTOR

Did any of these men talk to you?

RICHARD

They talked to the men who had brought us there. They made them all leave. The men in white stood all around us, but they never said anything. The two normal men spoke to us.

DOCTOR

The same as before?

RICHARD

Pardon?

DOCTOR

Did you just hear their voices in your head or did they speak to you orally?

RICHARD

They were normal. They spoke to us. They spoke to me and the woman. They were pleasant and they asked us how we felt and I said I felt fine.

DOCTOR

Did you feel fine?

RICHARD

No. I felt weak. I felt very removed. I was confused and I felt half asleep, as if not really there.

DOCTOR

Why did you say you felt fine?

RICHARD

I just said it. I didn't want to upset them.

DOCTOR

What did the woman say?

RICHARD

She didn't say anything. She just smiled.

DOCTOR

What did the men sound like when they talked?

RICHARD

They sounded normal. They were both speaking English. The younger man, the tall one, had a normal English accent—a sort of everyday American accent—and the older man spoke English like a foreigner. His English was very good, very good, but he had a strange accent.

DOCTOR

What sort of accent?

RICHARD

I don't know. It sounded a bit European. I think it might have been German.

DOCTOR

What else did they talk about?

RICHARD

They talked quite a bit. They wanted to know all

about us. Our names, our ages—things like that—and they were very polite. The older man was very distant. He watched more than he talked. I had the feeling he was older than he looked, and he seemed very cold. The younger man was more informal. I think he said his name was Aldridge. He kept asking us how we felt, if we were frightened, and he seemed very pleasant. The woman didn't say anything. I said I felt very tired. The man asked me if I knew where I was, and I just shook my head. He asked me if I'd like to know. I said that I would. He walked over to the wall and pressed a button and two white panels parted. There was a very large window there. I walked over and looked out. I thought at first that I was looking at a painted screen, and then I really got scared.

DOCTOR

It's all right. There's no need to be scared. Now what did you see?

RICHARD

Stars.

DOCTOR

Pardon?

RICHARD

Stars. Lots of stars. No real sky—just the stars. No up nor down, left nor right, just the stars in a blackness. Then the stars moved. The earth suddenly filled the window. The curved edge of the earth, wreathed in cloud, blue and white—like those movies the astronauts sent back . . . It all seemed like a dream.

DOCTOR

You were above the atmosphere?

RICHARD

Yes. I could see Brazil and the Argentine. We were way up in space.

DOCTOR

Are you sure this wasn't some kind of an illusion?

RICHARD

Illusion?

DOCTOR

You said that at first you thought it was a painted screen.

RICHARD

At first I thought it had to be. I think I was hoping that. I wanted it to be a painting or a film, because the other thing frightened me.

DOCTOR

What other thing?

RICHARD

Actually being up there.

DOCTOR

Did the man at the window say anything at this point?

RICHARD

I asked him where we were. He said we were up in space. He said we were landing briefly on Paraguay and then flying on.

DOCTOR

Flying on to where?

RICHARD

He didn't say. I didn't ask him.

DOCTOR

Didn't you want to know?

RICHARD

I didn't think of asking. I was frightened. I think I was frightened.

DOCTOR

You said before that you weren't frightened anymore.

RICHARD

I can't explain it. I wasn't as frightened as I should have been. I felt a bit unreal. I felt drugged . . . But there was fear. A sort of fear in the background. The fear was just there, very distant . . . I just wanted to please them.

DOCTOR

You say you felt drugged. Did you feel that they had some control over you?

RICHARD

I felt that I didn't control myself. I felt very strange.

DOCTOR

You were looking down at the earth. What happened next?

RICHARD

The man, the younger man, pressed a button and the two panels closed again. Then they took the woman away. I mean, the bald man took her away. I think I must have looked a bit worried because the younger man reassured me.

DOCTOR

The one called Aldridge.

RICHARD

Yes. He told me they wanted to examine the woman and that she wouldn't be harmed. He said that the bald man was going to examine her and that he—I mean Aldridge—wanted to examine me. He said it wouldn't hurt. He said it was just routine. I don't know why, but that really reassured me. It seemed a natural thing to do.

DOCTOR

You didn't wonder why he wanted to examine you?

RICHARD

I think I might have. I don't think I did much. I can't remember it clearly.

DOCTOR

Why can't you remember it clearly?

RICHARD

I just can't. I'm trying to think. I'm more tired. I'm suddenly feeling very tired and I just go and lie down on the bed.

DOCTOR

Are you still inside the spaceship, Richard?

RICHARD

Yes.

DOCTOR

Has the man told you to lie down on the bed?

RICHARD

It's more like an operating table.

DOCTOR

Has the man told you to lie down on it?

RICHARD

I think he must have. I can't remember. He passed his hand over my face and I lay down. I felt very tired.

DOCTOR

Go on.

(The patient does not respond.)

DOCTOR

I said, continue.

(The patient does not respond.)

DOCTOR

Can you hear me, Richard?

RICHARD

Yes.

DOCTOR

You are lying on the operating table. What happened next?

RICHARD

I woke up.

DOCTOR

You were asleep?

RICHARD

I woke up. I must have been asleep. I am in another room and the man, the one called Aldridge, is waking me up. This room is very small. It is relatively small. There are only two beds and the woman is in the other bed. She's unconscious. She's wearing a metal cap. There are wires running out of it.

DOCTOR

How long were you sleeping?

RICHARD

No time. There is no sense of time. I just feel very drowsy.

DOCTOR

So, the man shakes you awake.

RICHARD

No. He is there. I wake up. The man doesn't touch me.

DOCTOR

Yes?

RICHARD

He is very pleasant. He smiles at me. I am frightened because he is pleasant. It doesn't seem natural that he's pleasant, and I feel very frightened.

DOCTOR

Did he say anything?

RICHARD

He smiled and then asked me how I felt. I said I felt very tired. He said that was all right, that it was natural to feel tired, and that I had a very strong will, great resistance, and would have to come back. I didn't know what he meant. I said I didn't understand. He told me that I didn't have to worry, that I was going home soon. I said I didn't understand. I asked him where I was. I felt drugged and I asked this automatically, not thinking about it. I asked him where I was. He said if I got up he would show me. I got up and we walked out of the room and passed through a laboratory.

DOCTOR

A laboratory?

RICHARD

A laboratory. It looked like a laboratory. It frightened me because of what was in there and I tried not to look.

DOCTOR

What frightened you?

RICHARD

The big jars. The things in cages. All the things in the big jars. The big jars were filled with a clear liquid and these things were just floating there. I felt a bit sick. I started to feel really scared. I didn't recognize half of these things, but I still felt upset.

DOCTOR

You didn't recognize half of the things. What *did* you recognize?

RICHARD

Eyeballs. Tongues. Maybe brains—I'm not sure.
Things that looked like liver and intestines . . . things
that made me feel ill.

DOCTOR

Were these items from humans or animals?

RICHARD

I don't know. I didn't look much . . . There was a
corpse on a table, a human corpse, but its head was
all gone.

DOCTOR

Anything else?

(The patient does not respond.)

DOCTOR

Can you hear me, Richard?

RICHARD

Yes.

DOCTOR

You mentioned cages. What was in the cages?

(The patient does not respond.)

DOCTOR

It's all right, Richard. You have nothing to fear.
You are asleep, deep, deep in sleep, you are relaxed,
you will be calm. You have nothing to fear, you will
be calm, relaxed, you are calm. You are relaxed. Can
you hear me?

RICHARD

Yes.

DOCTOR

What was in the cages?

RICHARD

Heads . . . *Human heads!*

DOCTOR

It's all right, forget it, forget it, you have forgotten
it you are very calm, very relaxed, you are just passing through. Remember. I want you to remember.
Are you in the laboratory?

RICHARD

We passed through a laboratory. We went along a
curving corridor. The man was telling me that I would
come back some day and that I should at least see it.

DOCTOR

See what, Richard?

RICHARD

Where we were.

DOCTOR

You mean you were still in the mother ship?

RICHARD

No, I don't think I was in the mother ship.

DOCTOR

What made you think that?

RICHARD

The walls of the corridor were solid rock. They had been carved out of the rock. The corridor led into a large workshop with walls of sheer stone. The workshop wasn't large. It was really enormous. Not a workshop—a sort of factory or machine shop, filled with men and machines.

DOCTOR

What sort of machines, Richard?

RICHARD

I don't know. Large machines.

DOCTOR

You are in the machine shop. What else did you see?

RICHARD

The walls were stone or rock. The roof was stone or rock. I think it was under the ground. In the ground. In a mountain.

DOCTOR

Anything else?

RICHARD

I can't really remember. I can't remember it clearly. There were lots of machines, lots of people, hundreds of people, and there were catwalks running around the stone walls, catwalks above one another, running past what looked like giant computers, past brightly lit rooms. It looked like a factory. An underground factory. The people all worked like automatons. Hundreds of people.

DOCTOR

These people looked like normal human beings?

RICHARD

All the people looked normal.

DOCTOR

What else did you see?

RICHARD

Nothing. He showed me where we were. He took me up some steps to a platform and then pressed a button. There were steel panels on the wall. The steel panels slid apart. There was a really huge window, like a CinemaScope screen, and the panels slid away to expose it, and I saw where we were.

DOCTOR

Where were you?

RICHARD

I don't know. He wouldn't tell me.

DOCTOR

All right, Richard, what did you see?

RICHARD

Ice.

DOCTOR

I'll repeat the question: What did you see?

RICHARD

Ice. All ice. Hills and valleys of ice. The sun was shining and it flashed off the ice and the light nearly blinded me.

DOCTOR

Nothing but ice?

RICHARD

No. There was nothing but ice. Ice, maybe snow, a bright sky, very blue, the sun beating down and flashing off the ice and turning the ice into prisms. It was incredibly beautiful. It nearly took my breath away. There was nothing out there but the ice and the bright, flashing light. The ice went out to the horizon. The sky was very blue. I looked up at the sky and saw a green valley surrounded by more ice. The ice was everywhere—down below, in the sky—and I stared at it and thought it was beautiful and that really frightened me.

DOCTOR

Why did it frighten you?

RICHARD

Because I knew that it must be another world, that I was far, far away.

DOCTOR

It looked like another world?

RICHARD

It had to be another world. There was nothing like that on the earth. It was simply incredible.

DOCTOR

Did you ask the man where you were?

RICHARD

I asked him. I had to ask him. He wouldn't tell me.

DOCTOR

What did he say?

RICHARD

He said I would find out soon enough. He said we had to go back now.

DOCTOR

Back where?

RICHARD

I thought he meant back to the spaceship. I couldn't be sure.

DOCTOR

All right. What next?

RICHARD

He pressed the button and closed the panels. He said he thought I had seen enough. He said that I wouldn't remember this, that I might remember some of it, but that whatever I remembered would be confused and wouldn't mean much. He said I had great resistance. He said that was interesting. He said that most people forget it, but that I might be different. He thought I was interesting. He wanted me to come back. He said that when I ceased my resistance I would be very useful. After that, we went back along the corridor.

DOCTOR

Wait a minute, Richard. What do you think he meant by all that?

RICHARD

I don't know.

DOCTOR

You never thought about it?

RICHARD

I didn't remember it.

DOCTOR

All right. You went back along the corridor.

RICHARD

We went back along the corridor, through the laboratory, then into another room. There were a couple of surgical beds. The men in white smocks were there. The leader, the man called Aldridge—I think he was the leader—told me to lie down on a bed. It wasn't a bed: it was an operating.table. I didn't want to lie down. I lay down and the men all stood around me and pulled the metal cap lower. I didn't want them to do that. I didn't want them to *do* that! I tried to refuse, but I can't move and they're putting it on me. I don't *want* them to do that! *I don't want to I don't want to!* I don't want them to put that on my head, oh please God . . . *I don't want to I don't want to I don't want to!*

DOCTOR

It's all right, you are calm, you are relaxed, you are deep, deep in sleep, it's all right, are you calm now?

(The patient does not respond.)

DOCTOR

Can you hear me, Richard?

RICHARD

Yes.

DOCTOR

What happened next, Richard?

(The patient does not respond.)

DOCTOR

What happened next, Richard?

RICHARD

I am on the hill. I am cold. I don't know where I am. I—

DOCTOR

You are not on the hill, Richard. You are jumping ahead. You are on the operating table and they are

placing the metal cap on your head. Now tell me
what happened.

(The patient does not respond.)

DOCTOR

There is nothing to fear, Richard, you can tell me,
you will tell me what happened.

RICHARD

I am on the hill. I am cold. I don't know where I
am. I—

DOCTOR

Deep deep sleep, you are deep, deep in sleep, you
are relaxed, you have nothing to fear, you are very
relaxed . . . You are on the operating table. They are
placing the metal cap on your head. You have nothing to fear, you are relaxed, you can tell me what
happened. What happened, Richard?

(The patient does not respond.)

DOCTOR

You can tell me, you have nothing to fear, you are
relaxed, you can tell me. What happened, Richard?

RICHARD

No.

DOCTOR

You can tell me, you have nothing to fear, you are
relaxed, you will tell me. What happened, Richard?

RICHARD

I didn't want to lie down. I lay down. I didn't want
to lie down. I lay down and the men all stood around
me and pulled the metal cap lower. I didn't want
them to do that. I didn't want them to *do* that! I tried
to refuse, but I can't move and they're putting it on
me. I don't *want* them to do that! *I don't want to I
don't want to!* I don't want them to put that on my
head, oh please God . . . *I don't want to I don't
want to I don't want—*

DOCTOR

It's all right, you are calm, you are relaxed, you
are deep, deep in sleep, it's all right, you can tell me
. . . What happened, Richard?

(The patient does not respond.)

DOCTOR
    Can you hear me, Richard?
RICHARD
    Yes.
DOCTOR
    What happened next, Richard?
(The patient does not respond.)
DOCTOR
    What happened next, Richard?
RICHARD
    I am on the hill. I am cold. I don't know where I am. I—
DOCTOR
    All right, Richard, we'll leave it for now. You are in deep deep sleep, very deep, deep asleep, you are relaxed, you are very relaxed, you are sleeping, deep sleep. In a moment you can wake up. You will remember nothing that's been said between us. You will not remember until I ask you to remember, you are asleep, deep deep sleep. All right, Richard, you are wakening now, you are wakening, wakening slowly, you are very slowly wakening. You can wake up, Richard.

CHAPTER NINETEEN

Looking out of the rear window of the large, comfortable London taxi, the first thing that struck Epstein with pleasure was the peculiar beauty of the pearly gray afternoon light, falling now, through a drifting layer of clouds, on the stately grandeur of Parliament Square, on the Guildhall and Big Ben, on the tourists who milled about on the pavements dominated by statues. Epstein loved the English light. He had loved it since the war. There was something about that mild, misty gray that pacified the most fearful soul.

"How do you like being back?" Campbell said. "It's been an awfully long time."

"How long?" Epstein said.

"About ten years," Campbell said. "You came over quite a lot in those days. You were a regular tourist."

Epstein smiled and rubbed his eyes. The taxi was racing past the Cenotaph. He gazed at the Foreign Office, at Downing Street and the Treasury Buildings, saw the tourists around Horse Guards Parade, the soldiers stiff in red uniforms.

"There were a lot of conferences then," he said. "There isn't much happening now. The British are very secretive about UFOs, so there's no point in coming."

"It's better in America?"

"For good and for ill. But once you sort the wheat from the chaff, then, yes, it's better."

Campbell, sitting beside Epstein in the back of the taxi, wearing a pinstripe suit, black shoes and a flamboyant tie, studied the glittering ring on his finger and nodded judiciously.

"I know what you mean," he said. "We British are tight-lipped. The Official Secrets Act blankets all—we're not as free as we think we are."

The taxi was pulling out of Whitehall into the massed traffic of Trafalgar Square, the four lions staring eternally, flocks of pigeons above the fountains, Nelson's Monument soaring up to the sky, the National Gallery beyond it. Epstein studied the scene with sadness, remembering other days, better days, the days when he had felt more assured, his youthful innocence shielding him. Those days were gone forever and would never return. They had slipped away quietly, stealing dreams and good health, leaving him more restless and defeated, overwhelmed by his future. He didn't want to think of the hospital. He didn't want to be that brave. He coughed into his fist and looked out and saw the steps of the church.

"St. Martin in the Fields," Campbell said.

"What are those people doing there?"

"Some sort of demonstration," Campbell said. "They always demonstrate there."

The light was different here, darker, subtly tainted with carbon monoxide: the waste of the traffic that endlessly circled the square and caused chaos in the surrounding West End streets. Epstein rubbed his eyes wearily, slumping deeper into his seat, suffering the acute disappointment that comes to old men when they discover that the past has slipped away and cannot be recaptured.

"It's a pity about Stanford," Campbell said. "I'm really sorry he couldn't come. It's not like him to miss a trip to London. You must be keeping him busy."

"He didn't want to come," Epstein said.

"Stanford? You can't be serious."

"I'm serious. He didn't want to come. He's been a bit obsessed lately."

"Don't tell me he's in love."

"It's not a woman," Epstein said.

"With Stanford it's *always* a woman . . . and our young friend can pick them."

Epstein smiled understandingly. "You sound disappointed," he said. "Anyway, it really isn't a woman. He's obsessed with his work."

"You mean UFOs?"

"That's right."

"That doesn't sound like Stanford."

"Stanford's changed a lot," Epstein said. "He's not the man you remember."

"You think the UFOs are real?"

"Yes, I think they're real. And now Stanford . . . he thinks they're real as well, and it's made him obsessed."

The taxi slowed down at Cambridge Circus, inching carefully into the traffic, and Epstein looked out and saw the shuffling crowds, the gutters littered with rubbish. The city was dirtier, its buildings grim and unpainted, the pervading grayness no longer romantic, enshrining neglect. Everything changed, decayed, came to nothing, and he pulled his eyes away and stared inward, ashamed of his dark thoughts.

"Those transcripts were extraordinary," he said. "What's your assessment?"

"I agree with you," Campbell said. "I think it's a rather amazing story. I've gone over the tapes time and time again, but can't reach a conclusion."

"Why not?"

"I'm just confused. I don't know what to believe. It's the most incredible story I've ever heard under hypnosis, and I'm afraid it's just left me rather baffled."

"Is it a true experience or isn't it?"

"It's a true experience to *Richard*."

"But that doesn't necessarily mean that it actually happened?"

"No, I'm afraid it doesn't."

Epstein sighed and stared out at Tottenham Court Road, feeling weary after his journey from Kennedy to Heathrow, a slight nausea in his stomach, his head throbbing, a little dizzy from jet lag.

"It's a very elaborate story," he said. "He always returns

to the exact same story. If the story isn't true, what does it mean? Why does he *think* it's true?"

"I don't know," Campbell said. "I'm not sure. *Something* traumatic obviously happened to him when he was hitchhiking to Cornwall, and it's possible that he's just trying to conceal it."

"From himself?"

"Yes."

"Even under hypnotism?"

"Yes, even under hypnotism. They can get rather tricky."

Epstein sighed and glanced outside, saw the shops with plate glass windows, an abundance of tape recorders and televisions and stereo equipment, the audio and visual stimuli of a society increasingly divorced from its senses. There was input and output. The whole world was being programmed: plug in and turn on and forget that the real world exists . . . Yet what was the real world? Where did fact and fantasy join? Young Richard Watson's experience was very real—and yet may never have happened.

"All right," Epstein said. "Let's suppose he's hiding something. He's been shocked and he can't face up to it, so he creates a whole fantasy. Yet, if that's true, what would make him think of UFOs? He never *thought* about UFOs before, so why think of them now?"

"Not true," Campbell said. "He thought *occasionally* about UFOs. Like all of us, he'd read about them and discussed them now and then—not often, but he definitely did it, so they were there in his head."

"Hardly enough to make him switch on to UFOs when he suffers amnesia."

"Well, there *is* something else," Campbell said. "A few weeks back I had a quiet conversation with Richard's father, and he gave me some interesting information. It seems that his father—now an engineer with British Leyland—was a Royal Air Force navigational pilot during World War II, and that when Richard was a child his father used to tell him about the mysterious 'balls of fire' that were seen by a lot of pilots and have since gone down in UFO literature as the first genuine reports of contemporary UFO sightings. Now of course what we are told we remember—and Richard could have remembered that."

"Anything else?"

"Yes. According to Richard's father, he used to embellish these stories—just to scare the hell out of Richard—by telling him that the balls of fire were actually flying saucers, that they were piloted by extraterrestrials, and that the extraterrestrials had a secret base in the Antarctic, from where they made all their forays."

"That's an old UFO myth," Epstein said.

"Precisely."

"So you think that this might account for the landscape of ice and snow that Richard mentions?"

"Yes. There *is* a pattern there. First he remembers the balls of fire, immediately thinks of them as extraterrestrial, and then associates them with a landscape of ice and snow. It *could* account for his story."

"All right . . . But what would start it in the first place?"

Campbell shrugged. "Who knows? That's the area he won't discuss. As you could judge from the transcripts, there's a point in his narrative beyond which he refuses to go. That point, obviously, is the actual incident that kicked him off, but he just doesn't want to face up to it."

Epstein sat back, coughed again and rubbed his eyes, felt despair as they passed Regent's Park Station and headed toward Harley Street. The fantasy and the fact. The dream and the reality. He thought of the lights outside Galveston, of the enormous disc in the Caribbean, of the deaths and the disappearances and the contradictions in Air Force policy, and he realized that the dividing line was thin and could in truth be a mirage . . . And yet he had to know. His time was running out. He didn't want to take his last breath before the truth was revealed to him. Epstein felt a growing rage. He wanted to smash down all the walls. He wanted to do it for Mary, for Irving and for himself, for all the people who had suffered or passed away while the mystery remained. The taxi turned left into Harley Street, stopped in front of Campbell's office. Epstein climbed out, leaving Campbell to pay, and felt a rising impatience.

"Here we are," Campbell said. "The home of the brave."

"How long before Richard's appointment?"

"Twenty minutes. After you, sir."

Campbell opened the front door, ushered Epstein inside, then led him to the ancient elevator with its polished brass gate. Epstein felt trapped in the elevator, silently cursed its creaking lethargy, was relieved when they stepped out into the corridor and entered the office. Campbell had the same secretary. She had been with him for fifteen years. Epstein noticed how she had aged, said "You haven't changed a bit," shook her hand then followed Campbell through the door that led into his office. Campbell closed the door behind him, pointed to a chair in front of the desk, and Epstein nodded and gratefully sat down, breathing heavily, coughing.

"That's a bad cough," Campbell said.

"Yes," Epstein said.

"Did you eat on the plane?"

"Don't remind me," Epstein said.

"Then a brandy won't do you too much harm. A large or a small?"

"Make it large," Epstein said.

Campbell went behind his desk, opened a cupboard below it, and pulled out a bottle of Rémy Martin and two empty glasses. He poured two stiff shots, slid a glass across to Epstein, then sat back and put his feet on the desk, his glass to his lips. Epstein slowly sipped his brandy, felt it burning down inside him, making his head light and bright, his eyes watering slightly. It did him some good, warmed him up, eased his panic, but it didn't stop the growth of his rage, his increasing frustration. He coughed again and cursed mildly, remembering the hospital in New York: they had confirmed what he had known all along, but now the truth was pursuing him. One year, maybe two. The doctor who told him had actually smiled. Epstein thought again of what he had learned and then tried to forget it.

"You had another session with Richard," he said. "Did you manage to crack him?"

"No," Campbell said. "The same routine, the same

results. The minute you try to fill in the gaps, he refuses to answer."

"You tried to bully him into it?"

"Yes. He started panicking. He just won't face up to the missing period, and I can't push too hard."

"He's coming in twenty minutes?"

"Fifteen minutes. He's very punctual."

"I want to know," Epstein said. "I want you to give him the Pentothal. Believe me, James, it's very important . . . we must get him to talk."

"It could be dangerous," Campbell said. "He's not just frightened—he's terrified. I'm not sure what will happen if we force him, and that makes me nervous."

"Listen." Epstein leaned forward, placed his glass on the desk, clasped his hands together and spoke urgently, with a quiet, clipped precision. "This is the most remarkable encounter case I have yet come across. It *could* be true, and if it's true, it's important. It's more than important— it's vital—and we've got to find out. I'm not trying to *invent* UFOs. I actually know they *exist*. I don't know what they are or where they come from, but I know they're for real. I've seen one myself. Stanford and I saw it together. It was enormous and bright and very clear, and it was visible a long time. That UFO abducted a scientist. Stanford and I were the last to see him. Now the CIA is breathing down our necks, and their breath doesn't smell nice. They don't believe our story—at least they *say* they don't believe it—but I have reason to believe that they *might* believe it, and that their concern is caused by the fact that we actually saw it. Don't ask me why just yet. I'm begging you, just believe me. Apart from that, the CIA is hounding us, they're calling our story rubbish, so now, apart from natural curiosity, we have good cause to know. Richard might be what we need. He might unlock all the secrets. We've got to take the chance—we've got to crack him—because we've got to find out."

Campbell stared hard at Epstein, his eyes luminous and searching, then he let his feet fall to the floor and leaned over the desk.

"You've actually *seen* one?" he said.

"Yes."

"I don't believe that."

"Stanford and I saw it together—and we didn't imagine it. It was there a long time. There was an old boat beneath it. It cast light and shadow on the boat. It was there. It existed."

Campbell shook his head. "I can't believe this," he said.

"I'm not lying," Epstein said. "I don't lie. You *know* I don't lie."

Campbell sat up straight, cupped his hands beneath his chin, pursed his lips and shook his head wearily.

"It's too ridiculous," he said. "And I don't just mean the UFOs. Richard's whole story is like a dream—it's a typical dream."

"Typical? How?"

"Because Richard was *seeing* it. He wasn't involved in it—he was *watching* it. He was on the outside, looking in, surveying his own dream. He's not *active* in that narrative. He has no volition or will at all. All his actions are dictated by the other characters, and he never resists. He's not really a participant. He's merely an observer. At no point in the narrative does he display the slightest resistance to these men: what they will, he then does. It's a denial of responsibility, a repudiation of his own will. It's the classic dream of someone abdicating: the very heart of amnesia."

"And that's all it is?"

"Probably."

"All right, let's assume that it actually happened. Would his total lack of will be all that unusual?"

"I don't know what you mean."

"James, one of the most common aspects of contactee cases is the apparent lack of will, or resistance, on the part of the contactee. Contactees frequently talk of how, though frightened, they felt drawn toward the aliens, felt they were *obeying* the aliens—even when the aliens appeared not to have actually spoken. Again, just as in Richard's case, the common denominator seems to be a feeling of remoteness, of divorce from the self, with the contactees invariably behaving like zombies. Now, with this particular case we have the same thing. The woman, for instance, is initially terrified, but then, as soon as the beam of light hits her, she becomes extraordinarily calm. Likewise with Richard. The beam of light that hits the woman misses Richard and therefore leaves him unaffected. However, when the alien raises his hand, another beam of light hits Richard and temporarily renders him unconscious—and this time, when Richard awakens, he still feels the fear, but he's also dazed and feels a bit removed, without much resistance. Thereafter, whenever Richard feels frightened, these men simply wave a hand across his eyes and he goes limp and feels remote again. Also, as with other contactees, Richard does what the men tell him, but believes that they're not actually speaking to him . . . Now is that so impossible?"

Campbell leaned on the desk again, one hand folded upon the other, his cheeks slightly flushed, his gaze serious, his interest increasing.

"You mean hypnotism?" he said.

"Why not?" Epstein said. "There's nothing particularly extraordinary about that—and you know its effects. As you yourself have told me, once a person has been conditioned to accept the hypnotic state, a simple phrase or a gesture can be used to put them into a trance immediately. Thus, the alien just has to pass his hand across Richard's eyes, and Richard will immediately go into an hypnotic trance—but still awake, his eyes open."

"That's possible," Campbell said. "And you think the beam of light was some sort of hypnotizing device?"

"It could be," Epstein said. "There need be nothing particularly magical about it. Bear in mind that both light and sound can have extraordinary mental *and* physical effects on normal people. For instance, a light flickering somewhere in the alpha-rhythm range, between eight and twelve cycles a second, can cause extremely violent reactions in the person exposed to it, including jerking limbs, faintness, lightness in the head, or unconsciousness. It is scientifically possible, therefore, that the beam of light described by Richard was some sort of laser beam that simply flickered on and off at the particular rate which affects the brain's basic rhythmic patterns and encourages hypnosis. As for the strange humming, or vibrating, sounds that also appear to affect the listener, it's a scientific fact that infrasounds, which are just below the limit of human hearing—hence Richard's uncertainty about whether he heard or *felt* the noise—can effect humans in the same way as flickering lights; indeed, certain low frequency sounds can lead not only to a change in the brain's rhythmic patterns, but to actual *physical* changes, such as the breaking of glass or the killing of human beings by crushing their insides with pure vibration. Given this, I'm not being particularly farfetched when I suggest that the beam of light, combined with the vibrating sounds, could have led to the initial state of hypnosis."

"Yes, Frederick, that's feasible."

"Good. Now while we're still on this subject, there *is* one thing that constantly crops up in contactee cases and could possibly tie in with all this. Time and time again we are told of how the so-called aliens pressed the contactee on the side of the neck—either by hand or with a metal device—and thereby rendered the contactee unconscious or temporarily without will. Could this be related to hypnotism?"

"My God, yes, it could . . . in fact, it's a standard form of hypnotism: the instantaneous technique, or the carotid procedure."

"Which is?"

Campbell shrugged. "It's simple biology. You merely apply pressure to a blood vessel near the ear, thus inhibiting the heart rate, interfering with the circulation of blood to the brain, and rendering the subject dazed and confused, susceptible to suggestion."

"And is there such a thing as *waking hypnosis*?"

"Yes. The patient is wide-awake, knows where he is and what he is doing, but is actually doing what he has been told to do by his hypnotist. Incidentally, on the opposite end of the scale—and this could certainly apply in Richard's case—the subject can be hypnotized when sleeping quite normally. You simply attract the attention of the sleeping subject with some sort of physical contact, hypnotize him by repeatedly telling him that he can hear your voice, have him perform what it is you require of him, then very gently put him back to sleep. He will later wake up, as per normal, and know nothing about it."

"That could have happened to Richard when he awakened on the strange bed and found the man called Aldridge standing over him."

"Precisely."

"And what about posthypnotic suggestion?"

"What about it?"

"I just thought it interesting that according to Richard's narrative he was told that he would remember nothing that had occurred—or at least that he might remember *some* of it, but that the little he remembered would be confused and probably not make much sense. That seems to be what's happened: Richard still can't remember it—it only comes back under hypnosis; but even there, it's pretty vague and disconnected . . . and there's something still missing."

"Well, sticking to our hypothesis, yes, that's also quite possible. Assuming that Richard was hypnotized, any instructions to forget what had occurred would certainly make him forget."

"And there's nothing particularly mysterious about this type of hypnosis?"

"No. Quite routine." Campbell picked up his glass and had another sip of brandy, then licked his lips and set the glass down and folded his hands again. "You know, it *is* interesting," he said. "According to Richard, the man told him that he had a very strong will, great resistance, and that while most people forgot the experience, Richard himself might remember it."

"So?"

"For a start, the remark confirms that the experience has been undergone by other people."

"Yes. Richard's account certainly ties in with a lot of other such cases, most notably the Barney and Betty Hill affair of 1961 and the Pascagoula case of 1973."

"A great similarity there, certainly. I remember both cases."

"That was for a start. What else is there?"

"Well, dear boy, still leaning on our hypothesis, it is to be noted that when the woman was hypnotized by the beam of light—assuming, of course, that she *was* hypnotized—she went into what appears to be a trance, a wide-awake trance, and apparently experienced no further fear. On the other hand, when *Richard* was likewise affected by the light, he became more remote but did *not* in fact lose his sense of fear. Now this could account for that strange man's assessment of Richard: that he had a very strong will and great resistance. Accepting this, it is then possible that the woman, even if hypnotized, might not remember what happened to her; whereas a certain kind of person—a person like our Richard—would remember a certain amount under hypnosis. In short, while your so-called aliens can apparently make people forget their experiences, their success in this field is rather limited."

"And Richard?"

"Even with Richard, had he not come for hypnosis, he would never have remembered it at all."

"Yet his dreams were a sort of recall."

"Right," Campbell said. "Another clue to his resistance. Richard remembered some of the happenings in his dreams, but didn't know what they meant. It's also worth noting that his dream—and it was the same dream every time—involves a group of men standing around him while he's lying on a bed. From what he's told us, that can only be when he was forced to lie down on the bed and they put the metal cap on his head—the experience he refuses to detail further."

"Refuses to detail or simply can't remember."

"Okay," Campbell said. "Let's assume that his captors actually existed and that everything we've talked about actually happened. The man called Aldridge was obviously intrigued by Richard's unusual strength of will and told him that *he would have to come back*. Let us suppose, then, that the metal cap was a stereotaxic skullcap, that it was used to implant a minute electrode in Richard's skull to reinforce his inability to remember . . . Now, when one tries to force Richard to recall that particular incident in detail, he not only displays considerable stress, but also clutches his head and shakes it with great violence—and later awakens with an extremely bad headache . . . Is it therefore possible that Richard has been *programmed* to feel pain and fear when he tries to recall that event? And, further, that they want him to return in order to check out the relative success or failure of the implantation?"

Epstein rubbed his eyes and smiled. "We've just come full circle," he said. "Now *you're* the one asking the questions. You must be a believer."

Campbell grinned and put his hands up. "I accept defeat," he said. "Now you've got me as curious as yourself, another obsessed man."

"Good," Epstein said. "I like to hear that. So, is it possible?"

Campbell shrugged. "It's possible," he said. "Implantation of electrodes in the brain has been going on for years—overtly in animals, covertly in human beings, with the latter experiments kept rather secret. What *is* known is that electrodes implanted in the human brain have been used successfully to activate both paralyzed and artificial limbs, to control otherwise uncontrollable muscular spasms, such as in Parkinson's Disease, to pacify violent mental patients and prisoners, and even to initiate 'thought control' between a human controller and a computer. Now, given that any form of human brain manipulation can have frightening social and political possibilities, a lot of the experiments on human beings have been conducted behind closed doors, most notoriously in mental institutions and state prisons—and the results of these experiments are thus not widely known. Nevertheless, given what has already been accomplished, and what might have been accomplished in secret, it is safe to assume that the sort of programming we're talking about is well within the bounds of possibility."

"How are the subjects controlled?"

"Well, it's on the record that the reflexes and appetites of various animals have been controlled at a reasonable distance by a controller sitting behind a computer-linked console. Such an animal can be made to stand up, sit down, eat or starve itself to death, play, fight, collapse in terror—just about anything. Regarding human beings, we have, to date, only been able to stimulate specific areas of the brain, and do it, reportedly, under immediate visual control. Regarding long-distance control, it is reasonable to assume that the particular response required would be pro-

grammed at the time of the implantation—fed into the
brain via the computer—and would be limited to one or
two responses only. To put it at its simplest—and taking
Richard as our hypothetical case—yes, they could have
implanted an electrode in his brain and programmed him
to feel pain and terror each time he attempted to think of
a particular incident. In other words, it's quite possible
that when I try to force Richard to recall the skullcap incident, the very thought of it might stimulate the terror
and the crippling headaches—a terror and pain caused by
the implanted electrode."

"Another form of hypnosis," Epstein said.

"No," Campbell said. "Total mind control."

"You mean that by taking this technology to its ultimate
limits we could very simply steal a man's mind?"

"That's right," Campbell said.

Epstein sat up in his chair, suddenly excited and energetic, feeling that he was standing on the edge of a preci-
pice, about to leap across to the unknown. The possibilities
were boundless, the implications awesome, and the truth
was probably locked in Richard's mind. They had to pick
the lock, had to force the door open. The risk would be
great, but the rewards could be greater: the final unraveling of that mystery which now teased the whole world.
Epstein shivered and felt feverish, his head light and very
bright, no longer drained by fear and depression and
thoughts of his future.

"We've got to!" Epstein hissed. "We've got to use the
Pentothal! We've got to use it during this session and find
out what happened!"

"I'm not sure," Campbell said.

"*We've got to!*" Epstein hissed.

"It might be too early for that. Too early. Too dangerous."

"Damn you, James, it's important!"

"It's not *that* important, Frederick. You've been at this
game for thirty years—you can wait a bit longer."

"I can't," Epstein said, and felt ashamed as soon as he
said it. "I've got cancer. I've got two years at the most. I
won't live beyond that."

Campbell stared at him, shocked. Both of them: shocked. They stared at one another a long time, the silence enslaving them. Then Epstein looked away, kept his eyes on the floor. He suddenly seemed very old, very frail, his face lined with exhaustion.

"I've got to know," he said eventually. "I can't die without knowing. As you say, I've been at it for thirty years, but now I think I can solve it. It's the most important thing in my life. A lot of people have suffered for it. I can't get this close and let go . . . and every day it's more urgent. It's not just for me. It's not purely selfish. It's for Irving and Mary and all the others who were ruined trying to crack it. There's something going on, James. It's not an illusion; it's very real. Now my time is running out and I'm close, very close, and I can't sit back and hope that Richard remembers . . . I have to know *now*."

Campbell sighed and stood up, turned away, stared out the window, looked once at his watch and frowned slightly, his back still turned to Epstein.

"All right," he finally said. "I'll give Richard Pentothal. After that, no matter what he tells us, I'll have his head X-rayed."

He turned around and sat down. They stared silently at one another. The neat room was as quiet as a tomb and neither knew what to say. They both sat there, feeling stricken. They both checked their watches regularly. They both sat there for a very long time, but Richard never showed up.

CHAPTER TWENTY

When did Kammler and Nebe die? It was a long time ago. They were gassed as they slept in their rooms, and then I had them cremated. I didn't really have a choice. My implants were not perfected. We were still using the Death's Head S.S., and their obscene forms of discipline. It was shortly after the war. Kammler and Nebe showed much resentment. Power corrupts and they both had great power and started plotting against me. I could not let this happen. My life's work had reached fruition. Hidden deep in the immense, frozen wilderness, the colony functioned. Thus I had to get rid of them. Their room doors locked automatically. They never knew all the time they were there that the walls could spit gas. They died peacefully, in their sleep. The room was aired and they were removed. They were taken to the crematorium in the base of the mountain, incinerated, turned to smoke and ash, leaving me independent.

How ironic was their death. It was a death befitting them both. For how many had they themselves sent to the gas chambers during those nightmare years? I think particularly of Kammler. S.S. General Hans Kammler. Kammler planned the concentration camps, supervised the plans for Birkenau, was responsible for its four great gas chambers and its vile crematoria. A dark-haired, ruthless man. Energetic and decisive. His gross ambition, and his total lack of scruples, made him someone worth knowing.

August 1943. Himmler then was at his peak. His lust for power had increased every year and he was then almost godlike. Yet that wasn't enough. Himmler wanted more and more. Most particularly, he wanted control of the V-2 rockets and all those who worked on them. He had tried for that and failed. Then Peenemunde was bombed. Himmler suggested to Hitler that Peenemunde had been betrayed, and that his S.S. should take control immediately. Hitler agreed to this. Himmler now had full control. He immediately moved mass production of the rockets to the caves near Nordhausen. General Kammler was put in charge. He became Himmler's right-hand man. When that happened, I had to do something to protect my own project.

Those were dangerous years. The war was not going well. The Russian offensive was a disaster, Italy had fallen to the Allies, Hitler's physical and mental health was collapsing, and the Reich was in ruins. My own position was no better. As I remember, it was precarious. I now doubted Himmler's sanity and will, and this made me uneasy. The slaves were still being sent to Kiel. From there they went to the wilderness. The great caves were expanding under the ice, but they seemed far away. I wondered if I would ever get there. I no longer trusted Himmler. As disaster followed disaster for the Reich, I saw his brimming hysteria. I still wanted the wilderness. I knew I couldn't depend on Himmler. His hysteria was making him indecisive and that meant he was dangerous. I still wanted the wilderness, I didn't want Himmler there, and I met Kammler in 1943 and was drawn to his ruthlessness.

Kammler knew of my project. Himmler sent him to check it out. I was then at the BMW Platz near Prague, still working unceasingly. I knew the war would soon be lost. I was playing a double game. This game was very dangerous, very tricky, and I had to be careful. I still badly needed Himmler. His facilities were essential. Yet I knew that he now lived in fear of being found out by Hitler. After all, it was betrayal: Himmler was building his private empire. If the Fuhrer discovered his intentions, he would have Himmler executed. Thus Himmler became frightened. In his mild eyes there was frenzy. He had

promised to give der Fuhrer *great new weapons, and* der
Fuhrer *was restless. I didn't dare complete the saucer. Not
until I reached the wilderness. I was frightened that
Himmler's growing confusion might make him give it to
Hitler. That would mean the end of everything. The Allies
would take it over. As for myself, I would be classed as a
war criminal, and probably hanged.*

On top of this, there was Schriever. The Flugkapitan
*was ambitious. Yet another of Himmler's scientific pets, he
had the need to impress him. Schriever's eyes devoured my
saucer. He was in competition with me. I knew that if the
saucer was completed, he would take all the credit. Already I had seen him do this. He had the slyness of a
simple man. Himmler insisted that we share the whole
project, and I knew what that meant. I was Himmler's
secret. The* Flugkapitan *was not. Once the cause was completed I would simply disappear, and then Himmler could
offer* der Fuhrer *the saucer as a German achievement. So,
Schriever was a threat. He wanted credit for my achievements. Because of this, I withheld a great deal and understated my progress. Schriever worked from doctored
drawings. I gave him enough to make it credible. The
Schriever saucer could rise and hover briefly, but it didn't
yet fly. I had to let it progress slowly. Not much, but
enough. Meanwhile, in the BMW plant, I quietly finished
the real work.*

*My one thought was for the wilderness. The hangers in-
creased beneath the snow. Sooner or later I would have to
escape and join the vast, hidden colony. I could not depend on Himmler. His rising panic had made him treacherous. I could see, in his fear and indecision, that he might
never leave. I needed another ally. Another man of gross
ambition. I met Kammler in the BMW* Platz *and felt that
here was my man.*

*Kammler was an organizer. He was ruthless and deci-
sive. More important: his ambition was boundless, his
selfishness total. I worked on him very slowly. It took
months, but I was patient. Kammler's one thought, at the
time, was self-survival, and that's what I played on. He already knew of the hidden colony. He was startled and intrigued. I could see, as I unveiled further facts, that he*

was drawn to the notion. The Reich was crumbling all about him. There were plots and counterplots. The Nazis were devouring their own kind and survival was difficult. Then, of course, there were the Allies. Kammler knew the war was lost. He also knew that if the Allies took him prisoner they would certainly hang him. Kammler had to get out of Germany. He had to disappear completely. When I knew this, I told him my plan and he said he would join me.

That same month he went to see Himmler and blatantly lied to him. He painted me in a black light. He praised Schriever to the skies. He claimed that my own project was a mess, that I was stealing from Schriever. I was too old, he said. Flugkapitan Schriever was young and bright. He said that Schriever should be given his own project and encouraged much more. Himmler wasn't too sure. Kammler pressed home his point. He reminded Himmler that the Allied invasion had begun and that he should take precautions. Kummersdorft West should be evacuated. The American and Schriever should be separated. Kammler suggested that I be moved to the mountainous region of Thuringia, and that Schriever be moved to Mahren. It was better that way, he said. Schriever could then work unencumbered. Himmler, now dependent on Kammler, promptly gave his permission.

I was moved out shortly after. At last I was free of Schriever. In Kahla, in the mountains of Thuringia, I completed my major work. Himmler never knew about it. Kammler told him I was not progressing. Himmler eventually turned his attentions away from me and focused them all on young Schriever. That was just what we wanted. We were not concerned with Schriever. I had insured that Schriever's flying saucer project would never succeed.

June 25, 1944. In my office in the research center at Kahla, I talked to Kammler and Nebe. I remember it well. S.S. General Artur Nebe. A man whose very name suggested terror and the screams from the basements. General Nebe was ice and fire. He had the cunning of a rat. He was a man who did not show his feelings, who worked quietly and ruthlessly. An exemplary record in the Gestapo. Extermination squads in Russia. With such work he had gutted his soul and embraced the unthinkable. Nebe knew how to survive. He was a master of intrigue. He had trampled on the bones of countless comrades to protect his own skin. A dangerous man, certainly. Also, a cold realist. And that day in my office in Kahla his eyes were wide open.

General Nebe was escaping. There had been an assassination attempt. The Fuhrer had survived the explosion and was now seeking vengeance. The reprisals were terrible. Himmler's men were butchering hundreds. A lot of officers were fleeing for their lives, disappearing forever. General Nebe was such a man. He had been forced to desert. Kammler had told him of what we were doing and he now wished to join us.

Nebe controlled the escape route. His most fanatical S.S. men joined him. Those men formed the chain that stretched from Kahla to the port in the Baltic. I often watched the trains pull out. The S.S. cracked their whips. The dogs snapped at the feet of the children as they wept on the platform. Many came from the concentration camps. Others came from the Lebensborn. We stole children from all over Europe and marked them for slavery. The trains took them to Kiel. The ships and submarines devoured them. They vanished off the face of the earth and were not seen again.

Meanwhile, I continued working. My time was running out. The final components for the saucer were in production, but had not yet been tested. The Red Army was in Warsaw. Very soon it would reach the Oder. I had to complete the saucer and test it before the Russians arrived.

Kammler helped me all he could. His authority was considerable. What we didn't have, he took from other scientists and less powerful research centers. Hitler was dreaming of secret weapons. He spared no expense in getting them. All over Germany, even as the bombs were falling, the scientists worked night and day. There was an Atom Bomb project. There were electrical submarines. There were laser beams and infrared warheads and remote-control systems. The Kaiser Wilhelm Institut. The Forschungsinstitut of Lindau am Bodensee. From such places I stole what might help to enhance my own project.

The swirling energy of the Feuerball. *A porous metal called* Luftschwamm. *In the laboratories of the Kreiselgerate, not far from Berlin Britz, I solved the problems of gyroscopic control and Prandtl's infamous boundary layer. This latter proved to be the breakthrough. The boundary layer was the key. At the end of 1944 we had conquered it and started construction.*

The thought of Schriever amuses me. Perhaps it always will. I look out upon the glinting ice caps and think of what that man lost. Schriever lived for fool's gold. His saucer designs were all useless. While I finished the real work in Thuringia, he chased phantoms in Mahren. His flying disc was an abortion. All my guidelines were false. Nevertheless, Schriever thought it would work, and that's what we all wanted. Himmler rarely asked about me. He kept visiting Schriever. The Schriever disc could hover above the ground, but could do little else. No matter: it was impressive. Schriever thought he could make it work. He told Himmler that it only needed time, and the Reichsfuhrer believed him. That was just what we wanted. It was exactly what we had planned. As Himmler focused all his attentions on Schriever's disc we got on with the real one.

It was a miracle that we managed it. It was a desperate, frantic race. The skies overhead were filled with Allied planes, the horizon was smokey. The Ardennes offensive had failed. The Soviets had now crossed the Oder. The Allied armies were advancing in the south and our towns were in ruins. Hitler had moved into the Chancellery. He was preparing his Gotterdammerung. *His Reichsfuhrer, Heinrich Himmler, was in panic and had almost forgotten us. Himmler wanted a flying saucer. He wanted Schriever's flying saucer. Because of this, we were free to continue without interference. The war raged far away. The smoke thickened on the horizon. We stepped out of our caves to see this, and then went back to work.*

I remember it all vividly. The sounds of labor still echo. The great underground complex at Kahla represented my future. The caves were inside the mountain. From the air they were invisible. Inside them were thousands of slave workers and dedicated technicians. The bright lights stung our eyes. Walls of stone cast giant shadows. Machines roared and plates of silvery, porous metal dangled over our heads. The flying saucer was a skeleton. It grew large and filled the hangar. The technicians clambered under its steel ribs, their eyes covered in goggles. The hissing white flame of the welders. The laborers sweating beneath the dome. The lights beamed down and flashed off the cabin and hazed the slave workers. The great caves dwarfed them all. They were cathedrals carved from stone. The sounds of riveting and welding and drilling reverberated throughout. The men looked very small. They were like ants in their nest. They climbed ladders, crossed catwalks, stood on platforms and girders, now removed from the real world, isolated inside the mountain, working long hours and sleeping very little, supervised by Nebe's soldiers.

We kept working night and day. We heard the thunder of distant guns. Every night our trains snaked down the mountain and headed for Kiel. The flying saucer took shape. Its glittering mass filled the hangar. The final plates were welded around the pilots' cabin and the body was finished. The immense disc hung from chains. It was lowered onto the massive legs. The legs housed the four jet propulsion boosters that would aid its ascent. The disc locked onto the legs. The noise echoed throughout the caves. The slaves looked on in silence, their eyes dulled with exhaustion, while the technicians all roared and applauded, their hands linked in triumph.

An historic day. I will never forget it. I stood beside Kammler and Nebe and felt as if I were dreaming. The enormous hangar doors opened. Light and cold air poured in. The Kugelblitz, now supported on mobile blocks, had a quiet, serene beauty. We wheeled it out of the hangar. It was February 1945. The sun shone upon the base of the mountain, but was darkened by gray smoke. Then the rain and snow came. We had to cancel the test. Two days later, on February 16, the saucer soared to the heavens. It climbed vertically and gracefully, stopped abruptly and then shot south. It became a winking light above the battlefields, a bright star in the smokey haze.

The next week, we destroyed it.

CHAPTER TWENTY-ONE

The minute he saw the house the pain left, but the fear lingered on. Richard stood by the gate. The graveled path ran through the gardens. The moonlight fell over the flowers, over the Audi in the driveway, over the Italian tiles that led up to the front door, over the white, Georgian house. Richard pressed his head again. He couldn't believe that the pain had gone. The pain had pulled him from his bed, the voices whispering and urging, and sent him on the next train to Cornwall, determined to find her. Now he shivered with fear. The pain had gone, but the fear lingered. He glanced up at the house in the moonlight and wondered how he had found it. In truth it had been easy. She had told him she was from St. Nicholas. It was a very small village, very insular, and they all knew the lady.

He had asked about her in the local pub, feeling dazed, the pain blinding him, and the people with the large jugs of beer had all chattered at once. Aye, lad, they knew the lady, knew the expensive foreign car; the lady and her bloody great car were just outside the village . . . And so he had walked here, still dizzy, the headache monstrous, and now stood by the large, open gates and touched his head, not believing it. The headache had gone, but the fear lingered on. Richard kicked the gravel nervously with one foot and looked up at the large house.

Why had he come? He didn't know why he had come. Yes, he knew—because the headaches had destroyed him

and the voices had urged him. What voices? *The voices.*
Voices? Was he mad? Sitting slumped in the train, his
head throbbing, he had sensed his own lunacy. Not voices.
Couldn't be. He had gone to the bar car. The bar was
crowded and the smoke stung his eyes and made his throbbing head worse. And the voices. *I won't listen!* He drank
a double Scotch. It had burned down inside him, a thin
flame, and made him feel better. Yet the headache grew
worse. He returned to his seat and sat down. He closed his
eyes and tried to block them out, but the voices persisted.
What voices? *I won't listen!* He wanted to scream with
pain. The pain was killing and the voices were whispering
and making him dizzy. Five hours on the train. The
shadows creeping across the hills. He had glanced once at
the moors and closed his eyes and felt the fear breathing
over him. What voices? *I won't listen!* The train had
pulled into Bodmin. He had disembarked and walked to
the village like a man in a trance. Then the smokey pub,
the noisy clatter and ringing glasses. He had asked about
the lady with the Audi and they pointed the way. A short
walk through the darkness. The night silent, stars glittering. He had arrived at the gate of the house and then the
headache had gone.

The fear lingered on. It was with him right now. He
stood by the gates and kicked the gravel and saw lights in
the windows. The house was white in the moonlight. It was
a converted 18th century manor: elegant, romantic,
dreamlike, the stars glittering above it. Richard walked
through the gates, stopped again and felt the fear. Why
fear? There was nothing to fear, and yet he felt it and
shivered. Then he moved again, knowing he couldn't turn
back. When he thought of going back his head hurt and
the voices returned. He was imagining it, of course. He tried
to turn back and it started. He licked his lips and stared at
the house and then moved forward again.

Silence. A light breeze. The light breeze hissed through
the silence. Richard walked along the broad, curving
driveway toward the white Audi. It was definitely the same
car. There could be no doubt about it. Richard looked at
the car and felt a chill and remembered the white haze.

No, he should not have come. Yes, he had to go on. The voices whispering in his head confirmed the latter as he walked toward the gleaming car. He stopped once, stared above him, saw the black sky, the stars, felt fear and something else, a sense of wonder, then moved forward again.

He stopped when he reached the car. His fear and wonder had increased. He shivered, felt the ice in the breeze, and reached out to the car. He ran his fingers along the hood. He had to confirm that it was real. Satisfied, he gazed up at the house, the large windows in white walls. All the lights were on. The whole house was ablaze. He saw long velvet drapes, a chandelier, a rich mahogany table. There were lanterns about the door, the door made of natural wood. The door was open and he thought that was strange and it made him more frightened.

Fear. The inexplicable. He walked slowly around the car. The breeze hissed and chilled the sweat on his brow and made him shiver again. He walked across the Italian tiles. The fear grabbed him and held him. He had the urge to turn around and run away, but he just couldn't do it. Then he was on the porch. Italian tiles and potted plants. There were vines writhing along the balustrades that gleamed white in the moonlight. He stood there, uncertain, thinking of Jenny and the doctor, remembered them, forgot them, heard the voices, then walked toward the open door.

Why was the door open? He knew why: she was waiting for him. She had known he would come, somehow known that, and now she expected him. Fear. The inexplicable. The need to know and the fear of knowing. He reached out and touched the door with his fingers, lightly stroking it, testing it. The door was very real. A bright light poured out around it. He stepped forward and pushed it further back and then stepped into the house.

Silence. The hall was empty. Paintings hung from paneled walls. There was a chandelier glittering below the ceiling, illuminating the stairs. Rich carpets, shining glassware. Richard stood there, couched in fear. The stairs ran up to a balcony that was angled around the hall, closed doors concealing numerous other rooms and offering nothing but silence.

Richard licked his dry lips and looked slowly around him. Two varnished doors, one at either side, leading into more rooms. One of the doors was open. The light poured out around it. He knew it was the room that he had seen from the lawn, the room with the velvet drapes and chandelier and rich mahogany table. He took a deep breath, not alone, sensing someone, remembering the silhouettes in the white haze, the woman's red hair and green eyes. Then he walked toward the open door. The silence swam out and surrounded him. He pushed the door back and walked in and then stopped, feeling frightened.

She was sitting at the far end of the table, the red hair tumbling down, the green eyes very bright, even now, at this considerable distance. She was staring straight at him, perfectly still, almost frozen. She was wearing a black evening gown, flowery frills around the sleeves, and her right hand was curved around a glass of what looked like red wine.

Richard was frightened. Her green eyes were insane. She raised her glass and sipped at the wine and then set the glass down.

"I was expecting you," she said.

"Why?" Richard said.

"I just knew you were coming," she said. "Don't ask me why. I just knew."

Richard didn't move toward her. He was frightened and confused. He didn't know why he was here, couldn't believe that he was here, felt unreal and divorced from himself, not in charge of his actions. The woman just sat there, staring at him, not smiling. In the black dress, surrounded by antiques, she looked like someone from long ago. Another time, another age. Richard didn't know where he was. He had the feeling that he had stepped into a dream from which he might not escape. His headache had gone, but the fear lingered on. He stood there, near the door, staring at her, wondering who had informed her.

"How did you know?" he said.

"I told you not to ask that."

"I had to come," he said. "I just had to. I have to know why."

She smiled bleakly and raised her glass, sipped some wine, set the glass down. The glass made a sharp, ringing sound that made his heart leap.

"Why did you have to come?" she said.

"I'm not sure," Richard said. "I had forgotten—I was trying to forget—and then it suddenly came back to me. I started getting bad headaches. I thought the headaches were going to kill me. I heard voices, or I thought I heard voices, and kept thinking of you. I just had to come. It seemed imperative that I come. I had the feeling, I had this thing in my head, that said to come here would cure me. The headaches were terrible. They drove me out of my apartment. I didn't know what to do, I couldn't think of anything else . . . just the train—I thought of catching the train, and that made it seem better."

"And your headache has gone?"

"I think so. I hope so."

"How strange," she said. "My headache's gone as well. It's very strange . . . I'm not frightened."

Her declaration frightened Richard. He glanced nervously around the room. He didn't know what he was expecting to see, but he had to look anyway. A chandelier above the table. A long wall lined with books. Velvet curtains, large paintings, various trophies, the glint of bottles and glasses. The long table was illuminated. Her green eyes were slightly shadowed. The shadows deepened where they swallowed the corners, making strange, gargoyle shapes. Richard shivered and felt cold, wondered vaguely where he was, glanced around him and then stared at the woman, feeling frightened: in need of her.

"How are you?" he said.

"Pardon?"

"How are you?"

She looked at him, brow furrowed, not believing what she had heard, then she put her head back, her hair gleaming, burning red, tumbling over her bare, convulsed shoulders as her laughter exploded.

"What—?"

"Oh, my God!" Her laughter echoed around the room,

a barbaric sound, slightly insane, devoid of humor or warmth. "Oh, my God, what a question!"

Richard stood where he was. "Shut up," he said quietly.

"How are you?" she gasped, laughing dementedly. "What a question to ask me!"

Richard walked across the room, hardly knowing he was doing it, seeing bright light and shadow, glinting glass, flickering candles, the chairs stacked against the table, all empty, supporting ghosts, her laughter cutting through the silence, demented, a jagged sound all around him. He slapped her face. It was a single, precise blow. The laughter stopped as her head jerked to the side, and froze there, green eyes wide. She took a deep breath. She was staring straight at the wall, her eyes bright, her lips forming a tight line, holding in a cold fury. Richard stepped away from her, pulled a chair out and sat down. The woman stared at the wall, leaning over, turned sideways, then she straightened up and took a deep breath and touched her cheek with her left hand.

"You hurt me," she said.

"I'm sorry," Richard said. "I didn't know what else to do. You sounded hysterical."

She touched her cheek again, smiled ruefully, picked her glass up, sipped some wine and then put the glass down and pushed a bottle toward him.

"Have a drink," she said. "I think you need a drink. Before the night's out you'll need it more, but you probably won't get it."

"What does that mean?" Richard said.

"I don't know," she replied. "I don't know what any of this means . . . I just know that it's happening."

Richard poured himself a drink, noticed that his hand was shaking, set the bottle back on the table and then stared at the woman.

"How did you know I was coming?"

"I don't know," she said. "I just knew. I just had the feeling . . . a very strong feeling."

"You left the front door open."

"Yes, I left it open."

"You don't leave a door open for a feeling—it must have been more than that."

The woman looked at him and smiled. Her green eyes were very strange. They were bright, but they were looking straight through him as if not really seeing him. Richard felt himself shivering. He reached out for the glass of wine. He picked it up and turned it around and saw the light flashing off it.

"Drink it," the woman said. "It's not poisoned. It's not going to hurt you."

Richard smiled and drank some wine, set the glass back on the table. The woman watched him with that strange, bright intensity, her left hand tightly clenched.

"Where's your husband?" Richard said.

"He's not here," the woman said.

"Where is he?"

"I don't know," the woman said. "He left me five months ago."

"Left you? You mean for good?"

"Yes, I mean for good. The poor man thought his wife was going mad, so he packed up and left."

"And *are* you going mad?"

"I'm not sure. I think so." She picked her glass up and drank some more wine, licked the rim with her tongue. "I rarely sleep," she said. "I get nightmares when I *do* sleep. I get angry, start smashing things up, wreck the place, rip the phones out." She set her glass back on the table, lit a cigarette, inhaled, turned her head aside to blow the smoke out, slowly turned back to face him. "We had terrible rows," she said. "I never knew what I was saying. I just hated him—no reason—just hated him and wanted to get rid of him. I had to be on my own. I don't know why—I just had to. I wanted to be alone in this mausoleum, where I could wait . . . wait for something . . . Naturally he left me. I could hardly live with myself. I had headaches, like migraines, terrible dreams, really bad, then he left me and it all went away and I sat back and waited."

She exhaled cigarette smoke, let it swirl around her face, a blue haze disguising her fading good looks, the lines of tension and loss. Yes, she had changed. Her face advertised the fear. Richard stared and saw a woman grown much older, quietly mad, disappearing.

"Waiting?" he said. "Waiting for what?"

She shrugged, shook her head, studied her glowing cigarette, looked at him as if looking through him, nicked ash to the floor.

"I don't know," she said. "I just know that something's happening. Last night I had a headache, went to sleep and dreamed about you. I woke up and thought my head was coming apart, but I kept thinking of you. I knew then that you were coming. I knew that when you came I would be cured, so I opened the doors."

"That's crazy," Richard said.

"Is it? You really think so? And yet *you* had a headache, it drove you out of your apartment, it compelled you to take a train straight to Cornwall, it drove you right here . . . Are we both . . . ? Are we crazy?"

Richard glanced around the room. A nineteenth-century drawing room. The shadows swallowed the corners, crept along the bookshelves, crawled across the floor and faded out against a bright pool of light. Another time, another age. Another age, another place. He sipped his wine and felt the movement of his mind, slipping out through a black hole. He wasn't here; he was there—somewhere else, far away—here and there which was one and the same, divorced from reality. Then he stared at the woman. Her green eyes swam in the shadows: mad eyes, obsessed with what was coming, feeling more than they understood.

"What happened?" Richard said. "That day on the moors. I remember the silhouettes in the haze. Only that. Nothing else."

The woman licked her upper lip, green eyes wandering, returning, looking at him, looking through him and beyond him, going back, finding nothing.

"I don't know," she said. "I remember no more than you. I woke up three days later, in the car, the same place, and drove straight home, not understanding what had happened, not really believing it. I remembered the start of it. The huge aircraft in the haze. I remembered the saucers flying around us, the light beaming in on us. Then nothing. Oblivion. I woke up and you were gone. It was dawn and I thought I'd slept there all night, that I'd somehow passed out. So, I drove back here, went to bed and slept all day. I got up, had some food, watched TV, and found out that three days had passed. Then the headaches came. The nightmares, the fear. When my husband put his hands on my body, I flinched with revulsion. I couldn't understand it. I just knew I had to get rid of him. I had fits and started wrecking the house, and he left me eventually. It was better after that: no more nightmares, no headaches. Just people . . . I couldn't stand to see people, so I stayed in the house. I just hung around all day. I drank a lot and that helped me. I knew something was happening, *would* happen, but I didn't know what. No nightmares, no fear. That all started again last night. I knew then that it had happened, that it hadn't been a dream, and I knew that you would come here tonight and that soon it would end."

"*What* would end?" Richard said.

"I don't know. I just know it will end."

She stubbed her cigarette out, picked her glass up, drank some wine, set the glass back on the table, looked at it, then smacked it away. The noise made Richard jerk. He looked down at the table. The glass was lying on its side, reflecting light, shaking lightly, the red wine pouring out across the table and dripping down to the floor. Richard looked at the woman. She stood up and smoothed her dress. She was tall and very slim, her face pale and fatigued, still elegant, her hair gleaming in the light, pouring down the black dress.

"Did the police come?" Richard said.

"The police?" She looked puzzled. "No, not the police . . . some men came, wearing gray suits, briefcases . . . from the government . . . took notes."

"About a week after it happened?"

"No. About a month. They said it was just routine— they took notes—I haven't seen them since then."

"They came a *month* after the event?"

"That's right. A good month."

"What did you tell them?"

"I told them what happened. They obviously didn't believe me."

Richard stared up at the woman. She was still standing in front of her chair. The shadows fell across her eyes, across her face, across the swell of her breasts. Richard stared at her, mesmerized. The light fell upon her hands. Her fingers were locked loosely together, long and thin, a pale web.

"What did they say?" Richard whispered.

The woman shrugged. "Nothing much. They told me they had seen you, that you had told them what happened, that they just wanted to confirm that it was true. I told them what I remembered. It wasn't much, but they wrote it down. Two men, very quiet, quite polite. I haven't seen them since then."

"You confirmed that it happened?"

"I confirmed what I remembered. When I got to the beam of light they just smiled, not believing a word of it. They said I had seen the planet Venus. They got into their car and drove off and have not been back since."

She still stood there, staring around her, faraway, not really present, a ghostly lady in a long, flowing gown, the walls behind her in shadow. Richard didn't know what was happening. His fear blossomed in the silence. He looked up and saw her glittering eyes, their bright, unfocused depths. What was he doing here? What were they both waiting for? Richard thought of standing up and walking out, but his head tightened instantly. He knew then that he wouldn't leave. His gaze fastened on the woman's breasts. He breathed deeply and the threatened pain departed and his head felt more normal.

"This is crazy," he said.

"Yes," she said. "It's crazy."

"I'm frightened and I just don't know why."

"It's all right. It's all right."

Richard felt a sudden chill, remembering the blinding white haze, remembering that what she said at that moment had frightened him more. *It's all right. It's all right.* He recalled the words clearly. He now looked up at her green eyes, very bright, surveying the room, and he knew, even through his mounting fear, that in some way he needed her.

"We've been brought together," he said.

"Yes," she said. "I think so."

"Why?" he said. "I don't understand."

"It's all right. It's all right."

She gently bit her lower lip, staring above him, through the windows, looking up at the black, star-flecked sky, her eyes searching, appealing. A shiver ran down Richard's spine, made him feel more unreal. He saw the darkness lying over the lawns, a fine line of mushrooming trees. The stars were bright and multitudinous, offering silence, revealing nothing, and he turned back and looked up at the woman and felt the fear creeping over him.

"I feel tired," he said obliquely.

"It's very tiring," she replied.

"Do I stay here? Is that what I do? I *have* to stay here . . . the headaches."

The woman looked at him and smiled, a strange smile, not her own, raised her right hand and stroked her flaming hair, flecks of steel in her green eyes.

"Yes," she said. "The headaches . . . Something's happening . . . it's all right . . . Yes, of course, you have to stay here . . . We both have to stay here."

Richard stared at her, mesmerized. The black gown flowed on her body. She was tall, her skin white, very elegant, unreal in the shadowed light.

"Can I sleep here?" Richard said.

"Yes," she said. "You should sleep. You'll feel better."

They stared at one another. The wind groaned across the lawn. The candles flickered on the table, their light defeated by the chandelier, a larger pool of light around them both: a pool of light in the darkness.

"I'll take you up," the woman said.

"Thanks," Richard said. "I haven't actually brought anything with me . . . No towels. No clothes . . ."

The woman waved her right hand, a languid, eloquent movement. "Don't worry," she said. "It's all right. We're always ready for guests."

Richard stood up very slowly, his body aching and weak, glanced up and was blinded by the chandelier, looked away, his eyes sparkling. The corners of the room were dark. Glasses glittered in a cabinet. He saw his shadowy reflection in the glass, a gray ghost, nonexistent. Then he saw another reflection, a flowing form, incorporeal, felt a chill and turned around and saw the woman walking slowly toward him.

"This way," she said, touching him lightly as she passed, her long fingers outspread, brushing briefly across his chest, then falling back to her side as she walked on, the dress rustling around her.

Richard followed her out, stepping into the hall, a pulse beating nervously in his stomach as he walked toward the stairs. The hall seemed very large. It looked bigger than it was. They advanced across the carpet, the woman's gown rustling lightly, then the woman put her hand on the bannister and calmly walked up.

Richard followed her, feeling strange, more unnerved by her calm, confused, not really knowing what was happening, wondering if he was sane. None of this was real—not the house, not the stairs, not the lights that bled weakly from the walls and fell over the woman. He reached out for the bannister. It was smooth to his touch. He looked up at the woman, at the swaying of her hips, his gaze traveling along her arm to her wrist, the white flesh on the polished wood. She was real. It was happening. They both stepped onto the landing. The woman turned and looked over her shoulder and smiled enigmatically . . . then she walked away from him.

Richard followed her, feeling cold, along the balcony, through the shadows, the wall lamps hanging downward, glowing weakly, a modest aid in the gloom. The woman stopped at a closed door, put her hand out, turned the knob, gently pushed the door open and then stepped back, waving Richard inside. He glanced at her, saw the smile, a strange smile, not her own, then he shivered and brushed past her and stepped in, his shoulder grazed by her breasts.

"Will this do?" she said quietly.

Richard hardly saw the room, just the bed, the covers turned back, a lamp burning on a table beside the bed, a pool of light in the shadows.

"Yes," he said. "It's fine."

"You look tired," she said. "Exhausted. That other door leads to the bathroom. You'll find towels . . . pajamas."

Richard nodded, but said nothing, too nervous, confused, mesmerized by her eyes, by that green, opaque glittering, by the long line of her body, the black dress, the shadowed light all around her.

"Don't worry," she murmured. "It's all right, it's all right. Have a good sleep and then you'll feel better. We'll just stay here. We'll wait."

He wanted to know what she meant, what she thought they were waiting for, opened his mouth and then closed it again, now afraid of his own voice. The woman stepped forward and reached down, put her hand on the doorknob, stepped back and pulled the door as she went, disappeared, the door closing.

Richard stood there in the silence, in a noise that seemed like silence, his ears ringing, the closed door in his eyes, feeling tense and light-headed. He stood there a long time. He heard her walking away. She stopped walking, a door opened and closed, and then the silence was total.

Richard shook his head slowly, feeling dazed, a bit frightened, turned around and had a good look at his room, a large room, neat and comfortable. He studied it carefully, drank it in and saw nothing, just the bed and the lamp on the table with a window-framed darkness. He walked across to the window. Feeling nervous, he looked out. He saw the far edge of a patio, a low wall, a few steps, a flat lawn disappearing in the darkness, some trees, a small shed. He looked up at the sky. The moon glided beneath the stars. He shivered and turned away, feeling desolate, then went into the bathroom.

He turned the lights on. Blue and green tiles, blue rugs. A toilet, a marble bath and a shower, expensive and tasteful. He turned the lights off. He didn't feel like a shower. He walked over to the bed and stood there, then went back to the bathroom. He turned the lights on. They were bright and stung his eyes. He used the toilet and then took his clothes off and stepped under the shower.

He turned the water on to hot, let it scald him and revive him, remained there for a very long time, then turned it off, dried himself. He walked out of the bathroom, making sure the door was closed; naked, he walked over to the bed and lay down, sighing loudly. He lay there for some time, hearing the silence of the house. He heard the wind blowing outside the window, then he turned out the bedside lamp.

The darkness was divided. Moonlight fell through the window. Richard heard the blowing wind, felt the pounding of his heart, looking up, looking around, seeing the ceiling, the dark walls, his fears multiplying and joining and becoming a blanket. He suddenly felt claustrophobic, rubbed his face with his hands, saw the moonlight trickling over a cupboard and an empty white chair. He lay there, breathing deeply, forcing himself to stay calm. He wanted to get off the bed and leave the room, but he just couldn't do it. What was happening? *Why stay?* He rubbed his face and closed his eyes. He saw the moonlight—or he thought he saw the moonlight—and then it seemed like a dream.

The door clicked and then opened. Richard opened his eyes. He looked around—or he thought he looked around—and saw her shadowy outline. She was standing in the doorway, silhouetted in yellow light. She was naked beneath her nightgown, a short nightgown, transparent, and he saw her slim waist, her broad hips, her long legs parted slightly. She didn't say a word, simply stood there, looking at him. Richard rubbed his face and then licked his lips and stared up. The woman closed the door and walked toward him and lay down on the bed.

Flesh. The warmth of skin. There were dreams within the dreams: the moonlight falling on the white sheets, on the edge of a pillow, on a flash of red hair, the gleaming eyes, the pink tongue on the wet lips. They came together and merged, their limbs colliding, embracing, warm skin, willing flesh, her flattened breasts, his sweating spine, searching fingers, scratching nails, outspread thighs, thrusting groin, a dream within a dream, shadows writhing in the moonlight, rising up and falling down and rolling over and biting like animals . . . He had to have her, couldn't stop, either dreaming or awake, not caring, now knowing, seeking release from his fear, a child again, helpless, lips and tongue on the nipple, wanting solace, revenge, forgiveness, final answers, his hands searching for her breasts, his belly sliding on her belly, thrusting up, trying to hide himself inside her, sweat and blood, life's reality . . . Did it happen? Did it matter? The red hair across his eyes. Her face sliding down his chest, down his stomach, her lips open, receiving him . . . Release. No more fear. He looked up and saw the moonlight. He closed his eyes and let himself be devoured, flowing out, pouring into her.

The moonlight. The darkness. Stars swimming in the void. He lay back and dissolved and disappeared and defied space and time. To touch and be touched. The beating blood and pounding heart. To touch and to feel and to know and to drift toward peace. He remembered her touch. He awakened, still remembering. He blinked and rubbed his eyes and looked around him, his body still burning.

"It's all right, it's all right . . ."

Richard saw her in the doorway, her back turned toward him, naked beneath the white transparent gown, slipping out of the room. Then she was gone. He felt her flesh upon his flesh. He blinked again and looked hard at the door and saw the light on the balcony. Then the fear returned. He sat up straight on the bed. The moonlight fell into the room, met the light from the doorway, illuminating the necklace she had dropped before entering his bed.

The fear slithered in slyly, crept toward him, enveloped him, turned to ice that first froze and then burned and left him sweaty and shaking. He glanced wildly around the room. The moonlight fell through the window. He felt the fear and it forced him from the bed and made him run to the door.

He saw the woman on the stairs, walking down toward the hall, naked beneath the white, transparent slip, her lean body outlined. Richard stared at her, terrified. She walked as if in a trance. The nightgown rippled around her breasts, on her thighs, as she walked down on long legs. Richard grabbed hold of the bannister, seeing pale light on her face. He shouted at her—someone screaming, someone urging her to come back—but she continued to walk down the stairs, her eyes fixed on the front door.

Richard looked over the balcony. The lights in the hall were dim. The front door was open, moonlight falling on the hall, a small figure silhouetted on the porch, featureless, not moving.

The fear grabbed Richard and crushed him, made him move back from the bannister, press his spine to the wall and glance around him, paralyzed, his head spinning. Then he suddenly moved again. He felt a need to touch the woman. She was real, a vibrant presence, flesh and blood, and she was all that he had. Richard raced toward the stairs. He saw the woman in the hall. The figure standing on the porch had disappeared, but the moonlight poured in. Richard cried out again. The woman didn't look around. Richard ran down the stairs, his heart pounding, as she walked out the door.

Richard stopped, paralyzed. He held the bannister with one hand. He looked down at the door, at the moonlight, the fear slicing through him. Then he moved again, hardly knowing that he was doing it, his one thought for the woman, for her presence, for that touch of reality. He reached the bottom of the stairs. The moonlight fell across the floor. He stepped forward and saw the woman on the lawn, the darkness swimming around her.

Richard walked toward the door. The fear was choking him, draining him. He reached the door and stepped out onto the porch and saw the woman ahead of him. She was in the middle of the lawn. She stopped walking and just stood there. The wind blew her hair around her, pressed the white nightgown to her body, her hips and her legs emphasized in a singular beauty. Then she slowly turned around. She was looking directly at him. He saw her pale face, her streaming red hair, and her strange, haunting smile.

Richard stood on the porch, felt the wind and its ice. He was draining out of himself, the fear choking him, dulling his senses. The woman stood there on the lawn. Her red hair streamed in the wind. He heard the wind and then he heard the humming sound, *felt* the sound, was crushed by it. He stepped forward slowly, keeping his eyes on the woman. He saw the line of trees behind her, the light appearing beyond the trees, a hazy light that rose and spread out and became a pulsating fan.

"Oh, my God," Richard whispered.

After that, he said nothing. There was nothing to say. He knew that it had ended, that it was over, and that he could not turn back. No turning: the fear. No resisting: the pain. Richard shook his head and licked his dry lips and walked onto the lawn.

The woman was waiting for him, her arms hanging down by her sides. He stopped when he was halfway toward her, searched in vain for her green eyes. A trick of light and shadow. Richard blinked and looked again. He saw the smile on her face, that ghastly grimace, but her green eyes were missing. Richard shook his head and shivered. He stared hard at the waiting woman. He stepped forward and saw that her eyes were closed, that she was standing there dreaming.

Richard almost stopped breathing. He felt the pounding of his heart. He walked over to the woman and touched her, but her eyes didn't open. Then the fear really shook him. He stared wildly at the sky. He saw the moon gliding under the stars, a few dark, drifting clouds. Richard looked beyond the woman. He saw the light above the trees. The light pulsated and formed a hazy fan, a spectral glow in the dark night.

Richard started to weep. The tears rolled down his cheeks. He heard the sound, *felt* the sound, was crushed by it, and he clenched both fists. Then he saw them coming toward him. They were faceless in the darkness. There were three of them, all of them small, spreading out, walking slowly.

Richard stared at them. The fear slithered down his spine. He forgot the woman by his side, forgot the doctor and Jenny, thought of nothing but the dread that was embodied in the men walking toward him. The tears rolled down his cheeks. He saw his history dissolving. He watched the men spreading out, walking toward him, and he knew he must join them. His grief and fear combined. His head tightened and throbbed. The men walked out of darkness, the light spreading out behind them, their shadows hazy and falling before them, creeping over the damp grass. Richard stood there. The men approached him and stopped. They were small and they wore silvery masks and were dressed in gray coveralls. Richard stood there, transfixed. One of the men walked to him. The man reached up and touched Richard's neck and the fear fell away from him.

"Yes," Richard said.

CHAPTER TWENTY-TWO

New York in December was a bitch of a city, the wind blowing like ice along the canyons of concrete, stabbing at Stanford's eyes and raw face, his Californian blood frozen. He cursed and turned his collar up, saw the bright lights of Broadway, breathed the dust and the exhaust fumes of the traffic, appalled by the noise. He wasn't in a good mood, hadn't been for a long time; he now lived with a cold, suppressed rage that often threatened to strangle him.

"New York," he murmured. "Shitsville."

He didn't know what was happening to him, was lost in his obsessions, haunted by the lights of Galveston, by the girl on the porch, by the vision he had witnessed in the bay near St. Thomas, by the mysteries that increased every day and made sleep much more difficult.

Stanford felt the freezing wind. He cursed again and walked faster. The traffic ran along Broadway, lights flashing, horns honking, the pavements crowded with junkies and prostitutes and pimps, people tumbling out of cabs, out of restaurants and theaters, the neon signs flashing out against the night, a kaleidoscopic display. Stanford studied it with distaste. He had never liked New York. He cursed and then turned into the disco-bar, hurrying down the steep steps.

The disco was in a basement, beyond a silver-gleaming arch, past the blond girl who sat behind a desk and a glit-

tering cash register. The girl was wearing a negligible halter, her breasts ballooning dramatically, her tanned belly
exposed, her crotch emphasized by hot pants, long legs in
black stockings, crossed languidly; green lipstick, false eye-
lashes. Stanford paid her and walked through, passing a
man in black leather, the amplified rock music exploding
over him, deafening him, the strobe lights flashing on and
off the stage where a glitter group screamed.

"Are you alone?" someone hissed.

"What's that?" Stanford said. He looked around to see a
shock of purple hair, rainbow eyes, the girl looking like a
cross between an Apache Indian and a Buddhist monk,
her lips lined with glitter dust and pouting invitingly,
blowing smoke in his face.

"Thirty bucks," she hissed. "Make it fifty for all night.
We go to my place and I'll show you some tricks that
you'll never forget."

Stanford shook his head and left, pushing his way
through the crowd, brushing against creamy breasts and
jolting asses in tight pants, the air smelling of nicotine and
marijuana and sweat, the strobe lights flashing on and off
the heads that bobbed up and down crazily. Stanford just
kept on going, concentrating on the bar. He saw phos-
phorescent shirts and tight denims and sunglasses, the girls
elegant and tatty, displaying tits and belly buttons, the
men rattling with necklaces and bracelets, their talk loud
and pretentious. Scaduto wasn't at the bar. Stanford
moved on, looking elsewhere. He cut across the dance
floor, the band shrieking just above him, the dancers gy-
rating all around him, asses jolting like pistons, ducked
flying hands and long, whipping hair, and finally reached
the far side. A line of girls held the wall up, glittering
brightly, looking limp, and he avoided their eyes and went
past them, entering another large room.

The band seemed more distant here, the sound muffled,
the talk clearer, people crushed between a parallel line of
booths that led back to another bar. He saw Scaduto at
the bar, unmistakable, flamboyantly dressed, wearing a
fringed buckskin jacket, very tight purple pants, knee-
length boots, a mess of chains around his neck, hanging

over the bar. Stanford walked up behind him and grabbed his long blond tangled hair.

"What the fuck—?" Scaduto yelped.

"Hi, hotshot," Stanford said. "What the hell did you tell me to meet you here for? I can hardly hear myself speak."

Scaduto grinned and slapped Stanford's back. Stanford let go of his hair. "You old shitface!" Scaduto said, patting his hair down. "How you bin? Great to see you!"

Stanford smiled and glanced around him. "What the hell are you doing here?" he said. "You're getting a bit old for this, aren't you? I mean, these girls . . . they're all *kids*."

Scaduto rolled his eyes and grinned, formed his right hand into a tube, pumped it up and down above his groin and groaned loudly, theatrically.

"That's the idea," he said. "A guy doesn't get any younger. At forty they're ready to put you out to grass, and these kids soothe the pain. I like 'em tight, Stanford. Oh *fuck*, I like 'em tight. Some day I'm gonna find one so tight, they'll have to cut my dick off."

"You want a drink?" Stanford said.

"I've already got one," Scaduto said.

"Have another," Stanford said. "I'm only in town for one night. Let's have an old-fashioned reunion. We'll throw us a big one."

Scaduto rolled his eyes and grinned, slapped the counter with one hand. "Goddammit!" he exclaimed. "What a turn-up! It's been a long time, old buddy."

"What do you want?" Stanford said.

"I'll have a bourbon on the rocks. Fuck it, the night's just begun—let's have us a good time."

There was only one barman, moving fast but overworked, serving two or three groups all at once, his head down, his brow furrowed. Stanford tried to attract his attention, failed, tried again, started wondering if the barman was ignoring him or if the noise had just deafened him. Scaduto came to his rescue, getting off his tall stool, bending forward, his long body across the bar, his hair falling around him. "Hey, greaser!" he bawled. "What the fuck? Are you jerking off back there?" The barman glanced at him, face swarthy above a bow tie, glared and then recognized Scaduto and broke out in a grin. "Does it feel good?" Scaduto bawled. "You got blisters on your fingers? Two bourbons on the rocks, you fucking greaser, or I won't pay my bills." The barman grinned and shook his head, poured the drinks, disappeared, and Scaduto turned and grinned at Stanford and then laughed as if he just couldn't stop.

"Here's to you," Stanford said.

"Fucking right," Scaduto said. He had a drink and wiped his lips with his wrist, his glassy eyes sliding sideways. "Just look at it," he said. "All that tight stuff, all that honey. I swear, the world's coming to an end—they just can't get enough of it."

"You're kidding yourself," Stanford said. "You're just a middle-aged *roué*. You can't stand the thought of being forty and now you're making an ass of yourself."

Scaduto leered and glanced around him, almost falling off the stool, then he reached out and grabbed Stanford's shoulder and grinned like a lunatic.

"Fucking right," he said. "I stand unzipped and corrected. I'm a middle-aged prick, a wilting dick, and I'm having a great time. So how are you, Stanford? What the fuck have you been doing? How long's it been—five years, ten years? I hear you're still with that Epstein guy."

"That's right," Stanford said. "I'm still with Professor Epstein. You and I, we last met in '69—when you finally left NICAP."

Scaduto grinned and shook his head, his body swaying from side to side, his stomach flopping over the glittering belt, the shirt youthful, too tight.

"Great days," Scaduto said. "I had a fucking good time. Wandering over the whole country, meeting people, seeing places, chasing UFOs like they were going out of fashion—a great time, a fond memory." He almost fell off the stool, steadied himself, glanced around him, then stared at the bag on Stanford's shoulder and said. "Hey, what you got there?"

"Just a shoulder bag," Stanford said.

"Oh, yeah?" Scaduto said. "Carrying anything of interest? Anything I can swallow or smoke or inject? I mean anything, old buddy, to light my fire and get me through the long night?"

"No," Stanford said.

"Not to worry," Scaduto said. He closed one eye and waved a finger across his face, a stage Irishman, drunk. "We can always go back to my place. I've got a few syringes there. A little nip, a little jab and then it's Heaven, a slow glide through inner space. You fancy that, old buddy? We might even get some cunt. Something warm, something tight as a glove, to make the dawn look more pleasant."

"Who knows?" Stanford said.

They ordered more drinks. The smoke swirled all around them. The room was packed and noisy, people tugging and pushing, colored lights drifting over the walls in surreal, dreamy patterns. Scaduto drank very fast. He kept ordering more drinks. He was obsessed by the girls, by their legs and plunging necklines, his glassy eyes darting restlessly around the room, his wolfish leer unappealing. Stanford was shocked by him, found it hard to recognize him, was embarrassed to see this forty-year-old man in his juvenile clothes. In truth, he was ridiculous, pathetically trying to fool himself, and Stanford couldn't reconcile the man before him with the man he had known. Scaduto had been with NICAP for close to twelve years, had investigated UFOs up and down the whole country and had built up a strong reputation. He had left in 1969. He had been in Arizona then. He and Stanford had gone drinking, had painted Tucson red, and had then gone their separate ways and had not kept in touch. That's why Stanford was shocked: he couldn't recognize the old Scaduto. The man swaying on the bar stool, talking loudly, leering openly, was a pathetic, shocking shadow of his former self, obsessed with drugs and young girls.

"I'm still at it," Stanford said. "I'm still out there chasing UFOs. I guess I've been at it too long. Why did you give it up?"

"I thought, fuck it," Scaduto said. "That's all: I just thought, fuck it. There was too much coming down, too much flak, and I just didn't need it."

"What sort of flak?" Stanford said.

"Just flak," Scaduto said. "Flak from the left, right and center, every day, a real drag."

"I got a bottle," Stanford said. "Here, fill your glass up, I don't understand. What kind of flak? Who was giving you flak?"

Scaduto swayed from side to side, almost fell off his stool, held onto the counter and cursed, reaching for his glass.

"Everyone," he said. "Fucking flak from every bastard. Who needs them? Who needs the CIA, the FBI, the fucking Air Force? Couldn't take it anymore. Too much shit in the bathtub. When they started to pay me visits at midnight, I decided to quit."

"Midnight?" Stanford said.

"Would you believe it?" Scaduto said.

"Who started coming to see you at midnight? I don't understand that."

Scaduto nearly fell off his seat. Stanford grabbed him and held him up. Scaduto leered at the girl beside him, had a drink, smoothed his long hair, gazed down at the bar and started snorting like a horse at the starting post.

"Fucking CIA," he said. "Fucking bastards came to see me. Came at midnight, got me out of my bed, my cock still standing straight. No rough stuff. Just questions. A formality. A mere formality. Sat me naked in a chair, froze my balls and talked very polite, like we're having a business lunch. Very pleasant. Very quiet. Didn't mind if I poured a drink. Said it's your house, you do what you want, we're just here for a talk. Asked me some questions. About NICAP and our work. Said they'd heard from a friend of a friend that I was digging too deep. Then we had a little chat. Woke me up. Interesting. They said they hoped I wasn't feeling too tired, but could they make some suggestions. Suggest, I say; I'm breathless. They suggest I clip my wings. They say I shouldn't be mixed up with UFOs, that they don't really like that. I say it's a free country. They assure me that it is. They also say they saw some drugs in my bathroom, and that that isn't legal. I tell them it's a setup. I say you're setting me up. They tell me that's a nasty thing to say and that I could get ten years. You want me to leave, I say? You want me to leave

NICAP? We wouldn't dream of suggesting such a thing, they say. You can do what you want. A free country, they say. I can work where I want. It's just that they're worried about those drugs that they found in my bathroom. I say I'm sorry about that. I say I'm truly repentant. They say maybe it's the strain of chasing UFOs that's making me take them. You have a point there, I say. I say I'm gonna resign from NICAP. They say that's a wise decision, we respect you for that, and maybe, if you really leave NICAP, we'll forget what we found. That's real decent, I say. I confirm that I'm resigning. They both shake my hand, very pleasant, and walk out the door. So, I resign from NICAP. I get a job with RCA. I forget that I ever knew NICAP, and they never come back. Hallelujah. Peace, brother."

Scaduto burped and glanced around him, smiled beautifully and grabbed the counter, swayed dangerously from side to side, his eyes blinking, then reached out for his glass.

"Fuck," he said, "it's empty."

"I bought a bottle," Stanford said. "Here, have another, it's on me. What the hell were they worried about?"

Stanford filled Scaduto's glass, watched him put it to his lips, drink and then burp and put his glass down, his red eyes slipping sideways.

"Motherfuckers," he said.

"What bothered them?" Stanford said.

Scaduto closed one eye and waved his finger, playing up as an Irishman.

"Secrets," he slurred. "*Secrets!* I knew things I shouldn't know. Those sonsofbitches, they knew I'd been to Canada—and they didn't like that."

"Canada?" Stanford said.

"A fucking pisspot," Scaduto said. "Very cold in the forests, very quiet, and at night the wind haunted you."

"I don't understand," Stanford said. "What's Canada got to do with it? They accused you of digging too deep. What did they mean by that?"

Scaduto grabbed him by the arm, leaned closer, breathed in his face, his eyes darting left and right, melodramatically, hissing his words.

"What have you got in the bag?" he said.

"Nothing," Stanford said. "Some papers, a calculator, odds and ends—it's just a traveling bag."

"You're going somewhere?" Scaduto said.

"I just got here," Stanford said.

"Of course," Scaduto hissed. "Stupid of me. Forgot. What you got there?"

"Nothing," Stanford said.

"Jesus Christ," Scaduto said. "A little smoke, a little coke, a little something to shoot? What the fuck, we can't go on like this forever—I'll take just about anything."

"I didn't bring anything," Stanford said. "I'm only here for one night. Here, fill your glass, have a drink; we'll get something else later."

Stanford filled Scaduto's glass. Scaduto nodded his appreciation. He put the glass to his lips and drank deeply, shook his head, looked around him.

"Sonsofbitches," he said. "Those sonsofbitches made me leave. I had a good time at that time, but those bastards just killed it."

"Why?" Stanford said.

"My discoveries," Scaduto said. "Very cold up in Canada, the forests, all that shit in the forests."

"What shit?" Stanford said.

"The fucking truth," Scaduto said. "I found out and I braced them with the facts and then they paid me the visits."

"You took the facts to the CIA?"

"Whistled in like the breeze. You fuckers know all about it, I said. You fuckers knew all along."

"Knew what?"

"They kicked me out. They took my papers and kicked me out. They said don't come around again, you're fucking crazy, it's a lie, then they paid me those cute midnight visits and made me leave NICAP."

"What papers?" Stanford said.

"Hey, listen," Scaduto said, grabbing Stanford by the arm, leaning closer and hissing into his face, the red eyes darting left and right. "Let's get out of here, old buddy. Let's go back to my place. Fuck the cunt, they'll only give us the pox, let's get high the clean way. I've got some hot shit back there. Fucking blow your head off. I've got cable TV and we'll shoot us some stuff and then watch a blue movie and do it that way. Okay, buddy? Let's go."

He stood up and fell forward, tripping over his stool, crashing into Stanford's shoulder and spinning off and knocking into some people. Stanford reached out and grabbed him, held him up, shook him lightly, and he straightened his shoulders and looked around him, outraged by the angry stares. "Stupid cunts," he said. "You can't get out for the stupid bastards." Then he shook his head and grinned, threw an arm around Stanford, said, "Let's go, old buddy, let's get out, let's blow our brains through the roof." They pushed their way through the crowds, through the surreal, strobe-lit darkness, passed the dance floor, the long line of ladies, the rock music pounding. Scaduto waved to some friends, shouted out, his white teeth gleaming, still clinging onto Stanford, unsteady, his face a jigsaw of colors. It took a long time to reach the stairs, the crowds thicker than before, the pert buttocks and the bulging breasts teasing as they stumbled on through. Eventually they made it, stepping under the silvery arch, stumbling up the stairs, Stanford supporting Scaduto and stepping into the night.

"Jesus Christ," Scaduto said. "All the lights, they're fucking blinding me. Jesus, I just love it here on Broadway, I just love the Big Apple."

"Where do you live?" Stanford said.

"In SoHo," Scaduto said. "I got a little loft there in Broome Street. We'll be there in no time."

He started off along the sidewalk, swaying dangerously from side to side, and Stanford rushed up and stuck close beside him, not wanting to lose him. The neon signs flickered crazily, the cars roared and honked their horns, and the sidewalks were crowded, people queuing for the theaters, the whores standing at the side streets in their flame-colored clothes, hopeful customers silhouetted by the bright lights of the huge plate glass windows. Stanford saw it and ignored it, now obsessed with cracking Scaduto, just wanting to get him back to his loft, sober him up, get him talking.

"Those hookers," Scaduto said. "Those fucking bitches get me going. Just look at that black bitch wearing nothing—I mean, she's practically naked. What about it, old buddy? You think we should take one back? We'll take the Amazon and share her between us, shoot some stuff, have a threesome."

"I'd rather shoot first," Stanford said. "And I don't like to pay for it. Let's go back to the loft and shoot up and then I'll make a few phone calls."

"That's my Stanford," Scaduto said. "Always in there with the phone book. The most famous fucking phone book in the country, and it's always paid dividends. You had a reputation, Stanford. I'll have to give you that. When it came to getting the cunt, you could do it, no two ways about it."

They turned into Broome Street, stumbling along the sidewalk, passing art galleries and antique shops, health food stores and fresh food restaurants, the old warehouses converted, repainted, decorated, the fire escapes saluting the past, the noise falling behind them.

"Those sonsofbitches," Scaduto mumbled. "Those CIA sonsofbitches. I'm earning twice as much as I did before, but it's just not the same."

"A raw deal," Stanford said.

"Fucking right, a raw deal. Now I'm a salesman for fucking RCA, and that's why I'm so fucked."

"What worried them?" Stanford said.

"What I found out," Scaduto said.

"What did you find out?" Stanford asked.

"Fucking Canada. My *God!*"

Scaduto stopped at a converted warehouse, almost fell against the wall, straightened up and plunged his hands in his pockets and eventually pulled out a key. He had trouble finding the keyhole, kept cursing and mumbling, finally managed to push the door open and stagger inside. Stanford followed him in, opened the gates of the elevator, a large elevator once used for heavy goods, now used only by residents. Scaduto swayed as they went up, holding languidly to the gate, tried to open it when the elevator stopped, then had to let Stanford do it. The door opposite was large and ugly, the paint stripped, the wood flaking, but the loft behind the door was luxurious, a plush *Playboy*-styled penthouse.

"Wow," Stanford said. "Is this yours?"

"Fuck it," Scaduto said. "I feel ill. I gotta fix myself up."

He burped and slapped his belly, shook his head as if dizzy, then walked along the clean, polished floorboards of the enormous, rectangular loft. The walls and ceiling were white, stretching back to a wall-length window, the living area situated near the window, illuminated by spotlights. Stanford walked behind Scaduto, impressed by the decor, passing a vast spectrum-colored picture that covered the right-hand wall, its colors fading as they neared the large window where in daytime the light poured in. Scaduto stumbled and almost fell, grabbed a table of natural pine, straightened up and skirted around a modern couch and stopped beneath an arched Flors lamp.

"Christ," he said, "I feel shitty. I think my head's stuck up my ass. The room's spinning, the walls are closing in, what the fuck are we doing here?"

"I want to talk to you," Stanford said.

"You want to shoot?" Scaduto said. He took his jacket off and threw it on the couch and started rolling his sleeve up. "Those fucking sonsofbitches killed me. They put the fear of God up me. Very nice. Very polite. Regular gentlemen. Planted pot in my bathroom."

"I thought you took that anyway."

"I didn't have it at the time. I was clean as a whistle, the fucking bathroom was bare, and those bastards had me set for ten years because I hit them with Canada."

"I want to talk about that," Stanford said.

"No way, buddy, I'm not talking. That bathroom's not bare anymore and I want to shoot up."

"I'm not joining you," Stanford said.

"Have a drink," Scaduto said. "Relax, put your feet up, watch TV; we'll call some hookers and burn ourselves."

"I have to know," Stanford said.

"Fuck you, baby, I'm not talking. It never happened. I can't remember, I know nothing. I won't talk, it's not worth it."

Scaduto finished rolling his sleeve up, shook his head, glanced around him, licked his lips and then walked to the door that led into the bathroom. Stanford watched him disappearing, felt desperate and outraged, wondering what he could say to this lunatic to shake him out of his stupor. The loft had central heating. Stanford felt very warm. He felt dizzy with rage and frustration, and he wanted to smash something. It couldn't happen again: he couldn't let this one go. Stanford stood there and let the rage take him and shake him awake. Then he cursed and turned around, walked across the rush matting, stopped once, clenched his fists very tight, then walked into the bathroom.

Red walls. Mirrored panels. The bath unit was charcoal brown. Scaduto stood there with one foot on the bath, his knee supporting his elbow. He was tying the tourniquet to his arm. He had one end between his teeth. His fist was clenched and a vein throbbed in his neck, beads of sweat on his forehead. Stanford glanced at the dark brown unit. He saw the gleaming hypodermic. Scaduto grunted and tugged at the tourniquet and then looked up at Stanford.

"I have to know," Stanford said.

The tourniquet slipped from Scaduto's teeth. "What the fuck are you talking about?" he said. "Can't you see what I'm doing here?"

"I have a contact," Stanford said. "A strong CIA contact. He said that you had found something out that could blow this whole thing."

"Fuck off out of here," Scaduto said. "You sonofabitch, that's why you came. I must be fucking dumb. I should have known. Just get the fuck out of here."

"I have to know," Stanford said.

"I know nothing," Scaduto said. "If I knew, I would have blown it to the papers and made myself rich."

"You're frightened," Stanford said.

"Go to hell. Get out of here. I don't know what the hell you're talking about. Fuck off, Stanford. Just leave me."

"Tell me."

"I'm shooting up. Jesus Christ, I can't think straight. I've got my head in my ass, my nerves are singing, and you're just fucking killing me. I don't know anything, Stanford. I don't remember, I don't care. I'm shooting up and you're not going to stop me and that's all there is to it."

Stanford moved in very fast, his left hand swinging sideways, sweeping Scaduto's bent leg off the bath and making it slam to the floor. Scaduto's body jerked forward, following the line of his leg, and Stanford moved in and grabbed him by the hair and cracked the head on his knee. Scaduto yelped and jerked back up, his head shaking, mouth open, his hands flapping and trying to cover his belly when he saw Stanford's punch. A sluggish gesture, too late—Stanford's fist punched his belly; Scaduto doubled up and Stanford grabbed him by the hair and threw him into the wall. Scaduto gasped and seemed to dance, his arms waving, legs shaking, then he groaned, turned around, his hands reaching for the basin, leaned over the basin and vomited, his whole body shuddering.

Stanford stood there, feeling cold, far removed from himself, waited until Scaduto had turned around and then hit him again. It was another blow to the stomach, one blow, sharp and brutal, and Scaduto just grunted, doubled up, reached out for him, grabbed Stanford and slid down his legs and then collapsed on the floor.

Stanford knelt down, rolled Scaduto onto his back, grabbed him under the armpits and pulled him up and heard him mumbling and groaning. He dragged Scaduto toward the shower, stepped in backwards, laid him down, pushed him into a fetal position and then turned the shower on. Scaduto yelped and started flapping, still not fully awake, the water drenching his clothes, forming a pool all around him, as he groaned and kicked his legs and waved his arms, a fish flung on the shore. Stanford kept changing the temperature, first hot, then icy cold, and Scaduto opened his eyes and started bawling, slithering around on the wet tiles. Stanford kept the shower going, hot and cold, hot and cold, and Scaduto bawled a stream of colorful abuse and slithered around like a drowning rat. He finally stood on his hands and knees, shaking his head, pouring water, cursed and tried to crawl from the shower and was kicked back by Stanford. Scaduto howled and waved his hands. He managed to get up on his knees. He was gasping and he swayed from side to side, the water hissing down over him. Stanford turned the shower off. Scaduto groaned and flopped forward. Stanford grabbed him and dragged him over the bloodred tiles, past the path, through the door. Scaduto kicked and waved his arms, sluggish movements, devoid of strength, and Stanford dragged him across the living room, still struggling and protesting, then left him on the floor before the couch and stood there and just stared at him.

Scaduto lay there and shivered, shook his head, groaned and cursed, his fingers scrabbling at the squares of rush matting, the steam still rising off him. Stanford stood there, saying nothing, breathing deeply, fists clenched, feeling cold and removed from himself, determined to finish it. Eventually Scaduto moved, propped himself up on his hands, shook his head and struggled up on his hands and knees, a colt learning to walk. He shook his head and stared at Stanford, took a deep breath, turned sideways, then hauled himself up on to the couch, and slumped there, looking stunned.

Stanford walked across the room. He had left his traveling bag on the table. He picked the bag up and quickly unzipped it and pulled out a small tape recorder. He set the tape recorder on the table, threw the bag to the floor. Scaduto watched him, his glassy eyes wary, still red and unfocused. Then Stanford walked over toward him, knelt down right in front of him, reached out and grabbed him by the collar and shook him a little.

"You're going to talk to me," Stanford said. "You're going to tell me all you know. We're going to sit here all night, you're going to talk and keep talking, and we'll go over it again and again until I've got what I want. You don't have to be formal about it. Just lay it down as it comes. I'm putting it all down on tapes, I'm going to cross-check and edit, and when I've finished it will all be in sequence and sound quite intelligent. I'm not bullshitting, Scaduto. I want to drain your damned brain. I want everything, from your first day to your last, and I want no evasions. If you're a good boy, I'll reward you: I'll let you shoot up. If you're a bad boy, I'll knock the shit out of you and then start again. And don't try lying, Scaduto. Don't try leaving things out. If you lie, or if you leave anything out, I'll go straight to the CIA. I'll show them what you've given me. That should be enough to choke them. They'll be around here so fast, you won't know your balls from your ass. So don't mess with me, Scaduto. Talk long and talk well. If you give me what I want, if it's correct, I'll never mention my source. I'm turning the tape recorder on now. I'm going to sit down here beside you. Just relax, put your feet up and talk, and the night will soon pass."

Stanford went to the table, picked the tape recorder up, bent down and picked up his traveling bag and then returned to the couch. He sat down beside Scaduto. He reached into the traveling bag. He pulled out a lot of cassettes and set them down on the table, placed them on the table one by one until they formed a neat pile. Scaduto stared at all the tapes. He licked his lips and shivered slightly. Stanford picked up the first tape, slipped it into the small recorder, turned the recorder on and then sat down, looking right at Scaduto.

"That's it," he said. "Talk."

CHAPTER TWENTY-THREE

"My phone's been bugged," Epstein said quietly. "That's why we're out walking."

It was nighttime in Washington, and they walked through the streets of Georgetown, passing discos and restaurants.

"Bugged?" Stanford said. "You've been *bugged*? Why the hell would they do that?"

Epstein turned his collar up. He looked older and very frail. He coughed a lot and rubbed his eyes constantly, rarely raising his head.

"I'm not sure," he said. "It obviously happened when I was away. I think it's got something to do with London and young Richard Watson."

"No one knew about that," Stanford said.

"My passport," Epstein said. "It makes me nervous. They must be watching us carefully. I think it started in St. Thomas."

"Mr. Gerhardt," Stanford said.

"That's right," Epstein said. "They're disturbed that we saw what we saw, and I'd like to know why."

"Fucking CIA," Stanford said.

"Yes," Epstein said.

"Where we go, people just disappear. It's not a comforting thought."

They were in Wisconsin Avenue, passing kids wearing baubles, the vendors defying the weather and hawking their wares. Stanford hardly saw a soul, now buried inside his head, obsessed by the girl in Galveston, by his experience in the Caribbean, by the revelations of Goldman and O'Hara, by Scaduto's long story. Stanford knew he couldn't leave it; he was hooked right through the throat. No matter what might happen in the future, he now had to continue.

"You said Scaduto was sensational," Epstein said. "All right. Let me hear it."

Stanford shrugged. "I don't know where to start," he said. "The whole story's just fucking incredible—and it's pretty damned complex." He glanced briefly around him, his eyes stung by the bright lights, heard the sound of disco music pouring out from a crimson-lit doorway. "Okay," he said. "The basic background to Scaduto is that he was working for the National Investigations Committee on Aerial Phenomena way back in 1957 when they first started up."

"NICAP," Epstein said. "A civilian organization. Not too good a background at all: the outside looking in."

"They're an efficient organization," Stanford said, "and damned well you know it."

Epstein smiled gently, huddled up against the cold, almost lost in the thick, furlined coat, the street lights washing over him.

"Right," Stanford said. "I hope I can continue now. You know, of course, about the Levelland sightings."

"Of course," Epstein said. "Probably the most remarkable sightings on record. November 2, 1957. Seven different automobile drivers, all at different locations around Levelland, Texas, suffered at approximately the same time inexplicable car disablement and subsequent recovery after coming across large, egg-shaped, glowing metallic objects which were sitting on the roads and then ascended vertically and disappeared. The Air Force later caused themselves acute embarrassment by (a) not examining the reported landing sites, and (b) attributing the cause of the sightings to an electrical storm that was not in fact in the area of Levelland at that time."

"Full marks," Stanford said. "So, the Levelland sightings formed a sort of grand climax to the biggest UFO flap since 1952. Those sightings caused the Air Force a lot of embarrassment and led to NICAP pushing for congressional hearings. In August 1958 John McCormack's House Sub-Committee on Atmospheric Phenomena requested a week-long hearing in closed, secret session, but NICAP's pleasure at this was quickly guillotined. Any hope that the hearing would be a fair one was destroyed by the evidence of Captain George Gregory, then representing Project Blue Book, who came out with so many half-truths he made Menzel seem Christlike. Given this, as you can imagine, the House Sub-Committee decided to take no further interest in the matter."

"So?"

"NICAP was furious. And they were even more furious when, in December of that year, the Air Force published a staff study that came down heavily on the civilian UFO groups, accusing them of being biased and sensationalist. To make matters worse, it was during that same month that NICAP found out, through one of the more powerful members of the NICAP board, that the Robertson Panel, in making their recommendations back in 1953, had, when discussing civilian UFO groups then in existence, used the chilling phrase: 'The apparent irresponsibility and the possible use of such groups for subversive purposes should be kept in mind' and, further, when they discovered that both the FBI and the CIA had been keeping extensive records on people involved in UFO investigations, including quite a few members of NICAP."

Epstein smiled and nodded wearily, rubbed his eyes and coughed a little, looked away when an elegant prostitute started walking toward him.

"Now," Stanford said, "stories about the CIA's involvement in the UFO phenomenon had been circulating for years, but a lot of people put it down to paranoia. However, after Gregory's performance in front of the House Sub-Committee, and after learning about the Robertson Panel recommendations, some of the people at NICAP, including Scaduto, decided to check out the situation. Then, just after they started, one of the members of their board came up with a pretty amazing story."

The prostitute kept trailing them, swinging her shoulder

bag, looking prosperous in her long coat and boots, the breeze blowing her dark hair. Stanford glanced at her briefly, thought of the girl in Galveston, experienced a sudden, blinding lust, and then waved his right hand. The woman shrugged and turned away, a neon sign flashed green and red, and the snow drifted lazily along the ground as Epstein stared at his own feet.

"Apparently," Stanford continued, "just a few weeks earlier—this was 1959—the Office of Naval Intelligence had heard of a woman in Maine who claimed to be in contact with extraterrestrials and brought that fact to the CIA's attention. Since this seemed like a typical crank contactee case in which the woman, a psychic, had used automatic handwriting for communication with the extraterrestrials, the CIA naturally gave it a miss. However, the Canadian government had also heard about the woman and they sent their leading UFOlogist to interview her. According to the Canadian expert that woman, during a trance, had correctly answered highly complex questions about space flight. Surprisingly, when the U.S. Navy learned about this, they sent *two* intelligence officers to investigate. During the subsequent interview, one of the Navy intelligence officers, who had been trained in ESP, tried to tune in to the woman's contactee; this experiment failed, so he and his associate returned to Washington and informed the CIA. This time the CIA displayed more interest than before and arranged for the intelligence officer to try making contact in CIA headquarters. Six witnesses— two of them CIA employees and one of them from the Office of Naval Intelligence—got together in the office in Washington to observe the results of the experiment—and this time, when the intelligence officer went into his trance, he reportedly made contact with *someone*."

Stanford glanced at Epstein, trying to gauge his reaction, but Epstein was gazing down at the ground, looking frail in his heavy coat.

"At that point," Stanford said, "one of the men in the room demanded some kind of proof that they were in contact with extraterrestrials. The intelligence officer, still in his trance, said that if they looked out the window they would see a flying saucer over Washington. The other three men went straight to the window and were amazed to see a UFO in the sky—a description of which has never been released. However, it *has* been established that at the time of the supposed sighting, the radar center at Washington National Airport reported that its radar returns had been blocked out in the direction of the sightings."

Epstein glanced up at the sky, saw dark clouds drifting lazily, dropped his gaze and stared forlornly at the snow, rubbed his eyes, coughed again.

"So," Stanford said. "Major Robert J. Friend—who had since replaced Captain Gregory as head of Project Blue Book—was informed of these events by the CIA and asked to sit in on a later trance session during which, reportedly, nothing unusual happened. Nevertheless, Friend felt that Duke University's parapsychology lab should investigate both the psychic and the intelligence officer, which they subsequently did . . . but their report never materialized, Blue Book released no analysis of the sighting report, the government did nothing about the Washington radar blackout, and what the intelligence officer saw over Washington remained a tight secret. Not only that, but the CIA took 'punitive' action against the men involved, and had them all transferred to other positions."

"That story is authentic," Epstein said. "Major Friend wrote about the whole affair in a Memorandum for the Record—a memorandum that can now be found in the Air Force Archives at Maxwell Air Force Base, Montgomery, Alabama."

"Right," Stanford said. "And that's exactly what got Scaduto going. First, Scaduto wondered at the unusual amount of official interest displayed in a civilian female with supposed telepathic abilities. Scaduto was aware that both the Russian KGB and the CIA had been investigating the espionage potential of telepathy, psychic photography and other forms of parapsychology, and he therefore wondered if there could be any connection between that fact and the psychic from Maine. Since communication by telepathy had already been attained with moderate success both in Russian and American laboratories and between submarines and land bases, it was possible that the CIA was genuinely concerned with the woman's knowledge of the more complex aspects of space flight. It also stands to reason, since they themselves were interested in the espionage potential of telepathy, that they would have certain men trained in ESP—thus, they sent one of their men to attend the trance sessions."

"I don't see where this is leading," Epstein said.

"Patience," Stanford said. "The first thing Scaduto had to accept was that telepathic communication had been made with *someone* in that CIA office in Washington—and that the man in a trance, if not actually making it materialize, had been informed that there was a UFO in the sky. If he then kept in mind the fact that certain secret military laboratories had succeeded in training people in telepathic communication—which had been done in a primitive fashion years before—it then seemed more possible that the woman from Maine had actually been in contact with some telepathically trained *government* employee."

"Wait a minute," Epstein said, looking a lot more interested. "Are you suggesting that the UFO over Washington was a *government* aircraft?"

"Yes," Stanford said. "And for Scaduto, this possibility became even more intriguing when he thought of the U.S. Navy Intelligence's interest in the matter and, even more intriguing, when one of the members of NICAP's board of directors reminded him that the Canadian government and the U.S. Air Force had both acknowledged their involvement in supposedly unsuccessful flying saucer construction projects."

Epstein suddenly stopped walking, glanced up at the sky, then looked all around him, at the snow on the ground, at the discos and restaurants and bars, his eyes bright with excitement.

"I'm hungry," Stanford said. "Let's get something to eat. Also, I don't like all this walking and I want to sit down."

They went into Clyde's, enjoyed the warmth and the saloon atmosphere, sat down and gave the waitress their orders and didn't speak until she left. Stanford studied Epstein's face: he looked ill, but more alive. Stanford thought of them both, of Epstein's fate and his own obsessions, and he had to beat down the cold rage that now drove him relentlessly. His old friend was soon to die. The pains of cancer now assailed him. Stanford wanted to give him something—all the answers—before death cut him down.

"Okay," Stanford said. "Bear in mind that at least *some* kind of flying saucer prototypes had actually been built by the U.S. and Canada: first, the U.S. Navy's Flying Flounder and the Air Force's Flying Flapjack—projects reportedly worked on between 1942 and 1947—then the mysterious flying saucer that the Canadian government claimed they had aborted and passed over to the U.S. in 1954. Now the most interesting thing about those projects was that, one, the U.S. Navy claimed to have dropped their project back in 1947, but were known to be still involved in super-secret aeronautical projects scattered around the White Sands Proving Ground; and, two, the Canadian government, while admitting that the enormous UFO seen over Albuquerque in 1951 was similar to the one they had tried to build, claimed that they had passed their project on to the U.S. because they couldn't afford to continue it."

"So what you're saying is that the UFO over Albuquerque might have been a U.S. product based on the 1947 Canadian designs."

"Right . . . And that everyone's admitted that they had once tried building saucers, but all are now denying that they succeeded—which could well be a lie."

"I see," Epstein said.

"Now remember," Stanford continued, "that Scaduto had started to investigate these questions in the Year of our Lord, 1959. The first thing he remembered was that the first major UFO sighting—the Kenneth Arnold sightings of June 24, 1947—had taken place near Mount Ranier in the Cascades in the state of Washington—which divides Canada from Oregon—and that Arnold had stated that the *nine* UFOs had disappeared in the direction of the Canadian border. What is *not* so widely known is that on that very same day another man, Fred Johnson, prospecting about 4,000 feet above the Cascades, reported seeing six similar objects, and that three days before, on June 21, Harold Dahl, on harbor patrol in Puget Sound—which runs from the Canadian border to Tacoma—was following

the coastline of Maury Island when he reportedly saw five
UFOs maneuvering 1,500 feet above the coast before disappearing toward the open sea. Throughout that whole
month—even ignoring the crank reports encouraged by
the initial sightings—there was a disturbing number of
sightings over the northwest corner of the United States,
and by the first week in July there were reports of
'strange, luminous bodies' in the skies over the Province of
Quebec, Oregon and New England. The following week
those sightings spread to California and New Mexico, and
by the end of that year—the same year that the U.S. Navy
had, apparently, *dropped* their flying saucer project—flying saucers were being reported from all over the world."

"So you're suggesting that the U.S. Navy, the U.S. Air
Force and the Canadian government were all working together to build those saucers."

"Yes," Stanford said. "The next major flap was the
Washington flap of 1952. On reinvestigating that case,
Scaduto found that while the real flap had started on July
19, there was a record, dated June 17, of several unidentified red spheres that flew at supersonic speeds over the
Canadian Air Base of North Bay in Ontario and then
crossed over some of the southeastern states. He also discovered that nearly all of the subsequent Washington
UFOs were described as disappearing toward the south,
and that when the UFOs returned *en masse*, on July 26,
their disappearance in a general southerly direction also
applied."

"All heading toward the Canadian border," Epstein
said.

"Right," Stanford said.

The waitress brought their food, set it down and smiled
at Stanford, did not receive a smile in return and flounced
off in a huff. Epstein had ordered a Spanish omelet and a
glass of cold milk, drank the latter down in one thirsty
gulp and then stared at the former. Stanford stared at him,
perturbed, feeling sorry for his plight, then he picked up
his own bacon cheeseburger and sank his teeth into it.

"It adds up," Epstein said. "Lake Ontario and Lake Erie
are as notorious as the Bermuda Triangle for the unexplained destruction of hundreds of aircraft and ships, the

failure of gyroscopes and radio instruments, irrational behavior in normally sane crew members and, of course, the sighting of numerous UFOs. It's also worth noting that Canada, contrary to popular belief, is one of the greatest aeronautical powers in the world, that as far back as 1952 it had been described as the Promised Land of Aviation, that it has a truly remarkable range of world-famous aircraft companies, and that it also has vast areas of heavily wooded and uninhabited land—ideal for hiding secret aeronautical research establishments."

"That," Stanford said, "is what Scaduto found out. So, the next thing he had to ascertain was whether or not the Canadian saucer project had *really* been passed on to the U.S. Air Force and if the Air Force had then simply dropped the project."

"And the answer on both accounts was No."

"Correct. His research revealed that on February 11, 1953, the *Toronto Star* announced that a *new* flying saucer was being developed at the Avro-Canada plant in Malton, Ontario—"

"The word 'new' suggesting that it wasn't the first one."

"Exactly. Then, on February 16, the Minister of Defense Production, C. D. Howe, informed the Canadian House of Commons that Avro-Canada was in fact working on 'a mock-up model of a flying saucer, capable of flying at 1,500 miles an hour and climbing straight up in the air.' By February 27, Crawford Gordon Jr., the president of Avro-Canada, was writing in the *Avro News* that the prototype being built was so revolutionary that it would make all other forms of supersonic aircraft obsolescent. Next, the *Toronto Star* was claiming that Field Marshal Montgomery had become one of the few people ever to view Avro's mock-up of the flying saucer, and shortly after that Air Vice Marshal D. M. Smith was reported to have said that what Field Marshal Montgomery had seen was the revolutionary construction plans for a gyroscopic fighter whose gas turbine would revolve around the pilot, who would be positioned at the center of the disc."

Epstein winced with pain, ignored his omelet and swallowed a tablet, washed the tablet down with a glass of water and then looked right at Stanford.

"Good God," he said, "I think I remember it. The American press dubbed that then legendary machine the *Omega* and in 1953 the *R.A.F. Review* gave it a semi-official respectability by reprinting most of the unclassified Canadian research and including doctored drawings of the machine."

"What did it look like?" Stanford said.

"According to the sketches, it was a relatively small, horseshoe-shaped flying wing, with numerous air intake slots along its edge, ten deflector vanes for direction control, a single pilot cabin topped by a cupola of transparent plastic, and a large turbine engine that *revolved* around the vertical axis of the main body."

"Fantastic," Stanford said. "Now listen to this. In early November 1953, Canadian newspapers were reporting that a mock-up of the *Omega* had been shown on the thirty-first of October to a group of twenty-five American military officers and scientists; then, in March the following year, the *American* press was claiming that the U.S. Air Force, concerned at Soviet progress in aeronautics, had allocated an unspecified sum of money to the Canadian government for the building of a prototype of their flying saucer, that the machine had been designed by the English aeronautical engineer John Frost—who had worked for Avro-Canada in Malton, Ontario—and that it would be capable of either hovering in midair or flying at a speed of nearly 2,000 miles an hour. This hot bit of news was followed by Canadian press assertions that their government was planning to form entire squadrons of flying saucers for the defense of Alaska and the far regions of the North, and that the machines required no runways, were capable of rising vertically, and were ideal weapons for subarctic and polar regions."

"Did the Canadian government make any comment about all this?"

"Not until December 3, 1954, when they suddenly announced that the saucer project had been abandoned."

"Any reason?"

"Oh, yeah. Because, although it was believed that the saucers would fly, they would, quote, serve no useful purpose. The Minister of Defense then confirmed their decision, adding that the project would have cost far too much for something that was, in the end, highly speculative."

Epstein picked up the fork, poked distractedly at the omelet, set the fork down again and glanced around him, his eyes still excited.

"All right," he said. "All these facts merely confirmed what your friend Scaduto had known for some time: that the Canadian government had officially dropped their saucer project in 1954."

"I would stress the word 'officially,' " Stanford said.

"Why?"

"Because that announcement by the Canadian government was clearly contradicted on October 22, 1955, when U.S. Air Force Secretary Donald Quarles released an extraordinary statement through the press office of the Department of Defense. Among other things he said that an aircraft of 'unusual configuration and flight characteristics' would soon be appearing, that the U.S. government had 'initiated negotiations' with the Canadian government and Avro-Canada for the preparation of an experimental model of the Frost flying disc, and that that aircraft would be mass-produced and used for the common defense of the subarctic area of the continent."

Epstein rubbed his eyes, studied his omelet and shook his head, then looked back at Stanford and smiled, his hands flat on the table.

"So what am I to make of all this?" he said. "First, the Canadian government announces that they have abandoned their saucer project. Next, ten months later, the U.S. Air Force officially announces that such a project is still underway. Was it or wasn't it?"

"It was," Stanford said. "By February 1959 the press was receiving ambiguous Air Force statements about a revolutionary new aircraft that had been jointly undertaken by the U.S. Air Force, the U.S. Army and the Canadian government. Then, on April 14, during a press conference in Washington, General Frank Britten implied that the first test flight of the aircraft was imminent and that it was destined to revolutionize traditional aeronautical concepts."

"That doesn't necessarily imply a saucer."

"It did," Stanford said. "In August 1960 the Air Force, giving in under pressure, allowed reporters to view the very machine they had all been writing about. What the reporters were shown was the Avro Car, an experimental aircraft that combined the characteristics of air-cushion machines and airplanes—in short, a crude flying saucer based on the principles of the jet ring and barely able to rise above the runway. Small wonder, seeing this, that they experienced no surprise when, in December the following year, the Department of Defense announced that they were withdrawing from participation in the project."

Stanford finished off his cheeseburger, wiped his lips with a paper napkin, then sat back and stared intently at Epstein, not smiling at all.

"There the story of the *official* flying saucers ended," he said. "Scaduto spent months trying to work out what it all meant, but in the end he grew increasingly baffled. First, he tried to find a correlation between the fact that an awful lot of UFOs seemed to come from and return to Canada and the fact that the Canadian government had been engaged in trying to build flying saucers—but there could be no remote comparison between the capabilities of the unknowns and the pathetic performance of the government-sponsored saucers. On the other hand, there were a few lingering mysteries . . ."

"Let me try to guess," Epstein said. "Why did the Canadian government announce that they had dropped their saucer project when in fact, at least according to the U.S. Air Force, they were still working on it? And why did the U.S. Air Force Secretary announce that aircraft like flying saucers would soon be flying? And why, after that announcement, was there a four-year gap—with no sign of the magical air craft—before a remarkably similar announcement was made? And why, after this latest announcement, did the Air Force unveil their magical offering, let it be known that it was a failure, and then announce that they were dropping the project? And finally why, if the Canadians had genuinely dropped their flying saucer project, did the U.S. Department of Defense, in announcing the termination of their own project, state that they were *withdrawing* from *participation* in the project? Withdrawing from participation with *whom*?"

"Those were the burning questions," Stanford said. "The suspicion remained that both the Canadian government and the U.S. Air Force were still involved in the construction of flying saucers, that those saucers were vastly more advanced than the rubbish the Air Force had deigned to show us, that some of the supposed UFO landings on or around various top-secret military establishments were actually the products of Canadian-U.S. cooperation, and that the Canadian and American statements, with their contradictions and ambiguities, had been designed to deliberately confuse the facts and turn them into mere rumors."

"Good God," Epstein said.

Stanford didn't smile at all. He paid the check and stood up. Epstein followed him out into the street and turned his fur collar up. Neon signs flickered erratically. The snow was turning to slush. The street was filled with beaded youngsters and politicians and whores, with lush secretaries and generals wearing suits, all defying the biting cold. Stanford headed for M Street. Epstein coughed at his side. They both walked in a slow, casual manner, rarely looking around them.

"Anyway," Stanford said, "unable to solve the problem, Scaduto finally had to let it go. Then, in 1965, it all came back with a bang." Stanford glanced up at the sky, hardly knowing he was doing so; he saw a patch of glittering stars beyond the clouds, the black void all around them. "In 1964, 1965 and 1966 there were three singular events that really put the Air Force in a fix. It was the culmination of those events that finally stung the Air Force into getting rid of its much publicized Project Blue Book—and that also encouraged Scaduto into re-examining the whole Canadian mystery. The first of these events was the close encounter of the third kind in Socorro, New Mexico, in 1964, when Deputy Marshall Lonnie Zamora claimed to have seen two schoolboy-sized people in coveralls standing beside an egg-shaped, metallic craft that was resting on legs extending from its body. The machine took off with a roar, spitting flames and ascending vertically, before Zamora could get down there to investigate."

"An extraordinary case," Epstein said. "Witnesses, including Allen Hynek, later confirmed the four landing marks and the burned greasewood plants, a local verified that they had seen Zamora's squad car heading toward a strange, oval-shaped object that was descending in the direction of the sighting, and a check with NASA, the Jet Propulsion Laboratory and fifteen industrial firms to see if they were working with experimental lunar landing modules in the area received nothing but negative answers. Hynek later described the sighting as one of the major UFO sightings of all time."

"Jesus," Stanford said, "you're like a computer. Anyway, that was the first event. The second was when, on March 20, 1966, at Hillsdale College, Hillsdale, Michigan, *eighty-seven* women students and a civil defense instructor saw a glowing, football-shaped object hovering over an empty swamp a few hundred yards from the women's dormitory, repeatedly racing at and retreating from the dormitory, dodging an airport beacon light, and generally flying back and forth for hours before disappearing—and when, the next day, in Dexter, Michigan, five people including two police officers reported seeing the same. The third event was merely the fact that by 1966 a Gallup poll had indicated that approximately *nine million* Americans thought they had actually seen a UFO. It was these major events, plus the Great Northeast Blackout of November 9, 1965, that led directly to the infamous Condon Report and the final closing of the Blue Book. Now while the Great Northeast Blackout was actually the second incident, I've left it to the last because it was the incident that really resurrected the Canadian mystery at NICAP—particularly with Scaduto."

Stanford glanced at Epstein and saw him swallowing a tablet, passing the numerous people on the pavement as if they didn't exist. His old friend looked exhausted and ill, and Stanford felt angry.

"As you already know," he said, "there's a long history of UFOs being seen over power lines and of subsequent, unexplainable power failures. Now, during the first week of August 1965, thousands of people in Texas, Oklahoma, Kansas, Nebraska, Colorado and neighboring states witnessed one of the biggest UFO displays ever. Unidentified lights flew across the skies, in formation, were tracked on radar, and played tag with civilian and Air Force aircraft. This major display of UFOs eventually faded away, but a milder flap continued over the next three months until, on the night of November 9, 1965, unidentifieds were reported from Niagara, Syracuse and Manhattan. Then, that same night, all the lights went out—in Connecticut, Massachusetts, Maine, New Hampshire, New Jersey, New York, Pennsylvania, Vermont and a section of Canada—went out over a total area of 80,000 square miles and a population of twenty-six million people."

"I remember it," Epstein said. "The huge power grid that controlled all those blacked-out areas—an interlocking network linking twenty-nine utility companies, with hundreds of automatic controls and safety devices—was considered to be invulnerable . . . yet the cause of the blackout was never ascertained."

"Right," Stanford said. "They never found out what caused it. The only thing they knew was that the failure had occurred *somewhere* in the flow between the Niagara Falls generators and the Clay power substation, an automatic control unit through which the electric power flowed from Niagara Falls to New York."

"There was a UFO connection," Epstein said.

"Yes," Stanford said. "First report of an unidentified was made by the Deputy Aviation Commissioner of Syracuse, Robert C. Walsh, and several other witnesses, all of whom, just after the power failed at Syracuse, saw what resembled a huge fireball *ascending* from a fairly low altitude near Hancock Airport. Approaching for landing at that time was flight instructor Weldon Ross and his passenger, computer technician James Brooding, both of whom saw the same object, at first mistaking it for a burning building on the ground—something corroborating the fact that the fireball was at low altitude—then quickly realizing that it was something in the air: a single, round-shaped object about 100 feet in diameter, which they later described as a 'flame-colored' globe. And, according to Ross's calculations, that object was directly over the Clay power substation."

"So," Epstein said, "we're back with Canada."

"Yes," Stanford said with some emphasis. "For obvious reasons this whole fucking mess resurrected the Canadian mystery at NICAP, particularly with Scaduto. Now, more than ever, he was convinced that there was some sort of connection between Canada and the UFO phenomenon. He was further convinced of this when a friend pointed out that until the United States defensive radar network was extended to the Far North, which was in 1952, Soviet long-range reconnaissance planes from Siberian and subarctic bases had flown frequently over Alaska, the Yukon territory and the MacKenzie District areas to spy on what was supposed to be relatively uninhabited territory. This just didn't make sense. What the hell were the Russians spying on? And wondering this, Scaduto pulled out his Canadian files and started working again."

They walked across M Street, hypnotized by the traffic lights, turned left on the sidewalk and kept going, rarely looking at anything. Eventually they turned again. They both walked like blind men. The residential streets were empty and quiet, the snow gleaming in darkness.

"Scaduto found nothing new in the files," Stanford said, "but by accident he finally struck gold. One of the members of the NICAP board of governors had managed to run down one of the CIA agents who had been transferred after the Woman from Maine affair. This agent, who had been transferred to London before being eased out of the service, was naturally feeling embittered and was willing to talk as long as it was off the record. Consequently, Scaduto met him in a room in the Drake Hotel in New York, and what he told Scaduto knocked Scaduto out."

Epstein shivered with cold, rubbed his eyes and coughed painfully, cursed, but kept listening to Stanford.

"Apparently," Stanford said, "one of the agent's assignments in the CIA was to undergo specialized training in Duke University's parapsychology lab, the psychology department at McGill University in Canada, and a sensory-deprivation establishment at Princetown. The purpose of all this was to open his mind—a naturally responsive one—to mental telepathy, sightless vision and psychokinesis. The reason for this—it was explained to him—was that the U.S. was about thirty years behind the Soviets in this field, and that the Russians were already employing such skills for espionage purposes.

"After a year of training the agent found that he could, like Ted Serios, cause photographs to appear on a film by merely studying the camera. A year after that, in 1959, he was working with U.S. Naval Intelligence and having successful shore to ship telepathic communications with the U.S. *Nautilus*, the then famous atomic submarine. And that same year, when the press exposed the *Nautilus* experiments, he was transferred back to Washington to work with the female psychic from Maine.

"During his first session, in the presence of the psychic, the agent was unable to make contact. However, at the second session, in the CIA office in Washington, when the woman wasn't present, he went into a trance and made contact with *someone*. Now, like the woman from Maine the agent was scribbling down, automatically, what it was he was hearing in his trance. He never actually found out what he wrote . . . because by the time he awakened one of the senior officers present had spirited the message out of the office."

"So they didn't want him to know who he was talking to."

"Correct," Stanford said. "No matter: when he finally woke up he found everyone at the window, all excitedly scanning the sky where the UFO, apparently, had been. Intrigued—and annoyed because his notes had been stolen from him—the agent later had a clandestine meeting with one of his colleagues and asked him if the UFO had been real. His colleague, very drunk at the time, told him that it was real, that it was part of a top-secret government project, and that one of the crew on board had been ESP trained. The woman from Maine had picked his thoughts up by accident."

They were nearing Epstein's house, the streets were desolate and quiet, and Epstein kept his head down, breathing harshly, coughing often, his head filled with what Stanford was telling him, his heart pounding excitedly.

"That wasn't all," Stanford said, speaking almost in a monotone, his gaze fixed on the empty street ahead, on the tall, brownstone buildings. "According to the agent's colleague, the UFOs reported to have landed at Cannon AFB, Deerwood Nike Base, Blaine AFB and, apparently, Holloman AFB, actually existed. Those saucers were the products of years of highly secret activity between the Canadian and United States governments—but in no way did they resemble the aborted projects that were 'leaked' to the press. They were, in fact, highly advanced flying discs of the most extraordinary capability—and there was a total of about twelve in existence."

Epstein felt his heart pounding. He ignored his aching stomach. He didn't feel Stanford's rage, had no thoughts of betrayal, felt nothing but an exalting vindication of all he had lived for. The UFOs existed. He had not pursued a phantom. He could die without dwelling on failure, and that made it all worth it.

"Only twelve?" he said instinctively.

"Yes," Stanford said. "According to the agent, his colleague had previously been seconded to the Royal Canadian Air Force Intelligence where he was given the task of implementing internal security on the flying saucer project. The project, he discovered, had been in existence since 1946, and was being run jointly by the Canadian government, the U.S. Air Force and Navy, and a few high-ranking Army officers from the Pentagon. They had managed to maintain secrecy by locating the underground production plants in the vast, deserted regions of southern Canada between British Columbia and Alberta; by insuring that the production of the numerous components of the saucers was distributed between hundreds of different, international companies, none of whom could have guessed what they were for; by undertaking the more specialized research in the super-secret installations of the White Sands Proving Ground and similar establishments all over Canada; and, finally, by deliberately confusing the press and public with a continuous stream of ambiguous 'leaks' and misleading statements. In other words: those saucers are real and they're hidden in Canada."

Epstein stopped at the street corner, turned around and stared at Stanford, looking up, his eyes bright in the lamplight, white snow on his gray beard.

"You *do* realize," he said, "that this leaves a mere twelve saucers to account for all the sightings of thirty years?"

"Yes," Stanford said, "I realize that. But that's not what I'm saying."

"Oh? And just what *are* you saying?"

Stanford didn't hesitate. "It transpires that the Allied Air Forces had been harassed by UFOs—mostly in the shapes of balls of fire—from as far back as 1944. Then, shortly after the war, in the summer of 1946, the more familiar types of UFOs, mostly cigar-shaped, swarmed across Scandinavia, seemingly coming from the general direction of the Soviet Union. The conclusion at the Pentagon was that German scientists, seized by the Russians at Peenemunde where the V-2 rocket had been developed, were constructing advanced weapons for the Soviets, and that the unidentified 'missiles' were being launched from the rocket test site of Peenemunde which was then in the Russian-occupied zone of Germany. This suspicion became stronger when the British, who had also seized and taken back to Britain a wealth of Germany's top-secret scientific and weapons research material, announced that the Germans had been working since 1941 on extraordinary aeronautical projects and on processes to release atomic energy. Included in the former was a 'remotely controlled, pilotless aircraft' and a 'device that could be controlled at a considerable distance by another aircraft.' So, faced with this, and thinking of the supposed Soviet 'missiles' over Scandinavia, there was a sudden British-Canadian-United States alliance to beat the Soviets in the race to follow through the German designs and complete their extraordinary aeronautical projects."

They both stood there at the corner, a cold wind whipping around them. Stanford was totally humorless, his eyes bright and intense, and Epstein looked up at him in wonder, either dazed or still doubtful.

"Listen!" Stanford hissed. "As we've just been discussing, the actual concept of a flying saucer is not a new one. The U.S. Navy and the British Navy have both been interested for a long time in the possibility of constructing either a vertical rising aircraft or a simpler air-cushioned machine that would be particularly suitable for use at sea. Regarding this, the Navy Flounder and the Flying Flapjack were crude examples of the former, the normal Hovercraft a perfect example of the latter. However, what they were attempting to build in the underground plants in Canada was a machine with the extraordinary capabilities of the machines suggested in the incomplete German research material. They wouldn't achieve this goal for another twenty years, but the first, extremely crude versions of their saucers were successfully tested over the Canadian border on June 21, 1947: a total of five disc-shaped aircraft, two of them piloted and approximately fifty feet in diameter, the remaining three remotely controlled by the pilots flying nearby, these three a mere six feet in diameter. These particular flying saucers could reach an altitude of approximately 7,000 feet, could hover uncertainly in the air, and had a horizontal speed of about 600 miles an hour."

"That test flight," Epstein said, "could account for the Harold Dahl sighting of that same day."

"Right," Stanford said. "However, it was what happened *after* that test flight that really got the ball rolling. On June 24, three days after the first successful test flight of the five Canadian-U.S. saucers, a total of nine, highly sophisticated, *unknown* saucers flew down over the Canadian underground plants, hovered there for about twenty minutes, shot off toward the Cascades where they reportedly circled the test area, then returned, circled the plant for another twenty minutes, then shot off at an incredible speed. And from that day on—the day, incidentally, of the famous Kenneth Arnold sighting—those UFOs, and others, returned again and again, and eventually spread out across the whole world."

Epstein stepped back and covered his mouth with his hand, his eyes very large and very bright, his whole body shaking. Stanford watched him, saying nothing, waiting for Epstein to recover, finally saw him removing his hand from his mouth and shaking his head.

"My God," Epstein said, "are they Russian?"

"No," Stanford said. "The agent's colleague, during his tenure at the flying saucer plant in Canada, never found out who those saucers belonged to. What he *did* find out was that some time during the Cold War the Pentagon received proof that the unknown saucers didn't originate in Russia—and that the Russians were being harassed by the same objects. He also found out that they were *not* from outer space, that the Pentagon probably knew where they came from, and that Canada and the United States were racing to build similar machines because the unknown saucers, even as far back as the fifties, had the sort of maneuvering capability that made them virtually invincible."

Epstein stepped back, turned around and walked away, and Stanford followed him around the street corner and saw him stopping again. He seemed to be frozen. He was staring across at his own house. Three men were coming out of the house and walking toward a black limousine. Epstein offered a strangled cry. The three men all looked up. Epstein started to run across the road toward them, his overcoat flapping. Stanford cursed and ran after him. The men slipped into the car. The car's headlights flashed on, formed a dazzling pool of silver, and then the car roared and shot off down the street. Epstein stopped and stared at it. Stanford slid to a halt behind him. The car slowed down at the bottom of the street, turned the corner and vanished.

Epstein cursed and lurched forward, almost slipping in the snow. He and Stanford reached the brownstone together and found the door open. They both raced inside. The whole house had been ransacked. Epstein kept looking around him, his eyes dazed, uncomprehending, then he groaned and covered his face with his hands and slumped into a chair.

"Bastards!" Stanford hissed. "They've got us marked!"

He reached down and grabbed Epstein, pulled him up to his feet, shook him until his hands fell from his face and his eyes were wide open. He held Epstein by his shoulders, trying to keep his old friend steady, then he spoke in a low and murderous voice that gave Epstein his strength back.

"Listen to me," he said. "I didn't stop at Scaduto. I did some investigations of my own and this is what I discovered.

"I discovered that the mysterious fireballs seen frequently over Germany disappeared for good when the Second World War ended. I discovered that the Russians, the British and the Americans divided the scientific spoils of Germany between them, and that some of those spoils were rumored to be related to the mysterious German fireballs. I also discovered that the British had received the major portion of this booty, and that they had, in 1945, sent back secret German aeronautical equipment and papers to be distributed to their experimental center in Bedford, England, and to their complementary research centers in Australia and Canada.

"I discovered that by 1947 the British aeronautical establishment was experimenting with such bizarre German concepts as a supersonic 'flying wing,' a gyroscopically stabilized pilot's cabin surrounded by a revolving turbine engine, and a suction airfoil shaped like a meniscus lens—or like a fucking great mushroom. And finally, I discovered that in 1946, with the encouragement of the British government, there had been a mass migration of aeronautical establishments and their workers from their original English production centers to the vast, uninhabited regions of southwest Canada."

"So," Epstein said. *"What does it mean?"*

"What I believe," Stanford said, "is that the Canadian and American governments, quietly backed by the British, have been working jointly since the end of World War II on the development of supersonic flying saucers, that they now have a limited number of such machines hidden away in the wilds of Canada or in the White Sands Proving Ground, and that those saucers are based on aeronautical projects that originated in Nazi Germany—but aren't related to the vast majority of UFO sightings. What I also believe is that the U.S. government knows the origin of the more extraordinary saucers, that it is frightened of what the capability of those saucers might represent in military and political terms, and that its building of its own saucers is a race against time and its secrecy a means of avoiding national panic. Finally, what I believe is that the government has to keep its secret, that it will murder to do so, and that the deaths of Jessup and Hardy, of Dr. McDonald and Irving Jacobs, are examples of how far the government will go to keep the lid on the pan.

"The Canadian government has flying saucers. The U.S. government has flying saucers. But someone, *somewhere*, has flying saucers so advanced we can't touch them. Those saucers don't come from space. They aren't figments of imagination. They are real and they are right here on earth and their source is a mystery."

Epstein pushed himself away, spinning around, hitting a chair, then he walked across the wrecked room, past his pillaged belongings, and tore the curtains back from the windows and looked up at the stars. He stood there a long time, didn't once rub his beard, and when he finally turned around his eyes were glazed with a strange, haunted brilliance.

"I'm going to Paris," he said.

CHAPTER TWENTY-FOUR

*I owe Kammler and Nebe. Without them, I would not be
here. That I killed them was not a sign of malice but of
simple expediency. I think of it often. What I did, I had to
do. The deaths of Kammler and Nebe were necessary for
the good of the colony. They were both growing greedy.
They wanted power for themselves. They were more concerned with politics than science, and I knew what that
meant. Plots and counterplots. The introduction of intrigue. A dissension that would interfere with work and
thus hinder our progress. Such a thought could not be
tolerated. We had come too far for that. For that reason I
had them gassed in their sleep and then took over the
colony.*

*Yet I recognize my debt. Without them, I would not be
here. I never liked them, but they did what was required
and made good our escape. We left Germany behind us.
We embraced a world of ice. Beneath the ice, in the immense towering caves, thousands slaved to support us. The
colony grew quickly. Without dissension there was
progress. Our medical and scientific experiments led to
wondrous achievements.*

*I was racing against time. I was sixty-six years old.
What I did in the laboratories in the ice was a necessary
evil. What I did, I had to do. If I died before my work
was completed, the colony would flounder. I had to make
it self-sustaining. The workers had to be controlled. Sooner*

*or later, even the guards with the whips would have nega-
tive thoughts. This could not be allowed to happen. The
control had to be automatic. I was obsessed with the mysteries of the brain and biological mutation.*

*What I did, I had to do. The slaves writhed beneath my
knife. The gray matter of their brains was examined; lungs
and hearts were explored. Their blood was my life. What
they suffered was necessary. Vivisection on animals is useful, but has grave limitations. So, I operated. The experiments were not pleasant. Many died and many more
became useless and had to be terminated. Nonetheless, I
progressed quickly. Without law there are no boundaries.
The mystery of human life was unraveled as it writhed on
the tables.*

*I was aging every day. I felt the fluttering of my heart.
My skin was tightening across the cheekbones of my face
and my stomach was addled. This frustration was energiz-
ing. I spent months in the laboratories. The experiments in
the camps of Nazi Germany now bore splendid fruits.
Hearts and lungs were transplanted. Prosthetic arms and
legs flourished. Many died on the tables, those maimed
were terminated, but our gains quickly overcame the cost
and encouraged us further. Gerontology was a priority.
My own aging was the spur. We experimented with various drugs and surgical aids and had dramatic results.
Naturally we made mistakes. There was paralysis, palsied
limbs. Nevertheless, with application and will, we eventually met with success. At first it was modest. Vitamin pills
and various stimulants. They were, however, just a beginning and soon led to much greater things. I myself was
thus saved. The first injections renewed my vigor. Within a
year, with my heart at full strength, I could take the pacemaker. A tentative first step. The artificial stomach followed. Years later would bring the plastic surgery and the
minor prosthetics.*

*The means of control was urgent. This object obsessed
me next. I was aware that even the most fanatical guards
would soon yearn for the outer world. Human nature is a
curse. It is weak and quite irrational. What I wanted was a
method of control that would make the guards obsolete.*

I exposed the human brain. Once exposed, it is a blanc-

mange. No mystery: just tissue and fibers, blood and acid and water. I experimented with the brain. I specialized in living subjects. I discovered that by tampering with certain cerebral areas, the mental processes of the brain could be altered in any manner required. I inserted microscopic electrodes. I had them activated by computer. Thus, at the press of a button, I could induce pain or pleasure, craven fear or brute aggression, numb acceptance or insatiable curiosity, heightened intelligence or idiocy. This discovery was invaluable. It was quickly utilized. Within months, implantation of the workers was well underway.

We were masters and slaves. The latter were virtually robotized. The former were still controlled by Artur Nebe, but were clearly redundant. The slaves had all been implanted. The whips were needed no longer. The only danger of revolt now resided in the guards and technicians. Nebe recognized this danger. He gave permission to implant. We both knew that this could lead to resistance, so we had to work carefully. It took us two years. We performed the implants one by one. We anesthetized the men while they were sleeping and then stole them away. The operation was simple. The men were programmed to forget the implant. When they awakened, they would not seem any different to those still untouched. After two years it was finished. There were no untouched left. Only Kammler and Nebe and myself were allowed to go free.

Every member had his function. His every thought was controlled. Every child, man and woman was robotized and had his course mapped out for him. Their desires were my desires. Their needs were my needs. I ordained their pain and pleasure, their every hunger, and was worshipped accordingly.

The implantations were all different. Some severe, some less so. What mattered was that each individual would perform as required. To drain a mind is to kill it. One must drain just a little. One must leave free those cerebral areas that perform certain functions.

The technical staff were least effected. I left them the spur of discontentment. This discontentment only related to their creative urge and did not go beyond that. What I removed was their hostility. What I enhanced was their

*love for work. Given this, they were almost like normal
men, but lacked personal ambition.*

*Below the technical staff were the administrators. Such
men and women were more affected. Required for system-
atic work, uncreative and repetitious, they were programmed to be wholly positive thinkers, enthusiastic and
dedicated. They were drained of discontentment. Their
work triggered satisfaction. In frequent contact with the
scientists, who were almost like normal men, the administrators had minimal personality and no thought for themselves.*

*The lowliest workers were most affected. I could allow
them no personality. I think of Nebe's soldiers, of the factory workers and secretaries, of the drivers and laborers
and cooks who performed simple tasks. All were heavily
implanted. All were drained of personality. All were programmed to perform their given tasks without reason or
thought. In a real sense they were robots. They experienced few emotions. Much cheaper and more reliable than
cyborgs, they had a minimal consciousness.*

*What an achievement this was! The first perfect society!
No waste, no crime, no need for debate, no insubordina-
tion or rebellion, no conflict of any kind. Such a society is
a miracle. It is also highly productive. With no digressions
for politics or conflict, it can advance by extraordinary
leaps. It can and ours did. We rode the whirlwind and
conquered it. Within two years our saucers were creations
of an awesome complexity. Jet propulsion was obsolete.
Atomic energy was routine. And even this, given the bene-
fit of hindsight, was but a modest beginning.*

*I see the saucers as I sit here. They climb vertically
from the wilderness. As I watch them, they glide across
the skies and cast their shadows on mountain peaks. The
sun beats all around them. They seem to merge with the
flashing ice. They rise up and then hover in silence, their
inertial shields glowing.*

*I confess: I feel pride. Inhuman? I cannot be. As I sit
here on the mountain, as I gaze out through the windows,
the beauty of the saucers above the snow makes me feel
like a young man.*

A divided society could not have accomplished it. Cer-

tainly not in that brief period. I would not have accomplished it myself had I ignored Nebe and Kammler.

They both wanted to leave the wilderness. They wanted to regain what they had lost. Simple men, moved by normal, pointless hungers, they wanted cheap, instant glory. The saucers offered that opportunity. They knew the saucers were invincible. They wanted to use the saucers to plunder the earth and make it bow down before them.

I did not desire the same. I wanted no more than my work. My new cathedrals were made of ice and stone, my one religion was science. I did not want that changed. I knew that conflict could change it. I also knew that with patience and time there would be no need for conflict.

The saucers rendered us inviolable. Their very presence was our security. What we needed, we could get from the outer world if we handled it gently. Meanwhile, we could progress. We could increase our capabilities. If we did so, we would be in a position to gain much with no effort. The outer world would have to join us. We would slowly draw it in. Given time, the outer world would surrender, turning men into Man.

Yes, given time. But Kammler and Nebe had no time. Their brains untouched by the healing electrodes, they were still normal men. They still suffered from base emotions. They knew fear and resentment. They both yearned for the world beyond the ice, and for its decadent pleasures. Vengeance and power. Material gain and the means of squandering it. Like restless children, Nebe and Kammler were inflamed with the need for attention. No, they couldn't wait. They wanted a war of aggression. They wanted to use my extraordinary creations as their weapons of plunder.

I could not let that happen. Such a conquest would be short-lived. Such aggression would be met with the resistance of insane politicians. Why encourage a nuclear war? What real purpose would it serve? Already our resources were running low, our needs increasing dramatically. What we needed, the world had. We could get it without conflict. In so doing, we could progress even more and thus bide our own time. In the end, the rest would come. The rule of science was inevitable. A conflict such as *Nebe* and *Kammler* wanted could only lead to destruction. I could not let it happen. I had no immediate goals. My concern was for the future of science and Man's metamorphosis—I still wanted the Superman.

My intention was to trade. I needed mass-produced items: small components and tools, nuts and bolts, screws and nails, light bulbs and paper and pens and other modest essentials. So far we had stolen them. Our flying saucers had landed. We had often abducted men and machines where isolation protected us. But nuts and bolts were more difficult. Small items were large problems. What was shipped here throughout the war years was now diminishing rapidly. No colony can be self-sustaining. I had always understood that. So it was that in 1952 I had to form an alliance. There was really no alternative. I had no choice but to trade. What I had, the world needed; what the world had, I needed; and until I had the world on my side, I would have to negotiate.

Indeed, I had already started. I was negotiating with President Truman. After the mock invasion of 1952, he had agreed to a meeting. We eventually met in the Oval Room. My CIA contacts were present. President Truman was an intelligent man, and as such he was nervous. He kept fiddling with his glasses. His lower lip was not too steady. General Vandenberg was standing near the desk, his eyes filled with suppressed rage. The Oval Room was very crowded: General Samford and Professor Robertson; other members of the Robertson Panel, including Lloyd Berkner. The meeting didn't take long. They had already examined my brief. Most were specialists in the physical sciences and had no problem reading. I put forward my suggestions. Truman sighed and raised his hands. Generals Vandenberg and Samford were outraged and inevitably outvoted. The scientists knew what they were reading. They were aware of our capabilities. They put the facts clearly to Truman and we reached an agreement.

After that, I had no choice. Kammler and Nebe became a threat. Disgusted that I should trade instead of conquer, they started plotting against me. I have no proof of this. I just know it was inevitable. Their chance for immediate power and recognition had been ruined by my ac-

*tions. They were now trapped in the colony. In the outer
world they would be war criminals. The only way they
could return to the outer world would be to step down as
conquerors. So, they felt trapped. Thus they had to plot
against me. And knowing this, I had no choice but to remove them and take over the colony.*

*They had not been implanted. They were men of free
will. I could not, as I could with the others, suggest euthanasia. For that reason I had no choice. What I did, I had
to do. I could not concern myself with individuals while
the future was threatened.*

*Not shortly after the war, then. It was 1953. We had
dinner overlooking the plateau, the snow white, the stars
glittering. I served champagne and caviar. The meal was
followed with brandy. Such luxuries were rare in the
colony, but the night seemed to warrant it. Kammler
spoke of America. He reminisced about his visits. Artur
Nebe turned his glass between his fingers, his dark eyes
unrevealing. Kammler spoke of General Vandenberg. His
voice trembled with loss. He said that Vandenberg had reminded him of his past, of his days with the military. Artur Nebe was not attentive. His dark eyes surveyed the ice.
He gazed over the glistening plateau to the dark, frozen
wilderness. Kammler spoke of the V-2 rockets. He talked
of fighting in the Hague. He recalled his days with Walter
Dornberger and Wernher von Braun. The hours passed in
this manner. Artur Nebe's dark eyes were veiled. A large
saucer formed a glowing cathedral that ascended majestically. Artur Nebe did not look up. His eyes were fixed on
the wilderness. Kammler yawned and stood against the
large window and was framed by the starlit night. He
talked vaguely about the future. He said decisions must be
made. He walked away and I saw the white wilderness dissolving in darkness.*

*They both left shortly after. I had no sense of urgency.
The glowing cathedral dropped down from the heavens,
hovered briefly and disappeared. I gazed out and saw the
ice. The frozen wilderness stretched out below me. I stood
up and then went to my desk and turned on the two scanners. Nebe and Kammler were both in bed. They both*

looked like sleeping children. I reached down and pressed the button on my left and let the gas fill their lungs.

What I did, I had to do. What I do, I have to do. Above morality, above the sanctity of the individual, is my duty to science. I do not suffer guilt. They were of use and were used. Without them, I would never have escaped— thus I offer them tribute.

CHAPTER TWENTY-FIVE

Stanford climbed out of the car, closed the door and looked around him, listening to the crying of the wind as it crossed the large field. The sun was going down, the sky filled with crimson light, a few drifting clouds casting the shadows that would soon die in darkness. Stanford stood there for some time. The field was utterly desolate. The lights and the barbed wire had gone, but the scorched earth remained. Nothing would grow there anymore. The dead cattle had been buried. The dust drifted lazily across the ground, emphasizing the barrenness.

Stanford looked all around him and saw the mountains beyond the flatlands. He thought of what Scaduto had told him, and it made him feel lost. The saucers didn't come from space. They weren't figments of imagination. They were real and they were right here on earth and their source was a mystery. Stanford thought about that. To think about it made him shiver. He gazed at the desolate flatlands, saw the bloody sinking sun, watched the dust drifting over the field and then turned back to the car.

He sat in his seat, closed the door and stared ahead, thinking of the girl on the ranch and of what she might know. The lust grabbed him immediately, filled his mind with her presence, almost making him forget what he was here for, his groin flooded with heat. Damn it, he thought, starting the car, driving off, thinking of her eyes, their strangely vacant luminosity, of her breasts and her thighs and her brown legs, her thumb parting her wet lips. He couldn't understand himself, didn't know what was happening, drove blindly, hardly seeing the road, the field falling behind him. What was he really doing here? Was it the girl or what she knew? Stanford shook his head wearily, feeling nervous and excited, confused by his conflicting emotions, despising himself.

The surrounding land was desolate. The crimson sky was turning dark. Stanford drove through pools of shadow and light, over stones and potholes. He thought briefly of Professor Epstein, his good friend, growing frail, now obsessed because death was at his door and the mystery remained. He had to find out for Epstein. He didn't want to fail his friend. He couldn't bear to think of Epstein fading away, his eyes haunted by failure.

Yet that wasn't the only reason. It never had been and never would be. Stanford's throbbing groin insisted on the truth and stripped the mask from his face. He had to do it for himself, his own need was the main concern, and he drove toward the ranch, feeling shame, seeing only the girl.

Stanford felt a little crazy. He didn't feel like himself at all. His thoughts tumbled on top of one another and amounted to nothing. He was obsessed with the girl. His lust went beyond sex. He had to touch her, had to break through her silence, had to creep through her tunneled eyes. This need was bewildering, an irrational, compulsive lust; it was a need for the revelations of her flesh, for the source of her being. What she was, was what he needed. She belonged to what she had witnessed. The girl was alien, a human touched by the unknown, and that made her seductive.

It was that . . . and much more. She had known he would come back. She had known and she had told him with her smile, and with her luminous, empty eyes. Not empty: concealing. Eyes that shone and quietly darkened. She had looked at him and willed him to return and now he felt enslaved by her.

Stanford didn't know what was happening, and was powerless to resist. He felt as if the girl had hypnotized him and drained him of will. She had known he would come back. He had known it as well. They had both made the pact three years ago without speaking a word.

Inexplicable. Ridiculous. It couldn't happen and yet was happening: a web of mysteries and intriguing possibilities with the girl at its center. Her vacant eyes, suggesting all. Her languorous innocence, inviting lust. Stanford thought of her standing on the porch, gazing up at the sky. She had touched and been touched. She had observed and now knew. She was silent as the knowing are silent: secret, inviolate. Stanford wondered what she had seen. He wondered what they had done to her. And he wondered, with a strange, hallowed awe, what she had then done to him.

Stanford drove for five minutes, driving blindly and dangerously, bouncing over potholes and mounds of earth until he came to the ranch. He slowed down when he reached the gate, stopped the car, hesitated, then opened the door and climbed out and heard the wind's lonesome moaning. The ranch hadn't changed, was still sadly dilapidated, the dust blowing gently along the porch, the lights burning inside. The girl was not on the porch. There was no sign of the old man. Stanford sighed and then opened the gate and closed it quietly behind him.

It was now nearly dark. The wind moaned across the flatlands. Stanford walked very slowly toward the ranch, his eyes drawn to the windows. The lights were on inside. There was no other sign of life. The only sound was the moaning of the wind, and that made him feel strange. Eventually he reached the porch, looked up at the nearest window. He saw an oil lamp glowing fitfully between the curtains, a shelf of cracked plates and cups. Stanford looked up at the sky. The moon glided beneath the stars. Stanford shivered and then walked up the steps until he stood on the porch. There was no sound from inside. Stanford felt very strange. He stepped forward and knocked on the door and then stepped back again.

There was no immediate response. Nothing. Stanford waited for some time. Nothing happened so he knocked on the door again and then stepped back a little. Silence. The wind. Stanford felt very unreal. He stepped forward and knocked on the door again and felt his heart racing wildly. That annoyed him a lot: he wasn't used to being nervous. He cursed softly and willed her to come and then he heard a faint sound. A tin mug on a tin plate. A chair scraping on the floor. Stanford took a deep breath and let it out and kept his eyes on the door. The bolt made a rasping sound. The door creaked and opened slightly. A beam of light fell out over Stanford and he saw the girl's face.

She stared at him a long time. Her brown eyes were very large. Stanford looked at those eyes and saw the void that led into the unknown. The girl was sucking her thumb. Stanford thought she was smiling. Her long hair tumbled loosely around her face in a dark, uncombed tangle.

"Emmylou?" Stanford said.

The girl nodded her head.

"Do you remember me?" Stanford said. "I was here a few years ago. The night all the other men were here . . . the night the cattle were slaughtered."

The girl sucked her thumb silently. The door was barely open. The girl's body was pressed against the door, her head tilted around it. She was wearing a cheap cotton dress. Stanford saw a brown leg. The girl stared at him, possibly smiling, then she nodded her head.

"Can I come in?" Stanford said. "It's important that I talk to you. I want to talk to you and your father. Can you tell him I'm here?"

The girl just stared at him, her thumb still in her mouth, the brown eyes very large, strangely depthless, luring him in.

"Can I speak to your father?" Stanford said. "Is your father inside?"

The girl suddenly giggled, a high-pitched, childish sound, then she took her thumb out of her mouth and opened the door a bit wider. Stanford stared at her. He couldn't take his eyes off her. She was wearing the same dress she had worn three years ago, the buttons undone up her thighs, undone down to her breasts. Stanford wanted to put it into her. He suddenly saw himself doing it. The lust took him with immediate, startling force and stripped his senses away. He shook his head and checked himself. He was sweating and felt feverish. The girl was leaning in a languid fashion against the door, a distant smile on her face.

"Is your father in?" Stanford said.

The girl tilted her head slightly. Her eyes were staring up at him, very large, their brown depths strangely luminous. Then she giggled again. Stanford shivered a little. She stopped giggling and shook her head from side to side in a negative gesture.

"He's not in?" Stanford said.

The girl shook her head again. Stanford saw her belly pressed against the door, one breast thrusting around it.

"You mean he's not here?" Stanford said.

The girl nodded that this was so.

"Where is he?" Stanford said. "Do you understand? I want to know where he's gone."

The girl opened the door wider, slipped around it like a dancer, moving with a natural sensuality that made Stanford harden. He saw the curve of her breasts, the faint outline of her nipples, glanced down and saw a brown inner thigh, a film of dust on her bare feet. The girl pressed against the door, slid along it, moved toward him, then she passed him, brushing lightly against him, and stood out on the porch. Stanford watched her, fascinated, seeing the curve of her spine. She leaned back and then raised her left hand and pointed up at the night sky.

Stanford suddenly felt cold, raised his head and looked up. The sky was dark and the stars were very bright, the moon gliding beneath them. What did she mean? Stanford couldn't accept it. He shivered and then stepped toward the girl until he stood just beside her. She was still pointing at the sky. She turned her head and stared at him. She was smiling, a strange, distant smile, her brown eyes hypnotizing him.

"What do you mean?" Stanford said. "You mean your father's up there? In heaven? You mean your father has died and that he's now up in heaven?"

The girl smiled and then giggled, shook her head from side to side, indicating that Stanford was wrong, pointing up at the sky. Stanford wished she would talk to him. He was convinced that she could talk. He stared at her, and wondered if she was mad. The girl returned his stare. The wind pressed the cotton dress against her body, emphasizing her hips and breasts. Stanford glanced at the sky, saw the moon and the stars. He looked back at the girl and she nodded and kept pointing upward.

"He's not dead?" Stanford said.

The girl giggled and shook her head.

"He's up there?" Stanford said. "He's in the sky? Someone took him away?"

The girl nodded in agreement, dropped her hand and turned toward him. The wind blew the dress behind her legs. Stanford wanted to put it into her. He wanted no more than that. It was a mindless, brutally primitive desire, and he ached with his need for her.

"Who took him away?" he said. "Was it the men here that night? Was it the Army or the Air Force or the police? Who took him away?"

The girl raised both her hands, placed them together above her head, drew them apart and lowered them gently to describe something dome-shaped. Stanford shivered, feeling cold. He also felt a distinct excitement. He nodded to show that he understood, then the girl raised her hands again. She pointed to the sky. Her left hand was mushroom-shaped. She let the hand drop in a vertical line, knelt down and placed the hand on the porch and swept it up toward the sky again. It was an eloquent gesture, graceful, dreamlike, and then the girl turned around on her bare feet and slowly stood up again.

"They came back," Stanford said. "They came down in the strange aircraft. Your father was taken into the aircraft and then they all flew away."

The girl nodded and smiled, put her thumb in her mouth, brushed past him and walked back to the house and leaned against the doorframe. Her long legs were crossed. The dress blew around her hips. Stanford saw the shadowed area between her thighs, raised his eyes, saw her luminous stare. She was sucking her thumb, a child, perhaps insane, and Stanford flushed with a mixture of shame and primitive lust.

"How long ago?" he said.

The girl's brown eyes grew large.

"When did all this happen?" he said. "How many days? How many weeks ago?"

The girl made a V sign.

"Two days?" Stanford said.

The girl nodded, then giggled and turned around and vanished into the house.

Stanford followed her inside, feeling strange, not himself, haunted by what she had told him, and by what it might mean. The house was unchanged, the oil lamps still near the windows, casting shadows on the dusty wooden floor and the makeshift furniture. The girl stood near the table, smiling at him and sucking her thumb; the shadows fell down flaking walls, crept over the wooden chairs, danced fitfully on and off the girl's face, the rise and fall of her breasts. Stanford simply smiled at her. There was light in her brown eyes. Her left thumb was in her mouth and her right arm was folded behind her back, Stanford saw her parted thighs, saw her flesh as his salvation. The shadows flickered on her face, a pool of light around her eyes; and the eyes, which were vacant, were also bright with some vague, sly awareness.

"Who were they?" Stanford said. "Who took your father away? Can you describe the men who took him away? What were they like?"

The girl tilted her head slightly, her knuckles pressing against her nose, her dark hair hanging down across her face and covering her right eye. Stanford thought she was smiling, wasn't sure, just had that feeling: he then thought of what had happened, of the strange craft descending, of the men taking her father away, and wondered how she could smile. An idiot? Possibly. Stanford wasn't too sure of that. There was a light in the brown, vacant eyes that gave hints of awareness. The girl seemed to be teasing him, her languid carnality seducing him; silent, she spoke through her body with a sly, feline eloquence.

"Who were they?" Stanford said.

The girl giggled and walked up to him, stood very close to him, her breasts very close to his chest, the rising flesh lightly shadowed. She looked up at Stanford, still smiling, strangely mischievous, arched her spine and stood on tiptoes and raised her hand to his head. Stanford felt sick with longing; he had a hard, pulsating erection. The girl put the edge of her hand against his forehead and drew it down to his chest. Stanford followed the hand down. He saw the shadow between her beasts. She moved her hand in a cutting motion across his chest, as if marking a line.

"They were all that size?" Stanford said. "They were small? Is that what you mean?"

The girl nodded and stepped away. Stanford moved into the shadow. His erection was tight against his pants and he wanted to hide it. The girl moved closer to him. She cupped her left hand in the air. She indicated that the men had been five feet tall, her brown eyes more expressive. Stanford nodded that he understood. The girl smiled and touched her forehead. She placed her hands around her neck, probably indicating a collar, then ran the delicate hands down her body in two parallel lines.

Stanford didn't understand. He was finding it hard to concentrate. The girl's hands were on her breasts, on her belly, on her thighs, pressing her own hollows and curves and inciting his need. It wasn't what she intended. She was trying to tell him something. She waved her left hand in a negative gesture and then started again.

She moved her hands down from her throat, drawing them away from one another, rubbing them over the buttons on her dress as if trying to erase them. Stanford nodded that he understood. He saw the shivering of her breasts. The girl smiled and placed her hands on her shoulders and ran them straight down her sides. Her hands traced her gentle curves. She stooped down and ran her hands along her legs until they touched her bare feet.

"One-piece suits," Stanford said. "They were wearing one-piece suits. They were wearing some sort of coveralls and you didn't see buttons."

The girl nodded and stood up, a graceful movement, very sensual, the dress falling back over her legs, rippling over her breasts. She put her thumb back in her mouth. Stanford felt that she was smiling. She stared up at him, her eyes more expressive, now mischievous. Stanford looked her up and down. He couldn't take his eyes off her. He wanted to peel the dress from her body and press himself into her.

"Who were they?" he said. "I want to know where they came from. You know and I think you can talk and I want you to tell me."

Stanford stared at her, fascinated, his will destroyed by his erection, trying to gauge what her large eyes were concealing, the room dissolving around him. The girl looked like an adolescent, ragged, unkempt, her feet dirty, her legs burned by the sun. Stanford heard the moaning wind. He thought of the moon and stars. The girl stood there, beside the old table, her long legs slightly parted.

"You won't talk," Stanford said. "Did they order you not to talk? Did they do something? Why won't you talk to me?"

The girl smiled and sucked her thumb, started humming a tune. Stanford watched her, fascinated. He felt very unreal. The oil lamp on the table burned fitfully, flickering over her face. The girl sucked her thumb and hummed. She rocked languidly back and forth. She was leaning against the table, her hips forming a graceful curve. Stanford wanted to press against her, wanted to feel her tender flesh; he felt dizzy and tense with throttled lust, hardly knew where he was.

"Who were they?" he said.

The girl didn't reply. Stanford stared at the thumb in her mouth, at her breasts, her curved hip. The shadows flickered across her face, across the pale skin of her throat, across the cleft of her breasts, her rocking belly, the leg exposed by the open dress. Stanford felt choked with lust, finally walked over to her. He stood right in front of her, very close, almost touching, and looked down at her brown, expressive eyes, saw himself in their dark depths.

"Who were they?" he said. "I know you can talk. I want to know where the men came from. I know you can tell me."

The girl looked up and smiled, her thumb still in her mouth, still humming, her body rocking to and fro, her warmth flowing around him. He reached up and put his hand on her wrist and pulled her thumb from her mouth. The girl licked her lips. Her hand dangled indecisively. She smiled and slid the hand beneath her dress and lightly scratched her right breast. Stanford felt that he was choking. He saw the hand beneath the dress. Her fingers moved up and down, scratching lightly, her palm pressed to the white skin. Stanford's heart started pounding. His one truth was his erection. He raised his hand and pressed it down on the cloth right above the girl's hand. He saw her tongue at her lips, his own reflection in her eyes, then he felt her fingers slipping away and his hand cupped her breast.

"Who were they?" he said.

The girl made no reply. She was still humming quietly. Stanford felt the breast beneath the cheap cotton, very soft, very warm. He pressed gently and felt the nipple. The girl continued humming quietly. Stanford pulled the dress back and cupped the bare breast in his hand, his palm rubbing the nipple, sliding slowly, pressing down, trying to flatten it. The nipple hardened against his palm. He squeezed the warm, heavy breast. The girl hummed and rocked gently against him, her warmth flowing around him.

Stanford sensed the room dissolving. Shadows flickered across the walls. He looked down at the eyes looking up. Silence. A moaning wind. His own breathing was very harsh. He took the collar of her dress in both his hands and pulled the dress off her shoulders. The girl stopped humming, bit her tongue and smiled at him. Stanford slid his hands along her smooth spine, felt her sweat, pulled her to him. The girl continued smiling. Her belly was pressed against his erection. She just hung there in his arms, arching backward, her hands loose by her sides.

Stanford looked at her shoulders, very smooth, very white, dropped his eyes and drank in her milky breasts, the dark nipples erect. He didn't kiss the girl's lips. Her smile was distant, ambiguous. He bent over and pulled her hard against his groin and pressed his lips to her right breast. The girl quivered a little. Stanford kissed her heavy breast. He put his lips around the nipple and sucked it, his tongue licking and stroking. The girl quivered and writhed against him. He felt her hand on his head. She stroked the back of his neck and pulled him down, her breast filling his mouth.

Stanford didn't know where he was. He didn't stop to

think about it. He saw lights ascending quietly to the sky, blending in with the moon and stars. It was all one and the same. She had known it and belonged to it. Stanford wanted her, he wanted the answers, and the mystery was part of her. He felt the nipple between his lips, sucked and licked it like a child. Her warm groin was pressed against his erection, moving back and forth, teasing it. Stanford pressed her sweaty spine. He slid his hands down to her buttocks. He took his lips from her right breast, slid his tongue across her skin, then took the other nipple in his mouth and let it roll through his teeth. The girl gasped and writhed against him, both her hands at his neck. She ground her belly against his throbbing erection and pulled him down lower.

Stanford pushed her against the table, pulled the dress down her arms; she moved her arms and let the dress fall to her waist, her body sweat-streaked and white. Stanford sucked her breasts and nipples, soaked his lips with her sweat. The girl gasped and put her hands on his neck and sunk her nails in his flesh. Stanford felt her ridged spine, slid his hands up to her shoulders. The girl groaned and fell back and pulled him down, her thighs opening out to him. Stanford knew that he was lost. A void opened up to him. The girl was bent back against the creaking table, and he glimpsed the oil lamp. The light glowed in a darkness. Beyond the darkness there was nothing. The girl opened her thighs and clamped them tight around his hips, and Stanford pushed his erection against her belly, his hands gripping her buttocks. He didn't think of what he was doing: her writhing form was his whole being. He had lived with her flesh for three years and now its touch stripped his senses. He squeezed her buttocks and pressed upon her, kissed her nipples and breasts, slid lower and put his tongue in her navel, his lips sucking the creamy skin. Flickering shadow and light. A moaning wind in the distance. The girl lay back on the table, her thighs clamped around his hips, and he saw the dress tangled around her waist as his tongue licked her belly.

"Yes," Stanford groaned. *"Yes!"*

The girl reached up for his jacket, pulled it down around his arms, and he slipped his hands from under her naked spine and let the jacket fall off. The girl gasped and grabbed his shirt, her fingers tugging at the buttons, her legs coiling around him, her buttocks pressed against the table's sharp edge, her groin thrusting up into him. Stanford saw the burning lamp, flecks of light in brown eyes, the eyes wild and blind, the pink tongue at her lips, dark hair streaked across her tanned face, beads of sweat on her forehead. He groaned and ripped his shirt off. Her hands slithered along his chest. He saw the pale skin of her throat, the smooth shoulders, the heavy breasts, very white, the nipples dark and erect, the dress around the slim waist.

The girl writhed and grabbed his belt, undid the buttons on his pants. Stanford saw her parted legs, the golden down of her inner thighs, her dress split above the crotch and falling away from a red patch of panties. He groaned and unzipped his pants, spread his fingers on her belly, very smooth, soft and warm, felt the mound of damp hair, closed his fingers and slid them under her panties as she groped in his pants. Stanford groaned and muttered something. The girl gasped and shook her head. Stanford slid his fingers through the mound of hair, curled them back, felt inside her. The girl gasped and thrust down, her thighs opening and closing, then she tore at his pants and pulled them open and took hold of his cock. Stanford groaned and felt inside her, the wet warmth, the yielding lips, found her clitoris as she pulled his cock out, her fingers closing around it. Stanford felt her sliding fingers, lost himself, *became* her fingers, thrust himself into the soft glove of her hand, his fingers kneading her clitoris.

The oil lamp shone on the table. Around the lamp there was darkness. Stanford groaned and dissolved, flowed out in the darkness, became one with the darkness and the silence that was torn by her gasping. The girl pulled his foreskin back. Her fingers slid up and down him. He drained out of himself, flowed away and knew only her silken touch. Stanford felt deep inside her. She was wet and very warm. He jerked his fingers out and tore her panties off, the ripping sound jolting through him. The girl gasped and shook her head, rocking wildly from side to side, her thighs clamped around his hips, her hand tight around his cock, around his hardness, trying to guide him inside her, his tip rubbing her clitoris. Stanford groaned and shuddered violently, grasped her buttocks, squeezed and pulled; the girl pushed herself against him, opened for him, drank him in, became part of him.

"Yes," Stanford hissed. *"Yes!"*

He sank down and brought her with him, his hands clutching her buttocks, kneeling low, letting her slip off the table, her thighs opening out wider. Stanford grabbed her by the shoulders, pulled her down hard on his cock; the girl gasped and slipped her hands beneath his arms and then clawed at his ribs. Stanford pushed her shoulders back. Her spine was arched in a flowing line. Her breasts were pointing at the ceiling, her brown thighs locked around him, her legs bent back, her feet touching the floor, his cock still deep inside her. Stanford held her sweaty spine. His other hand caressed her breasts. He groaned and lowered her down to the floor and then pressed down upon her. She shook her head from side to side, her eyes closed, her mouth open. Her dark hair was coiled across her nose and lips, curled around her pink tongue. Stanford stretched out along her. She opened her thighs and writhed beneath him. She pulled her legs up, her knees level with his shoulders, slid her hands across his buttocks and squeezed him, trying to coax him in deeper. Stanford groaned and rolled his hips. He felt her melting around his cock. She was liquid and his cock dissolved within her and he felt himself burning. He shuddered and changed direction. He moved from one side to the other. He thrust deeper inside her, touched her center, set her loose, and she gasped and banged her head on the floor and started shuddering under him.

"Oh, God!" she gasped. *"God!"*

The words exploded over Stanford, ricocheted, filled his head, jerked him brutally back into himself and made him open his eyes. He saw the girl's bouncing head, her closed eyes, her open mouth, strands of dark hair stretched across her strained face, beads of sweat on her forehead. Stanford stared at her, startled. He raised himself up on his hands. He saw the smooth line of her shoulders, the stretched tendons in her neck, thrusting breasts, nipples

dark and erect, his own sweat on her belly. Stanford
looked along her body, saw his own heaving groin, her
thighs parted, his groin pumping up and down, his cock
thrusting, withdrawing. He was shocked, but couldn't stop,
felt a mounting excitement. He ceased moving and the
girl's torso shuddered and pushed up toward him.

"Who were they?" he said. "You can talk. You can tell
me. You hear me? I want to know who they were."

"No!" she cried. *"God!"*

Stanford held himself off her. He was propped up on his
hands. He looked down at her pale, writhing body and
then thrust deep inside her. The girl gasped and clenched
her fists, banged the fists on the floor. Stanford flattened
her breasts with his chest and grabbed her under the
shoulders. He pulled her tighter to him. She groaned and
thrust down. The girl gasped; they both gasped. Stanford
started to lose control. He slid his hands beneath her buttocks, along the bottom of her thighs, then pushed her
knees back toward her face and raised his hips and thrust
deeply. Stanford's head started spinning. He thrust in and
out in long, languid motions, his buttocks constricting.
Stanford thrust even harder, heard the liquid sounds of
sex, felt her heat, that jellied warmth around his cock, her
spasms building and shaking him.

"Who were they?" he hissed.

Stanford worked himself up onto his knees and grabbed
the girl by the hips. She was stretched out below him. He
pulled her buttocks off the floor. He slid his hands along
the soft down of her thighs and then pulled her tight to
him. The girl gasped and shook in spasms. Her body
flowed away from him. She was twisting on the floor,
rocking wildly, her legs over his shoulders. Stanford pulled
her even closer, thrust fiercely inside her. He saw the lights
in the sky, the dead cattle in the field, all the friends who
had died or disappeared, the pulsating, miraculous craft.
He had to crack the mystery. The truth must have dominion. He grabbed her by the hips and pulled her closer,
thrusting in to his limit. He touched her. She broke loose.
Stanford pushed his hips forward. The girl cried out as the
spasms whipped through her and took her apart. She

started coming, wave piling upon wave, her body twisting and shuddering.

"Oh my God!" she cried. "They were *Germans!*"

The last word cut through Stanford, exploded, made his head spin, and he shuddered, they both shuddered together, the room spinning around them.

They let it go and rolled apart, felt the floor, lay on their backs, breathing heavily, separated by a pool of light, both protected by shadows. Stanford stared up at the ceiling. The walls were spinning around him. He licked his lips and let the spasms pass away and then looked at the girl. She was lying on her side. Her hair fell across her face. The upper portion of her body was white, both her legs a dark brown. She lay just outside the light. Her eyes were hidden by her hair. She was breathing in deep, painful spasms, her breasts rising and falling. Stanford stared at her, speechless. He knew he had to ask her more. Then he felt a wave of hatred flowing toward him as the floor started shaking.

"*Jesus Christ!*" Stanford hissed.

The room roared and seemed to shake, the crockery rattling on the shelves, and Stanford felt a sudden fierce wave of heat and was blinded by white light. He thought he heard the girl screaming, blinked his eyes and saw stars, heard her screaming in a terrible manner and rolled over toward her. The floor beneath him was shaking. Cups and saucers were breaking. The glass in the windows blew apart and flew all over the room. Then the roaring stopped abruptly. The wave of heat passed away. Stanford opened his eyes and looked at the girl and saw her clutching her head. She was shaking her head from side to side. She wasn't screaming anymore. She took her hands from her head and stared at him and the hatred flowed out of her.

Stanford drew away from her. He didn't think—he just did it. Her brown eyes were very bright and intense, illuminated by hatred. The floor growled and then stopped shaking. The girl jumped to her feet. Stanford jumped up behind her as she grabbed at a knife, picked it up and turned around and started slashing. Stanford ducked and jumped away. "Get out!" the girl shrieked. She rushed at him, the knife raised high and glittering, swung it down toward his face. Stanford grabbed hold of her wrist. The girl hissed like a cat. The knife clattered to the floor and she clawed at him with her free hand, her nails raking down his right cheek and gouging lines in his face. Stanford felt the warm blood, felt the pain, a chilling fear; he slapped the girl with the back of his hand and pushed her into the table. The girl hissed and grabbed the oil lamp. "Get out of here!" she screamed. She threw the lamp and it flew past Stanford's head and crashed into the wall. A crackling roar, a wave of heat. The burning oil poured down the wall. Stanford cursed and swung his fist at the girl and knocked her into the wall. The flames raced across the floor. Stanford had to leap away. The girl hissed and then darted for the door, flung it open, rushed outside.

Stanford choked in the swirling smoke. The flames were racing along the walls. Stanford cursed and then ran through the door and saw the stars in the sky. Then the darkness exploded, became a sheet of fierce white light, blotting out the sky and flatlands and temporarily blinding him. Stanford stopped then staggered back, put his arm across his eyes, moved his arm away and squinted through his fingers, trying to see through the blinding light. He couldn't see, but he could hear. There was a steady bass humming. Stanford heard the sound and felt it—it was drilling through his skull—and he reached up and clutched at his head and then stepped forward blindly.

He missed the steps and fell down, hit the ground with his right shoulder, heard it snapping and felt a sharp pain that made him cry out. He rolled onto his back, spitting dirt, looking up, saw the brilliant striations of white light and closed his eyes again quickly. The ground shook beneath his back. His head was tightening, exploding. The sound was drilling through his skull, making his muscles seize up, and he shuddered, his body out of control, and then dropped down through darkness.

A light bored through the darkness, spread out and filled his vision. Stanford opened his eyes and looked up and saw the brilliant white light. This time he could look at it. He tried to rise, but couldn't move. He heard the roaring of flames and turned his head and saw the whole ranch house blazing. Stanford heard a noise behind him.

He turned his head in the opposite direction, saw a fierce white haze with brighter lights inside it, the lights forming a long line. Then he saw the silhouettes. They formed a semicircle around him. They moved closer and he saw the ragged girl, looking down at him, smiling. The girl's eyes were large and vacant. She was sucking her thumb. One of the silhouettes walked over to Stanford and knelt down beside him.

The man was wearing a gray coverall that seemed silvery in the bright light; his face was very pale and very smooth, smiling slightly, removed. Stanford couldn't see him clearly. The man seemed to be very small. He moved his head and the shadows disappeared and Stanford saw him more clearly. He wasn't an adult. He was about fourteen years of age. He reached out and touched the side of Stanford's neck and Stanford felt very calm.

"You shouldn't have come here," he said, his voice deeper than it should have been. "We don't know what to do about you, Dr. Stanford, because you shouldn't be here. We know all about you. We're not pleased with what you're doing. We are computing but we don't know what to do, because you shouldn't be here. We'll have to leave you for now. We have received no instructions. We will leave you and then, when we are gone, you will be able to walk again. You shouldn't be here, Dr. Stanford. We were not informed of this. We will leave you because we have no instructions and we cannot compute you. Close your eyes, Dr. Stanford. That's right, keep them closed. When we leave, you will open them again and be able to walk. Keep your eyes closed. *Auf Wiedersehen.*"

Stanford kept his eyes closed. He hardly knew he had closed them. There was silence and his head felt very light and he felt very calm. He heard the footsteps moving away. A film of dust fell on his face. He felt the earth beneath his back, very cold, eating through to his bones. Then he heard a humming noise. Something thumped the ground lightly. He heard shuffling, a hollow, metallic drumming, then the silence returned. Stanford lay there, not moving. He kept his eyes closed, feeling calm. He smelled smoke and heard the crackling of the flames that engulfed the ranch house. Then the ground started shaking. Stanford felt the vibrating noise. The vibrating noise grew stronger, seemed to fill his whole head, then it cut out, became a rhythmic humming that spread out just above him. The ground settled down again. Stanford lay there, feeling calm. The humming noise became fainter, climbed away and then cut out, leaving silence, the whispering of the dust, the wind's dull, lonesome moaning.

Stanford opened his eyes. He looked up at the moon and stars. He shook his head and climbed painfully to his feet and looked carefully around him. The whole ranch house was on fire. The flames spat at the sky. Stanford stood there, feeling dazed, gazing over the desolate flatlands, the flames crackling and illuminating the darkness, and thought of only one thing: the parting words of the boy.

Auf Wiedersehen.

CHAPTER TWENTY-SIX

Lying on the double bed in the lodge in Mount Rainier, Epstein dreamed of the lights in the sky, rising gracefully, silently. He tossed and turned in his sleep, felt a desolate sense of loss, wanting to follow the ascending lights, to drift up there through the darkness, to share in their serene, graceful majesty, to unravel the mystery. Then the dream changed. Epstein murmured and groaned out loud. He was on the flight back from Paris, flying high above the clouds, listening to the voice on the tape recorder, the revelations astounding him. Then the whole plane suddenly shook, rolling over, scattering passengers, a blinding white light pouring through it, temporarily blinding him. Epstein shaded his eyes, ignored the screaming, tumbling passengers. The plane leveled out again and he looked through the window and saw a flashing mass just above, gliding over the plane. It was the great mother ship, the one he had seen in the Caribbean, and Epstein watched it as it came down on the plane and then somehow swallowed it . . . In his sleep he tossed and turned. He looked down upon himself. He saw himself lying there on the bed, his eyes opening, frightened. He was surrounded by a group of men. They all seemed very small. They were wearing gray coveralls, they didn't say a word, and then one of them leaned over Epstein and reached out and touched him . . . Epstein groaned aloud. He returned to the streets of Paris. He was sitting in the restaurant on the

Rue de Rivoli, the old man talking into the tape recorder, sipping *cognac* methodically. The old man was English. There was dandruff on his shoulders. He talked slowly, with studied precision, and Epstein drifted away . . . He was just back from Paris, changing planes at Kennedy Airport. There were people all around him, rushing back and forth, shouting, and he felt very frightened to be there, but didn't know why. Then he was on another plane. The flight to Washington was uneventful. He glanced down at the clouds, a field of cloud, shifting slowly, and he checked the cassette tapes in his pocket because the fear was still with him . . . Epstein groaned in his sleep. He tossed and turned on the bed. He was in his office in Washington, putting the tapes in his safe, obsessed with the idea that he was being followed, that someone was watching him. The office was very quiet. The bright lights stung his eyes. He heard the traffic along Massachusetts Avenue, still there even at midnight. Epstein locked the safe. He read the message from Stanford: his young friend was up in Mount Rainier, checking some recent sightings. Epstein felt tired and frightened. The night faded into noon. He was in his car, driving up the mountains, the fear making him sweat . . . Epstein groaned and muttered something. He tossed and turned in his sleep. The lodge was empty and he found another message and lay down and felt frightened. The fear increased and became unreal. Epstein opened his eyes. He saw the small men standing all around the bed, very quiet, looking down at him. Epstein felt very cold. They weren't men: they were boys. Then one of them, about fourteen years of age, leaned over and touched him . . .

Epstein groaned and woke up, feeling cold and very frightened, thinking only of the tapes in the safe and of what they might mean. He licked his lips and rubbed his eyes, saw the wooden beams above him, the room no longer dark, the lights on, a chair creaking beside him. He turned his head, expecting Stanford. There was a stranger in the chair. Epstein sat up on the bed and rubbed his eyes and tried to keep himself calm.

The man was tall and sophisticated, wearing a black shirt and slacks, his eyes bright blue and intense, his hair silvery but plentiful, parted neatly on the left and falling down over an unusually seamless forehead. He sat casually in the chair, his hands folded on his crossed legs, staring straight at Epstein and smiling, a cold, remote smile.

"Who are you?" Epstein said.

"Aldridge," the man said. "You might remember me. Richard Watson mentioned my name. It was there in the transcripts."

"How did you know about the transcripts?"

"Richard told me," the man said. "We let him go and then we brought him back and he told us about it."

The fear shivered down Epstein's spine, made him numb, a bit unreal, and he rubbed his eyes and tried to wake up, still tired from his flights. The man was looking at him steadily. There was something odd about the man. He seemed to be in his early fifties, very handsome, extremely youthful, but the skin on his forehead was unlined, his chin smooth as a boy's.

"You remember the transcripts?" the man said.

"Yes," Epstein said.

"Then you should remember me," the man said. "I'm Aldridge. I was present."

Epstein shook his head slowly, feeling slightly disorientated, not sure that this was actually happening, his fear slowly subsiding.

"You're Aldridge?"

"That's right," the man said. "I know it must be something of a shock, but that won't last too long." He smiled in that bleak manner, glanced casually around the room, then turned his gaze back upon Epstein, his blue eyes very bright. "Stanford's on his way back," he said. "He's been up in the mountains. He's been checking on some UFO reports, but he hasn't found much."

"How do you know?" Epstein said.

"We've been watching him," Aldridge said. "It was *my* flying saucers that were seen—and they're up there right now."

Epstein felt very cold. He wondered if he was dreaming. After pinching his left wrist, he knew he wasn't, and he shivered a little.

"*Your* flying saucers?"

"That's right," Aldridge said. "Don't look so shocked—they're very real . . . and they're up there right now."

"Where?" Epstein said.

"Above the atmosphere," Aldridge said.

"Then our reconnaissance satellites will see them."

"They've been seeing them for years."

Epstein wondered what he meant, wanted to ask but couldn't do it, still dazed from being jerked out of sleep, a throbbing pain in his stomach. He coughed and rubbed his eyes. The room seemed very bright. Aldridge uncrossed his legs, placed his elbows on his knees, then rested his chin in his cupped hands, studying Epstein intently.

"How are you?" he said.

"What do you mean?" Epstein said.

"Your stomach," Aldridge said. "Is it hurting you? It must bother you a lot."

"How do you know about my stomach?"

"Cancer's a terrible thing," Aldridge said. "I myself have suffered ailments in the past, but all that is behind me now."

"Behind you?" Epstein said.

"Yes, behind me," Aldridge said. "I used to have bad trouble with my heart, but I've managed to mend it."

"What are you talking about?" Epstein said. "I don't understand. What are you doing here in my room? Who let you in?"

"I have a pacemaker," Aldridge said. "A very sophisticated device. It utilizes a piezoelectric crystal, a small balloon filled with water, and causes the heart's own pumping power to stimulate itself. It is, of course, maintenance free. It does not require batteries. The miracles of science, Dr. Epstein, are literally boundless."

"Plastic surgery," Epstein said.

"I beg your pardon?" Aldridge said.

"I was looking at the skin on your forehead. You've had plastic surgery."

Aldridge smiled and nodded slightly. "Most perceptive," he said. "Plastic surgery, pacemaker, various organs replaced . . . unfortunately I was one of the first—we are much more advanced now."

"Who's we?" Epstein said.

"My own people," Aldridge said. "We are very removed from what you know, but that, too, can be remedied."

Epstein coughed and rubbed his eyes. He thought that maybe he was dreaming. He blinked and glanced around the bright room and then turned back toward Aldridge.

"Who are you?" he said.

"I created the saucers," Aldridge said. "You've been trying to solve the mystery for twenty years, and I'm here to assist you."

Epstein rubbed his eyes again. He didn't have to, but he did it. He wanted to bang his head and wake up, but that seemed a bit foolish.

"*You* created the saucers?"

"Yes," Aldridge said. "They exist, they are right here on Earth, and I'm the man who created them."

"For the Air Force?"

"No."

"For the Navy?"

"No."

"I don't understand. I'm confused. I'm very tired. Who are you and what do you want with me? What are you doing here?"

"You don't believe me," Aldridge said.

"Of course not," Epstein said.

"I can't tell you where I come from," Aldridge said. "But I'm taking you back there."

The fear slithered down Epstein's spine. He couldn't believe that this was happening. He thought of Stanford and Scaduto, of his own trip to Paris, of the questions that writhed and collided as the facts were unveiled. He would have to keep his mouth shut. He would have to watch this man carefully. This man knew an awful lot about him, and that couldn't be good. He thought of the tapes in his safe. This man knew about the tapes. This man must be from the government or the FBI or the CIA; he already knew about the tapes and wanted to steal them and shut Epstein's mouth. Epstein felt very frightened. He didn't know what to believe. He stared at the man sitting in the chair and wondered if he were real.

"You're from the government," Epstein said.

"No," Aldridge said. "The government saucers are relatively primitive. My saucers are the ones you're looking for."

"I don't believe you," Epstein said.

"I was in the Caribbean," Aldridge said.

"The Caribbean?"

"St. Thomas," Aldridge said. "It was my ship that abducted Professor Gerhardt. You saw it—you and Stanford were on the beach."

Epstein's fear deepened considerably, made him hold his breath in, now starting to believe the man in the chair, having no other choice.

"You took Gerhardt?" he said.

"Yes," Aldridge said.

"Where do you come from?" Epstein said. "How do you know about me? I can't really accept what I'm hearing. This just doesn't make sense."

"I built the saucers," Aldridge said. "You've just found out how they started. You've got that information down on tape. I want you *and* the tapes."

Epstein licked his dry lips. He felt shaken and frightened. The man's eyes were very blue, almost steely with intelligence; he leaned forward and looked directly at Epstein, speaking slowly and clearly.

"We know all about you," he said. "We've been watching you for twenty years. You're a very tenacious man, you don't stop, and now you're dying of cancer. That makes you more dangerous. You'll be even more determined. We think you've found out too much already, so it has to end now."

"I've found nothing out," Epstein said.

"You're lying," Aldridge said. "You've just come back from Paris where you were seeing Professor Ronald Mansfield, an Englishman who worked for the scientific division of the British Intelligence Objectives Sub-Committee during World War II and who is currently working for the *Groupment d'Etudes des Phenomenes Aeriens*. That disturbed us, Dr. Epstein. That's as far as you can go. We want you and the tapes you brought back, which is why I am here."

The fear took hold of Epstein, creeping over him slyly,

paralyzing him, removing him from himself, not convinced this was happening.

"You want me?" he said.

"That's right," Aldridge said. "You will not see the dawn over Mount Rainier. You are coming with us."

Epstein didn't know what to say. He wished that Stanford would return. This conversation was bizarre, not quite real, and he felt very strange.

"I don't have the tapes," he said.

"Where are they?" Aldridge said.

"I didn't tape the conversations," Epstein said. "We just talked. He knew nothing."

"You're lying, Dr. Epstein. I respect it, but it's pointless. We will take you away tonight and then ask you—and believe me, you'll tell us."

"What about Professor Mansfield?"

"He hung himself yesterday."

"You mean you murdered him."

"That's a very emotive word," Aldridge said. "We simply did what we had to do."

"And what happened to Richard Watson?"

"An interesting case," Aldridge said. "He had very strong resistance, great will, so we wanted him back."

"You've got him now?"

"Yes. We were surprised at how much he told you. We implanted an electrode in his brain and he *still* showed resistance."

"He's alive?"

"He is functioning. We will send him back soon. He will do what we tell him to do—and he won't be alone."

"Who's we?" Epstein said.

"I can't tell you that now."

"And is that what you do? You pick them up and robotize them? Then you send them back into the world and make them follow your orders?"

"That's right," Aldridge said. "It's not as incredible as it sounds. Bear in mind that such work has been going on for years—in America, in Russia, in Europe—and it's highly advanced. Your people don't understand that, they don't know what's really happening; they only hear about *acceptable* experiments—they don't know the full extent of it. Electrocontrol is a growing industry, being expanded behind closed doors. In your own society it's relatively well advanced; in ours, much more so. Our own people begin in infancy—we take them out of the cradle. We implant electrodes in their brains, and at certain points in the spinal column, before they've even reached their fourth week. After that, they belong to us. They are developed in extraordinary ways. They are programmed for obedience, their capabilities are enhanced, and they never know the pain of discontentment."

Epstein closed his eyes. "The young boys," he murmured.

"Ah, yes," Aldridge said. "Stanford saw them. That must have confused him."

Epstein opened his eyes again. "And Richard Watson?" he said.

"It's different with outsiders. Their advanced age makes all the difference. With outsiders we have to be more careful—and aren't always successful. Richard Watson was such a case. A strong will, great resistance. We've inserted another electrode in his skull and now he seems to be functioning."

Epstein glanced around the room, feeling unreal, almost dreamy, glanced out through the window, at the darkness, heard the wind on the mountains. Stanford was out there. He was looking for UFOs. The irony of it made Epstein smile, but then the fear trickled back again. He looked at the man called Aldridge. The blue eyes were very bright. Epstein looked at the smooth skin on his forehead and felt very uncomfortable.

"I don't believe this," he said.

"What don't you believe?"

"I don't believe a damned thing you say. I think it's some kind of trick."

Aldridge smiled bleakly. "You'll believe soon enough," he said. "You've been working at the mystery for twenty years . . . your reward comes tonight."

"What do you mean?" Epstein said.

"We're taking you away," Aldridge said, "It doesn't matter where you go, where you hide . . . we'll just come down and get you."

"You're not taking me now?"

"It's not convenient," Aldridge said.

"And what happens if I don't leave this room?"

"We'll just open the door." Aldridge smiled and stood up, went to the window and gazed out, turned back and looked down at Epstein, his blue eyes bright and cold. "You were in the Caribbean," he said. "You know what happened there. If we want someone, we just come and take them—and nothing can stop us."

Epstein thought back on the Caribbean and remembered the howling wind, the hotel room going crazy, the bright light and intense heat, recalled Stanford's experience at the ranch about five months ago. White light and heat, fierce storms and shaking buildings: the symptoms were always the same, the causes unknown.

"Did you cause the storms?" he said.

"Yes," Aldridge said. "Advanced weather engineering. Something similar to your own various cloud-busters, but much more sophisticated. Our own cloud-busters are laser-based and highly effective. The larger saucers can whip the wind up—or disperse it if necessary."

"I don't believe this," Epstein said.

"Why not?" Aldridge said. "Cloud seeding is an established science. Orgone energy weather engineering is expanding every day—with floods and droughts engineered for political purposes. Of *course* we can cause a storm—so can the Russians and the Americans. Weather engineering is no longer a mystery—it's an effective new weapon."

"And the cattle?" Epstein said.

"For our laboratories," Aldridge said. "For various drugs and vitamins and advanced medical research—again, there's nothing outlandish about it . . . a simple question of theft."

"And the people . . . the kidnapped people?"

"Like the cattle," Aldridge said. "More complex, but essentially the same: they are there to be used."

"How do you mean?" Epstein said.

"It depends on the catch," Aldridge said. "Some are used as slave labor, some are robotized and returned, some are sent to the medical laboratories as guinea pigs for our research."

"That's horrible," Epstein said.

"The word 'horrible' is redundant. The spider eats the fly and in turn is devoured—all that lives in the present supports the future and has no other purpose. Nothing is horrible, Dr. Epstein. As a scientist you should know that. Blood and suffering is the constant of the laboratory—and is vital to progress."

"We're talking about human beings."

"Indeed we are," Aldridge said. "And human beings are no more than the rungs on evolution's great ladder. Science is all, Dr. Epstein. The mysteries of life must be uncovered. Science cannot progress as it should if it's held back by sentiment. Humans live and die anyway; they do so to no purpose; only science can stop this primitive wastage and make people useful. Free choice leads to conflict and wastage and is harmful to progress. Emotion is wasted energy. Moral judgment holds back science. There are too many people, there is too much human wastage, and we have to accept that human life is just cement for the future. To merely exist is not enough: what we need is a new *form* of being. We must learn to take the human being apart and reconstruct him as something else. A superior being. A creature devoid of contradictions. And the gulf between Man and Superman can't be bridged with emotions."

"That's still horrible," Epstein said.

"You're still a primitive," Aldridge said. "Where you are going, you will not feel the same: you will come to accept it."

"Where am I going?" Epstein said.

"You'll find that out soon enough."

"I don't believe this," Epstein said. "I *can't* believe it. It just doesn't seem real."

"Time will tell," Aldridge said.

Epstein closed his eyes briefly. He felt weak and light-headed. In the darkness behind his closed eyes he saw the void of the cosmos. Not a void: something else. The voids of space were filled with energy. Beyond the galaxies, in what seemed like a void, possibilities were boundless. Where would Man go? What would he become? Epstein opened his eyes again and tried to accept what he was hearing. He had searched for twenty years, had lived constantly with the mystery, and now, face to face with the answer, his fear overwhelmed him.

"The machines are real," he said.

"You know that," Aldridge said. "What you heard in Paris must have convinced you, so the question's superfluous."

"What are they?" Epstein said.

"You already have the basic facts. We've progressed enormously since then, but the basics remain. At present, apart from the systems which Mansfield doubtless told you about, we utilize advanced ion propulsion, electromagnetic propulsion, in certain cases nuclear fusion pulse rockets, and, for the carrying ships, an antigravity field. Ionization and electromagnetic discharges account for the plasmalike glow that so fascinates your witnesses, the antigravity accounts for the lack of turbulence and sonic booms, and you and Stanford have already discussed—reasonably accurately—the cause of the sudden invisibility."

"How did you know that?" Epstein said.

"We bugged your rooms," Aldridge said. "Nothing is new under the sun—we've simply made progress."

"And the antigravity shield accounts for your crews' apparent ability to withstand the extraordinary speed and direction changes of your machines?"

"Precisely. The gravity-field force applies simultaneously to the crew *and* the ship . . . and, since it provides a cushion of air around the ship, it also prevents the ship from heating up. Incidentally, I should point out—since you're looking so disbelieving—that antigravity is not as revolutionary as it seems. As far back as 1965 there were at least forty-six *unclassified* G-projects being undertaken in America alone—by the Air Force, the Navy, the Army, NASA, the Atomic Energy Commission and the National Science Foundation. Since these were the *un*classified projects, I need only point out that considerably more advanced projects are doubtless under way right this minute in the strictest of secrecy."

"Are you saying that you're connected with the U.S. government?"

"No, I'm not saying that."

Epstein couldn't think straight. He looked at Aldridge, at the blue of his eyes. Then he remembered Dr. Campbell, what he had related about hypnosis; remembering this, he thought he should try to get off the bed . . . but Aldridge spoke and that stopped him.

"It all right," Aldridge said.

"Yes," Epstein said, no longer worried, simply wanting to know more. "We keep receiving reports of different-sized machines, and that always confuses us . . ."

"The smallest discs are similar to your own CAMS—Cybernetic Anthropomorphous Machine Systems, either remote-controlled or programmed to react to certain stimuli, used mainly as sensing devices or probes. Taking the Richard Watson case, the beam of light that shone into the car was merely a laser beam on a wavelength that temporarily freezes skeletal muscles or certain nerves—thus producing either paralysis or a trancelike condition."

"And the other discs?"

"The first group are anything from five to fifteen feet in diameter. Again, these are highly complex Cybernetic Anthropomorphous Machine Systems, either flying with their long axis vertical or flying in the direction of their axis, used mainly for reconnaissance and basic manual tasks, such as the collecting of soil or water, and controlled by Remote Manipulator Systems not much different from normal ones. The second group, usually about twenty-five to thirty-five feet in diameter, are extensions of the former group, but revolving around their axis and controlled by extremely advanced cyborgs. The pilot that Richard Watson saw in the second disc was just such a cyborg: half man, half machine—the results of our thirty years of prosthetic experiment. The lungs of these cyborgs have been partially collapsed and the blood in them artifically cooled; since this operation renders their mouth and nose superfluous, these are sealed and completely nonfunctioning. The cyborgs' respiration and other bodily functions are controlled cybernetically with artificial lungs and sensors which maintain constant temperature, metabolism and pressure, irrespective of external environmental fluctuations—thus they are not effected by the extraordinary accelerations and direction changes of their craft. The third group of ships can range from one hundred to two hundred feet in diameter, can be up to several stories tall inside, are used mainly to pick up people and animals and machines, and have a crew of about one dozen men. The fourth category is the carrying ship—what you people call the 'mother' ship—a somewhat gigantic affair, approximately a mile in diameter, used for major operations of a long-term nature. The carrying ships are essentially self-generating airborne colonies, capable of drifting in outer space or of hibernating on the sea bed, manned by a large crew of humans and cyborgs, the heavy labor performed by programmed slaves, and containing workshops, laboratories, medical wards, cryonic preservation units, various hangars and all the other discs mentioned."

Aldridge smiled as he talked to Epstein, a slightly distant, cool smile, his lips dutifully performing the motions while his eyes remained icy. His eyes fascinated Epstein, repelled him and drew him in, unblinking, as clear as sunlit ice, making Epstein feel unreal. And yet the man sounded reasonable, talking quietly, precisely, explaining with the patience of a teacher, making everything simple.

"You must be very advanced," Epstein said.

"Yes," Aldridge said. "We are. Our society is based on masters and slaves, and exists just for science."

"Where is it?" Epstein said.

Aldridge smiled. "Just be patient."

"Tell me now," Epstein said. "I want to know."

"You'll find out soon enough."

They stared at one another, the silence broken by the wind outside, the light in the room very bright, the window framing the dark night.

"You said that the carrying ships can hibernate on the sea bed," Epstein said. "Is there a connection between that fact and the mystery of the Bermuda Triangle and the other areas reported to be like it?"

"Yes," Aldridge said. "We have permanent undersea laboratories in the Bermuda Triangle, the so-called Devil's Sea between Guam, Luzon in the Philippines, and the southeast coast of Japan, and another off the coast of Argentina. These laboratories are manned by cyborgs and a few programmed scientists, and are visited frequently by the carrying ships."

"And it's your carrying ships that cause the unusual magnetic disturbances in those areas?"

"Yes."

"I can't accept that you could construct such laboratories without being noticed by *someone*—by some ships or planes."

"Various governments know we're down there, and in fact cooperate with us. As for the actual construction of the laboratories at such depths, you have to appreciate the unusual dimensions and capabilities of the carrying ships. As I said, the average carrying ship is about one mile in diameter, which means that its interior space is considerable. The carrying ship simply settles near the sea bed and the laboratory is constructed inside it. The base of the carrying ship then opens up and deposits the laboratory, complete with crew, on the sea bed. The permanent fixing of the laboratory to the sea bed is accomplished with the aid of specially reinforced, remote-controlled CAMS, and then the carrying ship ascends to the surface, leaving the laboratory down there."

"And various governments *know* you're down there?"

"Yes."

"But you don't belong to any of those governments?"

"No."

"Will you explain that?"

"Not yet."

Aldridge smiled bleakly and turned back to the window, looked out as if searching for someone, glanced up at the night sky.

"Our reconnaissance satellites," Epstein said. "Is it true that they've seen you?"

"Yes," Aldridge said, turning back and looking at him. "Naturally. How could they miss us? They've seen us for years."

"Then they've been covering up for years."

"Of course," Aldridge said. "There's nothing particularly unusual about that—they've been covering up everything."

"I don't know what you mean," Epstein said.

"Don't you? What about all their secret research programs: their chemical warfare programs, their advanced weaponry programs, their secret achievements in aeronautics and communications and neurology, their covert operations against, and their clandestine agreements with, the Soviets and the Chinese and the Third World countries? The private citizen knows precious little. He knows only what they deign to tell him. Governments cover up everything, from their politics to science, and when it comes to something as big as our ships, they cover up even more."

"Why?" Epstein said.

"Because they don't trust the people. Because there isn't a government in the world that still believes in Democracy."

"What's your connection with them?"

"I can't discuss that," Aldridge said.

"You're not an extraterrestrial," Epstein said. "That much I know."

Aldridge stared at him, offered a faint, victorious smile, and Epstein flushed, thinking of the tapes in his safe, knowing that Aldridge had tricked him.

"Ah, yes," Aldridge said, "Professor Mansfield. He must have told you a lot."

Epstein burned and then cooled down, his throbbing stomach now peaceful, feeling bright to the point of unreality, removed from himself. He wondered where Stanford was, wished that Stanford would return. The wind moaned outside the window, sweeping over the darkened mountains, and he thought of the sightings over the Cascades, of what Scaduto had told them. The truth emerged in small pieces. It lay before him like a jigsaw. There were still missing pieces, gaping holes, and the clock ticked the time away.

"The harassment," Epstein said. "The suicides and disappearances. I take it that they're part of the cover-up—and that you engineered them."

"Some of them," Aldridge said. "It depends on the circumstances. The actual harassment was usually arranged by your government, but most of the deaths and disappearances are due to us."

"Most?"

"Not all. Occasionally your government steps in and does a job on its own."

"Then they work with you," Epstein said.

"On and off," Aldridge said. "As with all political situations, the agreements are tenuous and are prone to break down at any moment. We negotiate with the U.S. government. We also negotiate with the Soviets. We trade and play one against the other because we haven't much choice yet."

"Yet?"

Aldridge smiled. "The Nuclear Deterrent, the Balance of Terror, is a precarious business."

"And you're in the middle?"

"Yes," Aldridge said. "We straddle the seesaw . . . but we'll soon tip the other two off."

Epstein felt very calm now, divorced from himself, the pain in his stomach gone, the fear disappearing with it, the bizarre nature of the whole conversation making it unreal. He didn't know what to think, felt distant, almost placid, well aware that this man had done something to make him accept it all. The revelations were stunning, ambiguous, fascinating, and yet Epstein thought they sounded quite reasonable, down-to-earth, almost simple. He wondered if he was hypnotized, stood outside himself and thought this. He saw Aldridge standing right beside the window, gazing up at the night sky.

"You killed Irving," Epstein said.

"Irving Jacobs?" Aldridge said.

"Yes. Irving Jacobs. You killed him. Why did you do that?"

Aldridge walked back to the chair, sat down, stared at Epstein, not smiling, his blue eyes very bright, filled with icy intelligence.

"He was digging too deep," he said. "He had found out too much. Your own government was disturbed by his discoveries and wanted us to get rid of him. They didn't want to do it themselves. They didn't dare use their own men. They didn't want the FBI or CIA to get anywhere near him. So, we worked on him. We had him followed and harassed. When he grew frightened, when his resistance was low, we used long-range telepathy. We stole part of his mind that way. We made him think he was possessed. In the end we made him drive out to the desert where we came down on top of him. We didn't need him as a scientist—we have plenty in that field—so we simply stuck the gun in his mouth and made it look like a suicide."

Epstein should have been shocked, but he felt nothing at all. He thought of Irving and Mary and the old days, but it seemed far away.

"You use mental telepathy?"

"Yes," Aldridge said. "Certain brain implantations can enhance telepathic powers and actually lead to nonverbal communication. Some of the children, and all of the cyborgs, communicate that way."

"Were you involved with the woman from Maine?"

"Yes," Aldridge said. "We were experimenting and the woman from Maine picked us up and then told the CIA. The people she first informed knew nothing about us *or* their government's saucers; but the Canadian government, when they heard about her, were naturally more concerned, thinking she might have picked up some Soviet signals. Bearing in mind that only a limited number of government and armed forces personnel know about the existence of the saucers, it was unfortunate that the men who first interrogated the woman knew nothing about what was going on. However, at the second meeting, some of the officers present knew all about the saucer programs—and it was they who subsequently buried the incident and transferred the CIA men who were in the office but didn't know what was happening."

"Our informant said it was a Canadian–U.S. saucer."

"An understandable error. Unfortunately it was an error that led to your friend Scaduto spying on the Canadian plants. More fortunately, Mr. Scaduto recently died of a premature heart attack. You can blame that on Stanford."

The remark hardly effected Epstein. He felt calm and interested. The man speaking sounded exceptionally reasonable, the revelations quite commonplace.

"What about Irving?" Epstein said.

"I've already told you about him."

"You didn't actually tell me what he found out. I'd like to know that."

"Jacobs was interested in the deaths and disappearance of so many of his contemporaries, and this encouraged him to investigate the Jessup case. In doing this, he discovered that the U.S. Navy had, back in 1943, been experimenting with pulsating and vortexual high intensity magnetic fields which might alter the molecular structure of physical properties and render them temporarily invisible. This experiment became known as the Philadelphia Experiment, but contrary to popular belief it was a disaster. What in fact happened was that the Navy inadvertently created a source of electromagnetic energy that produced an infrasound of such intensity that it killed every sailor on board the ship and actually split the ship's hull. In short, the ship rumored to have disappeared actually sank—and naturally, since the Navy didn't want word of this to leak out, they whipped up a mass of rumors that acted as a cover-up and led to the contemporary myth . . . However, in investigating this, Dr. Jessup discovered that the Navy's basic scientific principles were valid, that the Navy and Air Force were involved in saucer projects, and that those projects were utilizing certain aspects of the original Philadelphia Experiment. Having found out about this, Jessup had to be removed . . . then Jacobs found out much the same thing and also had to be terminated."

"I see," Epstein said. "And those principles were also the principles underlying the invisibility-inducing properties of your craft?"

"Correct. A specific quantity of electromagnetic radiation creates a stream of escaping photons of the same wavelength and frequency, which leads either to a glowing, plasmalike shield or to a color source beyond the known spectrum that renders the saucer invisible."

"How does this relate to the annotations in Jessup's book—the ones that stimulated the interest of the Office of Naval Research?"

"That was something of a red herring," Aldridge said. "In 1955 the Navy was still experimenting with the possibilities of electromagnetically-induced invisibility. They were then, and remain today, unsuccessful. Nevertheless, they were disturbed by some of Jessup's published remarks—and the annotations in that copy of his book had been made by their own intelligence officers, and related only to the sections that discussed force fields and dematerialization. The Navy wanted to know the source of his information, Jessup naturally refused to tell them, then Jessup walked out of their office—and that's all there was to it."

"You had nothing to do with the annotations?"

"No. Not a thing."

Epstein closed his eyes, let himself drift away, drifting down through the darkness and the long years he had labored, feeling peaceful, then feeling confused, and drifting back up again. He thought of the tapes in his office, of the old man now dead, thought of everything the old man had told him, wondered what it might mean. He had to get the tapes to Stanford. If nothing else, he had to do that. He now knew that they would take him away, and that he would not resist. He didn't want to resist. His curiosity was too great. He opened his eyes and saw Aldridge by the window and felt a great peace.

"I have to go now," Aldridge said. "When I depart, you will sleep. When you wake up, you will do what you feel like—because the choice won't be yours."

"I'm confused," Epstein said.

"By what?"

"You're not an extraterrestrial, you're from Earth, and you created the saucers. That's what confuses me. It just doesn't make sense. The first genuine UFO sightings were in 1897—yet you say you're the man who created them."

"That's correct," Aldridge said. He turned away from the window, walked back to the bed, and stood there, staring intently at Epstein, his blue eyes very bright. "I am one hundred and seven years old," he said. "My real name is Wilson."

CHAPTER TWENTY-SEVEN

Approaching the lodge after his long day in the mountains, covered in snow and freezing, Stanford desperately wanted sleep, a respite from it all, an escape from the fear that now dogged him every day and was encouraged by his present exhaustion. The snow was deep and very clean, drifting lazily upon itself, sweeping gently around the trees, the moonlight making it glisten, the wind moaning and scraping at his nerves, the mountains looming above him. Stanford longed for the lodge, for its safety and warmth, but when he saw it, the fear increased greatly and made him stop walking.

All the lights were on. The front door was ajar. A beam of light fell from the door to the porch, illuminating the snow that drifted along the wooden boards. Stanford stood beneath some pines, not moving, his heart pounding, wondering why the lights were on, who was in there, his head spinning with fevered thoughts. He knew he was being foolish, felt ashamed of it, couldn't stop it, remembering the boys in gray coveralls, the burning ranch and the vanished girl, remembering Gerhardt's abduction and Scaduto's recent suicide, and the fact that *they* knew who he was and might come back again . . .

Stanford cursed and shivered slightly. He wiped snow from his face. He thought of the lights he had seen above the mountains, drifting up, shooting sideways. Not descending: ascending. Not meteors: unidentifieds. Stanford shivered and stared ahead, the panic emptying his mind, then he shook his head and realized it was Epstein, cursed again, started walking.

He climbed the wooden steps, pushed the door open, walked inside, glanced around the living area, seeing no sign of Epstein, wondered why he had left all the lights on, then went into the bedroom. Epstein was on the bed, wearing pajamas, looking sleepy, his hands folded primly in his lap, his gaze fixed straight ahead.

"You got my message," Stanford said.

"Yes," Epstein said.

"It's been a bitch of a day," Stanford said. "They've been all over the place."

"Unidentifieds?"

"Yes."

"What kind?"

"Just lights. They've been flying all over Mount Rainier, but they never came close."

"No possible landings?" Epstein said.

"None reported," Stanford said. "Most of the lights were high up, standing still, then shooting sideways, racing back and forward across the mountains, disappearing, coming back again. Then this big light came down. All the smaller lights went into it. Then the big light climbed vertically and disappeared and hasn't been seen since. That was an hour ago."

Epstein nodded judiciously, looking down at his folded hands, very frail in his pajamas, too frail, a man fading away. Stanford noticed the frailness—that and something else: a remoteness, a sort of dreamy look, that seemed very unnatural.

"Are you all right?" he said.

"Yes," Epstein said. "I'm fine."

"And how was Paris? What did you find out?"

"You were right. It was Germany."

Stanford was taking off his jacket, but he stopped and stared at Epstein, the shock mixed with fear and excitement, disbelief and wild hope. He shrugged his jacket back on again, took a deep breath, just stood there, the snow melting on the shoulders of the jacket and dripping down to the carpet.

"Germans?" he said.

"I don't know," Epstein said. "I thought so at first, but now I'm not so sure. I'm confused. I don't know what to think."

"What do you mean, you're confused?"

"I have some tapes," Epstein said. "It's vital that you hear them. From what the old man told me, it seems almost certain that the Americans and Canadians, and possibly the British, have their own flying saucers . . . But Scaduto was right: there's someone else involved. I don't know who they are or where they come from or what they're up to, but I *do* know that they're not extraterrestrial and that they're frighteningly advanced . . . It's vital that you hear the tapes. They're in my safe back in Washington. It's vital that you go back there right now and get them out of the safe."

"Right *now*?" Stanford said.

"Yes," Epstein said.

"That's ridiculous," Stanford said. "I'm exhausted. Just tell me what's on them."

"There's no time," Epstein said. "The tapes aren't safe anymore. They want me and the tapes and they'll probably get both before the dawn. You have to get there before them."

Stanford walked over to the bed and looked carefully at Epstein, thinking that his friend had gone mad, wondering what he was talking about. Epstein was leaning against the pillow, his hands folded on his lap, his gray beard more shaggy than usual, his eyes slightly unfocused.

"What are you talking about?" Stanford said. "I'm not sure I heard you right. *Who's* going to get you and the tapes? I don't think I heard right."

Epstein didn't look up. "I had a visitor," he said. "He killed the Englishman and Scaduto. Now he wants me and the tapes. He says he'll have both by dawn."

"A visitor?" Stanford said.

"Yes. He came here. He left just before you arrived. He knew all about Irving and Gerhardt and Richard Watson, about you, about me, about that girl on the ranch, and he said he wants me and the tapes and that he'll have both by dawn."

"And you believe him?" Stanford said.

"Yes, Stanford, I believe him. I don't think I'll be here long. He claims he saw you and me on the beach near St. Thomas, he knows about your encounter with the boys outside the ranch, and he knows about a lot of other things that he just shouldn't know. He's one of them, Stanford. He told me about the machines. He told me enough to convince me. I've no doubt that he'll get me."

Stanford sat down on the bed, the snow still dripping off him, and stared at his friend for some time before he managed to talk again.

"Tell me," he said.

Epstein recounted the whole story, his voice calm and remote. Stanford sat there, fascinated, both frightened and excited, his head filled with bright lights and pulsating coronas and glittering stars that moved majestically through black night and then blinked out and disappeared. Epstein's voice was very tired, almost toneless, abstracted, filtering through Stanford's head and out again. Stanford listened, hypnotized, the walls dissolving around him, not fully comprehending what he heard, overwhelmed and struck dumb. Then Epstein stopped talking, gave a sigh, looked at his hands, and the walls of the room reappeared as the real world crept back. Stanford glanced all around him, wondering where he was, who he was, then managed to take control of himself, looking back at his old friend.

"I don't believe this," he said.

"It's all true," Epstein said.

"Jesus," Stanford said. "It's too much. I just can't get a hold of it."

Epstein coughed into his fist. "You have to leave now," he said. "It's vital that you get all the tapes before they get me to talk."

"What makes you so sure you'll talk?"

"Because I think they'll hypnotize me. Either that or they'll put an electrode in my brain like they did to young Richard."

"You think they're coming back tonight?"

"Before dawn," Epstein said. "It's vital that you leave right this minute and get there before them."

"Me?" Stanford said.

"I'm not coming," Epstein said.

"What the hell do you mean, you're not coming? You can't sit here and *wait* for them."

Epstein's hands shook imperceptibly. "I don't want to go," he said. "I've been trying to unravel the mystery for twenty years and now it's right on my doorstep. They're going to take me with them. I can't miss that opportunity. I want to know who they are, where they come from, so I'll have to go with them."

"Are you crazy?" Stanford said. "If you go, you won't come back. Those bastards aren't doing you any favors— once you go, you'll be *gone*."

Epstein shrugged and smiled gently. "So what?" he said. "Look at me. I look like a ghost. I've only got a year anyway."

"You're crazy," Stanford said.

"I have to know," Epstein said. "I can't die without knowing the whole story—and this is my chance."

"I won't let you," Stanford said.

"Get the tapes," Epstein said.

"No, dammit," Stanford said. "I won't let you. Now get your clothes on."

Epstein shrugged and then looked up, smiling gently, remotely, staring directly at Stanford without really seeing him.

"It's pointless," he said. "If they want me, they'll get me. It doesn't matter where I go, where I hide, because they'll know where to find me."

"Don't bet on it," Stanford said.

"I would bet on it," Epstein said.

"Shut up," Stanford said. "I'm not listening. Now put your clothes on."

Epstein smiled and nodded gently, swung his legs off the bed, stood up and started dressing himself like a man still asleep. It didn't matter if they left. He was certain the man would find him. He was certain that whatever he did, the man would know he was doing it. This thought gave him some comfort, eased his pain, made him glow, now enraptured with the thought of the revelations that would soon set him free. He would not die defeated. Death would not have dominion. He would wait and they would come, the night would turn to blinding light, and he would blink and then open his eyes and see a world beyond reckoning. Epstein put his clothes on. When he had finished, he glanced around him. He had only been here a few hours and yet he felt a great sadness. It was not a painful sadness. His sense of loss was couched in joy. Epstein buttoned up his coat and smiled at Stanford, prepared for just anything.

"Okay?" Stanford said.

"Okay," Epstein said.

"Right," Stanford said. "Let's go. Let's get the hell out of here."

They walked through the lodge, stepped out onto the porch, felt the cold and saw the snow falling down as Stanford locked the front door. Stanford grabbed Epstein's elbow, guided him down the slippery steps. The snow was thin on the ground, drifting lazily, as they walked to the car. Stanford helped Epstein in, holding his arm, staring at him, then he closed the door and walked around the car and slipped into the driver's seat. Epstein said nothing, simply smiled and looked ahead, and Stanford started the car and headed out through the tall, snow-limned trees.

"Are you all right?" he said.

"I'm fine," Epstein said.

"Are you sure? You seem a bit quiet."

"I feel fine," Epstein said.

Stanford drove between the trees, the snow white in the darkness, the mountains jagged and silhouetted against the sky, rising up all around them. Stanford drove very carefully, squinting against the falling snow, his headlights picking out tree-trunks and rocks and high banks of green earth. He was nervous, excited, not sure what he was doing, glancing occasionally at Epstein, at his smile, and wondering what he was thinking. The car rolled down the narrow track, the trees gliding past silently, the snow drifting dreamily across the track, the darkness stretched out below them.

"You know, it fits," Stanford said. "A lot of what he told you fits. The application of an antigravity shield could result in a virtually massless body. Now, according to technical analysis, the lift-off of your average UFO would require as much energy as the detonation of an atomic bomb, would cause the body of the UFO to heat up to about 85,000° centigrade, and would naturally lead to intense deposits of radioactivity. However, with an antigravity shield reducing the mass of the UFO to almost zero, it would only require a very modest force to reach exceptionally high accelerations. That would account for the UFOs' ability to disappear in the blinking of an eye, for the fact that the UFOs can be brought to a very abrupt stop, and would explain why they can make such normally impossible right-angle turns. Since we can also assume safely that the inertial mass of such a UFO would decrease the higher it goes, we can then reason that such a mass would be reduced to almost zero by the time it reaches the limits of the Earth's atmosphere. That would explain why the UFOs invariably have what appears to be a two-stage take-off: a slow rise to about a hundred feet or so, then a sudden acceleration and disappearance. Finally, since the UFOs' performance is directly related to the Earth's gravity, and since the pull of gravity varies slightly from place to place, that would explain why a UFO in horizontal flight often appears to rise and fall slightly: the increase and decrease of gravitational pull would effect the inertial mass of the UFO and make it bob up and down a bit; it would also explain why the UFOs appear to be able to automatically follow the profile of the terrain below . . . So, the facts fit."

Epstein nodded and smiled, his hands folded in his lap, his eyes slightly unfocused and peaceful, fixed on the downhill road.

"Still," Stanford said, "it's pretty fantastic. And he said he was one hundred and seven years old . . . If that's true, he's not human."

"You don't think so?" Epstein said.

"No, I don't think so. If the guy comes from Earth, I can't buy that: it's just too incredible."

"I'm not so sure," Epstein said. "Bear in mind that whoever these people are, they're obviously extraordinarily advanced in their technology. Now, according to Aldridge that technology includes medical and psychological research, with no apparent restraint on the researchers.

They're definitely very far advanced in parapsychology and prosthetics, and they practice vivisection on human beings."

"Jesus Christ," Stanford said.

"Yes," Epstein said, "it's horrible. But no matter, that's certainly what they're doing. Now assuming that their medical and surgical research is as advanced as their other sciences, it is not unreasonable to assume that Mr. Aldridge is one hundred and seven years old. What I do know is that his face was reconstructed with plastic surgery, that he uses an extremely advanced pacemaker, and that he has had various organs replaced. He also pointed out that the work on him was performed at an early stage and that those methods were now considered to be relatively primitive. Presumably, then, it is possible that Mr. Aldridge is one hundred and seven years old."

"What does that make his date of birth?"

"1870."

"No," Stanford said. "I don't believe this."

"Think again," Epstein said. "A few people have actually managed to live to that age—and without medical assistance. Add medical and surgical assistance of the most advanced kind, and Mr. Aldridge could be exactly what he says he is."

"Okay," Stanford said. "But *who* is he?"

"He said his real name was Wilson," Epstein said.

"So?"

"Have you ever heard of a Wilson in relation to UFOs?"

"No," Stanford said. "I can't say that I have . . . No, it's too ridiculous."

"What's ridiculous?" Epstein said. "Don't be shy. I want to know what you mean."

Stanford shook his head wearily, squinting against the falling snow, his headlights boring through the darkness as the car moved downhill, the road winding around canyons and ravines, the land stretched out below them.

"The flap of 1897," Stanford said. "The first real modern sightings."

"Don't blush," Epstein said. "Just keep talking."

"Okay," Stanford said. "As you know, the first major

UFO flap was in 1896—about November of that year—
and continued until May 1897. This was five years *before*
the Wright brothers' experiments, but there were, by this
time, various airship designs on the drawing boards or in
the Patent Office. On August 11, 1896, patent number
565805 was given to Charles Abbot Smith of San Francisco for an airship he intended having ready by the following year. Another patent, number 580941, was issued
to Henry Heintz of Elkton, South Dakota, on April 20,
1897. However, I should point out that while many of the
UFOs sighted were shaped roughly like the patent designs,
there is no record of either airship having been built."

"But the airships looked like the UFOs?"

"At that time the general belief was that aerial navigation would be solved through an airship rather than a
heavier-than-air flying machine—so most of the earlier
designs looked like dirigibles with a passenger car on the
bottom."

"Cigar-shaped."

"Right."

"Please continue."

"Okay, what stands out in the 1896 and 1897 sightings
is that the UFOs were mostly cigar-shaped, that they frequently landed, and that their occupants often talked to
the witnesses, usually asking for water for their machines.
Now, the most intriguing of the numerous contactee stories involved a man who called himself Wilson. The first
incident occurred in Beaumont, Texas, on April 19, 1897,
when J. B. Ligon, the local agent for Magnolia Brewery,
and his son Charles noticed lights in the Johnson pasture a
few hundred yards away and went to investigate. They
came upon four men standing beside a large, dark object
which neither of the witnesses could see clearly. One of
these men asked Ligon for a bucket of water, Ligon let
him have it, and then the man gave his name as Mr. Wilson. He then told Ligon that he and his friends were traveling in a flying machine, that they had taken a trip 'out
of the gulf', and that they were returning to the 'quiet
Iowa town' where the airship and four others like it had
been constructed. When asked, Wilson explained that electricity powered the propellers and wings of the airship,

then he and his friends got back into the airship and Ligon watched it ascending.

"The next day, April 20, Sheriff H. W. Baylor of Uvalde, also in Texas, went to investigate a strange light and voices in back of his house. He encountered an airship and three men—and one of the men gave his name as Wilson, from Goshen, New York. Wilson then inquired about one C. C. Akers, former sheriff of Zavalia County, saying that he had met him in Fort Worth in 1877 and now wanted to see him again. Sheriff Baylor, surprised, replied that Captain Akers was now at Eagle Pass, and Wilson, reportedly disappointed, asked to be remembered to him the next time that Sheriff Baylor visited him. Baylor reported that the men from the airship wanted water and that Wilson requested that their visit be kept secret from the townspeople. Then he and the other men climbed back into the airship and, quote, 'its great wings and fans were set in motion and it sped away northward in the direction of San Angelo.' The county clerk also saw the airship as it left the area.

"Two days later, in Josserand, Texas, a whirring sound awakened farmer Frank Nichols, who looked out of his window and saw 'brilliant lights streaming from a ponderous vessel of strange proportions' in his cornfield. Nichols went outside to investigate, but before he reached the object, two men walked up to him and asked if they could have water from his well. Nichols agreed to this—as farmers in those days usually did—and the men then invited him to visit the airship where he noticed that there were six or eight crew members. One of these men told him that the ship's motive power was 'highly condensed electricity' and that it was one of five that had been constructed in 'a small town in Iowa' with the backing of a large stock company in New York.

"The next day, on April 23, witnesses described by the *Houston Post* as 'two responsible men' reported that an airship had descended where they lived in Kountze, Texas, and that two of the occupants had given their names as Wilson and Jackson.

"Four days after this incident, on April 27, the *Galveston Daily News* printed a letter from C. C. Akers, who claimed that he had indeed known a man in Fort Worth named Wilson, that Wilson was from New York, that he was in his middle twenties, and that he was 'of a mechanical turn of mind and was then working on aerial navigation and something that would astonish the world.'

"Finally, early in the evening of April 30, in Deadwood, Texas, a farmer named H. C. Lagrone heard his horses bucking as if in stampede. Going outside, he saw a bright white light circling around the fields nearby and illuminating the entire area before descending and landing in one of the fields. Walking to the landing spot, Lagrone found a crew of five men, three of whom talked to him while the others collected water in rubber bags. The man informed Lagrone that their ship was one of five that had been flying around the country recently, that theirs was in fact the same one that had landed in Beaumont a few days before, that all the ships had been constructed in an interior town in Illinois—which, note, borders Iowa—and that they were reluctant to say anything else because they hadn't yet taken out any patents. By May that same year, the sightings ended . . ."

The car rolled on down the mountain, the snow sweeping across the road, the forests rising up on both sides, white and ghostly in darkness.

"Interesting," Epstein said. "It's certainly beginning to add up. And this Wilson appeared to be in his early twenties."

"Exactly," Stanford said. "So assuming, as he claims, that he's one hundred and seven years old—your Wilson, or Mr. Aldridge—that means that in 1897 he would have been twenty-seven."

"It fits," Epstein said. "A lot of the facts fit. For instance, Aldridge, or Wilson, said that he had originally studied aeronautics at MIT and at Cornell, New York."

"You're kidding," Stanford said.

"No, I'm not kidding. He said he went to MIT and then left to study under Octave Chanute . . . Does that make any sense?"

"Oh, Christ, yes," Stanford said.

The snow swept across the headlights, the rising hills

sliding past, the sky forming a long, glittering ribbon between the towering trees.

"It's hard to believe," Stanford said, "but it's possibly true. Although there were no formal aeronautical courses at the Massachusetts Institute of Technology during the early 1890s, there were plenty of informal courses on propulsion and the behavior of fluids. Then, by 1896, instructors and students at MIT had built a wind tunnel and were experimenting with it to get practical knowledge of aerodynamics. Aldridge, or Wilson, could have attended these courses and then gone on to Sibley College, Cornell University, in Ithaca, New York, where, by the mid-1890s, it was possible to get a Bachelor of Science in Aeronautics."

They were coming out of the mountains, the road straightening and leveling out, a great drop on one side, the soaring hills on the other, the snow banked up at both sides of the car, gleaming white in the darkness.

"So," Epstein said. "Wilson, or Aldridge, was born in 1870. In 1890, at the age of twenty, he was studying propulsion and the behavior of fluids at MIT, after which he went on to Cornell to study aerodynamics. Let us say, then, that by the mid-1890s he had obtained his Bachelor of Science in Aeronautics. Assuming he is a genius, we can then assume that he left Cornell and went directly into designing and constructing flying machines. Now, bearing in mind the enormous interest there was at that time in the possibilities of such machines—and the fact that numerous researchers and inventors were obsessed with the possible theft or plagiarism of their designs—the need for secrecy would certainly have been predominant. Given this, it *is* possible that your Wilson, or my Aldridge, was financed by some stock company in New York to set up a secret research center in the uninhabited wilds of Illinois or Iowa. It is then also possible—still assuming that our friend is a genius—that he could have built the first airships by 1896."

"Christ," Stanford hissed. "Jesus Christ! Which gets us to your tapes."

"Correct," Epstein said.

"What's on them?" Stanford said. "Tell me what's on

the tapes. I can't wait until we get to Washington. I have to know *now*."

Epstein didn't reply. Stanford turned and looked at him. Epstein sat there with his head on one shoulder, his eyes closed, breathing deeply. Stanford smacked him on the shoulder, but Epstein didn't respond. Stanford cursed and looked out at the swirling snow and then looked back at Epstein. He was still breathing deeply, his eyes closed as if asleep, and Stanford shook him and got no response and felt a sharp, stabbing panic. He shook Epstein and called his name. Epstein didn't wake up. Stanford suddenly felt frightened, wondering what was going on, thinking Epstein might have had some sort of stroke, wondering what he could do. They were a long way from Washington. The mountains climbed up behind them. Ahead, on either side of the road, the hills climbed into darkness. Stanford cursed and stopped the car, turned around and shook Epstein. Epstein blinked and then opened his eyes and looked vaguely around him.

"Where are we?" he said.

"Nowhere," Stanford said. "I had to stop the car to awaken you. I thought something had happened to you."

"I fell asleep?"

"That's what it looked like. I just looked and you were gone. I've never seen anyone fall asleep that fast and it gave me a fright."

Epstein smiled. "My apologies."

"Are you sure you're all right?"

"Of course," Epstein said. "I feel fine. I don't know what happened . . . All the flying. Jet lag . . ."

"Can I go now?" Stanford said.

"Certainly. Please do."

"Good," Stanford said. "I'm relieved. I don't like it out here."

He turned the ignition key. Nothing happened and he tried again. Nothing happened and he cursed and tried a third time, but still nothing happened. He glanced briefly at Epstein. Epstein's eyes were slowly closing. Stanford cursed and then tried the car a fourth time, but still nothing happened. The engine was completely dead. Stanford couldn't understand that. He looked around him, saw the thick, spiraling snow, the hills covered in trees. Stanford turned to look at Epstein. The professor was asleep. Stanford opened the door and climbed out of the car.

The wind was light but very icy, and he shivered and went to the front of the car and lifted the hood. He beamed his flashlight on the engine, examined the spark plugs, the carburetor, the works, but couldn't find a thing wrong. Stanford shivered with cold. The snow was settling on the engine. He turned the light off and went back around the car to try the ignition again. He bent down to climb in, stopped, blinked his eyes, saw that the other door was open and that Epstein had disappeared.

Stanford straightened up quickly, feeling panic, his heart pounding, looking over the car, across the road, at the tree-covered slopes. The trees were tall and close together, blocking out the moonlight, the white snow disappearing into darkness where the slope became steep. Then he saw Professor Epstein, stooped over, coat flapping, clambering up the slope and heading through the trees, the snow swirling about him.

Stanford bawled Epstein's name. Epstein didn't glance back. He had passed the first trees, his feet buried in the snow, disappearing, reappearing, climbing up. Stanford looked up above him. A chill ran down his spine. He saw the light beyond the trees, rising up, spreading out, a glowing fan at the top of the hill that grew larger each second.

"Oh my God!" Stanford hissed.

He banged the car with his fist, ran around it, followed Epstein, his feet sinking into the snow as he crossed the dark road. The light wind was sharp and icy, blowing the snow into his face, and he put his hand over his face until he reached the first trees. Looking up he saw Epstein heading straight for the pulsating light that fanned out in the black sky. Then Stanford felt something, thought he heard it, wasn't sure, jerked his head back and looked straight above him and went numb all over. There was no sky above. There was just a total blackness: a blackness that wiped out the moon and stars and was utterly physical. Stanford kept looking up. He couldn't believe what was happening. The blackness went as far as he could see and seemed to bear down upon him.

Stanford looked up at Epstein. He saw him moving between the trees. The light fanned out above the brow of the hill, pulsating and glowing. Stanford screamed Epstein's name. Epstein didn't glance back. Stanford cursed and started racing up the hill, the air vibrating around him. He heard the sound or felt it, wasn't sure what was happening, slowed down and started slipping and sliding, his head tight, his lungs bursting. Then he fell and rolled over, looked up and saw the light, saw Epstein climbing up toward the light with unnatural energy.

Stanford lay there in the snow, looked up and saw the light spreading out and enveloping Epstein. Then two figures materialized. They were both silhouetted. They came up over the top of the hill, moving slowly, methodically. They stopped and stood still and were framed by the fan of light. Epstein stood up and walked toward the figures, and one reached out and touched him. Stanford lay there, looking up, unable to move. Epstein merged with the two silhouettes and then they all walked away, vanishing over the hill. Stanford lay there a very long time, the vibrating sound numbing him.

The snow continued falling. The fan of light started fading. It grew weaker and smaller, shrank to nothing, and then disappeared. Stanford lay there in the snow, watching the top of the hill. A line of white lights rose out of the darkness and climbed slowly and vertically. Then the vibrating stopped. The dark night was filled with light. Stanford jerked his head back and looked above him and shielded his eyes.

There was light in the blackness, a perfect circle, growing larger, spreading out and hurling down a radiant glare that turned the night into daytime. Stanford shielded his eyes. He squinted up at that pool of light. He saw the other line of lights gliding over from the hill and merging with the fierce light above him and then disappearing.

Stanford closed his eyes a moment. They were watering and stinging. He blinked and looked up again and saw the blinding white light. There was a black disc in the middle. The larger circle of light was shrinking. It kept shrinking until it swallowed the black disc and then the blackness was total.

Stanford kept looking up. He saw nothing but the blackness. He lowered his gaze and looked back along the road and saw a ribbon of stars. The blackness ended back there. The ribbon of stars was growing wider. The far edge of the blackness was receding and racing toward him. Stanford looked the other way. He saw the very same thing. He saw a ribbon of stars growing wider as the blackness raced toward him. Then he looked up again. He saw nothing but the blackness. He looked around him and saw the emerging stars as the black mass kept shrinking. It shrank as it ascended. The stars raced in on all sides. Stanford looked up and saw the dwindling darkness with the stars all around it. It finally became a small black disc. The disc shrank and disappeared. Stanford looked up and saw the starry sky, the moon wreathed in the clouds.

The tightness left Stanford's head. He stood up and then walked up the hill until he stood at the top. He looked down the other side, saw a white, empty field. He turned around and stumbled back down to the car, feeling grief and outrage. He turned the ignition key. The car roared into life. Stanford drove back to Washington, the loss of Epstein tearing at him, now determined to get the tapes in the safe before he, too, was taken.

CHAPTER TWENTY-EIGHT

February 22, 1945. The guns roared in the distance, the skies were filled with smoke, and we had to destroy the Kugelblitz and make good our escape. I remember it well. I had to wrap my heart in ice. The sleek saucer stretched across the broken stones at the base of the mountain. We had removed the new components. We had to leave the rest behind. We couldn't let what remained fall to the enemy, and so we had to destroy it. I stood near the hangar doors. General Kammler was not present. The forested hills of Kahla stretched around us and were veiled in a thin mist. I glanced at General Nebe. His swarthy face revealed nothing. My fellow scientists and technicians were just behind me, their eyes fixed on the saucer. The guns roared in the distance. The saucer glittered in the sunlight. Nebe's demolition men were standing beneath it, grouped around the four legs. One of the men waved his hand. General Nebe nodded quietly. All the men walked away from the saucer and returned to the hangar.

I no longer accepted pain. It was a redundant emotion. Nonetheless, as I gazed at my creation, I had to harden myself. The saucer seemed enormous, its sloping walls a seamless gray, sweeping up to a steel-plated dome and reflecting the sunlight. It looked very beautiful. It also looked quite unreal. What I felt was a fleeting sense of loss, but I rigorously stifled it. I just stood there, saying nothing. General Nebe nodded quietly. A kneeling ser-

geant leaned forward and pressed a plunger and the saucer exploded.

Fierce flame and whirling smoke. We were crouched behind the sandbags. The explosion reverberated through the hangar and then faded away. We all stood up slowly. The smoke was swirling toward the sky. Where the saucer had been there was a dark hole, filled with debris and smoldering.

I found myself speechless. I turned away and faced Nebe. His dark eyes and humorless face displayed no sign of sympathy. He just shrugged and surveyed the hangar. It was vast and filled with workers. The workers were lined up against the walls, being guarded by soldiers. Nebe's dark eyes were watchful. He murmured an order to his sergeant. The sergeant barked further orders to his troops and they all raised their guns. The prisoners moved immediately. They put their hands on their heads. Silent, their eyes dead as the moon, they started leaving the hangar.

The destruction began. We would leave little to the Allies. All that day the ground rocked to explosions and the shrieking of bullets. A dark smoke boiled from the hangar. The long tunnels were filled with flame. The technicians stood outside, bemused, as their laboratories crumbled. Soldiers darted to and fro. Hand grenades curved through the air. The flames daggered through the black smoke and splashed down on the ground.

Other guns roared in the distance. The horizon was smokey. The enemy was advancing every minute and our time became precious. We all rushed to pack the trucks. The large crate was first to leave. In the crate were the numerous new components, without which we were lost. I climbed in beside the crate. I glanced out and saw the prisoners. They were kneeling in their hundreds on the ground, the smoke all around them. I did not look very long. They were destined for Buchenwald. When they turned to smoke and ash in the crematoria, what they knew would die with them. I reached out and touched the crate. General Nebe waved from the murk. The truck growled and then rumbled down the hill as the destruction continued.

The darkness was descending. The Allied guns roared in the distance. The truck started rocking from side to side

*and the large crate swayed dangerously. I reached out and
touched it. I thought briefly of Rudolph Schriever. The
Flugkapitan was still working in Mahren, trying to finish
his saucer. As the guns roared, I smiled. Schriever's saucer
could never work. I stroked the large wooden crate with
my fingers and felt a great peace. The truck shuddered
and then stopped. I heard the hissing of steam. I looked
out and saw the mass of milling workers, getting close to
the train.*

*We unloaded in darkness. The crate was moved with
great care. A battalion of S.S. troops marched by, their
guns and knives gleaming. They were all young fanatics.
They were General Nebe's disciples. They had deserted after the attempt on Hitler's life, and were now going with
us. The war raged in the distance. The train clanged and
spat steam. The slave workers were stripped to the waist,
sweating under the cracking whips. I watched the crate
being loaded. It bumped against the long carriage. I cursed
the man who was operating the crane and he lowered his
head. The crate dropped down more slowly. Blackened
hands pushed it in. The doors were closed and the slaves
were pushed away as I walked toward the platform.*

*Allied planes growled overhead. I heard the crack of a
rifle. A dog snarled and a man began to scream as I
reached the dark platform. The train's steam swirled all
around me. Troops were entering the train. The earth shuddered and I saw flames in the distance, flaring up in the
black night. Men were shouting and jostling. A torch
shone in my face. General Nebe materialized from the
murk, his dark eyes unrevealing. He pointed up at a
nearby carriage. I saw the peaked caps of the officers. I
nodded and we both climbed on the train and closed the
door hard behind us.*

*The carriage was packed and noisy. A sweating corporal
pulled the blinds down. Once finished, he turned on all the
lights and I felt my eyes stinging. The officers were all disheveled. Their ties were loose and their shirts were
soaked. The air was blue with cigarette smoke, smelled of
ash and fresh sweat. General Nebe murmured something.
Two men jumped to their feet. They saluted and then
marched away, leaving two empty seats. Nebe indicated*

one of them. I sat down and he sat beside me. The two officers sitting opposite froze visibly and then dropped their eyes. Nebe yawned and glanced around him. His rough face was expressionless. Shortly after, with a clanging and groaning, the train started to move.

The night was long and miserable. The train stopped and started often. Allied planes growled continuously overhead, the guns boomed in the distance. The officers smoked and played cards. Their ears cocked when they heard explosions. Nebe slept with his mouth pursed and whistling, his head hanging heavily. General Kammler was not present. He was busy elsewhere. That same night he was moving the scientists from Peenemunde to the mine shafts of Bleicherode. He had suggested the move to Himmler. It was a cunning thing to do. Its purpose was to distract Himmler's attention while we made our escape. The Reichsfuhrer was in a panic. He had forgotten about the wilderness. He was now more concerned with the V-2 rockets, and with young Schriever's saucer. The guns roared as I smiled. I thought of Shriever back in Mahren. That fool would still be working on his saucer when the Allies surrounded him.

We were bombed a few hours later. I remember my streaming fears. The sudden roaring almost split my eardrums as I plunged to the floor. The bending tracks shrieked. My one thought was for the crate. The whole carriage climbed up and crashed down and then rolled on its side. The noise was catastrophic. Men screamed as seats buckled. I went sliding along the floor and hit a wall and rolled over a flailing form, flying wood and spinning chairs. A smashed head pouring blood. I turned around and saw the windows above me, glass shattered and glinting. Men screamed and bawled curses. I jumped back to my feet. A bloody corporal formed a stirrup with his hands, and Nebe planted his boot in it. The corporal heaved the general up. I saw a mass of dangling legs. More bombs fell and exploded around the train as I found a cleared space. I pulled myself up through the window. The night roared and spewed flame. I crawled away from the window and rolled off and crashed down to the ground.

My one thought was for the crate. I ran toward the long carriage. Men were falling off the train and crashing down and then rolling away from me. The night spewed flame and smoke. A silhouette was bawling orders. I clawed two or three men from my path and then saw the long carriage. General Nebe was already there. There were three trucks near the train. A dozen men were laboring under my crate, their eyes large, their necks straining. Another bomb fell nearby. Nebe stepped forward and barked an order. The men heaved the crate onto the truck and then quietly collapsed. General Nebe's jackboot glistened. He kicked one of the lolling men. The men jumped up and grabbed at their weapons and climbed into the truck. Nebe waved his right hand. I climbed up beside the driver. Nebe climbed in beside me, barked an order, and the truck started moving. The planes passed overhead. A gray dawn began to break. There was another truck in front, one behind, and we kept moving forward.

The breaking dawn was filled with smoke. The landscape was devastated. Charred trees and smoldering buildings and corpses, ragged columns of refugees. The refugees were going the other way. Allied planes flew overhead. The trucks growled and bumped along the dusty roads and the smoke cleared away. A drab country: anonymous. The devastation remained. The black buildings were no longer smoldering; the ash had turned cold. We stopped and started often. Darkness fell and brought a stark, chilling silence that gave way to the murmuring sea.

We stopped just outside Kiel. The fields were flat and barren. I saw a hangar, a series of low bunkers, a few bleak, concrete buildings. There we stayed for five weeks. The crate was hidden in a bunker. Every day I went down to inspect it, wanting desperately to leave. Each day was the same. The men played cards and drank. Allied planes rumbled over our heads, but always kept going south. Long days and freezing nights, I toyed with mathematical problems. It was wet and the S.S. men were drawn to the flickering ovens. General Nebe kept to himself. His dark eyes were unrevealing. He slept soundly, his mouth puckered and whistling, his legs outstretched and heavy. Dawn drifted into dusk. The Allied planes flew overhead. I often *studied the S.S. men in the bunkers, wondering what they were thinking. They were mostly very young. All were handsome and sweet-faced. All had dipped their hands in blood and tortured flesh, few would suffer from sleepless nights. I wondered how we could take them all. I didn't think we had the space. A cold wind came and chilled us to the bone and Nebe said we were moving out.*

We drove down through Kiel. A fine mist veiled the darkness. I was sitting in the back of a truck, the wooden crate towering over me. I thought of Kammler in Oberammergau. I wondered if he had escaped. I thought of Wernher von Braun and Dornberger and wondered what would become of them. Kammler might be with them still. He might be down there in Kiel. I ran my fingers along the length of the crate and then we came to the docks.

The trucks squealed to a halt. The crate shook and then was still. General Nebe's dark eyes appeared from swirling mist and he motioned me out. I jumped down, feeling weary. The docks were very quiet. The black water reflected the lamps beaming down on the submarines. I glanced vaguely around me. Nebe was murmuring to some troops. The men formed up in a neatly spaced line against the wall of a hangar. Other men were at my crate. They worked slowly and carefully. I glanced down at the submarine just below me: U-977. There were men on the deck grouped around the hold. Chains rattled and I saw my precious crate dangling over the water. There was a moment's hesitation. The crate jerked and started spinning. Hands reached up and guided it down until it dropped out of sight.

General Kammler appeared on deck. He was accompanied by Captain Schaeffer. Both men climbed up the ladder to the dock and walked toward General Nebe. Kammler talked in a low voice. He kept glancing along the docks. His shadow trailed out along the wet stones and smothered my feet. General Nebe turned away. He murmured something to his sergeant. General Kammler took a torch from his pocket and flashed it three times. I glanced along the dock. I saw the lights of another truck. The truck growled and then started coming toward us, its headlamps turned down. General Kammler walked toward me.

He introduced me to Captain Schaeffer. We shook hands as the truck pulled up near us and turned toward the water.

The S.S. troops were silent. They formed a line along the hangar. The sergeant stepped back and bellowed an order and they all faced the wall. I heard their guns rattling. Their boots rang on the stones. The truck stopped, overlooking the water, and its ramp was thrown down.

A shocking noise split the silence. I stepped back and shook my head. The men lined up along the tall hangar were jerking and dancing. My eyes swung toward the truck. I saw a barrel spitting flame. The machine gun was roaring and rattling as the men screamed and died. When I blinked, there was silence. A gray smoke drifted lazily. The tall wall of the hangar was filled with holes, and splashed with fresh blood. The men all lay on the ground. They were sprawled across one another. Their large pupils reflected the lamps beaming down on their faces.

Captain Schaeffer turned away. I saw Kammler's tight lips. General Nebe took his pistol from its holster and then cocked the hammer. He nodded to his sergeant. They both walked toward the bodies. Most were silent, but a few were still whimpering, their fingers outstretched. General Nebe fired the first shot. The sergeant fired the second. They took turns, bending over the bodies, the gunshots reverberating. It seemed to take a long time. It did not take long at all. When they had finished, General Nebe turned away and gently waved his left hand.

Some men jumped out of the truck. The machine gun barrel clanged. General Nebe returned his pistol to its holster and walked slowly toward us. There was no sweat on his brow. His dark eyes were unrevealing. He nodded and we all turned away and climbed down to the submarines.

We pulled out shortly after. We did not go very far. I stood with Nebe and Kammler on the deck and watched the men on the dock. There were only four men. They worked long and very hard. They put the bodies of their comrades in the truck and drove it into the hangar. The dock seemed very quiet. The lamps beamed down on the wet stones. More Allied planes rumbled overhead as the four men emerged again. They were not in the truck.

They merged gradually with the darkness. They climbed down the steel ladder one by one and dropped into a dinghy. The oars splashed in the water. The distant lamps showed desolation. After what seemed a very long time the men arrived at the submarine. They were all pulled aboard. The dinghy drifted into the darkness. I stared back across the water at the docks and saw the lamps on the hangar.

The explosion was catastrophic. The whole hangar disintegrated. The flames shot up in jagged, yellow lines that turned the night into daytime. The noise was demoniac. A black smoke billowed out. The flames swirled and turned into crimson tendrils that embraced one another. Then the smoke drifted sideways. Behind the smoke was rubble. The flames leaped across the charred, broken beams and filled the road with great shadows. The flames burned a long time. The harsh wind made them dance. They were still burning brightly when we submerged and disappeared in the Baltic Sea.

CHAPTER TWENTY-NINE

EDITED TRANSCRIPT GER/0023/DEC 3 77
TAPED INTERVIEW BETWEEN DR. EPSTEIN &
PROFESSOR RONALD MANSFIELD OF THE
GROUPMENT D'ETUDES DES PHENOMENES
AERIENS
LOCATION: PARIS, AS ABOVE
INTERVIEW DATE: NOV 27 77
EPSTEIN EDITED OUT

Tape 1:

"Yes, Dr. Epstein, it is of course true that we in the British Intelligence Objectives Sub-Committee were particularly interested in German scientific progress in the Second World War. It must be borne in mind that from the moment Hitler took power, in 1933, a gross militarism prevailed and all outstanding German scientists were forced willy-nilly to work for military laboratories. Now most of that work was concerned with producing various kinds of advanced weaponry, but as early as 1934 there was talk coming out of Germany about even more disturbing projects such as aerial torpedoes, pilotless aircraft, remote-controlled rockets, long-range guns and mysterious death rays—so quite naturally we worried. Our anxiety was increased when, in 1942, various resistance groups informed us of the flying bombs and giant rockets being

constructed at a secret research establishment at Peenemunde, and then we started receiving reports, from very
experienced pilots, of mysterious 'fireballs' that were harassing them on their bombing runs.

"Confirmation that the Peenemunde experiments had
been successful came on June 13, 1944, when the first V-1
flying bombs fell on England, and, more forcefully, on
September 6 the same year, when the first of the V-2 rockets devastated areas of Chiswick and Epping. Since these
fearsome inventions were dropping on London, the populace were quite obviously aware of them; however, what
the populace did *not* know—and what we were not about
to tell them—was that many Allied pilots had started returning from bombing runs with wild tales of being pursued by mysterious 'fireballs' that made their aircraft's
ignition and radar malfunction.

"The first recorded incidence came from Lieutenant Edward Schlueter of the 415th U.S. Night Fighter Squadron.
Apparently, on the night of November 23, 1944, Lieutenant Schlueter was flying in a heavy night fighter over
the Rhine, about twenty miles from Strasbourg, when he
and Air Intelligence Lieutenant Fred Ringwall glanced out
of the darkened cockpit and saw 'ten small balls of reddish
fire' flying in formation at what they claimed was amazing
speed. The lights followed the aircraft for some time, were
pursued and disappeared, returned and seemingly caused
the aircraft's rader and ignition to malfunction. The 'balls
of fire' eventually vanished over the Siegfried Line.

"Four days later, on the night of November 27, pilots
Henry Giblin and Walter Cleary submitted an official report stating that their airplane had been harassed over the
vicinity of Speyer by 'an enormous burning light' that was
flying 1,500 feet above their plane at about 250 miles per
hour and seemingly caused their radar to malfunction.
This report was followed by a sudden spate of similar reports, most of which agreed that the objects were large,
bright, orange lights, that they appeared to *ascend* from
low altitude, and that when they leveled out and followed
the aircraft there were inexplicable radar and ignition mal-
functions. Finally, when on January 12, 1945, several

bombing squadrons *simultaneously* reported seeing the lights, we decided to open a dossier on the subject.

"Naturally, when the war ended, our major priority was to take under our control as much as possible of the documents, drawings and actual components belonging to German scientific and military research. Regarding this, the Red Army moved into the enormous underground rocket factory in Nordhausen in the Harz Mountains, where they immediately took charge of almost-completed flying bombs and rockets, numerous precision tools and parts, and over 3,000 research workers from Peenemunde, including leading scientist Helmut Grottrup and quite a few other rocket experts—all of whom disappeared into the Soviet Union to create God knows what. The Americans, on the other hand, managed to get their hands on over a hundred V-2 rockets, five cases of hidden and highly secret Peenemunde documents and, of course, the very famous Wernher von Braun, a few hundred of his V-2 specialists, and another hundred-odd scientists who were intimate with the various Peenemunde projects.

"I give you these figures not just to impress upon you the fact that both the Soviets and the Americans gained from this division much of the material, human and otherwise, vital to advanced weaponry research and the exploration of space, but also to impress upon you the sheer *size* of the German projects.

"And the British? It was our intention right from the start—as it was doubtless the intention of the Soviets and the Americans—to complete the picture on the state of development of German research on guided missiles, supersonic aircraft and other secret weapons. Appropos of this, we sent teams of specialists belonging to the Ministry of Aircraft Production all over Western Germany and Austria, their brief being to locate every cave, disused mine, tunnel, ravine or forest where secret German establishments might be hidden, and, once having located them, to dismantle and return to England the most valuable or enigmatic equipment, even including the Germans' quite extraordinary wind tunnels.

"Since the British zone of occupation extended from the Dutch frontier to Prussia, centering on the invaluable port of Hamburg and including a large part of the eastern Alpine massif in Austria, we really did quite well out of the deal. The movement of this mass of captured documents and equipment was discreetly controlled by the British Intelligence Objectives Sub-Committee, and in general it was transported to Hamburg, shipped from there to England, and from there distributed to various interested parties such as the experimental center then being built at Bedford, the Royal Radar Establishment at Great Malvern, the Telecommunications Research Establishment, and to other top-secret establishments in Australia and Canada.

"Working under British Intelligence, my job was to organize the Anglo-Canadian teams of scientists who would scrutinize every aspect of the captured German technology. Our main concern was with unraveling the mystery of certain German secret weapons which may, or may not, have existed. These would have included the Foo Fighter or 'ball of fire' that apparently harassed so many of our pilots; the 'circular German fighter without wings or rudder' which, according to one reliable source, crossed the flight path of a four-engined Liberator at very high speed, gave off a number of little bluish clouds of smoke, and thereby caused the Liberator to catch fire and eventually explode; and the 'strange flying machine, hemispherical or circular in shape' which reportedly flew at incredible speed, attacked a whole convoy of twelve U.S. night fighters, and destroyed them without using visible weapons. Naturally, being British, we approached our task with a certain skepticism—but such skepticism would be shortly dispelled and replaced with amazement.

"Let me briefly summarize what we found. First, whether or not the mysterious aircraft that sprayed those bluish clouds of smoke over the unfortunate Liberator was 'a circular German fighter without wings or rudder,' it certainly could have caused that aircraft to explode without using its guns. We came to this conclusion when we discovered that documents recovered from the technical departments of factories hidden in the forested areas of the Schwarzwald contained details of experiments conducted with a liquid gas that would, when blown with considerable force over an aircraft, catch fire from the aircraft's exhaust fumes and cause that aircraft to explode. The existence of this gas was confirmed when one Dr. Rosenstein, an organic chemist and Jewish collaborator who, when interrogated by members of the American Aslos Mission in Paris in 1944, stated that the Germans had succeeded in perfecting a new gas whose use would have caused 'strong vibrations and even breakage in aircraft engines' by encouraging immediate and repeated self-ignition.

"In this context it is worth noting that in April 1945, on the outskirts of the Hillersleben testing grounds west of Berlin, members of the Intelligence Technical Branch of the 12th Army Group found the rusty remains of a rather odd item called the *Windkanone*—a cannon that shot gas instead of shells—and another odd item called the *Wirbelringkanone*, or whirlwind annular vortex cannon, which was designed to shoot, and then ignite, a gas ring that would spin rapidly on its own axis and form a rather fierce 'ball of fire.'

"Regarding the possibility that the 'circular German plane without wings or rudder' might have been some sort of remote-controlled flying device, we discovered that as far back as 1939 Dr. Fernseh of Berlin, in collaboration with Professor Herbert Wagner of the Henschel Aircraft Company, was working on the development of a television component that would enable pilots to control bombs and rocket bombs *after* they had been launched; that Fernseh was also involved in the development of a microtelevision camera that would be installed in the nose of an antiaircraft rocket and guide it precisely to its target; and that similar projects were quite commonplace in Germany— and, more important, highly successful.

"Naturally such information led us back into an investigation of the apparently remote-controlled German 'fireballs.' What we found was that Messerschmitt had developed two workable radio-controlled interceptor planes—the *Krache* and the *Donner*—that these were initially designed to be controlled from the ground by a television receiver installed in an armored console, but that certain negative aspects to the system led to the development of numerous very advanced electromagnetic, electroacoustical and photoelectric fuses, and to even more advanced warheads which were sensitive to the natural electrostatic fields that surround aircraft in flight. Indeed, some of those devices were incorporated into 'automatic' aircraft weapons, with the result that all a German pilot had to do was fly his plane a few hundred yards beneath or above his target and the automatic firing mechanism would operate. Thus, by installing similar devices in a pilotless interceptor rocket, the Germans could engage in aerial combat without using human pilots.

"The devices I've just mentioned led inevitably to a more solid version of the original wind-cannon idea. By 1945 a Luftwaffe experimental center in Oberammergau in Bavaria had completed its research into an apparatus capable of short-circuiting the ignition system of an aircraft's engine at a distance of about a hundred feet by producing an intense electrical field. Their intention—aborted by the ending of the war—was to expand the field greatly, but certainly by the middle of 1944 they had incorporated the device into a weapon actually called the *Feuerball*, or 'Fireball.'

"The *Feuerball* was first constructed at the aeronautical factory at Wiener Neustadt. Basically, it was an armored, disc-shaped object, powered by a special turbojet engine, which was radio-controlled at the moment of take-off, but then, attracted by the enemy aircraft's exhaust fumes, automatically followed that aircraft, automatically avoided colliding with it, and automatically short-circuited the aircraft's radar and ignition systems. During the day this device looked exactly like 'a shining disc spinning on its axis'—which may account for the first Allied newspaper reports of 'silver balls' observed in the skies over Germany—and by night it looked like a 'burning globe.' The 'burning globe' was actually a fiery halo around the solid device, caused by the very rich chemical mixture that over-ionized the atmosphere in the vicinity of the target and thus subjected it to extremely damaging electromagnetic impulses. It is also worth noting—with regard to the fact that the *Feuerballs* reportedly flew away when attacked—that under the armored plating of the *Feuerball* was a thin sheet of aluminum which acted as a defensive 'switch': a bullet piercing the armored plating would automatically establish contact with the switch, trip a maximum acceleration device, and cause the *Feuerball* to fly vertically out of range of enemy gunfire. In short: the *Feuerball* really existed, it was described accurately by our pilots, and it was used with great effect from about November 1944, to the end of the war.

"At this point I feel I should remind you that from as far back as 1942 the German military establishment had encouraged every kind of research and experiment in the field of jet propulsion and advanced remote-control systems. However, after the attempted assassination of Hitler on July 20, 1944, Hitler, in a bout of fury, turned control of the planning and construction of these astonishing new weapons over to Himmler's dreaded S.S. I mention this because the S.S. were, by that stage of the war, a self-ruling and highly secretive body with their own research centers and construction plants and factories, many of which even Hitler didn't know about. In other words, from that point on, the fate of many of the secret weapons was even more difficult to trace—and indeed, in many cases is not known even to this day.

"What we *do* know is that many of the leading scientific establishments were evacuated totally and transferred to vast underground complexes scattered all over Germany, most notably in the area of the aborted Alpine redoubt. Once transferred, they were virtually sealed off from the outer world, rigidly controlled by the S.S., and forced to concentrate their attention on nothing other than advanced military projects. Given that this work went on twenty-four hours a day, that even the scientists worked in shifts, and that thousands of slave-laborers from the concentration camps were at their disposal, there can be little doubt that some extraordinary advances were made in those secret research plants.

"Unfortunately the S.S., when retreating from the Allies, destroyed much of this remarkable research. Unfortunate because what we often found were highly advanced but frustratingly incomplete documents, isolated parts of obviously complex components, and a wealth of other odds and ends that could have belonged to just about anything. Even more disturbing was the fact that thousands of slave workers who had been used in such establishments had, with their S.S. overlords, simply disappeared by the time we got there—and few of them were ever found again.

"So, my evaluations are incomplete. Nevertheless, regarding the 'wingless' aircraft so often reported, we did collect enough material to tantalize us and keep us involved for years. Found across the length and breadth of Nazi Germany were not only the V-1 flying bombs and V-2 rockets, the gas cannons and *Feuerballs*, and the quite extraordinary variety of automatic flying devices and infrared warheads, but also a considerable number of highly advanced U-XX1 and U-XX111 submarines, almost completed ME-262 jet fighters, a nearly completed atom-bomb project, the prototypes for various vertical-rising aircraft and even, in the immense underground Riva del Garda research complex, the manufacturing process for a metallic material which could withstand temperatures of about 1,000 degrees Centigrade. So, as you can imagine, the Germans were on the verge of some truly extraordinary developments."

Tape 2:

"There are two problems standing in the way of a supersonic, completely circular aircraft: one is the need for gyroscopic stabilization and the other is control of the boundary layer. It is therefore worth noting that scientists of the Kreiselgerate at Berlin Britz had, in 1943, worked on the construction of mechanisms employing gyroscopic phenomenon and succeeded in reducing the oscillations of a violently shaken body to under a tenth of a degree. This was, of course, a most important achievement—and added to control of Prandtl's 'boundary layer' it would have led to some extraordinary advances in aeronautics.

"Let me briefly explain this 'boundary layer.' While being four or five thousand times less viscous than oil, air *is*, nonetheless, viscous. Because of this, the air sweeping in on the solid body of an aircraft forms imperceptible stratifications of resistance and consequently decreases the speed of the body in flight. These layers of air are therefore known as the 'boundary layer'—and the boundary layer increases its resistance in direct proportion to the increasing speed of the flying object.

"In layman's terms, therefore, the major problem regarding supersonic flight was to somehow or other move this negative air as far to the rear of the aircraft as possible, thus minimizing the expenditure of energy required to propel the aircraft through the sky. Further: it is possible that a revolutionary type of aircraft could—by not only *completely* removing the boundary layer, but by somehow rerouting it and utilizing it as an added propulsive force—fly through the skies using little other than the expelled air itself. Should this be accomplished we would have an aircraft capable of remarkable speeds while utilizing the barest minimum of fuel.

"By 1945—or so our captured German papers indicated—both the L.F.A. at Volkenrode and the research center at Guidonia were working on a revolutionary new type of aircraft that was devoid of all obstructing protuberances, such as wings and rudders, was devoid even of the normal air intakes, and was powered by a highly advanced turbine engine. In short, that new aircraft was a 'flying wing' that offered the least possible air resistance, sucked in the 'dead air' of the boundary layer, and then used that same air, expelling it at great force, to increase its momentum.

"Whether or not that aircraft was actually developed and flown is not known. What we *did* know, however, was that the *Feuerball* really existed, that it took the form of a circular 'wing,' and that that wing was in a sense wrapped around the suction pump and that the pump was part and parcel of the engine. In other words, the *Feuerball* was a perfectly symmetrical disc devoid of all surface protuberances—the first small flying saucer.

"Nevertheless, with the *Feuerball* the boundary layer would still have been present, albeit drastically reduced. In order to get rid of the boundary layer completely—and in order to make use of the 'dead air' not only for acceleration, but for maneuvering as well—what was required was a porous metal that would act like a sponge and remove the need for air intakes altogether. This need led scientists into the exploration of what would henceforth be called, in the words of the German engineer Schrenk, 'frictionless air flow' and which would result, according to Sir Ben Lockspeiser, in an aircraft that would 'slip through the air in the same way as a piece of wet soap slips through the fingers.' I mention this because certain documents discovered by us in both Gottingen and Volkenrode indicated that between 1943 and 1944 the German scientists had been completing their research on just such a metal—a compound of magnesium and aluminum—and had given the resultant material the name of *Luftschwamm*, which translated means 'aero-sponge.'

"Let us assume, then, that by early 1945 the Germans had combined all the aforementioned discoveries into one complex experimental flying machine. First, we have a small flying disc known as the *Feuerball*. This disc not only spins around its vertical axis, but automatically follows its target, makes its target's radar and ignition malfunction by filling the vicinity with a gas which when burning creates a damaging magnetic field, then automatically flies away when attacked.

"Now let us enlarge this flying 'fireball.' The new, enlarged disc will also spin on its own axis, but with the addition of direct gyroscopic stabilization, a pilot's cabin can now be placed on that axis, with the main body—or engine—of the disc spinning around the cabin. We then add to the enlarged, pilot-carrying disc a form of radio that can cancel at the pilot's discretion the return signals, or blips, from the enemy's radarscope and thus render our flying disc undetectable to that enemy. Next, we have electromagnetically or electroacoustically controlled firing weapons, we have cannons that spit ignition-damaging gas instead of shells, we possibly have various laser or pulse-beam weapons, and we have devices that insure that our flying disc will automatically retreat from enemy attacks. Add to all this the fact that the disc is made of an alloy that can withstand enormous pressure and a temperature of 1,000 degrees Centigrade and that, being porous, can take the air in like a sponge and then use it to enhance its own propulsion to almost unbelieveable speeds . . . Add it up and what have we got? What we *might* have is the

German *Kugelblitz*, an offspring of the *Feuerball*, a piloted machine in which a single mass of wing, tail and fuselage is formed into one gyroscopically stabilized, vertical-rising, possibly supersonic flying disc.

"Did such a machine exist? I think it might have. What I *do* know is that a machine very much like it, and called the *Kugelblitz*, was apparently test-flown sometime in February 1945, in the area of the underground complex at Kahla, in Thuringia, that the test was marked as successful, and that from incomplete notes found in the Kahla complex when the Allies took it over, that machine reached a height of about 40,000 feet at a speed of approximately 1,250 miles per hour.

"Regarding the possibility that what we found in Germany was later utilized by the Allies, I can only point out that shortly after the war the British and the Canadians between them began to develop some revolutionary kinds of aircraft that were rumored to be based on designs discovered in Germany after its collapse. Included in these were the Armstrong Whitworth Aircraft Company's AW-52-G all-wing glider and the AW-52 Boomerang—both of which were similar in appearance to the German 'flying wing' designs and, incidentally, to the enormous 'flying wing' seen over Albuquerque in 1951. Also, during that same period, there was much talk going around British and Canadian aeronautical circles about research into 'porous' metals and vertical take-off jet planes—and, of course, there were an enormous amount of UFO sightings. Finally, as you yourself have reminded me, both the Americans and the Canadians made numerous mentions of official flying saucer projects. From all this, Dr. Epstein, I think you can draw your own conclusions."

CHAPTER THIRTY

The noon sun was scorching, the humidity suffocating. The river rippled and flashed, curving away in the distance, shadowed by the conifer trees and the banks of red mud as the sun beat on the forests, on the creaking gunboat, draining Stanford and making his eyes sting as he clung to the railing. He could not grasp where he was, had lost track since his arrival, stunned by the heat, by the stifling humidity, alienated by the noise and dusty streets of Asunción, now gazing across the Paraguay River and wondering where he was going. Stanford normally liked the heat, had grown up with it, was used to it; but here, on the gunboat, the forests looming across the river, the heat was unearthly, unreal, totally monstrous, a sodden heat that clamped all around him and threatened to strangle him. Stanford took off his hat, wiped the sweat from his forehead, put the hat back on and glanced around him, his clothes soaked, his boots burning.

"Have a beer, *Señor* Stanford. It will help to cool you down. You must not let the sun dry you out. You need plenty of liquid."

Juan Chavez was smiling, a sly, gap-toothed grimace, his dark eyes as unrevealing as the forests that slipped past the gunboat. Stanford nodded and took the beer, the bottle cold in his sweaty palm, drank and wiped some beer from his lips, stared uncomfortably at Chavez.

"How much longer?" he said.

"Not long, *señor*." Chavez grinned and then spat over the railing, his open shirt fluttering.

"*How* long?" Stanford said.

"Not long," Chavez said. "Five, maybe ten or fifteen minutes. It is just around the bend in the river. It will not take much longer."

Stanford gazed along the river, saw it curving around the forests, flowing lazily, rippling out around rocks, slashed by sunlight and shadow. The sight of it chilled him, made him feel more unreal, filled with foreboding and with vague, nameless fears that lanced through him for no apparent reason and drained him of courage. He despised himself for it, tried to fight it, failed constantly, tumbled back into fear and confusion like a child having bad dreams. In a sense that's what it was—his recent memories were all nightmares: the strange boys outside the ranch, the suicide of Scaduto, Epstein willingly clambering up the darkened hill and not seen since that evening. Stanford felt crushed by it all, dogged by incomprehension, dreaming frequently of the lights that pulsated and merged, and then awakening to an alien world in which nothing was constant . . . And now here he was in Paraguay, the sun blinding him, the heat draining him. He had been on the shuddering gunboat for four or five hours, passing banks of red mud and sleazy waterfront cafes and great forests that soared on either side and seemed totally impenetrable. Stanford shivered and gazed ahead, saw the muddy, rippling water, raised the bottle to his lips and drank more beer, seeking some kind of solace.

"Good," Chavez said. "You must drink. You must never dry out." He was eating from a cone of paper, dipping into it with his fingers, and he grinned and held the cone out to Stanford, his brown eyes faintly mischievous. "Here, *señor*," he said. "You must eat. You should have some *camarónes*."

Stanford fought back his revulsion. "No thanks," he said. "I can just about stomach the beer. I don't think I can eat."

"You are feeling ill, *señor*?"

"Not really," Stanford said.

"Ah, yes," Chavez said. "This stinking boat. And the heat . . . You're not used to it."

Stanford didn't reply. He gazed around the crowded gunboat. The Ache Indians were still crouching at the aft end of the deck, small, emaciated, their narrow eyes dulled by fear, dressed in rags and huddling close to one another as if for protection. Two *Federales* were guarding them, wearing jackboots, carrying rifles, both gaunt-faced and bored, chewing gum, their eyes hooded beneath peaked caps. Stanford studied them at length, feeling helpless and ashamed, remembering how they had been herded onto the boat from the village some miles back. He knew what was happening to them. They were being sold into slavery. They would end up in the Bolivian tin mines, in the ranches of Boqueron, in the brothels of Argentina and Brazil, in the cotton fields of Guatemala. Stanford shivered when he thought of it. The eyes of the women and children haunted him. He turned away and gazed along the muddy river, drinking beer, the heat draining him.

"This is your first time in Paraguay, *Señor* Stanford?"

"Yes," Stanford said.

"You must get used to these things," Chavez said. "You must not be upset by them."

"I won't get used to them," Stanford said. "I won't be staying that long. Once I talk to the German I'm leaving. I won't get used to anything."

"You disapprove," Chavez said.

"That's right: I disapprove."

"Disapproval is a luxury," Chavez said. "An American luxury." He grinned and glanced around him, his jaws chewing on *camarónes,* drank some beer and then looked back at Stanford, his brown eyes slightly mischievous. "You know the German?" he said.

"No," Stanford said.

"It is very strange, *señor*," Chavez said, "that you should know he is here."

"Why strange?" Stanford said.

"The German doesn't have many friends. He has been here in the forest for thirty years, and is a man of great mystery."

"That's not unusual," Stanford said. "There are a lot of Germans here. They own and operate the *estancias* and are all well protected."

Chavez sipped his beer and grinned. "You do us wrong, *señor*," he said. "These rumors about us harboring Nazis have no basis in fact."

"Really?"

"Really."

"That's bullshit," Stanford said. "Your whole economy is based on slavery and drugs—and on harboring Nazis."

"Lower your voice, *señor*." Chavez's eyes flicked left and right. "It is not wise to speak of such things in so open a manner."

"I'm an American," Stanford said.

"That won't help you, *señor*. The *Federales* are devoted to General Stroessner and will not make allowances."

Stanford glanced across his shoulder, saw the lounging *Federales*, most of them lingering around the rusty gun-mounts, chewing gum, smoking cigarettes. Stanford didn't like the look of them. They looked simple and brutal. There were Kalashnikov rifles slung across their sweating shoulders, and their jackboots, which were covered in mud, made him think of the Nazis.

"Okay," Stanford said. "What's *your* connection with the German? Note: I don't call him a Nazi. I'm a very good tourist."

Chavez grinned and shrugged. "The Ache," he said. "I round up the Ache and deliver them to the German, and he gives me a percentage of what he makes on the ones that he sells."

"And what happens to the ones he *doesn't* sell?"

Chavez shrugged laconically. "At our worst, we are patriotic. The Ache are vermin, filthy and diseased; they cannot look after themselves and they cause us much trouble. So, if they cannot be sold, we look after them in other ways . . ."

"You exterminate them," Stanford said.

"A harsh word, *señor*. Let's say we put them out of their misery and leave it at that."

Stanford finished his beer, crushed the can, threw it

overboard, watched it glinting as it bobbed along the river and was swept out of sight. He glanced again at the Indians. They were huddled pathetically on the deck. He tried to reconcile this world with the world he had come from: with the pilots and astronauts and the control towers of NASA, with the jet planes and the space probes and the orbiting satellites, with the UFOs that haunted man's thoughts and mapped out his future. He couldn't reconcile the two. This river carried him through history. The gunboat and the forest, the *Federales* and the Indians, all existed in a primitive, frozen past far removed from the modern world. And what *was* the modern world? It was what he had come from. It was a world of technology, of relentless, searching science, racing blindly into a future not yet even imagined, a future in which men would be numbers and facts would rule feelings. Yet was that such a bad thing? Stanford felt sure that it was. He looked at the squatting Indians, saw them bought and sold as meat, and then wondered if the future conjured up by the man called Aldridge was in any sense a better world than this, less cruel, more just. No, it was not. The human lot would not improve. The cruelty and injustice and inequality would remain, changed only in their areas of distribution and in who would most suffer. The advance of science ignored that fact. The two worlds were very similar. The future being built by Aldridge, and represented by his technology, was as savage and emotionally primitive as the world this boat drifted through.

Stanford shivered and looked ahead. The river curved out of sight. He saw a jetty thrusting out from the riverbank, the water rippling around it.

"There it is," Chavez said. "Your journey is ended, *señor*. You will soon feel the ground beneath your feet, and can talk with your German friend."

"He's not a friend," Stanford said.

"My apologies, *señor*. A man like you would not have such friends. Your appearance confirms that fact."

Stanford ignored the sarcasm, his eyes fixed on the wooden jetty, watching intently as the boat approached and the waterside village slid into view, thrusting out from the tangled shrubs and liana at the edge of the forest. There were people on the jetty, men in filthy fatigues, looking suspiciously like *contrabandistas*, pistols stuck through their belts. The boat growled and shuddered violently, turning in toward the village, crept forward and then bounced against the tires along the edge of the jetty. Stanford glanced over his shoulder. One of the Ache women was wailing. A *Federale* slapped her brutally across the face and screamed a stream of abuse. The woman's wailing became a whimper. Stanford flushed and turned away. One of the crew had thrown a rope to a man on the jetty and this man was tying the rope around an upright, bending low, shouting loudly. The boat's engine cut out. A crew member removed the gate. A plank was thrown across the space between the deck and the jetty, then tied to some flaking uprights to form a crude gangplank. Stanford moved toward the plank, wanting desperately to get off, but Chavez tugged at the sleeve of his shirt and motioned him back.

"No," he said. "First the Ache."

Stanford stopped and stared at him, saw the sly, gaptoothed grin, stepped back as Chavez went to the *Federales* and shouted out his instructions. The *Federales* were quick to move, venting their boredom on the miserable Indians, screaming abuse and kicking them to their feet and herding them toward the gangplank. The Indians were not so quick, weak from hunger, confused, and the *Federales* encouraged them along with vicious blows from their rifles. The women wailed and held their children, cowering away from the swinging rifles, while their menfolk, uncommonly small and frail, tried in vain to protect them. Stanford had to throttle his rage, turning away and surveying the gangplank, saw the first of the Indians stumbling across it with their hands on their heads. Chavez was leading them down, his shirt unbuttoned and flapping loosely, his broad hat tilted over his eyes, a bright white in the fierce sun. Stanford burned and looked away, let his gaze roam over the village, a drab collection of leaning huts made from *palmetto* trunks and vines, hogs and goats sniffing lethargically at the dust, babies lying on corn

shucks. The poverty was total, the old and young emaciated, sunlight falling on scattered gourds and woven bas-
kets and banana leaves, on the giant rat that raced across
the clearing and disappeared in the forest. Stanford looked
along the jetty. The Ache Indians had just left it. They
were now at the edge of the clearing, the *Federales* surrounding them. Chavez waved both his hands. He was sig-
naling to Stanford. Stanford choked back his rage and
walked over the gangplank, looked down once at the
muddy, oil-slicked water, then stepped onto the jetty.

One of the nearby men approached him, a big man,
broad and muscular, a pistol stuck through his belt, a
knife flapping against one hip, his shirt open and exposing
a leathery chest, his trousers tattered and greasy.

"The *Americano*?" he said.

"Yes," Stanford said.

"You speak Spanish?"

"No," Stanford said.

"Okay. Come with me."

"You're from the German?" Stanford said.

"You have no luggage, *señor*."

"I don't intend staying," Stanford said. "All I need is in
here."

Stanford indicated his shoulder bag. The big man just
stared at him. He had narrow eyes and very fat lips and
his head had been shaved.

"Okay," he said. "I see. Come with me."

"You're from the German?"

"Yes."

"Where is he?"

"Over there." The man pointed impatiently toward the
village. "Let's go. He expects you."

They walked along the creaking jetty, past the staring
contrabandistas, the air smelling of urine and sewage and
diesel fuel, the sun glinting off the oil in the water, off pistols and knives. Stanford took note of the weapons, could
scarcely credit the sheer amount of them, had the feeling
that he was in a war zone, death ready to pounce on him.
This thought heightened his tension, swelled his sense of
unreality, and he blinked and wiped the sweat from his

face, tried to keep his head clear. The big man was just
ahead, the knife bouncing against his hip, stepping down
into the dust of the clearing, chickens scattering around
him. Stanford followed him down, feeling drained and exhausted, breathing dust, the heat burning his skin, the light
dazzling his eyes.

There were two trucks in the clearing, their paint flaking, the rust showing, and the Ache Indians were now
grouped just in front of them, being prodded and poked.
The Indians were being examined. The *Federales* were
watching them. A tall man in gray slacks and white shirt
was walking up and down, studying them. This man was
very thin, almost cadaverous, brown eyes in a sunburned,
brown face, brown hair graying and thinning. He did not
touch the Indians, merely looked on with distaste, standing
back while Chavez extolled their virtues, showed their
teeth, stripped their clothes off.

"*Quatsch!*" the tall man sneered. "This is rubbish you
bring me. Old men and sick women and children, not
worth ten *guaranis.*"

Chavez spluttered his protestations, his hands waving
theatrically, then he stripped the blouse off a woman's
shoulders and held her breasts high. The woman's narrow
eyes widened, filled with fear and terrible shame, as
Chavez jiggled her breasts in his hands as if bouncing two
balls.

"Look, *señor,*" he said. "They are ripe and filled with
milk. Still a good breeder, *señor.* And so soft, *señor. Soft!*"

"*Dreck!*" the tall man sneered. "They are unwashed and
diseased. They are not fit to work in the fields. You should
bury them now."

Stanford glanced at the Indians, saw the terror and
shame, shook a little and stared at the tall man and
wanted to murder him. Chavez glanced over his shoulder,
saw Stanford, grinned slyly, pointed in Stanford's direction
and then glanced at the tall man. Stanford stepped forward. The tall man walked toward him. They stopped
about a foot from one another, the dust drifting between
them.

"You are Stanford," the tall man said.

"Yes," Stanford said.

"You have the money?"

"I have half the money. The rest is in Asunción."

"You don't trust me," the German said.

"I can't afford to," Stanford said.

"Good," the German said. "That is intelligent. I cannot deal with fools." He grinned bleakly and turned away, looked at Chavez, waved at the trucks. "All right," he said. "I have no choice but to take them. Put the *schweine* into the trucks and get them out of my sight."

Stanford stood there, enraged. He knew he had to control the rage. There was nothing he could do for the Indians, not now and not ever. Still, it made him burn. He heard the shouting and saw the blows. The *Federales* punched the Indians, thumped them brutally with their rifles, forced them up into the backs of the trucks, the women and children all wailing. The tall German hardly saw this. He was negotiating with Chavez. Their hands were waving and they hissed at one another and then came to agreement. They actually shook hands. Stanford stood there, disbelieving. The trucks roared and kicked up the red dust and drove out of the clearing. Stanford glanced around the village. The huts were primitive and filthy. Hogs and goats wandered freely, babies sucked at sagging breasts, Indians squatted around fires of glowing ash, staring at him with dulled eyes. Chavez waved at the tall German. He turned around and walked toward Stanford. He stopped to offer his sly, gap-toothed grin, his brown eyes slightly mischievous.

"Keep your eyes and ears open," he whispered. "*Adiós, compañero!*"

He walked back toward the boat, his shirt flapping about him, and the German walked over to Stanford, his gaunt face dark and sweaty.

"So," he said. "You came."

"Yes," Stanford said. "I came."

"And how do you like Paraguay?"

"I'm not very impressed."

The German laughed at the remark, a high-pitched, barking sound, then the laughter turned into a ragged coughing that made his whole body shake. The German

cursed and turned aside, covered his mouth with a handkerchief, kept it there until the coughing had subsided,
then wiped blood from his lips.

"*Scheisse*," he hissed dramatically. "This filthy forest is
killing me. I must return to Europe as soon as possible for
some civilized care."

"Germany?"

"Where else? I need a civilized doctor. The Paraguayans
have the surgical skills of butchers. I would not let them
touch me."

"I thought you liked it here," Stanford said. "You've
been here for thirty years."

"Not by choice," the German said. "As you well know.
I do not require sarcasm."

He gazed steadily at Stanford, his dark eyes hard and
searching, then he sniffed and turned his gaze on the large
man who had brought Stanford to him. The large man
moved forward slightly, his knife and pistol flashing, and
stopped when he was right beside Stanford, his thick arms
hanging loose.

"This is Atilio," the German said. "He is from Argentina. He is now what we call a *cuchillero,* and is very reliable."

"What's a *cuchillero*?" Stanford said.

"A knifer," the German said. He turned his head and
glanced around him, his eyes moving in jerking movements, his lips curling back in distaste at the sight of the
village. "*Diese Halunken,*" he hissed. "Unbelievable. Come
. . . let us go."

He led them across the clearing, scattering children and
chickens, Atilio just behind him, Stanford just behind
Atilio, their feet kicking up the red dust, the fires smoldering about them. The fires were not for heat. The Indians
were roasting sweet potatoes. The German glanced down
and spat on a fire as he passed the drab huts. He stopped
at the edge of the forest. The trees shadowed the waiting
jeep. The German climbed in the back, Stanford climbed
in beside him, then Atilio sat behind the steering wheel
and turned on the ignition.

"Where are we going?" Stanford said.

"To my compound," the German said. "You want information and shall have it—but I must have my comforts. It is not too far away. Ten kilometers from here. I feel safer when I'm deep in the forest where the planes cannot see me."

The jeep roared into life, kicking up earth and stones, lurched forward and headed into the forest where the trees kept the sun out. Stanford thought it would be cooler, was shocked to find that it wasn't: the humidity was much worse, overpowering him, almost making him choke. He glanced around him, feeling ill, seeing a riot of vegetation, tangled vines and soaring trees in a chattering green gloom, isolated shafts of sunlight beaming down on the steaming banana leaves. The narrow track was very rough, hacked by hand and pitted with holes, winding left and right between the trees and disappearing ahead of them. The tall German said nothing. Stanford glanced at him briefly. The German looked like a skeleton, his cheekbones too prominent, his dark eyes buried deep in his head, his lips thin and disdainful. The jeep roared and kept going, bouncing up and down roughly, rushing through the shafts of sunlight that bored down through the trees and illuminated the steaming vegetation. Stanford felt suffocated. He was sweating and felt feverish. He glanced again at the German, saw his dark, remote eyes, shivered and licked his parched lips and wished the journey would end.

"So," the German said. "You want to know about the saucers. You have come a long way for your information. You must want it quite badly."

"I brought the money," Stanford said. "I want it that much."

"Why?" the German said. "Why this interest in the saucers? Everyone wants to know about the saucers, but it does them no good."

"You've had others?" Stanford said.

"Of course," the German said. "Did you think you were the first to locate me? Such vanity, *mein Herr*!"

The German laughed at his own joke, the same high-pitched, barking sound, and again the laughter turned into a coughing that made him spit blood. He cursed and wiped his lips, shook his head and muttered something, his thin body being jolted by the jeep as it bounced through the forest.

"How many others?" Stanford said.

"Just a few," the German said. "Three or four over the past ten years or so—all wanting the same thing."

"Who were they?" Stanford said.

"Men like you," the German said. "Men with a great need to know, two Americans, a Russian . . ." The German coughed and cursed softly. "It will do you no good," he said. "Those who know what I know will not admit that it is true; those who don't know will refuse to believe it . . . It will do you no good."

Stanford didn't reply. He thought the German might be right. He looked around the forest, at the steaming vegetation, saw the pillars of light in the gloom and felt as if he were dreaming. Then the jeep burst into sunlight. He saw a clearing in the forest. Lines of barbed wire formed a fence around a large wooden building, its sloping roof covered in vines and banana leaves and supported by tree trunks. The jeep skidded to a halt. Clouds of dust swirled up around them. Stanford coughed and covered his eyes with his hands and let the dust settle down again.

"*Sehr gut,*" the German said. "We are home. I live humbly, *mein freund.*"

Stanford followed the German down, the dust settling around his feet, the heat monstrous, pouring down on the clearing as if through a huge glass. He rubbed his eyes and glanced around him, saw the curved line of the trees, the large, L-shaped hut right before him, surrounded by barbed wire. The compound was busy, filled with Indians and *cuchilleros*, the latter keeping an eye on the former, their guns and knives flashing.

"The barbed wire is electrified," the German said. "Make sure you don't touch it. Over here. Come this way."

They walked across the dusty earth, past the Indians and *cuchilleros*, reached the house and climbed up some wooden steps and stopped under an awning. There was a table and some chairs. An Ache woman stood by the table. She was wearing a white blouse and long skirt, a

towel over her right arm. She bowed low to the German.
He simply grunted and sat down. He waved his right hand
at Stanford who sat down at the table, saw two glasses and
a bottle of brandy, a clay cup full of wriggling worms.
The worms were white and fat. The German reached over
and grabbed one. He bit off its head and held it up and
said, "*Koro* worms! Try one." Stanford shuddered and
shook his head. The German chortled and swallowed the
worm. He put his feet up on a stool and the Ache woman
knelt down and laboriously pulled off both his boots,
wiped his feet with the towel. When this was done, she
shuffled backward. She didn't get off her knees. The German barked and the woman stood up and filled the glasses
with brandy. Stanford watched her, saying nothing. The
German clapped his hands loudly. The woman bowed and
disappeared inside the hut, her bare feet making sucking
sounds.

"So," the German said. "We are home. We are relaxed.
We can talk."

He picked up his glass, sipped some brandy, set it down,
stared at Stanford with a humorless smile that made his
flesh creep. Stanford picked his own glass up, drained it
dry, set it down, then he pulled the leather bag from his
shoulder and placed it between them.

"Your money," he said.

"And the rest?"

"When you've told me. One of your men can take me
back to Asunción and I'll give him the other half."

"You might not do that," the German said.

"Then your man will kill me," Stanford said.

"Good," the German said. "You understand that. That
makes me feel better."

He finished his brandy, refilled both the glasses, then
leaned back in his chair and looked at Stanford with that
humorless smile.

"There's something else," Stanford said, wiping the
smile from the German's face. "I didn't just come for information. I also want proof."

The German sat up straighter, leaning forward on his
knees, stared at Stanford with steely, suppressed anger,
licked his upper lip slowly.

"Proof?" he said quietly.

"You heard me," Stanford said. "I know for a fact that you can prove it—and that's what I want first."

The German stared at him a long time, hardly moving, expressionless, then his lips slowly curled into a smile as he sat back again.

"We have a jungle up north," he said.

"I know that," Stanford said.

"That jungle is hell," the German said. "You can take it or leave it."

Stanford pushed his chair back, took his glass and stood up, then went to the leaf-covered railing and looked over the compound. The sun was sinking behind the forest, the sky violet and serene, the conifers and cypress turning dark as the twilight descended. A faint breeze stirred the dust up, blew it lazily across the barbed wire, let it drift around the Indians and *cuchilleros*, their shadows stretched out and merging. Stanford stared at the forest. It seemed dense and vaguely threatening. Stanford shivered and turned away, let his rage defeat his fear, then he grinned and held his glass up to the German who was sitting in shadow.

"Here's to Hell," Stanford said.

They moved out the next morning, in the dawn's bloody haze, heading into the forest, following a narrow, dwindling path, shafts of crimson light boring through the gloom between the dense, soaring trees. The Ache beaters were out ahead, their knives hacking and slicing, clearing a path for the short line of men stretched out behind them. Stanford marched beside the German, the huge Atilio protecting them both, a few disheveled *cuchilleros* behind them, their guns and knives rattling. The forest was cold, the dew glistening and dripping, the leaves underfoot damp and treacherous, branches whipping and spitting. The forest rustled and chattered. Stanford heard the noise and loathed it. The morning sun was fighting through the soaring trees and bleeding into the chilling gloom.

"*Sehr gut*," the German said. "A good morning. It will soon be less cold."

Stanford marched with some care, a small pack on his back, feeling cold and almost ill from lack of sleep, still not fully awake. He had slept in the German's hut. The German's snoring had haunted him. He had tossed and turned uncomfortably on the hammock, the forest sounds in his ears. The forest never slept. The long night had taught him that much. He had heard jagged cries, staccato cackling, distant growling, the leaves rustling with a life of their own, the ground shifting and sliding. It was not much different now. Stanford glanced around him nervously and saw the tangled vegetation in the gloom.

"How long will it take?" he said.

"All day," the German said. "It is a very long walk, my American friend, and will possibly kill you."

"I'll make it," Stanford said.

"I'll make sure of it," the German said. "You are worth the second half of the money, and that makes you worth helping."

Stanford tugged at the pack straps, felt the tingling of his skin, sweating even in the chill of the morning, dreading the heat to come. He saw Atilio just ahead, his gross hips rolling rhythmically, a pistol and a couple of knives stuck behind his broad belt. The forest seemed to be endless. It grew deeper and darker. The path dwindled to nothing and disappeared and the forest closed in on them. Stanford fingered his pack straps. His shoulders had started aching. He looked ahead and saw the knives of the Ache beaters hacking down the banana leaves. Stanford felt tired already, heard the bellowing of his lungs. He looked briefly at the German, saw his gaunt, weathered profile, and wondered how that frail, gangling body could endure such a punishment.

"You are with us?" the German said.

"I'm still here," Stanford said.

"*Sehr gut*," the German said. "You must survive. It is part of your penance."

"What penance?" Stanford said.

"Why ask me?" the German said. "But a man does not come to this place just because of the saucers."

"The saucers are a mystery."

"And you came here for a mystery?"

"I came because I lost a couple of friends and I want to know why."

The German nodded and smiled. "Ah," he said. "I see. And these friends were involved in the saucers. *Ja?* Am I right?"

Stanford didn't reply. He didn't want to think about it. The forest chattered and slithered all around him, and he felt his flesh creep. He couldn't find an answer. There were too many questions. He tried to think, but the sweat dripped in his eyes and reduced him to pettiness. All right, think: he would think. He thought of Epstein in the mountains. He closed his eyes and saw the blackness rushing at him and exposing the stars above. His old friend had gone away. The months since then had not been pleasant. During the day, at night, when awake or deep in sleep, he had known the dreams of those who were haunted and lived with their helplessness. Stanford knew he was being followed. He wasn't sure and yet was certain. He had sat back and studied it objectively, then collapsed into lunacy. He now understood paranoia. He knew what the frightened felt. He had turned into an old man overnight and might never recover. Stanford fingered his chafing pack straps. He glanced nervously around him. The forest rustled and slithered with mysteries that did not offer comfort.

"Your friends disappeared," the German said.

"Yes," Stanford said.

"That is not so unusual," the German said. "It happens here all the time."

"You mean the Ache," Stanford said.

"Just so," the German said. "The Ache disappear in their hundreds, melting into the trees."

"You do it," Stanford said. "You make them disappear. You sell them or use them as slaves and then you bury them deep."

"You disapprove," the German said.

"Damn right, I disapprove."

"You're a guilt-ridden American," the German said. "And your conscience is pricked."

"Fuck you," Stanford said.

"*Sehr gut*," the German said. "Nevertheless, there are many disappearing that we cannot account for."

"*Wunderbar*," Stanford said.

"I am serious," the German said. "The Ache disappear too fast. We cannot account for their numbers and the saucers are blamed for it."

They came out of the forest. A broad savannah stretched before them. Stanford blinked and felt an awful blast of heat that almost sucked his lungs dry. He rubbed his eyes and looked ahead, saw a sea of waving grass, a few barren trees here and there, the sky white, the sun dazzling. Stanford felt himself melting. He drained down into the earth. He stared across the sea of grass, saw it shimmer and undulate, and longed for the comforts of a city and its luring parameters. He fingered his chafing pack straps, licked his parched, drying lips. The heat was monstrous and it closed in around him and he gulped like a drowning man.

"Beyond that is Boqueron." The German spoke with calm indifference. "It sits between Argentina and Bolivia and Brazil, and within it is the jungle I mentioned—a place to avoid."

"That's where we're going," Stanford said.

"You will remember it," the German said. "What you want is buried deep in the jungle, and you must pay the price."

The German seemed pleased. He smiled at Stanford and moved forward. Stanford gulped and felt the heat burning through him and then stumbled ahead. The air was hot and clammy. He put on his sunglasses. The Ache Indians were already in the savannah, their knives flashing in sunlight. Stanford walked beside the German. The huge Atilio was just ahead. The *cuchilleros* were moving out around them, beating down the tall grass. The sun blazed down on the grass, on the scorched, scattered trees, turned the sky into a sheet of white steel that radiated tremendous heat. He tried to think, but his thoughts slipped and slid as if out of control . . . Epstein clambering up the hill. The black sky peeling back. The dark globe shrinking high in the sky, flaring up, disappearing . . . He was doing it for Epstein. He would not let Epstein go. He would not be defeated by Aldridge and his fellow conspirators . . . Stanford wiped sweat from his brow. He was waist-deep in the grass. The field of grass shimmered and stretched out to a silvery haze.

"The Ache," Stanford said. "What do you mean, they disappear? You said you can't account for their numbers. What did you mean by that?"

"They disappear," the German said. "We are not the ones taking them. We go to their villages, we find the huts empty, we search the surrounding forests and find nothing—they have just disappeared."

"Other traders?" Stanford said.

"No," the Germans said. "We all know each other quite well—and all suffer the same way. They are not removed by traders. Such a theft would be impossible. Paraguay is a very small country and is strictly controlled. The Ache disappear in their hundreds. They disappear overnight. The only way out is along the rivers, but they've never been seen there."

"Airplanes?" Stanford said.

"They can't land in the forests. *Nein*, it cannot be airplanes, so we think it's the saucers."

Stanford heard the rustling grass, felt it brushing around him, had visions of the life beneath his feet, of the snakes and giant rats. He shivered and kept going, trying not to look down, the muscles tightening in his stomach, the sweat pouring down his face, the dark glasses inadequate protection against the sun's fierce white glare. The grass snapped and broke around him. The Aches' long blades were flashing. The *cuchilleros* formed a loose protective circle, their knives and guns rattling. Stanford felt that he was choking, his breath burning in his lungs. The pack jumped up and down on his back and made his whole body ache.

"Lots of saucers," the German said. "We see the saucers all the time. They come down on the Chagres, on the Gran Chaco and the Mato Grosso, and afterward all the Ache have disappeared and are not seen again."

"They actually *land*?" Stanford said.

"*Ja*, they land," the German said. "They descend into the forests. They descend where there is nothing but swamps, and yet they always take off again. They must hover above the swamps. We cannot explore such areas. But they appear to descend above the swamps and take the Ache away."

The sweat poured down Stanford's face, soaked his armpits and body; his feet were burning in the canvas jungle boots, his throat dry, his head tight. He tried to think of the reports, shook his head, tried again . . . dark skin, narrow eyes, very small, Oriental . . . the most common characteristics as described by the numerous contactees. Such descriptions fit the Ache. They were small and Mongolian. Stanford marched through the tall grass, half blind and exhausted, the muscles in his stomach growing tighter with excitement and tension.

"You feel good?" the German said.

"I feel rotten," Stanford said.

"You're an American," the German said. "That makes you weak. You should thank me for this."

"Thanks," Stanford said.

"Don't thank me," the German said. "Just stay on your feet until we get there. It is still a long way."

The savannah seemed endless, a rustling, yellow sea, the tall grass bending under his feet, springing back up around him. Stanford blessed the Ache beaters. He saw their blades flash in the sun. They worked hard and the sweat soaked through their shirts and streamed down their dark faces. Here and there were lonely trees. The blazing sky was a white sheet. The air was hot and very humid, suffocating, a giant glove slipping over him. Stanford wiped sweat from his eyes. His shirt was sticking to his body. The light shimmered and distorted the waving grass and played tricks with his eyes. He blinked and licked his lips. Pains were shooting up his legs. The heat swam all around him, scorched his skin, sucked his lungs dry; the brightness of the sky was overwhelming, a vast, silvery furnace.

One of the Ache Indians screamed, waved his hands and fell down, disappearing into the rustling, waist-high grass while the others all scattered. Atilio cursed and raced ahead, tearing his pistol from his holster, a knife jumping up and down on his left hip, the grass parting around him. Stanford stopped and licked his lips. He heard the screaming of the Indian. Another Indian raised his blade above his head and swept it down through the shifting grass. The hidden Indian kept screaming. Stanford shrank from the sound. The German muttered and rushed toward Atilio, the *cuchilleros* surrounding him. Atilio bawled and waved his pistol. Stanford caught up with the German. They both stopped beside Atilio and looked down at the Indian on the ground. He had been bitten by a snake. He was wriggling about and shrieking. Another Indian stood beside him, his long blade dripping blood, the snake's amputated head at his feet, the headless body nearby.

"*Scheisse,*" the German hissed. "We have no time for this. Fix the Indian."

It was over very quickly. Stanford hardly knew what was happening. He saw the Indian on the ground, pouring sweat and shivering badly, holding on to the leg that had been bitten and screaming dementedly. Then Atilio knelt down, grabbed the Indian by the hair, jerked his head up and poked it with the pistol and then squeezed the trigger. The sudden bang made Stanford twitch. He saw the Indian's head jerking. Blood and bone splashed on the ground beneath the head, and then the head itself fell. Stanford blinked and looked again. Atilio stood up and blocked his view. Atilio shouted at the watching *cuchilleros*, who then turned on the Indians. They were all shouting at once. The *cuchilleros* pushed the Indians forward. The Indians moved out and swung their long blades and started hacking the grass down. The *cuchilleros* formed a circle. Atilio marched on ahead. Stanford looked down at the ground, saw the snake's bloody head, saw the brains of the Indian spilling out, his eyes open, his arms outstretched. Stanford blinked and licked his lips. He hurried after the marching German. The *cuchilleros* surrounded them both as the grass swayed about them.

"You killed him!" Stanford said.

"*Ja,* that is correct."

"He could have been saved," Stanford said.

"We haven't the time, *mein freund.*"

Stanford looked at the German. "What does *that* mean?" he said.

"Be quiet," the German said. "We can't carry him. It is too hot for that."

"You bastards," Stanford said.

"*Sehr gut*," the German said. "At least you still have enough energy to display your resentment."

"It was a swinish thing to do."

"You are here of your own free will. That makes you a collaborator, *mein freund*, so don't offer me pieties."

Stanford couldn't deny it, felt ashamed, kept his mouth shut, bent forward and pushed against the tall grass, wondering when it would end. The sun crossed the burning sky. The heat increased and dissolved him. He bled down through himself, through the earth, and lost touch with reality. The long blades flashed up ahead. The *cuchilleros* surrounded him. Atilio walked on in front, his hips rolling, his gun and knives flapping. Time slowed and then stood still. Stanford tried to stop thinking. His thoughts scattered and spun. The white sun started sinking in the sky, became gold and then violet. Stanford saw the yellow sea. He blinked his eyes and looked again. He saw a dark line between the sea and sky and wondered what it might be. A sea: a yellow sea. Not a sea: a scorched savannah. Stanford blinked and saw the dark line as a snake that crossed the line of his vision. He heard the snake and felt it. He tried not to look down. He thought of the *capibara*, the giant rats, and a cold chill slid through him. Stanford shuddered and kept walking. He saw the German beside him. The German's gaunt frame was hazed in silvery light, the yellow sea of the tall grass. The sun shifted in the sky. It sank lower, turning purple. The dark line divided the grass from the sky and took shape as a forest. Stanford almost sobbed for joy. He felt as if he were on fire. He was burning and his body seemed hollow and drained of all feeling.

"There it is," the German said.

"Thank God," Stanford said.

"You will not thank God once you are there. That's the Devil's playground."

Stanford tried not to listen. He didn't want to believe it.

He did not believe it possible that he could feel worse than
he did, did not believe that any place could be worse than
the blistering savannah. Those trees formed a forest. Not a
jungle: a forest. In there, in the shade of the trees, it
would have to be cooler. Stanford felt a great joy. He followed Atilio toward the trees. The Ache beaters were out
ahead, their blades flashing, the grass snapping and falling
down. Stanford wiped sweat from his brow. The white sky
was streaked with violet. Stanford grinned and walked faster, felt the pack on his back, ignored it, ignored the sweat
and pain, and stumbled into the forest.

His spirit plunged down and died. He couldn't believe
the heat was real. His lungs burned and he felt that he
would drown in his own pouring sweat. He hadn't known
he could sweat so much. He wondered where it all came
from. He rubbed his eyes and glanced around the green
gloom, saw it steaming and glistening. Stanford felt a deep
dread. Here everything was outsized: the tangled vegetation, the huge plants and swaying leaves, the crawling in-
sects and chattering birds and monkeys, the great rats in
the undergrowth. Stanford felt his flesh crawling. He felt
trapped and suffocated. The forest chattered and shrieked,
hissed and growled, the steam curling in faint light.

The long knives flashed in the gloom, slashing branches
and leaves, the Indians ripping the shrubbery aside, their
brown bodies sweat-slicked. Stanford choked back his
sobs. He felt petty and childlike. His despair was a void at
his center and it threatened to swallow him. Something
crawled across his foot. He looked down and saw a spider.
It was huge and very black, its body covered in gleaming
hairs, and he kicked out with his foot, almost screamed,
saw it flying away from him. He shuddered and wiped his
brow. He saw the German smirking at him. He felt rage
and the rage drove him forward and brought back some
strength. A bat flew above his head. Its beating wings
merged with the leaves. Stanford shuddered when the
leaves brushed his face with the feel of warm slime. He
cursed softly and moved faster. Tangled vines trapped his
feet. He knelt down and tore the vines from his boots and
saw a lot of large ants. They were devouring a dead rabbit. Not a rabbit: a huge rat. Stanford shivered and then

something stung his hand and he slapped the ant off. He stood up and walked on. The forest steamed and dripped around him. It was chattering and shrieking, alive with crawling things, the undergrowth rustling and shaking, furry forms racing back and forth.

"You are all right?" the German said.

"Yes, I'm all right."

"You do not look too good," the German said. "You seem a little bit shaken."

"I'm all right," Stanford said.

"You have tenacity," the German said.

"Just get me there, you fucker," Stanford said. "I won't crack until you do."

The forest opened around a swamp. A crimson light poured through the trees. He saw the bones of various animals in the clearing, the swamp steaming and stinking. The Indians led them around it. The *cuchilleros* cursed and groaned. Atilio slapped one of the men across the face and then kicked him ahead. Someone screamed and started sinking. His dark eyes were round and frightened. The slime oozed and bubbled up around his knees as he waved his hands wildly. Atilio cursed and bawled some orders. A few Indians rushed toward him. They formed a chain and reached out for the sinking man and pulled him out of the mud. The man rolled onto his back. Atilio walked across and kicked him. The man yelped and then leaped to his feet and was quick to move on. Atilio followed, bellowing orders. The forest closed in again. The heat clamped around Stanford, suffocated him, drenched him, and he choked back his nausea, stumbled on, his eyes scanning the green gloom.

The forest opened out again. He saw a village in crimson light. He saw a river of blood on his left as they passed through the village. The natives stared at them silently. They had dark, haunted eyes. Children played in the dust, swallowed worms, their flesh almost transparent. The *cuchilleros* ignored them. They drove the Indians on ahead. The forest closed in again, a green gloom filled with steam, the heat monstrous, the humidity suffocating, the depths shrieking and chattering .

Stanford felt that he was dead. He hardly knew why he

was here. His body burned and was covered in slime and he felt his flesh peeling. He was nothing. He was now. He was in and of the forest: the snake and the spider and the rat and the teeming, unseen life. The huge leaves dipped and dripped. The vegetation hissed and steamed. He was boiling blood and aching bones and filth, but he soared above all of it. The trees held him and protected him. The green gloom was his sustenance. He swallowed bile and drank in the scalding air and rubbed his eyes and saw shooting stars. Then the gloom. Shafts of sunlight. The distant cries of the Indians. The trees parted and let him walk through and he saw streams of crimson light.

They were in another clearing. A towering cliff blocked their way. The sinking sun was a huge bloody globe that filled the air with a crimson light. The cliff face was steep and jagged. The rock looked like flowing lava. The *cuchilleros* and the Indians, Atilio and the German, all were frozen in that swimming crimson haze, staring up at the bleeding rock.

Stanford followed their gaze. He shook his head and stared hard. He saw tree trunks and planks, knotted vines and banana leaves, all piled up to block off the entrance to a cave in the cliff face.

"This is it?" he said.

"This is it," the German said. "It's a shrine. The natives worship at this shrine. And the shrine is your proof."

He stepped forward and barked some orders. The Indians swarmed across the cliff face. The *cuchilleros* moved back and raised their rifles and did not look too happy. Stanford watched them, feeling dazed. His throat was dry and he felt ill. The Indians worked at the vegetation, pulled the leaves and vines away, removed the planks and then tackled the leaning tree trunks, knocking them over. The debris crashed to the earth. A shower of dust billowed up. The dust sparkled in the swimming crimson light and turned the Indians to specters.

Stanford stared through the dust. He saw the dark mouth of the cave. He stepped forward and saw a dull, metallic gleaming behind the red haze. The last of the tree trunks were pushed away. They crashed down and raised more dust. The Indians looked at the cave with frightened

eyes and then hurried away. Stanford stepped forward
again. His senses suddenly rushed back. His heart was
pounding and he saw the metal gleaming in the spiraling
dust.

The crimson light filled the cave. Stanford almost
stopped breathing. He saw a jigsaw of coiling black lines
and metallic gray pieces. He stepped forward and looked
again. He saw a solid sphere of metal. It was thirty-five
feet long, it rose up to a dusty dome, and the black lines
were a coiled mass of snakes, all asleep on the saucer.

"Oh, my God," Stanford whispered.

He stood there for some time. He couldn't believe what
he was seeing. There were at least a hundred snakes on
the saucer, their bodies coiled, intertwined. Stanford felt
his flesh creep. He saw the gleaming gray metal. The
smooth perimeter swept up to the dome and looked incredibly beautiful. The natives thought it was a shrine.
Stanford understood the feeling. His fear collapsed and
made way for a deep and overwhelming exhilaration. The
saucer was magnificent. Its polished surface seemed
seamless. It stretched across the mouth of the cave and
was bathed in the crimson light.

"What happened?" Stanford said.

"It crashed years ago," the German said. "The natives
thought it was a gift from the gods, and they dragged it in
there."

"Was there anyone in it?"

"I think so. I presume so. But there's no way to open it
up—and now the snakes keep us out of there."

Stanford felt his heart pounding. He saw the lovely,
sublime machine. He saw the snakes coiled around the
dusty dome, still and silent, a tapestry. Stanford started to
shake. He couldn't bear it any longer. He stepped forward
and walked toward the saucer, determined to touch it.

A single shot rang out. The bullet ricocheted off the
saucer. Stanford gasped and jumped back and whirled
around and saw the men looking at him. They were frozen
in crimson light. They looked hazy and unreal. The tall
German had a pistol in his hand and was waving it gently.

"Don't do that," he said. "Don't try to touch it. If you
do, you'll be dead."

Stanford looked at the gleaming saucer. His flesh crawled at what he saw. The snakes were all awake, slithering through one another, wrapping themselves around the dome, dangling over the edges, hissing and spitting and sliding along the smooth, seamless surface. Stanford started to shake. The exhaustion suddenly swept over him. He stood there in the jungle, the dust drifting about him, staring through the swimming crimson haze at the snakes on the saucer.

"Your proof," the German said. "Now I talk."

CHAPTER THIRTY-ONE

"Let me begin at the beginning. In 1933, when Hitler took power, the greater part of German science was totally subordinated to the creation of new military weapons. Thus, by 1935, research on rockets and other forms of aerial warfare had advanced by spectacular leaps. Now the common assumption is that most of that work was being done by Walter Dornberger, Karl Becker, Klaus Riedel, Helmut Grottrup and Wernher von Braun, but such was not in fact the case. Most of the fame attached to those gentlemen resides in the fact that they all worked on the V-1 and V-2 rockets, that the majority of them went to America after the war, and that once in America they became even more well known for their NASA work on space exploration. *Sehr gut.* However, the real pioneer of Germany's World War II achievements was the American you now know of as Wilson.

"In 1935 most of the German rocket research was being undertaken at the experimental stations in Reinickendorf and Kummersdorft West, not far from Berlin. It was to Kummersdorft West, where I was then scientific administrator, that Himmler personally came to introduce Wilson. And what really astonished me, apart from the fact that he was an American, was the extent of the powers that Himmler intended giving him.

"By the middle of 1935 it had been decided that the Reinickendorf and Kummersdorft research centers were no longer big enough to house the rocket projects. That same year, Wernher von Braun had suggested using an island in the Baltic, named Usedom; this island was situated close to Szczecin at the mouth of the Oder River, and it was densely wooded, sparsely inhabited and relatively isolated. It was therefore decided to move the two research centers to the northern promontory of Usedom, near to the small village of Peenemunde . . . And this mysterious man, Wilson, this stranger from America, was to take over Kummersdorft West when the rocket teams left.

"It was an unusual situation, but not as impossible as it might seem. While Germany was not a nation under constant surveillance, that surveillance was carried out by the Gestapo and the S.S., and those organizations were strictly controlled by Himmler. Himmler's S.S. were unique, a law unto themselves; they answered neither to Hitler nor to the German High Command, but only to their beloved *Reichsfuhrer*: their demigod, Heinrich Himmler. In fact, Himmler controlled Germany. He did it quietly and surreptitiously. He quietly took over schools, universities and factories, and soon he had his own research centers scattered all over Germany. Thus Himmler controlled Germany—he controlled the flow of information—and his projects were shrouded in a secrecy that would never be broken.

"Wilson's project was such a secret. It was known only to a few. His research centers were filled with meticulously chosen technicians and constantly patrolled by the S.S. He was a genius, almost certainly. I don't doubt it at all. He was cold and brilliant and relentless, and nearly inhuman. His one passion was science, his knowledge was beyond belief, and he rarely discussed anything but his work and the need to complete it. That's why he was in Germany. Only Germany could meet his needs. He had limitless facilities and slave labor and Himmler's personal support. That's what he wanted. He didn't care about anything else. He needed money and muscle, and he didn't give a damn where they came from.

"So. Given carte blanche by Himmler, Wilson quickly strengthened his project: pulling in other departments, utilizing other research centers, and stealing more technicians

wherever he found them, working through the S.S. Now
while this had many obvious advantages, it also meant that
Wilson was forced to take on some engineers whom he
didn't really care for all that much. Included in these were
the German scientists Habemohl and Miethe, the aging
Italian, Dr. Bellonzo, and the ambitious Luftwaffe engineer, Rudolph Schriever. Most of those men were actually
there to watch Wilson, and their presence around his project really annoyed him. He therefore kept them busy by
letting them work on various designs, which they could
then forward at regular intervals to Himmler. Few of the
designs were worth the paper they were drawn on, but
they kept Himmler happy, soothed the vanity of his four
scientists, and enabled Wilson to get on with the real work
without too much interference.

"Determined that his project should be the most advanced then in existence, Wilson traveled all over Germany, visiting the other research centers, and utilizing any
innovation that could enhance the possibilities of his own
project.

"At this point you must understand that while it is true
that the German scientists as a whole were then working
on some extraordinary innovations, it is equally true that
their separate projects were rarely coordinated. So great
were the rewards in Nazi Germany, and so terrible the
penalties, that even formerly cooperative scientists were
reduced to seeking favor by competing ferociously with
one another. In this sense, the Peenemunde situation was
typical: while we had the cream of our rocket engineers
working on the V-1 and V-2 at Peenemunde, the V-1 was
a Luftwaffe project, the V-2 was an Army project, and
both sides competed with one another instead of putting
their heads together. Similarly, while various establishments scattered all over Germany and Austria were working separately on gas turbines and jet propulsion, heat
resistant and porous metals, and gyroscopic mechanisms
and boundary layer-defeating airfoils, it was not until the
arrival of the relentless, gray-haired Wilson that someone
had the sense to link these innovations together in one astonishing, revolutionary aircraft. Wilson did that—he com-

bined the cream of German innovations—and in five years he had completed the prototype of his first flying saucer.

"Now, Himmler was very excited by the possibilities of the flying saucer, but he never mentioned the saucer to Adolf Hitler. Indeed, the only thing *der Fuhrer* knew about Kummersdorft West was that it was one of many aeronautical research centers and that it was probably engaged in producing conventional aircraft. Regarding technological matters, Hitler knew very little, since he expected Himmler to keep him informed. That was a mistake: Himmler kept a lot to himself. So Hitler knew about Peenemunde, about the V-1 and V-2, but otherwise he only heard about 'secret' weapons that were still being processed.

"Himmler had good reason for his secrecy. Back in 1938, Hitler, anxious for a foothold in the Antarctic, had sent an expedition commanded by Captain Alfred Richter to the coast due south of South Africa. Daily for three weeks two seaplanes were catapulted from the deck of the German aircraft carrier *Schwabenland*, with orders to fly back and forth across the territory which Norwegian explorers had named Queen Maud Land. The Germans made a far more thorough study of the area than the Norwegians had done—believed to be the most extensive aerial study undertaken up to that time—finding vast regions which were surprisingly free of ice. Their planes covered 230,000 square miles in all, photographing almost half of this area. They also dropped several thousand metal poles, each marked with the swastika and pointed at the tip so that the poles would dig into the ice and remain upright. This job done, they renamed the whole area *Neuschwabenland* and then claimed it as part of the Third Reich.

"From that moment on, men and equipment were shipped regularly to Neuschwabenland for the purpose of building a secret underground military base. Most of these men were either specially trained S.S. troops or slave workers from the concentration camps. Now, while Hitler was aware of the fact that Himmler was shipping his men to the Antarctic, he thought of it as a purely military endeavor. As far as *der Fuhrer* was concerned, the secret base in the Antarctic—being constructed underground—was merely an S.S. training base designed to acclimatize scientists and soldiers to those rigorous conditions in preparation for explorations after the war. However, what Himmler was in reality doing was pursuing a dream that did not include Hitler, would supersede the Third Reich, and would then place Himmler up there with the immortals as the Lord of Atlantis.

"Let me clarify that. Himmler's obsessions were numerous, bizarre and totally mad: sorcery, mesmerism, clairvoyance, reincarnation, faith healing, Lemuria, Atlantis, the mystic strength of the *Volk*. Himmler also believed absolutely in Hoerbiger's fanciful doctrine of Eternal Ice—that a world of ice was the natural heritage of Nordic men—and he therefore also believed that a return to such a world would lead to men who were like gods.

"It was because of this dream that Himmler, when he was given the task of organizing the S.S., did not envisage it as a normal police force but as a real religious order devoted to the creation of the perfect man. Indeed, right from the start it was his intention to eventually isolate the 'élite' of the S.S. from the world of ordinary men for the rest of their lives. It was also his intention to create special colonies of the 'élite' all over the world, answerable only to the administration and authority of Himmler's New Order.

"For this, the first step was the creation of special schools in the mountains of Bavaria where the S.S. élite were indoctrinated in Himmler's ideals and firmly convinced that they were the unique new men 'far finer and more valuable than the world has yet seen.' The second step was the creation of the *Ahnenerbe*—the Institute for Research into Heredity—whose function was to finance and publish Germanic researches and to supervise the hideous 'anthropological' medical experiments in hellholes like Auschwitz and Dachau. The third step was to eliminate the Jews from the face of the earth, and to transport all subhumans—the Poles, Czechs and Slavs—to the numerous concentration camps and keep them there, generation after generation, as slaves to the Reich. And the fourth and most important step was the *Lebensborn*—Spring of Life—which would, through the controlled mating of élite S.S. men and pure Aryan women, breed out the 'imperfect' German types within one hundred years.

"A world of ice and fire: the Antarctic and the S.S. This dream obsessed Himmler night and day and then became a reality. He had his colony: the Antarctic. He had his masters: the S.S. He would send his slaves to the Antarctic, use them for labor and as guinea pigs, and in time, with scientific application, the Superman would be born.

"You do not believe, Herr Stanford? You do not think it possible? Then think of the *Ahnenerbe* and the *Lebensborn*, of the medical experiments and controlled breeding, of Belsen and Buchenwald and the S.S. torture chambers, of the millions who were processed like battery hens and emerged as warm ash. The concentration camps were no accidents. They indulged in imitative rites. They were the prototypes for the social order of the future: that world of masters and slaves . . . And think again, Herr Stanford, of the *Lebensborn*. Apart from arranging matings between the S.S. élite and fine blond ladies and adopting 'racially suitable' children for childless parents, the *Lebensborn* also kidnapped thousands of 'suitable' children from the occupied territories and had them raised in special S.S. institutions . . . And a lot of those children—indeed, thousands of those children—simply disappeared from the face of the earth.

"So, it was Himmler. Hitler never knew about it. Himmler wanted his secret colony, he wanted his world of ice and fire, and he wanted the extraordinary flying saucer for his future protection. Thus it was that by 1943 more concentration camp prisoners and children kidnapped by the *Lebensborn* were being shipped to the Antarctic, and that a lot of valuable equipment, including components for the flying saucer, were disappearing via the South Atlantic route in S.S. controlled submarines.

"Alas, Himmler's dream then collapsed. By 1943 it was clear to us all that the war would eventually be lost. This awareness put Himmler in a panic, made him yearn more desperately for some extraordinary new weapons, and finally encouraged him to look fondly at the V-1 and V-2 rocket projects. Then, after the August 17 bombing of the Peenemunde research centers, Himmler persuaded Hitler to hand the whole project over to the safekeeping of the S.S. A month later, on September 3, 1943, S.S. General Hans Kammler was put in charge of the transfer of most of the Peenemunde development works—not including Wernher von Braun—to caves in the mountains near the Traunsee in Austria, and mass production of the rockets to the underground factory in Nordhausen in the Harz Mountains. This effectively gave Himmler a new pet project and distracted him from Wilson.

"By early 1944, Wilson, now working at the BMW *Platz* near Prague, had replaced his original flying saucer's turboprop propulsion system with a new, highly advanced jet propulsion system, thus completing the first truly operative machine. It was Wilson's intention to test fly the machine as soon as possible, but increasingly darker thoughts about Himmler put him off this idea.

"Bear this in mind about Wilson: As a child in America he had, like our von Braun, been obsessed with the potential of space flight. A genius himself, he had secretly worked with the genius Goddard, and had observed how that gentleman was mistreated by the country he helped. Because of that—and because of his experience in Iowa—Wilson was obsessed with the need to avoid a similar fate and find absolute freedom regarding his work. That freedom was in the Antarctic. It was in a master and slave society. And Wilson wanted that society to succeed more than anything else.

"By 1943, however, it was Wilson's belief that Himmler was basically insane, that he would eventually fall apart, and that he would then represent a threat to Wilson's plans for escaping. Knowing that this view was shared by a few other high-ranking officers, Wilson waited until the time was ripe—when the forthcoming defeat was very evident—and then approached them with a separate escape plan. One of those officers was myself, another was S.S. General Hans Kammler, and a third was S.S. General Artur Nebe, a very secretive man. It being that both Kammler and myself had been directly responsible for the utilization of the slave labor, and that Nebe had been in the Gestapo and had also headed an extermination squad in Russia, we were all well aware of our fate should the Allies get hold of us. Needless to say, we fell in with Wilson's plan.

"The crux of the plan was to make Himmler forget our project and turn his attention elsewhere. Consequently, Wilson started to lie about his project and submit incomplete drawings to Himmler and one of his favored engineers, namely *Flugkapitan* Schriever. While never going far enough to make Himmler suspicious, Wilson nevertheless understated the actual progress being made and told Himmler of bad setbacks, involving labor and equipment, that never for one minute existed. This worried Himmler—he desperately wanted an extraordinary weapon—and as anticipated, he turned away from Wilson and started looking elsewhere.

"This brings me back to Wilson's unwanted associates, particularly *Flugkapitan* Rudolph Schriever. Now remember that it was mostly the unworkable drawings of Schriever that had been passed on to Himmler, and *not* the more advanced Wilson drawings. Therefore, in accordance with Wilson's plan, Hans Kammler, shortly after the Allied invasion of Europe, intimated to Himmler that the Schriever drawings were more advanced, that Wilson was maliciously holding Schriever back, and that Schriever should be given his own research center and allowed to continue his work without interference. Kammler further suggested that because of the terrible bombing raids over Berlin and its surrounding areas—and because of the Allied invasion—the research center at Kummersdorft West should be evacuated to a more inaccessible, secret area. He suggested that Wilson's project be moved to Kahla in the mountains of Thuringia, and that Schriever's new project be located in a desolate area of Mahren. Himmler agreed to this.

"On June 22, 1944, shortly after having fitted his saucer with jet propulsion, Wilson's project was moved from

Kummersdorft West to Thuringia. A week later, with Schriever in charge, the remaining staff of Kummersdorft West was moved to a secret location in Mahren. Thus, while Schriever's progress would be watched closely by Himmler, Wilson could complete the genuine flying saucer under the protection of Hans Kammler and myself.

"What we now needed was a tightly controlled escape route that would take us from Kahla to Kiel in the Baltic. The best man for such a job was obviously Artur Nebe, an S.S. general with a keen sense of survival and sound training in all kinds of intrigue. Unfortunately, while Nebe had once been one of the most favored of the S.S., he was now under suspicion from those closest to Hitler and knew that he was being watched all the time. Nebe had to disappear—he would have to work in anonymity—and his chance came on July 20, 1944, after the attempted assassination of Hitler.

"That assassination attempt led to the most terrible reprisals, and a great many of our officers, in fear of their lives, fled and then disappeared for good. One such officer was General Nebe. He had a lot of fanatical followers. Nebe fled straight to Kahla, took a lot of his men with him, and those men organized the escape route from Kahla to Kiel. Thus it was that by early 1945 important men and materials were being quietly moved from the research complex in Thuringia to sympathetic submarines and ships in Kiel Harbor on the Baltic Sea—the moves officially authorized by favored S.S. General Hans Kammler and tightly controlled by the anonymous General Nebe and his other 'missing' S.S. men.

"Kammler was in the perfect position to arrange all this. Now trusted implicitly by Himmler—and therefore revered by his S.S. troops—Kammler could move men and equipment anywhere without being questioned. More so because by this time he had been placed in full charge of the V-2 program and that program had become Hitler's final hope. Naturally, since the job gave Kammler the freedom to travel at will around the German-occupied territories, he worked like a demon on the launching of the V-2s and made sure that all his movements were noticed.

In this way, Wilson could assemble the complete prototype of his flying saucer in the underground factory at Kahla—undisturbed by the increasingly disillusioned Himmler, ignored by the V-2 obsessed Hitler, and otherwise protected by General Nebe and his runaway S.S. subordinates.

"Kammler had another useful job at this time. While the infamous Alpine Retreat had never really existed, Hitler was still dreaming of forming a last redoubt in the mountains of Germany. Since his chosen area was to include the metaphorical arc that ran from the Harz Mountains to Thuringia, south of Prague and across to Mahren, Kammler was put in charge of all the important research centers hidden deep in those areas. This again made it easy for him to protect Wilson's project in Kahla and insure the continuing shipment of men and supplies to the ships and submarines in Kiel Harbor.

"By early February 1945, Wilson had completed a truly advanced flying saucer and a test flight was arranged for the fourteenth of that month. Unfortunately, when the saucer was wheeled out of its hangar during the early hours of that morning, bad weather, including rain and snow, caused the test to be canceled. Two days later, however, a resoundingly successful test flight was made.

"The machine tested near Kahla on the morning of February 16, 1945, was known as the *Kugelblitz*. Basically, it was a triple-layered, disc-shaped machine with a diameter of 14,400 millimeters and a height from base to canopy of 3,200 millimeters. The central body was made from heat-resistant nickel-based alloys and titanium; and the top and bottom discs of this circular body rotated at varying speeds around the two-pilot control cabin which was molded to the solid body that housed the engine. While the spinning discs were devoid of all surface protuberances such as wings and stabilizers, their porous metal composition would suck the air through the machine and utilize it as an added propulsive force.

"As with the previous turboprop version, this saucer's four legs also functioned as downward thrusting, swiveling tail pipes used for lift-off—but now activated by low and high pressure compressors generating an enormous thrust and including a new vaporizing fuel injector system that rendered the jet thrusters smoke-free. The jet burners lifted the *Kugelblitz* vertically, at modest speed, to a height of just over one hundred feet; once there, the downward thrusting tailpiece would swivel up through the bottom disc and be locked into position in the molded central body. Four similar boosters, situated at equal distances around the immovable central body, would then be used for horizontal propulsion and direction control, while the upper and lower discs, with their porous composition, would revolve at high speed to utilize the boundary layer and achieve unprecedented high speeds.

"The *Kugelblitz* was in fact a giant-sized *Feuerball*—the most recent spin-off from Wilson's endeavors—and as such was remarkably sophisticated. During the test flight it reached an altitude in excess of 40,000 feet at a speed of approximately 1,250 miles per hour. Not yet capable of the extraordinary maneuvers of the modern UFO, it nevertheless incorporated a special inertial shield for the protection of the pilots; an automatic control system that utilized the profile of the terrain below; high frequency, omnidirectional automatic navigation; and a few primitive, but fairly effective pulse beam weapons.

"Naturally, with the flying saucer project completed, our most urgent task was to transfer the project to the Antarctic, obliterate all signs of our work, and insure that nothing was left for the advancing Allies. Bear in mind that we had, as each separate section of the machine had been successfully tested, been shipping those parts to the Antarctic, component by component, throughout every year of the war. Now, the only components that had to be shipped out were those belonging to the redesigned jet engines. Within a week of the test flight those components were removed from the *Kugelblitz*, the machine itself was blown up, and then Wilson, accompanied by Nebe and other S.S. personnel, made his way by truck and train to the port of Kiel. Two days after that, on February 25, 1945, the remaining slave workers of the underground Kahla complex were driven back to Buchenwald where they were gassed and then incinerated in the crematoria. The Kahla complex was then a deserted shell.

"Himmler never knew about the evacuation of Kahla since he was too obsessed with the rapid Soviet advance. To distract him further, General Kammler suggested that the scientists still at Peenemunde be made to join the others in Nordhausen, pointing out that a new research center was being built in the Bleicherode mine and that accommodations had been prepared for the technicians and their families in the surrounding villages. Himmler promptly agreed to this move, and not long after, Wernher von Braun and his associates were moved by train, truck, private car and barge to their new quarters deep in the Harz Mountains.

"By this time, precisely as Wilson had anticipated, Himmler was falling to pieces. No longer trusted by Hitler, and having just made a fool of himself by allowing the Russian army to reach the outskirts of Berlin, he was then spending much of his time in Dr. Gebhardt's sanatorium at Hohenlychen, seventy-five miles north of Berlin, and idiotically planning his private surrender to the Allies.

"At the end of February, while Wilson and General Nebe were hiding just outside Kiel and Kammler was transferring the Peenemunde technicians to Nordhausen, I paid the *Reichsfuhrer* a visit. Babbling dementedly, he told me that his peace negotiations were not progressing, that he was going to try to approach Eisenhower, and that he intended using Schriever's flying disc as a bribe to the Allies.

"Following Kammler's instructions, I informed the *Reichsfuhrer* that the Wilson project had made no progress, that Wilson had been shot while trying to escape toward the Allied lines, and that the research complex at Kahla had been evacuated and then blown up to prevent the equipment from falling into Allied hands. I also told him that since the enemy would soon be reaching Hohenlychen, there was little chance of escaping to the Antarctic and that his peace negotiations were therefore our only hope. Himmler, terrified by this news, asked me to inform Kammler that the last redoubt was to be held at any cost. Meanwhile he, Himmler, would arrange for the Schriever disc to be tested as soon as humanly possible.

"Knowing that the Schriever disc could not possibly fly, I returned to wait for Kammler at Nordhausen. At the end of March, Kammler returned from the Hague where he had, ostentatiously, been firing the last of the V-2 rockets on London. Unfortunately, just before we could join Wilson and Nebe in Kiel, Kammler received orders from Himmler stating that the Americans were approaching Nordhausen and that the whole complex therefore had to be evacuated. Determined to insure that no suspicion fell upon him, Kammler went ahead with this order.

"However, Kammler did not go with the evacuees. Seeing a more surreptitious way of making his escape, Kammler, on April 2, took about 500 V-2 experts to the Bavarian Alps in the region of Oberammergau, traveling with them in his private S.S. train. Once there, the technicians were housed in army barracks and guarded by some S.S. fanatics. Included in these scientists were Wernher von Braun and General Dornberger—and shortly after they were imprisoned, General Kammler quietly disappeared for good . . .

"Did I go with him? Obviously not. On April 2, when Kammler was on the train to Oberammergau, I returned to Berlin to check out the general situation. However, once in Berlin I found myself buried in plots, counterplots and other intrigues. As for Himmler, he just wouldn't let me go. Now totally hysterical, hiding out in his sanatorium, he was studying his horoscope, still trying to negotiate a separate peace, and babbling constantly about Schriever's flying disc and how it could save us all.

"In the end, it was Schriever's worthless saucer that got me trapped in Britain. Now believing that the Wilson project had been terminated and that Wilson had been shot, Himmler insisted that I supervise the test flight of Schriever's supposedly completed prototype. Reluctantly I did this—I arranged the test flight for mid-April—but the test was called off in the face of the Allied advance, the prototype was destroyed by the retreating S.S., and Schriever's few worthwhile drawings were stolen from him and burned in my presence. After that, Himmler collapsed, he eventually killed himself, and I fled the holocaust of Berlin and finally ended up here.

"And the others? On April 25, 1945—five days after Hitler's birthday, two days after the first meeting between Soviet and U.S. troops on the banks of the Elbe, three days before the Allies crossed the Eastern Bank, and five days before Hitler killed himself in his bunker in Berlin—General Kammler joined Wilson and General Nebe aboard submarine U-977—bound for the Antarctic."

CHAPTER THIRTY-TWO

April 26, 1945. We had left Kiel illegally, not daring to ask for fuel, so we pulled into Christiansund South to fill up the tanks. The war news was bad. The Soviets were in Berlin. The Americans and Russians had finally met at Torgau on the Elbe. The end was in sight. The submarine submerged the next day and kept hugging the coastline. I often went to the hold to check the crate, but I knew this was pointless. General Nebe kept to himself. His dark eyes revealed nothing. General Kammler was obsessed with the radio and passed on the news. None of this news was good. The Reich was obviously crumbling. When the death of Adolf Hitler was announced, we all knew it was over.

Captain Schaeffer called a meeting. Nebe and Kammler sat together. General Kammler was tense and energetic, Nebe was totally expressionless. The war was over, Schaeffer said. That presented certain problems. There would be no submarine tankers in the South Atlantic, which meant no food nor fuel. We would have to change our plans. We would never make it to the Antarctic. With luck, we might reach Argentina, but we couldn't go further.

I confess: I was shocked. My one thought was for the wilderness. I glanced at Nebe but his dark eyes were expressionless, so I then looked at Kammler. The general's eyes were bright. He mentioned Colonel Juan Peron. He reminded us that Peron was a man who could not resist geld. Kammler smiled when he said this. He was an or-

ganized man. He then added that he had already discussed the matter with the necessary people. General Nebe did not smile. Captain Schaeffer looked relieved. We agreed to head straight for Argentina at no matter the cost.

Not quite straight: a digression. Some of the crew were rebellious. The war was over and they wished to return to Germany, and Schaeffer agreed to this. We hugged the Norwegian coastline. We only surfaced at night. A few days later we reached the mountain coast of Bergen and let the men off.

I climbed up to the deck. I had to breathe the cooling air. I saw patches of stars between the clouds, the dark water, the jagged cliffs. The men shivered on the deck. General Nebe surveyed them coldly. The men shuffled their feet on the deck and shook hands with their comrades. I looked across the dark water. The coastline was featureless. The sea lapped against the submarine as the men clambered overboard. I felt a great yearning. It was a yearning for dry land. After this, we would spend months in the submarine, mostly submerged.

May 10, 1945. The real journey began. My strongest memories are of constant heat and stench and the engine's bass rumblings. It was too long for sanity. We were living on top of one another. First a day, then a week, then two weeks, the submarine like a tomb. The North Sea and the English Channel. The blackened breast of Gibraltar. When we surfaced, our freedom was brief and the planes made us fearful. In truth, we hardly surfaced. The hatch was opened to let air in. We would see the glittering circle of sky, and then the hatch would be closed again. Then along the coast of Africa. A brief glimpse of sun and sand. Then sixty-six days under water, a nightmare of sweat and noise.

By June the crew was restless. There were arguments and fistfights. Once a man took his knife from his dinner plate and slashed the face of a friend. Captain Schaeffer gave them beer. He was a careful, thoughtful man. There was peace for at least another week, and then more fights broke out. General Nebe's dark eyes were watchful. His hand often stroked his pistol. He started walking up and down the submarine, murmuring words here and there.

His words stilled some restless souls. Nebe's dark eyes chilled their rage. They would stare at his eyes, at his pistol, and remember his history. After that, it was easier. It was miserable, but less dangerous. We turned away from one another, faced the walls, and let our own thoughts sustain us.

We surfaced six weeks later. We were in the middle of the South Atlantic. A fierce sun burned a hole in the sky, and the green sea was placid. This reprieve was a blessing. The next month was more bearable. We alternated between floating on the surface and diving back to the depths. Then the Cape Verde Islands. We went ashore on Branca Island. The men frolicked on the burning white sand and washed themselves in the dazzling sea. That day was all too brief. The droning of aircraft made us leave. The submarine dived back to the depths and our journey continued.

Nevertheless, life was easier. We started surfacing almost daily. Once we stayed on the surface for a week by disguising the submarine. False sails and false funnel. From the air, we were a cargo steamer. The planes droned overhead but ignored us, not suspecting a thing. The men waved at the planes. They fought their boredom with such humor. They would watch the planes flying away, and then lie down and sun themselves.

Nebe usually remained below. He liked the claustrophobic depths. Kammler paced the deck and searched the horizon like a man with no time to spare. Eventually we saw land. It was the coast of Rio de Janeiro. Kammler smiled and climbed down through the hatch to listen in on the radio. The news was not good. Kammler relayed what had happened. Another fleeing submarine, Captain Wehrmut's U-530, had recently put into the River Plate with unfortunate consequences. The whole crew had been taken prisoner. They had been handed over to the Americans. Kammler told us this, studied us, enjoyed our despair, then grinned and mentioned a place called Mar del Plata and went back to the radio.

August 17, 1945. We pulled in at Mar del Plata. Four months after we had stepped aboard at Kiel, we stepped off in the Argentine. We had no need to worry.

*An arrangement had been made. From here, we were to
be transported to a secret airfield in Bahia Blanca, and
from there flown directly to the Antarctic.*

*The thought filled me with pleasure. I looked up at the
crowded dock. The Argentinian officials crossed the gangplank, their medals flashing and jangling. They did not
look too happy. They were mopping their sweaty brows. I
sensed immediately that something was wrong and crossed
over to Kammler. He shook hands with the officials. The
man with the most medals whispered. Kammler's lips
formed a single, thin line that expressed his concern. He
then smiled at Captain Schaeffer. He introduced us to the
officials. We all had wine and biscuits on the deck, the sun
blazing upon us. A small delay, someone said. An unfortunate mishap regarding transport. We would have to spend
some days on the submarine before we could leave. Captain Schaeffer agreed to this. He was a reasonable and
thoughtful man. The Argentinians all smiled and bowed
low and then left in a hurry.*

*I spoke to Kammler and Nebe. We met at midnight on
the dock. It was dark and I saw the moon reflected in
Nebe's depthless eyes. Kammler spoke in an urgent whis-
per. He told us what had really happened. He said that
British and American Intelligence had picked up the information that Hitler and Martin Bormann had escaped.
Reportedly they had fled in a submarine. They were
thought to be heading for the Argentine. It was the British
and American wish that the Argentinians report the arrival
of any German submarines in their waters. Thus the Argentinians were in a panic. They felt that something must
be done. What they wanted was to offer the Allies a little
something to chew on.*

*General Nebe lived by intrigue. It was bread and meat
to him. His dark eyes offered no pain or pleasure as he
outlined a compromise. We three alone would leave. We
would take the crate with us. But to save the Argentinians
embarrassment, we would leave all the rest behind. They
would be held as political prisoners. The Argentinians
would hand them over. That way, the Argentinians would
look good and we would save our own necks.*

Ruthless? Yes. But then the three of us were ruthless.

We had lived in the Third Reich a long time and had learned to survive.

We agreed to Nebe's plan. It could not possibly fail. The fate of Schaeffer and his crew did not concern us and could hardly effect us. It didn't matter what they told the Allies. By then it would be too late. By then we would be hidden in the Antarctic, our whereabouts unknown. The Allied forces would then be helpless. They would never find our underground base. They would know that the underground base existed, but they wouldn't dare mention the fact. How could they mention it? It would only lead to panic. And so, aware of this, knowing the Allies would be helpless, we decided to drop Schaeffer and his crew and go on by ourselves.

We unloaded the crate the next day. This aroused no curiosity. Schaeffer assumed that we were simply unloading it for safekeeping on shore. That same night we slipped away. Some army officers were waiting for us. I saw the crate in the back of their truck and I climbed up beside it. Nebe and Kammler quickly followed. We looked back at the submarine. We saw the other troops moving along the dock, their rifles aimed at the submarine. Then the truck drove us away. We left the submarine behind us. The flat plains of Argentina swept around us and the stars glittered brightly. Kammler looked at me and smiled. Nebe pursed his lips and slept. The night passed and a pearly dawn broke and then we reached Bahia Blanca.

The airfield was heavily guarded. The plane's engine was already running. The truck drove up to the hold of the plane and the crate was unloaded. General Kammler climbed in first. I let Nebe go ahead of me. I glanced briefly around the airfield, at the soldiers and barbed wire fences, at the flat plains that stretched out to the sky, and then I boarded the plane. The doors of the hold were slid together. The steel locks made a clanging sound. I sat down beside Kammler and Nebe and stared up at the wooden crate. Then the plane roared and shook. It taxied slowly along the runway. Then it roared even louder, raced along the runway, jolted, leaped off the tarmac, and climbed into the sky.

Perhaps I slept then. I do not remember the journey. I

remember Nebe's dark, depthless eyes and the plane's constant rumblings. It did not take very long. My spinning thoughts destroyed time. Kammler smiled when the wheels touched down again and the crate bounced disturbingly. I reached out and touched it. The plane shuddered and stopped. The doors opened and a bright light rushed in and brought with it the shocking cold.

All white. Everything. The frozen wilderness stretched out before us. I stepped down and felt the snow around my boots and breathed the pure, icy air. We were on a small, modest airstrip. Our own plane was waiting for us. We transferred the crate to this plane and then clambered in after it. The doors closed again. The plane's skis chopped through the ice. We took off and flew above the white wilderness and headed inland. All white. Everything. The plains and mountains were as one. My impatience was a hand upon my heart, my exultation was boundless. Then at last we dropped lower. I saw the enormous, encircling plateaus. We flew down below the mountains, below the glittering ice peaks, and then the great caves opened out to embrace us and carry us home.

Here we are and here we stay. The ice glitters in the sun. History changes and the world surrenders to us. We are here. We exist.

CHAPTER THIRTY-THREE

Stanford arrived early, deliberately so. Slowing down at the crossroads, just before the meeting place, he turned off the road and drove between the trees, comforted by the darkness and moonlight, feeling safer that way. He stopped the car, turned the lights out, killed the engine, took a deep breath; looked out at the darkness, glanced up at the sky, half expecting, as he now always did, to see glowing lights merging. When had Epstein disappeared? November 1977. Since then, a whole year had passed and a new year was dawning. Stanford shivered at the thought of it. He didn't think he would survive it. He reached into the glove compartment, carefully pulled out a pistol, checked it, then got out of the car and closed the door very quietly.

The skies of Virginia were starry. There was no wind at all. Stanford smelled the wet grass, felt the chill in the air, marveling at how soothing it was after the furnace of Paraguay. He checked the pistol again, checked the time, shivered slightly, then he walked back through the trees to the road, his eyes moving from left to right.

The road was still deserted. Stanford glanced up at the sky. He grinned automatically, more self-mocking than amused, thinking of himself as a fugitive and wondering how it had come to this. The road remained deserted. Stanford checked his watch again. Satisfied, he knelt down on the grass behind some thick, tangled brambles. The hills were covered in trees. He thought of Epstein in Mount Rainier. His lips tightened and he looked along the road and heard a sound in the distance.

Fuller was on time. He had always been reliable. Stanford got up off his knees, but stayed low, cocked the pistol, looked along the road and saw Fuller's lights coming out of the darkness. The road was flat and very straight. The car approached the crossroads. Stanford watched it as it slowed down and stopped, its engine still purring softly. Fuller flashed his headlights twice. He didn't get out of the car. Stanford looked along the road and saw nothing, listened carefully, heard nothing. Fuller flashed his lights again. He was expecting a response. Stanford turned and loped back through the trees and cut around in a circle. He emerged behind the car. He looked back along the road. There was obviously no car behind Fuller and that made him feel better. He stepped out from the trees. The gun felt heavy in his hand. He walked up to the car, bent down, knocked on the window, and Fuller rolled the window down and looked up and saw the gun in his face.

"Stanford?"

"That's right."

"What the fuck are you doing? You asked me to meet you and I'm here. What's the fucking gun for?"

"Are you alone?" Stanford said.

"What the hell do *you* think? Take a good look. You got eyes in your head. I'm all alone, for chrissake."

"Get out of the car," Stanford said.

"I don't believe this," Fuller said. "I came because you asked me, and now you're sticking a pistol in my face. Have you gone fucking crazy?"

"I'm sorry," Stanford said.

"We're old buddies, for chrissake!"

"I'm sorry. I'm a little bit nervous. Now get out of the car."

Fuller sighed and rolled his eyes, killed the engine and headlights, climbed out and put his hands up in the air as if praying for mercy.

"I don't believe this," he said. "You must have lost your fucking marbles. Who the hell do you think you are? Elliot Ness? Get it out of my face."

"This way," Stanford said.

"It's a joke," Fuller said. "He drags me out of my bed to stick me up. An old buddy from way back."

Stanford waved the gun gently. "I'm not joking," he said. "If I have to use this pistol I'll use it. Over there. Through the trees."

Fuller sighed and shook his head, not believing it, forced a grin, then he sauntered across the road toward the trees, the pistol prodding him on.

"In here, old buddy?"

"That's right," Stanford said.

"It's a picnic," Fuller said. "A midnight treat. I can't fucking wait."

Stanford kept the gun on him, still fond of him, not trusting him, not capable of trusting anyone anymore, not even his oldest friends.

"Can I stop now?" Fuller said.

"That's right. You can stop now."

"I take it that's your car," Fuller said.

"That's right. Get inside."

Fuller sighed and shook his head, ran his fingers through his gray hair, opened the door and lowered himself onto the seat, looking cramped in that small space. Stanford walked around the front. He kept the gun aimed at the windshield. He opened the door and slid into the driver's seat, the pistol still aimed at Fuller.

"Where are we going?" Fuller said.

"Nowhere," Stanford said. "We'll just sit here and have our little talk and then I'll let you go home."

"Most generous," Fuller said.

"I'm sorry," Stanford said.

"My old buddy's sorry," Fuller said. "I feel better already." He was a big man, all muscle, his face rough as they come, and he ran his fingers through his gray hair, his blue eyes very sharp. "Okay," he sighed. "I'm impressed. I can't believe it. We're sitting here in the middle of nowhere and you're pointing a gun at me. What the fuck's going on?"

"It's the saucers," Stanford said. "I want to talk about the saucers."

"I figured that," Fuller said. "You always do. Only the pistol is new to me."

"I've had a bad year," Stanford said. "I have the impression I'm being followed. My room's been wrecked twice, my phone's been cut off, and a hit and run driver smashed my car . . . I just don't feel too safe."

"This is a very dangerous country," Fuller said. "I thought you knew that." He looked down at the pistol, shook his head and grinned laconically. "I'm putting my hand in my pocket," he said. "I'm not smoking. I need chewing gum."

Stanford nodded and watched him. Fuller pulled out some gum. He unwrapped it and popped it in his mouth and proceeded to chew.

"So," he said. "You're nervous. You're being harassed. And you think we're the bogeymen."

"That's right," Stanford said. "Those are CIA trademarks. You bastards have been following us since we went to the Caribbean, since we told you about Gerhardt's disappearance. You accused us of lying."

"Us?" Fuller said.

"Me and Epstein," Stanford said.

"Epstein's gone."

"That's right. Epstein's gone. And you haven't done anything."

Fuller shrugged and chewed his gum. "What the hell could we do?" he said. "You say the guy's been abducted by a UFO and expect us to wear it. It was too much to ask."

"Why?" Stanford said.

"Don't talk shit," Fuller said. "You come up with a story like that and you can't *expect* much."

"You believed me," Stanford said.

"You're talking shit," Fuller said.

"You've known me too long *not* to believe me . . . you know I don't invent things."

"Your story was ridiculous."

"Then where's Epstein gone? He's been missing for over a year and you haven't asked why."

"It's a police case," Fuller said.

"Police, my ass," Stanford said. "I told the police and

they laughed me out of the station and forgot the whole thing."

"What the fuck did you expect? You said a UFO stole your friend. You came on like a crank in a gabardine, so of course the cops laughed."

"Fine," Stanford said. "But Professor Epstein's still missing. He's a pretty important name and now he's gone and no one seems to be bothered. I think that's pretty strange. I mean, it doesn't make sense. A famous man disappears for a year and they don't bat an eyelid. That strikes me as strange."

"So, he's missing," Fuller said. "A lot of people are missing. He was an old man, he was on his last legs, and now he's probably dead."

"I was there," Stanford said.

"Yeah, I know. A UFO took him."

"You believe me," Stanford said. "I know that. That's why you're not searching."

Fuller stopped chewing his gum, stared at Stanford, not smiling, then slowly started chewing the gum again, his jaws working methodically.

"So," he said, "we're at an *impasse*. What the hell are we talking for?"

Stanford watched Fuller carefully. His old friend seemed like a stranger. The pistol was very steady in Stanford's hand, and he was ready to use it.

"You believe me," Stanford said. "You believed me then and you believe me now. You've been following me and you know what I found out and now it's making you nervous."

"Oh?" Fuller said. "And what was that? Just what did you find out?"

Stanford felt very hot. He wanted to roll the window down. He was frightened to roll the window down because of who might be out there. His eyes flicked left and right. He felt foolish as he did it. He licked his lips and put the gun in his other hand, wiped his right hand on his trousers. Then he transferred the gun again. He kept it pointed at Fuller. His old friend, his old CIA buddy, could no longer be trusted.

"The saucers exist," he said. "You've known about them

for years. You have your own, but you're keeping them quiet for political reasons. There are other saucers as well. They're extraordinarily far advanced. They represent a threat to this country, and you're running a race with them. You're frightened of those saucers. You're frightened of public opinion. You don't want the word to leak out and lead to mass panic. Those saucers are very powerful. The people who made them are very powerful. They have weapons we never dreamed about, and they're willing to use them."

Fuller raised his eyebrows. "I don't believe this," he said. "I think maybe I'm not hearing too good. My old buddy's gone crazy."

"You have your own," Stanford said. "There's no point in denying it. The original concepts came from Germany, you've been building them for years, the work was carried out at White Sands and in the wilds of Canada, but now the people who built the original saucers are displaying anxiety."

"I don't believe this," Fuller said.

"You believe it," Stanford said. "You just want to keep it quiet. You killed off Project Blue Book, you harassed all our best researchers, and you've deliberately spread confusion through rumor for the past thirty years. You knew you couldn't keep it secret—you could just confuse the issues—so when something leaked out you just twisted it and wrapped it in myths. Take Cannon AFB. Take Deerwood Nike Base. Take Holloman and Blaine Air Force Bases and then tell me they're rumors. They weren't rumors, you shitface. The saucers seen there were your own. People talked and you let the talk lead to tales of extraterrestrials. But the extraterrestrials don't exist. Something much worse exists. It's a bunch of wizards down in the Antarctic, and you know all about them."

"The Antarctic?" Fuller said.

"You're not so innocent," Stanford said. "There's a bunch of men in the Antarctic, they created the original saucers, and now they're so advanced you can't touch them and the government's shit-scared."

"This is crazy," Fuller said.

"No, it's not," Stanford said. "The Antarctic's a very big place, and those people are hidden there."

"Where?" Fuller said.

"I don't know," Stanford said.

"No," Fuller said. "You don't know. You're just spouting hot air." He shook his head slowly, chewed his gum, looked disgusted, stared sympathetically at Stanford and shook his head again, wearily. "What horseshit," he said. "I mean, I thought you had more sense. That's one of the oldest stories in UFO mythology—and one of the worst."

"What story?"

"Fucking holes in the poles. UFO bases in the Antarctic. Underground cities beneath the ice . . . Atlantis, Lemuria."

"I've heard the stories," Stanford said. "I never believed them for a minute . . . But then I never believed in the saucers either. It turns out I was wrong."

"So they come from the Antarctic?"

"So you admit that they exist?"

"We don't have flying saucers," Fuller said. "Nor does anyone else." He tried to grin at Stanford. It was not a successful grin. "Let's assume they're in the Antarctic," he said. "I might clarify you that way."

"They're in the Antarctic," Stanford said. "They're in underground plants. They're the same as the hidden factories of Nazi Germany, and they're under the ice."

"That's ridiculous," Fuller said. "You can't get beneath that ice. Don't give me that hollow earth shit. That's a theory for hacks."

"Is it?" Stanford said.

"You know fucking well it is. There aren't any holes at the poles. Don't talk like a crackpot."

"I don't know," Stanford said. "What about the ESSA 7 satellites? The photographs taken by those satellites caused a sensation."

"It's beneath discussion," Fuller said.

"Tell me anyway," Stanford said.

"You're a scientist. You know the facts well. I don't have to tell you."

"Tell me anyway," Stanford said.

Fuller shook his head wearily. "Okay," he said. "You want to play games, we'll play games. I'll tell you about the photos that conned all the fucking UFOlogists." He took out some more gum, unwrapped it, stared at it, popped it in his mouth and started chewing, looking thoroughly disgusted. "Those famous NASA photos were released to scientific journals, most of whom could have been expected to understand them. Unfortunately, and as usual, the ESSA 7 satellite photos found their way into the hands of certain commercial writers. The enormous holes in the poles, so clearly shown on the photos, were described, through what can only be termed ignorance, as being just what they looked like: goddamned holes in the poles." Fuller shook his head sadly, chewed his gum, glanced around him, saw nothing but the darkness beneath the trees and then turned back to Stanford. "Of course they weren't holes," he said. "You know that as well as I do. Those photographs were obtained by onboard Vidicon camera systems, and as such were not normal pictures. They were, in fact, photomosaics. They were reproduced from processing the signals from a lot of television camera frames obtained over a twenty-four hour period. Those signals were processed in a computer and transformed to a polar stereographic map projection with latitude, longitude and the outlines of land areas superimposed electronically. The areas in which camera frames were missing—due to the fact that the pictures were taken during the dark polar winter and the ESSA 7 camera systems lacked infrared facilities—were shown in solid black or white, which accounts for the famous 'black holes.' However, current polarorbiting satellites use a two-channel scanning radiometer instead of the Vidicon camera system, and this radiometer is sensitive to energy in both the visible and infrared spectrums. If you, being the ignorant scientist you're so obviously pretending to be, care to return to my office, I'll show you some polar stereographic satellite images from the NOAA 5 satellite in which the visible channel data over the poles during the polar winter shows *holes* at the poles—whereas the *infrared* channel data for the same period shows the land as it actually exists. There are no holes in the poles and you know it, so let's just fucking drop it."

Stanford knew he was right. He just wanted him to talk. He wanted to loosen Fuller's tongue before he pulled his ears off.

"Okay," he said. "Let's change the subject. What do you know about Admiral Byrd?"

"Oh, Jesus," Fuller said.

"Tell me," Stanford said.

"I'm going crazy. My ears are playing tricks. We're in the land of the freaks."

"Tell me," Stanford said.

"Just ask me," Fuller said. "My imagination doesn't stretch as far as yours. I can just about answer you."

Stanford didn't laugh. He kept the gun aimed at Fuller. Just occasionally, he glanced out of the car, scanned the dark, silent forest.

"Okay," Stanford said. "Accepting that there's no enormous hole at the South Pole, the next great UFOlogist theory is that the land around the pole actually dips down considerably, forming a sort of giant doughnut, and that this land mass is therefore greater than we commonly think it is and could actually be a lot warmer than the surrounding Antarctic."

"Right," Fuller said. "And being so immense, hidden from us and quite warm, that land could be fertile and inhabited: the home of your saucer people."

"It's possible," Stanford said.

"It's not possible," Fuller said. "You're going to quote Admiral Byrd's remarks about a continent in the sky."

"Right," Stanford said. "It's been widely reported that Admiral Byrd penetrated a land extent of 2,300 miles *beyond* the pole and saw a mass of land reflected in the sky. Okay, since we now know about Antarctic conditions, we can assume that it *was* a reflection."

"Or a mirage," Fuller said.

"Or a mirage. That still begs the question of how, given where Byrd turned back, he could have reported traveling 2,300 miles *beyond* the pole."

"He didn't," Fuller said. "The origin of that figure is a mystery and did not come from Bryd. Go to your newspaper morgues and you'll find that the actual stated figure was a journey covering approximately 10,000 square miles, with only 100 of those miles beyond the pole. As for the 'Great Unknown beyond the Pole,' that statement —which the UFOlogists have picked up as solid proof of their 'hidden continent' theory—is merely the very understandable remark of a man who was, in 1947, looking for the first time at a land mass that had not yet been explored. The 'Great Unknown' was simply the Great Uncharted—but it *has* been crossed and photographed since and is no longer 'unknown.' "

Stanford started to speak, but Fuller waved his large hand, now involved in what he was saying and determined to finish it.

"Let me continue while I'm eager," he said. "I can't bear your sweet ignorance . . . It is to be noted, regarding Byrd's *other* much abused remark about 'that enchanted continent in the sky,' that Byrd *also* stated that during the flight both he and his crew had no oxygen equipment, that they were suffering from anoxia, and that they were therefore not quite themselves—a point conveniently ignored by our UFOlogists. As for the 'enchanted continent in the sky' being a reflection of a land mass not covered in ice, this isn't as extraordinary as the UFOlogists pretend it is. There are in fact, and contrary to the ignorant assertions of many UFOlogists, many well known ice-free areas in the Antarctic—and any one of these could have been the reflection, or mirage, viewed by Byrd. Another popular so-called 'fact' is that there are no volcanoes in the Antarctic, and that the dust sometimes found in the Antarctic must therefore come from the 'hidden' continent. That's a very neat theory except for one thing: there *are* volcanoes in the Antarctic."

Fuller grinned and chewed his gum. Stanford moved closer to him. The gun was still steady in his hand and he felt pretty high.

"Okay," he said. "That gets right to my point. I just want to clear up a little matter and then we'll call it a day. There are lakes in the Antarctic. There are also ice-free areas. There are mountains and volcanoes, the ice can be a mile deep, and it's believed that the ice beneath the surface is actually joined to the sea. That suggests certain things. It suggests hidden valleys. It suggests canyons and caves and other ice-free hidden areas in which a colony of people could exist in comparative safety. I never *thought* the earth was hollow. I *know* we've charted the Antarctic. But I also know that we've only charted it from the air and that there are vast, unknown areas. You know the bastards are there. You probably know where they are. I want to know what they're doing, I want to know just where they are, and I want all the facts here and now and no pissing around."

Fuller stared hard at Stanford. His large body was quivering. Stanford knew he wasn't quivering with fear, but with cold, suppressed rage. Stanford kept the gun on him. Fuller looked down and studied it. He looked at the gun a long time and then he stared straight at Stanford.

"I'm getting out of here," he said.

"Don't try it," Stanford said.

"You wouldn't know how to fire that fucking thing. *Adiós*, kid. I'll see you."

He started turning toward the door. Stanford raised the pistol higher. He tapped the pistol against Fuller's head, then slipped it into his ear. Fuller froze immediately. The gun barrel filled his ear. Fuller sat there and stared at the dashboard and took a deep breath.

"You wouldn't do it," he said. "Who the fuck do you think you're kidding? You're a scientist. You don't play with those things. Now get it out of my ear."

"It's cocked," Stanford said.

"I noticed," Fuller said.

"Talk or I'll blow your fucking brains out."

"No way. You won't do it."

Fuller jerked his head away. He started opening the car door. Stanford turned the pistol around, used the grip as a hammer, hit Fuller across the side of the head and on the back of his wrist. Fuller's head seemed to spin, hit the dashboard and bounced back, and he grunted, his wounded hand flapping, trying to wipe off the blood. The hand dropped down to his side. His good hand started swinging. Stanford swept the hand away with his gun, jerked the gun down and over. He hit Fuller's hand again. Fuller gasped and flopped forward. He lay there with his head on the dashboard, dripping blood, breathing deeply.

"Talk," Stanford said.

"Get fucked," Fuller gasped. "If you didn't have a gun for a fist, I'd have your balls in my teeth. I'm not talking, you little prick. You've gone too far too quick. If you want me to talk you'll have to suck me, and you're just not the type."

"I'll do it," Stanford said.

"I bet you would," Fuller said.

"Okay, Fuller, that's enough, the joking's over. Just talk. It's less painful."

Fuller started to raise his head. Stanford smashed it with the pistol. Fuller's head cracked against the windshield and bled even more. Stanford watched himself in action. He was standing outside himself. He didn't recognize himself anymore, now driven only by anger. His hidden self had stepped forward. He knew what the hunted felt. He was desperate and it lent him a rage that overrode his old nature. He remembered the girl in Galveston, remembered beating up Scaduto; remembered his journey through Paraguay, the Ache Indians, the cold, brutal German. Yes, he had changed. He knew it now as he looked at Fuller. His old friend, who was breathing harshly and bleeding, could no longer be trusted.

"Talk," Stanford said.

"Fucking Christ," Fuller gasped. He gripped the dashboard with his thick, hard-ridged fingers, as if trying to bend it. "You've sure learned a few tricks," he said.

Stanford smashed Fuller's hand. Fuller yelped and jerked his head up. Stanford pushed the head back down with the pistol and saw the blood flowing.

"I've changed," Stanford said. "I'm not a scientist anymore. I was never a good scientist anyway, but now you bastards have finished me. I won't sit back and take it. I want to get Epstein back. I don't know why it's all that important; I just know that it is. I have to find Epstein. I have to know what happened to him. That old man means a lot to me now, and I don't understand it. He said I refused to make decisions. I made a decision when he disappeared. I decided to track this filthy business down and let no bastard stop me. Now I want you to talk. I think you'll just have to talk. If you don't talk, we'll sit here all night and I'll hurt you much more."

Fuller cursed and jerked upright. Stanford thumped him in the stomach. He grunted and flopped forward again, his good hand on the dashboard. Stanford smashed the hand. Fuller screamed and then whimpered. He was propped up with his forehead on the dashboard, dripping blood to the floor.

"Jesus!" he hissed. "Oh my God, fuck, it hurts. Okay, Jesus Christ, I'm fucking dying, you win, Christ, it hurts . . ." He shook his head but kept it down. He was staring down at his own feet. The blood was dripping off his head and lips, and splashing onto his shoes. "Okay," he said, "you're right. It was the Second World War. The fucking Krauts built a saucer. We found components and various drawings: the British, the Canadians and us, we all found bits and pieces. It was enough to get us going. We all put our heads together. You already know most of the details, so I'll save my breath there. The main work was done in Canada. Other work was done at White Sands. A lot of the UFOs seen over those areas were our very own saucers."

"Fine," Stanford said. "I know all that. What about the Antarctic?"

Fuller groaned and shook his head. "It's all on Epstein's tapes," he said.

"That was Germany," Stanford said. "You're confused. What about the Antarctic?"

"You went to Paraguay," Fuller said. "You went to see that old Kraut. We know what the old fucker told you . . . he told us the same thing."

"When?" Stanford said.

"A long time ago," Fuller said. "That old vulture, he should be dead by now, but we just can't get near him."

"The Antarctic," Stanford said.

"He told you the background," Fuller said. "That was the beginning of it all: those Nazis went to the Antarctic and that's where it began." He shook his head and wiped his lips. He could hardly use his hands. He groaned and let his hands fall down again, his head still on the dashboard. "We knew they were there," he said. "Captain Schaeffer told us that much. He said they had gone to Neuschwabenland to build flying saucers. We were inclined to believe him. We had plenty of evidence to support his statements. We had drawings and components, and we found a few people who talked. That's why we launched Operation Highjump. That was in January '47. It was a military mission disguised as an exploratory expedition, and its true purpose was to find out where the Germans were."

"They docked near Neuschwabenland," Stanford said.

"No," Fuller said. "You can discount that rumor. We had to bluff the whole fucking world, so we did it with style. We circled the whole continent. We really covered that mother. We split up into three separate groups and flew all over the place. The Central Group, based at Little America on the Ross Sea, covered the area between Marie Byrd Land and Victoria Land, moving inland, in crisscrossing patterns, as far as the South Pole. Meanwhile, the East and West Groups girdled the whole continent, moving out in opposite directions and actually coming in sight of one another's planes. The East Group reached the Weddell Sea. The West Group went as far as Princess Astrid Land. Some planes from both groups then flew over Queen Maud Land, including the area that the Germans had called Neuschwabenland. They saw ice-caps like mountains. Their compasses went crazy. They got lost and then they saw some flying saucers that appeared out of nowhere. The flying saucers sort of buzzed them. The planes' ignition systems malfunctioned. Four of the planes went down and the others just cut out, and the crews then told Admiral Byrd about it. The expedition was cut short. The official explanation was hurricane winds. Byrd returned to America, made some indiscreet announcements, then we told him to shut up, we killed all talk of the saucers, and we decided to treat the Antarctic with considerable care. About three months later, in June 1947, we tested our own saucers over Mount Rainier in the Cascades—and then the saucers we had seen in the Antarctic paid their first visits."

"How did you find out where they were?" Stanford said.

"We didn't," Fuller said. "They found us. They started to play tag with our jets and airliners, just to let us know what they could do. They hammered the point home by harassing our top-secret test centers and driving our interceptor pilots nuts. After three years of this there was no doubt in our minds about who those flying saucers belonged to. Naturally we kept it quiet: we were shit-scared of panic. We killed Project Grudge, tried to ridicule all sighting reports, and generally confused the whole issue to turn it into a myth. For the most part this worked. It also worked for our *own* saucers. The Lubbock sightings, for instance, were sightings of our own saucers—and a lot of other sightings were the same."

Fuller kept his head down. He was bleeding much less now. He talked like a man in a trance, his breathing more steady.

"They approached us in 1952," he said softly, "and they did it just like regular politicians, through all the right channels. The approach was made by a man called Aldridge. He got in touch with the CIA. We met him and he told us the story, and we couldn't believe it. Aldridge proved his point. He was talking to one of our top men. He already knew the guy's address and he told him that the next night he would send a flying saucer over his home. The CIA chief lived in Alexandria, Virginia, he was having a garden party on the night in question, and during that garden party both he and his guests saw a UFO directly over the house."

"That was when the Director of Intelligence, General Samford, called Ruppelt to a secret meeting in Washington."

"Right. But Ruppelt didn't know about that Antarctic colony—and we never did tell him."

"So, why the meeting?"

"After the UFO sighting over the CIA chief's home, he had another meeting with Aldridge. Aldridge told him more about the colony, told him what they were capable of, and then said that he didn't want any interference and would trade with the U.S. Apparently, even with *his* awesome genius and his hundreds of workers, he was in

constant need of various mass-produced components and
equipment. His idea, then, was that he would form a clandestine partnership with the U.S., trading certain secrets of
his technology in return for what he required to advance
the same. A seesaw arrangement, right? A tricky maneuver. But that's what he wanted."

"And?"

"He was asked what would happen if we decided to say
no, and he pointed to various disasters, on land and at sea,
that we had not, at least up until he told us, been able to
explain. Aldridge explained them. He told us how he had
caused them. We still didn't believe him, so he told us that
his saucers would invade Washington. When they did, we
believed him."

"That was in 1952."

"Yes."

"And the meeting between Ruppelt and General
Samford?"

"That was after Aldridge had told us about his planned
invasion. Samford never told Ruppelt anything about Aldridge, but he wanted to know about the extent of the
UFO sightings. Ruppelt, not knowing about our conversations with Aldridge, confirmed that there had been a massive build-up of UFOs around Washington throughout that
whole month. He also made it quite clear that he was expecting a UFO invasion over the capital. That invasion
came, we decided to sit tight, and one week later the
bastards came back and we had to tell Truman."

"And then you came to an agreement with Aldridge."

"Right. But the first thing we did was form the Robertson Panel. The purpose of that panel was twofold. The
first purpose was to convince the public that a proper
scientific body had investigated the UFO phenomenon and
found it to be fucking nonsense. Also, regarding this, it
was our intention right from the start to use the panel's
recommendations as an excuse for suppressing all UFO reports. I think you know how we went about it . . ."

"Yes," Stanford said.

"Okay. The second, and equally important purpose of
the panel was to examine what Aldridge had told us and

shown us, and to assess his viability as a threat to the nation. Our assessment was that his technology was so far advanced, it constituted an unprecedented threat to the nation—and probably the world. It was therefore decided to come to an agreement with Aldridge."

"I see," Stanford said. "So that explains why the Robertson Panel was made up of men specializing in atomic research and advanced weaponry, why it was chaired by a CIA-classified employee, and why it included Lloyd Berkner, who had accompanied Admiral Byrd to the Antarctic in 1937."

"Yes. It also explains why, when Ruppelt found out that the UFOs were intelligently controlled, we had to get rid of the bastard."

"And anyone else who was like him."

"Right."

"Then you made your agreement with Aldridge."

"Right. The agreement, simply put, was that we would have a step-by-step trade, negotiating as and when required for what we both wanted. What Aldridge wanted was access to our mass production industries—and what we wanted was everything he knew. Naturally he didn't buy this. He fed us a spoonful at a time. And with neither side trusting the other, we built up a relationship. That relationship grew more complex. Like all relationships, it had its faults. And the biggest was that Aldridge was also trading with our good friends, the Russians."

"He played one against the other," Stanford said.

"You're still awake," Fuller said. "He's still at it right now. We all trade, we all lose. We keep trying to catch up with his technology, but he keeps just ahead of us. So now the pattern's changed. We're all creeping across the Antarctic. The Antarctic is a vast, untapped treasure-house of oil, coal, gold, copper, uranium and, most important, water. The whole world now needs water. Ninety percent of all the world's water is in the Antarctic. In short, the Antarctic is where the future of the world will be decided, so we just can't keep out of it any longer. We all pretend it's not political, that we're just there for research, but the logic, or lack of logic, in politics is leading straight to a clash."

"It's political leapfrog," Stanford said.

"That's right. A kid's game. But somebody's going to trip and get hurt—and then all hell will break loose."

"Are they Nazis?" Stanford said.

"No," Fuller said. "They're a society of masters and slaves, but they're no longer Nazis. That Aldridge is a genius. His genius extends to manipulation and he runs that whole place. He's into parapsychology, electrodes and prosthetics. He has his people implanted when they're born, and they grow up like zombies. There's never more than a thousand of them. The system is based on euthanasia: when someone ceases to be of any use, Aldridge has him put down. There's no possibility of resistance. They're all disciplined with electrodes. They all exist just to work, and that work is for the glory of science. Human beings are vivisected. What he doesn't have, he steals. We know he steals people from us, but we discreetly ignore that fact. We can't afford to rock the boat. We have to stay on the seesaw. That colony represents the balancing power, and we just can't catch up with it."

"So the Americans and Russians actually *work* with him?"

"In truth, it's what we need. The whole world's out of control. We all need what that fucking bastard has, but he's buried down there. So, we continue trading. He lies to us, we lie to him. We keep building more satellites, pulse beam weapons, more powerful saucers, and we think that in a couple of years we might be ready to tackle him. The Russians think the same. Aldridge knows what we're both thinking. When we slip up, he demonstrates his power and then we quickly correct ourselves. It's like I said: it's a seesaw, a tricky maneuver, but sooner or later, it's bound to explode—and I don't like to think of that."

"So," Stanford said. "That explains the secrecy about UFOs. It also explains why the Russians and Americans cooperate in the Antarctic."

"You've hit the nail on the head, kid."

Fuller raised his head slowly, put it back against the seat. He took a deep breath and just sat there, staring out at the darkness.

"Where are they?" Stanford said.

"Don't even think about it," Fuller said. "You go there and you'll never come back, and that's all there is to it."

"Where *are* they?"

Fuller sighed wearily. "They're in Neuschwabenland," he said. "You fly along the zero meridian, straight in to Queen Maud Land, and about two hundred miles in from the coast, you'll find a range of low mountains. It's really Norwegian territory. It's really part of Queen Maud Land. You usually only find it marked in German atlases, and they call it Neuschwabenland. The Antarctic colony is in those mountains. They've hollowed out the base of the mountains. There's an area where the ice forms a huge circle that resembles a volcano. The carrying ships are down there. They come up out of there. Beneath the circle of ice is solid rock, now honeycombed with long tunnels. The tunnels lead into the colony. They all live and work there. The whole area is protected with a force field that makes aircraft malfunction. We found that out to our cost. We stopped trying years ago. That whole area is like the famous Area of Inaccessability—and our pilots avoid it."

"I'm going there," Stanford said.

"You're going nowhere," Fuller said. "I once liked you, but you can't walk away with this. Understand? You're a dead man."

Stanford suddenly heard the noise. He glanced out automatically, saw the light flashing on and off the trees, beaming down through the darkness. Then Fuller made his move. Stanford turned back and saw him. Fuller had opened the door and was falling back, one hand inside his jacket. The pistol bucked in Stanford's hand. The roar filled the whole car. Fuller bawled as his body hit the ground, but then he rolled over quickly. Stanford dropped across the seats, heard the roaring helicopter, saw Fuller rolling away from the car, a pistol clenched in his right fist. Stanford fired and Fuller jerked, dropped his pistol and flopped over. Stanford sat up and turned the ignition key as the roaring grew louder.

He didn't bother to close the far door. A cloud of dust and stones swept over him. The chopper roared and dropped down through the trees and bathed the car in a fierce light. Stanford cursed and put his foot down, reversed, the wheels squealing, shot forward and made a tight turn as Fuller staggered toward him, swaying weakly from side to side. Stanford couldn't avoid him. He heard a sickening thud. Fuller bounced across the hood of the car, limbs akimbo, his eyes large and his mouth hanging open, waved crazily, rolled off again. Stanford put his foot right down. He raced straight at the trees. He swung the car wildly from left to right and stayed away from the road.

First the darkness, then the light: the helicopter was right above him; it came down through the trees, whipped the dirt up, whipping and roaring. Stanford cursed and swung the wheel. He hit a tree and bounced off. The car shrieked and then shot forward again, crashing through vegetation. The chopper roared and deafened Stanford. It was just above the trees. It was whipping the dirt up on his right and forcing him back to the open road. Stanford cursed and kept going, weaving left and right furiously, tearing branches and bark from the trees, the car howling dementedly. He kept away from the road. The forest suddenly opened out. The roaring chopper dropped down through the clearing and smashed the car with its skids. The impact blinded Stanford, made him let go of the wheel. The car shot to the left and started skidding and he grabbed at the wheel again. He drove into the skid, shrieked around in a circle, was blinded by the chopper's spotlights, almost choked in the dust. The car raced toward the chopper. The chopper jerked up and shuddered. A rotor snapped against a tree and flew away as the chopper tipped over. The car raced right beneath it, shot back into the trees, was shaken by a thunderous explosion, bathed in fierce, jagged lightning. Stanford managed to glance back. A ball of fire filled the clearing. The fire swept across the field and up the trees, the flames hissing and spitting.

Stanford pulled hard on the wheel, headed straight for the road. He bounced back onto the road, took the right fork to Washington, glanced across the road and saw the

blazing trees illuminating the forest. The flames quickly
dropped behind him. He slowed down and drove more
carefully. He saw the dark night all around him, the
moon, the glittering stars, and he knew that he would have
to leave the country and never return.

CHAPTER THIRTY-FOUR

Awakening, in that biting cold dawn of January 28, 1979, still not believing where he was, Stanford shivered and closed his eyes again and thought of how he had come here . . . He saw the harbor of Manzanillo on the western coast of Mexico, the 125-foot ship, its wooden hull creaking rhythmically, moving out in the gray, early December afternoon, its engines and generators and air-conditioners filling his ears with a muffled roar. Then due south to Easter Island, the gray waves rolling slowly, the frigate birds sailing by on their fluttering black wings, the swarm of Galapagos storm petrels like a dark cloud of locusts. Blue-gray flying fish, the sea's monotonous rise and fall, the sun rising as orange fire, turning into a dazzling white, the pink sunset, then sharp, abrupt darkness, the stars glittering in velvet sky. The slow death of December. The dawn an eerie green glowing. The sun forming an arc, arched across the horizon, first green and then turning to red and setting the clouds on fire. The clouds shifted and changed, tinged with pink and orange-yellow, touched here and there with glinting gold, the sea violet, languorous. America was no more. Other worlds were now beckoning. The South Pacific, Cape Horn, the seas rough and uninviting, flocks of whalebirds with blue and white plumage, then the Tropic of Capricorn. White-breasted, dark-backed shearwaters, gliding through the troughs of waves, the southern latitudes with their long ocean swells, the smaller waves in between. The great wings of the albatross, their graceful soaring and gliding, then past the southern coast of South America, rain and fog, the winds moaning. Buoyant Magellanic penguins. More birds, high and low. The barren, forbidding rocks of the Ildefonso islands, the Beagle Channel, its dark, humpbacked islands, brown and bleak and forlorn. Then the New Year coming in, the sea foam-flecked and grim, giant petrels and skuas overhead, the cold winds unrelenting. Farewell to the Old World. No escape from the future. The primeval forests and glacier-encased peaks of Tierra del Fuego. Then the stormy Drake Passage, the current driven by the westerlies, waves fifty to a hundred feet high, the green water smashing over the bow and sweeping back out again. The New Year, a new person: Stanford losing himself. Over the Antarctic Convergence, past Elephant Island, the great blocks of rock and ice, flashing ribbons of snow, a shroud made of dark, drifting cloud, a sudden upthrusting glacier. Time passing and stopping. Stanford's gloved hands on the railing. Then the ice-encased mountains, seals and whales and pelagic birds, the air dazzlingly clear, the cascading ice blue, the mountain ridges of Gibbs Island, the penguins circling the ship, the crevassed ice cliffs sliding past as if not really there. Stanford's gloved hands in the air. A bird fluttering on the deck. More islands, more snowbanks, the penguins crowding on the rocks, Greenwich Island, green waves exploding fiercely, the spray drifting and settling. Then a white line in the distance. The approaching Antarctic Peninsula. Then the glaciers and icebergs, huge umbrellas and arches, flat white islands of sea ice, the grottoes and canyons and fjords reflecting sun on the green sea. A world like no other. Silent. Majestic. Sweeping plains of packed snow, soaring peaks of bright ice, the peaks yellow and pink and sometimes black, a blue sheen over all . . . Stanford opened his eyes again. He looked around him and shivered. He was now at the bottom of the world and could still not believe it.

He sat up on the bunk, yawned and blinked, glanced around him, saw that the other bunks were already empty, the Norwegians out at their work. He sat there for some time, staring through the window opposite, seeing nothing but the wall of the dome that surrounded the base. Stanford couldn't believe it. He had finally arrived. He swung his legs off the bunk and stood up and dressed himself very quickly.

The Nissen hut was long and bleak, a converted Army barracks, the blankets rumpled on the bunks, clothes and boots scattered all over the place, the walls covered in pin-ups. Stanford zipped up his jacket, shivered again and grabbed his gloves, then he walked along the hut, between the bunks, and went into the washroom. He splashed water on his face, combed his hair, put his hat on, made sure that his ears were well covered, and then looked in the mirror. A stranger stared back at him, a long-haired, bearded man, his eyes very hard and intense and possibly mad. Stanford wondered about that. The thought didn't bother him much. Then he turned and walked out of the hut and looked around the Norwegian base.

The whole camp was in an enormous, glittering geodesic dome that shielded it from the wind and drifting snow. Beneath the dome there were mess halls, administration huts and living quarters, power plants and machine shops and garages. All the buildings were painted red, were square and rectangular, took the form of cylindrical Quonset huts, were made of corrugated steel. The generators were whining, the power plants humming quietly, as Stanford walked past the research laboratories for meteorology and atmospheric physics, past the library and medical center and radio masts, and stopped in front of the mess hall. He looked directly above him, studied the immense, glittering dome, then shrugged and went into the mess hall for a strong cup of coffee.

It was a self-service canteen, the food stacked behind glass, plastic trays piled up beside the steel urns and the white plates and saucers. Stanford poured himself a coffee, studied the food and decided against it, turned away from the steel-framed glass cabinets and looked around the mess hall. Most of the tables were empty, the men already out at work. He saw the pilot at a table near the wall, a large mug at his lips.

Stanford went to join the pilot, wending his way between the tables, a pulse beating nervously in his stomach, feeling bright and unreal. The pilot looked up and grinned, wiped some coffee from his beard, his hair, just like Stanford's, very long, a wild gleam in his eyes.

"Hi, ho," he said. "How's my buddy? He don't look too good."

Stanford shrugged and pulled a chair out, sat down facing the pilot, noticed that his pupils were enlarged and did not feel encouraged.

"I'm fine, Rocky," he said. "Just wind me up and I'll go. One coffee—just one cup of coffee—and the day has begun."

Rocky grinned and scratched his beard, inhaled luxuriously on his cigarette, blew the smoke out and filled the chilly air with the sweet smell of pot.

"Oh, my," he said. "Beautiful."

"You're stoned," Stanford said.

"Fucking right, I'm stoned," Rocky said. "A man needs a good breakfast."

Stanford shrugged and sipped his coffee, let it burn down inside him, neither angry nor pleased about the pilot, knowing what he was like. Rocky was a free lance, working on commission for the Norwegians, a kid with scrambled brains and a history of Vietnam and the ability to fly just about anything under any conditions. The Norwegians called him the Mad Bomber. He lived up to his reputation. He would do things that no one else would do, and that's how Stanford got him. The other pilots avoided Neuschwabenland. It was forbidden to fly there. Stanford had learned that fact pretty quickly, and had thought he was sunk. Then he heard about Rocky. He started to get stoned with Rocky. He told Rocky where he wanted to go, and Rocky giggled with pleasure. Rocky liked the forbidden. He was just out for kicks. They had scrambled his brains in Vietnam and now he lived like a wild man. Still, he could fly. He had his own plane and crew. It was an old transport plane with skis attached, and Rocky knew how to handle it. He had loved the idea of the trip, had wanted to see them goddamned UFOs. He had, like everyone else in the Antarctic, seen them flying around. Now he could see them up close. He couldn't wait to get in there.

Rocky wanted to go down in a blaze of glory, stoned out of his skull.

"What's it like outside?" Stanford said.

"Minus fifteen degrees Fahrenheit. I hope you've got your balls wrapped in velvet—you might lose them out there."

Rocky grinned and scratched his nose, inhaled some more marijuana, the pupils of his eyes very large, shielding sweet, secret dreams.

"Can you fly?" Stanford said.

"Zip your lip," Rocky said. "I could fly that fucking airplane through a pinhole with a girl on my cock."

"You must have tried it," Stanford said.

"That's my secret," Rocky said. "Finish your coffee and let's get on the road. I don't want them to check us."

"What did you tell them?" Stanford said.

"That we were flying to Cape Norvegia. I said we were picking up some supplies, and the dumb cunts believed me." Rocky giggled at the thought of it, finished his smoke and stood up, looking large in his boots and padded clothes, a pair of gloves in his right hand. "Okay," he said, "let's get the fuck out of here and have us a good time."

Stanford gulped down his coffee, grabbed his gloves and stood up, then he and Rocky walked out of the mess hall and headed straight for the airstrip. Stanford glanced around him constantly, still not used to being here, the geodesic dome soaring above him, sunlight pouring down through it. They passed the power plants and garages, saw a line of snow tractors, cut around a cylindrical Quonset hut, approached a door in the curved wall. They both put their gloves on. Stanford followed Rocky out. His boots sank into snow, a glaring brightness stung his eyes, then the cold clamped around him like a vise and rushed into his lungs.

Ice. All ice. Hills and valleys made of ice. The sun was shining and it flashed off the ice and the light almost blinded him. It was incredibly beautiful. It nearly took his breath away. There was nothing out there but the ice and the bright, flashing light. The ice went out to the horizon. The sky was very blue. He looked up at the sky and saw a green field surrounded by more ice. The sky acted as a mirror. It reflected the land below. The green field was an ice-free mass of land twenty miles to the west. Stanford looked all around him. The view never failed to stun him. The ice was everywhere—at his feet, up in the sky—and he stared at it and thought it was beautiful and mysteriously frightening.

They both walked across the snow, both bulky in their heavy clothes, putting their gloves on and breathing clouds of steam, a light frost on their beards. The airstrip was fairly close, nestling under a towering ice cliff, the lowest peak two hundred feet above the planes, the sky a white haze above.

"Fucking crazy," Rocky said. "I can't believe we're really doing it. I mean, you say we're going to see some flying saucers, and that's it; we're off. We must both be fucking mad. You must be as mad as me. What the fuck are you going to do if you see them? Just answer that question."

"I'm going in there," Stanford said.

"From what I've heard, that would be nuts."

"You can land about ten miles from the mountain and I'll take the snow tractor."

"It's really true then?" Rocky said.

"It's really true," Stanford said. "All the UFOs you've seen were real, all the rumors you heard were true: there's a colony buried deep in those mountains, and they've got flying saucers."

Rocky shook his head with wonder. "Oh, boy," he said, "that's great. That's absolutely fanfuckingtastic and it's blowing my mind." Rocky giggled with pleasure, rolled his stoned, crazy eyes, the frost thickening on his bushy red beard, the sun flashing around him. "I just can't wait," he said. "What a wild, fucking gig. What a story to tell when I'm senile. I won't believe it myself."

They were on the edge of the airstrip, a wall of ice towering above them, a fine snow drifting lazily around their feet, their eyes watering with cold. A helicopter was taking off, its rotors whipping the snow up, its image reflected in the wall of ice as it climbed past the cliff. They walked across to Rocky's airplane, an old and battered transport, its green fuselage decorated with pinups and colorful comments. The plane was sitting on long skis, the door open, the ladder down, and a couple of men were standing in the doorway, their fur collars turned up.

"All set?" Rocky said.

"Smooth as butter," one of the men said. "But we better take off pretty quick. I think they're getting suspicious."

"Norwegian shitheads," Rocky said.

"They're okay," the man said. "They've just had a few complaints from the Russians—those fuckers said you'd been buzzing them."

Rocky giggled and shook his head. "Lord have mercy," he said. "Them Ruskies weren't telling any lies; I buzzed Novolazarevskaya."

The man in the aircraft grinned. "That's what you did," he said. "The Russians said you were lower than their radar, almost pissing on top of them."

Rocky giggled again. "What the fuck?" he said happily. "A man needs a little action now and then to keep boredom at bay."

"You were stoned," the other man said.

"Happy days, I was stoned."

"Some day they're gonna boot you in the ass and send you back to Alaska."

"Some day," Rocky said.

He climbed up into the airplane, followed closely by Stanford, and they made their way along to the cockpit, past the heavy snow tractor. Stanford heard the ladder rattling, the door shrieking and then slamming, the sound echoing around the aircraft and making his ears ring.

"Here we go," Rocky said. "You can sit in the copilot's seat. The guys there, they'll sit in the back and look after the tractor."

Stanford nodded and sat down, strapping himself into the seat, his eyes taking in the control panel, the mass of switches and indicators in front of him, above him, to his right, the engineer's chair behind him. Rocky sighed and pursed his lips, flicked a couple of switches, and Stanford looked out through the glass and plastic windshield at the strange world before him. All white. Everything. The sun flashed off the ice. The airplane suddenly bellowed and shuddered and roared into life.

"There's no traffic control," Rocky said. "That's the

blessing of this burg. They just tell you what time you can leave, and then you get up and go. Hold on to your cock, kid."

The plane moved forward slowly, the strip running between banks of snow, a broad line narrowing down to a pinpoint at the base of a towering cliff. The cliff was made of ice, the sun flashing off its face, the peaks sharply defined against the sky that changed from white haze to blue. The plane shuddered and roared, picked up speed, started racing, passing trucks and sun-reflecting radar bowls that were framed by the glistening snow. Then the strip was racing around them, the white cliff spreading out, growing taller as the plane rushed straight at it as if about to go through it. Stanford took hold of his seat, took a deep breath, nearly panicked, then Rocky giggled and the plane jumped off the runway, going into a steep climb. Stanford kept hold of his seat. The plane was shuddering and rattling. He saw the wall of the cliff, the blinding eye of the sun, then the glistening white peaks passed below and the plane leveled out.

"Jesus," Stanford hissed.

"Hi, ho," Rocky said. "Nothing like a little bit of action to get rid of the cobwebs."

The panorama was immense, a sweeping vista of packed ice, snow falls and glinting glaciers, low mountain peaks framed against a sky of unbelievable clarity. Nothing moved in that landscape, nothing broke its frozen silence; the fierce light of the sun poured down on it and was then devoured by it. Earth and sky became one—the sky reflected the ice below—and the rays of the sun were distorted and formed luminous arches. All white. Everything. The towering glaciers were like prisms. The light flashed and swept out in white lines that merged with dazzling white snowfalls.

"Queen Maud Land," Rocky said. "We're flying along the zero meridian. We should reach Neuschwabenland in forty minutes if we don't get lost first."

"What happens if we keep going?"

"We cross the fucking South Pole. Then north becomes south, fucking east becomes west, and we have us a smoke and say our prayers until we run out of gasoline."

"Don't get lost," Stanford said.

"I'll do my best," Rocky said. "We'll circle over the mountains, we'll try to find that hidden base, then we'll turn back and land five miles away and go in with the tractor."

"You're coming with me?" Stanford said.

"Fucking right," Rocky said. "I'm not giving you this goddamned trip for free—I want to see all them saucers."

"It might be difficult," Stanford said. "There's supposed to be a force field around the area. It's designed to make engines malfunction and bring down the aircraft."

"It might be true," Rocky said. "A lot of planes were lost out there. That's why we're not allowed there anymore—and why I lied to those bastards."

"So what do we do?" Stanford said.

"We just stay at high altitude. That means we won't see very much, but it's better than nothing. We'll land near the mountains anyway. We'll go in on the snow tractor. We just have to see that circle of ice caps to know where we're going."

Stanford looked down below, saw the dazzling white landscape, the peaks of glaciers merging with the snow, revealed only by flashing light. He felt tense and excited, a pulse beating in his stomach, closed his eyes and thought of where he had come from and still couldn't believe it. He had left the past behind him. He could never return. He had found out too much, was a threat, and would have to be wiped out. Stanford opened his eyes again. A sweeping white plain filled his vision. Looking at it, he realized that he had come to the end of the road. There was nowhere else to run to. There was nowhere to hide. If he managed to return from the Antarctic, he would find no safe place. Finally, he was trapped. He was one of the hunted. He was at the lowest point on the Earth and could travel no farther. So what about Epstein? What would he do if he found his old friend? The contracts would be out on them both and the hunters would find them. Stanford sighed and looked below. He saw a boundless white terrain. It was a wilderness of drifting snow and ice, and might yet be his resting place. Stanford didn't really care.

It didn't matter anymore. He saw the white world sweeping out to meet the sky, and suddenly felt a great peace.

"Holy fuck," Rocky said.

Stanford followed his pointing finger, saw the radiant blue sky, great circles of white light spreading out and forming luminous patterns. He was used to that by now, knew the tricks of the Antarctic, leaned forward and looked even harder at what Rocky was pointing at. Something flashed and disappeared. The rings of light framed the blue sky. He kept looking and he saw the flash again about nine o'clock high. It came and went in an instant. Before he blinked, it came again. This time it was much further down, a brief flash and then nothing.

"Over there," Rocky said. "It's changed position . . . Jesus Christ, *now there's two of them!*"

Stanford followed his pointing finger. He saw two pulsating lights. They were west of the plane, flying level with it, pacing it, two dime-sized pulsating white lights in the light-streaked blue sky. Stanford shook his head and stared. The two lights were now three. The third light had just suddenly winked on as if it had always been there. Rocky whooped with excitement. The lights were flying in formation. They formed the three points of a triangle and kept abreast of the plane.

"It might be nothing," Stanford said. "It might be atmospheric phenomena."

"No way," Rocky said. "Those lights are *moving.* Those motherfuckers are pacing us . . . There they go . . . *Jesus Christ!*"

The three lights broke apart, moving slowly, serenely, one climbing and one dropping down until they formed a long line. It was a precise, vertical line, pacing the plane, pulsating brightly, the three lights about a hundred feet apart, one on top of the other. Rocky whooped with excitement. Stanford just stared, entranced. The lights pulsated against the vivid blue sky and outshone the fierce sunlight.

Then they suddenly exploded—not exploded: disappeared—were suddenly over and under the plane as two large, silvery discs. The plane vibrated violently. It was sandwiched between the saucers. The saucers glittered

above and below the plane and were a hundred feet wide.
Then the plane just cut out. Rocky wrestled with the controls. Glancing down, Stanford saw a curving stretch of
metallic gray; looking up he saw the base of the other saucer, a black hole right above him. It was a stark, total
blackness, denying definition, so deep that it was more like
a hole than anything solid. Stanford blinked and it was
gone. The silent plane plummeted downward. Stanford
saw the brilliant snow, the glinting peaks of the glaciers,
two lights streaking down to join a third, the whole sky
disappearing. The plane dived and Rocky cursed, fighting
vainly with the controls, then the engine suddenly roared
back into life and the plane leveled out. Stanford saw the
sky again, swinging down and then steadying, saw the
lights streaking toward a line of mountains and then winking out.

"Holy shit," Rocky said.

"What the hell's happening here?" One of the men had
come up from the rear, wiping blood from his nose. "We
nearly lost the snow tractor. I nearly got my head
smashed. What the fuck are you doing, diving like that?
That fucking place was bananas."

"We had an accident," Rocky said.

"What the hell does *that* mean? This fucking plane went
as dead as a doornail and damned nearly killed us."

"It's okay," Rocky said. "I made a little mistake. Stop
worrying. It won't happen again. Don't get your balls in a
knot."

"You're fucking crazy," the man said.

"That's right, I'm fucking crazy. Now get your ass back
in that plane and keep your eyes on the tractor."

The man vanished back inside. Stanford stared straight
ahead. Rocky pulled the plane up, climbing gradually,
gaining altitude, glanced at Stanford, his eyes large and
wild, beads of sweat on his forehead. Stanford stared
down at the mountains, saw the snow-swept brown peaks,
stark shadows breaking up the white cliffs where great
canyons divided them.

"That's it," Rocky said. "And that's where the fuckers
went. You were right, holy shit, you were right: they're
hiding somewhere down there."

"You better climb," Stanford said.

"Just what I'm doing," Rocky said. "Though I don't know that it'll do any good if those bastards come back again. Did you see how fast they moved? And they definitely killed the engine. The plane was dead, but it just kept on going as if by pure magic. I still can't believe it. I just don't believe it's possible. But those fuckers killed the engine, they carried us along somehow, then they just moved away and let us drop—and I don't understand that."

Rocky shook his head in wonder, pulled the plane up, kept climbing, leveled out when he felt that it was safe, muttering under his breath. They were approaching the mountains, flying high above the peaks, saw the sunlight flashing on and off the ice and forming faint, shifting rainbows. There was more color there: the peaks were tinged with pink and green, the light beating off the ice and making arches of yellow and gold. The mountain peaks were free of snow, thrusting up to the sky, the sky a white haze that faded into violet and then became brilliant blue. Stanford felt overwhelmed, his eyes glued to the terrain, seeing the shadows of canyons and ravines as black scars on the glaring white.

"Fuck," Rocky said. "We're too high. We won't see a damned thing."

They were above the mountains now, turning west and flying along them, gazing down on a ribbon of black shadow and flashing light, an indication of ravines and ice peaks, a ribboned scar through pure white. Then the plane started coughing, started spluttering and vibrating, dipped down and then picked up again, the engine dangerously malfunctioning. Rocky cursed and glanced at Stanford. They both looked down at the mountains. They saw the ribbon of shadow and light splitting in two, the two ribbons curving out and then returning to form a shadowy circle.

"*That's it!*" Rocky screamed.

"Yes," Stanford said, "that's it. And we're just on the edge of the force field. You better go higher."

"*Jesus Christ, can you see it?*"

"Yes, Rocky, I can see it. Now let's get the hell out of here and land somewhere safe."

Rocky shook his head in wonder, started changing direction, circling around and heading back where they had come from, muttering under his breath. Stanford sighed and looked down, saw the circle passing below them, saw the boundless white terrain all around it, a blank, frozen wilderness. Then he blinked and looked again, saw two lights fanning out, streaking up in opposite directions from the glaciers, fanning out at incredible speed and then just disappearing. Stanford looked down on the mountain, shook his head and then looked up, saw a light shooting away to the west, blinking out, leaving nothing.

Stanford couldn't believe it, turned his head and looked east, saw a light rising vertically, then stopping, then racing toward him. He shouted something at Rocky. He didn't know what it was. The light ballooned into a massive, flaring disc that shot past them and disappeared. The plane shrieked and rocked violently, was bathed in radiant light, the light racing away and shrinking in the west and then shooting up vertically. The plane steadied down again. Rocky glanced around him wildly. The man came out of the rear and said, "Hey, what the fuck?" and then the light from the west raced back again and shot past and was gone. "Jesus Christ!" Rocky said. A light shot out of the east and then exploded and shot by them and disappeared. The man behind them was thrown sideways. The lights exploded over the plane and passed each other and disappeared on both sides of them. The man behind them was cursing. Equipment shot off the walls and flew around and formed a shocking cacophony. Rocky fought with the controls. Stanford looked east and west. The lights were pinpoints in the distance, racing in at incredible speed, suddenly ballooning above the plane as massive discs of flaring light, rocking the plane, then racing away in opposite directions, becoming pinpoints again.

"Holy shit! We can't beat them!"

Rocky fought with the controls, tried to keep the plane steady, was defeated every time the discs shot past and stopped as pinpoints some miles away. The plane shrieked and rocked wildly, the holding bay now in chaos, the man behind them screaming incoherently as he rolled on the floor. Stanford looked east and west, saw the pinpoints of light, blinked and saw the huge, flaring discs exploding overhead, shrinking. The plane rocked even more. It was coughing and spluttering. The discs raced back and forth, from east to west, and kept passing each other.

Stanford watched them, amazed. He hardly thought of the bucking plane. He was fascinated by the speed and capability of the two flying saucers. They raced in and rushed away. Stanford tried to see them properly. He put his head back and looked straight above him, but it didn't help much. The flying saucers were too fast. They passed faster than he blinked. He saw nothing but a flaring mass that divided and disappeared. Then he looked east and west. He saw the pinpoints of light. They climbed vertically, then dropped down again and then flared out above him. The plane rocked when they passed, the engine spluttered on and off, and the two men in the holding bay were screaming as equipment fell over them.

"We're going down!" Rocky bawled.

The horizon shot above the cockpit, the white plains spreading out, sunlight flashing on and off the iced peaks around the edge of the mountains. Rocky tried to pull the plane up, fought the control column, cursed as the plane spiraled downward, heading straight for the mountains. The fierce light flared out above them, seemed to race through the cockpit, disappeared as the plane shrieked and shook and went out of control. The discs appeared out of nowhere. This time they passed over and under before shooting away. Stanford couldn't believe it. They had sandwiched the falling plane, had passed so close he thought they must crush it, were now pinpoints again. The plane roared and kept plummeting. The shadowed mountains spun below them. He heard Rocky screaming a stream of abuse as the mountains rushed at them.

First the sky, then the white plains, then the spinning black shadows, then the flashing of glaciers and ice caps and the dark, jagged canyons. The plane kept diving down, its engine roaring, then dying, the mountains spreading out and then spinning and becoming a jigsaw.

Rocky screamed his abuse. The men were bawling in the rear. Stanford looked down, mesmerized, seeing light-reflecting ice, the great snowfalls leading down to dark canyons of brown earth and ocher rock. It spread out and spun around. Walls of ice shot up around them. Dazzling light flared up and swept through the cockpit and then became darkness.

The plane lurched and leveled out, raced along an ice-free canyon. A glowing disc, about a hundred feet wide, was keeping pace just below it. Stanford stared down, blinked his eyes and looked up. There was another enormous disc above the plane, a black silver-edged, whirlpool. The plane didn't make a sound. The saucers made a whipping noise. They were so close to the plane, they almost touched it, and they swept it on forward.

Then the black hole was gone. The sky exploded above them. The plane roared and climbed steeply toward the snow and then was out on its own again. It left the canyon far below. There was no sign of the saucers. The plane leveled out and raced across a gleaming ice cap that surmounted a mountain ridge. Rocky whooped and grinned wildly and grabbed the control column. Stanford looked down and saw a round shadow racing over the ice cap. "Shit, no!" Rocky howled. Stanford jerked his head back. He looked up and saw a dime-sized, glowing disc, growing bigger, descending.

"Not again!" Rocky bawled.

First the sky, then the saucer, a black whirlpool above them, stretching out fifty feet on either side, a swirling silver-edged glowing mass. The plane's engine cut out. The swirling mass pressed them down. Rocky fought with the control column and then screamed more abuse. Stanford looked up at the saucer. He couldn't define what he was seeing. He was looking at a swirling dark mass that pulsated and glowed. It defied the laws of science. It was black and filled with light. It glowed and was devoid of all color, had no depth and seemed hollow. Stanford looked up and was foiled. He didn't know what he was seeing. Then it flared up and changed, became a dull, metallic gray, possibly spinning, its rim glowing and pulsating, racing in, shooting skyward. Stanford blinked and it was gone. He looked down when Rocky screamed. The plane was just above the ice cap, racing across the glassy surface, the ice rushing up and spreading out around them and becoming a white blur.

"Hold on!" Rocky screamed.

The skis touched down and screeched, chopped the ice and sent it flying, a white storm that howled and raged all around them and pummeled the fuselage. The plane bounced up and down, the skis chopping and screeching, blocks of ice and great chunks of packed snow sweeping past in fierce white clouds. The noise was hellish, almost deafening, reverberating around the cockpit as the skis chopped through the ice and dug deep and finally buried themselves. Stanford saw the spinning sky, his head exploding, stars streaming, heard screeching and hissing and bawling, felt breathless and bruised. He opened his eyes and saw Rocky, swirling snow beyond the windshield, Rocky jackknifed, slumped forward, hanging over his safety belt, jerking upright and shaking his head, the snow settling down again.

"Jesus Christ. We've just landed."

Rocky grinned and stared at Stanford, a wild light in his eyes, shook his head again, unsnapped his safety belt, slithered out of his seat. Stanford quickly did the same, felt the pains shooting through him, twisted out of his seat and followed Rocky back into the holding bay. He saw the eyes of the other men, four large eyes, glazed with shock, floating hopelessly in the gloom of the holding bay, a scene of chaos behind them. Rocky waved his hands and bawled, pushed the men, took command, not giving them time to think about it, moving quickly and ruthlessly.

"Okay!" he bawled. "Get that fucking ramp down! Let's get the hell out of here!"

The ramp crashed down to the snow, a dazzling brightness pouring in, the two men silhouetted in glaring white, the plane filled with an icy chill. Stanford stepped forward slowly, his bones aching, head spinning, saw Rocky's hands waving in the air, felt the cold creeping into him.

"Right!" Rocky bawled. "Fucking great! You're doing

fine! Now let's get the snow tractor out! Okay! Move your asses!"

The silhouettes became men, moving back toward the tractor, light flashing in striations all around them as they unsnapped the clamps. There was a sharp, metallic sound, the clamps banging on the floor, as Stanford passed the men and went to the ramp and looked up at the sky. A white sheen filled with blue, stunning clarity, no clouds; he looked and saw a gray sphere in the sky, very high, hovering silently. Rocky bawled, his voice echoing, blending in with screeching steel, then the snow tractor, gray and unwieldy, slid down the sloped ramp. Stanford shivered, felt the cold, saw the men filing past him, stopped Rocky and pointed at the sky, saw his bearded friend nodding. They both walked down the ramp, then climbed up into the tractor. Stanford studied the other men, their large eyes, the glaze of fear, then the tractor suddenly roared and lurched forward and headed east, going nowhere.

There was nowhere to go. They were on a high plateau. The ice cap was a flat white terrain that stretched around them for miles. The tractor whipped the snow up. It swirled around them and froze them. Stanford saw a white ribbon of land between the sky and the ice cap. That land was thousands of feet below them. There might be no way down. Stanford thought about that and felt nothing but a cold, blinding rage.

"Jesus Christ!" Rocky hissed.

First the light, then the gloom, the snow blowing around them, a humming, a vibrating, a savage jolting sensation, a black hole one hundred feet in diameter hovering quietly above them. Someone cursed, someone screamed, the tractor slid to the left, Rocky hissing a stream of abuse. The saucer stayed there, kept humming, its base a black hole, letting the tractor move, quietly forcing it forward. Stanford felt a fierce pressure, grabbed a handle, looked behind him, saw the gray metallic surface of the saucer sweeping up to a glass dome. Maybe glass, maybe not; it didn't really make much difference: the saucer was huge and awe-inspiring, looming over the tractor.

"Fucking cunts! They'll just bury us!"

Rocky bawled his defiance, pushed the tractor to its limits, racing over the ice cap, fighting through the snow, heading into a featureless white haze that offered them nothing. Stanford looked up at the saucer, saw the rotating black base, its surface sweeping up to the dome and reflecting the sunlight. The saucer appeared to be motionless, always stayed the same distance, was not motionless, was inching forward slowly, whipping the snow up. Rocky cursed and tried to lose it, swung the tractor left and right, the snow whirling and hissing and devouring them and forming a curtain.

The tractor raced across the ice cap, not knowing where it was going, pushed forward by the fiercely swirling snow that the saucer whipped up. It raced right through eternity, time frozen, all frozen: the men and the tractor and the landscape and the saucer above them. Rocky cursed, Stanford stared, saw the other two men, one cracking and screaming and shaking and waving his hands. He tried to leap off the tractor, was pulled back by his friend, both falling down and rolling on the floor. Stanford shivered and glanced up, numbed by cold, filled with rage, saw the black base of the saucer as it came down upon them.

Then the laser beams shot down, burning through the snow, two beams of pulsating yellow light that split the ice right in front of them. The ice cracked in jagged lines, spewing steam and spinning diamonds, hissing and snapping and exploding with an earthquake's fierce venom. Rocky cursed and whirled around, was flung forward, hands outstretched, as the tractor crashed down into a crevice and the laser beams vanished. Rocky spinning, Stanford saw it, his own body jackknifing, rolling over and exploding with pain, his feet finding the floor again. The tractor roared and whipped the snow up, tilted downward, going nowhere, a much stronger, more devastating storm howling wildly around them. Stanford stood up, felt lost, heard a wretched, shocked sobbing, saw the dark mass of the saucer just above, now obscured by the swirling snow. The sobbing turned into a scream, a pair of hands waving wildly, the man pushing his friend to the floor and clambering over the side. Stanford saw him, did nothing, thought of nothing, felt dreamlike, was pushed forward by a pair of strong hands and urged over the side. He dropped down into the snow, was whipped by it, numbed totally, saw the dark mass in the sky, the three shadowy forms just ahead, stumbling blindly and bawling.

First the wind, then the snow, then the dark mass, then the whiteout, then the running, crouched low, seeing nothing, then the beam of bright light. The beam swept across their path, and they ran, leaping forward, heard a scream and turned around and saw a man sinking down, disappearing. The ice snapped and the chasm widened, falling down a thousand feet, and they turned away and plunged into the storm, the dark saucer above them. Stanford heard a shocking scream, couldn't tell one man from the other, saw a rigid beam of light shining down upon a dancing black shadow. The man quivered and spun around, his face briefly illuminated. Then he jerked and fell back, his eyes bright in the light, and the snarling ice split and opened wide and then swallowed him whole.

Stanford turned back and ran, turned right and saw the other unknown man as a shadowy form. They ran together, as one, moving blindly, not thinking, pushed forward by the dark mass above them, each in love with the other. Then the beams of light shot down, the lasers cutting the ice, the ice snapping and hissing and streaming and exploding around them. They both stopped, feeling trapped, both alone with a shadow, then they moved, running around the beams of light, the snow shredding their skin. Too late: they saw the end. A beam of light shot between them. Stanford jumped back and stumbled and fell and heard the other man screaming. Then darkness, the snapping sound of ice splitting, the dying echo of the man plunging down a thousand feet to his death. Then the silence. And nothing.

Stanford lay there on his back, the snow settling down, his flesh numb, his bones aching, head spinning, the brilliant daylight returning. He watched the saucer descending, no longer glowing, enormous and very real in the sunlight, descending gently and quietly. Stanford sat up, fell back, pressed his hands into the snow, gasped loudly and turned around onto his belly, saw the radiant blue sky. He was near the edge of the ice cap, two thousand feet above the lowlands, his eyes drinking in a stunning panorama of white, frozen wilderness. It was too much, too blinding, too remote to be real, and he sighed and rolled over on his back and then forced himself upright. The saucer swept out before him, an enormous steel dome, resting lightly on the snow of the ice cap, the sun flashing around it.

Stanford studied the saucer. He felt cold and very calm. He sat there on the ice, in the snow and the silence, a white wilderness two thousand feet below, a radiant blue sky above. Stanford sat there and waited.

CHAPTER THIRTY-FIVE

Stanford waited a long time, his eyes fixed on the gleaming saucer, the snow drifting lazily around him, the silence unbroken. The saucer seemed enormous, its sloping walls a seamless gray, sweeping up to a dome of what looked like opaque yellow glass. The dome was thirty-five feet high, the saucer three times that in length, sunlight beating down and flashing off the gray steel and turning it white. All white. Everything. The land and sky looked the same. There was no definition, no sense of direction; just a glaring, white void all around him, a stark, total silence.

The saucer didn't move, made no sound, offered nothing, was simply spread out across the ice cap as if actually part of it. Stanford sat there and studied it, feeling cold and very calm, occasionally glancing at the white haze all around him, a light frost slowly covering him. The saucer didn't move. It made no sound at all. After a long time, feeling the cold eating at him, Stanford climbed to his feet.

His bones were bruised and aching, his flesh numb, his head light, and he stood there for a moment, uncertain, the snow drifting around him. Then he walked toward the saucer, feeling smaller, more unreal, stopped a few feet away from its near edge and saw it towering above him. He stared at it with wonder. The steel swept up to the dome, very smooth, totally seamless, curving down and then under at its edge, becoming part of the base. There were no doors or windows, no visible lights. He looked up at the opaque yellow dome, but it was vague in the white haze. Stanford stood there, bemused. The saucer filled his line of vision. He stepped forward, stopped close to the curved edge, then reached out and touched it.

The metal felt like sandpaper. Stanford ran his fingers across it. He felt air, or he thought he felt air, and then he stepped closer to it. The metal was porous, the holes smaller than grains of sand, scraping imperceptibly against his fingers and releasing trapped air. Stanford smiled and looked closer, examining the curved edge, saw very fine, almost invisible lines crisscrossing each other. The lines formed various rectangles, some small and some large, swept up to the opaque yellow dome, were dissected by other lines. Stanford studied them carefully. There was a low-pitched, humming sound. Panels slid up around the curved edge to reveal hidden lights.

Stanford stood there, not moving. The lights were covered with convex glass, various colors, the glass thick and opaque and rippling slightly. None of the lights were on. The low-pitched humming sound grew louder. A series of panels slid up where the sloping surface was almost vertical, revealing a very long, rectangular window that curved around the whole saucer. The windows glowed with violet light, then this changed to whitish yellow. A group of shadowy forms were lined along the window, obviously staring at Stanford.

Stanford stood there, waiting patiently. There was a muffled, hissing sound. A large section of the curved wall moved forward, tilting back from its top edge. It slid out on large white hinges, tilting back, moving forward, the front edge finally touching the ground, the back edge in the saucer. The section of wall was now a ramp. It led up into the saucer. Stanford stared at the large, rectangular opening and saw a white wall beyond it. The men at the windows were looking at him. The windows were well above the door. Stanford smiled and then walked up the ramp and found himself in a corridor.

The inner wall was white and blank. There were windows on the other wall. These windows were behind the gray shell of the saucer's body. The corridor curved away

from him and obviously ran around the saucer. Stanford
then heard a sharp, hissing sound as the door closed behind him.

He stood there in the corridor. He waited, but no one
came. There was a muffled sound all around him, above
him, below him. Intrigued, he started walking. He felt no
fear at all. The humming sound was filling his head and it
made him relax. The corridor curved around the saucer,
the white walls and ceiling arched, then a door slid across
the space in front of him and forced him to stop.

There was a room to his left, the walls white, a perfect
circle, broken up by the rectangular windows at which the
men had been standing. A small hunchbacked man walked
forward, waved a beautiful white hand. Stanford stepped
into the circular room and stopped close to the hunchback.

"You're all right?" the hunchback said.

"I think so," Stanford said.

"I'm Rudiger," the hunchback said. "Please don't worry.
We will take you down now."

Stanford stared around the room. It was shaped like a
large dome. The walls were covered with control panels
and consoles and what looked like computers. There were
eight men in the room. They were mostly very small.
Some were young boys and some were Ache Indians, three
were fair-skinned and middle-aged. About half of them
wore masks, the masks made of thin metal, covering their
noses and mouths, molded close to the skin. Stanford
stared, fascinated. The boys and Indians were at the consoles, sitting down in chairs fixed to the floor, the control
panels flickering. The other men looked at Stanford, not
smiling, their eyes cold, then they turned away and sat in
other chairs, turning knobs, flicking switches. The computers started flashing. The muffled sound grew louder.
Stanford felt a light vibration, thought he felt it, wasn't
sure, then he looked down at the small man with the
hunchback, saw his luminous brown eyes.

"Come," the hunchback said. He was smiling and waving his hands. The hands had an extraordinary delicacy, a
feminine grace. "Come," he said. "I will show you."

He led Stanford across the floor, up some steps to a
raised platform, the floor running right around the dome,

above the computers and consoles. The long windows were
there. Stanford stood beside the hunchback. The ice cap
was shrinking beneath him, blending in with the mountains, the glittering snowfalls of the wilderness spreading
out until they touched the horizon. The saucer was ascending, climbing vertically, leisurely, then it stopped, or
seemed to stop—Stanford didn't feel a thing—then it
moved horizontally, as if backward, and then dropped
down again.

There was no sense of motion. The saucer dropped
down at the speed of an elevator, falling into the mountains. The mountain peaks climbed up around them, first
the rock, then blocks of snow, then the sheer, towering
walls of blue ice, turning green, disappearing.

They were moving faster now. The saucer was flying
horizontally. Walls of algae and plankton, green rocks
splashed with white, were sweeping past on both sides of
the saucer as it raced through a canyon. There was no
sense of motion. He thought he felt a light vibration. He
looked down and saw the rim of the saucer, metallic gray
in a glowing haze. Then he looked ahead again, saw the
canyon walls parting, opening out around a lake, the lake
whipping out of sight, more snow, more brown earth, a
dazzling green spreading outward, then an enormous,
round valley, the white cliffs soaring skyward, the ice
flashing and fading away above the earth and becoming
pure rock. The saucer swept across the valley, the green
earth rushing at them, then the rushing earth slowed down,
almost stopped, then rose gently to greet them.

Stanford didn't feel a thing. There was no sense of
movement. The saucer drifted, or appeared to drift, across
the broad valley, heading toward the towering cliffs that
surrounded it and cast monstrous shadows. The hunchback
raised a hand and pointed. Stanford stared straight ahead.
He saw the mouths of large natural caves at the base of
the ice-free cliffs.

"We go in there," the hunchback said.

Stanford glanced at the rim of the saucer, saw the pulsating glow dying, saw the panels around the rim opening
to expose all the lights. Then the lights started flashing, left
to right, right to left, a kaleidoscope of green and blue and

orange and violet, flashing right around the rim of the saucer as it moved forward slowly. The caves expanded as
they approached, became enormous dark tunnels, and the
saucer drifted into a tunnel, its colored lights flashing on
and off. Stanford saw natural rock, the glint of moisture
and moss, saw a pinpoint of light far ahead, growing bigger each second. First a pinpoint, then a dime, then a
glowing balloon, then an enormous round exit racing at
them and pouring light over them.

Stanford saw another valley, almost roofed in with
cliffs, the rocks forming an umbrella above, the sun flashing through crevices. The valley floor was far below, broken up by silvery domes, some minute, some looking quite
large, the ground around them a deep brown. The saucer
hovered and then descended, dropping slowly, almost leisurely; it appeared to bob up and down gently, yet Stanford felt nothing. He looked down on the silvery domes, at
first mistook them for geodesic domes, watched them rising up and growing larger and taking shape as more saucers. Stanford stared at them, bemused. The valley spread
out around him. The saucer dropped past a soaring wall of
glinting gray metal, and Stanford looked back up and saw
a flying saucer as big as a cathedral: one of the legendary
carrying ships.

The saucer touched down gently. The hunchback looked
up and smiled. Stanford gazed through the window, saw a
large square steel platform, the flashing lights around the
saucer's rim winking out one by one. The metal panels slid
back down. The rim looked smooth and seamless. The
steel platform was above the ground, thrusting out from
the cliff face, fronting a tunnel from which a group of
men emerged, bareheaded, wearing coveralls. They were
all very big, their lower faces in silvery masks, and they
pushed a mobile lounge against the saucer as the door
angled down. The door was swallowed by the mobile
lounge. The lounge was pushed against the saucer; its
angled edge had been perfectly contoured to the saucer's
sloped surface.

"We go out now," the hunchback said.

He led Stanford down the steps, across the dome-shaped
white room, past the adolescents in coveralls, the Ache cy-

borgs in the chairs, their mouths and noses sealed and rendered useless, their narrow eyes dulled and fathomless.
Stanford looked at them, accepted them, left the room
with the hunchback, followed him back along the curving
white corridor with its row of sealed windows.

They turned onto the ramp, the tunnel-shaped lounge
sweeping over them, the walls white, the floors white, the
windows framing nearby rock, passed through the lounge
and walked along a tunnel that had invisible lighting. The
tunnel was fairly long and had been hacked out of the
rock; it obviously ran into the bowels of the mountain,
and was surprisingly warm.

Stanford followed the hunchback, studied his strangely
lovely hands, was struck by their feminine delicacy, the
crude contrast of powerful arms. Then they both left the
tunnel, stepping into brilliant light, crossed a catwalk that
loomed above a workshop of massive dimensions. Stanford
saw jibs and cranes, the enormous roaring machines,
sheets of metal, dull gray and all shapes, being swung to
and fro. There were hundreds of workers down there, long
steel tables, steaming vats, blast furnaces and tall,
screeching drills, immense, saucer-shaped skeletons.

Stanford stopped to survey it, was pushed forward by a
cyborg, saw an oblong metal plate in his fist, let it touch
him, was shocked by it. It was a sharp, electric shock,
jolting fiercely through his shoulder, and he jumped away
and followed the hunchback, his arm stinging and burning.
They passed through another tunnel, crossed a steel-plated
room, rows of frosted glass cabinets on the shelves, naked
bodies inside them. Stanford stared at them, startled, felt
the chill in the room, then recovered and followed the
hunchback through a door that led into another room.

This room was a laboratory, steel-plated, very large, the
walls climbing to a ceiling of chiseled rock that was part
of the mountain. The staff looked quite normal, men and
women in white smocks, reading and writing, peering
down through microscopes, checking printouts and gauges
and thermometers, working quietly, intently. What was
different were the specimens in the cages and glass jars:
human heads, pumping hearts, floating brains and intestines, the naked body sitting upright in a chair, a wire

frame where its head had been. The frame was shaped like
a human head, was made from crisscrossing wires, contained flashing bulbs and fuses and copper coils, wires and
tubes running out of it. The wires and tubes ran to a console, were plugged into various sockets, the console flashing and buzzing, activating the headless body, its arms
rising and falling, legs kicking: a puppet of flesh and
blood. Stanford looked and turned away, saw the hunchback smiling at him, felt the sting of the electric fist in his
back, and followed the dwarf through another door.

They passed through a sort of warehouse, its walls
hacked out of the mountain, refrigerated and couched in
semidarkness, filled with tables and cabinets. Stanford tried
not to look, felt horrified and fascinated, his head level
with the cabinets, the tables all around him, his eyes drawn
against their will to what was present: the nightmare of
progress.

The cabinets kept the meat frozen, arms and legs, hands
and feet, wires extending from bloody necks and stumps,
electrodes sprouting from sliced skulls. The tables were
much worse, the human subjects not completed: here a
steel chin and nose, there a woman with plastic breasts,
here a torso with metal legs, valves and tubes instead of
genitals, there a chest with the flesh peeled off the bone, its
hydraulic heart gleaming. Other cabinets contained the
hardware: the exoskeletons and pacemakers, the percu-
taneous power connections, the bifurcated blood vessels
and aortic valves and silicone boosters, the orthopedic
braces and cobalt joints and piezoelectric generators—the
stainless steel and chromium, the meat and bone, of those
picked to be cyborgs.

"Jesus Christ," Stanford said.

The metal fist thumped his spine, the electric shock
stabbing through him, and he gasped and followed the
hunchback past the tables, the cyborg padding behind him.
They walked through another door, passed more bodies in
cabinets, the glass frosted, the graph needles not moving,
and then came to another door. The hunchback stepped
aside, bowed low, waved one hand, and Stanford walked
through the door and was dazzled by bright light and plate
glass.

He was in a dome-shaped room, its white metal walls gleaming, enormous windows running right around the wall, framing clear sky and mountain peaks. Between the windows there were doors, steel-plated, all closed, large consoles jutting out just above them, their lights flashing on and off. The room was fifty feet wide. There was a desk in the middle. On the desk there was an intercom, a Micro-film viewer, a pile of books, pens and pencils, notepaper, a black panel of switches. There were chairs in front of the desk, three white chairs, deep and comfortable; there was no other furniture in the room and the floor was cold plastic. A man sat behind the desk. He was staring steadily at Stanford. He was handsome and white-haired and slim, and he waved Stanford forward.

Stanford walked across the cold floor, his footsteps reverberating. It seemed to take a long time to reach the desk, but he got there eventually. He stopped and stared at Wilson. There was no doubt it was Wilson. Stanford stared at the unusually seamless forehead and knew who he was talking to.

"Mr. Wilson," he said.

"Take your pick," the man said. "Mr. Aldridge or Mr. Wilson—I don't mind. You've come a long way to see me."

Stanford didn't try to smile. He hadn't smiled for a long time. He rubbed his beard and looked at Wilson's blue eyes and thought of the Antarctic ice.

"This is it," Wilson said. He waved his hand in a careless manner. "Those doors lead out to the colony, to all the different departments; the consoles tell me what's going on and I control it from here. The colony forms a sort of circle. The tunnels run right through the mountain. The tunnels are the spokes of the wheel, and this room is the hub. We're on the top of a plateau. The tunnels lead down to the bottom. The saucers and construction plants are down there, and can't be seen from the sky. This room constitutes the highest point. An overhanging rock protects it. I have lived here for more than thirty years and I find it inspiring."

Wilson offered a bleak smile, his blue eyes very cold, filled with a luminous intelligence that did not know emotion. There was no malice in him. Stanford sensed that immediately. The man knew neither malice nor fear: he had gone beyond all that.

"You know who I am," Stanford said.

"Naturally," Wilson said. "We've been watching you and Epstein for years: you were both too persistent."

"Where is he?" Stanford said.

"You'll see him soon," Wilson said. "Dr. Epstein is healthier than he was—and is really quite happy."

"Happy?" Stanford said.

"Yes, happy," Wilson said.

"What the fuck did you do to him?" Stanford said.

"I just offered him life."

Wilson smiled and stood up, walked across to the window, his movements excessively slow and careful, then stopped and looked out. All white. Everything. The Antarctic was stretched out below him. He turned away from the window and looked at Stanford, his face smooth and expressionless.

"Why did you come here?" he said.

"I came for Epstein," Stanford said.

"No," Wilson said. "I don't think so. That just doesn't make sense."

"Why not?" Stanford said.

"You must have known you couldn't go back. You knew you couldn't get in here unless we let you—and you knew you couldn't escape. You must have known that and yet you still came . . . It wasn't just for your old friend."

"Partly that," Stanford said.

"And the other part?" Wilson said.

"I don't know," Stanford said. "I'm not sure. I guess I just had to finish it."

Wilson smiled without humor. The smile never reached his eyes. He walked back around the desk and sat down, his gaze still fixed on Stanford.

"You're living dangerously," Stanford said.

"I'm not sure I understand."

"We're all alone," Stanford said. "I could kill you. And I think I might do it."

"I don't think so," Wilson said. "You didn't come here

for that. Besides, it would serve little purpose: it would not affect this place."

"You're not concerned for yourself?"

"Not really," Wilson said. "I've had a long life, a full life, but it can't last forever."

"You're a cyborg," Stanford said.

"Not quite accurate," Wilson said. "I have an artificial heart, a few joints are prosthetic replacements, my face has undergone plastic surgery, but I'm hardly a cyborg. Not that it makes much difference. Even cyborgs pass away. We still haven't conquered the liver, and that means we're still mortal."

"How long have you got to go?"

"A few more years," Wilson said.

"Then what? What happens when you die?"

"This place will continue."

He stared steadily at Stanford. His eyes radiated no feeling. He displayed neither malice nor warmth, his soul destroyed by intelligence.

"Man is simply a tool," he said. "He is the seed of evolution. He exists to explore and create, and has no other value. But men alone are self-destructive. Without discipline, they rot. Take the history of man and examine it and you come up with lunacy: wasted time and opportunity, self-indulgence and corruption, material greed and self-pity and vanity: all negative impulses. The will to freedom has never worked; every success has been matched with failure; we step forward and then we step back and wallow blindly in pettiness. Our superiority is in thinking. Only the mind has any value. But our animal needs, our appetites and fears, keep us chained to the floor. We must leave the cave behind us. We must reach for the stars. We can't do that while Democracy persists and lets freedom destroy us."

"Freedom leads to creativity."

"No, it doesn't," Wilson said. "Freedom leads to boredom and conflict and waste—and perpetuates stagnancy."

"The world hasn't stagnated."

"It hasn't advanced much," Wilson said. "Or at least, it's only advanced on one level and is now dangerously imbalanced. We have advanced scientifically, have made extraordinary leaps forward, and now we stand on the brink of the miraculous and can reshape man's future. But that advance was intellectual. We are still emotionally retarded. The other face of man is still as primitive as it was in the cave. That face remains unchanged. It masks the dire results of freedom. It disguises mindless greed, political suspicion and social fear, pointless hatred and the boredom and resentment that lead to destruction. The world is wallowing in bloodshed, the seas are being polluted, we're gradually gobbling up our natural resources and inviting a barren earth. We do this because of greed, because of politics and war, and these things are the consequences of so-called freedom, the fruits of Democracy. Man must have a purpose. He must be disciplined and driven. Only then will the world become sane and save itself from destruction."

"Totalitarianism," Stanford said. "A world of masters and slaves. The people will be content because they're zombies . . . and the earth will be peaceful."

"You disapprove," Wilson said.

"Fucking right, I disapprove. It's obscene and it's been tried before and it just never works. A man needs free choice. Without that, he's not a man. To steal a man's will and contradictions is to steal his humanity."

"That's sentiment," Wilson said.

"I'm a sentimentalist," Stanford said.

"You're a primitive," Wilson said. "You're self-destructive. That's why you came here."

"Fuck you," Stanford said. "What you're saying is shit. And you won't get away with it forever—the world out there won't let you."

"Won't it?" Wilson said. "How naive you are, Stanford. The world out there is part of the conspiracy, and has been for years. The United States knows about us. The Soviet Union knows about us. The British and the Germans know about us, and all of them deal with us. What I have is what they need. What I'm doing is what they want. The world is out of control, freedom has led to revolution, and now Democracy is no more than a name to keep the innocent happy. You think your people are any different? No, Stanford, they're not different. Totalitarianism creeps over the world and is stifling resistance. Regimentation is increasing. People are numbers instead of names. The world is now ruled by a selected few, and suppression is spreading. Surveillance is widespread. Every citizen is on file. The salient facts of every individual human have been fed to computers. Television mesmerizes them. Piped music fills their factories. Credit cards and employment cards and passports have rendered privacy obsolete. All these people are numbers. Their so-called freedom is an illusion. Their politics, their cultures, their religions have no bearing on anything. Let them demonstrate occasionally. Let them criticize and abuse. Feed them issues that will keep them engaged while the real work goes on. In the end they will be passive. They won't really have any choice. Their credit cards and employment cards and passports can be withdrawn at any time. Such items make or break them. A select few decide the issue. The mass of men are guided through various channels and they don't even know it. That's your freedom, Mr. Stanford. That's your precious Democracy. The world is a chess game, the pieces are property, and the game is only played by the select few who hide behind closed doors."

"A neat theory," Stanford said. "It just has one glaring flaw: your players will fight amongst themselves, and you'll still have world conflict. The Americans want you out of here. The Russians want you out as well. They're human beings and they're filled with the suspicion and fear that you loathe. You won't have peace on earth. They're just playing for time. When they're ready, or when they *think* that they're ready, they'll come at you with everything. You just said it yourself: they're not logical people; they're human beings and they're moved by primitive fears—and that's the flaw in your scheme. Sooner or later, they'll try it. It might be madness, but they'll try it. Then the war that will come, caused by you, will be the war to end wars."

"You're wrong," Wilson said quietly. "I've made allowances for that. I'm not so naive as to imagine that this race can continue. But the race will *not* continue. It will end in ten years. Within ten years every major government post will be run from this colony. We have people everywhere,

in every country, in every government, and those people
have electrodes in their heads and will do what we tell them.
They are currently in the Pentagon, in the CIA and the
FBI, in NASA and the Cheyenne Mountain Complex, in
the Army and Navy and Air Force, in every top-secret
project. It's the same all over the world. We have people
everywhere. We're robotizing important people every year,
and every year it gets easier. They don't know they're robotized. They think they're making their own decisions.
But every new law of suppression, every new surveillance
system, every action that changes the course of world
events is dictated by us. We grow more numerous every
month. We're gradually climbing up the pyramid. In ten
years—or possibly less—all the rules will be our rules.
Your world is ending, Stanford. It will soon be no more.
If I sent you back out there tomorrow, it would do you no
good."

Stanford didn't know what to say. There was nothing
left to say. He hadn't felt emotion for months, but now he
felt it returning. That emotion was fear. It might well
have been despair. He gazed down at the man behind the
desk and saw the ice of his blue eyes. The eyes were devoid of feeling. No malice, no resentment, no greed . . . it
was organization.

Stanford thought this and was shocked. He thought of
the world beyond the mountains. That world, his own
world, was procreating and becoming too complex. The
cities couldn't be controlled, the great suburbs were a
mess; inequality and boredom and frustration were leading
to madness. Increasing violence and civil strife, increasing
wealth and attendant poverty; the contradictions of society
were exploding and crippling whole nations. The politicians were defeated: freedom foiled them every day; more
and more they were introducing legislation that encouraged suppression. They didn't appear to have much choice.
Increasing chaos overwhelmed them. Categorization and
surveillance and harassment were all they had left. Stanford thought of it with woe. He desperately wanted an alternative. He was human for the first time in months, and
he paid the full price. The fear chilled him and shook him,

turned into quiet rage. He stared at Wilson and felt the faint stirrings of a cold, hard defiance.

"Where's Epstein?" he said.

Wilson reached across the desk. flicked a switch and then stood up, led Stanford across the room to a door, not saying a word. Stanford looked above the door. A red light flashed on the console. He turned his head and looked out through a window at the sweeping Antarctic. The panorama was stupendous; the white plains stretched to the sky; the jagged mountain peaks were just below, their rocks ringed with blue ice. Then the steel doors slid open. Wilson waved Stanford in. They stood together in a white-walled elevator and the doors closed behind them.

The elevator fell very quietly. It dropped down through the mountain. Stanford thought of what the German had told him about Hitler's teahouse. He saw a window on one wall. Floors shot up and disappeared. There was hardly any sound, no sense of motion, and the elevator was quite warm. Wilson didn't say a word. He stared at Stanford with detachment. Stanford saw a huge cavern, littered grottoes and caves, various workshops and storerooms and offices, people working in silence. The elevator door slid open quietly. They stepped out into an office. The walls were painted white, the shelves were crowded with books, and Professor Epstein was sitting behind a desk, looking up, smiling gently.

"Hello, Stanford," he said.

Stanford looked at his old friend. Epstein seemed very healthy. He had put on some weight, his gray beard had been trimmed, and he was wearing a shirt and tie, a white coat, his cheeks ruddy, his eyes clear.

"I'll leave you now," Wilson said. "I hope you are agreeable. You will have to make a decision, Dr. Stanford, and I hope it's the right one."

He turned back to the steel door, the door opened and he walked in, then the door closed and Wilson was gone, leaving silence behind him.

Stanford looked at his old friend. Epstein stayed behind the desk. His hands were clasped under his bearded chin, his eyes clear and steady.

"It's good to see you," he said.

"Is it?" Stanford said.

"It's been a very long time," Epstein said. "It seems more than a year."

"What happened to the cancer?"

"They cured me," Epstein said. "They're really quite extraordinary that way. I must say I was grateful."

"Grateful?" Stanford said.

"A new life," Epstein said. "Not just that, but new purpose, new work—something worth living for."

Stanford looked at his old friend, felt a deep, searing anguish, a pain that came out of his bowels and made him feel lost.

"What did they do to you?" he said.

"They did nothing," Epstein said. "They cured me of cancer and explained what they were doing, and I realized that the work was important and decided to stay."

"They did an implant," Stanford said.

"Not on me," Epstein said.

"Either you're lying or you simply can't remember. They must have done something."

"They did nothing," Epstein said.

"Jesus Christ," Stanford said.

"Believe me, they didn't do a thing. They just talked and I listened."

"And this is what you want?"

"Yes, it's what I want. They took me up above the Earth and showed me things that I just can't forget."

"They implanted," Stanford said.

"Not in me," Epstein said.

"They do it to everybody," Stanford said. "They must have done it to you."

"They didn't," Epstein said.

"You don't remember," Stanford said.

"I don't remember. I know they didn't do it. I just want peace and quiet."

"I'm taking you out," Stanford said.

"I won't go," Epstein said. "The very thought of it gives me a migraine. I just don't want to go."

"A migraine?" Stanford said.

"The thought of outside," Epstein said.

"They did an implant."

"No, they didn't," Epstein said. "I just don't want to go."

Stanford felt hot and clammy, swept with anguish and despair, a hopelessness that threatened to drown him and kill his resistance. He thought of Jacobs and Gerhardt, of the girl near Galveston, of Scaduto and Epstein and himself and all the years now behind them. The mystery was resolved. The nightmare was manifest. The world was being saved from itself and taking on a new face. Stanford wanted no part of it. He didn't want to lose himself. He wanted to live with contradictions and conflict and the pain of free choice. Yet the price was too great. He didn't know if he could pay it. He looked down at his old friend, Dr. Epstein, and the pain slithered through him. Dr. Epstein was no more. His placid eyes were all-revealing. He stared at Stanford without malice or friendship, offering nothing and everything. Stanford shook with grief and rage. He let his senses fly away. The pain stripped him and put him back together and gave life to defiance.

"You must stay here," Epstein said. "We need people like you. You will work and know great satisfaction and never know discontent."

"I don't want it," Stanford said.

"You must accept it," Epstein said.

"You're not Epstein," Stanford said. "You're someone else. You're not the person I knew."

"I'm the same," Epstein said. "They just cured me of the cancer. Now I do the sort of work I always dreamed of—and feel wonderful with it."

"They've stolen your mind," Stanford said.

"That's ridiculous," Epstein said. "I know you. I remember my past. I know just who I am."

"They've stolen your will," Stanford said.

"They've stolen nothing," Epstein said. "They just talked and I listened and that's all: they did not operate."

"You can't remember," Stanford said.

"I'm getting a headache," Epstein said. "We really must stop talking about this. You must stay. You can't leave here."

Epstein's eyes were placid. His hands were folded on

the desk. He looked at Stanford with a calm, remote interest, talking quietly and patiently.

"You can't leave here," he said. "There's really no place to go. You can walk out whenever you wish, but you'll freeze to death out there. Here you'll live a painless life. Your life will take on some meaning. You might be deprived of your imagined freedom, but think of the blessings. No more discontentment. No decisions to be made. You will work and take pleasure in that work, and never know doubt or fear."

"I'll be robotized," Stanford said.

"They won't do that," Epstein said.

"They did it to you," Stanford said.

"No, they didn't. They didn't."

Stanford knew it was useless. His sense of loss was overwhelming. He let the grief and the rage shake him loose and make him fight for his freedom. It didn't matter where he went. He didn't give a damn what happened. The point was to make a decision and then follow it through.

"You said I can leave," he said.

"That's correct," Epstein said. "We won't stop you, but we won't help you either. The decision is yours."

"I want to leave," Stanford said.

"You'll freeze to death," Epstein said.

"Fuck you," Stanford said. "Fuck you all. I won't submit to this shit."

Epstein sighed and stood up. He walked across to a wall. There were large curtains drawn across the wall, hanging down to the floor. Epstein pulled a sash cord. The large curtains drew apart. A dazzling light poured through a massive plate-glass door and washed over them both. Stanford blinked and rubbed his eyes. He was looking along a huge glass hall. Through the glass walls he could see the glaring white of the immense, frozen wilderness.

"The choice is yours," Epstein said. "You can stay or you can leave. However, once the decision is made there can be no turning back. You just have to touch this glass. It will open and let you through. Once you step into the hall the door will close and trap you in there. You can only leave by the other door. It's at the far end of the hall.

That door opens by contact from inside, and leads out to the wilderness. You can't open it from outside. If you step out, you must stay out. You can leave or you can stay—as you wish—and you must decide now."

Stanford looked at his old friend, at his gray, remote eyes, mutely prayed for some sign of emotion and received calm indifference. The sense of loss was overwhelming, the pain unprecedented, shaking Stanford and making his heart pound, leaving nothing but rage.

He would hold the rage and use it. He would make his decision. Neither old friends nor memories nor hopes would make him bend to their will. He was not a machine. He would not be a cipher. Stanford looked along the hall, saw the blinding sunlight, saw the white haze running out to the sky and then pressed on the plate glass. The large doors slid apart. The glass hall was filled with light. Stanford stared at his old friend, at his gray eyes and beard, thought of all that they had been through together and dissolved into anguish.

"You're not Epstein," he said.

He stepped into the hall. The large doors closed behind him. Sunlight blazed through the glass walls and roof and formed dazzling mosaics. Stanford zipped his jacket up. He covered his ears with the woolen hat. He plunged his hands in his pockets and walked forward, determined not to look back. The past was now behind him. The hall stretched out to the future. Stanford saw a globe of fire fill the sky with lines of silver and pink. He walked quickly along the hall. The flashing glass was all around him. He reached the door at the other end of the hall and stopped a few feet away from it. Stanford wanted to say something, wanted to speak to the silence. He stepped forward and the glass doors slid open and the fierce cold rushed in.

All white. Everything. The cold was appalling. Stanford leaned into the wind and stepped forward and the doors closed behind him. He didn't stop or look back. The white wilderness stretched before him. The wind blew the snow in languid, glinting clouds across the pack ice and glaciers. Stanford kept moving forward. He didn't care where he was going. He saw an arch of light above a horizon that forever receded. All light. Flashing light. A unique and dazzling vision. The light flashed and made his eyes sting and weep. Stanford didn't give a damn. He felt defiant and proud. He was alive and he kept moving forward to disprove all their theories. He saw a monstrous balloon. It was floating there before him. The balloon was transparent and shimmered and framed a pink sky. Stanford shivered and stumbled. He had to clench his chattering teeth. The wind moaned and made the snow swirl around him and settle upon him. He ignored it, kept going. His teeth started to ache. The snow settled on his beard and his hair and then formed a light frost.

All white. Everything. Definition was lost. The wind moaned and the snow blew all around him and made him a part of it. He fell down and stood up and stumbled forward again. He thought of Epstein and Wilson and the colony and the great flying saucers. The future was here and now. His own history had passed. The snow formed huge darkened portals that were luring him in. He stepped in and saw a light, stumbled forward and saw it grow. The snow hissed and swirled and then the bright light exploded. All white. Everything. He let the wilderness embrace him. Glinting glaciers and flashing pack ice and streams of yellow and violet. The frost thickened on his face. He couldn't feel his numbed lips. The hands plunged deep in his pockets had vanished and left singing nerve ends. Stanford laughed as he froze. The icy air filled his lungs. He stumbled forward, heading into the wilderness, and could not be defeated.

He walked out a long way. The mountains fell far behind him. The white wilderness stretched out all around him and offered no exit. Stanford didn't give a damn. He thought of what he had left behind. The future that would rise from the ice held no promise for him. Stanford's lips cracked when he smiled. The blood froze on the instant. He moved forward with his weeping eyes stinging, his hands and feet missing. No feeling. All numb. The ground shifting and sliding. A great rainbow formed across the horizon and framed a fierce whiteness. Then a luminous balloon. A mirage: a sun dog. He saw miracles of blue ice and light, the dazzling wastes of the snowfalls. Stanford stumbled on, regardless. He started talking and singing. He heard a voice that was offering comfort and coaxing him onward. He followed the Pied Piper. He let the sun and ice dissolve him. He fell down and saw the great slabs of pack ice that drifted and glittered.

He would travel, he would move. He crept along on his belly. His missing fingers found the snow and dug in and his body inched forward. Stanford saw the drifting ice. He sang and muttered under his breath. Jagged black lines on white glare. A giant jigsaw in the sun. Stanford felt a fierce defiance and exultation that would not let him die. He crawled across the frozen earth. He dragged a dead thing behind him, his body, and would not let it go. Stanford slithered across a crevice. His fingers touched a slab of ice. The ice glittered and reflected the sun as the snow settled down. Stanford murmured and sang. He heard someone singing somewhere. His fingers touched and felt nothing and bent as his body inched forward. Stanford saw streams of light. The light flashed and beat about him. Stanford slithered onto the slab of pack ice and rolled onto his back.

All white. Everything. Stanford saw lights in the sky. They were very high up, very small, pulsating and glowing. He knew what the lights were. He smiled when he saw them. The lights were like stars in the white sky, very bright and intense. Stanford lay there on the pack ice. The ice drifted imperceptibly. Stanford lay there and let the frost encase him and turn into more ice. The lights drifted across the sky. They defied the sky's bright haze. The ice drifted and flashed blue and yellow and became part of Stanford. He lay there and smiled. The ice carried him away. Stanford felt a fierce defiance and exultation that would not let him die. The frost thickened and hardened. It molded Stanford to the pack ice. He turned around in the sun, a glass figure, quite beautiful, the light flashing on and off him, exploding, streaming skyward, slowly turning him into a glacier, a prism: a star.

END

Author's Note

While *Genesis* is very much a work of fiction, it *has* been based on certain facts which this author feels are worth bringing to light.

In the course of researching a different novel altogether, I obtained, through the Imperial War Museum in London, two short but intriguing articles which immediately captured my interest. The first one was a routine war report by Marshall Yarrow, then the Reuters special correspondent to Supreme H.Q. in liberated Paris. This article had been published, among other places, in the *South Wales Argus* on December 13, 1944, and it stated: "The Germans have produced a 'secret' weapon in keeping with the Christmas season. The new device, which is apparently an air defense weapon, resembles the glass balls which adorn Christmas trees. They have been seen hanging in the air over German territory, sometimes singly, sometimes in clusters. They are colored silver and are apparently transparent." The second article, an Associated Press release extracted from the New York *Herald Tribune* of January 2, 1945, illuminated the subject even more. It said: "Now, it seems, the Nazis have thrown something new into the night skies over Germany. It is the weird, mysterious 'Foo Fighter' balls which race alongside the wings of Beaufighters flying intruder missions over Germany. Pilots have been encountering this eerie weapon for more than a month in their night flights. No one apparently knows what this sky weapon is. The balls of fire appear suddenly and accompany the planes for miles. They seem to be radio-controlled from the ground, so official intelligence reports reveal . . ." Apparently those 'unknown' objects made their final appearance in May 1945, when the end of the war was in sight.

Intrigued by these reports, I conducted some more research and discovered a highly technical but little-known book called *Intercettateli Senza Sparare* (see "Sources" for details), by Renato Vesco, in which the author claims that the "Foo Fighter" actually existed, that it was originally called the *Feuerball,* and that it was first constructed at the aeronautical establishment at Wiener Neustadt, with the help of the *Flugfunk Forschungsanstalt* of *Oberpfaffenhoffen* (FFO). According to Vesco, the *Feuerball* was a flat, circular flying machine, powered by a special turbojet engine, which was used by the Germans during the closing stages of the war both as an anti-radar device and as a "psychological" weapon against Allied pilots. Says Vesco: "The fiery halo around its perimeter—caused by a very rich fuel mixture—and the chemical additives that interrupted the flow of electricity by overionizing the atmosphere in the vicinity of the plane, generally around the wing tips or tail surfaces, subjected the H2S radar on the plane to the action of powerful electrostatic fields and electromagnetic impulses." Vesco also claims that the basic principles of the *Feuerball* were later applied to a much larger "symmetrical circular aircraft," the *Kugelblitz* (or Ball Lightning Fighter), which was the first example of the vertical-rising "jet lift" aircraft.

Further intrigued, I continued my research in West Germany and came up with a surprising number of newspaper and magazine clippings—all from the 1950s—about one *Flugkapitan* Rudolph Schriever. One clipping stated that this former *Luftwaffe* aeronautical engineer had designed, in the spring of 1941, the prototype for a "flying top," and that the device was tested in June 1942; another stated that the same *Flugkapitan* Schriever, with "three trusted colleagues," had actually constructed, in August 1943, a "large specimen" of his original "flying disc," but that in the summer of 1944, in the East Hall of the BMW plant near Prague, he had redesigned the original model, replacing its former gas turbine engines with some highly advanced form of jet propulsion; and a third, which reiterated the above information, added the interesting news that original plans for the flying disc had been drawn up by the "German experts," Habermohl and Miethe, and an Italian physicist, Dr. Bellonzo. According to other reports (and, subsequently, to Major Rudolph Lusar's indispensible book, *German Secret Weapons of World War II*, English language edition, published by Neville Spearman, London, 1959, and the Philosophical Library, New York, 1959), Habermohl and Schriever had designed a large ring plate with "adjustable wing-discs," which rotated around a "fixed, cupola-shaped cockpit," while Miethe had developed a "discus-shaped plate in which adjustable jets were inserted." Reportedly the flying saucer had a diameter of 42 meters (137.76 feet), a height from base to canopy of 32 meters (104.96 feet), and had reached an altitude of approximately 40,000 ft, with a horizontal flight speed of 2,000 kilometers per hour (1,250 mph).

So far, so good . . . But what I now came to was a series of small and puzzling contradictions.

Shortly after the war, *Flugkapitan* Schriever was living at Hokerstrauss 28 in Bremerhaven-Lehe from where he announced that the flying disc had indeed been constructed, that it had been ready for testing in April 1945, but that with the advance of the Allies into Germany, the test had been cancelled, the machine entirely destroyed, and his papers either mislaid or stolen. Schriever's story was, however, contradicted by alleged eyewitness Georg Klein, who later stated that he had actually *seen* the test flight of the Schriever disc, or one similar, on February 14, 1945. A certain doubt may be cast on Klein's date since, according to the War Diary of the 8th Air Fleet, February 14, 1945 was a day of low clouds, rain, snow and generally poor visibility—hardly the conditions for the testing of a revolutionary new kind of aircraft. Nevertheless, according to author Renato Vesco, in his thoroughly documented book, *Intercept UFO,* the test flight of a machine called the *Kugelblitz*—which was rumored to be a revolutionary kind of supersonic aircraft—was successfully conducted over the underground complex of Kahla, in Thuringia, *some* time during that February of 1945.

By 1975 *Luftfahrt International* was stating that a certain World War II *Flugkapitan* Rudolph Schriever had died in the late 1950s, and that found among his papers were the incomplete notes for a large flying saucer (most of them technically out of date), a series of rough sketches of the machine (some of which had obviously been redrawn and updated just before his death), and several newspaper clippings about himself and his supposed flying saucer. Now, while none of the designs would have led to a workable flying saucer, *Luftfahrt International* did include reproductions of the designs of both Schriever and Dr. Miethe and also pointed out that Schriever, right up to his death, had been convinced that the UFO sightings since the end of the war were proof that his original ideas had been taken further with successful results.

Could this be true?

Let us examine the possibilities. According to Schriever, what appears to have been the final version of his flying saucer was constructed at the BMW plant near Prague in the early months of 1944 and was ready for testing in April 1945. According to Georg Klein, a similar flying disc was actually flown near Prague in February 1945, and according to the Italian author Renato Vesco—who seems unaware of the existence of the Schriever legend—an extraordinary new flying machine called the *Kugelblitz* was tested sometime that same month over the complex of Kahla, in the mountain region of Thuringia.

Tying in with this information is the fact that the gas turbine section of BMW was originally located in the suburb of Spandau, near Berlin—where, according to Renato Vesco, a lot of research on the *Kugelblitz* was undertaken—that it was later moved to the underground plant of Wittringen, near Saarbrucken, but that it finally ended up, as from 1944, in seven enormous underground

complexes in both Thuringia and Nordhausen in the Harz
Mountains.

That whole area, running in a metaphorical arc from
the Harz Mountains, down through Thuringia, Bohmen
and Mahren, was to form the Germans' last redoubt, and
as such was littered with a staggering number of underground military and scientific complexes, including the
enormous and invaluable Mittle-Werke factories and the
personnel and equipment from the experimental center at
Peenemunde. Certainly, while history was to decree otherwise, it was from there that Hitler intended to defend the
remnants of the Third Reich with "a whole underground
army" and the "secret weapons" he had been promised for
so long.

In May 1978, at Stand 111 in a scientific exhibition in
the Hannover Messe Hall, some gentlemen were giving
away what at first sight appeared to be an orthodox technological tabloid paper called *Brisant*. This paper contained two seemingly unrelated articles: one an article on
the scientific future of the Antarctic, the other an article
about Germany's World War II flying saucers. The flying
saucer article reiterated the information mentioned above,
but added that the research centers for *Projekt Saucer*
had been located in the areas of Bohmen and Mahren.

Regarding this, it should be pointed out that Prague is
in Bohmen, and that Bohmen is more or less surrounded
by the metaphorical arc of the Harz Mountains, Thuringia
and Mahren—all of which areas contained vast underground research complexes, none of which were more than
a few hundred kilometers from Prague.

The article also included a detailed drawing of a typical
World War II flying disc, did *not* mention the designer's
name, and claimed that the drawing had been altered by
the West German government to render it "safe" for
publication. Adding weight to his argument, the unknown
author then pointed out that during the Second World
War all such inventions, whether civilian or military,
would have been submitted to the nearest patent office
where, under paragraph 30a and 99 of the *Patent-und
Strafgesetsbuch*, they would have been automatically

stamped "Secret," taken away from their rightful owners, and passed on to Himmler's research establishments . . . and, according to the article, at the end of the war some of those patents disappeared into secret Russian files, others into equally secret British and American files, and the remainder disappeared with various "missing" German scientists and S.S. men. (Since neither the British, the Americans nor the Russians are ever likely to reveal what, precisely, was discovered in the secret factories of Nazi Germany, it is worth noting that in 1945 Sir Roy Feddon, as leader of a technical mission to Germany for the Ministry for Aircraft Production, reported: "I have seen enough of their designs and production plans to realize that if they had managed to prolong the war some months longer, we would have been confronted with a set of entirely new and deadly developments in air warfare." And by 1956 Captain Edward J. Ruppelt, then head of the U.S. Air Force's Project Blue Book, was able to write: "When World War II ended, the Germans had several radical types of aircraft and guided missiles under development. The majority of these were in the most preliminary stages, but they were the only known craft that could even approach the performances of the objects reported by UFO observers.")

The same article went on to point out that in 1938, Hitler, anxious for a foothold in the Antarctic, sent an expedition commanded by Captain Alfred Richter to the coast due south of South Africa. Daily for three weeks two seaplanes were catapulted from the deck of the German aircraft carrier, *Schwabenland*, with orders to fly back and forth across the territory which Norwegian explorers had named Queen Maud Land. The Germans made a far more thorough study of the area than the Norwegians had done, finding vast regions which were surprisingly free of ice. Their planes covered 230,000 square miles in all, photographing almost half of the area. They also dropped several thousand metal poles, each marked with the swastika and pointed at the heavy tip so that they would dig into the ice and remain upright. This job done, they renamed the whole area *Neuschwabenland* and claimed it as part of the Third Reich.

According to *Brisant*, German ships and U-boats continued to prowl the South Atlantic Ocean, particularly between South Africa and the Antarctic, throughout the whole of the Second World War. Then, in March 1945, just before the end of the war, two German provision U-boats, U-530 and U-977, were launched from a port on the Baltic Sea. Reportedly they took with them members of the flying saucer research teams, the last of the most vital flying saucer components, the notes and drawings for the saucer, and the designs for gigantic underground complexes and living accommodations based on the remarkable underground factories of Nordhausen in the Harz Mountains. The two U-boats duly reached *Neuschwabenland*, more correctly known as Queen Maud Land, where they unloaded. Finally, two months *after* the war, the same U-boats surfaced mysteriously off the coast of Argentina where the crews were handed over to the American authorities, who interrogated them at length and then flew them all back to the United States.

About a year after this, the United States launched the biggest operation ever known regarding the Antarctic. While the stated purpose of the operation was to "circumnavigate the 16,000-mile Antarctic coastline and map it thoroughly," *Brisant* felt it odd that Operation Highjump, under the command of Antarctic veteran Admiral Richard Evelyn Byrd, included thirteen ships, two seaplane tenders, an aircraft carrier, six two-engine R4D transports, six Martin PBM flying boats, six helicopters and a staggering total of 4,000 men. It was also considered odd that when this virtual assault force reached the Antarctic coast, they not only docked, on January 27, 1947, near the German-claimed territory of *Neuschwabenland*, but then divided up into three separate task forces.

That expedition became something of a mystery. Subsequent official reports stated that it had been an enormous success, revealing more about the Antarctic than had ever been known before. However, other, mainly foreign reports suggested that such in fact had not been the case: that many of Byrd's men were lost during the first day, that at least four of his airplanes inexplicably disappeared, and that while the expedition had gone provisioned for six to eight months, the men actually returned to America in February 1947, after only a few weeks. According to *Bristant*, Admiral Byrd later told a reporter (I could find no verification on this) that it was "necessary for the USA to take defensive actions against enemy air fighters which come from the polar regions" and that in the case of a new war the USA would be "attacked by fighters that are able to fly from one pole to the other with incredible speed." Also, according to *Brisant*, shortly after his return from the Antarctic, Admiral Byrd was ordered to undergo a secret cross-examination—and the United States withdrew from the Antarctic for almost a decade.

What was being suggested, then, is that throughout the course of the Second World War the Germans were sending ships and planes to the Antarctic with equipment for massive underground complexes, that at the end of the war the flying saucer project's team of scientists were taken from Germany by submarines U-530 and U-977, that the Americans interrogated the crews of those submarines when they docked in what they had thought was a friendly Argentina, that the Americans then, upon hearing of the Antarctic base, organized a military task force disguised as an exploratory expedition, that that expedition was subsequently put to disarray when it came up against the extraordinary German saucers, and that the United States then pulled out of the Antarctic temporarily, in order to build their own saucers based on the designs found in Germany after the war.

The second article was also of modest interest. It was in point of fact a rather crude propaganda statement masquerading as a scientific review of Antarctic potential. Dusting off the already well-known topographical facts, what one was left with was an insistence that the Democratic Republic of Germany should claim back their rights to that part of the Antarctic which the Nazis stole from the Norwegians and arrogantly renamed *Neuschwabenland*.

Taking note of the National Socialist leanings of the article, bearing in mind the fact that *Brisant* was a one-shot publication whose origins were untraceable, and reminding myself that the whole theory had suspicious parallels with the more farfetched "Holes in the Poles" UFO myths, I nevertheless checked up on other aspects of the article and discovered that the Germans had, in fact, been patroling the Antarctic regions of the South Atlantic Ocean throughout the war. Indeed, two years after the Richter expedition, a couple of large Norwegian whaling ships were seized by boarding parties from the German raider *Pinguin* as they rested at anchor in their own territorial waters just off Queen Maud Land. Within hours of that incident, a Norwegian supply ship and most of the nearby whaling convoy had been lured into the German trap— and the war in the Antarctic was underway. In May 1941, HMS *Cornwall* located and sank the *Pinguin*, but not before *Pinguin* had captured a whole string of Allied merchant ships totaling more than 135,000 tons. What is also historical fact is that *Pinguin*'s sister ships, appropriately named *Komet* and *Atlantis*, continued to prowl the Antarctic shores until the end of the war.

Regarding the two submarines, I also came across some startling information. U-977, under the command of Captain Heinz Schaeffer, did in fact leave Kiel Harbor in the Baltic Sea in April 1945, stopped in at Christiansund South on April 26th, left Christiansund South the following day, and was not seen again until it surfaced at Mar del Plata, Argentina, on August 17, 1945—a period of nearly four months.

Where was the submarine all that time? According to Captain Heinz Schaeffer, they had left with the intention of patroling the South Atlantic, had docked for fuel at Christiansund South the following day, and had then, several days later, heard over their radio the news that the war was over. Convinced that he would not be treated too kindly by the Allied Command, Schaeffer gave his crew the option of being put off along the coast of Norway or traveling on with him to what he thought was a friendly Argentina. Since some of the crew preferred to return to Germany, the next few days were spent in hugging the Norwegian coastline until, on May 10, they dropped some of their men off on the mountain coast not far from Bergen. This done, according to Schaeffer, he and the remaining crew embarked upon what surely must have been one of the most remarkable feats of the war: a total of sixty-six days under water—through the North Sea and the English Channel, past Gibraltar and along the coast of Africa, and finally surfacing, all of sixty-six days later, in the middle of the South Atlantic Ocean. During the next month they alternated between floating on the surface and diving back to the depths, once even surfacing off the Cape Verde Islands and going ashore on Branca Island, another time going so far as to "disguise" the submarine when it was on the surface by rigging up false sails and funnel to make it look like a cargo steamer. Finally, when close to Rio de Janeiro, they heard over their radio that another fleeing German submarine, U-530, had put into the River Plate and that its crew had been handed over to the United States as prisoners of war. Disturbed by this, they nevertheless put into Mar del Plata on August 17, 1945—nearly four months after they had put out from Kiel Harbor.

This rather fantastic story was recounted by Captain Schaeffer to the Argentine authorities when they interrogated him on three specific issues: (1) Where had U-977 been when the Brazilian steamer *Babia* had been sunk? (2) How come U-977 had arrived in Argentina so long after the war had finished? and (3) Had U-977 carried anyone "of political importance" during its voyage to the Argentine? Schaeffer denied that he had been anywhere in the area of the *Babia* when it was sunk, explained his late arrival in Argentina with the fantastic story I have just recounted, and stated that no one of "political importance" had ever been aboard U-977.

Now what is really intriguing about all this is that a few weeks later an Anglo-American commission, composed of high-ranking officers especially flown to the Argentine to investigate "the mysterious case" of U-977, spent a great deal of time interrogating Schaeffer regarding the possibility that he might actually have taken Hitler and Martin Bormann aboard his U-boat, first to Patagonia and then to a secret Nazi base in the Antarctic. Indeed, they were so insistent on this that they subsequently flew Schaeffer and

his crew—*and* Otto Wehrmut, commander of U-530—
back to a prisoner of war camp near Washington where
for months they continued their interrogations. While I
could find no record of the fate of Commander Wehrmut,
what I did authenticate is that Schaeffer repeatedly denied
having shipped anyone anywhere . . . Nevertheless, he
was handed over to the British in Antwerp and *again* interrogated for many months.

Assuming that Schaeffer was telling the truth and that
the Allies found nothing unusual in Schaeffer's U-boat, it
seems rather strange that the Americans would later send
the submarine back to the United States where, under
direct orders from the U.S. War Department, it was blown
to pieces with torpedoes. As for Schaeffer, he was eventually returned to Germany, did not feel comfortable as one
of the conquered, and then went back to join some fellow
Germans in the Argentine.

The possibility remains that Schaeffer might have been
lying. For a start, it is decidedly odd that two insignificant
German U-boats should have stirred such monumental interest among the Allies. It is also worth considering why
the Allies would even have *imagined* that Hitler and Martin Bormann—or anyone else for that matter—would have
fled to such an unlikely place as the Antarctic. Finally, it
is worth noting that Schaeffer had spent much of his
career protecting the research centers at Regen and Peenemunde, that he was highly experienced at patroling the
South Atlantic and the polar regions, and that he was one
of a select group of Naval officers who were sent to the
Harz Mountains to study the highly advanced XXI submarines. Schaeffer was, in other words, a man familiar
with the "secret" underground establishments of the Harz
Mountains, and a man familiar with the Antarctic sea
routes.

Now let us review the situation. It is not confirmed, but
it is very possible that the German *Feuerball* existed, that it
accounted for the first modern UFO sightings during the
Second World War, and that an extraordinary flying machine, the *Kugelblitz*, was successfully test-flown in Germany a few weeks before the war ended. The *Feuerball*,
therefore, could have been the forerunner of the small,

seemingly remote-controlled UFOs observed frequently throughout the final months of the war, while the *Kugelblitz* could have been the first of the larger, pilot-controlled flying saucers.

The unsigned flying saucer designs reproduced in *Brisant* (and in a great many more orthodox journals) mentioned materials not in existence, as far as we know, during the war years. This suggests that they could have been reproductions of the original plans which *Flugkapitan* Rudolph Schriever updated just before his death in the late 1950s. Assuming, then, that Schriever's "mislaid" or "stolen" notes and designs were actually in the hands of the S.S., it is possible that they were secretly developed in one of the many underground complexes in the area of the aborted last redoubt—either the Nordhausen complex in the Harz Mountains or at Kahla in nearby Thuringia—that the completed saucer was test-flown in the early months of 1945, and that it was then destroyed in the face of the Allied advance.

We know from reproductions of the drawings of Schriever, Bellonzo and Miethe that a flying saucer project, no matter how primitive at the time, was definitely on the list of German military priorities. Regarding the fact that the only evidence of such machines is the evidence mentioned above, it should be borne in mind that the most fanatical of the Nazi S.S. were controlling the research centers in the areas mentioned, that as they retreated they attempted to destroy as much as possible of their most important scientific papers and inventions, and that thousands of slave workers and their S.S. overlords—who could have revealed a great deal more—disappeared in the chaos of the liberation and were not seen again.

Could some of them have gone to the Antarctic?

Contrary to the accepted view, it is actually quite possible that the Nazis continually shipped and flew vital men, material and documents to the Antarctic throughout the war years.

Regarding the possibility of the submarines of that time being able to complete such a lengthy journey, it is to be noted that the normal U-boat could cover 7,000 miles on each operational cruise, that the Germans had submarine

tankers spread across the South Atlantic Ocean at least as
far as south of South Africa, and that any one of those
tankers, which had a displacement of 2,000 tons, could
have supplied ten U-boats with fuel and stores, thus
tripling the time that those U-boats could stay at sea.

Regarding the possibility of the Germans building self-
sufficient underground research factories in the Antarctic,
it has only to be pointed out that the underground
research centers of Nazi Germany were gigantic feats of
construction, containing wind tunnels, machine shops, as-
sembly plants, launching pads, supply dumps and accom-
modation for all who worked there, including adjoining
camps for the slaves—and yet very few people knew that
they existed.

Given all this, it is in my estimation quite possible that
men and materials were shipped to the Antarctic throughout the war, that throughout those same years the Germans were engaged in building enormous underground
complexes in *Neuschwabenland* similar to those scattered
around the last redoubt, and that the American, Russian
and British "cover-up" regarding saucer sightings could be
due to the reasons given in this novel.

Skeptics would argue that the major histories of the
Third Reich either ignore or pass off as "ridiculous" any
stories about German "secret" weapons, but such an argument can be countered by reminding the reader that most
of the secret weapon projects *were* highly secret, usually
controlled by the dreaded S.S., and were therefore beyond
the reach of later historians. While Albert Speer, as Minister of Armaments and War Production, was openly skeptical about the "secret weapons" in his otherwise eloquent
book *Inside the Third Reich* (Weidenfeld & Nicholson,
London, 1970), he *does* admit that there was increasing
speculation about such weapons during the closing months
of the war—and that while he himself had stated at the
time that there were not enough basic materials for the production of such, he had, in his own words, "underestimated
. . . the large stocks of material that had been accumu-
lated in the factories." Speer was equally skeptical when
Robert Ley, the Minister for Labor excitedly told him, in
April 1945, that his German scientists had invented a

"death ray" (possibly a laser weapon); this is interesting when one considers the fact that Heinz Schaeffer, captain of the submarine U-977, stated in his book *U-boat 977* (William Kimber, London, 1952) that in April 1945 an S.S. associate had offered *him* a demonstration of a so-called "death ray." It is unfortunate that Schaeffer, in a hurry to return to Kiel for his famous last voyage, had no time to remain in Berlin and check out the validity of his friend's claim.

For the purposes of fiction I have utilized the real-life personages, S.S. generals Hans Kammler and Artur Nebe. Readers might therefore be interested to know that while Nebe was placed on the Nazi "death list" after the attempted assassination of Hitler, his death was never actually confirmed and many felt that he had simply fled for his life. As for General Hans Kammler, his history with the S.S. and the V-1 and V-2 rockets is well documented, but what became of him after he disappeared from Germany in April 1945 remains a mystery to this day. Regarding the members of the German flying saucer team, Schriever and Bellonzo are now dead, Habermohl was reported to have been captured by the Russians (thus the American military's fear of *Russian* saucers shortly after the war), and—perhaps most interesting—Miethe, who stated to the press that he had worked on *Projekt Saucer,* went to work for the Americans and Canadians. Finally, for the record, the prototype for the AVRO flying saucer, which was handed over to the U.S. and loudly proclaimed to have been a failure, is now in the U.S. Air Force Museum in Fort Eustis, Virginia.

While *Genesis* is a work of fiction, the fiction is based on various facts—and those facts could do with further examination. A list of sources is given overleaf.

Sources

Information about *Flugkapitan* Rudolph Schriever and his fellow officers on *Projekt Saucer* came mainly from the following articles: "Untertassen—Flieger Kombination," *Der Spiegel,* March 30, 1950. "Fliegende Untertasse in Deutschland erfunden," *Sonderbericht der Deutsche Illustrierte,* S.1350, 1951. "Fliegende Untertassen—eine Deutsche Erfindung," *Criticus,* No. 26, June 27, 1952. "Die Deutsche Fliegende Untertasse," *Das Ufer—die Farb-Illustrierte,* No. 18, September 1, 1952. "Flugscheibe flog 1945 in Prag," interview with Georg Klein, *Welt am Sonntag,* April 25, 1953. "Wunderwaffen 45," *Bild am Sonntag,* February 17, 1957. "Die UFOs—eine deutsche Erfindung," *Das neue Zeitalter,* October 5, 1957. "Flugkreisel, irdisch," *Geun & Welt,* No. 14, April 2, 1959. "Deutsche UFOs schon 1947/48 einwandfrei beobachtet," *Das neue Zeitalter,* February 6, 1965. "Projekt Flugkreisel," *Bremerhavener Zeit* (undated photocopy); and "Deutsche Flugkreisel," *Luftfahrt International,* No. 9, May–June, 1975. Major Rudolph Lusar's book, *German Secret Weapons of World War II* (see "Author's Note"), which was an invaluable reference work regarding both completed and uncompleted secret German projects, also contains a detailed section on *Projekt Saucer.*

The other major source of information about Germany's World War II aeronautical innovations, and also about the postwar history of British, American and Canadian uti-

lization of those innovations, was Renato Vesco's *Intercettateli Senza Sparare*, first published in 1968 by E. Mursia
& Co., Milan, Italy, later English-language edition published in 1971 by Grove Press under the misleading title of *Intercept—But Don't Shoot,* and then reissued in 1974 by
Zebra Publications Inc., New York, under the even more
misleading title of *Intercept UFO.* Unfortunately, while
Vesco bases most of his technical information on very
strong official sources, most notably the numerous reports
of the Combined Intelligence Objectives Sub-Committee
(H.M.S.O., London, 1945–47), the reports of the American Alsos Commission in *Alsos* (Schuman, New York,
1947) by Samuel A. Goudsmit, and similar reports from
other World War II scientific investigators, he offers no
real substantiation for the existence of the *Kugelblitz*
which is meant to be the pivotal subject of his argument.
However, Vesco's book remains indispensable on two
counts: (1) It is the most detailed history yet published of
the lesser known, but revolutionary German aeronautical
innovations; and (2) while the author makes no mention
of Schriever or his saucer project, he *does* state that a
machine called the *Kugelblitz*—or the "Ball Lightning Automatic Fighter"—was first test-flown in early 1945 over
the great underground complex at Kahla, in Thuringia,
and suggests that both the *Kugelblitz* and the remaining
Feuerballs were then destroyed by the retreating
S.S.—details which have remarkable parallels with the
Schriever story.

Apart from the books mentioned above, the following
books were of real value: *Hitler's Last Weapons: The Un-
derground War Against the V1 and V2* by Josef Garlinski
(Julian Friedmann, 1978); *V2* by Walter Dornberger
(Hurst and Blackett, 1954); *The Birth of the Missile: The
Secrets of Peenemunde* by E. Klee and O. Merk (Harrap,
1965); *German Secret Weapons of the Second World War*
by R. Luser (Spearman, 1959); *History of the German
Guided Missile Development* by T. Benecke and A. W.
Quick (Brunswick: Verlag E. Applehans, 1957); *German
Guided Missiles* by R. F. Pocock (Ian Allen, London,
1966); *Raketon-Flugtechnik* by E. Sanger (Edwards, Ann

Arbor, Michigan, reprint of 1933 edition published by
Oldenbourg of Munchen); *Soviet Rocketry* by Michael
Stoiko (David & Charles, 1971); *The Papers of Robert H.
Goddard*, edited by E. C. Goddard (McGraw-Hill, New
York, 1970); *The Rise and Fall of the Third Reich* by
William L. Shirer (Secker & Warburg, 1960); *Adolf Hitler*
by John Toland (Doubleday Company/Ballantine, New
York, 1976 and 1977 respectively); *Gestapo* by Edward
Crankshaw (Putnam & Company, 1960); *Children of the
S.S.* by Clarissa Henry and Marc Hillel (Hutchinson & Co.,
London, 1976); *Himmler als Ideologue* (Gottingen,
1970); and *The Occult Establishment* by James Webb
(Open Court Publishing Co., La Salle, Illinois), the only
reliable book I have read so far on the Nazis and the Oc-
cult.

There are literally thousands of so-called "factual"
books on UFOs, many of which are well worth avoiding.
Since this author has obviously not read all of them, he
must acknowledge his debt to the following: *The UFO
Experience; A Scientific Inquiry* (Corgi) and *The Hynek
UFO Report* (Sphere), both by Dr. J. Allen Hynek; *The
Report on Unidentified Flying Objects* (Doubleday & Co.,
New York, 1956) by Edward J. Ruppelt; *The UFO Con-
troversy in America* (The New American Library, 1976)
by David Michael Jacobs; *Project Blue Book* (Ballantine)
edited by Brad Steiger; *The Interrupted Journey* (Berkley
Medallian Publishing) by John G. Fuller; *The Crack in
the Universe* (Neville Spearman, London) by Jean-Claude
Bourret; *UFOs From Behind the Iron Curtain* (Souvenir
Press, London) by Ion Hobana and Julien Weverbergh;
UFOs: A Scientific Debate (W. W. Norton & Co., New
York), edited by Carl Sagan and Thornton Page; *Worlds
Beyond* (And/Or Press, Berkeley, California), edited by
the New Dimensions Foundation; and *Ufology* (Celestial
Arts, California), a fascinating analysis of the possible
physical properties of the UFOs by James M. McCamp-
bell.

The famous monthly magazine *Flying Saucer Review* is
mandatory reading for anyone interested in the subject,
but should be perused with a very selective eye.

I am indebted to NASA's *Exploring Space With A Camera* and to their reproductions and analysis of the much abused ESSA 7 satellite photographs. I am also heavily indebted to Eliot Porter's *Antarctica* (Hutchinson, London, 1979), in which both text and photographs are magnificent.

Should some of my readers think that the physiological and psychological horrors presented in certain chapters of *Genesis* are solely the products of the author's feverish imagination, I must recommend the following factual books: *As Man Becomes Machine* (Sphere) by David Rorvik; *Man Modified* (Paladin) by David Fishlock; *Manipulation* (Fontana) by Erwin Lausch; *The People Shapers* (Futura) by Vance Packard; *Supernature* (Coronet) by Lyall Watson; *The Immortalist* (Panther and Abacus) by Alan Harrington; *Inside the Black Room: Studies of Sensory Deprivation* (Pelican) by Jack Vernon; *Hypnotism: Fact and Fiction* (Pelican) by F. L. Marcus; *PSI; Psychic Discoveries Behind the Iron Curtain* (Abacus) by Sheila Ostrander and Lunn Schroeder; *Future Science* (Anchor Books, Doubleday, New York), edited by John White and Stanley Krippner; *Future Facts* (Heinemann) by Stephen Rosen, and *Mysteries* (Hodder & Stoughton) by Colin Wilson.

My thanks to the following libraries and universities for their kind assistance in gathering further research material: Cornell University, New York; the Massachusetts Institute of Technology; the University of London; the British Museum Library, London; the Imperial War Museum, London, the Landesbibliothek, Wurttembergische; the Universitatischebibliothek, Freiburg Im Breisgau; the Landesbibliothek, Stuttgart; and the Staatsund Universitatsbibliothek, Hamburg.

Personal thanks to Stephanie Trudeau (New York); Willi Mayer, Reinhold Stoll, and Rudiger and Hannelore Vogt of West Germany; Marc Williams of *Lookout* magazine, Spain; Martin Atcherley for his kind assistance regarding Paraguay and Argentina; James Webb, for his very authoritative response to my inquiries about the S.S. and the Occult; Richard and Iris Grollner, my literary agents; Nick Austin, for his generosity with certain books; and finally, Alan Earney, for so enthusiastically backing this whole project.

W. A. Harbinson,
London, 1980.

Imagine yourself finally settled into your large Victorian home. Life in your charming, quaint New England village is a dream come true...until the dream turns slowly into a nightmare. And you must confront evil forces *you don't even believe in*...and cannot stop.

Just like the families in these 3 novels of horror and suspense. By the *master* of supernatural terror,

DUFFY STEIN

Looking for some scary novels that really will leave you limp? Here are three by the new name in nerve-wracking suspense.

JOANNE FLUKE

Her terrifying novels of psychological suspense are in the tradition of Mary Higgins Clark, John Saul, and Patricia J. MacDonald. They will not disappoint you!

COLD JUDGMENT	11311-3-10	$3.50
STEPCHILD	18408-8-19	2.25
WINTER CHILL	19617-5-30	3.50